THE
IMMORTAL
RENSHAI

THE IMMORTAL RENSHAI

The Renshai Saga: Volume Three

Mickey Zucker Reichert

DAW BOOKS, INC.

DONALD A. WOLLHEIM, FOUNDER

375 Hudson Street, New York, NY 10014

ELIZABETH R. WOLLHEIM
SHEILA E. GILBERT
PUBLISHERS

www.dawbooks.com

To Carly Moore,

Our last great hope.
Luckily, she is up to the task.

ACKNOWLEDGMENTS

Sheila Gilbert, editor extraordinaire, and Jody Lee of the unmatched cover art.

Also Caesar Moore without whom my life would be far less golden.

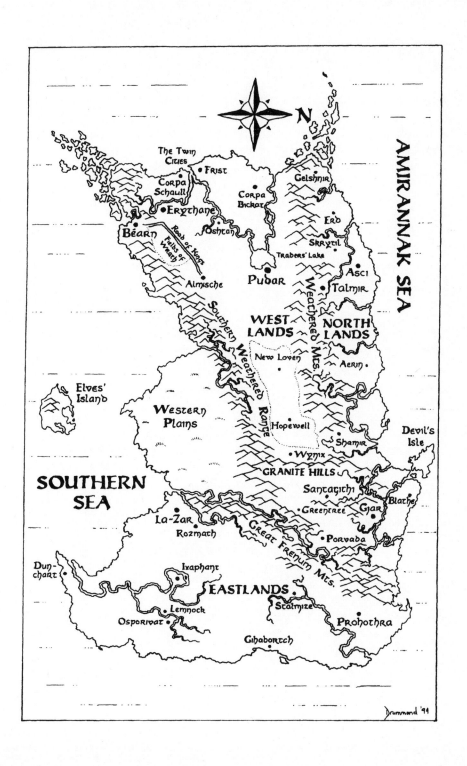

CHAPTER 1

The larger the enemy, the larger the victory.

—Renshai proverb

THE SOMBERNESS OF BÉARN'S STRATEGY ROOM seemed to pervade Saviar Ra-khirsson's bones to their marrow. Men representing every corner of the continent sat around the massive table, the only article of furniture in the room other than the multitude of chairs on which they sat. The walls, usually filled with maps, now held lists of names grouped by homeland and arranged in alphabetical order. The north wall bore those of the confirmed dead, the other three the more than a thousand missing in the magical blast that had ended the war.

Saviar looked around the table, recognizing most of the others from previous meetings which had taken place between the two wars that had rocked the continent in less than a year. The high king of the Westlands, Griff, took his usual place at the head of the table, massive and bearlike, with black curly hair and eyes nearly as dark. The first of his three wives, Queen Matrinka, sat at his left hand and his bard and bodyguard, Darris, at his right. The captain of his palace guards, Seiryn, hovered behind him.

A single man represented all nine of the Northern tribes, the only one they could possibly have agreed upon, the hero Valr Magnus. Pale, with white-blond hair, a muscular torso, and legs like tree trunks, he sat attentively, his handsome features radiating charm. Saviar appreciated that the North had agreed on a single representative, particularly one of the few Northmen who did not despise all Renshai inherently and beyond all reason.

Two men representing the Eastlands had remained in Béarn, though only one was in attendance. Despite the irritation currently coloring Saviar's every utterance and action, he could not help smiling at the sight of Weile Kahn, the most complicated man at the meeting. He had a strange ability to organize the most deadly and dangerous criminals on the continent, and they granted him a loyalty of which most would not believe them capable. Though he lived a quiet and titleless life, mostly in hiding, Weile was quite probably the most powerful man in existence. The other Easterner in Béarn, King Tae Kahn, was his only child.

As usual, the oldest of the elves represented his kind, a tall, slender, auburn-haired creature with canted amber eyes called Captain.

The Westlands had a larger host of representatives. Sir Harritin of the Knights of Erythane took the place of Knight-Captain Kedrin, Saviar's paternal grandfather, while he recovered from injuries sustained in the war. Though resplendent in his uniform and meticulous in every detail, Harritin's eyes displayed a hint of nervous discomfort. He was not used to taking such a high-level leadership role. Thialnir was the official leader of the Renshai, though he relied heavily on Saviar, whom he had chosen as his successor. The West also had General Sutton, a master strategist from the eastern portion of the Westlands and General Markanyin, who hailed from the West's largest city, Pudar.

Young pages flitted through the background, adding or subtracting names from the lists at the whispered requests of the representatives and prepared to chronicle every word of the meeting in the Sage's library.

King Griff had provided baths and his most comfortable rooms for all the representatives, and a single night of sleep, before insisting on this meeting. Despite the common exhaustion and the solemn occasion, Sir Harritin had no choice but to preside over all the ancient rites and rituals attendant upon such an important meeting. Saviar felt certain nearly everyone would have preferred to forgo them, but the Knights of Erythane were sticklers for formality.

However, the moment the introductions, flourishes, and announcements had concluded, King Griff rose and went right to the heart of the matter. "I know you're all understandably tired and saddened by the events of the last couple of months and, particularly, of the last few days. I will try to keep things as brief as possible and still answer all your concerns and questions. Please feel free to approach me at any time with any issues needing my attention. If there is anything reasonable you need or desire while you are my guests, be sure to ask any of the servants."

Aware Griff had added the word "reasonable" after a visiting Northman had demanded one of the maids spend the night with him, Saviar bit his lower lip to quash a cynical grunt. Béarn had never abided slavery, and though well-paid, the servants were under no obligation to fulfill any perverse requests or commands.

Griff continued, "First, I want to thank each and every one of you, and all of the peoples you represent, for any and all contributions to the wars. I plan to refer to the first as the Pirate War and the second as the World's War."

Murmurs swept the room, but no one argued. Saviar supposed wars needed some kind of name for historical reference, and the "Great War" was already taken for a battle some three centuries earlier that had pitted the Eastlands against the Westlands. Saviar might have considered calling this one the second Great War, but he could see why Griff had avoided it. Doing so might offend the people of the Eastlands, allies in the current conquest.

"I know the sacrifices you have all made in time and travel mean disruptions in planting and harvest, in the production of goods, in the mining and distribution of luxuries and necessities. I have no authority over the North or the East, but over the next year, there will be no taxes demanded from Béarn. My ministers assure me I will have to gradually phase them back in over the following few years, but we will do so gently and with consideration. My artisans are working on the plans for a memorial at the site of the World's War, and we will provide as much assistance as possible to the twin cities, which will need to be entirely rebuilt."

Heads bowed at the oblique mention of Corpa Schaull and Frist, leveled by their enemy, the *Kjempemagiska*, magical giants from an island in the seas far west of the continent beyond their maps.

"At the moment," Griff continued, "our most pressing issue is the brave soldiers carried away by the magic that ended the war."

Memories descended upon Saviar of the vicious, unnatural storms that had wracked the armies when the horrors of the combined magic of the *Kjempemagiska* had smashed into the joint defenses woven by the elves. The backlash had slaughtered the giants en masse, victims of their own offense, but the raw chaos into which the elves' defensive magic had degenerated did not kill instantly. Instead, it developed into a tempest of unimaginable proportions, threatening to tear the elves apart from the inside outward, to buffet every living thing on the continent with unsurvivable force. Deadly winds slammed people into breaking trees, flung living bodies like leaves until the elves managed to open multiple, random gates to other planes of existence. Released into these openings, the chaos dispersed, carrying the destructive force—and many of the warriors— onto unexplored worlds.

"As I understand it," the high king said, "the elves had no way of knowing to which worlds these gates might lead. They had no choice but to throw the ways open blindly in order to spare as many lives as possible." Saviar saw the king's gaze shift toward Captain. Clearly, he wanted the elf to take over the explanation, but he also knew elves did not like human attention.

Unfortunately, most of the gazes in the room focused on the elf, even without the king's gesture.

Captain handled it remarkably well. Rumored to be several millennia old, he had lived on Midgard, the world of humans, for most of his life, unlike the others of his ilk who had only arrived in the last two decades. "King Griff is correct. It is extremely difficult to open gates to other worlds under the best of circumstances. It requires controlling and shaping a large amount of power. In this case, we had more raw chaos than we could handle, but working with it . . ." He paused to consider. "Rather like trying to carve a statue from a block of marble while you're being attacked from every side by a phalanx of enemies. It might be barely possible, but only if you know your life and others' hangs on finishing that statue. And it's not likely to be your most exquisite piece."

Saviar saw nods and winces all around the table. Most of these men identified with a half-decent fighting analogy, and the Béarnides' pride and joy were the statues crafted by their master sculptors. They had carved the castle itself from a mountain.

Captain explained further. "Aimed gates can only be created with someone or something familiar on the other side to hold our focus. We were basically punching arbitrary holes in the fabric between universes, with no way to know what was on the other side. Had we not vented the winds this way, everything living on Midgard would have died." He added emphatically, "Everything."

If possible, the solemnity of the room increased. Several representatives dropped their weary heads to the tabletop. General Sutton, always thinking strategy, asked the pertinent question first. "The soldiers sucked onto these other worlds . . . Captain, is there a way to get them back?"

Captain squirmed a bit. He tented his long fingers in front of his angular face. "Some of them, yes. And believe me, General, we are as eager as you to do so. As a percentage, more elves were whisked away than humans." He did not add it was a greater catastrophe for the elves as well. It was a poorly kept secret that elfin births were limited to the recycled souls of elves who died of old age. Every elf who perished unnaturally meant one less elf for all eternity. Saviar did not know whether an elf who succumbed to age on another world could still become reincarnated as an infant on this one, and he doubted Captain would tell him if he asked.

"Some of them?" Thialnir pressed. Unlike elves, Renshai could procreate at will, but they numbered barely over three hundred prior to the war. Every member of the tribe was a warrior, including the women and children. That, in and of itself, resulted in low fertility and high mortality. To make matters worse, their fearsome reputation, not wholly undeserved, caused many other peoples of the world to hate them, particularly Northmen who would be only too happy to see the entire Renshai tribe exterminated.

"Some of them," Captain repeated. "The Outworlds are . . . different. Many cannot support life of any kind, and others can't support life as we know it. Some are . . . dangerous, inhospitable. We believe an infinite number of worlds exist, and each one is unique in some way."

General Markanyin shifted his bulk in his chair. "Are you trying to say we may not get anyone back alive?"

Captain swallowed hard, a remarkably human gesture for an elf. "I'm trying *not* to say it. Mostly because I don't think it's true. I believe the majority of the Outworlds are capable of supporting human and elfin life. Some may even be more comfortable than Midgard. Some may be virtually indistinguishable."

General Sutton spoke again, still strategically. "Can you give us some statistics? Percentages perhaps?"

Captain worried his lower lip with his teeth. "If you're asking how many Outworlds I've personally visited, the answer is very few and all of those were part of the nine main ones studied by religious scholars. Alfheim, the world of elves, used to be an Outworld before it got destroyed during the *Ragnarok*. I've also been to Asgard, the abode of the gods. Once. I've heard secondhand stories about Hel, still one of the nine, and Chaos World, which isn't. I can give you rough percentages based on information I've overheard, read, and extrapolated, but it would only be a guess."

"Guess," Sutton encouraged.

"I'd say about ten percent would be instantly fatal to elves or humans. Another ten percent might be survivable by elves but not humans due to certain immunities and the ability to tame raw chaos. Of the remaining eighty percent, about three-quarters would have some sort of potential life-threatening hazard or danger."

"Such as?" Sutton asked.

Captain shrugged. "As you know, the last group who had to negotiate Outworlds ran into, among other things, spirit spiders, shape-changing magical creatures who feed on souls. Some worlds have giants, gods, monsters, oddities, or even hostile human or humanlike societies. Other hazards might include shifting terrain, rugged mountains, geysers, volcanoes. There are more strange things on the Outworlds than my meager imagination can conjure."

The room erupted into conversation. Thialnir tried to engage his successor, but he found Saviar lost deeply in thought. His twin brother was among the missing, and his thoughts about Subikahn, at the moment, consumed him, fiercely negative. The brothers had parted on the worst possible terms.

Sir Harritin made a broad gesture to claim the floor, waiting until Griff acknowledged him before speaking. "What is rescuing our brethren likely to entail?"

Saviar knew six of the twenty-four Knights of Erythane had died in the war or its aftermath, but none had gotten sucked to the Outworlds. When Harritin spoke of "brethren," he meant the soldiers of every army representing the continent.

Captain lowered his head with a suddenness that implied weariness, at least when a human did it. "I don't know, exactly," he admitted. "We've discussed it on the trip here, of course, but . . . other issues . . ."

Saviar knew elves were capricious and difficult to direct at the best of times. He also realized Captain was avoiding saying that, not wishing to paint his people in a deleterious light or to denigrate the significance of the lives driven to the Outworlds.

When the silence remained after several moments, Captain finally felt compelled to fill it. "We had the same issues as every one of you to distract us, too."

Several leaders nodded. The focus for the human groups had been separating the dead from the missing, preparing the lists that now covered the Strategy Room walls and tending to the injured and exhausted.

Griff reassured the elf. "We all certainly understand that, Captain. All of your people are welcome anywhere they wish to go inside or on the grounds of Béarn Castle. If they require anything, they need only ask any of the staff."

Captain seemed grateful to speak directly to the king. "Thank you, Sire. We will need a large meeting room and the use of the Pica Stone."

The greatest artifact of the known worlds, the Pica currently belonged to the ruler of Béarn, used to test the worth of subsequent heirs and determine the next king or queen. It was one of a scant handful of items ever known to contain any amount of permanent magic. Nevertheless, Griff did not hesitate. "Let's plan to meet over supper, you and I. I'll find the best room to accommodate your needs and turn the Pica over to your care."

"Thank you, Sire." Captain retook his seat.

Griff reclaimed the meeting. "I have one more item of business, if you'll all indulge me."

No one spoke or moved, not a single sign of impatience or disgruntlement, though they were all tired and hungry for fresh, kitchen-prepared food.

"I need to introduce you all to an important visitor who will make everyone uncomfortable. I assure you he means us no harm; he's a politician of sorts and was never a soldier."

Saviar tipped his head, curious. He could think of no individual who could bother every person in such a diverse group, except perhaps an Outworlder or god. Every giant had perished in the war; and, this time, they had come to the continent without their man-sized servants. Even had they not, experience told Saviar they would have killed themselves rather than allow capture.

Griff did not make them wait long. He said something to one of the pages who threw open the large door to the Strategy Room. King Tae Kahn of the Eastlands entered first, his nearly-ever-present silver tabby cat on his shoulders, beckoning to someone unseen behind him. Then, the other stepped through the portal, ducking deeply to spare his head. When he cautiously rose to his full height, his wavy brown hair scraped the ceiling. His blue-green eyes looked enormous and his mouth, above a lantern jaw, large enough to swallow the cat whole. He wore a short-skirted coat, loose trousers and a cloak with a silver clasp, all more finely woven than any cloth Saviar had ever seen. The top of Tae's head barely reached his waist.

Nearly everyone in the room, including Saviar, sprang to their feet, leaving only the sprawled pages, Captain, Griff, and Matrinka sitting. Fighting men could not help reacting to such an obvious threat. The giant looked askance at Tae who spoke in a language Saviar did not understand. The tone of his voice was soothing.

Griff made the introduction. "Everybody, this is Kentt. As I understand it, he's a fairly high-ranking member of *Kjempemagiska* society, though not involved in the military in any capacity. The army dropped him off to swim to Béarn while they moved on to the twin cities in the hope of flanking us. He came in search of his missing daughter, a toddler named Mistri."

Saviar did not understand; and, from the looks on the other faces, no one else among the human representatives did, either. Only Weile Kahn remained poker-faced, though he rarely displayed emotion unless it suited him. Valr Magnus asked the question on nearly every mind, "How could his toddler daughter have gotten here?"

Griff explained. "As you know, we sent scouts to Heimstadr, the island of the *Kjempemagiska*, three people in this room among them." He indicated Tae, Matrinka, and the elfin Captain. "They discovered Prince Arturo alive there. The girl had formed a deep attachment to my missing son; and, when the scouts rescued him, she followed. They could not safely return her, so she accompanied them home."

Saviar knew the explanation was much more complicated, but, at least for the moment, it did not matter. Tae, Matrinka, and Captain would never have brought the giant toddler back to Béarn without a logical reason.

Griff summed things up, "Kentt and his daughter have been reunited, and they have promised to assist us in establishing diplomatic ties with the giants who did not invade our shores."

General Markanyin's eyes narrowed. "In exchange for what?"

"In exchange for taking him and his daughter safely home. He also believes such ties will benefit the *Kjempemagiska*. Trade of goods and information goes both ways."

Valr Magnus pointed out, "As I understand it, their intention was to kill all of us and steal our land because they had run out of room."

Griff had a patient answer for that as well. "With a huge number of them killed in the war, they no longer have an overcrowding issue. Kentt also now realizes we're intelligent beings whereas, before, they looked upon us as some sort of . . . human-shaped animals who mimic rational behavior."

Darris took his seat, as did Weile. The rest still remained standing, wary.

General Sutton studied the giant. "I assume he doesn't understand our common language." The words served as a warning and a test. If Kentt knew what they were saying about him, they needed to do a better job of guarding their tongues.

Tae responded, "Not a word, General. I'm here to translate both ways, when appropriate."

"But you haven't said anything until just now," Sutton pointed out. "Other than a couple of words before the introduction."

Tae rearranged the cat on his shoulders. "Nothing needed translating yet. Also, not all their language is verbal. It has a mental component much like the elves' *khohlar*. Kentt and I could carry on an entire conversation, and no one would know it but us." He added with a toss of his head. "You may speak freely."

"I have something to say," Thialnir growled. "In the first war, the one we're calling the Pirate War, the enemy brought along only one of these magical giants." He did not attempt the term the enemy and King Griff had used: *Kjempemagiska* pronounced kee-YEM-pay-muh-JEES-kah. "That single giant nearly destroyed our combined armies by himself. As I understand it, we had a couple of elves and one of those magic humans . . ."

Thialnir glanced at Saviar who supplied woodenly, "A Mage of Myrcidë." The so-called "magic human" at the Pirate War had been Chymmerlee, Saviar's girlfriend who had left him in a rather abrupt and angry manner, another issue he had not wished to consider at the moment, perhaps ever.

"Two elves and a *mage*," Thialnir corrected. "Without them to prevent that *one* giant casting magic, we might have all lost our lives."

Valr Magnus nodded vigorously. "Even then, it required special weapons just to fight him." He and Saviar's youngest brother, two of the continent's most persistent and competent warriors, had managed to bring that *Kjempemagiska* down; but they could have achieved nothing without the swords gifted to them by the immortal Renshai, Colbey Calistinsson. Neither man had escaped the battle unscathed.

King Griff reminded them, "That giant was a warrior trained to battle whereas Kentt is a noncombatant who wishes to help us establish peaceful relations between Heimstadr and our continent. He's here with his young daughter."

Saviar was not wholly convinced. From the actions of the other soldiers, still standing, they were not, either.

Always blunt, Thialnir put their suspicions into words. "But if he decided to avenge his people, or became angry for other reasons, he could cause a catastrophe with magic."

Saviar knew it was truth more than anyone. He had watched the *Kjempemagiska* of the Pirate War, Firuz, creating a massive tidal wave that could have destroyed most of Béarn and all the human soldiers gathered on her beaches had the elves and Chymmerlee not locked his magic with their own. Saviar's own enchanted weapon, *Motfrabelonning*, had allowed him to see the formation of magic that was invisible to normal human vision.

Griff could not deny it, even if he were prone to lies. "He could, but I believe he won't. During the Pirate War, we had no idea of the capability of the giants or how to counter them. Now, we do. Furthermore, we had one mage and only one elf, my second wife. Currently, we have more than a hundred." He meant elves, Saviar knew. All twelve of the Mages of Myrcidë who had reluctantly joined them in the battle were missing, presumably blown to the Outworlds with the other absent soldiers. The fourteen remaining mages were cloistered in their magically-concealed citadel, unwilling to admit their existence let alone show their faces to the rest of humanity.

The twelve Myrcidians had been sneaking away from the war when one of the *Kjempemagiska* had found and nearly slaughtered them. Saviar's twin, Subikahn, had come to their rescue. He killed the giant but was also mortally wounded. It was then he had made a terrible confession to Saviar, the one that placed Saviar into the foul mood he seemed incapable of shaking. When Saviar had last seen them, the mages were trying to heal the dying Subikahn with magic, and Saviar knew they might succeed. They had once rescued him from certain death as well.

This train of thought sent a swell of rage through Saviar, so he swiftly discarded it, focusing instead on the plight of those trapped on Outworlds through no fault of their own. Unlike the men and woman in this room, they had no idea how they had come to be wherever they had landed and little to no concept of magic.

Finally, the last of the warriors sat, leaving only Saviar and the men without chairs still standing.

Griff continued, "Kentt is my guest in Béarn. I understand if anyone chooses not to interact with him, but I expect the atmosphere in my city to remain civil at all times."

Saviar sat but found his hand steadfastly attached to his hilt.

Tae addressed Captain, "Did you receive Kentt's reply?"

The elf shook his head. "I didn't. Can he *khohlar*?" He referred to a process elves often used to communicate. It planted a "voice" directly into the head of either one listener or everyone within range, at the discretion of the "speaker".

"No," Tae explained. "The intelligent life of Heimstadr has a mental language they all understand, but it's not *khohlar*. Humans can't hear it, and my studies suggested elves can't either. Now we know for sure."

"But he did receive my *khohlar*?"

"Yes," Tae confirmed. "He said you greeted him and asked if he might assist with helping the elves bring the missing elfin and human soldiers back from the Outworlds."

"Said?" Saviar surprised himself by interrupting. When all eyes shifted to him, he continued, "He still hasn't spoken."

"Aloud," Tae confirmed. "But he did use what they call *anari*, their mind-language. We've been communicating that way ever since we entered." He glanced around the room, though he clearly knew the answer to his own question. "Did anyone besides me hear it? It can't be directed to just one receiver the way *khohlar* can, and it doesn't automatically translate, so it would sound like mental gibberish."

Murmurs and head shakes were the only answers Tae received. Clearly, no one had heard Kentt's *anari*.

Tae did not seem surprised. "It's the reason they considered us animals. In their world, anything that can't hear *anari* is, by definition, of trivial intelligence and fair game for slaughter. They believe language is a singular concept, a gift from the gods; and so our speech is, to them, nothing different than the lowing of cows or the squealing of pigs."

While the others mulled over this revelation, General Sutton pointed out a significant fact that should have been blatantly obvious. "King Tae, how is it you hear and send *anari* when even elves can't?"

Darris added facetiously, "Perhaps it requires a large, furry animal sitting on one's shoulders."

If Saviar had not turned to look at the bard, he might have missed Matrinka's reaction. She stiffened, and her eyes and nostrils widened a bit. Swiftly, Saviar turned his attention to Tae; but, if the wiry Easterner had shown any similar response to the joke, he immediately suppressed it. It made Saviar wonder whether or not the cat did play some sort of role, though that seemed like utter madness. Only the fact that Matrinka loved cats so much she had once filled Béarn Castle with them kept the suspicion alive. *Is it just possible cats really do have something to do with it?*

If so, Tae did not admit it. "If you remember, General, I took several enormous risks to learn their language. I didn't hear *anari* at first, either, but I figured out I was missing huge swathes of conversation by listening only to their spoken words. Over time, I started hearing it, although I'm not consistent. Sometimes I can't hear *anari*, either, especially if I'm not concentrating on it. I've come to believe the same weird process that allows me to quickly learn new languages also allows me to sometimes hear *anari*."

Saviar had to admit Tae did learn tongues with a speed that had always shocked and amazed him. It had something to do with the dangerous and varied peoples Weile had surrounded his son with from a very young age.

Griff's attention returned to the elf. "Captain, how long do the elves need to figure out how best to retrieve the missing soldiers?"

Captain hesitated only briefly before his canted amber eyes swung around to the king. "With the Pica in hand, two days should do it, Sire."

"We'll meet back here immediately after supper in exactly two days." The high king looked at every person around the strategy table individually, including the guards and pages. "Is that a problem for anyone?"

No one responded, and Sir Harritin made the ponderous pronouncements to officially end the meeting.

Itching for a fight, Saviar waited only until Kentt, King Tae, and King Griff had exited the chamber before slipping out the door and heading for the sparring room.

CHAPTER 2

Renshai aren't known for their sweet dispositions.
—*Thialnir Thrudazisson*

PRINCE ARTURO OF BÉARN searched the closet and storage trunk of the guest bedroom with exaggerated interest before pulling aside the dust ruffle and peering under the bed. Two enormous blue eyes looked back at him from a broad face. Mistri giggled and announced, "Found me!"

"Found you!" Arturo returned in ebullient *usaro*, the spoken language of the *Kjempemagiska* and the same one the three-year-old daughter of Kentt and Hortens had used.

Arturo scooted backward to give Mistri room to scramble out from under her bed. They had started playing as soon as Kentt left for the meeting, but the game had lost some of its fun as they soon discovered only three places in the room large enough to hide the enormous toddler or a full-grown Béarnian man. Still, Arturo had indulged her long past that realization. While they played, all troubles melted away and his mind returned to the carefree, heady days when he had been her pet, Bobbin, and she his loving mistress.

During the Pirate War, a shipboard battle against the *Kjempemagiska*'s servants, the man-sized *alsona*, had resulted in the deaths of every man aboard. Arturo had fallen into the ocean during the fight and, somehow, wound up floating, more dead than alive, to Heimstadr. Mistri had discovered him washed up on the Beach of Flotsam and insisted on keeping him. Indulging his daughter, as always, Kentt, his wife, and relations had saved Arturo's life with magic, although he had awakened entirely without memories, with no identity or any idea of his previous life.

Mistri and Arturo had spent most of a year together, learning the spoken language, although Arturo had never heard *anari*. He knew he was missing large pieces of conversation, but he could not fathom the reason. Strangely unconcerned about his amnesia, he had served as Mistri's loyal protector, considering himself lucky to have such a sweet and wonderful owner who also served as his constant companion. Then, playing with her had been the joy and highlight of his existence, and he had even saved her life on one occasion.

Now, most of the details of his former life had returned to Arturo's memory. He was the second child of Queen Matrinka but the fourth of King Griff, who had three wives. Arturo's full sister, Marisole, was the oldest. Then came Ivana from Griff's second wife, the elf Tem'aree'ay. Though eighteen, she suffered disabilities, including the intellectual development of a one- to two-year-old child. Barrindar, the son of Griff and his third wife, came next. Only then had Matrinka borne Arturo. Three more princesses followed, two courtesy of Barrindar's mother, Xoraida, and one more via Matrinka.

Arturo had never considered himself temperamentally suited for the throne nor likely to ever sit upon it, so he had focused on becoming a naval warrior, perhaps Béarn's admiral someday. His amnesia had made it impossible for him to participate in the World's War, so he had remained at the castle with healers to tend him and help him remember his past.

Mistri sat on the bed, then patted the spot beside her, a plea for Arturo to join her. He did, as he had so many times before. Like most Béarnides, especially those of the royal line, Arturo was tall, well-muscled and broad for a human, yet Mistri already nearly matched him for height and weight. As he joined her, she snuggled against him, and the rest of the world disappeared. He felt strangely safe in the arms of the child, as though nothing and no one would dare to disturb them.

"When Poppy and me go home, you come, Bobbin? Yes?"

Prince Arturo sighed. At the moment, he did not want to think about anything but the contentment of their closeness, the consummate love of a child. "Can't, Mistri. Can't." Not for the first time, he wished for the fluency he worried he would never gain with the island language.

Tears welled in the toddler's eyes, turning them into pale pools of blue. This was not the first time they had had this conversation. "Me will miss my Bobbin. Miss Bobbin too much." She nestled closer.

Arturo wrapped his arms around the girl. He did not want to let go. "Me will miss Mistri, too. Not want you go." He stopped short of suggesting she stay. That might cause friction between her and her father, which seemed not only grossly unfair but also quite dangerous.

They sat in silence a long time, entwined in one another's arms. Shameless tears glided down the child's face, while Arturo shaded his moist eyes, convinced grown men never cry. The *Kjempemagiska* had considered him something akin to a dog, an animal with apparent loyalty that could never be fully trusted because it still had teeth and nails and might, one day, attack their precious child. But Mistri had known for certain, in all her innocence, she had nothing to fear from her pet. She had always loved him unconditionally, defending him whenever she could from those who would have preferred him dead.

In hindsight, Arturo understood their fear. They must have realized he had not originated from the mostly red-headed, smoother, more slender-built *alsona*. His curly mane of black hair, his hirsutism and dark eyes made it clear he arose from another source, most probably from the continent across the sea that harbored only what they considered unintelligent or, at least, lesser intelligent life. He was the enemy; and, in their experience that made him savage, violent, unworthy. For all of his docility and protectiveness when it came to Mistri, they believed he could snap at any moment.

If not for Kentt, the *Kjempemajiska* would have slaughtered Arturo without a pang of regret. That Kentt indulged his only child was obvious, but Arturo now also realized the father had actually shared Mistri's affection for her pet. Kentt had been the only giant besides the girl who ever touched him, usually a hair ruffle or back pat accompanied by a smile of honest fondness. Kentt had a clear interest in fauna and flora as well as in the development of young creatures and the relationships between the natural world and civilization. When the giants eventually discovered Arturo had learned to talk, albeit pidgin *usaro* only, Kentt had taken a certain strange delight in the knowledge.

Prince Arturo could not help smiling at the realization. *Kentt likes me, and he's fascinated by our peoples and civilizations.* He doubted the other giants would warm to them as quickly, but it did suggest Kentt was no more likely to became abruptly aggressive than Arturo, as Bobbin, had been. It seemed a shame the relationship might come to a sudden and permanent end when Captain found time to sail Kentt and Mistri back to Heimstadr. *I can't allow that to happen.* He spoke the rest aloud. "We friends forever, Mistri. Will visit lots."

Mistri raised her tear-streaked face. "Really?"

"Really," Arturo said firmly. "Promise."

A smile forced its way past the tears, and Mistri buried her enormous face into the prince of Béarn's ample chest. Arturo wrapped his arms fully around her, contented.

As previously arranged, King Griff met Captain in the private quarters assigned to the ancient elf. His own people called him Arak'bar Tulamii Dhor, He Who Has Forgotten His Name, because he had outlived all of them and for so long none of them had ever heard his given name. Several millennia ago, the Cardinal Wizards nicknamed him "the Captain" because the gods had burdened him with the task of ferrying them across the seas. Humans could never grasp his original name; they had enough difficulty with the eight syllable one the elves used, so he introduced himself as Captain and never looked back.

Captain's creator, Frey, had granted him some six thousand years to learn the ways of elves and men; and, currently, he suffered from a combination of wariness, weariness, and dark anticipation. Nevertheless, he managed a smile for the guileless king. "Good evening, Sire."

"Good evening to you, Captain." Griff carefully shut the door behind him and sat on the edge of Captain's bed. The elf had claimed the room's only chair, a hard, wooden construct that would not have suited royalty. The king said nothing about the arrangement. He abandoned formality whenever possible, and he knew the ways of elves from his one true love, his second wife, Tem'aree'ay Donnev'ra Amal-yah Krish-anda Mal-satorian. His other two marriages had been demanded by his advisers and the populace, women who met the proper criteria for producing heirs to the throne of Béarn. Elves preferred forests to plains, outdoors to indoors, and, when indoors, wooden floors and furniture to padded.

"I brought the Pica Stone, as promised." From the folds of his massive robe, King Griff produced the brilliant, round sapphire. Many peoples claimed rightful ownership of it, but the gods had decreed it remain in his possession. The Pica-selected ruler of Béarn was the fulcrum of the nine worlds, maintaining their balance and, hence, their existence. If that delicate arrangement tipped too far toward good or evil, toward law or chaos, it would herald their ultimate destruction.

Captain wished he could refuse. The Pica belonged in a secure location known only to the current king or queen of Béarn. The elf had used it before in dire circumstances; without it, this task would prove far less successful and more difficult. As it was, rescuing those sent to the Outworlds would require the combined power of the remaining elves. Without the Pica Stone, they would have to operate with several unnecessary handicaps. Its solid, permanent magic would make the difference between rescuing a handful of soldiers at great peril to others or bringing back large numbers, potentially without losing additional lives. The elves could not afford another death, and the humans would want to avoid it. "Thank you," he said simply.

Griff laid the nearly head-sized, shimmering blue ball gently on the coverlet. Clearly sensing Captain's discomfort, he tipped his head in question. "This will be easier than the last quest to the Outworlds, yes?" He tapped the Pica with two fingers.

Captain knew Griff was referring to the time most of the elves had formed a massive *jovinay arythanik* to find and reunite the remnants of the Pica Stone, destroyed hundreds of years earlier by a mistake of the Cardinal Wizards, its pieces scattered throughout the Outworlds. Then, the massed elves had needed to blindly send a group of humans and elves to the proper locations to physically retrieve the largest shards. Once the party was gated to the Outworld, they then had at least one elf on the opposite side, allowing the *jovinay arythanik* to more easily bring them home. Lives had been lost in the process, and an elf and a human had each lost their souls to spirit spiders.

Having the now-intact, clairsentient Pica Stone should allow the elves to create a more powerful pooling of magic, despite having fewer elves, and might also allow some scrying ability. "It should be technically simpler, Sire."

Griff's head tipped even further. Captain had to restrain the urge to turn his own head to look at the king full-featured. "But . . . ?" Griff encouraged.

Captain realized the king could read his mood too well to bluff. "But we're dealing with innocent lives rather than volunteers. Experience tells me we can't save them all. Some have already died, and we will lose others to the process. It is inevitable."

"To suffer anxiety over that which is inevitable . . . is folly."

"Yes, Sire." It was good advice but did not strike to the heart of Captain's concern. "When it comes to the Outworlds and the desperation of the situation, too much is random. We can't know who got sent to worlds where life is impossible and who to ones with various degrees of danger . . . or none at all. There is a tendency of humans—" Captain broke off, knowing he was treading on hazardous ground.

Griff's head reverted to its normal position. "A tendency of humans," Griff repeated. "It's just the two of us, Captain. You can speak freely, safely."

"Yes, Sire." He knew Griff would never accept anything other than the truth. "Humans tend to see bias where it doesn't exist and to think in conclusions. Mom just hugged my brother. I could use a hug. Therefore, she loves my brother more than me. Dad just gave my sister three copper pieces. I could use three copper pieces. Dad favors my sister."

Griff studied the elf. Clearly, the point eluded him, but he patiently waited for Captain to finish.

"We're still working out the details of the process, and the Pica Stone will help a lot, Sire. But so much depends purely on happenstance. I'm just a bit concerned about what will happen if we rescue more elves than humans, more Easterners than Westerners or, gods forbid, more Renshai than Northmen."

Griff still seemed confused, but he clearly sensed Captain had nothing to add, so he mulled over the information thus far imparted. "Humans understand happenstance, and I think we have a good assortment of representatives."

Captain did appreciate that the Northmen had left Valr Magnus, rather than the more bellicose and less reasonable Captain Erik, in Béarn. The delegate group did seem to consist of levelheaded leaders, but the elf could not shake his discomfort.

Apparently aware of this, Griff added, "I believe if we prepare them for the worst possibilities when we meet tomorrow, they will understand whatever happens and appreciate every life saved regardless of the proportions."

Though his anxiety was still not assuaged, Captain nodded. He could not help worrying that any issue, whether foreseen or unforeseen, would become negatively attributed to the elves.

Griff placed an encouraging hand on the other's arm. "You worry about the magic. Let me handle any repercussions. I believe you're underestimating human perception and gratitude; but I do value your concerns. Nothing bad will happen to any elf under my authority and protection."

Though riddled with fatalism, Captain appreciated Griff's words and gesture. "Thank you." He managed a smile and, at least, a tone of appreciation. He hoped, with all his heart, the wise and simple king was right.

Most of the Renshai had eagerly returned to the Fields of Wrath, having regained its possession only days before they had to leave it again for war, so Saviar had hoped to find Béarn's practice room mostly empty. Constructed for visiting warriors and for Renshai stationed in Béarn to guard its heirs, the enormous area held a wide variety of simulated terrain: from woodlands to closets, boulder-strewn clearings to a winding staircase.

The moment he opened the heavy door, Saviar realized his miscalculation. Most of his people had returned to the Fields of Wrath, but nearly every Renshai who planned to remain in Béarn, or who had not yet left for the Fields of Wrath, was here. Some, he suspected, had delayed their departures purely for the pleasure or privilege of practicing in this specially designed room. Many had heard tales but never had an opportunity to use it. Others had fought in it before and wanted another chance. In all, Saviar estimated nearly forty Renshai practiced sword forms or sparred on and around the various types of equipment, including Thialnir and the last person Saviar wanted to see—his younger brother, Calistin.

In the past, Calistin had mostly ignored his twin brothers. Naturally gifted and driven to become the best swordsman in the world, Calistin possessed a potential recognized and nurtured by the tribe nearly since birth. He was expected to practice and to teach, nothing else. Throughout childhood, he had reveled in tormenting his brothers by not just besting them, but humiliating and hurting them. Calistin had seemed utterly devoid of empathy or any desire other than perfection with his swords. A devoted Renshai, their mother had delighted in Calistin's accomplishments, which only made the twins dislike him more. They soon learned to avoid him.

Since the Pirate War, Calistin had gradually changed, becoming strangely more human to Saviar's judgment. Neverthless, when Calistin approached him now, Saviar had to suppress the instinct to run. His mind clicked through possible excuses, though politeness had never been necessary with the youngest of Kevral's three sons. Until recently, Calistin had displayed little or no understanding of social conventions and wrote off any type of behavior as beyond his ken. This time, Saviar leaned against a table covered with various practice weapons, things no Renshai would ever use, and clamped his hands to the edges of the table, well away from his hilts. If Calistin wanted a spar, he would have to ask for it.

To Saviar's surprise, Calistin made no attempt to violently engage his brother. Instead, he asked, "How did it go?"

Saviar stared a moment, blinking. He had no idea what his brother was asking. After a moment of tense silence, he prodded, "It?"

Calistin scratched a finger through his feathered, blond hair, considering his question and the nonsensical response. "The meeting. How did it go? Is Subikahn alive, and how do we rescue him?" His voice contained more than just curiosity or excitement about a possible dangerous mission. Calistin sounded as if he really cared about Subikahn, and that brought back the memories Saviar had tried so hard to suppress.

Too sick to remember what had brought them to the hidden home of the Mages of Myrcidë, Saviar had relied on Subikahn's memory. But his beloved twin had mostly dodged the details, leaving Saviar to believe he had suffered a wound during a skirmish with enemy Northmen that festered. To die of illness or infection would doom his soul to Hel, a fate no Renshai could tolerate for himself or any other in the tribe. Saviar should have viciously attacked Subikahn, forcing his brother to kill him and, thus, assuring himself a death in valiant combat and a permanent place in Valhalla.

Yet, somehow, Saviar had wound up in the care of those secretive mages who had inexorably pulled him from the very brink of death. During the months of recovery, Saviar had learned the mages only showed themselves to Subikahn because they had mistaken the "aura" of Saviar's sword for magical blood, believing the twins to be distant relatives who could help them reestablish their bloodline. The mages despised other humans, and Renshai in particular, so Saviar and Subikahn kept their true origins hidden. Saviar had plied Subikahn with questions, needing to understand why he had not died in combat, concerned he had behaved like a coward unworthy of Valhalla. Subikahn's avoidance of the subject only convinced Saviar of his own disgrace.

At the World's War, Subikahn's dying confession had finally revealed the truth. Saviar's twin had caused the injury, a careless sword stroke during an angry spar. Saviar had tried to die in combat, attacking repeatedly, but Subikahn had refused to battle, insisting the fever was not dangerous, even as he knew it was, even as Saviar fell into coma. Had it not been for Subikahn's chance meeting with Chymmerlee, Saviar's soul would have become forever trapped in Hel. And it was all Subikahn's doing.

It was the most unforgivable crime in Renshai culture to damn the soul of any worthy warrior to a coward's death. As Subikahn lay dying from a war injury that guaranteed him a place in Valhalla, he gasped out the story of a treason beyond belief, beyond understanding, beyond pardon. Had the other Renshai heard the story, they would have punished Subikahn with a painful coward's death: starvation, deliberate infliction of a mortal disease, staking him out for animals to devour. In the entirety of his life, Saviar had never heard of any Renshai committing such a heinous crime, especially against his own brother.

Reliving the horror drove Saviar to incoherent rage. As answer, he drew both swords and plunged toward Calistin.

Fast as fire, Calistin met the attack, parrying both blades, then riposting in an instant. Limited by the table at his back, Saviar spun away, only to find the tips of Calistin's swords at his throat. That should have stopped him cold. An undeclared spar assumed first would-be fatal stroke as the endpoint. But Saviar harbored too much anger to quit after a single strike. With a howl of fury, he flung himself at Calistin again.

Again, Calistin parried and riposted; but this time Saviar managed to retreat far enough to keep the battle going. He attempted to use his superior size and weight against the irritating little fly speck, but Calistin moved like a snake, striking and retreating, never in one place long enough to slice or skewer. If Saviar's misplaced fury led to Calistin's death, no one would blame him, especially Calistin who believed a man not quick enough to save himself did not deserve to live. If Calistin killed Saviar, however, it would diminish him in the eyes of the other Renshai. A *torke* of Calistin's skill should have the ability to avoid harming another, even someone who seemed determined to die. If Saviar suffered from a mortal injury or illness, Calistin would not hesitate to take him down. In the absence of those things, he would do nothing worse than deliver some well-deserved nicks and bruises.

This time, Calistin did not seem interested in leaving his brother aching, at least not yet. He appeared almost to be humoring Saviar, which only fueled his rage. Saviar became a ruthless flurry of attack, while Calistin carefully rerouted the deadly assault, dodging rather than parrying, which allowed him to avoid the pounding strokes against his swords and delicate arms. When feasible, he darted through the most miniscule of openings to score light touches against various parts of Saviar's anatomy. In a real fight, Saviar would be dead ten times over, but he ignored these opportunities to end the spar.

Before Saviar knew it, Calistin had herded him into a faux forest clearing littered with debris. As he made a hard-edged lunge that forced Calistin to retreat, Saviar's foot came down on a branch that bruised his instep and rolled awkwardly. It upset his balance momentarily. Like any good Renshai, he instinctively found it almost instantly, but not quite fast enough for Calistin. The youngest of the brothers dove for the tiny opening just as Saviar veered forward, still on the attack even as he attempted to regain stability. Realizing he was about to impale himself, Saviar tried to shift mid-movement.

Sent three ways at once, he had no choice but to die or fall. He chose the latter, one knee touching the ground as he swung wide to save himself. He wound up in a crouch with the tips of Calistin's swords at his neck again.

Saviar froze. Any other action was suicide. Then, abruptly, he sheathed his weapons, rose, and brushed dirt from his britches with stiff strokes.

Calistin also sheathed his swords and waited, clearly uncertain what to say or do.

Thialnir rescued them both from speaking. He stood at the highest point, the top of the spiral staircase, which gave him an excellent view of every person in the room, currently all Renshai. "Could I have everyone's attention for a moment?"

Gradually, the clang of swords diminished, then stopped. All eyes found Thialnir.

As always, Thialnir went straight to the point. "I'm sorry for interrupting the spars and *svergelse*." They all knew everyone in the room wanted to listen to what he had to say. Otherwise, they would still be practicing. "When Béarn asked the Renshai for a representative, I was selected. The reasons don't matter now. At the time, any Renshai would have sufficed, and I mostly just listened to whatever they had to say and relayed it back to the tribe." He added with a twinkle in his bright green eyes, "When I had an opinion, I just gave it without any regard to procedure or what anyone else wanted to hear."

"Hear, hear!" someone shouted; Saviar could not tell who. He seized the opportunity to move away from Calistin to avoid having to talk or think about Subikahn.

Though he sported the standard Northern features that revealed the background of the Renshai, including fair skin and blond hair worn in multiple braids, Thialnir stood taller and broader than any other member of the tribe. Saviar had often suspected that was why he had been chosen rather than for any oratory skill. Renshai maneuvers relied on wiry quickness and skill rather than bulk, but the generals and leaders of other peoples tended toward great size. They would perceive a small or female Renshai as weak, regardless of ability. "As you know, Saviar and I just returned from a meeting. You all know about the missing soldiers, and thirty-seven Renshai are on that list: lost on the Outworlds, possibly alive. I know you want to know what we're doing to bring them home."

Saviar expected murmurs, but it only grew more silent. Everyone wanted to know.

Thialnir glanced at Saviar. "I've served as leader for a long time. When I started, it was a title without authority or even real meaning. Renshai fight without strategy or pattern; we don't obey orders. We just needed someone who could stand as our agent, and it didn't matter who we chose. But times have changed. Now, I find the tribe looking to me for real guidance, if only because I know things from those endless meetings I have to attend. Those occupy more of my time and require more wisdom, wile, quick-thinking and the ability to speak well. Those are not my strengths."

Thialnir left an opening for laughter or comments, but no one took it. If they felt he had not done a good job as leader, they chose not to express it. "I'm old now, and I want nothing more than to go back to being a regular Renshai. I have chosen to step down as leader, and I'd like to pass the mantle to my successor, Saviar Rakhirsson. He can tell you all what occurred at the latest meeting."

A sprinkling of applause met this pronouncement. All attention turned to Saviar, and a path opened for him to claim the high point of the room.

Saviar did not oblige. The last thing he wanted was attention, and it bothered him Thialnir had dropped this duty on him without any chance to think about it, to prepare. He felt bewildered, utterly overwhelmed, plagued by a barrage of ideas and emotions he doubted he could ever sort. All of his life, he had felt torn between his constant and overwhelming Renshai training and his desire to become a Knight of Erythane like his father and grandfather. He still harbored an innocent—most would say desperate—hope of doing both, though it seemed beyond impossible. To accept the position Thialnir offered meant permanently abandoning the dream he had clung to since childhood, and he was not ready to let go.

Too many terrible things had befallen Saviar in the last few months: his mother's death, which he had only just learned was essentially murder; the banishment of the Renshai from nearly all corners of the known world, hounded by armies of murderous Northmen; the inexplicable loss of his first and only girlfriend in the most awful way he could imagine; his own near-death experiences. That all seemed like more than any man should have to face in a lifetime, yet the most brutal of all his burdens was the most recent revelation: Subikahn was gone forever. *Gone.* Dead, he hoped, and by all rights. If the Mages of Myrcidë managed to haul him back to life, if he survived the Outworld, Saviar would have no choice but to kill the once-beloved brother who had betrayed him in a way no Renshai could ever possibly forgive.

It was a secret Saviar felt unable and unwilling to share with any-one, at the same time a burden he did not feel strong enough to bear alone. The terrible irony was that Subikahn was the one and only person with whom, in the past, he could share the worst moments of his life. If the other Renshai learned what Subikahn had done, they would be obliged to utterly destroy him. They would hold Saviar and Calistin blameless, but the shame would still affect them, especially the twin who had shared all the highs and lows of his life, the bright-est and darkest revelations. As much as he hated Subikahn at the moment, Saviar found himself incapable of shedding a lifetime memory of love and closeness, and that bothered him nearly as much as the treason itself. It seemed grossly unfair to share that pain and shame with Calistin, who was only just learning social conventions and how to feel and display emotions, or with their father, who was just emerging from the dark pit of despair after Kevral's abrupt and terrible death.

Every Renshai eye was riveted on Saviar, and the silence hung over him like a lead-weighted cloak. Overwhelmed by his own thoughts and feelings, fighting to hold himself together, Saviar kept the explanation terse, "We learned there's a friendly *Kjempemagiska* named Kentt, who is currently staying in Béarn with his three-year-old daughter. The elves are figuring out how to rescue the missing and will report back in two days. That's all we know."

The Renshai continued to stare at Saviar, some with open mouths. He had imparted significant information in just two sen-tences and with no outward display of emotion or any suggestions. "I appreciate your confidence in my abilities, but I am declining the honor. I cannot be your leader."

Thialnir's face went blank with shock; he resembled a lost tod-dler. After a moment, he regained enough composure to say, "Then I'll hold onto the title a bit longer until I can find and train a suitable replacement." That said, he rushed down the stairs toward Saviar.

Worried he might break down in front of everyone, Saviar turned and headed for the door as Thialnir ran after him. "Wait, Saviar! I need to talk to you."

Saviar saw Thialnir glance at Calistin as he passed. Either he questioned aloud or merely with an expression, but whatever he said or did elicited a broad shrug and head shake from Calistin. Before Thialnir could reach him, Saviar slipped out the door, found the nearest exit, and escaped into Béarn's courtyard.

CHAPTER 3

We are a product of our experiences, no matter how hard we try to escape them.

—*Knight-Captain Kedrin*

AT KING GRIFF'S ORDER, Béarn's great hall had been emptied of all its furniture. Though Tem'aree'ay had lived in the castle for nearly two decades, she still reveled in the wide-open spaces usually found only outside of human constructs. Griff had won her over with his inherent thoughtfulness and empathy. He always tried to assure the maximal comfort of any guests, be they city folk, farmers, elves, or Renshai. The sturdy palace had walls of mountain stone, but the great hall contained wood paneling carved into intricate patterns by Béarnian craftsmen. The elves also appreciated its bare floor boards.

The inherent magic of elves made them chaotic at the best of times. In their natural habitat, they flitted and danced through the woodlands, tossing spells at will and copulating whenever the mood struck, which was often. They needed no permanent shelters; weather had barely existed on Alfheim and they were created impervious to wind, rain, and cold. They worried nothing for family units, and pregnancy occurred only after the natural death of an elf, the soul recycled into the fetus. No one knew or cared about biology. They all shared the parenting for their rare infants and children.

Frustrated by the impossibility of keeping all of the elves focused on one task simultaneously, Captain had broken them into groups. But even that seemed doomed to failure. Tem'aree'ay could see one bunch engaging in pirouettes, another in mating rituals, and her own unit's discussion had devolved into the oddities of human illness and healing processes when compared to the elves' immunities. Like many of the groups, Tem'aree'ay's had formed because of a shared specialization, in their case healing magic, and she seized the moment of distraction to discuss the matter that had occupied her mind, day and night, for the last eighteen years.

First, Tem'aree'ay glanced around the room to assure herself that Captain was not in the vicinity to steer them back to the proper topic: brainstorming for the rescue mission. Finding him engaged in conversation with a group on the far side of the room, she asked her companions, "What do you think about the possibility of tearing down the wall that prevents Ivana Shorith'na Cha-tella Tir Hya'sellirian Albar from hearing *khohlar*?"

The other six elves in Tem'aree'ay's group stopped speaking to turn and stare at her. The shortened form of the half-elfin, half-Béarnian princess' name had become synonymous with anathema in elfin culture. They referred to the prospective progeny of elves with humans as "ivanas" and not in homage. They hated Ivana from the moment her extensive abnormalities became known, and they had avoided any contact with humans as a result. Only the war had finally brought them, reluctantly, together.

Shortly before the war, Tem'aree'ay had finally persuaded the elves to examine Ivana, though most had avoided her, and the others had done it without hiding their revulsion. They had confirmed Ivana was the one creature in all the nine main worlds who could not receive *khohlar* and also Tae Kahn's belief this stemmed from some type of congenital barrier in her mind. Then, the war had intervened.

Now, the other elfin healers stared at Tem'aree'ay in silence. For a change, their canted gemlike eyes conveyed more confusion than bitterness.

No longer willing to pussyfoot around her peers, Tem'aree'ay reminded them: "You all know she deserves your help. If not for Ivana, we would all be dead."

The others still studied Tem'aree'ay curiously. Although she believed they all knew, she explained into their silence. "When the *Kjempemagiska* figured out how to combine their magic and assaulted us in a single wave, they nearly broke us. We all surrendered to panic and despair except for Ivana Shorith'na Cha-tella Tir Hya'sellirian Albar. She alone remained focused, and we rebuilt our *jovinay arythanik* around her. She never wavered, not for an instant, because she had no understanding of defeat. She did what she had to do; and, had she not, the *Kjempemagiska* would have destroyed us all: elves, humans, and Myrcidians alike. If not for Ivana, elves would no longer exist."

The other healers could not deny it. They owed an enormous debt of gratitude to the disabled half-breed they had so long reviled.

Ghy'rinith Ha-tarian Exar Myrintus Ashon'tae responded first. "Several of us have touched the wall in your daughter's mind that shields her from *khohlar*." It was an odd way to describe the situation. *Khohlar* was merely a form of communication, of no danger to any creature. "As you know, we attempted to remove it but were unable. It cannot be banished."

Myr-intha Tariash El'bar Kay Torrin'arka explained further. "It's . . . semi-solid. When you punch a hole in it with magic, it . . ." She struggled for words and used her hands to simulate flowing motions. "It *glorbits* and gloops in to fill the gap." She invented words to describe an action she better explained with the *khohlar* that accompanied her speech. The image reminded Tem'aree'ay of overly wet clay.

Tem'aree'ay recalled Tae referring to the barrier as "mudlike." She asked softly, "Then it's impossible to remove?"

Several of the healers exchanged glances that suggested there was more, but they did not want to vocalize it.

"Tell me," Tem'aree'ay insisted. Though she, too, used mostly healing magics, she specialized in exterior injuries as well as human and animal illnesses. Only a handful of elves could use their magic to pierce a skull, and she was not one of them.

Myr-intha raised her eyes to the ceiling, as if studying words written there. "Perhaps not impossible."

Several of the others made motions as if to shush her, and Tem'aree'ay could almost feel the direct *khohlar* they sent to her fellow healer. Myr-intha glanced at Tem'aree'ay, but it was too late to change her mind. Her last three words had clinched it. Tem'aree'ay would not stop pressing until she had the answer, and they all knew it.

Myr-intha continued, "We have heard that human healers, on rare occasions, have worked inside a skull." She hesitated, her emerald eyes now fixed on Tem'aree'ay. "Yes?"

King Griff's first wife was an accomplished human healer, and Tem'aree'ay had held discussions with her about many areas of medicine. Matrinka had once mentioned that pounding a metal spike through a warrior's skull had relieved pressure inside the brain cavity and saved his life. The resultant permanent hole in his head did not appear to diminish his life in any way. Tem'aree'ay knew little more about the process, but she nodded anyway. Any other response might impede the flow of information. "I've heard of such a thing, yes." The implications struck her suddenly. "Are you suggesting I find a human willing to break open Ivana's skull?"

Myr-intha shifted from foot to foot.

Though the idea rankled, Tem'aree'ay refused to put Myr-intha off. Once she had the full explanation, Tem'aree'ay might find a different and better way to use it. "I'm certain Matrinka would know where to find such a healer, but he or she would certainly need elfin guidance. Are you saying you'd be willing to assist? To work with this human?"

Myr-intha seemed to shrink a bit. For a moment, Tem'aree'ay thought she might disappear.

Ghy'rinith stepped up. "I would."

Tem'aree'ay felt certain *khohlar* pelted Ghy'rinith; but, unlike Myr-intha, she did not wither beneath it. "We owe Ivana Shorith'na Cha-tella Tir Hya'sellirian Albar that much, but you need to understand. Such a procedure is not without danger."

"Danger," Tem'aree'ay repeated. She had forced herself to focus on keeping her fellows talking and deliberately thrust details aside. Now, the realization of what they were contemplating struck her fully. *Cut open Ivana's head and remove something from it.* She had once seen a man walk into a healer's tent with a spear tip protruding from behind his left ear and its shaft jutting from his forehead. Though upset, he seemed in no apparent pain. That changed when the healers pulled it free, and he abruptly exsanguinated. "You're saying Ivana might die."

Myr-intha nodded. "She might. We don't know how frail an—" She stopped herself from saying "ivana." "A hybrid creature with an elf and a human as parents might be."

Tem'aree'ay understood. Some declared mongrel dogs and mules more resilient than their pureblooded peers, while others dismissed the notion. Ivana was the only creature in existence born of an elf yet not fully elfin. They had no way to know if she would prove hardier, the same as one of her parents, or more fragile than both of them. Though she had significant congenital abnormalities, she had not yet developed any of the illnesses that plagued humans. "You're saying we'd be risking her life for only the benefit of allowing her to hear *khohlar*."

Ghy'rinith and Myr-intha exchanged glances.

Tem'aree'ay stepped between them. She would not give them the opportunity to converse privately too long. It might result in a mutual pact of silence on the issue. Neither did she attempt *khohlar*. The indirect type would carry to everyone in the room, and the direct would only reach one mind. Right now, she wanted the instant attention of both. "Tell me," she fairly hissed. "Tell me everything."

Both of the other elves nodded agreement, and Myr-intha explained, "Other than the wall, we can find nothing abnormal about the brain of Ivana Shorith'na Cha-tella Tir Hya'sellirian Albar. If the wall were removed . . ."

It was a sentence destined to never be finished. In such a unique situation, no one could guess the result, but the implications were enormous. *Is it actually possible Ivana could become . . . normal?* Tem'aree'ay did not dare to hope.

Ghy'rinith added, "The wall has changed since the first time we scanned her. It has grown and become less cohesive, more mushy. We believe this process has been going on since her birth and suspect we might have been able to remove it with magic in its early stages had we only known to look for it."

Tem'aree'ay froze, the knowledge overwhelming on several levels. Ivana could have developed normally, might still be capable of doing so or, at least, not worsening. It also meant even if every half-breed was born with such a barrier, magic might remedy the problem at the time of birth. "Beloved Frey," she whispered, then returned to the necessary. "If we attempt to remove it, she might die. If we leave it there . . ?" She stopped, hoping one of the others would finish the thought.

Ghy'rinith complied, "I believe it will continue to grow and change, but I don't know what that means for her future. If we could remove even a piece of it, we could examine it directly and with magic. We would learn so much more."

Tem'aree'ay's options became terrifyingly real. Risk her daughter's life to save her, a difficult enough decision; but so much more lay at stake. Examination of this substance could help determine if it was something uniquely Ivana's, an assured side effect of combining human blood with elfin or something in-between. And that had implications for the tiny new life taking shape in her womb.

For eighteen years, Tem'aree'ay had refused King Griff a second mixed-breed child, at first focused solely on her daughter; then, as Ivana's problems became clear, worrying about bringing another child like her into the world. Tae Kahn had finally convinced Tem'aree'ay the only way to know for certain whether Ivana was an anomaly or the classic face of interbreeding was to create another baby and deal with any consequences.

The subject changed abruptly, as it often did among elves, but Tem'aree'ay could not channel her thoughts in any other direction. Fixated on the possibilities, she mulled over them long after Captain finally brought the group back to the issue at hand. She and Griff had a choice to make, and no one could possibly envy it. Two young lives, one unborn, now hung in the balance and the future relationship of elves and mankind with them.

Saviar had no idea where he intended to go until he found himself at the edge of Erythane's Bellenet Fields. Surrounded by woodlands and weeds, he listened to the crash of steel and the shouts of the armsmen as the Knights of Erythane practiced battle maneuvers with a multitude of weapons. Peering around copses and between trees, Saviar was able to locate his father. Ra-khir wielded a wooden approximation of a short-hafted battle-ax against a polearm substitute Saviar could not identify in the hands of Sir Edwin.

Besieged by emotion, Saviar had instinctively gone to his childhood place of comfort. So often, he had escaped the constant swordwork of the Renshai and their unrelenting *torke* who were never satisfied with his attempts to perfect the intricate maneuvers. "Again!" they would roar. "Again!" His mother had been the worst of them, hounding him toward the perfection his younger brother naturally displayed. Always a level behind Calistin, then two, thrilled and embarrassed by his brother's passing all the tests of manhood long before Saviar or Subikahn were prepared to try a single one.

The worst moments of his life had driven Saviar to the Bellenet Fields to watch his father and the other knights learn lessons not only in warcraft but morality, riding, grooming, judgment, decorum, and other disciplines that meant less than nothing to the Renshai. So many times, Saviar had imagined himself on a well-muscled white charger riding in resplendent formation beside the father and the grandfather he loved and admired. Erythane's boys gathered on benches and crates, perched on fences, or hunkered down to stare in awe at the knights, nearly all of them with the same desires and dreams as Saviar. Becoming a knight was the pinnacle achievement for Erythane's youth; now, with six lost to the war, actual openings had appeared to fuel what was, for most of them, unattainable fantasy.

The training would prove too grueling, the commitment too extreme, their wits or bodies not swift enough. For Saviar, the Renshai training had undone him. Every moment of every day, he was Renshai first, and no one would allow any Renshai to forget it. He had had barely enough stolen time to learn manners and ethics from his father. No weapon other than a sword, the only one revered by Renshai, had filled his hand.

Apparently finished, Ra-khir and Edwin stepped back with grand gestures of appreciation and exchanged bows of acknowledgment.

Ra-khir turned to face his squire, Darby. The boy eagerly leaped from his perch on a fence rail supporting several practice weapons, from which he had been watching intently. Edwin exchanged his polearm for a practice battle-ax, which he proffered to Darby.

With a crisp gesture of gratitude, Darby accepted the weapon. Ra-khir crouched, waiting for the imminent attack. Darby's first sweep was clumsy, sending him off-balance, and opening him to a gentle tap from Ra-khir. The exchange looked ridiculously slow to a man trained to the exacting standards of Renshai from the moment his chubby toddler fingers could close around a scaled-down hilt. Though too far away to hear the words, Saviar could see his father's mouth moving. A slight smile touched Darby's lips, and he nodded appreciatively.

Saviar could scarcely imagine that sort of teaching, clearly not the scalding look and spat insult he would have received from his *torke* had he made any move so awkward. But the method seemed to work for Darby. His next attack demonstrated more confidence and the one after still more. Apparently inspired by Ra-khir's words, Darby's attacks became more competent as well.

Not for the first time, jealousy welled up in Saviar. He had so long wanted to work with Ra-khir, to train with the father who seemed to have boundless patience. He would never forsake his Renshai training, the finest in the world, but he could not help wishing it had granted him more time to work with Ra-khir, more chances to sample the life of a knight. Saviar had accompanied his father and grandfather on a few missions, just enough to ignite a craving for more. And now that Saviar believed he might finally have the time, Ra-khir's attention had riveted on a stranger. Worse, Ra-khir had clearly fallen for Darby's mother. When they married, Darby would become his son, and Ra-khir would have no more need for a child who talked of the knight's life but could not spare the effort to chase it. Darby, on the other hand, happily devoted his life to becoming a Knight of Erythane and had no other responsibilities to stand in his way.

For several moments, Darby and Ra-khir exchanged thrusts, the elder pausing to demonstrate a different hold, another technique. Saviar always knew his father would make a great teacher. He watched as Darby grew more sure-footed, as his assaults became more furious and directed. His skill had visibly improved by the time Ra-khir claimed both weapons and set them against the rail with the others. After they exchanged bows and gestures, Ra-khir tousled the boy's mouse-brown hair, speaking softly, and they both laughed with abandon.

The gleeful sound pierced Saviar like a knife. Unable to stand another moment of the bonding that should have been his, he whirled, charging into the forest. Ra-khir had spoken to him about the situation, had assured Saviar that Darby had not usurped his place, that apprenticeship was not a prerequisite for becoming a Knight of Erythane. Because he had a low upbringing and no previous knowledge of weapons, Darby needed far more training and experience to pass the necessary tests. In any case, Ra-khir had told Saviar, he would never have taken his own son as his apprentice. But, given the obvious affection developing between Ra-khir and Tiega, it all seemed like a lie.

Saviar whipped by trees at a dangerous pace. Vines seized his ankles. Thistles tore at his clothing and striped his hands with blood. Something lashed out at him from the brush. Even as the world whipped by him in a vast green haze, Saviar recognized hostility in the movement. Drawing his sword, he spun to face it. Something heavy slammed his knuckles, and his sword flew from his hand.

With a lurch, Saviar caught the hilt before the blade could touch the ground and be dishonored. As he leaned forward, a hand lashed out and slapped him, hard, across the face.

Though less painful than smashed knuckles, the barehanded attack was raw insult. Rage flared to a bonfire. Saviar loosed a battle cry and charged his opponent, a man-sized shadow awash in greenery. His sword, *Motfrabelonning*, slashed the foliage, showering Saviar with bits of leaf and stem. But his opponent's sword was faster, weaving through Saviar's defense like a swarm of black flies, stinging here and there but never wounding.

A red fog filled Saviar's vision, and fire seemed to course through his veins. He knew of only one swordsman skilled enough to treat him this way. "Calistin, you bastard child of *wisules*!" Rage made him oblivious to the personal insult. He had just referred to his own parents as the world's most cowardly rodents. "Leave me alone!" He retreated far enough to force his opponent into the open.

The other did spring from the sheltering copse. Enveloped in a tight-fitting cloak with raised hood, he, or possibly she, was unidentifiable. Average-sized and lacking Saviar's muscular bulk, the figure lunged at Saviar with the speed of a straight-shot arrow. Saviar managed a swift dodge. A second sword appeared in the other's hand, as if magically summoned from the air. It slammed Saviar's shin hard enough to bruise.

With a howl, Saviar also drew a second sword, assaulting his attacker with hammerlike blows intended to drive him to the ground.

Instead of parrying, the other slid in and out of the attacks, wraith-like. A foot darted between Saviar's, hooked an ankle, and pulled. Fighting for balance, Saviar found it, against all odds, then the toe of his boot wedged under a tree root. Off-balanced again, Saviar fell prey to a measured push from his opponent that sprawled him. The tip of two swords found Saviar's throat before he could roll to safety.

Saviar froze. The enemy swords hovered at his neck. Wind swept down the other's hood, revealing gold hair flecked with silver, blunt cheekbones, and a wizened unfamiliar face. It made no sense. Saviar knew every one of the three hundred odd Renshai, and this man was not one of them. Yet he had definitely used their techniques and maneuvers with a skill only Calistin might match. "If you're going to kill me, do it already."

The swords retreated, and the stranger stepped back. Saviar had used the common tongue, but he replied in Renshai, "If I were going to kill you, I would have." He sheathed his swords.

Saviar leaped to his feet. The proper retort died on his lips. Suggesting it would take this man and more to do so was clearly false and would only make him appear foolish. "Who in deepest, coldest Hel are you?"

"You've seen me before, Saviar Ra-khirsson, though I wouldn't expect you to recognize me. It was during the war, and you were too engrossed with your own battles to take much notice of mine."

The only possible answer sprang into Saviar's mind as if placed there. "Colbey." Swiftly, he sheathed his swords and dropped to one knee.

Colbey's face opened in surprise. "What are you doing?"

Saviar glanced up. "Showing you proper deference," he explained. "You're an immortal. You live among the gods."

Colbey's tone hardened. "Stand up, or I really will run you through!"

Saviar clambered to his feet.

"Elves are essentially immortal, too. Do you kneel at their feet?"

Saviar did not bother to answer the clearly rhetorical question. He waited for Colbey to reveal his purpose.

Instead, he received philosophy: "Anger is a dangerous master. It saps a warrior of sound judgment and bodily control, both necessary in war."

Saviar had heard the same words from his mother, who had frequently quoted Colbey Calistinsson. Hearing them from the mouth of their original speaker spiraled chills through his entire being and reminded him of something Ra-khir had once said, *A man of honor never allows emotions to control him.* "You're right," Saviar admitted. "I would have fared far better in that humiliating exchange if I had kept control of my temper."

"Indeed," Colbey said. Then, as if to contradict his own point, he continued. "Anger has its place and its purpose, Saviar. It can change the world. The problem is it's far too easy; anyone can become angry. But rare is the man who can channel it properly, who can use it to make himself stronger, better, wiser. Do you understand?"

Saviar shook his head. "Not yet, but I'll think on it. I'm sure it will come."

Colbey nodded. They both knew he did not need to say anything more about the matter. Saviar would, eventually, realize the point the immortal Renshai wished to make and it would stick with him better if he discovered it on his own.

Worried to lose an opportunity he might never have again, Saviar asked the question that had plagued him for years. "In the war, I saw your charger. You really are a Knight of Erythane. A *Renshai* Knight of Erythane."

"For centuries. And yet, that's the first time I've ever gotten called to duty."

Ra-khir had come up with the idea, when the battle had seemed lost. Ultimately, that action had changed the tide of the war. Saviar could understand why the knights had never called Colbey up before. He had earned his title back in the days when slaying a Knight of Erythane in fair combat won the victor his slain foe's position in the ranks. Early on, the knights had probably been relieved Colbey had taken his charger and gone. Over time, he was forgotten or presumed dead. Any leader who did remember him probably believed it safer not to command service from someone as powerful and dangerous as the immortal Renshai. "Do you think it's possible, in this day and age, for a Renshai to also become a knight?"

Colbey did not hesitate or resort to riddles. "I believe anything is possible. Do you wish to become a knight, too?"

"Yes?" Saviar said.

Colbey's eyebrows inched upward just a hair.

"Yes," Saviar said, more firmly. "I do."

"Then why haven't you?"

Saviar launched into the familiar explanation. "You know Renshai training doesn't leave time for anything else. Then we were banished from the West. As we traveled eastward, we were repeatedly attacked by Northmen. I nearly died of blood poisoning, and it took months and magic to recover." Mentioning that reminded him of

Subikahn's betrayal, and pain lurched through his jaw. His teeth clenched so tightly, it became difficult to talk. "As soon as we got back, we went straight to war."

Colbey's brows continued to rise. "And now?"

"Now?" Saviar repeated.

"Why are you wasting your time dithering with a withered old man when you could be passing your tests of knighthood?"

Saviar managed a chuckle. "I find it safest to respond when I'm attacked, and what Renshai could resist matching his skill against a superior foe?" He needed to add, "Besides, becoming a Knight of Erythane has become a bit more complicated over the centuries. Most train for years to pass the proper tests; and, even then, they only allow a total of twenty-four."

"Twenty-five," Colbey inserted.

"Twenty-five." Saviar acknowledged Sir Colbey, who had gotten left out of the child's rhymes and historical texts at least for the last couple of centuries. "So the trainees have to wait for an opening that may never happen." Even as the words emerged, Saviar realized how silly they sounded. Currently, finding voids was not an issue.

The pale arch of hair over each of Colbey's stolid blue-gray eyes now nearly reached his hairline. His face opened, accentuating four parallel lines of scar tissue marring one cheek, directly in front of his ear. "Have you not yet mastered the necessary sword skills, son of Kevral?"

Colbey had chosen his words carefully, to remind Saviar of his mother's obsession with everything Renshai. "Of course I could pass the hardest test of sword skill the knights could throw at me. But their tests include mastery of several other weapons. Also, arduous decisions that assess ethics and judgment."

"Renshai learn swords of every length and type, how to best use them in any situation, even two at a time without belittling one to the status of a shield. We sweep, we strike, we thrust. We block, parry, disarm, and riposte. We even learn uses for the sides along with the edges and tip."

Knuckles still smarting from Colbey's attack, Saviar did not need another demonstration.

"Do you really believe the techniques we learn don't apply to other weapons? That battle ethics and circumstance change depending on the hilt in your hand?"

Saviar stared at the immortal Renshai, his words near to sacrilege. Renshai considered other weapons inferior at best, cowardly under certain circumstances. No self-respecting Renshai would ever touch a polearm or a bow of any kind. No Renshai learned to hurl a stone, dart, or dagger. Killing from a distance stole the ability of worthy opponents to earn themselves a rightful place in Valhalla.

Colbey laughed at Saviar's reaction. "If you want to become both knight and Renshai in the current age, you will have to learn to behave as one or the other under the proper circumstances. A knight can wear armor, Saviar; there are times he must. A Renshai would die before donning anything that could turn a weapon and is never constrained by rigid morality or decorum."

Colbey had an undeniable point Saviar had worried like a dog with a bone so thick he could barely mark it. He knew he possessed the skills and mindset to become a Knight of Erythane, but he struggled with the day-to-day details. There was no such thing as half a Renshai, and Knights of Erythane were at the beck and call of their captain and their kings at all hours of every day. "How can I possibly mesh the two?" Saviar aimed the question as much at himself as Colbey, and when he received no answer, he became more direct. "How do *you* do it?"

Colbey's eyebrows finally fell to their neutral position. "Mostly by being forgotten. I've gotten called to duty exactly once in three hundred years. Even then, I received no specific command other than to assist in the battle, which I did using nothing but my swords in my own unencumbered Renshai way." His eyes twinkled, and a half-smile wreathed his lips. Even after so long, he still loved the thrill of pitting his skills against those of enemies, the clash of steel against steel, the excitement of risking his life for the greater good. Saviar suddenly realized the old Renshai rarely got the chance to participate in a true fight anymore. Surely, he sparred with his son, the *Valkyries*, and the gods. He might even skirmish with the *Einherjar* in Valhalla when the whim took him, but it was not the same as mortal war.

Saviar doubted the Knights of Erythane would grant him the same leeway as Colbey. Instead, the combination could become a balancing act doomed to failure. "Do you truly believe I could pass the knight's weapon testing today?"

Colbey shrugged. "I can't imagine why you couldn't. In the process of practicing counterattacks to every type of weapon, you inadvertently had to learn their proper function. Besides that, I know you spent many hours watching the knights learn those techniques, and you had to absorb some of that knowledge as well."

Saviar stiffened. "How do you know that?" His words emerged more defensively than he intended.

A grin appeared on Colbey's face, accentuating his ancient scars.

"Every son of Erythane spends hours studying the Knights of Erythane, and you love your father and grandfather. Also, in addition to being a Knight of Erythane and a Renshai, I was once the Western Wizard and the world's champion of Law. In inheriting that power, I learned to read minds."

"History claims you represented chaos."

"History is wrong," Colbey said mildly. "And that misconception ultimately destroyed the system of the Cardinal Wizards and broke the Pica Stone." He did not wait for that revelation to sink in before returning to their original tack. "And as far as morality and appraisal, I find it difficult to believe Kedrin and Ra-khir did not teach you all you need to know to confront the most grueling test."

Saviar could not deny it. Less than a year ago, they had even allowed him to pass judgment on a conflict between two Westerners over ownership of a foal and had praised his handling of the situation. He did not mention the incident to Colbey. It might seem like bragging, and it hardly mattered anyway if the immortal Renshai could really read his mind.

Saviar shoved aside his self-serving web of thought to address the issue more significant to the continent. "Colbey, are you aware more than a thousand warriors and elves have become trapped on random Outworlds?"

Colbey nodded, lips pursed grimly. "I am, Saviar. A difficult situation, indeed."

Saviar shuffled a toe through the leaf mold, uncertain if he had the right to ask, if doing so might offend the immortal Renshai. "If Knight-Captain Kedrin called you up again, would you be able—"

"No." Colbey did not allow Saviar to finish the thought. "I'm an immortal now. I consort with gods . . ." He quashed a smile. "Well, a goddess at least, on a daily basis. My actions among mortals, even ones as small as this, can have consequences on the great balance of the universe."

"But," Saviar started. "You assisted in the World's War when he called you."

"I did." Colbey sucked in a lungful of air and released it slowly. "I'm not up for a days'-long lecture on timing, Saviar. You just need to understand there are times when I can step in and times I just can't or I simply shouldn't. It's not really that different than when humans call upon the gods who choose to answer or ignore their pleas. I'm less powerful . . ." He winked, "Or so they believe. I also have a better and closer understanding of the great Balance, having championed it. I'm more likely to intervene because I'm more interested in the affairs of mortals, having been one for a great deal of time; but even I can't muck around on Midgard without causing more problems than I solve."

Saviar nodded. He did understand, and he felt blessed to have the immortal Renshai find him worthy of one of his rare visits.

Colbey added, almost apologetically. "In this case, I couldn't help anyway. I don't have any real magic, just enough to get me where I want to go. You're far better off with Captain." He gave Saviar only a moment to consider before finally addressing the reason for his presence. "Can you do me the favor of arranging a meeting with Calistin?"

Discomfort rose in Saviar at the mere mention of his younger brother's name. Growing up, he had found Calistin a burden beyond endurance, often the reason he had sneaked away to spend his off-time watching Ra-khir and the other knights. Now, his annoyance seemed misplaced, so he discarded it and granted Colbey a smile. Though still inhumanly competent with a sword, Calistin was clearly struggling to become more socially adept as well. More and more often, he was daring to let his weaknesses show and nearly always to Saviar.

A man of honor never allows emotions to control him. Abruptly, Saviar realized he had become a victim to rage, to jealousy, to bitterness far too many times in the last few days. *Anger is a dangerous master. It saps a warrior of sound judgment and bodily control, both necessary in war.* "I'd be happy to relay any message from you to Calistin, and I'm certain he would relish the chance to meet and spar with you."

Colbey laughed. "Oh, we've matched swords on several occasions, and I'm not so certain he's eager to do it again. But I would appreciate your telling him to meet me at the easternmost edge of the Fields of Wrath at sundown."

Saviar had no idea Colbey and Calistin had met, other than the time most of the tribe, given the right to return to their homes on the Fields of Wrath, had been confronted by self-named Paradesians who had declared themselves the proper owners. Saviar had not been among them, but he had heard the stories, including the fact that Colbey had bested several Renshai simultaneously but had deftly dodged confronting Calistin sword to sword.

Colbey turned, heading back the way he had come, then stopped suddenly. "One more thing, Saviar."

Saviar nodded, certain he would receive more sage advice, though he currently had plenty to mull.

"If you ever refer to Calistin's parents as *wisules* again, you may not fare as well as you did today." Then, Colbey was gone.

Knuckles and shins aching, covered with stinging welts from Colbey's sword, remembering both blades at his helpless throat, Saviar could hardly imagine faring worse than he had. The threat itself confused him. Even at his most irksome, Calistin had always ignored Saviar's verbal insults, especially when they maligned their shared parents rather than Calistin himself. He could not shake the feeling Colbey was warning him of something more dangerous even than Calistin's wrath; but whatever he might have meant was currently lost on Saviar.

As he walked back toward the Fields of Wrath, Saviar's thoughts went to the more pressing matter of his mood and actions. Everything upset and annoyed him now; anger and envy had plagued him since the day Chymmerlee's love had turned to hatred only because she had discovered he was Renshai. Of course, many discomforting things had arisen out of that situation that could ruin anyone's mood: tasked with winning over Chymmerlee's people, Ra-khir and the other knights had warned and threatened Saviar away from her; she had attempted to kill Saviar; her people had imprisoned him, swordless, in a solitary manner that had driven him to madness. Chymmerlee and the other Mages of Myrcidë had accused Saviar of raping her, even though he had stolen nothing more intimate than an occasional, readily-returned kiss.

Upon his eventual return home, Saviar had discovered slothful, hate-filled Paradesians had taken over the Renshai's ancestral home and stolen all of their possessions while nearly all of the Renshai languished in Erythane's dungeons. With the substantial assistance of Weile Kahn, Saviar had remedied the situation, only to face magical giants in a war that had nearly claimed the lives of every human and elf on the continent.

Now, with the war over and his people put essentially to right, Saviar needed to return to his usual strong, contemplative and sociable self. In the past, it came naturally to him. Now, he found it more often than not an uphill battle. Resentment drove him to escape the responsibility thrust upon him by Thialnir, Ra-khir and, formerly, himself. It was taking far too much effort to free himself from negative emotions, so much easier to surrender to adolescent angst and escape the bonds of society and adulthood.

Guilt added itself to the boiling mixture. Saviar loved the world, and his place in it, too much to withdraw. The Renshai needed him, his father craved his attention and his blessing, Calistin required a guide in the new world that had opened since he developed a primitive form of what Saviar could only describe as empathy. And Subikahn . . .

A smile crawled onto Saviar's face instinctively, from nearly two decades of experience loving his twin, then disappeared beneath a torrent of anger. This, Saviar recognized, was the true source of his current torment. All the terrible things that had happened to him paled in comparison; he had weathered them all and only come out stronger, or would have, had it not been for his brother's unforgivable betrayal. Most likely, Subikahn was dead. He had already made what he had believed to be his dying confession, clearing his own conscience at the price of Saviar's reason. Saviar's recent difficulty letting go of past hurts, his inflexibility, his pointless resentments all came down to the agony of knowing the person he had always trusted, to whom he had bonded in the womb, the one he had loved most in the world had committed the cruelest of all crimes against him, had nearly assured his eternal condemnation in Hel.

For the sake of others, for his own sanity, Saviar knew he had to find a way to let it go. He could not forgive or forget, but he could relegate the knowledge to a deeper corner of his mind and not allow it free rein to control his emotions, to poison every part of his life. *Anger is a dangerous master.* Colbey was right, regardless of what name Saviar gave it. Any or all of the negative emotions had the power to pollute his thoughts, dreams, and actions, to destroy his future and his relationships, to hurt those around him who did not deserve to suffer.

But realization was not enough. Saviar knew he had to free himself from the tyranny of his emotions, yet actually doing so took more than just understanding. He would have to fight it with the same tenacity and attention he had given his sword training. He only hoped it would not take nearly as long.

CHAPTER 4

Humans tend to see bias where it doesn't exist and to think in conclusions.

—*Arak'bar Tulamii Dhor*

EVEN THE ENORMOUS GREAT HALL with its wooden paneling and floorboards seemed confining to the elves, especially after the servants had replaced much of its furniture. Captain stood in front of a small but sturdy table that held the Pica Stone, his hands resting on its smooth surface, the other elves massed behind him. Humans sat on benches around multiple long tables, mostly those who had attended the meeting. Tae Kahn was there from the start this time, his hands absently stroking the cat sprawled across his lap. Several of Béarn's heirs had joined the throng, too, along with their Renshai bodyguards. King Griff and Queen Matrinka attended, of course, and his second wife joined the *jovinay arythanik*. The last of Griff's wives, Xoraida, rarely took part in any political process, including the current proceedings. The giant, Kentt, was also conspicuously absent, to Captain's relief. He made the humans apprehensive and the elves even more so because unknown magical abilities made the *Kjempemagiska* dangerous in ways the humans could not understand.

The Pica Stone felt warm and familiar against Captain's salt-stained, callused palms. He remembered the effort it had taken to reconstruct it, dragging the smaller bits and pieces in to join the larger shards rescued from the Outworlds, shaping and steadying with all the power of the *jovinay arythanik* flowing through him. He still reveled in the joy that had spiked through him when he felt the first tingle of magic returning to the savaged sapphire. Only the gods knew where the power of the worlds' greatest artifact originated; history suggested the Cardinal Wizards had infused it as a team, before their differing charges had turned them into enemies. Its destruction had been a tragedy few had the means to contemplate.

Now, as Captain stroked the Pica, he experienced a mixture of pride and sorrow. He could feel the chaos it contained, the vast potential of its power beyond even the combined might of all the elves massed as one. This much, the elves had restored to it; yet he could also feel rare thready disruptions wound around and through its core, those tiny nagging places where the smidgens had not perfectly fused despite their best and longest efforts. He knew the Wizards had mostly used the Pica for scrying during the Tasks of Wizardry, which had determined the suitability of their successors. The presence of the Pica, and all four Cardinal Wizards, had been necessary to construct the other rare items with permanent magic. It was an artifact of vast beauty and power, and Captain wished he understood it fully, worried his imperfect fix might, someday, cause a problem. Something so special deserved flawless reparation; thus far, however, the gods had shown no interest in assisting.

The elves began their chant, their voices rising and falling, flowing seamlessly through one another in a sound that had come to define the intertwining of magic. Captain drew in that chaos, channeling it through the Pica Stone and directing it to three others. Ladori Ma'hellorian Naf-talis Ark Venarith Te was the most suited for locating traces of elfin magic. Buoyed by the *jovinay arythanik* and the Pica, she could find evidence of elfin existence beyond the nine explored worlds. Two others would collaborate on creating a gate, while Captain stabilized the doorlike shape that would cue any elves on the opposite side of it.

Gradually, the gate took shape, at first a single spark. At length, a spindly form appeared against an empty area of wall. Focused on funneling magic, Captain barely heard the sharp intake of human breath. He had warned them to stay away from the place the elves planned to put the gate to prevent them from bumbling into the way. They would not even be capable of seeing it until it reached its most formed state, and then only as a vague outline that required nearly as much imagination as vision. Only the rare few armed with magical weapons, all but one of them Renshai, would be capable of perceiving it as fully as the elves did.

Captain concentrated on keeping his breathing even and his mind focused, despite the myriad of emotions grinding through him. Expectation drove him to hold his breath, fear of the unknown to hide, concern for the missing to weep. Need overcame them all. He had to stand his ground and maintain control of the vast chaos flowing through and around him. To do otherwise meant dooming every soul in the room.

Finally, a welcome whisper of elfin magic added itself to his burden. Somewhere far away an elf touched the gate from the opposite side, adding his or her own chaos to the mix. Nothing appeared different, but everything had changed. The door was now open, allowing anyone to step through it in either direction. A few of the elves shifted position, sending an all but imperceptible wave through their fused magic, the only sign they, too, had detected the change.

Something poked through the gate and swiftly withdrew. A moment later, a long-fingered hand appeared, attached to a slender wrist and a barely larger forearm. Murmurs swept the human observers. The hand explored the wall blindly, tentatively. The elves could do nothing to assist; losing their concentration would instantly close the gate. Only one human had the presence of mind to lunge forward and clasp the hand gently: Tae Kahn, king of the Eastlands, though he had to dump his feline companion to the floor to do so. Imorelda hissed her displeasure, tail outstretched and fur fluffed, making her appear twice her normal size.

Tae released the hand within moments, and it disappeared back inside the gate. Then, part of a head emerged, allowing a canted saffron eye to sweep the room. It paused briefly, apparently long enough for its owner to inform others of its findings, then the entire elf stepped through the gate and away from it to clear the way for those behind him.

Captain recognized this elf, as well as all of the ones who followed. As they came through, each rescued elf blinked away the transportation magic before studying the room and skittering toward their fellows. Tae reclaimed his seat, scooping up Imorelda and attempting to placate her with scratches behind her ears and under her chin. She seemed mostly unimpressed, slashing at him as he lifted her and emitting a long, warning growl that seemed endless. However, once she reached his lap, she remained there stiffly.

At length, sixteen of the missing elves emerged. The moment the last glided through, the gate disappeared. Captain gave the proper signal, and the *jovinay arythanik* died.

The human commanders looked quizzically from their lists to the utter lack of new men in the room and back. One of Béarn's ministers leaped to his feet, the picture of outrage. "Where are the people?" He pirouetted to take in the entire room. "You've rescued nothing but elves!"

A glare from King Griff silenced him, but the humans took up the cry in grumbled comments to their neighbors. Captain lowered his head. He had anticipated this problem. "Sire, we will go outside and allow you time to speak to one another in private. That will also give me a chance to quiz these elves."

Griff gave Captain a reassuring smile, though, under the circumstances, it seemed strained. "Please, Captain, no. There are far fewer humans in this room, and it's much easier for us to leave. You stay. Make yourselves comfortable, and let me know if you need anything. I'll reconvene the leaders in the Strategy Room. Please join us at your leisure."

Captain bowed, avoiding the usual jokes about the difference between an elf's leisure and a human's. The king of Béarn had left the way open for him to wait years to report. "Thank you, Sire. We need nothing but a bit of time alone, and I'll head for the Strategy Room as soon as I have some answers."

"Thank you." Griff gestured toward the door. Still murmuring, the humans filed out, leaving the elves to their own devices. Captain sucked in a deep breath, held it longer than necessary, then let it out with fanatical slowness. If the elves noticed this delay, they gave no sign. Time meant little to beings who lived for centuries or, rarely, millennia, who had scant understanding of stress. For the moment, they simply rejoiced in having sixteen of their companions back safely, sixteen elfin souls rescued from permanent and fixed oblivion. Captain singled out one of the no-longer-missing from the group and started the questioning.

This time, King Griff limited the meeting to only those officially representing their districts: Valr Magnus for the North, Tae Kahn and his father for the East, Thialnir for the Renshai, Sir Harritin for Erythane, General Markanyin for the western Westlands, and General Sutton for the eastern Westlands. The soldiers and various ministers of Béarn were barred, as was Queen Matrinka. The only additional participants were the king's own bodyguard, Bard Darris, and the ever-present recording pages, none of whom had a right to add anything to the discourse even if they dared.

After Harritin made the appropriate formal gestures, King Griff started the meeting with a weary wave. "You may all speak freely here."

Tae stroked Imorelda absently. The room was filled with reasonable, tolerant, intelligent men, yet he still felt an undercurrent of injustice and righteous rage. Silence reigned. No one wanted to be the first to point out the obvious.

General Markanyin finally did. "We knew from the start they

had to focus on elves, but no humans rescued at all? We can't stand for this!"

Heads bobbed around the table, faces grim.

Valr Magnus spoke next. "Convincing the elves to assist us in this war was difficult enough. We promised to do everything in our power to protect them, to prevent the deaths of any one of them; and I believe we kept our vow to the best of our ability. Not a single elfin life was lost to violence. If any have died, it's as a result of their own magic."

Imorelda bumped Tae's hand with her head, twining through his lap. She had always demanded his attention, but never more so than since becoming pregnant. He increased the volume and intensity of his stroking, sending dislodged hairs flying. At the time of the elves' recruitment, Tae had gone off on a spying mission against the *Kjempemagiska*, so he had missed it. Still, he had some insight. "The elves worried about assisting us in the war because of the danger. Whether magical or physical, dead is dead; they could have avoided both by refusing to help us." The point required making to avoid a tangential argument; ultimately, however, it did not matter. "I don't believe the elves wanted or expected to rescue only their own kind. They seemed just as surprised as us by the results, and our dissatisfaction only increases their risk, at least in their minds."

General Sutton did not seem as certain. "Or maybe they just didn't consider the effect it would have on us. Perhaps they were so focused on saving their own, ours did not concern them."

"Elves don't think the same way we do," Valr Magnus pointed out, rightly. "They don't . . . seem to have the same . . ." he chose his words carefully, ". . . depth of concentration."

Tae could not deny it. Elves acted far more impulsively and superficially than humans most of the time. They considered people ponderous and slow with a propensity to overthink simple situations.

Sir Harritin gestured for recognition and waited until King Griff acknowledged him before speaking, a convention none of the others had honored, surely to his chagrin. "Ethically, it's wrong for the elves to have use of the Pica Stone and our facilities if they aren't going to give our missing soldiers equal attention."

"Or any at all," Thialnir added, nearly subvocally.

Tae suspected the elves would prefer to pursue the whole operation outdoors and on their own territory, though Harritin made a point about the Pica. Until they heard from Captain, it was all just speculation; but they could do nothing else until the elf finished his own business and arrived. Although Griff had given the leader of the elves unlimited time, Tae did not think he would take long. Captain had lived among humans long enough to know allowing them time to stew would not help his cause.

Always the strategist, General Sutton spoke carefully. "Whatever the elves meant to achieve, the way they're approaching this situation needs to change. Ascribing bad intentions won't fix the problem, but . . ."

No one interrupted. Sutton did not speak frequently. When he did, he was nearly always right.

". . . we need to make certain they understand the consequences of what happened today. If we act as if nothing catastrophic occurred, they have no impetus to correct the problem."

Valr Magnus pressed. "And by consequences, you mean . . . ?" He let the question hang.

Without Magnus' addition, Tae might not have pondered the situation the same way. There were, of course, the natural consequences: humans became irrevocably trapped, families permanently and unnecessarily broken. They could hope the elves saw and corrected the problem without the need to point it out, or they could parade weeping widows and orphans in front of the elfin assemblage to create the proper guilt. There were also indirect consequences: human rage against the elfin mistakes or oversights could result in incidents ranging from uncomfortable to vicious to lethally violent.

Sutton barely turned his head toward his fellow general to answer. Clearly, he intended his words to reach all of them equally. "Well, that's what we were called here for, wasn't it? To determine what consequences should befall the elves?"

Tae found his head bobbing without conscious effort; when he glanced around the table, he found nearly every other leader doing the same.

Imorelda flopped onto her side in Tae's lap, purring loudly. *Wouldn't Captain know the best way to handle that?*

It always amazed Tae when the cat, who seemed wholly absorbed with herself, demonstrated her knowledge of the subject at hand. *Of course, my love. But we need to decide how to handle Captain.*

He's the oldest two-legs in the world, and he knows things none of us even knows we don't know. You don't handle him; he handles you.

As usual, Imorelda had an undeniable point Tae did not dare to acknowledge. He was five times Imorelda's age, but he doubted she would agree he had any authority over her. He knew some wise el-

ders and others with the intellectual ability of a swampstone, and he
had come across plenty of youngsters, both brilliant and stupid.
However, in his millennia, Captain had amassed experiences far beyond anything a human lifespan could allow.

Ultimately, the orders had to come from Griff, the acknowledged
highest ranking king. "I do not think . . ." he started.

The knock on the door could not have come at a less appropriate
juncture. Like many of his predecessors, Griff had a tendency to
come across as simple, sometimes even as he rendered immediate,
exceptional judgments teams of wise men might have taken weeks to
ponder. He gestured at one of the pages seated in a row on the floor,
their backs against the wall. The boy jumped to his feet, pulled the
door open a crack and slipped into the hallway. A moment later, his
head reappeared and he announced in a small, nervous voice, "Your
Majesty, it's the elf known as Captain."

King Griff called through the chink, "Please join us, Captain."

The door opened wide enough to admit the tall, slender elf.
Though weathered by salt and rime, he still seemed ageless, his
reddish-brown hair speckled randomly with white. An androgynous
figure and canted amber eyes completed the picture. He seemed to
float as much as walk through the door. The page pushed the heavy
panel shut and sat back down with his fellows.

Silence accompanied Captain's entrance. All eyes followed him
to Griff's side where he executed a short, agile bow. Griff pointed to
an empty chair between Bard Darris and General Sutton, and Captain obliged by taking his seat.

The silence grew disquieting until, at length, the elf broke the
hush. "I'm sorry."

When he did not explain further after several moments, all eyes
went either to him or to the high king. A couple of the leaders cleared
their throats, but none of them spoke.

Griff asked the question on every mind. "Exactly what are you
apologizing for, Captain?"

The answer was quick. "For disappointing all of us."

Tae found that response interesting. "All of us" clearly included
the elves, who should have been celebrating the rescue of sixteen of
their own missing.

Captain added, "For not bringing any humans home."

Griff asked the significant question, one no one seemed to have
considered. "Were there humans to bring home?"

Captain made a helpless gesture. "We . . . don't believe so, but we
can't be certain." He paused without the human need for delaying

fillers such as sighs, grimaces, or wordless noises. "The elves sent to that world saw no humans there."

Thialnir appended the obvious, "But they didn't look, either?"

Captain studied his long-fingered hand. "Not as such, no. However, they located one another using *khohlar*, and humans do hear *khohlar*. They could have joined up with the elves, but none did."

Tae imagined himself in the same situation: one moment in battle, the next bombarded by a massive storm, then finding himself in an unrecognizable place. If he heard *khohlar*, he would go toward it; but he had some experience with it. Most humans did not.

Valr Magnus spoke the concern aloud, "Assuming they knew what *khohlar* was. Most of my men had never heard it until after the storm, after the missing were already gone, when you sent it to explain what had happened."

Captain lowered his head a bit. "Yes." He sighed. He clearly did not want to say what came next. "Also, *khohlar* can be difficult to triangulate for the inexperienced. Or so I'm told."

The leaders stared at Captain. Tae had some idea what he meant, but he had spent weeks with Captain aboard his ship on two occasions and asked a lot of questions.

Markanyin guessed, "Are you saying it's difficult to find the source of the *khohlar*?"

"Not for elves," Captain said. "Our infants usually start with *khohlar*, then move on to spoken language. They're bombarded with it from birth, and they usually quickly learn how to determine its location and source. It's as inborn as reaching for objects or assuming an upright stance. As I understand it, humans can usually determine who is sending the *khohlar* if they are within visual distance, but they rely mostly on expressive clues: facial appearance, gestures, and the like. When they can't see the sender or senders, they have difficulty figuring out where it's coming from. And, unlike elves, they can't send answering *khohlar* to help them navigate."

Again, heads bobbed as they considered the significance of Captain's description. The elves and humans had started out in different locations during the war. The former had remained hidden in the woodlands, working their magic, while the human warriors took the frontline positions. The explosion had created vicious winds that sent living creatures flying, and the desperate elves had opened their gates blindly, randomly. It certainly seemed reasonable some gates might have sucked in only elves, others only humans and some various combinations of both. Once there, the elves would seek one another out, and the humans would do the same; but they would not necessarily look for members of the opposite group.

While the leaders contemplated the situation, Captain summed up the pertinent details. "It's unlikely any humans wound up on that particular world. However, if any did, they got left behind."

Thialnir had the ready answer. "Can't we just go back and get them?"

Captain grimaced. "To open a gate, we need willing magic on both sides. Once the last elf came through, the gate we created closed permanently. Having left no elves behind, we can't go back."

Markanyin added, "But we can change the way we operate in the future."

That popped a question into every mind. The only one in the room who ought to know the answer was the first to speak it. "How?" Captain asked.

Every eye went instantly to the elf. Captain's gemlike gaze swept the room in challenge.

Weile cleared his throat, and several of the leaders stiffened. He had remained so silent, they had apparently forgotten him. "I believe our friend is trying to say the elves are already using every bit of their combined magic, and their link with the Pica Stone, to locate the missing and create a gate to them. Anything more would have to come from us."

The leader of the Renshai asked incredulously, "But what could we possibly do?"

Tae had one answer, based on his previous experience as part of the team that had fetched pieces of the Pica Stone. "One or more of us could go through the gates to the Outworlds and search for humans."

Sutton scowled. "We're trying to save as many lives as possible, not add to those missing and in danger."

"You're right, General," Tae admitted. "It would add to the number off-world briefly; but if it saved multiple lives, it might be worth the risk."

Imorelda reminded, *Whoever went in would first have to make sure an elf stayed on the Outworld side to keep the gate from closing.*

It was such an important detail, Tae echoed it verbatim and aloud.

Sutton's glower deepened. "That leaves a lot to chance. There could be as few as one elf on the Outworld to start with, and none of them are soldiers. Even if the elf or elves listens to a human, we risk them getting antsy or fearful and running through to our side."

Captain broke in. "I also have concerns about sending more people to the Outworlds, but I do have a solution to that particular problem. We could spare an elf from the *jovinay arythanik* to accompany whoever went through the gate."

Tae suspected Captain would choose Chan'rék'ril who, along with El-brinith, had accompanied Tae and his companions on their trips to the Outworlds. Chan'rék'ril had lost his soul to a spirit spider; if something lethal happened, his loss would not affect the elves to the extent any other would. He had proven himself a calm and competent companion, and Tae would trust him not to abandon any humans sent through the gates.

Weile spoke again, which surprised Tae. When not fully in charge, his father usually remained as still and quiet as a shadow. "I have read that the Cardinal Wizards used the Pica Stone to observe distant action."

The subtext was obvious. He wondered if the elves could get a view of any situation or even make contact with their brethren on the other side of the gate.

Captain made an uninterpretable gesture. "It's true. And, with a minimal *jovinay arythanik*, we have used it to scry on an individual located on the same world. To see what's happening on an Outworld, we would need the gate in place and secured from both sides. That, in and of itself, strains the combined magic of just about every elf we have. We could spare a few, especially with the sixteen more we just added, but I'd prefer to keep them in the *jovinay arythanik*, if possible. It may look easy, but all magic is shaping and controlling chaos, and it takes a huge amount to make a gate. If we lost control . . ." He shuddered. "Let's just say it would risk the lives of everyone in the room or worse. I'm not convinced being able to see a small portion of the Outworld would be worth it."

Sutton said thoughtfully, "But if it allowed you to communicate with the elves on the other side, it might save a lot of lives. You could instruct them to seek out any humans and to make sure at least one elf remained on the other side until we could send in and retrieve a rescue party."

Captain made another purely elfin gesture that was meaningless to Tae and, surely, the others. "Speaking through the Pica is not within our repertoire of magic. I'm not sure it's even possible."

Griff prodded, "Are you saying some creature with a different concept of magic might be able to do it?"

Captain fidgeted, notably agitated, particularly noticeable since elves rarely showed obvious concern. "That's not entirely impossible, Sire."

The same name had to come to every mind, and several spoke it aloud in unison. "Kentt."

"Do you think he would assist?" Griff asked Tae.

"I know he would." Tae harbored no doubt. "He's said so on several occasions. The hesitation seems to come on the part of the elves." He hated to throw the impetus back on Captain, but it belonged there.

Captain did not hedge. "He did say he would help, but the elves are terribly afraid of him, Sire." He added defensively, "It's one thing to allow an enemy to walk among you, trusting you have the numbers and firepower to subdue him if he causes trouble. It's quite another to grant him access to your survival secrets. To learn how his magic works, we would need to explain ours to him, to essentially meld our minds with his through *jovinay arythanik*. It would give this dangerous stranger the means to our annihilation."

"Our?" Thialnir wanted clarification.

Captain clearly knew exactly what the old Renshai wanted. "Elfin and human, too. Without elfin magic reining in the *Kjempemagiska*, they would have destroyed all of you. Wasn't that the very reason you begged our help?"

It was, and they all knew it.

Sutton brought up a clever point Tae had not considered. "But wouldn't he be giving up the *Kjempemagiska* secrets as well? Doesn't that negate any advantage?"

Captain hunched his shoulders, then smiled. "I suppose that's true, General, and you know I'll use that in my argument. I believe I can convince the elves to do it, if King Griff truly believes it's best. However, it will take time to exchange information and figure out the best ways to combine our abilities. Are you willing to allow the missing to wait on the Outworlds while we do?"

Now, all attention went to the high king. Griff pursed his lips, clearly weighing the options. "How long are we talking about?"

"By human reckoning, two to three weeks should do it."

Griff ran his fingers through his beard.

Weile spoke again, "That would give me time to convince the remaining Mages of Myrcidë to help you as well. They don't have a lot of magic yet, but they could at least contribute to your *jovinay arythanik* and, maybe, they could add something to the discussion at the least."

The mages had proven even more difficult than the elves to convince to assist the war effort. Most had remained in their hidden citadel.

Matter-of-factly, the leader of criminals added, "Of course, I would need the Pica. Can you spare it for some of that time?"

Captain answered without consideration of the more important factors that came immediately to Tae's mind and, surely, those of the other leaders. "We would need it eventually, but not for the first week or two."

Only secondarily did Weile address the actual owner of the artifact. "Your Majesty, would you be willing to trust the Pica into my hands again?"

Griff nodded easily, but Markanyin expressed the concern the king of Béarn should have. "Sire, are you sure that's wise? It's the most significant item in the world, and we can't risk it . . . becoming . . . lost." He did not add the usual "or stolen," which would have sounded offensive, although it struck Tae as more appropriate.

Despite the seriousness of the situation, Griff chuckled. "General Markanyin, I have learned that it's best to indulge Weile Kahn. If you force him to talk you into things, and he inevitably will, he might decide to ask for more simply from spite. I'd prefer to loan him the Pica than the Pica plus my undergarments."

You know he's right. Imorelda's tail curled back and forth, flashing the white tip that was the only unstriped spot on her entire body.

Tae also grinned, though no one else in the room joined him or the high king in their amusement. *Griff usually is.*

Valr Magnus tried not to offend. "If it's all the same to you, Your Majesty, I'd like to know to what use he plans to put the Pica Stone. It's not the sort of thing one should loan to others, especially someone who intends to remove it from the kingdom."

Though he had addressed Griff, Magnus clearly wanted the answer from Weile.

Tae's father did not oblige. In fact, Weile gave no sign he had heard the Aeri general.

Griff used an informal gesture to request Weile's attention before speaking directly to him. "Would you mind explaining your intentions for the representative from the North? He wishes to know to what use you plan to put the Pica."

Weile replied breezily, suggesting he would have answered Magnus' concern immediately had it been addressed to him, rather than obtusely through the king. "The lair of the mages is not visible without magic in hand."

Apparently, he got the point, because Magnus questioned Weile this time. "Would a sword do? I would be willing to loan you mine in order to keep the Pica safely here."

Weile did not equivocate. "It would."

Tae wondered how he knew, but he did not ask. If Weile wanted to tell the group, he would. Tae would get more cooperation if he asked later, in confidence.

Weile continued, "Thank you for the generous offer, General. Bringing an elf with me would also work. I prefer the Pica for several reasons, but mostly because it's the object most likely to convince the Myrcidians to cooperate. If it pleases you, Your Majesty?"

Griff made a throwaway gesture. "As long as Captain can spare it, and you bring it back, you may take it with my blessing."

"Thank you, Your Majesty." Weile sounded suitably appreciative.

The matter was settled, but it clearly did not please most of the leaders. Tae could understand their consternation over lending the Pica Stone to an untitled man of dubious morals known to consort with the basest criminals. However, he also realized what Griff had to know. For all his power, Weile had simple tastes. He had usurped a kingdom, only to renounce his leadership and hand it to his son. If he wanted the Pica for himself, Weile would already own it; this was not even the first time he had borrowed it. Like the others, Weile was wise enough to know the world would collapse without the proper Béarnian king or queen in power, one chosen by the Pica test.

Griff moved on to other issues. "Are we all agreed to delay the rescue for two to three weeks?"

Tae considered. They had leaped into the mission without proper preparation to prevent such a delay, and they might have paid with some human lives.

Sutton spoke carefully, "Your Majesty, it's obviously not ideal, but it seems necessary." He addressed his next words to Captain. "Can you tell us a bit more about the Outworlds? Is a two-to-three-week delay likely to result in even more fatalities?"

Captain looked directly at the general as he replied. "It's impossible to know. We believe the gods created the Outworlds as places to banish problems and park miscreants, mistakes, and miscalculations. In some cases, the Outworld itself *is* the error. To my knowledge, no god or goddess has ever verified this idea, but it seems to work as a model." He paused briefly. "As far as risking more fatalities, that's harder to answer. It will probably depend on the cleverness and competence of the people sent to the Outworlds as much as luck. Obviously, anyone who went to a world that can't support life will die regardless of our timing. I would think the only situations where delaying rescue could become an issue are those where food and water are scarce, the local flora or fauna is hostile, or time passes at a much quicker pace." He added pointedly, "Of course, your supposition is as good as mine. Remember, I can count the number of worlds I've visited on three fingers."

Griff asked the question no one else would. "What's the preference of the elves, Captain?"

Captain managed a weak smile. "Of course, we'd prefer to work quickly. That might allow us to rescue every elf sent to a survivable Outworld, and we would not have to collaborate with a sworn enemy."

King Griff attempted to soften the information, "But the elves understand our dilemma and are willing to compromise if we believe it's best."

Captain's already meager grin wilted. "Sire, I can't lie to you. I hope you'll understand our limited and rapidly shrinking population adds a certain . . . value to our lives, at least in the minds of our people. It's simple fact there are many more humans, and they have no limitations on procreation." He raised a hand to forestall arguments that never materialized. This particular group held their titles and positions partly because they did not allow impulsiveness or emotion to rule them. "Having said that, a couple or three weeks is no time at all to an elf, and we need the Pica. I believe I can convince them the information we glean from the *Kjempemagiska* could make us safer and stronger and our comrades have the skill and sense to keep themselves alive for that short a wait even on an unexplored Outworld."

The room fell silent as the leaders weighed the possibilities. The result seemed inevitable to Tae. Whatever his intentions, Captain had practically baited the leaders to prove the missing humans also had the strength and fortitude to survive whatever the Outworlds threw at them. At the least, it seemed better to rescue the hardiest and smartest than to allow random chance to make the determination. They might ponder the situation for hours, but, ultimately, Tae felt certain the delay was going to happen. And it seemed to him like the wiser choice.

CHAPTER 5

To equate shared blood with love is to doom all of us to marrying our mothers and sisters.

—*Colbey Calistinsson*

POISED BETWEEN TWISTED *HADONGO* and gnarly herbont trees, Colbey watched the orange ball of the setting sun touch the western horizon, spraying rainbow colors in its wake. Where the sun touched, the ground seemed to have burst into flames, scarlet tendrils rising upward to merge with wispy patches of amber, muting to green, then clinging fiercely to daylight blue. Beyond and to the east, he could see the dying vestiges of purple mutating to black as the trees blocked his view of the heavens.

Against the background of color, two golden figures engaged in a *svergelse* that seemed more of a dance than preparation for lethal combat. One male, one female, both small and lithe, they flitted around one another like courting butterflies, their swords catching and throwing red glimmers from the setting sun. Colbey appreciated the lines that defined them both, his attention naturally focused on the conformation of their musculature: the origins and insertions, their reach and reflexes, the quickness of each movement. Both had great potential for competent, deadly swordwork.

Currently, the male was the superior master. That made sense, as the aptitude of Calistin Ra-khirsson had been recognized early and nurtured even beyond the excessiveness accorded all Renshai sword training. Nothing else had ever been expected of him other than to dedicate his life to the sword, a task he took on eagerly. To describe him as one-dimensional would have been understatement. He had neither had, nor desired, a social life, not even the normal attachments of a son to devoted parents and near-age siblings.

Change had come late and from an unexpected source. With the magical eyesight of a Cardinal Wizard, Colbey could see the flicker deep inside Calistin born of the donated soul of Treysind, a boy who had literally dedicated his life to his hero. Treysind had attached himself to Calistin like a son, though only six years separated them in age and Calistin had considered the boy more parasite than companion. Though his sword skills could barely be defined as meager, Treysind had sacrificed his life for Calistin's in the war. When the Valkyrie came to take Treysind's soul to Valhalla, he had chosen instead to have it replace the one Calistin had lost in-utero when his mother was bitten by a spirit spider.

Still coming to grips with what he had gained, Calistin never spoke of it to anyone, yet Colbey knew what had transpired from a superficial reading of Calistin's memories. When he had first discovered he had no soul, he had despaired of ever reaching Valhalla. Obtaining one had rekindled that perfect dream, yet the changes that came with incorporating a life-force that had once defined a kind-hearted and empathetic individual upset him and upended the simple, wholly sword-driven life he had built for himself in his first eighteen years.

Unbeknownst to Calistin, Treysind had started changing him long before the soul transfer. Where his brothers had written off Calistin's coldness and cruel sense of humor, Treysind had seen it as an opportunity for improvement. He taught Calistin that certain emotions existed in others he had never felt or understood. Now, they had comingled in this odd and intimate manner, and Calistin was discovering those feelings had always lived deep within himself as well. He found them a curiosity and a torment.

As the first tip of sun edged below the horizon, a haze settled over the scene, dampening it to dull gray. Colbey stepped from the forest to the Fields of Wrath, the home of the Renshai. The *svergelse* ended abruptly, and the couple whirled to face him as one, stances wary, hilts still clutched in their hands.

"Is that him?" the young woman asked.

Calistin nodded and sheathed his sword. "It's Colbey." His tone expressed no doubt, despite the shrouding twilight. As an adept *torke*, a teacher of Renshai, he did not rely on appearances to identify others instead knowing them by their forms, movements, and potential.

"Introduce us."

Calistin seemed confused by his companion's suggestion. He stood there in uncomfortable silence, knowing something was expected of him but not sure how to go about doing it.

After a moment's pause, Valira demonstrated. "Colbey Calistinsson, I'm Valira Eltorsdatter." She smiled at Calistin. "His girlfriend."

"My girlfriend," Calistin repeated stupidly. Apparently, he had never uttered those words before. He turned suddenly to face Valira. "My girlfriend?"

Valira rolled her eyes. "Of course, Calistin. What else could I be?"

Calistin addressed Colbey. "I have a girlfriend. Her name is Valira."

Colbey laughed at the awkward interplay. "Beautiful." Usually, he avoided scanning minds, believing it intrusive and rude. However, this time, he needed to know. He found Valira's thoughts delightful. She was a bright and dedicated Renshai with more than sufficient skill who genuinely loved Calistin and had the desire and patience to take up his emotional education where Treysind had left it. "And talented. An excellent choice. I highly approve."

Valira beamed. "Even if you disapproved, I'd consider it an honor and pleasure to speak with the immortal Renshai." She threaded a hand under Calistin's arm and along his waist, squeezed momentarily, and released him. "I'll be waiting over there when you're finished."

The trace of a smile crossed Calistin's face at her touch, but he clearly did not know how to respond to it. "All right," he said as Valira sheathed her sword and headed into the gathering dusk. He turned back to Colbey. "Do you really like her?"

"I really like her," Colbey affirmed. "You can learn from her and she from you."

Calistin shook his head. "She's a few levels below me still, but she is learning quickly."

"I wasn't talking about swordplay."

Calistin's cheeks reddened, and he looked at the ground. "I'm . . . not the same man I used to be. Not since . . ."

When it became clear Calistin had no intention of finishing the sentence, Colbey did. "Not since you gained a soul."

"Yes," Calistin admitted.

Colbey stated the obvious because Calistin clearly needed to hear it. "That's a good thing, Calistin."

"Is it?" He met Colbey's solid, blue-gray gaze. "Don't misunderstand; I do appreciate it. I mean, Treysind sacrificed his life and his afterlife for me. Without a soul, I wasn't complete. The focus of my existence, my dream of spending eternity in Valhalla, could never have become real. And yet . . . since I got it . . . I feel blessed, but cursed at the same time."

Colbey always kept his advice to mortals short. For anyone who lived among gods to do otherwise risked the balance. "Have you discussed this with your brothers or your father?"

Calistin's hands went instinctively to his hilts. Threats and discomfort in the past always heralded violence. He did not draw, however. "My . . . father?"

Colbey did not like the direction the conversation was headed. "I mean your real father, Calistin. The one who claims and raised you."

"If they knew, most people would consider Ravn my *real* father and you my *real* grandfather."

"Most people are stupid." Calistin had struck a raw nerve. Colbey carried the blood of Thor and a nameless mortal woman in his veins, but he had never considered anyone but the couple who loved and raised him, Calistin's namesake and Ranilda, as his parents. "A *real* parent is the one who's there for you. You've never even met Ravn, and I only sent him because I couldn't ignore your mother's fervent prayers." Few knew the king of Pudar had held Kevral captive and made his reluctant son sleep with her to assure an heir. At the time, an elfin sterility plague inflicted on all humans made the future appear doomed. Once a woman had her courses, she was rendered infertile, so female children and the few, like Kevral, who had just given birth seemed the only hope for mankind. Desperation had driven otherwise good people to commit horrible and vicious acts. "For all intents and purposes, you are, and will always be, Ra-khir's son."

"And yet," Calistin pointed out, "I can't help but notice you're here."

Colbey wished he had never revealed the truth to Calistin. At the time, it had seemed necessary. Calistin had just learned he had lost his soul, and Colbey offered the only possible solace: with the blood of gods flowing through him, Calistin might find the same sort of immortality Colbey had, given the right circumstances. He had no idea Treysind would find a way to remedy the situation in his own inimitable way. "I'm here to collect the gems I lent you for the war."

Calistin stiffened. Slowly, carefully, he drew the sword on his left hip, leaving the right one sheathed. He held the ancient Sword of Mitrian across his palms, a curiosity the Renshai had preserved for centuries. The hilt formed the face of a wolf; and legend stated the eye sockets had once contained magical gems. Long ago, those had been broken and lost, and any power the sword had contained disappeared with them. Just before the war, Colbey had replaced them with small diamonds he "borrowed" from his wife. Those had granted the sword enough magic to reverse its deterioration and allow it to cut the otherwise blade-impervious *Kjempemagiska*.

Without removing the sword from Calistin's hold, Colbey plucked the diamonds from the sockets and placed them gingerly into separate pockets of his tunic. When Freya had discovered them missing from her prized possession, the Necklace of the Brisings, she had made his life a misery as only those most beloved can.

The sword dulled to its familiar darkly pitted and rusted appearance, unusable in battle. The Renshai had done everything to preserve it, but time had taken its toll. The magical diamonds had given the Renshai's revered relic a new life that died with their removal. A sadness filled Colbey, and he sensed the same wafting from the much younger man.

Calistin held the Sword of Mitrian, unable to dishonor it by allowing it to touch the ground, yet clearly worried sheathing it in its current condition might damage it. "Did you have to?"

"The diamonds belong to Freya. I took them without her permission, and she . . ." Colbey did not think it wise to detail his married life and knew it would take a huge number of words to explain the situation in a way Calistin would understand. ". . . is not happy with me. Valira can explain it to you."

Calistin nodded, his gaze still fixed on the decaying weapon. "Subikahn has my sword." Those four words spoke volumes. Any Renshai would rather surrender an arm than his sword, and the one Calistin had loaned to his older brother was special. Originally one of Colbey's, he had passed it to Kevral when she required a magical sword to strike a demon. Its enchantment arose from its long proximity to an immortal and the gods, as well as the extent of the sacrifice. Subikahn had promised to return it to Calistin after the war, but he could no longer do so if he was missing on another world and, quite possibly, dead.

Colbey could have given Calistin one of his current blades, and Calistin probably expected to him to. Instead, he passed along some more advice. "Take the sword to a jeweler and have the sockets filled. The originals were yellow. I don't know enough about gems to suggest a specific type, but I do know the Cardinal Wizard who gave them to Mitrian accepted the Pica Stone in payment. To her, the Pica was a bauble; she just wanted a sword. But the wizard knew its value, and he wasn't a swindler. The fact that those eyes contained magic explains some of their value, but not all of it. They were probably expensive in their time."

"But the ones I put in won't be magical."

"Is that important?"

Calistin went on the defensive. "If magic would enhance my skill or defense in any way, I would refuse it, as all Renshai must. You know that! But it takes magic to keep this ancient sword from crumbling, and no sword can touch the worst of our enemies without it. If I'm called upon to help retrieve missing soldiers from the Outworlds, no amount of sword skill will matter if my blade passes right through without harming them."

He had an undeniable point, but Colbey had an agenda of his own. "For now, you should only carry, not wield the Sword of Mitrian. There may come a day when you earn special powers of your own, and you can use that sword again. Until then, you should think twice before volunteering to assist the missing."

The expression on Calistin's face made his thoughts clear. He could scarcely believe those in power would not want the best mortal swordsman on Midgard to join any rescue party. He had the presence of mind not to give voice to the idea, self-control he would not have displayed mere months earlier. "Colbey—"

Colbey waited, curious about what would follow but not wishing to invade the youngster's mind unless it proved necessary.

"You once said I might find a place in Valhalla even without a soul. Now, you say I might earn 'special powers.' Is it because my father is a . . . a . . . ?"

Colbey turned Calistin a sharp look. "A Knight of Erythane? No. Becoming a knight requires intense dedication, wisdom, and a great deal of time and study, but it does not convey the potential for mystical abilities upon their offspring."

Calistin flushed and started over. "I meant is it because I have a certain amount of god blood inside me?"

Colbey dropped the lesson. "Yes. Your blood sire isn't a god; as Freya's son raised on Asgard, however, he will almost certainly become one in time. Only a quarter of his blood is mortal, and he has lived among the gods since birth. It took eighty years for the gods to allow me to walk among them. I had to earn that privilege and survive long enough to do it."

"How?" Calistin asked eagerly. "What do I do?"

Colbey smiled. "That, Calistin, is something you will have to figure out for yourself." Buffeted by the emotions radiating from Calistin, ones that scared the young man more than guiding him, Colbey added helpfully, "Treysind and Valira can help you. Let them." With that, he left Calistin alone with his confusion.

Thialnir Thrudazisson sat at the small desk in the room Béarn provided for his visits, the document he needed to sign spread across its surface. In the older, unenlightened days before Saviar had joined him, he would have trusted King Griff and his legal experts, signing without hesitation or bothering to read it. Since Saviar had dissected the agreement that had, ultimately, led to the Renshai's banishment from the Fields of Wrath, Thialnir had become far more cautious. In the past, that caution usually took the form of having Saviar read any papers or documents and explain them. Now, Thialnir scrutinized the same sentence for the third time and wished the younger man had accepted Thialnir's pronouncement, allowing him to retire and leave the Renshai leadership in far better hands.

The document seemed straightforward. It simply codified what the representatives had discussed in the meeting: they all agreed rescuing the missing soldiers took priority and, despite a short delay, waiting until the Myrcidians arrived and the elves attempted to work through any magical glitches with Kentt seemed most prudent. They needed to understand not everyone could or would be saved and situations would arise where sacrifices and compromises would need to happen in order to assure the rescue of others. Categorizing just a few of the possibilities took multiple pages and did not begin to cover the full scope, only what a handful of men could imagine.

The meeting had bored and confused Thialnir, who did his best thinking on the battlefield, lightning quick, where mistakes were lethal. He felt certain most of the document would not matter. The decision making would mostly come in moments of desperate crisis: by elves as they worked their magic, by anyone sent to assist the lost, by the trapped soldiers themselves. Nothing he and the other representatives signed would change what happened. Still, he understood their need to discuss and consider alternatives; they were leaders accustomed to making decisions. At least they felt as if they had this tiny measure of control.

So they organized into writing things that seemed obvious to Thialnir: groups took precedence over individuals, the healthy-minded over the feeble, the able over the critically wounded. They also considered the relative risks of the rescuers or of dragging Outworld monsters to Midgard, thus placing all of humanity in peril. Every eventuality seemed to add a half or quarter page to the document, and Thialnir seemed incapable of wading through the first one without falling asleep or becoming prey to his own thoughts. More than anything, he wanted to just sign the blasted thing and go exercise his mind and body in the practice room.

Thialnir had just started his fourth reading of the same sentence, willing himself to concentrate long enough to get the gist of it, when someone knocked at the door. Gratefully, he shoved the papers aside. "Please come in!"

A squat, well-muscled Easterner opened the door in careful increments, peered at Thialnir and then around the entire room, muttered something, and stepped aside.

Weile Kahn entered then, with all the confidence of a king strolling down his courtroom carpet. "Good morning, Thialnir. If I'm disturbing you, I apologize."

"Not at all." Thialnir tipped his head toward the only other chair in the room, a padded monstrosity meant to hold Béarnides. A large example of his own people, Thialnir appreciated its size, but it seemed destined to envelop the smaller Easterner. Too late, he considered sacrificing the desk chair to take it.

Weile's two ever-present bodyguards entered and closed the door, examining the room minutely, paying particular attention to the single window. Weile Kahn chose to perch on one of the wide armrests. He gestured at the document on the desk. "Amazing how bureaucrats can reduce the most interesting things to tedium."

Thialnir grunted his agreement. "Have you signed yours yet?"

"Me?" Weile laughed. "Not my problem. Tae's the king. I dumped it on him."

"Wish I had someone to dump it on," Thialnir grumbled.

Weile said nothing, but a slight smile touched his features.

"Hard to believe wars have been fought by people eager to become leader of some place or other. I'd pass it off in a moment if I could only find another Renshai as foolish as I was when I accepted the position."

"Unfortunately, it's usually the ones least competent to rule who want it most." Weile reassured, "You've done a fine job representing your people, and you have an adept successor, I thought. What's wrong with passing the mantle to Saviar?"

Thialnir sighed. "I tried. He refused."

Weile's shrewd dark eyes rarely revealed his thoughts, and now was no exception. "Last time I spoke with him, he seemed keen enough. What changed?"

Thialnir merely shrugged. "I thought the same thing. But when I asked, he refused not only the position but an explanation."

Weile made a thoughtful noise. "Do you know where he is?"

"Any Renshai in Béarn spends as much time as possible in the practice room. I haven't seen him there in the last couple of days, so I'm assuming he went home." That reminded Thialnir of his burden. "Except me, of course. I'm stuck trying to make sense of this . . .

this . . ." He could not think of a sufficient word to describe the frustration the document caused him, so he just waved in its general direction.

Weile rose.

Thialnir did not want to lose his distraction so quickly. "You're always welcome to visit, of course; but I'm assuming you came for a reason. What can I do for you, Weile Kahn?"

Weile did not head for the door, but he did not sit back down either, to Thialnir's disappointment. "I came to ask if I could borrow Saviar, but if he's no longer your . . . apprentice . . ."

It seemed as good a description of their relationship as any, though Saviar had taught Thialnir nearly as much as he had the younger man. Uncertain why, Thialnir opened up to Weile in a way he had not done with anyone else. "According to him, maybe. I'm not giving up hope he'll change his mind. In fact, I'm depending on it."

Weile sank back onto the armrest. "How so?"

"I told the tribe I'd find a replacement, but Saviar's the only one qualified to lead us." Thialnir added before he could stop himself, "Much more so than I ever was."

Weile leaned forward. "You're being too hard on yourself, Thialnir. From what I've heard and seen, you started out a bit . . . raw, but it suited your job and you did a fine job representing your people who tend to be . . ."

Thialnir finished with a smile. "A bit raw?"

"All right." Weile did not argue. "And you've mellowed with age. Tae can't recall the last time someone argued you didn't belong in a meeting of leaders."

Thialnir did not take that as the compliment Weile probably intended. "It's not safe for Renshai to 'mellow.'"

Weile chuckled. "One can mellow without losing one's edge."

Thialnir did not agree. "No matter how much you work them, reflexes slow over time. I'm not as physically strong or agile as I used to be, gods damn it."

A ghost of a smile touched the corners of Weile's lips. "The trick is to make up for what time steals. A crafty old man can best a powerful young one. And usually does."

Thialnir had to admit Weile only seemed to become more powerful and dangerous as he aged. "Not often on the battlefield."

Weile turned Thialnir a look that forced him to reconsider.

Now, Thialnir managed a smile. "I suppose I have outmaneuvered more than a few eager young bucks in practice."

"Not with strength or agility surely."

Thialnir considered. "Sometimes. But more and more often with experience and wisdom. I often know what they're going to do before they do, and that knowledge gives me the time age has stolen."

"Clever," Weile said, as if Thialnir had come up with the explanation entirely on his own. "Are you sure you're not the best leader for the Renshai?"

Thialnir refused to be manipulated. He had considered this exact situation too many times. "Second best, maybe. I can keep doing it for now, but I'm feeling my age and not going to live forever. We need Saviar." That brought his thoughts full circle. Weile had managed to pry more information from him without revealing any of his own. Thialnir intended to rectify that. "For how long do you intend to borrow my apprentice?"

Weile raised a brow.

Thialnir clarified. "My *reluctant* apprentice."

Weile did not argue semantics. "I would like to take him with me to visit the Mages of Myrcidë."

"Why?" Thialnir focused on that word, determined not to allow the tricky Easterner to derail his thoughts again.

Weile replied directly, "Because Saviar has a relationship with the mages, albeit not always a friendly one. He's also the only one, besides me and my crew, who knows how to get to their citadel. It's extremely well hidden. I've only been there once to Saviar's twice, so I trust his memory more than mine."

More disarmed by Weile's candor than his secretiveness, Thialnir went momentarily speechless.

Weile added into the silence. "I also happen to enjoy Saviar's company."

Thialnir snorted.

That drew Weile's full attention.

"I usually enjoy his company also, but not recently. He's changed, and not for the better."

"How so?"

Thialnir did not have the words to explain it. He knew swords, not people. "If you find him, and if you can convince him to join you, you'll see for yourself."

Weile rose again. "So I have your consent to take him?"

He did, but Thialnir paused to consider. He wanted the Saviar he remembered back at his side, but he had no real authority to stop the younger Renshai from doing anything he wanted. Furthermore, in his current state, Saviar would only make his situation more frustrating and difficult. "On one condition."

Weile seemed more amused than bothered by Thialnir putting stipulations on a situation he had already admitted he did not control. "And that would be?"

Thialnir softened it to a plaintive request. "Please, Weile. Try to convince him the Renshai need him as our leader."

Weile headed toward the door. "I'll see what I can do." He paused at the desk, picked up Thialnir's quill, flipped the document to its last page, and made a mark. Neatly replacing pen and parchment, he said, "If I were you, I'd sign it." A moment later, he and his bodyguards were gone.

Thialnir waited until the door closed behind them before looking at the change Weile had made. The paragraph began: "This accord agreed to and signed by the legal representatives of the entire Northlands, Eastlands, Westlands, and the Renshai this 17th day of the month of Engen in the year . . ." The Easterner had neatly crossed out "and the Renshai."

Thialnir stared at the paper for several moments in deep consideration. Weile had turned to the proper place too quickly and easily to have simply passed the document on to his son as he had claimed. Clearly, he had read and studied every word in enough detail to find exactly what he wanted at the moment he wanted it. If he chose to delete exactly three words from something so massive, he had a reason. Doing so benefitted Weile Kahn in some fashion or, at least, did him no harm. The question remained whether it, in some way, aided or hurt Thialnir. That the chosen phrase actually contained the word "Renshai" suggested it certainly did.

But which one? Thialnir knew no one more cautious or wiser than Weile Kahn. Most people hated Renshai on a primal level, their reasons based solely on rumors, with limited analysis of facts or only a distant glimmer of truth behind them. Weile Kahn was not one of them. To Thialnir's knowledge, he had always dealt with them fairly. His missing grandson, Subikahn, was Renshai; and Weile had gone out of his way to help Saviar reclaim the Fields of Wrath. Thialnir wondered if crossing out "and the Renshai" would allow his people free rein to ignore the terms of the agreement despite their leader's signature, but he doubted it.

Thialnir turned the pages back to their beginning and started to read. The document had not changed in any other way. The words were in the common tongue, yet there was nothing common about how the bureaucrats had put the thing together. It might just as well have been written in Eastern, a language he did not speak or read. Thialnir trusted King Griff not to deliberately put anything in it that might damage the Renshai, or anyone else, but Saviar had taught him words and phrases could be twisted or misused. A clause meant to protect you could wind up protecting your enemy instead.

With just one simple change, Weile had pronounced the document safe. Thialnir felt certain that, if Weile truly believed it so, then it was. It only remained to decide whether or not to trust the lord of all criminals.

Thialnir Thrudazisson clutched the quill tightly. And signed.

CHAPTER 6

*When it comes to beings of magic, wise men never choose to anger
or detain them unnecessarily.*

—*Knight-Captain Kedrin*

TENSION FILLED THE SMALL MEETING ROOM chosen by
Captain, at least it seemed that way to Tae Kahn. Five elves sat on
the floor on one side, he and the enormous *Kjempemagiska* on the
other, like adolescents at their first dance. Captain squatted between
the two groups, but even he showed signs of distress that he attempted to hide by clasping his hands and drawing his arms tightly
to his body. His gaze flitted around the room as if he could not decide where it should alight.

Tae focused on his job. To compare magical abilities, the elves
and the *Kjempemagiska* first needed to find a way to communicate.
As the only one on the continent who spoke a significant quantity of
Kentt's language, Tae had been conscripted to assist. For his part,
Captain had chosen elves who knew the common tongue for this
initial meeting, which, at least, spared Tae from needing to draw on
his scant vocabulary of elvish.

The elves were clearly terrified of the giant stranger, loath to
share the room with him let alone their magical secrets. For all his
ability with languages, Tae knew little about magic, which seemed
like an insurmountable barrier to mediation between the two groups,
assuming he could even bridge the communication gap. It occurred
to him they might find their varied telepathic languages more compatible; but he had not, thus far, found a way to link them. Like humans, Kentt had no difficulty hearing and understanding elfin
khohlar. But, also like humans, the elves could not hear Kentt's *anari*.
Even Tae could only receive *anari* when Imorelda tethered their
minds and drew his to the correct "level."

The cat had not deigned to join Tae, which left him feeling diminished and abandoned. Over the past week, she had spent increasing amounts of time away from him. Even when she chose his company, she seemed irritated with everything he did: his petting was inadequate, his attempts to engage her insulting or stupid, his choices always wrong. Once, when he attempted to physically move her out of his way, she had hissed and clawed his hand deeply enough to draw blood. Attributing her mood to her pregnancy, he meekly accepted it, treading lightly to avoid as much confrontation as possible and allowing her to decide when and if she wished to accompany him.

Kentt and Mistri knew Tae's ability to receive their mental language was inconsistent, but his otherworldly interaction with Imorelda was a secret he shared only with Queen Matrinka. The cat's absence hampered him now, leaving him no way to even attempt connecting the magical beings unless one group learned the other's spoken language. If he could find a way to link them mentally, they could instantaneously send pictures, concepts, and emotions that transcended words. Without Imorelda, however, Tae was mind-deaf to anything but *khohlar*. To make matters more difficult, the elves could code their *khohlar* into their own tongue, which they were doing for most of their sidebars, and he found it distracting.

"They're afraid of me." Having already established that Tae was not currently able to hear *anari*, Kentt used *usaro*. "Can't you reassure them I mean them no harm? I want to help, and sharing our magical knowledge would be advantageous to all of us."

Tae understood the elves' hesitation. The *Kjempemagiska* soldiers had considered elves and humans savage animals worthy only of extinction. Tenderhearted and remarkably curious, Kentt was more akin to a naturist or scientist. Tae had spent significant time in conversation with him and Mistri, an experience the elves did not share. He had learned to read the giants' gestures and expressions, their tone of voice and the emotions inadvertently sent with their *anari*. Kentt was clearly sincere about assisting, but even that did not make sharing magical secrets safe. Whatever Kentt's proclivities, he intended to return to his family on Heimstadr as soon as Captain or the Béarnian navy was free to take him, bearing whatever information the elves and humans dared to reveal.

"I've told them," Tae said, cursing Imorelda's moodiness. He needed her as a go-between to have any chance of coordinating their telepathic abilities or, at least, allowing them to evaluate one another's motives without relying entirely on nonverbal expressions and gestures. Without her, he could only act as a verbatim translator. "I think I have their leader convinced, but he's having trouble bringing the others on board. If I could only find a way to get you talking directly to one another . . ."

Kentt pursed his massive lips and nodded. "It's hard to deceive using a*nari*. You can mask your state of mind, somewhat; but the act of doing it suggests deliberate deceit. If they could only hear it . . ." He looked askance at Tae, though they had discussed the situation before. Kentt believed the Easterner when he claimed he had little control over when he could or could not hear and send *anari*; but, in the past, Tae had always been able to talk Imorelda into assisting when doing so was truly important. Now, he was entirely at her mercy. *She knows lives are at stake, including my son's. Why isn't she here?* The thought evoked his own bad temper. Imorelda had a right to become prickly, especially carrying kittens she had not wanted in the first place. She had become pregnant only to appease the queen of Béarn whom she loved and who desperately wanted a replacement for Imorelda's mother. But she had no right to risk Subikahn and the other missing soldiers.

As if on cue, Imorelda stuck her face through the open doorway. *Come!* she commanded.

Tae was in no mood for games, and he let every bit of his pique leak through the contact. *You come here. You know I need you!*

Imorelda disobeyed, disappearing back into the hall. In a moment, he could see only the white tip of her tail, then nothing at all.

Damn it, get back here!

Receiving no reply, Tae tempered his sending. *Imorelda, please. You're the most wonderful of all beings, and you know I can't function without you.*

Tae's humbling also earned him no reply, which only made him angry. *What in all of Hel does she want? Do I have to sacrifice myself on an altar to appease her?*

Captain looked at the empty doorway, apparently trying to figure out what fascination it held for Tae. Clearly, he had not spotted Imorelda's momentary appearance. "The elves want to know what type of magic Kentt can share with us."

Dutifully, Tae put the question to Kentt.

The *Kjempemagiska*'s response contained long strings of words that Tae could not translate. He knew enough *usaro* to communicate with ease in common situations, but explanations of magic defeated his knowledge. Usually, when things became complicated, the switch to *anari* allowed them both to fill in details using pictures and concepts. Without Imorelda, he could not figure out what Kentt intended to convey.

The cat's head reappeared. *Come!* she said.

I will, Tae promised, fighting frustration and rising rage. *As soon as I'm free. That will happen much sooner if you could just help me. Please.*

Again, Imorelda left his sight and mind, this time with a vague trail of displeasure. She was at least as upset with him as he was with her.

Imorelda, I really need you, and it's very important. I promise I'll devote the rest of the day to whatever you want if you'll just help me.

Again, Tae got nothing back from the cat. He gritted his teeth, knowing he had to rein in his temper. He could not afford to explode on Kentt or Captain. He deferred to the cat on most matters trusting that, when he really needed her, she would be there for him. She had always vexed and pushed him; but, in the past, she seemed to recognize her limits. This went far beyond them. *Imorelda!* He addressed Kentt. "You're going to have to repeat that, more slowly. There's too much I just don't understand."

The cat reappeared suddenly, ran directly to Tae and dropped a newborn kitten into his lap. She fixed her gaze on him.

Gently, Tae picked up the tiny creature. Its eyes were tightly closed, its gray-pink ears folded flat against its head. Its tabby pattern seemed imprinted onto skin as much as fur, and a piece of umbilical cord dangled from its belly like wet, pink string. It made a soft moan of protest. In an instant, Tae was on his feet, following Imorelda to the door, the kitten cupped in his hands. He managed only a terse, "Excuse me," before dashing into the hallway, afraid to lose sight of her.

Despite his concern, Tae had no difficulty following Imorelda to his room. Not knowing her location and hoping she would join him, he had left his door open. She dashed inside, Tae trailing, and he paused only to shut it behind them for privacy, the kitten cupped between his fingers and his chest for warmth and security. Imorelda hopped onto his bed, greeted by tiny mews of distress. Beside her, something moved slowly and sinuously. Cautiously, Tae sat on the edge of the bed and placed his burden beside its mother, watching it wriggle toward Imorelda.

Apologies would not satisfy Imorelda, so Tae merely asked. "How many?"

Imorelda rose, and a kitten dropped from her belly to the bedcover. She stepped aside to reveal three, including the one Tae had carried: one silver tabby, one calico, and the third off-white and conspicuously abnormal. Smaller than the other two, who barely spanned the length of Tae's palm, its paws curled under its legs, its tail was stubby, and its ears crimped.

"Congratulations," Tae said, grinning. "You're a mother!"

Imorelda clearly did not share his excitement. She had claimed from the start that she did not like or want kittens. She had proclaimed them dirty and annoying, saying she would have them only if Matrinka cleaned and fed them. To Imorelda's surprise and dismay, Matrinka had agreed to those conditions. Certain Imorelda's maternal instincts would take over, Tae had observed the arrangement with amusement. Up until the last week, Imorelda had seemed content with her pregnancy, and she had clearly performed the instinctive acts at birthing. Other than a single wet spot, a few small blood smears, and the kittens, she had left no evidence. Despite her stated revulsion to consuming the afterbirths, she had either done so or done a spectacular job of hiding them. The kittens appeared clean, their fur appropriately groomed.

Imorelda's voice entered his head like a moan, *Don't tell Matrinka.* *

The request made no sense. It was only because of Matrinka these kittens existed. Tae forced himself not to laugh. "Imorelda, you told her you were pregnant. She knows more about the process than any human." *Clearly more than me. I didn't expect them for months.* "She'll be watching for kittens, and she'll want to help you as much as possible."

More angst assaulted Tae's brain. *No one can help me. It's hopeless.* * Imorelda walked a circle, then lay down. Two of the kittens dragged themselves toward her belly, grunting and squeaking. The third tossed its bulbous head and attempted to manipulate its paddle-paws.

Tae carried the misshapen kitten to Imorelda's teats to join the others. "It happens, Imorelda. One abnormal baby's not the end of the world. We'll work with it, and there're still two perfectly normal—"

Imorelda fairly howled her grief. *You stupid two legs! You don't understand.* *

That silenced Tae. His concern for the elfin-*Kjempemagiska* negotiations had driven him to rush this situation, acting and speaking on assumptions. Imorelda was trying to tell him something important. He sat on the edge of the bed, careful not to disturb the feeding newborns. "I'm sorry, Imorelda. You're right; I don't understand. Please explain it to me."

The distress that had only risen since Tae followed Imorelda to his room finally receded a bit. No longer bombarded by the cat's misery, Tae found himself calmer, able to think more clearly. *None of these kittens are acceptable.* *

Tae shook his head. He still did not get it. "Two of them look perfectly normal to me." He watched them suckle eagerly. "And they seem to know what to do." Even the third one managed to latch on, though it did not flail its paws or twitch its ears like the others did as they drank.

Imorelda ran her tongue over the tabby, as if to lick away all contact with Tae's hands. *This one looks normal, but he's not right. He's . . .* She seemed to struggle with the concept as well as the words. *. . . Ivana as a kitten.*

Tae did not like Imorelda's description. They had only just gotten the elves to stop using "ivana" as a general, negative noun. "Mentally underdeveloped?" Tae tried.

Though she did not respond directly, Imorelda seemed to accept the terminology. *The girl is normal . . . for a cat.*

Tae blinked, uncertain how to respond. If "cat" had become an insult in Imorelda's mind, he had no idea how to refer to her. He considered all the information Imorelda had given him. The kittens lacked adequacy. The best of them was normal for a cat. "Are you telling me . . ." It finally came together. "None of them has inherited your genius? Not one of these three will be able to communicate with humans?"

Imorelda sent him nothing but waves of sorrow and a decidedly uncatlike and mournful expression. *Don't tell Matrinka.*

Now, Tae finally understood. Matrinka had spent years breeding Imorelda's siblings and their offspring, trying to create another Mior. She had felt certain Imorelda was the key, that the ability must be passed from mother to child, perhaps only through the firstborn, like the bard's curse. "They're freshly born. It's impossible to know what the future holds."

Imorelda continued to lick the tabby. She did not look at him.

Tae kept talking, "You were nearly two months old before Mior offered you to me. I don't think she knew you had the ability to communicate until then. You were all too young to tell."

Imorelda continued to focus on the kittens. *I know.*

Tae doubted it. He worried Imorelda's inexperience with infants might cause her to do something dangerous or foolish. "Matrinka has to know about the birth of the kittens, but I won't tell her you don't think any of them can replace Mior. Give it some time. Why quash her hopes before we know for certain?"

I know, Imorelda repeated.

Tae refused to argue. It would only spur Imorelda to cling more tightly to her position. "Promise me you'll take care of them, regardless of their presumed . . ." He used Imorelda's word, "Adequacy. And you'll share them with Matrinka."

Do something for me. Imorelda's mental voice had a purr in it that Tae recognized. She would not allow him to refuse, but Tae also knew better than to make an unconditional promise to anyone.

"What do you want me to do?"

If Imorelda detected any hesitation in his voice, she gave no sign. She had become adept at reading tones of voice and deciphering human expressions, but verbal responses gave her less information than mental ones did. *For me to make kittens, Matrinka agreed to some conditions.*

Tae remained cautious. Some of those provisions were reasonable. Others, such as Matrinka feeding, cleaning and mothering the kittens, he would strongly discourage. "At the time, Béarn Castle was overrun with cats. You had her build two sheltered pens, one for the males and the other for females, to discourage breeding. It was hoped the elves would have a magical way to sterilize most of the cats so that they could run freely."

Do they?

Tae had not found the opportunity to ask and had no idea whether Matrinka had done so. "I don't know. The war and its aftermath still take priority. When we've settled the fates of humanity and elfinkind, I'll ask them."

Though it suggested two-legged creatures were more important than Imorelda's own kind, she did not complain. Tae believed her personal hierarchy placed herself on top, followed by various individuals before concerning herself with groups. He believed he was second on her list, though she would never admit it. *I had her make a separate place for the cats pregnant at the time. Go there now and find a mother with young kits, preferably whose eyes have not yet opened. Bring her and her offspring here.*

Wary, Tae considered his assignment. "I'm not going to allow another cat to harm these kittens."

Buffeted by a familiar wave of scorn, Tae knew Imorelda found him stupid and tedious at times. And this was one of them. *Cats share and steal kittens from one another all the time. She won't harm them. I just want to demonstrate something to you.*

Acutely aware of time passing, Tae sighed. "I have to get back to the elves and Kentt. I promise I'll do what you asked as soon as I'm finished."

Imorelda stared at him with angry eyes and a lashing silver tail.

"It's important," Tae explained.

The yellow-green orbs narrowed, and Tae realized his mistake. He had essentially called Imorelda's problem with her own children of lesser significance than his need to help establish communication between two unrelated beings. Though probably true, he would never convince her. Rather than wasting more time arguing, it made sense for him to appease her. It would still leave him plenty of opportunity to bridge the elf/*Kjempemagiska* communication gap, and her cooperation would go a long way toward solving the problems that had plagued him earlier.

Tae amended. "I'm sorry. You're right, as usual. I'll be happy to do this favor for you now with a promise that, once you make your point, you'll help me find a way to connect the elves and Kentt so they can talk to each other."

The rage left Imorelda's eyes. *Agreed.*

Moments later, Tae gently placed the wrapped bundle of strange cat and kittens on his bed. The mother looked wildly around her new surroundings and tensed, her five blind kittens mewling their protests. Tae spoke to her quietly, stroking her sleek black head. "It's all right, Mama. I won't hurt you."

The black cat settled down on the blanket, purring. She flopped onto her side. Two of her black-and-white kittens snuffled up to her belly to latch on, their diminutive claws opening and closing as they kneaded the fur around her teats. Two others curled around one another to sleep, while the last one continued to cry pitifully. The mother eeled her head around the feeding kittens to check on the complainer. Then, apparently satisfied it was safe, she closed her eyes and continued to purr.

Imorelda had claimed the chair, leaving her tiny kits sleeping on the bed. Tae had deliberately positioned himself between them and the new family. *Give her the girl.*

Tae twisted toward Imorelda's kittens. He had not sexed them, but he knew from Matrinka that all calicoes were female. Imorelda had told him the healthy kittens were a girl and boy; so, unless she meant the anomalous kitten, she was talking about the calico. Dutifully, he rolled the tiny creature into his palm and presented it to the black cat.

The mother cat half-rose, dislodging her progeny to sniff Imorelda's kitten in his hand. She loosed a loud meow, then stood up fully as her own babies released multiple noises of complaint. Reaching into his hand, she seized the kitten by the scruff of its neck.

Imorelda! Tae sent, worried for its safety.

Unperturbed, Imorelda remained in the chair, sitting up attentively. *It's all right. She's not going to hurt it.*

Tae allowed the black cat to pick up the kitten, though he remained warily poised. It would only take a moment, barely a movement, to kill something so delicate.

The black cat set the calico down near the others. Lying back down, she set to work licking it vigorously, purring all the while. Soon, the calico crawled away to join the sleeping kitten pile.

Now give her the boy.

Less nervous this time, Tae did as Imorelda instructed, watching the same scenario play out. Unlike its sister, the tabby kitten worked his way to an empty teat and suckled. Neither it, nor the black cat, seemed concerned this kitten had become so intimate with the wrong mother.

Now the last one.

Tae gingerly placed the last of Imorelda's kittens into his hand and held it out to the black cat. This time, when she leaped up and sniffed at the bundle of fur, she made an odd noise that sounded like a combination of growl and purr. Where the other two kittens had gone limp and silent as she hefted them, this one let out a squeak of distress. She carried it a few steps away from the others, dropped to a crouch and started gnawing at it.

Horrified, Tae grabbed the abnormal kitten from her and cradled it in his lap. As she headed back toward the kittens, he jumped up to rescue Imorelda's other two babies.

Leave them, Imorelda commanded calmly.

"She'll kill them," he protested.

No she won't. Leave them. She'll mother them.

Tae hovered over the litter, but the black cat simply returned to the seven kittens, all interspersed now, and curled up beside and on top of them. Some of the black-and-white ones mewled when she dropped on them. She repositioned herself, and they managed to move into a safer position.

"She was going to kill *this* one." Tae would not accept a lie.

Nor did Imorelda give him one. *Yes. She would have eaten it, a far less painful way to die than the slow withering you want me to inflict on it.*

Tae studied the malformed infant in his hand. "This kitten has defects incompatible with life?"

Yes. Why waste milk on it when you have others to feed? Some mothers would just push it away and let it die of starvation, but most would put it out of its misery by eating it. Like the afterbirths, it's good meat her body could convert to the energy she needs to take care of her brood. ★

Tae understood, though it bothered him. "Why didn't you eat it? I'd have assumed you only had two kittens."

★What a revolting thought! Would you have encouraged Tem'aree'ay to eat Ivana?★

"No," Tae admitted. "But she didn't eat the afterbirth, either."

Imorelda wrinkled her nose. *★Don't remind me. Instinct took over there. At the time, they seemed irresistible, but don't you dare mention that to the cooks. ★*

"Is that the point you wanted me to get?" Tae could scarcely believe it. "I wouldn't have liked killing it, but I would have done it knowing it would otherwise die in pain."

Imorelda knew Tae better than he knew himself. *★No, you wouldn't have. You'd have made me take care of it until you were absolutely certain. By that time, Matrinka would have learned about it and insisted on doing everything possible to try to keep it alive. ★*

Imorelda made a reasonable argument.

"So you want me to let this cat handle the situation for you."

Imorelda's tail lashed around and through the chair. *★Why not? She can use the extra nourishment. ★*

It did not feel right to Tae.

★And we'll let her keep the other two. She'll take good care of them, and they'll have normal cat lives. ★

Tae looked at the mother cat and her family. Had Imorelda's kittens not sported entirely different colors and been a bit smaller and younger, Tae could not have told them from the others. Neither they, nor the other kittens, nor the mother seemed to notice they had not been together since birth. "And what would we tell Matrinka?"

★We can say my pregnancy failed. It happens. ★

"It happens," Tae repeated, thinking. "You know Matrinka wouldn't allow it to end there. She'd insist on you having another litter."

Imorelda's tail stilled. *★I could do that if I had to. Maybe with a different father . . . ★* The cat did not finish, but her intentions leeched through their contact, and not all of it on purpose.

Tae could sense Imorelda's reluctance. Matrinka would probably find herself confronted with a whole new set of conditions. It was possible the ability to communicate with human minds was transferred from mother to firstborn kitten or from mother to daughter. The calico or the tabby might still develop that skill, even if Imorelda could not sense it yet. They could not afford to lose track of the blood babies of Imorelda. Another thought seized Tae. *What if it's this kitten?*

He looked at the one in his hands and asked casually, "What was the birth order of your kittens?"

Imorelda gave no indication she followed the train of Tae's current thoughts, and his use of verbal communication made it less likely. *Boy, then girl, then . . . monstrosity.*

Tae rolled the creature over and spread its hind legs, which were surprisingly stiff. It appeared swollen in the genital area. He could not establish gender.

Imorelda clearly knew what he intended. *I couldn't tell, either.* Apparently, she followed Tae's other consideration as well. *We don't know if or how this mind thing gets passed. You're all speculating based on my mother and me. Maybe she could have given birth to ten geniuses over time. Maybe she and I were flukes, and it has nothing to do with bloodline. All I know is the kitten in your hand will die sooner than later and none of these three has the intelligence to understand more than a few words of human speech.* She added forcefully, *And I doubt the boy will even manage that. He's no more intelligent than this chair I'm sitting in.*

Tae did not believe any human mother could make the cold assessments about her own children Imorelda just had; he doubted he would want to know anyone who could. But Imorelda was not human. He suddenly believed he understood her reticence to produce kittens, why Mior had waited so long in life and had had only one litter. Intelligence was an amazing, gods-given gift, but it had its downsides as well. It allowed for contemplation, for the speculation and consideration of information most animals took for granted. Humans could fear death and disability, could worry over the future of themselves, their progeny, their friends. For a normal cat, the world was relatively simple: find food and avoid things that harm or eat you. Regular cats did not worry over their offspring other than keeping them alive for the first couple of months, at which point they became a nuisance worthy of abandonment. Soon afterward, they were entirely forgotten. If they met again, they were treated like any other stranger. They might play, fight over food or territory, even mate.

Tae had found it difficult to deal with Subikahn's attraction to other men, a stance incompatible with Eastern mores and laws, punishable by death. As much as he tried to care about Ivana, to understand Griff and Tem'aree'ay's love for her, she repulsed him. He had learned to accept their differences, to love them, and he would do whatever he could to support Subikahn and Ivana; but his discomfort could never be fully banished. He could scarcely imagine deliberately bringing children into the world knowing most, if not all, of them would lack basic human intelligence.

Many people, including Matrinka, insisted Tae had a way with children. He enjoyed playing with them, and they tended to gravitate to him. He found their immaturity charming, but a lot of their appeal stemmed from the realization they would grow more responsible, wiser, and skilled. Introducing them to new games, new thoughts, and new experiences was a joy every parent appreciated. To attach oneself to creatures who shared your blood but were severely limited in what they could ever possibly do or know was another matter entirely. Helpless infants were enchanting; helpless adults were difficult, often repulsive, especially when one shared no ties to them.

Tae realized any future Imorelda had with her children would prove frustrating at best, most likely deeply painful. For six or ten weeks, she would watch over and love them, forming the basis for a lifelong emotional bond they could never share. They would forget her as she never could them. Once they left her, and they would, the concept of familial ties would elude them. No wonder she had not wanted to produce them, why she preferred that another mother raise them. She had only agreed to do it to appease Tae and Matrinka and, probably, with the hope at least one of the kittens would share her genius. Rightly or wrongly, she believed none did, and she understandably wanted to shed herself of them before she became too attached.

The urge to give in to Imorelda was strong, but Tae knew he could not. Anyone could tell the third kitten was abnormal; all current human societies would condone compassionately destroying one of their own with such problems in infancy. When it came to normal-appearing babies, however, even highly-experienced mothers sometimes went months or years before noticing certain innate problems. Tem'aree'ay, for example, did not realize Ivana's oddities until even long after the servants did. Tae attributed some of her blindness to the fact that elves did not suffer birth abnormalities or illnesses of any kind, so she did not know to look for them. Also, no one knew the proper developmental course for a human-elf hybrid. And, of course, Tae would never discount the same parental love that caused people to worry over every bump and bruise could also make them overlook the incurable simply because they did not want to see it. To Tae, it was way too early for Imorelda to plan the trajectory of her infants' intellects.

Tae searched for the best compromise. "Imorelda, if I allow this mother to dispose of the kitten I'm holding, will you raise the other two?"

There's no point . . . Imorelda started, but Tae could feel her wavering.

"Please, Imorelda. For Matrinka and for me. I just think it's too soon to make assumptions about anyone's intelligence or competence. They were only just born today."

Imorelda jumped down from the chair and onto the bed. The black cat turned her head to look at Imorelda and let out a single hiss of warning. *It would be the first time, but maybe you could be right.*

Tae smiled. It was the most characteristic thing Imorelda had said in longer than a week.

Imorelda lifted her chin and fixed her eyes on the deformed kitten. *Give it to her.*

Tae hesitated, his mind still bombarding him with unlikely supposition. *Imorelda . . .*

She read his concerns easily. *It's not the one,* she reassured him. *In addition to other problems, it does not have a fully developed heart or brain.*

Tae blurted out, "How can you possibly know that?" It seemed far too specific and technical for her to intuit.

Imorelda studied the other mother, apparently trying to find a way to safely extract her offspring. *Perhaps if humans ate their infants' placentas, they would have a better understanding of their children's potentials, too.*

Though intrigued, Tae had no intention of suggesting it to anyone.

Now give her the monstrosity, so I can reclaim my children while she's dealing with it.

Tae placed the kitten between himself and the black female. She rose immediately, once again dumping those lying on or attached to her into a pathetically mewing pile. Delicately, she stepped over them to sniff the newcomer. Moments later, she made deep growling noises as she set to work dispatching it.

Tae moved to the chair and watched Imorelda grab first the calico, which she dropped onto his thigh, then the tabby. That one, too, she put on his leg before leaping into his lap. The kittens made a few soft noises, then settled in against her. The abnormal kitten made no sounds, but the crunching noises of its demise made Tae uncomfortable. He talked over them. "Do you know why your litter came out . . ." He finished lamely, "The way it did?"

Imorelda did not appear to take offense. *I can't say why none of them have "the gift." However, I do know, in cats, first litters are often small and the likelihood of abnormalities is higher.*

Tae wondered how she knew this. He believed she could communicate with other cats but not at a sophisticated level. He supposed Matrinka might have told her, having witnessed hundreds of kittens born over the years.

It surely doesn't help I'm blood-related to all the cats in Béarn and that they've been interbreeding for generations.

Tae had learned King Griff also believed blood ties caused birth defects. His parents had been banished from Béarn for their illegal relationship, and he had blamed their close blood ties for what he considered his own intellectual lapse. He and Matrinka were cousins. The law allowed their marriage, and the populace had demanded it; but Griff had worried about any offspring they might produce. That had worked out for the best, since Matrinka loved the bard, Darris, whom Béarnian law forbade her to marry. Ultimately, Darris had sired her children, Griff claimed them, and the problem was solved to everyone's satisfaction. The ruler of Béarn, whether male or female, was expected to have multiple spouses; that left him free to marry his true love, Tem'aree'ay, who, as an elf, slipped through a carefully researched loophole in the law. Ironically, his child with the most blood-diverse of his three wives was the one who had suffered congenital abnormalities.

Tae accepted Imorelda's explanation without comment. It made as much sense as anything else, and he did want to believe her next litter, if they could convince her to have one, would not be plagued with the same issues as this one. He tried not to notice as the strange mother cat finished crunching, calmly licked the blood from her whiskers, and returned to her healthy brood.

CHAPTER 7

*When hatred is strong, when generation after generation has
distorted it far beyond truth and made it seem as if aggressors
were victims, it can spawn a hatred so intense that it defies any
logic*

—Sir Ra-khir Kedrin's son

BY THE TIME TAE KAHN returned the mother cat to her pen and
arrived at the meeting room, he found Kentt and the elves engaged
in spirited discussion. Surprised, he stood in the doorway watching
them for several moments, trying to figure out what language they
were using and how they had discovered it.

As far as Tae could tell, Kentt was speaking *usaro* and the elves
elvish, yet they seemed to understand one another. Though accustomed to being the only one in the room who grasped multiple languages, the conversation dizzied him. He had limited knowledge of
those two languages in particular; they had no overlap he could discern, and both sides were using words and concepts foreign to him,
apparently relating to magic.

Captain paused long enough to gesture Tae to him. As he fully
entered the room, Tae deferred to Imorelda perched on his shoulders. *Are they using some sort of mental communication?*

Imorelda disengaged for a moment, scanning various levels Tae
could not reach without her. Tae walked all the way to Captain before she finally replied, *Not that I can find. They're doing a lot of out-
loud jabbering, though.*

Tae could hear that for himself. He addressed the elf in the common trading tongue. "Are you . . . talking to one another?"

A smile wreathed Captain's face. "Amazing, isn't it?"

Tae could scarcely believe it. "But how?" Now that they had
bridged the gap, the elves no longer cowered at one end of the room.

Whatever Kentt was saying, it fascinated them enough to overlook the danger.

"It's difficult to explain, but you deserve to know. The hard part was convincing him other languages besides his own exist and make sense. That was your doing, and we appreciate it."

Tae accepted the compliment gracefully. He had placed himself at great risk on several occasions to learn the rudiments of the Heimstadr language, oral and mental. Without knowing it, he could never have demonstrated that sounds are just symbols and can substitute for other sounds. Even then, it had not proven easy. "But when I walked out of here, none of you knew a word of the others' language. Kentt could receive *khohlar*, but he couldn't respond to it in any comprehensible way."

Captain nodded. "All true. We used *khohlar* and gestures for a while. As we got more comfortable, we applied magic to the problem. The *Kjempemagiska* manipulate chaos very differently than we do, which we knew; but chaos is chaos. Organizing it, however you do it, takes magic. Turns out, Kentt knew a way to translate he would never have discovered if not for your convincing him of the reality of other languages and our desire to find a way to share chaos-organizing techniques. I think, once we learn how, elves can use it to bridge any and all communication gaps between intelligent beings with a concept of language."

The possibilities staggered Tae. Currently, all societies taught the common tongue and all diplomats were required to speak it fluently. However, few used it as their primary language. Literal, certain translation might prevent so many misunderstandings and render agreements ironclad. Whenever they came upon new groups of people, such as elves and *Kjempemagiska*, the world currently relied on Tae and his uncanny ability. He would no longer find himself trapped in Béarn as de facto translator. *I could go back to the East!*

The idea thrilled Tae more than he expected. It was his home, of course but he had traveled so much he no longer felt tied to it. His things were there and the throne he rarely sat upon, which often seemed more burden than honor. He always knew he needed and wanted to return, but he could not fathom what drew him with such a relentless pull.

Imorelda answered with a single word. *Alneezah.*

The sending startled Tae. He had not intended to broadcast his thoughts, but Imorelda knew him too intimately not to notice. *Alneezah.* Tae repeated the name of the castle maid who found ridiculous excuses to air the fluffiest blankets beneath him when he recklessly climbed the castle walls. Her love for him was pure and innocent, devoid of any malicious intent. Raised in an era when nobility never intermingled with peasants, she had no hope he would ever return her devotion. Yet, with Imorelda's help, he had noticed her. And, now, he realized, he wanted to get to know her a lot better. The idea of taking a queen, of building a family and remaining in the East with them suddenly seemed desirable, even to one as risk prone and adventuresome as Tae Kahn Weile's son.

Lost in his own thoughts, Tae suddenly remembered Captain. "That's wonderful! So . . . you don't need me?"

Captain made a throwaway gesture. "It would seem we don't. Kentt thinks he can use the same magic to talk to humans, but he has requested someone to bridge the types of communication gaps that have nothing to do with literal words." Now, he seemed to struggle. "Differences in . . . cultural expectations. Words, gestures, suggestions that may seem perfectly fine in one language but don't translate exactly and might come across as threatening or offensive. It doesn't have to be you, though."

Tae considered. Arturo had been taking lessons in *usaro* from Tae with the stated aim of becoming a diplomat between the two worlds. Tae knew Arturo and Kentt had familial affection for one another, and they both loved Kentt's daughter. He also felt certain Matrinka would prefer her son take up negotiations rather than the naval military position he had aspired to before the wars. He smiled broadly. "I know just the person."

Although Saviar Ra-khirsson arrived at the Myrcidian compound with only Weile Kahn for company, he knew a host had assisted their journey. He had seen only a few, but hints and experience told him a vast network existed. He and Weile spent each and every night in a new location, never an inn or an open clearing, like he and the other Renshai would have chosen. Saviar and Weile had spent some nights in well-camouflaged caves, others in hidden underground bunkers, a few more in forest brush and thistle that appeared impenetrable. They had even once slept in the cradling branches of a broad-leafed tree.

When others joined them, Weile spoke to them in a language Saviar did not understand. Usually, he recognized the gruffness of the Eastern tongue, but sometimes the voices sounded more lyrical or standard, the accents more or less familiar. They shared other forms of communication Saviar did not understand: hand signals and wordless noises, some animal and others wholly different and carrying long distances. Often, Weile would halt and look around, clearly seeing something invisible to Saviar. The Renshai suspected Weile's men left him symbols: branches, sticks, and stones arranged in intelligible patterns.

They had traveled mostly in silence, which had suited Saviar's mood, though he appreciated banter when his thoughts took him places he did not want to go. Occasionally, Weile deferred to him on what direction to take. Saviar did not know whether the Eastern leader truly needed his advice; Weile seemed far more savvy when it came to travel. However, Saviar could think of no other reason why Weile had requested his company. Obviously, it was not for idle chatter or protection. Saviar still practiced his sword forms daily, as Renshai training demanded, but he made sure to do it far enough from Weile he did not alarm the crime lord's protectors.

To call Weile Kahn cautious was gross understatement; his life depended on it. He had organized the most dangerous people on Midgard, the type even their own mothers would never trust, and he had angered several of the most powerful royals. He had elevated wariness to an art, yet he never appeared inconvenienced by it. Of course, he never appeared particularly anything; Saviar found him nearly inscrutable most of the time.

Now, they had arrived at the usually magically-undetectable home of the Mages of Myrcidë, and it amazed Saviar how he had no difficulty whatsoever visualizing every part of it. He had spent several months here convalescing after his wound had gone septic. At that time, the mages had nursed him back to health, with the most involved being Chymmerlee. According to Subikahn, she had fallen in love with his unconscious form, watching over him constantly, feeding him through a tube, and using her magic to gradually overcome the massive infection. As he healed, they had gone on walks together and played in the nearby creek; his fondness and appreciation for her had grown as well. She had even intervened when the mages refused to allow the twins to leave, accompanying them to the Pirate War and assisting when all of the other mages had refused.

Now, she despised him, and Saviar's prior attempts to find out why and change her mind had resulted in displeasing his father and the other Knights of Erythane, Saviar's capture and isolated confinement by the mages, and, ultimately, his rescue by Weile Kahn. His feelings for her had become as confused as the ones for Subikahn and nearly as disturbing. En route, he had considered the possibility of reuniting with her. On arrival, more complex thoughts assailed him, and he wondered if he should have refused Weile's invitation, assuming such a thing were even possible. When the leader of the world's criminals called, a wise person answered.

"Ready?" Weile asked.

More for delay than any need to know, Saviar asked, "Why is it so clear this time? I could always see it with sword in hand, but never in such detail."

Weile's face showed nothing, but he did quietly explain. "The Pica's reach is farther."

That Weile had gotten his hands on a priceless artifact twice in a matter of months did not surprise Saviar. He could waste more time pretending it did, but he suspected his companion would see through the tactic. Weile appeared to trust him and his competence, and it seemed like lunacy to put that in jeopardy. Saviar merely nodded in response. "Ready as I can get."

The two men approached the long, squat building housing the Mages of Myrcidë. The last time they had come, a guard nervously met them outside, prepared to pepper them with magic if they displayed any hostile intentions. This time, they walked all the way to the door without seeing anyone other than a few curious eyes at usually invisible windows. Weile gestured toward the door, and Saviar knocked firmly. The sound echoed. Though he listened carefully, Saviar could not hear any movement; the heavy stonework did not allow sound to penetrate.

After several moments, Weile motioned for Saviar to repeat the action. Saviar retrieved a stone from the ground and used it to rap against the door significantly louder. Then, Saviar dropped the stone so anyone watching would know he did not intend to use it as a weapon. He kept his hand away from his hilt, although he did not go so far as to remove the weapon. Weile appeared unarmed, though Saviar knew the Easterner had a knack for hiding easily accessed knives beneath his clothing.

Again, the knock received no answer. Saviar drew breath to suggest opening the door themselves. He could smash the lock if it had one, and he hoped the Pica would thwart any magic cast upon it. Before he could speak, however, the door eased open. Blenford's familiar face peered through the crack.

Saviar had met nearly all of the mages during his convalescence, when they had still believed him a descendant of Myrcidë. He had gotten to know them a bit better during the time they had kept him prisoner. The second youngest of the mages, after Chymmerlee, Blenford looked to be well into his thirties. He wore his orange hair halfway down his back and sported a matching spray of freckles.

Like most of the mages, who rarely or never ventured outside their compound, he had pale, sallow skin. "Saviar, Weile, what can I do for you?" Though his unwillingness to fully open the door hampered him, Blenford attempted to see beyond the two men on the unmarked doorstep, apparently to assure himself they had not brought an army.

Saviar knew it would not help. If Weile had brought one, even Saviar did not know about it, and no one would spot it with a casual examination. "May we come inside, please? We need to talk to you about Jeremilan and the others."

Blenford fidgeted, clearly unnerved by the suggestion, but surely aware he had no real choice. The Myrcidians needed to know the status of their leader and the eleven mages who had accompanied him to the war. "You have no violent intentions?"

"None at all," Saviar promised. "We came only to help you."

Though Weile made no similar vow, Blenford threw the door wide and allowed them to enter the familiar room where they had previously haggled. Then, Weile had returned the three Myrcidians he had kidnapped in order to rescue Saviar. The crafty Easterner had convinced the mages to send a dozen from their very small group of people to aid the war, a feat Saviar had desperately attempted and failed at on two separate occasions.

As the two entered, Blenford quietly closed the door and turned to face them. The room had not changed since their last meeting: a space filled with several matching wooden couches, benches, and chairs. Arinosta perched in the chair Weile had chosen the last time, a sturdy construct heaped with pillows that seemed to swallow her ancient, withered frame. Beside her on a slightly smaller chair sat Roby, another elder. A nearby couch held Chestinar, a skeletal man with brittle, colorless hair missing in random patches. He sniffed almost constantly, the heel of a scabby hand brushing the tip of his nose from long habit. Beside him sat Janecos, a middle-aged woman who had survived the indignity of being one of Weile's prisoners. Another, Paulton, a small blond, watched them warily from a bench on the opposite side of the room, between two exit doors.

A lanky white-haired man Saviar knew as Eldebar stood next to one of those doors as if prepared to bolt through it at any moment. Seven mages in the room meant another seven elsewhere in the compound, including Chymmerlee. Exactly twenty-six mages currently existed, twelve of them trapped on another world and half of the remainder assembled in this room to meet with Weile and Saviar.

Arinosta apparently served as leader with Jeremilan in absentia.

She was old and frail, Saviar knew, and tended to cling to Roby when she walked, an odd choice as he used a staff himself. She made a broad gesture that urged the newcomers to sit but did not specify a location, allowing them to choose.

Weile selected a well-pillowed chair that placed him in easy sight of every exit with minimal movement of his head. He did not seem troubled that it put his back to the bench holding the sickly Chestinar and also Janecos. Saviar took longer, making certain to pick a spot that allowed him to see all the areas Weile could not while still facing Arinosta, though it placed him on the only unpadded bench. He already towered over every other person in the room, so he did not need the added height, and was still young enough not to have to worry about comfort. Though his intensive practices and training often left him sore, he never suffered from positional aches and pains.

Unhurried, Arinosta waited until everyone was seated before speaking. "What news have you brought us of Jeremilan and the others?"

Now, Saviar deferred to Weile. He had watched the Easterner disarm a king with a few well-chosen words and dominate a conference of nobles with twice his experience. "I will tell you about Jeremilan and the others after we have made arrangements for my companion to meet with Chymmerlee in private."

Arinosta's wrinkles deepened, if possible. "We have violated Jeremilan's orders merely by allowing you entrance. No one who is not one of us will visit with Jeremilan's granddaughter, particularly not a . . ." She spat the word, "Renshai."

Saviar schooled his features, prepared for a withering rejoinder from Weile that never came. Instead, the Easterner clambered to his feet. "Very well. Saviar, it's time to go. They don't want their companions back."

Saviar rose obediently.

"Wait," Arinosta shouted before they could take a single step. "That's not what I said."

"It is," Weile assured her, explaining the entire situation with those two words. He had information the mages desperately needed and could obtain no other way. They had little choice but to agree to his terms, no matter how heinous.

Saviar almost felt sorry for the Mages of Myrcidë. Currently weak, but with the potential to amass great power, they had chosen to hide from the world. Jeremilan had cautiously gathered everyone he could find who appeared to carry a hint of blood left behind by the long-dead mages. Though he had intended to lead and breed them, hoping to train, grow, and strengthen the mages over time, his plans had gone awry. They had had trouble producing healthy children. Too few woman had conceived; too many children had died or lacked any potential for magic. The tribe grew dangerously older, sequestered, and convinced common humans would deliberately destroy them out of ignorance or fear. Most of the mages never left the safety of their compound.

It had taken masterful arguments, threats, and promises to induce nearly half the reluctant mages to assist in the war. The most significant pledge had been to protect them at the expense of all others, to bring Jeremilan and his companions home safely. Saviar could see how the mages might feel dishonored and deceived, why they might not wish to cooperate in any way. Yet they truly had no choice in the matter because Jeremilan and the others could yet be saved, unharmed. Their own actions—or lack—might doom their fellows.

Weile headed for the door, and Saviar dutifully followed.

The mages shifted uneasily. "Wait," Arinosta shouted again. "Please sit. We may be able to find a compromise."

Weile hesitated, his back still to the mages, head bowed as if deep in thought.

"You have information we need, but you must know we cannot grant unlimited or open-ended demands."

Weile finally raised his head. "I don't believe I've asked anything unreasonable."

Yet, Saviar added silently. He knew the mages would deem leaving their compound too dangerous and frightening for consideration, yet that was exactly what he and Weile had come to ask.

"True." Arinosta gestured for the men to retake their seats. "But you're not finished, are you?"

"Actually, I am." Weile's response surprised even Saviar. He retook his seat but only on the edge, as if he suspected he would not remain there long. Taking his cues from his twin's grandfather, Saviar slid back into position on the bench. "My only request is that Saviar has the opportunity to meet in private with Chymmerlee. Once that has been arranged to my satisfaction, I'll give you all the information you need regarding Jeremilan and the other mages."

It was a game even Saviar could not predict, and he believed he already had all the facts and knew exactly what Weile had come to accomplish or, at least, what he had promised King Griff.

Arinosta chose her words carefully. "You must understand our esteemed leader, Jeremilan, left us with specific orders. He believed it imperative none of us leave the safety of our compound, we not allow others to enter it and, most of all, we not allow any outsider, most especially young Saviar, to find, see, or talk to our Chymmerlee."

Though it made sense Jeremilan would demand these exact things, Saviar also knew, by the end of the negotiations, all of them would require violation. If he had had to guess exactly what words Jeremilan had spoken as he prepared to leave, Saviar would have missed nothing except, perhaps, the reference to himself by name.

Weile shrugged. "You can arrange the meeting, or we can leave. It is nonnegotiable."

Saviar was tired of being discussed. He no longer felt attracted to Chymmerlee; her ability to believe terrible things about him with no proof, her unwillingness to listen to his explanations, her cruel treatment of him had killed the romance they had once shared. To him, the meeting was entirely negotiable, but he knew better than to contradict Weile Kahn. "Chymmerlee and I spent hours alone together, and no one cared. I have never meant her any harm, still don't, and you all know it. I just need to talk to her." He wondered exactly what Weile wanted him to discuss with Chymmerlee and doubted it was about their prior relationship. Though only eighteen, she had the most experience outside of the mages' compound and did not assume every other human who discovered what they were would wish them all dead.

Arinosta tipped her head. "You will guarantee, when their meeting is finished, Chymmerlee and her baby will be unharmed?"

Weile laughed.

The incongruous reaction drew every eye, including Saviar's. Arinosta addressed it with venom. "Our desire to keep one of our own safe is a joke to you?"

Although he did not smile, humor danced in Weile's eyes, more passion than he usually revealed. "I find it amusing you're reading the situation backward. Saviar would never hurt anyone who did not attack him, and even some who did. Chymmerlee, however, has viciously assaulted Saviar and Subikahn on several different occasions. The savage, warrior Renshai you claim to fear—" He made a motion in the Renshai's general direction "—suffered the worst pain of his life when you captured and imprisoned him."

Weile added quickly, "I can assure you Saviar will cause Chymmerlee and her offspring no physical injuries. But we have no way to predict how any woman will emotionally react to a man she used to love."

Weile had a point Saviar could not deny. Chymmerlee had gone from adoring him to despising him seemingly overnight. He had believed this came from her discovering his Renshai background, something he should have told her but could not because he had been bound by a promise to Subikahn. Centuries earlier, according to history, the Renshai had wiped out the Myrcidians, so they were understandably predisposed toward disliking Renshai. Saviar had attempted to apologize and explain his lapse, but she had not allowed it.

Arinosta looked around the room, presumably for help from the other mages. Accustomed to deferring to Jeremilan, however, they did nothing. "May we discuss this amongst ourselves?"

Weile made a gesture that included every mage in the room. "Feel free, but our time is not unlimited. There's an emergent situation in Béarn that requires our attention."

Arinosta had probably meant for the discussion to occur in private, but Weile made no move to leave so Saviar did not either. Clearly, the other mages intended for Arinosta to make the decision, and they would not interfere with her choice. She looked last and longest at Roby who gave her nothing more than a single shoulder shrug.

Left to her own devices, Arinosta took control. "Eldebar, arrange a private room for Chymmerlee and Saviar and take her there. You and the others may watch through the window and intervene if anything potentially violent occurs, but you may not listen. Come back and let us know when the arrangements have been made." She swiveled her attention from Eldebar at the far side of the room to Weile. "Is that sufficient?"

Weile glanced at Saviar, who nodded. Any arrangements that suited Weile's specifications would more than work for him. He did not seriously worry Chymmerlee would harm him. Though she had magic he could not predict, he would never admit or even assume he could not take care of himself in any situation. "That is sufficient."

Without comment, Eldebar hurried through one of the exits to obey.

Arinosta returned her attention fully to Weile and Saviar. "What has become of Jeremilan and the others?" She reminded tightly, "You promised to bring them home safely."

Weile was quick to point out, "I, personally, made no such promise." Saviar did not bother to think back, certain Weile spoke truth. He rarely made pledges of any kind and did not allow himself to become beholden.

Arinosta did not argue. "Nevertheless, the promise was made. Are you saying it's been broken?"

"I said no such thing," Weile replied calmly, but his tone conveyed a spare hint of threat. Saviar knew it unwise to ever put words into the Easterner's mouth or make assumptions about what he intended. "I do not believe anyone is ever foolish enough to promise no harm could possibly befall someone they do not personally control. When Jeremilan and the others followed our advice, they were entirely safe. It was not until Jeremilan made a foolish decision, without informing any of us, that he became endangered."

Saviar wondered how Weile knew such a thing, then remembered the intensive spying that had played such an important role in keeping track of the *Kjempemagiska*. Weile Kahn had eyes nearly everywhere, at least within any reasonable distance of his person and anywhere he wished to examine.

Arinosta's nostrils flared. "Are you say—?" She caught herself before repeating her previous mistake. "If I'm interpreting correctly, you're suggesting Jeremilan deliberately placed himself in danger and paid a price for doing so."

Weile just stared back at her, expressionless. It was not a suggestion; he had said exactly that.

Arinosta's features reddened, but she made no hostile move. Saviar doubted the elderly woman could do anything swiftly without risking the integrity of her bones. "So he's . . ." The color left her face, restoring its normal pallor. ". . . dead?"

"No," Weile said. "He's alive and, as far as we know, unharmed."

"As far as you know?"

Weile hedged. "I have not had the occasion to speak or meet with him recently."

Eldebar returned to the room. "Chymmerlee is ready."

Arinosta dismissed him with a wave. Saviar glanced at Weile to assure his twin's grandfather had no difficulty with him leaving. Weile responded with a slight head tilt toward the door, and Saviar went toward Eldebar, surprised to find himself feeling more numb than excited. Only a couple of months earlier, he would have leaped at the opportunity. Now, his feelings for Chymmerlee, and the entire situation, confounded him. Everything had changed.

As he followed Eldebar through the door, down a short hallway, and to another opening, Saviar found himself uninterested in contemplating how love could turn to hate so swiftly. He had encountered it himself, when Subikahn had voiced his betrayal, yet Saviar still struggled with it. He despised what Subikahn had done with every fiber of his being, yet he found himself nearly incapable of loathing his twin. As much as he wanted to, it eluded him. Any Renshai worth knowing would seek revenge, if only on the traitor's broken body, pyre, or by showing disrespect to the swords he had not deserved to carry. Chymmerlee, on the other hand, did not grapple with conflicting emotions. She seemed to have no difficulty hating Saviar, treating him cruelly, and that made him certain she had never truly cared about him.

Realization struck Saviar hard. For as long as he could remember, people had described him as strikingly handsome. Most intended it as a compliment, but it never ceased to embarrass him. He had worked lifelong at becoming a competent swordsman and a moral person and wished others would focus on those efforts instead. He had done nothing praiseworthy to earn his appearance and gave it no particular attention. Simply, he closely resembled his father and grandfather: tall and muscular with strawberry-blond hair, classical features, and a square chin. Males and females remarked most on his eyes. Rather than his father's green or his mother's deep sky blue, he shared the pale azure of Knight-Captain Kedrin.

Ra-khir, too, seemed to have trouble dealing with people's reactions to what he called his "outer shell." He had warned Saviar some people would treat him differently based solely on his appearance, but Saviar had never taken the advice to heart. On several occasions, Subikahn had sarcastically called him "pretty boy" or claimed women were flirting with him and laughed at his obliviousness. Subikahn had always seemed a bit wary of Chymmerlee's attraction to Saviar. Only now, Saviar understood why. She had fallen for him while he lay in a coma, ravaged by sepsis, long before she knew anything about him in any way that mattered. His features alone had charmed her, and a love based on looks did not have the profundity to endure.

That sudden insight became more fuel for the irritation and anger Saviar was doing his best to overcome. How could he ever settle down, find love, create a family when he could never trust anyone's motivations again? He could not even complain about the situation; it would only incite ire. If the beautiful, the wealthy or the talented grumbled, they were instantly reviled. Their problems, no matter how painful or life-threatening, were automatically dismissed amid rolled eyes and sneers. It distressed him to realize he had even done his share of smirking when Marisole had dared to moan about the life of a princess.

All of this flashed through Saviar's mind as he hesitated at the door Eldebar held open. When Saviar finally glanced through the opening, he saw Chymmerlee standing alone in a room with a long table and two dozen chairs, her lower lip clamped between her teeth and her arms folded across her chest. Her mood did not appear open for discussion. Nevertheless, Saviar stepped through and remained silent until Eldebar closed the door behind him.

"Hello," Saviar said.

Chymmerlee looked older than when he had last seen her. She insisted she was eighteen, a year younger than Saviar, but he had no idea if she had told him the truth. Magic had kept Jeremilan alive for longer than two hundred years. Surely, all of the mages slowed their aging, if they could. Saviar noted a hint of a belly on her otherwise slender figure, and her breasts seemed larger and more pronounced through her shift. The mahogany hair she used to wear down was now bound up in the back. He could barely discern her oversized lips sucked into a scowl, the lower one still trapped between her teeth. He remembered her eyes as a playful blue-gray; now they just seemed steely. She was not pretty in a traditional way; but he still found her attractive, though not particularly so at this moment with hatred for him stamped across her features. "I have nothing to say to you, demon. Rapist. And I refuse to listen to you."

Many peoples considered Renshai demons, but the "rapist" epithet annoyed him more. He had no intention of losing his virginity before his wedding night and had never seen or touched an uncovered female body part. The mages had impregnated Chymmerlee, wiping her memory with magic, then convinced her Saviar had done it. Weile believed her own grandfather was the baby's father in a desperate attempt to enrich the infant with the maximum amount of magical blood before he passed away or lost the opportunity. Weile had confronted the mages, and they had agreed to tell her the horrible truth she certainly deserved to know. Apparently, they had not kept this vow.

Though angered, Saviar understood their reasoning. No woman would react well to learning such a terrible thing. Her distress alone might cause a miscarriage or she might seek to inflict one on herself, and the mages truly believed their future hinged upon this infant-to-be. Worse, Chymmerlee might run away, stealing not only the child but herself, the only fertile female who carried mage blood, Jeremilan's own granddaughter. Though beyond despicable, their decision had a weird logic Saviar understood but could never allow them to justify. Whether or not they believed they had reason, he could not allow them to use Chymmerlee or him in this wretched manner.

"I would never rape any woman, especially you."

Chymmerlee whirled, showing him her back, a gesture more disrespectful than any other she could have chosen. Even spitting on him, which she had done at their last confrontation, was not as aggravating as this. Renshai considered it a denigration of their martial skill.

"I . . . cared about you." Saviar found himself incapable of saying "love." He had never couched their relationship in those terms, not even to himself. He had begun to wonder, but it had not gone quite that far before she discovered his heritage and her pregnancy.

Chymmerlee clamped her hands over her ears.

"Chymmerlee!" he shouted, needing her to hear him.

Chymmerlee started singing at the top of her lungs, "Skip through the compound, skip, skip, skip! Keep it slow so you don't slip . . ."

"Chymmerlee," Saviar tried again.

"Weave through the doorways and watch the cracks. Careful you don't hurt your backs!"

It did not surprise Saviar a childhood rhyme of Myrcidians would contain two danger warnings in the first stanza despite the simplicity of the actions described. It was clear to him she had no intention of allowing him to speak, so he opened the door and retreated into the hallway. Eldebar waited for him there to lead him back to the sitting room.

Everything appeared exactly as Saviar had left it, the mages and Weile still sitting in the same locations. Tension wrapped the room, and Arinosta's expression bespoke irritation and concern simultaneously. When Saviar and Eldebar entered, she turned her attention to them. "Did it go all right?"

Eldebar shrugged. "That depends on how you define 'all right.'" He added the bit she would most wish to know. "There was no violence."

Weile caught Saviar's eye, but he had no idea how to explain what had happened with a gesture or two, so he merely shrugged hopelessly.

Arinosta cleared her throat. "The mages will need to discuss this . . . situation."

Saviar felt certain she referred to what Weile had told her, not what had happened or, more accurately, not happened between him and Chymmerlee.

Nimbly, Weile hopped down from the piled pillows. "Saviar and I will step outside so you can meet in here. I believe you understand the plight of the missing limits the amount of time we can give you to . . ." He selected the next word carefully and gave it clear emphasis, "ruminate."

Saviar felt his lips edging into a smile and stopped them. Granted unlimited time, the mages would chew the facts for eternity and never come to a decision.

Weile headed for the door, and Saviar followed him outside.

The sunlight beamed down on them, preternaturally bright after the self-inflicted gloom of the mages' dwelling. They strolled more than walked to a concealing line of trees before Weile finally turned to confront Saviar. "How do *you* define 'all right'?"

Saviar leaned against a tree trunk, addressing the intent of the question. "She called me a demon and a rapist, then refused to let me speak. The only word I said that she heard was 'hello,' and that was only because I managed to slip it out before she plugged her ears and started singing."

Weile chuckled, a sound that added nothing positive to Saviar's mood.

Still, the Renshai managed a faint smile. "Perhaps . . . *you* could speak to her?"

Weile drew in a deep breath, then let it out slowly. "Saviar, if you were Subikahn, I might consider it."

Saviar could scarcely believe what he had just heard. Ra-khir and Tae had always taken great pains to treat the twins similarly, never worrying about who carried the blood of which father. Most of the time, Ra-khir referred to all three boys as his sons, though he always deferred to Tae when it came to issues involving Subikahn. In their youth, when Kevral had taken the boys to visit the East, Tae had never favored one twin over the other. The last person in the world Saviar had expected to break that tradition was Weile Kahn. Saviar had always had a good relationship with Subikahn's grandfather, and they had grown much closer over the last month. "Oh," he said, trying to keep disappointment from his voice, though he doubted Weile missed anything.

"As you know, Renshai are not well-liked. Even people who believe themselves champions of morality and fairness blithely display vicious bigotry when it comes to Renshai. They always have a justification, of course, usually lies, rumor and innuendo, rewritten history, contexts deliberately twisted. Once upon a time, the Renshai needed no leader. When the world demanded one, any one would do. Now, things have become more nuanced, and the Renshai's future relies on having a leader who can handle the most difficult situations, who can find the hidden traps in treaties and covenants, whether written or verbal. A leader who can deal with anything."

Saviar's cheeks grew hot. He did not want to think about how badly he had treated Thialnir when he had still allowed anger to rule him. "I turned down that position."

Weile continued as if Saviar had not spoken, "I will convince the mages to accompany us back to Béarn because that's the task I agreed to undertake. As far as winning over Chymmerlee, that's your challenge. The approach you take will be up to you."

Saviar's jaw set, but he said nothing and kept his hands away from his hilts. Even a Renshai could not afford to look as if he were threatening Weile Kahn.

"The world is not as black and white as the Knights of Erythane make it appear; sometimes, the choices that confront you are all, in some way, bleak."

Saviar remained in place, contemplating Weile's advice which went far beyond the situation he faced with Chymmerlee. The Easterner's dark eyes seemed to flay him open to reveal the rage and betrayal and uncertainty he was trying so hard to control. Those words, spoken by a man most people considered a criminal, if an uncommon one, went to the heart of his turmoil over Subikahn, over his future, over his interactions, or lack thereof, with Chymmerlee. Even his conversation with the immortal Renshai had not touched him as deeply.

Only one thing had become absolutely certain. Saviar's life had fallen apart, and he could rely on no one but himself to bring the pieces back together.

CHAPTER 8

To believe that all life is predestined and all fate inescapable means denying the control of body and mind I have striven for too long. It reduces decision to meaninglessness and takes all glory and principle out of the hands of mortals.

—*Colbey Calistinsson*

QUEEN MATRINKA OF BÉARN sat on her canopied bed vigorously stroking a purring Imorelda in her lap, a long stripe of sunlight from the window falling directly and warmly upon them. Though keeping Tae's cat happy was her first priority at the moment, she could not take her eyes from the two kittens snuggled and sleeping in a hollow of her pillow, their tiny eyes closed, their ears occasionally twitching.

Despite Tae's warning not to get her hopes too high, Matrinka could not help wondering which of the kittens would replace Mior as her full-time companion, daring to hope both would develop the intelligence and communication talent of their mother and grandmother. She could imagine her heart soaring every time one or the other deigned to speak with her, would delight even in their sibling rivalries. If only one evolved to the proper level, she suspected and hoped it would be the calico, though she would love the other just as much. Her beloved Mior had been similarly colored; thus far at least, only females had demonstrated the talent. In fact, Imorelda had been the only girl in her litter.

"Thank you," Matrinka said, right fingers scratching beneath Imorelda's chin, left hand stroking her from side to flank as she rolled around to give access to whatever portion of her anatomy she wanted touched at the moment.

Why are you thanking me this time? Imorelda sent through her vibrant purring.

Matrinka smiled. "Thank you for having kittens, even though you didn't really want to be a mother. I promised to take care of them for you. You need only let me know what you want me to do. Also, thank you for letting me see and touch them. Most mother cats hide their babies, you know."

You've already thanked me for both of those things, Imorelda pointed out.

Matrinka switched to mental communication. *And I probably will several more times. I don't want you to ever doubt my appreciation. I understand you did this for me, and it's a lot to ask of anyone who's not your spouse. I really will do anything for them, even feed and clean them.*

Irritation accompanied Imorelda's sending, along with something else Matrinka could not identify. It resembled grief or, perhaps, deception. She dared not ask because just absorbing unintended emotion across the link felt like eavesdropping. She did not want to discourage Imorelda from communicating with her for fear of revealing something the cat would rather keep hidden. *And I've told you I'll let you know if I want your help. For now, babysitting occasionally is enough. Having humans watching out for them when I'm away means I don't need to hide them from predators or from wayward shoes on the feet of oblivious people.*

Matrinka understood but still felt guilty about the arrangement. At the time, she had even agreed to dispose of the afterbirths, stimulate their urinary and fecal systems, as well as feed them in order to get Imorelda to agree to the pregnancy. Now that the kittens had arrived, the cat had demanded none of these services.

Tae had stated his belief that motherhood would grow on the cat and the natural love and protectiveness mothers felt for their offspring would develop, even against her will. He was usually correct, and it seemed so this time as well, but Matrinka still worried. She had no real assurance either of these two kittens would be "the one," and she might have to cajole Imorelda into more pregnancies. It would prove far more difficult after the cat took all the burdens onto herself and found she still did not like the chores or the infants. Imorelda had stated her opinion that the world, and Béarn in particular, had too many cats already.

Someone knocked timidly at the door. Matrinka drew breath to invite the visitor in; before she could, the door whipped open and Marisole stepped inside, smelling of wind and tears, her gittern draped over one shoulder. Alarmed, Matrinka sat up straighter, but she did not rise to embrace her daughter for fear of dumping Imorelda. "What's wrong?"

A direct question required a simple answer, but Matrinka knew she would not get one. The bardic curse had come into fruition, and Marisole could not respond except in song.

As expected, Marisole swept the instrument into her hands and began to play. The music was sweet and soft, conveying anxiety and betrayal, fear and anger directly to Matrinka's heart. The emotional state of her gifted daughter became instantly clear, but the causes for it eluded her. Song, Matrinka realized, had two parts for a reason. The melody engaged her emotions, but she also needed lyrics to understand the motivations invoking them.

Years of loving Béarn's bard had made Matrinka patient about the curse. When she and Darris had traveled with Kevral, Ra-khir, and Tae, the others frequently found him tiresome. Yet Matrinka never had. She loved him for who and what he was. His music crept into her soul until it, and he, became a part of her. Now, she could hardly sleep until he came back to their bed at night to sing of the events of his day with King Griff, when his mood allowed, and of his undying devotion to her.

To Matrinka's surprise, rather than sing her troubles, Marisole merely asked, "Mama, have your courses come?"

Startled by the question, Matrinka's hands stilled on the cat and she dumbly repeated. "My courses?" She considered the point behind the question as she replied. "They've come and gone. I'm nearly halfway to the next—" Realizing the possible reason for the query, she cut off with a gasp. The two of them had synched up perfectly the past eighteen months. "Have yours not started?"

Marisole shook her head ever so slightly, as if she feared even that tiny bit of information might drive her back to song.

Either oblivious to or discounting the turmoil, Imorelda sent, *Pet me!*

Matrinka resumed stroking the cat absently.

"Oh, kittens!" Marisole said.

For a moment, Matrinka thought she had received a cryptic answer before she followed Marisole's gaze to her pillow.

"They're so tiny." The younger woman added wistfully. "I miss having kittens all over the palace."

Matrinka did not admit that she did, too. It would upset Imorelda, and she also knew they were probably the only two humans who did. The servants had tolerated the cats because they loved their queen, but placing the animals outside had made their lives far easier. It was difficult not to adore kittens, sweet curious playful kittens, but all of them grew into cats. And a castle overrun by any sort of animal was inconvenient, difficult to maintain, and even dangerous.

She recognized Marisole's tactic for what it was: delay. "Is there any chance you're . . ." She found herself scarcely able to speak the word. ". . . pregnant?"

Marisole opened her mouth, then closed it. She sighed, lifted the gittern, and played. This time she sang, her voice higher and not yet as sure as Darris', but all the same beautiful and with a talent beyond that of older and far more practiced minstrels. It had first appeared to Matrinka that the gift had come upon Marisole abruptly, her ability wholly and completely magical.

Later, Matrinka discovered Darris had been training Marisole from a very young age. He had kept it secret so as not to upset his lover by reminding her that her firstborn would inherit the bardic curse, and their deception about who had fathered Matrinka's three children would become transparent to anyone who gave it suspicious, deliberate thought. Whether or not the curse also granted the bard supernatural talent was a mystery no bard in recent history dared to test, fearing the curse would force their offspring to inflict atonal, unaccompanied song onto royals and commoners alike.

These thoughts disappeared as Marisole's song enraptured her mother. It dragged Matrinka to another time, anchored her to her youth in Béarn Castle when her love for Darris, and his for her, had been devastatingly raw. The bittersweet remembrance of that first, fiery attraction brought stars to her eyes and a bemused smile to her lips. Her hands drifted from Imorelda and across her chest to grasp her own shoulders. She felt warm and safe in Darris' arms and also terrified because she knew their love was forbidden, barred by law from ever reaching fruition.

As the last notes faded, Matrinka came back to herself. She found Imorelda bumping her elbow with her furry head and Marisole staring at her hopefully.

It had been decades since Darris had needed confirmation. Over time, he had learned when he could speak and when he needed to sing, had become so talented he never questioned what messages his music had conveyed. Marisole's uncertainty brought Matrinka back even more fully into her own adolescent past, when she and Darris had been young and hesitant and foolish, giddy with the joy of what they had discovered and sure no one else had ever experienced what they felt for one another.

Matrinka lowered her arms. One hand went back to petting Imorelda, the other she placed on Marisole's thigh, only then realizing the girl had joined her on the bed, her legs folded and her gittern cautiously cradled. Though the possibility her daughter had defied her burned like fire through Matrinka's veins, she knew she needed to reassure Marisole to allow her to continue before the answer would become clearer. "I know how you and Barrindar feel about each other. It must be difficult for you to believe, but Darris and I felt the same way when we were your age."

"You must have," Marisole said. "Or you would not have gone to so much trouble to skirt the laws."

Béarn's codes were strict and inviolate regarding marriage and heirs to the throne. Matrinka sighed. Now was not the time for reminiscence. "We got very lucky, but you must understand your situation is different. The law forbade Darris and me from marrying, so it simply could never happen. A wayward kiss would earn us frowns and warnings, but it was not a crime. Barrindar is your brother."

"Not really," Marisole shorthanded the situation. They had discussed it before. Since Griff was not Marisole's blood father, they were, at closest, distant cousins.

Matrinka saw no reason to hash out familiar ground. "As far as the populace and ministers of Béarn are concerned, you are siblings. If you remember, when this came up before with Darris, I was the one who spoke on your behalf. But that was with the promise you would not engage in any activity that could result in—" Once again, she found herself nearly incapable of speaking the word, so she used another. "—discovery." She added forcefully, needing to know and no longer patient, "What did you do?"

Marisole's gaze dropped to her callused fingers. Supporting the gittern, she slipped into song. Again, the music struck directly to Matrinka's heart, discordant and dangerous, evoking a fear near to panic. As words joined the notes, images filled her mind, flashes of war and blood and corpses. The earth trembled and terrible slashes, more brilliant and cutting than lightning, upset her vision. Her nose filled with the odors of sea wrack, infection, and storm and her ears with a roaring so intense it shook the walls around her. Amid this certainty of sudden and agonizing death, two figures clung to one another, their love enduring. For the moment, they were safe; but the morning, they felt certain, would bring the demises of everyone and everything they knew, including their own. How could it hurt to consummate their love?

The song ended, and Matrinka found Marisole's gaze upon her, willing her to understand. Imorelda had curled into Matrinka's lap, eyes closed, apparently sleeping and no longer demanding attention. Matrinka had to admit, "There were times, Marisole, when I also worried the *Kjempemagiska* would kill us all. But I forced myself to believe in your father." The deception no longer worked for Marisole, so she clarifed. "In Griff and his strategy and the other warriors to keep us safe."

Marisole looked stricken, and Matrinka found herself adding, "But the odds were tipped against us from the start." It was vast understatement. "And I can understand why anyone could lose hope."

Marisole strummed again, and Matrinka went silent, dragged into another whirlwind of sound and emotion. This time, Marisole sang of the grip of the promise she had made to her mother. Even at death's door, the vow would not be broken. The lovers would do nothing that placed their secret at risk.

Relief flooded Matrinka. The concern for pregnancy disappeared. If the act had never happened, then they had nothing to fear. Other things caused courses to come late, especially in the young. Strong emotions, weight loss, sometimes no explanation at all. She also had to consider the possibility of an illness, and that raised an anxiety all its own, but most medical causes for the delay or cessation of menses were treatable.

Marisole's song continued, and Matrinka found herself paying more attention to the words than the music. One couplet stuck, and she found herself repeating it even as Marisole continued singing: "Two virgins cannot a baby make; So they safely indulged in the give-and-take."

The tune took an abrupt turn, from sublime to raging. The female lover worried for betrayal, that the male had lied about his virginal status and it explained the delay of her courses.

Matrinka placed both hands on Marisole's arms, pressing firmly until the music stopped in the middle of a stanza. Marisole had not sung out anything resembling sex, or its accompanying sensations, though whether because copulation had not occurred or from modesty, Matrinka did not know. And she had to. "By 'give-and-take,' are you referring to . . . intercourse?"

Marisole met her mother's gaze. And nodded.

It felt as if an icy hand suddenly gripped Matrinka's heart. "Two virgins cannot a baby make," she repeated.

Marisole's nod became more vigorous.

The cold fingers clenched tighter, inducing nausea. Matrinka swallowed the bile crawling into her throat. "Marisole, two virgins cannot make a baby. But once those virgins engage in intercourse, they are no longer virgins."

Marisole's head stopped bobbing and tipped sideways. Her nostrils flared.

"We've talked about this, Marisole. Babies come from intercourse, not every time, but anytime. Even the first time."

Marisole's voice emerged as a squeak. "But two virgins . . . if it's the first time . . . for both . . ."

Matrinka shook her head sadly.

"So Barrindar didn't lie to me. This is not his fault."

"Not exclusively," Matrinka pointed out.

Marisole sounded so plaintive, if Matrinka shut her eyes, she could imagine she spoke to a four-year-old. Things had been so much simpler then. "Oh, Mama. I've been so mean to him." Her dark eyes grew round as coins. "What are we going to do?"

Matrinka swallowed her urge to shout, to lecture. Now was not the time. "First, we need to find out for certain if you're . . ." As a healer, it bothered Matrinka she kept finding the word so difficult to speak, especially since "intercourse" had tumbled so smoothly from her mouth. ". . . with child."

"How?" Marisole asked glumly, hands clenched over her gittern.

This time, Matrinka had an immediate answer.

Matrinka and Marisole found Tem'aree'ay sitting cross-legged on the floor of her room, her head cradled in her hands, golden curls cascading over her dainty arms. Though she had bade them to enter, Matrinka felt like an intruder. Clearly, the elf was dealing with issues every bit as significant as her own. Before she could think to do otherwise, she ran to her fellow wife, crouched beside her, and drew her into an embrace. "Tem'aree'ay, are you all right?"

Tem'aree'ay looked up, wiped away a tear, and even managed a smile. "I will be. I just have a difficult decision to make, and it's haunting me."

"Would you like to talk about it?"

Tem'aree'ay pursed her heart-shaped lips in consideration. For several moments, she remained still before finally saying, "I . . . think I might like to share with you, if you don't mind."

This surprised Matrinka. The elf did not usually talk about her concerns with any human. She never appeared particularly troubled about anything, although Matrinka knew Ivana caused her mother more than a bit of angst.

"But later." Tem'aree'ay looked toward Marisole and brightened. "After your visit. Please join us, Marisole."

Marisole looked askance at her mother before crouching to the side of and level with the other two. She and Tem'aree'ay had had little interaction in the past. Though seemingly ageless, Tem'aree'ay spent most of her time with Ivana and her status as Griff's wife meant she moved most easily through Griff, Matrinka, and Xoraida's generation. During Ivana's childhood, though, Tem'aree'ay had spent a significant amount of time silently watching Marisole. Matrinka had always believed that came of comparing her to Ivana as they grew. Less than a year apart in age, the two girls could not have grown more similarly nor developed more differently.

"Thank you so much for sharing your time," Marisole said sincerely and with appropriate royal politeness.

Tem'aree'ay's smile broadened. This expression looked so much more natural on her face. "My thanks to you for the same."

Matrinka got right down to business. "I'm ashamed to say this isn't really a social call. We were wondering if you would check something for us."

Tem'aree'ay's smile never wavered. "It would be my pleasure."

Matrinka glanced at Marisole and back. "Before you agree, I need to tell you that part of the favor is a promise not to share what we discuss, or the outcome, with anyone else. Including Griff."

Several moments passed in silence, which Matrinka appreciated. It would not be fair to burden Tem'aree'ay without allowing her the chance to consider her options and whether or not she felt comfortable participating. "Ah," the elf finally said. "You want me to check for a baby."

Marisole whimpered, which stole any chance for playing it cool and close.

A happy light flashed through Tem'aree'ay's eyes, chasing away the last of her previous discomfort. "Don't worry, my dear. I'm certain Griff would welcome a grandchild. He loves children."

"I'm certain he would," Matrinka said. "And if you find one exists, I promise I'll talk to him about it. But, for now, it's best if only we know it's even a possibility. Please."

Tem'aree'ay reached for Marisole, planting her long-fingered hands on the rich fabric of the dress covering her abdomen. "I won't tell anyone either way. If there is no baby, no one needs to know we checked. If there is one, it's your news and up to you how it gets announced." She stopped speaking and closed her eyes.

Marisole remained quiet but glanced at Matrinka, who motioned her to stay still and silent. She had requested Tem'aree'ay's help in the past to assist with medical issues. The elf had a magical ability to see inside humans to look for internal injuries as well as pregnancies. The amount of time it took varied.

After several moments, Tem'aree'ay sat back on her haunches. "It's tiny, and I've never been able to determine gender, but it seems normal."

Marisole moaned louder, dropping to the floor. Matrinka's heart sank. She closed her eyes, fighting the influx of information that threatened to overwhelm her. There was too much to think about, so she asked the only question Tem'aree'ay could answer. "Can you . . . terminate the pregnancy?"

Now, Tem'aree'ay made a wordless noise. Matrinka opened her lids to find the elf's sapphirine eyes filled with pain and shock. They had done it once before. A woman had come in badly injured from a fall. While searching for deep injuries, the elf had found a baby growing in the womb unbeknownst to the frantic husband and, presumably, to the woman as well. Matrinka and Tem'aree'ay had worked together to mend several dangerous wounds, including three horrific pelvic fractures. Passing a baby so soon would not have allowed for them to heal, risking her life as well as the infant's, which was already tenuous. If she survived the birthing, she would never have another child. However, if they eliminated the baby, the woman had an excellent chance to live a normal life span and have as many more children as she wished.

The choice seemed obvious to Matrinka, but Tem'aree'ay had struggled with the idea of ending a life. It was something elves never needed to do; they only conceived after the death of an elder to natural causes and they never experienced birth defects. Eventually, Matrinka had convinced her, and Tem'aree'ay had reluctantly done the deed. The woman survived and recovered. She and her husband returned to their home never knowing about the potential child.

It took Tem'aree'ay so long to answer that Matrinka became certain she never would. Finally, the elf said in a rusty voice, "Certain herbs can do the job, right?"

Matrinka sucked in a deep breath and let it out slowly. "They're all poisons, dangerous to the mother. And they don't work more often than they do." She acknowledged Tem'aree'ay's discomfort. "I know it's an awful lot to ask." She added quickly, "Too much. I'm sorry. I shouldn't have." She started to rise, but Tem'aree'ay waved her back down.

"I'll do it for you and you alone because I know your heart. If you want this done, it needs doing, and your reasons must be sound."

Matrinka sank to the floor boards, suddenly desperately weary. "It's not wholly my choice. Marisole and I will talk about this, and there are others, men, who have a right to their say, too. I'll let you know what we decide."

"Do not take long," Tem'aree'ay cautioned. "If you do, even I cannot help you." Her head dropped to her chest, as if she had become suddenly too weak to hold it upright. The gesture was so utterly unelflike it awakened every sympathetic and healing instinct Matrinka possessed.

Matrinka took Marisole's hand, and they rose together. "Sweetie, you need to explain this to . . ." Not wishing to burden Tem'aree'ay with more information and practicing the need for secrecy, she hedged, ". . . the father and apologize for treating him with anger when he did not deserve it. I don't believe he tried to deceive you."

Marisole nodded. She rarely spoke anymore, since too many situations had forced her into arias.

Matrinka believed Marisole understood the need to restrict the information, but she chose to make the point unerringly clear. Adolescents were not known for making wise decisions, and Marisole had already made one outrageous mistake. "Explain it to him and *only* to him. At this point in time, no one else can know about . . . your slip." She stressed, "*No one.*" Soon enough, they would need to bring Darris and Griff into the circle, but Matrinka planned to be present when that happened. Darris, in particular, would not react well.

Marisole turned her mother a black look that suggested she found the advice unnecessary, but she did not speak. Realizing the cantankerousness that often afflicted budding women, especially when it came to their mothers, Matrinka felt a sudden appreciation for the bardic curse. The princess headed for the door, left the room, and closed the door behind her.

Only then, Matrinka turned her attention fully on Tem'aree'ay. "Thank you so much for your assistance."

Tem'aree'ay managed a smile. It fit on her face as naturally as the creases on a human palm. Matrinka rarely saw her without one, although usually it seemed more simple and honest, less forced. "You know I'm glad to assist you, Matrinka. You've always been so good to me."

Matrinka tried to treat everyone well, but she had to admit she had gone out of her way to make Tem'aree'ay comfortable through the years. The marriage between Griff and herself had been one of convenience, and she appreciated he had been the one to suggest Darris warm her bed instead of him. Tem'aree'ay was his true love, and Matrinka so appreciated Griff's gesture she had always had a soft spot for his second wife. She had helped the elf find her place in the strange and unsettling world of humans and the hubbub of Béarn Castle. "Please let me return the favor. Tell me what's troubling you."

As Matrinka expected, the problem concerned Ivana. She listened intently as Tem'aree'ay outlined the problem: the strange mutating substance that filled the half-human head and would probably eventually kill her, the possibility of cure, of normalcy, the need for a human healer with experience working within the skull to join forces with the elves. For the most part, Matrinka remained silent as the details unfolded, occasionally offering an empathetic noise or asking an edifying question. In the end, uncertain whether Tem'aree'ay wanted assistance with the decision, a recommendation for a surgeon, or only a sympathetic ear, Matrinka held her fellow wife and waited.

Silence filled the room, tangible, far more than just a lack of sound. For other elves, ones who had not spent much time among humans, they might sit and wait for days before speaking. Tem'aree'ay had lived in the castle too long not to understand the human discomfort that came from pauses that lasted longer than a few moments. She had learned that humans tended to fill them, even if it required them to babble. Matrinka also knew Tem'aree'ay, so she waited patiently for the elf to speak again.

After several moments, Tem'aree'ay asked, "What should I do, Matrinka?"

Matrinka drew breath to reply, but Tem'aree'ay forestalled her by suddenly disengaging from the queen's arms and speaking first.

"And don't give me the healer's non-answer that 'it's my decision to make.' Believe me, I'm all too aware of that. I want to know, as a friend, what would you do if you had to make this choice? For Marisole or Halika."

Disarmed, Matrinka sucked in a deep breath and let it out slowly. Tem'aree'ay was right. She had been about to give the pat answer. Healers weighed the odds all the time. When the patient could not advocate for himself, and no family emerged, they used their best judgment to decide the course of treatment. When the choice was obvious, they frequently steered the sick and injured to proper treatment without presenting the alternatives. The more evenly balanced the scales, or the more dangerous the remedy, the choice had to shift to the sufferer or their loved ones. "Tem'aree'ay, you know I can't tell you what to do here. What if I give you the best advice I'm capable of giving, and it results in . . . ?" Matrinka found herself too distraught to finish.

Tem'aree'ay had no difficulty. ". . . Ivana becoming even less capable? Dying? Don't you think I've considered those possibilities?"

She paused, looking askance at Matrinka. "I know there are no good answers, no guarantees. Griff says he'll support whatever I decide, and I know he will. The final decision is mine, however. You have experiences and information I don't. Matrinka, please. I want your opinion."

Matrinka's healer training drove her to throw the question wholly back at Tem'aree'ay, but her conscience would not allow it. This was not a stranger's child or a situation she could not possibly understand. Though a splendid source of support, Griff could not help in the way Tem'aree'ay needed it most. He had a layman's knowledge of injury and illness. He could predict most people's reactions to situations and words in a courtroom, in a Strategy Room, even on a battlefield, but he knew nothing of the body's struggles against evil humors, festers, damage. Even the most experienced surgeons did not understand why some strong patients died under the knife while some frail ones thrived on doses of medication that would kill a mule. As always, he would remain neutral. It was his talent, his saving grace and also his bane.

It suddenly occurred to Matrinka why Tem'aree'ay needed her opinion so desperately. Tem'aree'ay had only an elf's knowledge to draw upon, but Ivana was demonstrating flaws only humans could. As Matrinka understood it, elves were immune to the capriciousness of weather, so they never developed heat stroke or frost bite, and they never caught the illnesses that laid humans low, temporarily or permanently. Birth defects, organ failures, contagions did not plague the elves. They had developed a thousand ways to handle injuries, their greatest threat because an elf who died of unnatural causes meant one less soul, one less elf for all eternity.

Tem'aree'ay's thoughts must have gone the same route as Matrinka's because she explained. "To my knowledge, only one elf has ever been . . . mad. Khy'barreth Y'vrintae Shabeerah El-borin Morbonos became damaged by grasping a pair of magical items too powerful for his psyche." The gemlike eyes pinned Matrinka. "We keep him confined for his own safety as well as ours. He receives food and water, of course, but there's nothing more we can do for him. We have no choice but to keep him alive until old age catches up to him, sooner I hope than later. Still, many worry about the state of his soul. How will it affect the elf who inherits it? Will he or she suffer the same insanity? Have any of the memories from the previous elves who borrowed that soul survived?" She shook her head. "Many elves claim never to have been visited by a single prior thought, but most get at least glimpses of those who came before them and others remember whole incidents." She shivered at the idea of someone having to relive parts or all of Khy'barreth's life.

It surprised Matrinka someone so attentive to her own abnormal child could find such horror in the suffering of another. Yet, Matrinka realized, it was the way of living beings to deftly handle their own offsprings' secretions, excreta, and behavior they would never tolerate from anyone else. The truth was that Matrinka had no more experience with situations like Ivana's than Tem'aree'ay. Severely abnormal children were humanely slaughtered or left to die in the elements. Animals treated their flawed issue similarly. All human societies currently believed it was nature's way of weeding out those who used up scarce resources without any potential to contribute. Children like Ivana did not exist—not because they did not happen, but because rightly or wrongly they were not suffered to live.

Matrinka cleared her throat. She needed to say something, but the right words refused to come. She did the best she could. "If nothing is done, Ivana will at best remain as she is. More likely, she will become less and less capable until she dies."

Tem'aree'ay acknowledged the description with a nod.

"The elves believe they can intervene, with the help of a human healer or surgeon. It would be dangerous to the point of life-threatening, but it could result in a cure. Ivana might get a normal or, at least, more normal life. And a chance to live it fully."

Again, Tem'aree'ay nodded.

Matrinka had merely restated the facts in a succinct fashion. As Ivana's situation had never happened before, the elves could give them no odds. The decision would become so much easier if they knew whether the chance for cure was 10% or 90% and the likelihood of life, whether it was the same, worse, or improved versus death.

Tem'aree'ay asked timidly, "Do you think Ivana is suffering? Does she have any understanding of her . . . differentness? And does it cause her pain?"

Matrinka considered. "Older people sometimes develop something we call senility. It usually starts with them losing words or names, a mild annoyance. But it progresses. Soon, they begin to forget recent actions, how to perform complex, and eventually even simple, tasks. That frustrates them, often to rage and aggression or plunges them into the depths of despair. They are clearly suffering."

Tem'aree'ay's expression turned thoughtful, but Matrinka knew she was hiding discomfort.

"But, unlike Ivana, they had prior knowledge of what it's like to be in full control of their faculties. Perhaps when someone has never known normal, they do not regret what they never had." Matrinka added reassuringly, "Ivana hasn't seemed particularly unhappy to me. She clearly loves you and greets people she knows with excitement. And you have done everything to make her life as pleasant as possible."

Tem'aree'ay sighed, a most unelflike sound. "You haven't seen her at her worst. Few have, other than me. When she rages violently or howls her troubles to the moon, it tears at my heart. It used to only happen a few times a week. Now, it's every day."

Matrinka winced. Tem'aree'ay had kept her affairs mostly private since arriving at Béarn Castle, and everyone attributed that to elfish nature. Matrinka had access to the family quarters, had seen Ivana act out at times, but Tem'aree'ay always promptly removed her daughter from these situations. What horrors had Tem'aree'ay witnessed and endured that family and servants barely knew? How much worse had it become as Ivana grew and became larger and far heavier than her elfin mother? When it came to making the decision of whether or not to muck about in Ivana's brain, the scales had seemed relatively balanced. When Matrinka added in Tem'aree'ay's adversity, they tipped dramatically. "If Ivana were my daughter, I would do whatever was necessary to give her that chance, even one in a million, to have a normal life. I would call in the best western surgeon from Pudar to assist the elves and have the procedure done."

"Even if it killed her?"

Matrinka did not allow any doubt to enter her voice, tamped down any misgivings. "Even if. If I could take the danger onto myself, I would, but life doesn't work that way. I would miss Marisole or Halika, but I would sleep well knowing I tried everything, gave her every chance." Knowing elves tended to consider circumstances longer than human endurance, and the elves involved would gleefully do nothing until Tem'aree'ay pressed them, she added. "Time is not on our side. Every day you delay, the growth inside Ivana's head degenerates further until there may come a time when nothing can be done."

The smile returned to Tem'aree'ay's face, and determination filled her eyes. "Thank you, Matrinka. I appreciate your candor. The decision is difficult enough without . . ." She placed her hand on her belly in a characteristic gesture.

Matrinka thought her own eyes might pop out of her head. "You're pregnant?"

Tem'aree'ay's grin faded at the edges. "I am. It seemed like a good idea at the time, but now I'm not so sure."

Matrinka's smile made up for whatever Tem'aree'ay's lost. "Of course it's a good idea. Griff must be thrilled."

"He is," Tem'aree'ay admitted. "He's wanted it a long time. But what if—"

Many conversational beats went by, and Tem'aree'ay did not finish. Matrinka considered the possibilities. They might have a normal child, which could only tighten relations between elves and humans. Reportedly, it was Ivana's abnormalities more than their differences that had kept the elves at bay. They worried their freely sexual culture would cause many elfin-human interbreedings resulting in populating the world with what they once interchangeably called anathema or ivanas. Knowing they could create viable mixed offspring might help stem the gradual attrition of elfin souls or, at least, assure elfin blood did not disappear entirely. If Tem'aree'ay and Griff made another abnormal child, it seemed unlikely to make the situation any worse, other than on Tem'aree'ay herself. "We will find a way to deal with 'if' if it happens. There are many more 'ifs,' Tem'aree'ay. Happy 'ifs'."

"Happy 'ifs,' " Tem'aree'ay repeated. "Thank you, Matrinka. You always know how to put a positive spin on everything."

Matrinka rose. "If you decide to go through with the procedure, let me know. I'll send for Tonaris in Pudar. He's the most competent surgeon I know and has more experience than most with opening skulls."

Tem'aree'ay floated to her feet, the smile still in place, though not nearly as broad as usual. "Please," she said. "Send for him."

CHAPTER 9

*The world is not as black or white as the Knights of Erythane
make it appear; and, sometimes, the choices that confront you are
all, in some way, bleak.*

—*Weile Kahn*

DUSK PAINTED THE SKY a fiery red that started at the horizon
and flared irregularly into the blue-gray net of clouds. Leaves of
myriad colors rained from the trees with each puff of wind. Dressed
in warm cloaks, wool hats, and knitted mittens, Ra-khir and Tiega
scarcely noticed the cold. Earlier, he had thrown himself into his
knightly training, and the time had flown past in anticipation of his
time alone with his beloved.

Now, they strolled through the forest on the edge of Erythane,
talking, laughing, kicking up leaves. Even though or, perhaps, because they came from such different backgrounds, they never seemed
to run out of things to talk about nor did anything become off-limits.
Tiega was the first person Ra-khir found with whom he could talk
about Kevral without feeling strangled with grief, and she chatted
just as easily about her late husband, Emmer.

Ra-khir leaped over a deadfall, then reached out to assist Tiega.
She took his mittened hand with both of hers as he hoisted her,
steadying her with a muscled arm around her waist, then placing her
gently onto the mostly barkless trunk. She looked beautiful: her smile
broad and genuine, her cheekbones high, her eyes long-lashed and
striking as a bluebird's plumage. She was taller than Kevral and not
as slender or sinewy, though nearly as pale. He appreciated Tiega's
curves; they made her seem warmer, kinder, and the touch of her
brought a longing to his loins he had worried he might never feel
again. She shivered.

Ra-khir sat down beside her, looped his arm around her back,
and drew her closer. "Are you cold?"

"A bit. But I don't want to leave. I love this." Tiega added carefully, "I love you."

Warmth grew inside Ra-khir, and joy tingled through his chest. Her closeness, her words, made him happy. He could have sat here all night with her, unspeaking, unmoving. Instead, he slid from his perch, untwining his grip from Tiega, to land on one knee in front of her, as if bowing to a queen. "I love you, too, Tiega. Will you do me the honor of becoming my wife?"

Tiega's eyes widened. Her nostrils flared. She peered deeply into Ra-khir's green eyes, and her sweet moist lips moved soundlessly for several moments that passed for him like hours. The dampness of the leaves seeped into the knee of his britches, chilling. Finally, she managed speech. "I can think of nothing in my life that has ever made me happier. Yes," she said. "Yes. I accept you as mine."

Ra-khir gathered her into his arms and kissed her mouth, salty with tears of joy. "When," he asked joyously. "When?"

They parted breathlessly.

Ra-khir swung Tiega from the deadfall to the ground, wanting nothing more than to run all the way back to the Knight's Rest Inn in Erythane, to shout the news from every balcony. He seized her hand, then practicality took over and he stopped mid-movement. "We need to tell our children first."

Tiega waited until Ra-khir clambered back to her side. "All at once, so none of them feels less favored."

Ra-khir added softly, his words slowing. "All five at once." He brushed honey-brown hair from her cheeks. "Which means we have to wait until Subikahn's . . ."

"Rescue," she chimed in. "Yes."

Tiega made it sound simple. Ra-khir had learned patience in spades through his knight training, but eagerness and the need to hide an exciting secret were not really the issue. Subikahn's fate was still uncertain. He might already be dead, or the elves might not find a way to bring him home. Even if they did, he might have changed in some substantial and dangerous way. Ra-khir's thoughts went back to the days when he had traveled the Outworlds with Kevral, Tae, and others to seek the shards of the Pica Stone. The things they had encountered could never be unseen, the changes in them negative and positive, every one permanent and, in its own way, terrible. So many times, he had felt certain they would not survive.

Ra-khir studied Tiega. By everything she did and said, she loved his boys as much as her own two children. He saw no need to worry her. "Rescue, of course. We can keep this to ourselves until Subikahn's rescue." He glanced at his feet, then back at Tiega. "Can't we?"

"We can," she assured him. "And it will make the announcement all the sweeter."

Ra-khir hoped so. He knew the news would excite Darby and Keva. The boy already considered him a father, and the girl adored him. His own boys worried Ra-khir more. Calistin had accepted Tiega in his usual seemingly uncaring way, but he had also once assaulted Darby in what resembled a jealous rage. Usually, Saviar was the most predictable and reasonable, but his recent mood had become so irascible the knight had breathed a sigh of relief when his eldest had ridden off with Weile Kahn. Saviar also seemed even more uncomfortable than Calistin with their father's growing closeness with Darby. And Subikahn's reaction was utterly unpredictable, assuming the elves managed to save him.

Uncertain what to say, Ra-khir scooped Tiega into his arms once more to deliver a more passionate kiss.

This time, nearly all of the remaining Mages of Myrcidë chose to accompany Saviar and Weile back to Béarn, surprising Saviar beyond words. Before each war, he had exhausted his every power of persuasion trying to coax them from their communal dwelling. Jeremilan had kept them so cowed and terrified of outside humanity most had never left it, even to gather food or enjoy the feel of the sun or the wind in their faces. They had grown so fearful of anyone discovering they existed that, when Saviar and Subikahn had coaxed Chymmerlee to Béarn to assist in the Pirate War, none of them had dared follow, even to rescue her. Or so he had believed. Now, he felt certain most of the reason they had allowed her to leave was the opportunity, upon her return, to convince her one or both of the twins had raped her.

Indignation rising again, Saviar put that thought out of his head to contemplate the change in heart of all but three of the mages. Arinosta had remained behind. Though not nearly as old as Jeremilan claimed he was, she had not aged nearly as well. Even if she survived the trip, it would slow their pace to a crawl. Chestinar also stayed. Eternally sickly, he clearly would not weather change well physically or, probably, emotionally. The third was a sexless, faceless figure so terrified of strangers he or she had never appeared within Saviar's sight during any of his visits. If the third member of the trio had a name, Saviar had never heard it spoken.

Those three had agreed to watch over the common house until the others returned, presumably with Jeremilan and the eleven other missing mages. Though he had made no actual promises, Weile had assured them he would do what he could to keep all the Myrcidians safe in a tone that made it clear he had the means and authority to do so. Some of that, Saviar knew, came of his staggering charisma, but much more in this case because he carried the greatest artifact in the world. Venerating the Pica Stone was the closest thing to a religion the mages had, and Saviar suspected they would be far more inclined to follow anyone who possessed it.

However, once the trip began, all the mages, aside from Chymmerlee, sought out Saviar's company. They cajoled him for information and guarantees, concerned they were being led into a trap yet seeing no other option. Without Jeremilan, they were as lost as puppies. The old man had brought them all together, had kept them safe lifelong, had honed whatever magic each of them possessed. They worried their companions had been murdered or were being held prisoner, that they were being lured to a similar fate. One thing became utterly clear to Saviar: Jeremilan had successfully instilled his fears into every one of his followers. Though based on logic he could not wholly dispute, this attitude was not serving them—or the rest of humanity—well.

Their behavior was teaching Saviar something shocking as well. When he had spent days trying to solicit their help on three separate occasions, he had believed his words no more effective than banging his head against granite. He had implored, and they had ignored, or so he had believed. Ultimately, it had taken Weile, with the help of the Pica, to induce any of them to come to Béarn. Now, Saviar realized his efforts had not wholly gone for naught. He may not have persuaded them to accompany him, but he had managed to convince them of his personal honor and credibility. It had taken extreme measures. They had imprisoned him for months and tested his honesty with magic. But, ultimately, it had won him their favor. The Mages of Myrcidë, those bastions of paranoia, had come to trust a Renshai.

Except for Chymmerlee. The irony seared Saviar. At one time, she was the only one whose opinion truly mattered to him. He had risked his life on several occasions, endangered his relationship with the Knights of Erythane, including his father, just to get her to listen. Now that seemed worse than foolish, though the relationship he had established with the rest of the mages made up for all of it. He believed he now understood the phrase "losing the battle but winning the war."

As the days went by without incident, and all interactions with Weile's followers and passersby remained friendly, the mages seemed to relax a bit. They engaged Saviar in actual conversation, questioning him about Béarn and other parts of the world they had never had the opportunity to see. Immersed in these exchanges, Saviar forgot to consider his many issues and even lost track of Chymmerlee. If she still made a show of snubbing him, he no longer took any notice.

They were still a day out from Béarn when Chymmerlee finally approached Saviar. She waited until the sun had slipped below the horizon. The evening meal was eaten; Saviar had completed his sword practice, rolled out his blanket, and settled down for the night. She sidled up to him quietly, cautiously, clearly uncertain. Trained from infancy to remain always alert to his surroundings, Saviar watched her approach but remained silent. His many and varied attempts had not worked; it was her turn to initiate and control the situation.

Achy and exhausted from his practice, Saviar wanted nothing more than rest. The urge to sink down flat, to let his lids close, to drift into a deep and restorative sleep became nearly unbearable. Too tired to field emotions, he did not even suffer from annoyance or impatience. He allowed instinct to take over, hammered into him by his parents and a myriad of *torke*. For the moment, he simply waited.

Finally, Chymmerlee stopped near enough they could converse without the others easily overhearing yet far enough he would have to rise and take a few steps to catch her. As he had no intention of doing so, Saviar remained in position, looking in her direction but making no other sign he noticed her. If experience held true, she would do nothing other than cruelly berate him, but he kept a hand casually draped across his sword. Its magic allowed him to see the outline of light that defined her aura; any flare in it would alert him to impending magic.

"Why?" she asked, her voice rusty, as if she had not spoken to anyone in a long time.

Saviar stared at her quizzically, the question too vague to warrant an answer.

Chymmerlee cleared her throat. "I'm eighteen years old, unmarried, carrying a baby I never asked for or desired."

Saviar wanted to express his sympathy without implying he had any responsibility for the problem. His thoughts waded through the mud of fatigue, making it hard to find the right words. "It's a bad situation, Chymmerlee. I wish you didn't have to suffer it." He added carefully, "Is there something I can do to help you through it?"

"Explain it." Darkness hid her expression, and she kept her words too clipped to reveal much emotion.

Saviar hesitated. "I'm—not sure what you're asking. If you're seeking a lesson on procreation, you've come to the wrong person. I'm still a virgin and extremely uncomfortable even discussing . . ." He whispered the last word, ". . . sex. I had to steel myself just to hold your hand, more so to kiss you."

Chymmerlee shifted in place, unspeaking, for several moments. "I thought I was a virgin, too." She placed her hands on the small but definitive bulge. "How can I be pregnant?"

Saviar knew the answer. He wanted to leap to his feet and shout it at her, to force Jeremilan and the others to take responsibility. If they truly felt preserving and enhancing the lineage of the Mages of Myrcidë was worth tormenting a loved one, they should have to justify it to the innocent victim of their decision.

Though Saviar despised what they had done to Chymmerlee, he attempted to give them the benefit of his doubts. It was just possible they had explained what they needed to Chymmerlee in advance, that she had consented, but the horror of it had forced her into a denial so deep her mind could never accept the truth. How could anyone ever believe the people who were supposed to protect her, who professed to love her, the only ones who shared her very blood could do something so heinous, even in a time of desperation? Perhaps the only possible reaction was for her mind to shut down and disallow any contemplation of the unthinkable.

Saviar could only surmise what he would do in a similar situation. He felt certain he would want to kill them, but when he visualized the actual faces of his family members, he could never imagine them doing such a thing. A thought intruded: *Subikahn tried to steal my eternity in Valhalla and nearly succeeded.* Rage boiled through him. He did know what it felt like to have the person he felt closest to in the world betray him. Unlike Chymmerlee, however, he had no intention of denying it or inflicting the punishment on someone innocent.

Except that's exactly what I've been doing. Although Saviar had not accused anyone else of Subikahn's misdeed, his uncertainty about how to handle it had made him lash out at everyone around him. He had to stop, and so did Chymmerlee. She might never come to accept the truth, but he was not going to take the blame for a crime he had not committed. Weile's words came back to Saviar then: *Sometimes, the choices that confront you are all, in some way, bleak.* He refused to leave her believing him the rapist, but her denial protected her from lifelong pain. She needed the other mages in order to survive.

Oblivious to the storm of ideas whirling through Saviar's mind, Chymmerlee awaited his explanation.

Saviar tried parable. "I believe you know Colbey Calistinsson is our patron."

Chymmerlee gave no reply, but Saviar thought he saw a slight nod. Encouraged, he continued.

"We believe he was conceived when the god, Thor, had a tryst with a mortal Renshai. When Colbey's blood mother died in battle with him growing inside her, it's said Thor's wife secretly saved him, placing him into the womb of a barren Renshai who had pleaded to her for a child."

Chymmerlee took a moment to consider before asking, "Are you suggesting this was a sexless conception? That a divine being implanted this baby inside me for some immortal reason?"

Saviar shrugged. "I'm just throwing out a possibility."

"Based on a fairy tale."

Saviar swallowed his anger. "That was rude."

"You're right." Chymmerlee's head drooped. "I should have said it's something I don't believe."

Saviar did not dispute semantics. He had waited so long for Chymmerlee to listen to him, yet now that he had her ear, he wanted only for her to let him sleep. "You can't tell me you don't believe in magic. Surely, there are . . . nontraditional ways to make a baby."

"Even in your story, the god used sex to make the baby."

That was not Saviar's point. "But Colbey's mother didn't participate in . . . it."

"Virgins don't beseech goddesses for babies. Surely she tried the regular way first."

Saviar sighed. "Not 'it' meaning she never did it; she was married. 'It' meaning the exact, particular act that caused his conception."

Chymmerlee persisted, "So it's possible Colbey was actually conceived by his mother and her husband through the act of sex."

Saviar shook his head to clear it. It was all he could do not to tell Chymmerlee to go away and bother someone else. If not for her predicament, he probably would have. "I'm not going to justify my faith to you, other than to say I've seen more than enough evidence to convince me. You asked me for possible explanations; I gave you one. Here's another." This one struck closer to the truth. "You participated in sex, willingly or unwillingly, with someone who has magical abilities. He either made you sleep through it or forget it afterward."

"Demons have magical abilities."

They had returned to the crux of the matter. Chymmerlee believed the ancient claims that Renshai either were or descended from demons. "Assuming they exist, I know nothing about demons. I've already proven that to the other mages." He gestured vaguely toward the center of camp. "They used magic to bind me to the truth."

Chymmerlee did not refute Saviar's claim; apparently, she had discussed the matter with at least one of them at some point. Clearly, though, she still harbored doubts. People who have learned something as fact from childhood do not abandon it easily, even when confronted with proof. "There are herbs that can cause someone to sleep through anything, ones that can make a person forget, and a few that can cause both of these things to happen."

Saviar nodded briskly. "Another possibility."

"Anyone could have done it that way. Including you."

Saviar's head shook back and forth of its own accord before he realized he was doing it. "Not me. I have morals, integrity, honor. No one with those qualities could ever do such a thing. And I believe, deep down, you know both to be true."

Chymmerlee crumpled. Saviar half-rose to catch her, then realized it was a controlled fall. She sat down hard but deliberately. "You didn't . . . rape me?"

"No."

"Nor your brother?"

The idea nearly made Saviar smile, but he resisted the urge and did not qualify. Saying something like "definitely not" would only make his initial denial sound weak, and smiling might make it appear as if he trivialized this horrible injustice. "No."

It was not over, but Chymmerlee blaming a random outsider was, at least, preferable to her believing he or Subikahn had raped her. Perhaps she could even live with that idea, hating circumstance rather than people she knew and relied upon. Had she listened to him sooner, allowed him the opportunity to assert his innocence rather than so easily leaping to the certainty he could and had done such a thing, he might have suggested marriage. Now, he realized, it would legitimize the baby at the cost of tying them together for life. She would never truly trust him, and he would never love her. They both deserved better.

"I believe you," Chymmerlee said. It was too little too late. "And I guess I don't hate you anymore."

"I appreciate that." Saviar found himself adding without thinking, "I hope, someday, you will find the forbearance to stop hating my people as well."

To Chymmerlee's credit, she did not resort to the tired justification. That the Renshai had destroyed the Mages of Myrcidë centuries ago could be a historical fact, but it held no relevance to him or to the current day. She said nothing, but the sneer that slipped across her features and the glimmer that sparked in her eyes spoke volumes. Prejudice ingrained since birth and fortified throughout childhood might never be fully overcome. Tomorrow, they would reach Béarn. The mages would team up with the elves, fully focused on retrieving the lost warriors, and they would no longer be Saviar's problem.

Without another word, he snuggled into his travel blanket and fell asleep.

It took Matrinka nearly a week to catch Darris in a proper mood; buoyed by the success of Weile Kahn's mission and the safe return of the Pica Stone. They sat in matched chairs in his room, as they had so many times before, holding hands over the armrests and relaxing. Soon, he would unsling his lute and sing her the story of his day, which would perfectly parallel King Griff's. It did not happen every time. Often, his duties intervened, or he preferred to brood and scowl as he had the last five nights. But most evenings, his day gushed forth with all the inherent beauty of his music, filled with highs and lows, joys and sorrows. And always, his love for her shone through.

Matrinka wanted to wait until they both basked in the afterglow of his composition: unique, hasty, yet with the talent of the ages, infused with information and emotion, knowledge and concern, hope and affection. Darris was always at his best when he performed, even for an audience of one eternal admirer. Most other times, he bore the weight of the kingdom on his shoulders. Anxiety seemed to wash off Griff like water; few things distressed him. It often seemed to Matrinka as if Darris took onto himself all the worry the king did not. And it rarely, if ever, seemed necessary.

When Marisole's time came, Matrinka hoped she confined her guardianship to the current king or queen's body rather than feeling the need to emotionally immerse herself into every situation. It made Darris a superlative bodyguard and adviser at the expense of his own tranquility, his own happiness. *Marisole.* Matrinka knew her current line of thought about their eldest daughter was delay. As Darris rose to unsling his lute, Matrinka tightened her grip on his hand, keeping him in place.

Darris turned her a curious look. She had grown accustomed to his face: fine Pudarian features swept by soft brown curls that had faded over time. The darker hairs still outnumbered the white, but it was a losing battle hastened by his tendency to fret. Lines scored his features, some like sharp slashes across her memory of his broad lips and full cheeks. An age spot marred the generous nose, and the eyes had lost their youthful glow. Though he had aged more quickly than the rest of their friends, she still found him wildly attractive.

Matrinka cleared her throat. "I have something I need to talk to you about."

Darris stiffened and looked at Matrinka with an expression that bordered on pleading. He wanted good news but always anticipated the worst.

Matrinka did not keep him waiting. "Marisole is . . ." As she spoke each word, she could actually see Darris' face growing visibly redder, his fingers clenching tighter. ". . . pregnant." As the last word left her mouth, she found herself cringing, awaiting the inevitable explosion.

Darris merely dropped back onto the bed beside her. His hand went limp in hers. He had every right to shout and blather. He had warned both women any relationship besides siblings between Marisole and Barrindar was depraved and dangerous. He had forbidden it and warned them to keep their distance from one another. It was Matrinka who had taken the side of young love, promising to oversee it. She had extracted vows from them that they would keep their attraction a secret and would do nothing that put them at risk.

Matrinka waited for something to emerge from her lover's mouth. He could remind her he had anticipated this problem. He might demand to know why she had allowed it to happen despite her many promises. He could insist on a solution. All of these would have seemed normal and appropriate. His silence did not. It unnerved her in a way none of the other possible reactions would. "Please, Darris. Say something."

Darris rose again and released Matrinka's hand. He moved to the window and stared out at the town below. "Who knows about it?"

"Marisole and I, of course. Barrindar, you, and Tem'aree'ay."

Darris turned back to face her. "Tem'aree'ay?"

"She's sworn to silence, but we needed her confirmation." Matrinka added the last piece carefully, "She can end it if we decide swiftly." She did not mention the six days already lost. According to Tem'aree'ay, they still had a week to decide.

Darris' entire body went taut. He tipped his head in thought, then relaxed. An unreadable expression eased onto his features, then disappeared. "Griff has a right to know. And Xoraida."

"Xoraida?" Matrinka repeated. She had not considered the need to involve Griff's third wife.

"She's Barrindar's mother," Darris reminded. "She has as much right to the knowledge, and to the decision, as you and I."

Darris was right, of course. Matrinka had little in common with Xoraida, other than royal blood and a husband, but she had always seemed like a kind and reasonable person. Griff would never have agreed to marry a harridan.

Matrinka did not know what to say. She had expected a more extreme reaction from Darris, and his aloof precision left her cold. Tears welled in her eyes. "I'm sorry," she whispered, and her own words wrenched forth the sobs she had not realized she was holding back. "I'm so sorry, Darris. They promised not to . . . but you know what forbidden love is like . . . and they thought they were going to die. They thought we *all* were going to die."

In a flash, Darris had Matrinka in his arms. Though smaller than her, he felt warm and powerful against her ample chest and stomach. She clung to him, weeping like a child, displaying all the grief and confusion and sorrow she had hidden from Marisole so as not to worsen the situation for their daughter. No more words passed between them as they held onto one another, nor did they need them. Matrinka had nothing left to say, and Darris would have had to sing. At the moment, neither of them felt like music.

CHAPTER 10

We are a product of our experiences, no matter how hard we try to escape them.

—*Knight-Captain Kedrin*

BÉARN'S MAIN DINING HALL seemed an odd place for a strategy meeting, but it was needed to accommodate the crowd attending. Saviar had come mostly because Weile had suggested it. Thialnir and Ra-khir had also requested his presence, but Saviar could have resisted them. When Weile spoke, wise men listened, and defying him was rarely an option.

The servants had arranged the seating in a pattern Saviar had never seen before. During feasts, it took the form of parallel rows of long tables. It had never occurred to him those might actually consist of smaller tables laid end to end beneath brilliantly-dyed blue-and-gold cloths. Now, one short table sat in the precise center of the room, surrounded by enlarging circles of more and more short tables, like ripples on a pond.

Captain, Griff, and his two-man entourage of Darris and Seiryn, and the representatives from their respective countries took up the middle table: Valr Magnus for the North, Tae for the East, Thialnir and Saviar for the Renshai, General Sutton of Santagithi for the far West, General Markanyin for the western Westlands and Knight-Captain Kedrin for Erythane. Bruises marred the knight's handsome features, and a splint made his left arm bulge beneath his uniform, but at least he finally seemed fully alert and reasonably well. Chymmerlee had found a place at the table as well, between Darris and Tae Kahn, as the representative of the Mages of Myrcidë.

Though Saviar technically did not belong, no one had complained when Thialnir patted the extra chair and invited him to join them. As far as they knew, he was still training to become Thialnir's replacement. Though Thialnir had not mentioned it again, Saviar felt certain the leader of the Renshai still held out hope he would change his mind. The only one still conflicted was Saviar himself.

The first circle of tables contained Béarn's ministers and guards, secondary diplomats, including Matrinka, Ra-khir, and Weile Kahn, various Béarnian princes and princesses accompanied by their Renshai guardians, and whichever mages and elves chose to occupy those seats. Farther out sat those curious enough to listen but not entitled to contribute such as lesser royalty, soldiers of various denominations, prison guards, untitled visitors, servants, and the more timid elves. Kentt sat on the floor in one of the corners, clearly attempting to remain as unintimidating as a giant possibly could, Mistri at his side. Though a prince in his own right, Arturo crouched with the *Kjempemagiska*, presumably to translate and explain the proceedings.

King Griff waved a hand, and all conversation eased into respectful silence. "We all know why we're here, so I won't prolong this. I'm going to ask our elfin ally to address you all via *khohlar* so even those of you on the fringes can hear clearly without need for translation. If anyone has difficulty with this mode of address, you are welcome to leave now, and we can discuss the highlights later. Otherwise, I will pass the mantle to Captain."

Murmurs followed, but not a single person rose to leave the room. There was nothing painful or distressing about the elves' mental language.

Captain waited briefly, allowing anyone present to finish his considerations and make the final decision about whether or not to remain. When no one still made any motion to leave, he stood. His voice touched every mind in the room, steady and accompanied by a wash of sincerity that seemed heartfelt and personal, as if it wafted through the contact unintentionally. Tone of voice and expression could be faked, of course, but Saviar found it difficult to believe anyone could simulate internal emotion. However, he had no real understanding of *khohlar*, either. *The elves, mages, and Kentt have pooled all of our resources to try to find a way to retrieve every missing soldier.*

Again, a scant rumble of conversation filled the room, which did not stop Captain. *Khohlar* did not require him to speak over noise. However, when he continued, the low din ceased because of the difficulty in trying to talk and listen at the same time.

We have tried to anticipate every possible problem and craft the best possible solutions to each of them. However, I must confess our resources are finite, our magic fallible, our ability to anticipate . . . imperfect. We have promised High King Griff Petrostan's son of Béarn to do everything within our power to rescue as many of the missing as possible, and we will. However, we must ask your forbearance in this matter. Some lives are surely already lost. * Grief accompanied his sending, clearly unfeigned. *Elves and humans alike, and we share your burden and your loss.* *

This time, Captain paused to allow his audience to commiserate. He looked at Griff, apparently for guidance, and the king nodded for him to continue. The elf complied, *It would take me years to explain magic in a way that makes sense to those who don't use it, so I'm not going to try. Instead, I will state some facts about what we can and cannot do and how we are planning to proceed. Rest assured we have discussed this amongst ourselves, our magical brethren, and several human advisers, including your king, to find the best course of action. However, if anyone has questions or suggestions, we would be all too happy to hear, answer, and consider them.* *

Saviar glanced around, though he did not speak. A few conversations broke the hush, but they were mostly whispered. At least in his vicinity, everyone seemed interested and open to what the elf had to say. Captain's caution slowed his explanations, but he did seem legitimately caring as well as worried about how his words would be received.

The Outworlds are farther away than most of us can conceive of: beyond our time, space, and understanding. The magical signatures given off by our companions are like grains of sand in comparison. We can find them only by focusing enormous quantities of magic. As we add more rescued elves to the mix, we become more powerful, more adept. We also insert the personal abilities of each of them into our mix, which gives us more to work with both in terms of overall power and also, possibly, new skills. *

Captain gave his words a moment to sink in before continuing, *At the current time, we only have the capacity to locate . . .* * He struggled for a word, probably one that did not exist in the common tongue since humans did not need terms defining magical constructs. Obviously unable to find the right word, he went back to the one he had previously utilized, * . . . magical signatures. Auras, the mages call them. The natural propensity for beings who shape chaos to radiate bits of it.* *

That was a concept Saviar understood. When he touched his magical sword, he could see a shimmering light around mages, elves, and *Kjempemagiska*. He could also see brilliant flares when they worked their magic. Under ordinary circumstances, these remained invisible to him and to all nonmage humans who did not carry an object of magic.

*Opening a gate requires magical intention on both sides working to-

gether. Because of these two issues, we are only able to locate and place gates where there are—

"Elves!" someone shouted out accusatorially.

The room fell silent. Saviar winced, understanding Captain's caution. He had surely presented this information before and not liked the reaction. It also explained why the previous attempt at rescuing soldiers had brought home only elves.

Captain continued, his mental voice still espousing honesty but also a wariness that had nothing to do with secrets. *We know the original gates appeared randomly, that gale-force winds stirred the battlefield, scooping up elves and humans alike. While proximity must be taken into account, who went through which hole is not entirely predictable. One thing we know for certain: we can only fixate and create gates where there are elves, but humans will be scattered among them. We have found ways to assure these humans, at least, are rescued. And, as we add more elves, we may find a way to locate and gate to pockets composed of only humans. *

Though the earnestness persisted, it was tempered by something akin to hopelessness. Saviar believed he rightly understood those humans stranded with no elves among them were almost certainly lost for good.

Although Captain had assured time for questions at the end, General Sutton did not wait. "How?" he asked in his booming voice. "What changes have been made to make sure any humans lost on the same Outworlds as elves will be brought home?"

Captain had a ready answer. *The Pica Stone can be used as a device to see others distant from ourselves. We knew that. Until very recently, however, we did not have enough combined power to scry across worlds. Now that we have several more elves, two Kjempemagiska, and the mages, we believe we do. The next time we locate a group on one of the Outworlds, we will also be able to see them. *

The volume of the mumbling that followed this pronouncement suggested it raised many questions. Saviar could think of several of his own, but he sat back, certain Captain would answer them if given the opportunity.

*It's not a wide or complete picture. We will only visualize the single being we focus on and anything in his or her close proximity. We can hold this image only until we have to divert our combined power into crafting the gate. However, it may help us in several ways. We might get lucky enough to see humans in the same frame. We could get a clearer picture of their situation, so we could figure out a way to help them or make sure no creature of the Outworld comes into our world. *

That possibility had not occurred to Saviar. It brought images of an enormous monster leaping through the opening and devouring elves and humans by the mouthful.

At the least, we'd have some idea of who we're rescuing and his or her emotional state. We even considered the possibility that knowing their positions might give us more leeway with gate placement, so one or more of us could slip onto the Outworld before they escaped in order to give them instructions regarding the need to find and rescue any humans before the last elf leaves the Outworld.

Now, the din became so loud even an elf using mindspeak could not ignore it. Saviar got the gist of most of the comments; they wanted guarantees, not possibility.

Captain raised a hand for forbearance. *That was not satisfactory, so we battled our understandable fears of the Kjempemagiska to try merging magical types.* He turned Kentt and Mistri an apologetic look and received a slight nod in response.

The noise subsided.

There was no precedent, and we don't even speak similar languages, so the difficulty cannot be overstated. Once we bridged the communication issues, which required heretofore unknown enchantments working from both sides, Kentt has proven a valuable ally. With his extraordinary help, we believe we can send simple verbal messages through the Pica Stone to the trapped elves. That should be enough to inform them of the need to locate all humans and bring them through before allowing the gate to close.

Once again, the muttering changed to a lower volume and more positive timbre.

Unfortunately, like the images, the sound travels only one way. The receivers would not have a Pica to look into or the proper merged spells to respond. They couldn't tell us if they had a potentially fixable complication or needed assistance until it was too late. We had hoped that by bringing this issue to all of you, we might find the solution.

Full-volume conversations broke out around the room, but it was King Griff who voiced the first possibility, and his booming voice brought the room back to silence. "Princess Ivana can't speak with words, but she can make some simple needs known with hand signals. Perhaps a modified version of that might allow some basic communication with elves who you can see but not hear."

The simplicity of the suggestion made Saviar wonder why none of the elves had thought of it. Then, a moment later, why the thought had not occurred to him, either, until Griff had spoken it. The answer came swiftly. Elves and Kjempemagiska could communicate farther than they could see using their mental languages. They had no use for visual signals, thus did not consider or employ them. He had less explanation for his own lapse, especially since he had traveled with Weile Kahn on two occasions now and knew he and his men sent messages with carefully placed twigs and stones, noises and sound effects, as well as gestures.

Captain tipped his head in clear consideration. At length, he used *khohlar* again, **Doesn't it require . . . learning? Training?**

Griff made a grand gesture toward Tae Kahn. "I defer to the expert. King Tae?"

Saviar stifled a smile, certain Tae's father was the more adept at this particular skill, but he said nothing. Tae could determine for himself whether or not to reveal one of his father's secrets.

Tae rose uncomfortably. He did not like attention any more than his father did, but he did not present the same danger as the leader of the world's criminals. "I wouldn't call myself an expert, but I did construct Ivana's language." He paused a moment in thought. "Depending on how limited your view is, I think we could find a way to communicate a few basic things. You could, for example, tell the person in the picture to raise both hands if his life was in imminent danger or turn in a circle if he needed some additional time to locate all the humans. That sort of thing."

Captain switched to verbal speech in the common trading tongue, his lilting accent a treat to Saviar's ears. "Would it be too much to ask for you to assist us in this, Your Majesty?"

Saviar suspected the elves had little understanding about how to proceed with such a project. Without Tae's help, it would take an inordinate amount of time, and they might not get the best information.

Tae nodded. "If you'll stop calling me 'Your Majesty,' I'll come up with the most important questions in the fewest words and clear ways to interpret the nonverbal responses immediately after this meeting."

Captain grinned the way only an elf can, using his entire face. "Thank you."

Tae waved off the gratitude and spoke loudly enough for everyone to hear. "We all have reason to be entirely invested in the success of this project."

Sounds of agreement rose from all around the room.

Griff took the meeting over again. "Captain, if we manage to create this rather limited two-way communication, does that mean you could open the gate for some of us to go to the Outworld and help them?"

Smaller voiced than the high king, Captain returned to using indirect *khohlar* to respond. *We could presumably tell the elves to stand aside and let an individual or group come through, yes?* He glanced at Tae for confirmation and received it.

That opened a lot of possibilities, Saviar realized.

King Griff continued with his thought, "So if the Outworld elves indicated they were all dangerously menaced, or humans were on the Outworld but required convincing in order to accompany them off . . . we could send a diplomat or rescue party to assist?"

Tae bobbed his head slowly in consideration, and Captain made the same motion more definitively. "I believe that could be accomplished, Your Majesty. In fact, we would be able to send one or two elves along. That would assure that, even if all of the elves currently on the Outworld panicked or left it for any reason, there would still be someone to hold the gate or open a new one."

King Griff looked around the room, as if seeking volunteers, then back to Captain. "How many humans could we have in the rescue party?"

Captain made an unreadable gesture. "No limit on our part, Your Majesty. The gate is like a magical door. It has to be entered and exited in single file, but the number who do it doesn't matter." He paused before adding, "Whoever volunteers for this mission does need to recognize its danger. First, if we need to send them in at all, it's because the elves and humans already there can't handle the situation for one reason or another. We need to remember that, while none of the elves stranded on the Outworld had combat experience, nearly all of the humans did. And, aside from Renshai warriors and mages, they're all relatively young, healthy males. That may decrease your pool of volunteers a bit, Your Majesty."

"I'll go, Sire, if you'll allow it."

It took Saviar a moment to locate the speaker, his father, Ra-khir.

"I was part of the team sent to various Outworlds to retrieve the pieces of the broken Pica. We were sent blindly, with no idea of what to expect, and we were successful."

King Griff's attention went immediately to Kedrin. He would have to agree to allow one of his knights on such a mission. Saviar expected him to take his time in consideration, to weigh the pros and cons of sending one of Erythane's elite into peril, especially his only son, when the Knights of Erythane had already lost six of their minute number to war.

To Saviar's surprise, the Knight-Captain did not even take a moment before waving his assent.

Seated beside Ra-khir, as always, his faithful squire spoke next, his voice so comparatively soft Saviar had to strain to hear it. "I'll accompany you, of course, sir."

Ra-khir turned his gaze directly on Darby, which put the back of his head to Saviar, but he could see the neatly-coiffed red hair moving to and fro in a negative. Darby nodded and slumped ever so slightly in his seat. Saviar did not know what Ra-khir had said, but the knight had clearly just condemned Darby to remaining behind in Erythane. It was a mission far too dangerous for someone still in the early stages of learning weapons' craft.

Tae looked up from a paper onto which he had started scribbling notes. "Then I'm going, too. I was part of that same successful mission and, without me, Ra-khir would have gotten his fool self killed."

Frowns scored several faces, particularly Kedrin's and Ra-khir's. Weile's only reaction was to whisper something to one of his bodyguards. No one spoke out against Tae's decision, though. No one had the authority to rebuke a king.

Darris jumped in next, though he seemed far more reluctant, looking from Griff to Seiryn to Matrinka before speaking, "I was also on that mission, and both of them need me, if only to mediate between them."

Matrinka studied her toes, clearly unhappy but not wanting the world to know it. She did not have Weile's experience with schooling her features.

Thialnir rose, towering over those around him. "You'll need a Renshai. As their representative, I volunteer myself."

Saviar felt as if someone had struck him with a whip. Thialnir had been a highly competent warrior in his time, but that had long passed. Ra-khir and Tae were no longer young men, but Thialnir had both beaten by at least two decades.

"No!" Saviar heard himself shout. He composed himself before continuing. "I'll go. I'll represent the Renshai in Thialnir's place."

Thialnir challenged him, "By whose authority?"

Having turned down the position of leader, Saviar had none; but he was damned if he would allow the old man to risk his life doing something better and more properly suited to himself. He also realized he needed to dedicate himself to something as important and worthy as the rescue efforts to help him keep his emotions properly focused. He could challenge his leader to a spar, but it seemed counterproductive. Thialnir could win; he had in the past. And, if Thialnir lost, it might diminish him in the eyes of the other Renshai. Saviar changed his tack, softening his tone. "I worded that poorly, and I'm sorry. I would very much like to represent the Renshai in your place, should you allow it." He came up with a legitimate reason that would not offend Thialnir. "You see, my mother accompanied Sir Ra-khir and Bard Darris to the Outworlds on the last mission, but she is no longer with us. It's a matter of . . . family honor." It wasn't, but it sounded good and the idea of working closely with Ra-khir, in the absence of Darby, excited him even more than he expected. He braced himself for a verbal battle, probably followed by a rousing spar.

To Saviar's surprise, Thialnir spent several moments in consideration. To his further amazement, the leader of the Renshai stepped aside without further argument. "Very well, then. If it is a matter of family honor, I will allow Saviar to go in my place."

Smiles from a few key individuals around the room left Saviar wondering if Thialnir had somehow played him. He dismissed the thought as madness. Renshai, in general, displayed little subtlety, and Thialnir in particular didn't. Yet, Saviar supposed, the old man might have learned a few tricks through the years.

A silence followed as no one else immediately volunteered. King Griff glanced around the room, reading it. His gaze stopped on Valr Magnus. "General Magnus, did you wish to add someone who would stand for the North?"

Addressed by the high king, Magnus rose. "Sire, Béarn's Northern representative is happy with the choice of Saviar."

No response could have startled the room more. Someone with a singsong Northern accent stammered out, "But he's Renshai!"

Saviar had not seen the speaker, but apparently Magnus either did or recognized the voice. He turned to look directly at a soldier in the farthest circle dressed in the colors of Nordmir. "Sigurd, surely you still have a scant bit of history rattling around that big head of yours. The Renshai were one of the original twelve Northern tribes . . . when we still had twelve tribes." There was the barest hint of bitterness in the final phrase. Constantly squabbling over borders, the North had eventually subsumed, banished, or annihilated three of its tribes, including the Renshai.

Sigurd looked around, seeking allies. When no one else spoke, he stepped back in. "But the Renshai are . . . demons. They're our . . . direst enemy."

Magnus laughed. It started as a low rumble of movement, then became a snicker that grew to great, booming guffaws. Saviar found himself smiling, despite the topic, and several others were swept into the laughter, including King Griff. After several moments, it finally became quiet enough for the Aeri general to explain himself. "We just fought a war more terrible than anyone could have imagined against beings twice our size with magic that rivals the worst nature has ever brought to bear. We banded together: East, West, and North; elves; and hidden mages and won only because of that cohesion and because our enemies made a terrible mistake. Even then, we find ourselves in the situation of hunting down many of our colleagues on Outworlds we never knew existed containing unknown dangers and monsters beyond our most terrifying stories. And you want me to seriously consider the claim that those two men . . ." He gestured toward Saviar and Thialnir. ". . . seated calmly among us are our direst enemies?"

The room grew completely quiet. Valr Magnus' point seemed as obvious as a scream, yet so few had considered it in those terms, it rendered them speechless. From infancy, people from every quarter of the world learned about the demonic Renshai, their inhumanity, their reign of terror that had lasted a single year and occurred centuries earlier. Those who had never met an actual Renshai feared or despised all of them with the same vehemence as a lethal storm or a rabid wolf, speaking of them in whispered tones lest the objects of their fear overhear them in some supernatural way. For those with experience with the Renshai, it morphed into a murderous hatred lacking boundaries or logic. It was a prejudice so ingrained not even a true apocalypse seemed capable of shaking it. Otherwise intelligent people found convoluted ways to hate humans who disagreed with their views of the world even more than true monsters hell-bent on slaughtering them.

Magnus' words had cut through the hypocrisy, pointing out the foolishness that so often underlay such biases. Coming from nearly anyone else, the Northmen would have discarded the words as madness or stupidity. Such is the nature of true believers, no matter their politics, no matter their religion. But Magnus was their hero, their true or ersatz leader, their champion and conqueror of Renshai and monsters alike. What he said truly mattered.

Saviar realized he had the chance to become part of history in a way he had never before considered. He would not have believed it possible the rift between Renshai and their haters could be mended in his lifetime or that he would have a direct hand in it. He made a deep and flourishing bow of the type his father and grandfather had taught him, usually reserved for the highest royalty, men and women currently in the room. But this bow was for a general from Aerin.

"Valr, you honor me and also my people. I would be proud to stand in for all of the North, and I assure you I will represent every one of her tribes with honesty, courage, and competence. I will not forget for an instant the trust you placed in me, and I hope this will begin to reforge the bonds that once existed between all of our peoples. I cannot possibly thank you enough for the opportunity." He retook his seat.

The silence deepened, as if carved statues had suddenly replaced every living thing in the room. No one even seemed to breathe.

Then, Kedrin rose, still pale and scarred from his injuries. He broke into slow applause, his features grim and serious. Almost at once, the other knights in the room leaped to their feet, joining him. The king of Béarn came next, and when he stood, every Westerner in the room rose with him, joining the applause. In dribs and drabs, the others came, some with slow deliberateness, their claps grudging, others springing up enthusiastically and slapping their hands together with wild abandon. Even the elves and Kentt joined in, studying their long-fingered hands as if surprised they could make such noises. The Renshai banded with the others, then, at length the mages and, last, the Northmen until the entire room swelled with the thunder of it and cheers rose over the arrhythmic noise that became a thunder of applause.

It wasn't the world, Saviar realized. It was just the people in the room; and, when they related it, those who listened would bring their own biases and libel to the mix. For the moment, all prejudice was banished from Béarn Castle although not yet from the world. That would take time, a lot of it. Still, they had taken an enormous step forward today, and no one present would forget the lesson of it.

A long time passed before Griff found himself in control of the room again. "Does any other leader wish to add someone to our rescue party?" His gaze swept the highest officers and diplomats of the varying groups. Despite the enormous size of the Eastlands, they came together under a single high king. The entire North had given itself to the judgment of Valr Magnus. Only the West still remained fractured into various lower kingdoms, fiefdoms, baronies, and democracies. Currently, they had chosen to place themselves into three main categories: those closest to the city of Pudar, those who united under the auspices of General Sutton of Sangtagithi, and the southern areas of the West, currently best epitomized by King Griff. As the current party stood, the last area had disproportionate representation: Darris for Béarn itself, Ra-khir for neighboring Erythane, and even the Renshai had recently become official citizens of Béarn.

General Markanyin spoke next, "The Northwestern branch of the West is content with the current arrangement and feels confident with whoever the high king chooses to represent the Westlands, no matter his or her origins." With a wave, he passed the mantle to Sutton, who accepted it by standing and speaking. "I can't deny the urge to personally join the group, to help them strategize as well as see places few humans ever have the opportunity to visit." He sighed deeply. "However, my current job is to return my soldiers to their farms, homes and shops, or no one in the eastern half of the Westlands will survive the winter."

Nods went around the room. Everyone understood the need to save the missing warriors but not at the expense of the sick and injured, the women and children left behind. It did no good to rescue these missing men if they had nothing to come home to.

"Upon your leave, Sire, it is my intention to lead my people home as soon as you can spare us."

King Griff nodded somberly. "Any leader or representative who chooses to stay will be treated as my honored guest, along with his followers. However, other than the elves, mages, and those who compose the rescue party, anyone must know you have my blessing to leave at any time. In fact, most of you have already done so. Rest assured, your continued presence or absence will have no bearing on who is saved or the order of it. We will bring home every possible warrior, no matter his or her origin. We will send notice whenever one of yours is found, whether dead or alive, handle any injuries, and assure a safe homecoming whenever possible. I ask only that you let me know when you are going so I can have my staff provision you properly."

The other leaders had not made their departure so public, but Saviar felt certain they had received the same assurances. All good leaders were fanatical about bringing every man in their command home, and it had to pain any and all of them to leave before the rescue. But the war had brought out nearly every man, from king to soldier to poorest peasant. Their families needed them, and the economies of the smallest villages and largest cities depended on them to return. The dead would leave holes enough, the missing more. To keep the survivors away under those circumstances might leave gaps from which they could never recover.

Griff had already moved onward. "Tae, Captain, how long do you need to figure out how to communicate with the trapped elves?"

Tae spoke for them both. "We can have something workable by morning."

King Griff nodded. "Very well. We will reconvene in the great hall immediately following breakfast. Anyone who wishes to attend is welcome." With that, he adjourned the meeting.

CHAPTER 11

Sometimes, right depends on where you're standing.
—*Subikahn Taesson*

MATRINKA HAD HAD EXTRA CHAIRS brought to her chamber, though Darris barely spent a moment in his before rising to pace incessantly. Tem'aree'ay perched delicately on the edge of her wooden seat. Barrindar and Marisole sat beside one another, clasping their nearest hands, alternating between darting, nervous glances and gazes so meltingly dewy they defined young love. Xoraida and Griff sat quietly in their chairs, contributing little to the discussion. The woman watched her son's interaction with Marisole as if seeing him for the first time, and the king stroked his beard in pensive silence. Imorelda's kittens lay in a pile on the bed while their mother made herself at home in Matrinka's lap, and the queen appreciated her presence. The soft fur, the warm body, the gentle motion of stroking kept her calm.

Matrinka had already explained the situation in detail and mouthed the proper apologizes for not putting a definitive end to the relationship and watching the youngsters more closely. She made no excuses for her lapse, though they all knew the war had occupied everyone's attention and driven even the most level-headed people to desperate actions. The time for Tem'aree'ay's intervention was rapidly closing. They would have to make a decision today.

Matrinka had expected the young couple to keep their profile as low as possible while the parents discussed their situation, so it surprised her when Barrindar broke the terrible silence first. "We will, of course, bow to whatever choice is made. I realize I'm ill-prepared for fatherhood and know we will have issues of law to confront if this pregnancy is allowed to continue. But I have to wonder. What will become of the bard's line if it's ended?"

Matrinka stiffened. So consumed with the horror of the situation, she had not considered that one glaring detail. She found herself staring at Darris, who froze in his tracks. Surely, he had given the matter plenty of thought, though he had not raised it once in their many conversations.

Griff said patiently, "How would you know to ask that question?"

Barrindar hesitated. It was clearly not the tack he had expected. "I'm an educated man," he reminded his father. "I know how the curse of the bards works, passed always to the eldest child. Darris is the current bard, and Marisole has already shown signs of being next in line. That means she is his blood daughter and her firstborn child . . ." He trailed off, suddenly unsure of himself. "Did I say something wrong?"

Xoraida jumped in. "I don't think it's obvious to the populace, if that's what worries you. Most don't believe in magic outside of fairy stories. Although the presence of the elves contradicts it, their magic is relatively small compared with a multigenerational curse." Xoraida flushed and looked at Tem'aree'ay. "No offense intended."

"None taken," Tem'aree'ay reassured. "What you have said is true. Magic that spans generations is strong and complicated, limited to gods or, possibly, something otherworldly. All of us working together might manage to inflict such a thing on one man, but it wouldn't taint his blood or pass to his children." She added quickly, "Of course, we would never do such a thing. It's too—"

Matrinka believed she had been about to say "evil," then realized it might insult Darris and Marisole to categorize it that way.

Encouraged, Xoraida continued, "Of those who do believe in magic of this caliber, most either don't know or don't believe the bardic line is a magical curse. They think Darris has selected Marisole for the honor of succeeding him. Even those who do know seem willing to remain in denial."

Matrinka nodded, threading her hands more vigorously through Imorelda's fur. She had not expected the conversation to go in this direction, at least not so swiftly.

"I am a wife of the king, so it behooves me to know where he spends his nights." Xoraida turned Griff a smile, and a flush filled his cheeks. Despite his age and experience, he was still a farm boy at heart. "I'm sure some of the servants gossip, but Darris and Matrinka have been discreet. Even after so many years, there is still true love in their eyes if you think to look for it." There was a bare hint of regret in Xoraida's tone, so tiny Matrinka could convince herself she imagined it. Xoraida had a charmed life, and she clearly appreciated it; but she would never know the depth of devotion shared by Matrinka and Darris, by Griff and Tem'aree'ay and, now, by Barrindar and Marisole. Her marriage to Griff was one of convention and convenience. Still, they cared for one another, and it allowed her to live a life of luxury without responsibility or expectation, other than to produce heirs.

Matrinka knew the secret was never supposed to spread beyond Darris, Griff, and herself. Marisole had figured it out based on certain physical features and the same chain of logic Barrindar had used, but she had promised never to share what she had learned. Of course, she had also promised not to risk pregnancy. Matrinka turned her attention to her eldest daughter.

Marisole caught her eye and grew immediately defensive. "I didn't tell him, Mama. I swear I didn't tell anyone. And you know no one told me." It bordered on imparting unknown information, and she squirmed, apparently twinged by the curse.

Still clinging to her hand, Barrindar explained. "We figured it out together, a couple of years ago. It was only after we became certain we shared no parental blood that we . . ." He trailed off again, clearly embarrassed. "Well, we started to see each other in a . . . different . . . nonsibling way."

Marisole's lips twitched as she fought a smile.

Abruptly, Darris snatched up his lute, his features tense, his cheeks dark with suppressed anger. He launched into a song without preamble, the words and music intertwining to create an atmosphere of deep, almost primal, credibility. He sang of responsibility, not the simple superficial types that all humans share but the ones that bow the heads of kings: the decision to go to war, to mete out justice based on conflicting testimony, to fling oneself into lethal danger to rescue the life of another, to place the lives of husbands, sons, daughters in peril.

Darris sang of morality, of taboos so ancient even the most ignorant barbarians would never violate them: murder, betrayal, and— most of all—incest. The inherent wrongness of these things, the horror and humiliation they brought upon the participants, the shaking of the very foundations of civilizations.

Tears dripped from Matrinka's eyes, unbidden. She found herself huddled, her arms wrapping her chest, her thighs hugging Imorelda so tightly, the cat let out a yelp of protest. Claws swept the back of Matrinka's left wrist, then the cat leaped free of her grip to join its offspring on the coverlet.

Darris brought the themes together: shaming Marisole and Barrindar for violating not only the laws of Béarn but of humanity itself.

Either one of them could be the next high ruler, Marisole the body-guard to whomever the Pica chose regardless of her own potential status, and they needed to act appropriately. The king or queen had a duty not only to country but to world, and both needed to make sacrifices, no matter the price, no matter the personal pain. Many riches accompanied the title but many more obligations of the type most peasants would never comprehend. A monarch worthy of the title did not embrace the privileges and forsake the duties. To expect one's followers to follow the law while flouting it oneself was the very definition of hypocrisy. And a hypocrite did not deserve his or her crown.

Overwhelmed by feelings of patriotism and morality, Matrinka barely noticed Marisole rising and lifting her gittern from its case. She wove a harmony through her father's melody, finding the tune and perfecting it before adding her voice to the mix. She seized upon the theme of hypocrisy, reminding Darris that he and Matrinka had violated law in much the same way he condemned the fresh-faced lovers. She sang of love itself, defining it with sound and song as simple words could never do, then presented it as a predator who selected its prey with no regard to law or justice or convenience. It inspired foolishness, but also acts of courage and desperation. It was sometimes stronger than the human psyche could endure, more significant than life and crueler than death.

Darris answered mournfully, acknowledging his defiance, then condemning it. He made it clear he appreciated what Griff had done, that he believed the king's motivation was kindness and understanding, making the best of a terrible paradox. He delivered the highest of compliments to the king, even while berating himself for accepting the sacrifice. It had been the king's choice not to sleep with his queen, but Darris should never have accepted the offer to take his place.

Marisole's chords soured, deliberately harsh in rebuke. She sang of herself, of Arturo, of Halika, the three children born of their consorting. She refused the premise that they were mistakes; they were products of perfect passion, not immorality and shame. If the three were unworthy, Griff would never have accepted them as his son and daughters, Darris would have left them, Matrinka would have schooled them harshly. She sang the praises of her siblings, of Arturo's stamina and courage, his unwavering dedication to Béarn. She sang of Halika's unshakable faith, her fondness for animals, her gentleness toward any and all who worked at, lived in, or visited the city.

Darris' turn to respond came and went. Both continued to weave flawless melodies and harmonies around one another, fast and furious, but no one spoke for several stanzas past what they had clearly intended. Marisole, it seemed, had silenced her blood father.

But it did not last long. When Darris jumped back in, he made no attempt to contradict Marisole's point. To do so would argue his love for Matrinka meant nothing, that Marisole and her siblings did not deserve to live. He bowed as he played, symbolically granting her the win. His fingers slowed on the strings, plucking out a different sort of mood, his music old-fashioned and evocative of history. He sang of the first bard, though not the classic and well-used song Matrinka knew by heart. That one spoke of Jahiran's curiosity and how it drove him to spy on goddesses. The gods had punished him by heightening his need for knowledge still further, to a relentless hunger for every piece of information the world could ever yield, at the same time preventing him from imparting what he learned to others. They further cursed his firstborn children through eternity.

Already competent with a lute, Jahiran had appealed to the goddesses with song. They enhanced his musical talent to allow him a way to communicate. They also granted him a facility with weapons so that he could protect himself from those who would torment him for his strangeness.

The gods and goddesses in the song were the ones of the now defunct Western religion, which suggested either they had existed and no longer did or the story was apocryphal or just plain wrong. Whatever the case, the bard's curse was certainly real enough, and the line that descended from Jahiran's firstborn all suffered it in time. The bond to the King of Béarn had come later. Darris believed the Cardinal Wizards had made the connection centuries ago in order to grant the king a skilled and unwaveringly faithful bodyguard and knowledgeable adviser for all eternity.

Darris' current song made reference to the well-known story but touched it only lightly in order to make a more significant point. He sang of the desperate craving for knowledge, how it existed in each bard's eldest child, how it burned and tore and stabbed worse than any wound a weapon could wreak. He sang of having to make all his points with music, how it kept him silent when he would rather speak, forced him to sing while others rolled their eyes or listened, enraptured, incapable of forming their own opinions because the passion inherent in music made it impossible not to become influenced by his own. It granted him power but also left him in dangerous ignorance. The influence of music, while strong, is finite. Distanced from the tune, the others might act or think entirely differently than they had in his presence, might despise him for manipulating their emotions.

Through all this, Darris made it clear the bardic inheritance was,
indeed, a heavy burden despite the easy talent that accompanied it.
His previous Outworld experience had given him the opportunity to
drink from the Well of Mimir, which would have granted him all the
knowledge in the universe. As he described it, Matrinka managed a
glance at Marisole, could easily read the excitement overtaking her.
In that same situation, she would have gulped the water without a
thought, driven by a desire she could not control.

Matrinka knew Darris had fought his every instinct and yearning
to resist. It had been a trap, one he would have fallen into if not for
Jahiran himself. The first bard had shown him through example what
happens to someone who achieves the goal to which all with the bardic curse strive: a terrible madness from which there is no escape.
She expected Darris to recount that story, to demonstrate how even
a desire god-driven can be thwarted; but he did not. Instead, he
asked the question that had plagued him through eternity. If a bard
dies without procreating, if that first child never exists, can the curse
be broken? It all went back to Barrindar's musing: "What will become of the bard's line if this pregnancy is ended?"

Darris attempted to answer with more questions: Would it have
no effect at all because the curse is to the first *born* and this potential
baby would never be born? Would it simply go to Marisole's next
child? Or was it just possible the curse could finally be broken?

Griff interrupted the song. "You speak as if breaking the curse is
a good thing, but I don't agree. I rely on you, just as other kings have
relied on your predecessors."

Darris lowered his lute. "The curse is still on me and on Marisole. And there is convention, of course. The bards have protected
and advised the ruling monarchs of Béarn for hundreds of years, and
I see no reason why that needs to end just because it could. If you
wish, we could draw up a contract to replace the curse with an apprenticeship."

Tem'aree'ay made a gesture that suggested she had something to
add. As she rarely spoke unless addressed and never interrupted, the
movement caught every eye. "I understand you're well-versed in
lore, Darris, but your words demonstrate a dangerous ignorance of
magic."

Absolute silence followed her declaration. If anyone moved or
breathed, Matrinka could not hear it, and Imorelda had long ago
stopped purring.

Tem'aree'ay explained, "I don't doubt this is gods' magic we're discussing, which makes it powerful beyond human ken. A curse of that magnitude will not break easily or without backlash. There's no way to know how it will affect you or Marisole; but, I'm absolutely certain if I perform any action that risks breaking gods' magic, I will find myself embroiled in a battle with chaos I have no hope of winning."

Matrinka rushed to Tem'aree'ay and took both hands into her own. "Oh, Tem'aree'ay," she said breathlessly, "I had no idea. Please believe I would never have asked if I thought it posed any risk at all to you."

Tem'aree'ay intertwined her long fingers with Matrinka's and bestowed a soothing smile on her. "I know that, Matrinka. There's not a bit of malice in you. Ignorance is not a crime."

Barrindar broke the tenseness with a joke. "Except, perhaps, to the bard and his heir."

Nervous chuckles followed. Marisole and Darris put their instruments down and took their seats.

"It would seem," Griff said significantly, "our decision has been made. This baby is going to be born, and we need to prepare for its arrival."

Barrindar looked up quickly. "But, Papa, what about the law? We'll be forever banished."

Griff shook his head. "We can't allow that to happen."

All eyes went to the high king. Matrinka hoped he had the answer that defied the rest of them. King or no, he had no authority to change the ancient laws of ascension. That had become abundantly clear when he tried to marry Tem'aree'ay. The solution had only come because the ancient laws had not taken elves into account, which allowed Darris to perform some deft maneuvering. On siblings, though, the law was incontrovertible and clear.

Seeming not to notice the others' expectant stares, Griff sighed heavily. "My parents . . . were banished." It was a point of history they all knew. Helana had told her grandchildren tales of her life, as frightening as any fairy story designed to keep children on the proper paths, but hers were all personal truth. Accustomed to Béarn Castle and a life of royalty, she and Petrostan had found themselves ill-prepared for foreign locales and poverty. They had suffered harrowing sicknesses, vicious attacks, and starvation. Untended by healers, unprepared for the whims of weather, unable to speak the languages of the townspeople and never accepted in their midst, they spent the first several years in anguished turmoil. Not long afterward, Petrostan had died in a plowing accident, and Helana found herself utterly alone with no one but young Griff to keep her company. For fear of losing her son as well, she had all but smothered him, never allowing him far from her sight, to interact with others or perform any action that might place him, even slightly, at risk.

"We can't allow that to happen," Griff repeated more firmly, his gaze distant, clearly lost in memory.

Springing from her chair, Tem'aree'ay threw her arms around her husband. It looked rather like a kitten attempting to hug a bear, but it clearly soothed him. His enormous hands enwrapped her, and they went from deflated limpness to gripping strength. "The lives and well-being of my children—of my grandchildren—are too important to risk; but, more so, we cannot jeopardize the future of Béarn. The balance of the world relies on it." He released Tem'aree'ay.

More graceful than any dancer of the court, Tem'aree'ay slid to the floor at Griff's side, one hand comfortingly resting on his thigh.

Griff pointed out what they all knew and should have considered. "By law, no child I create with Tem'aree'ay can sit on the throne. Whatever the populace believes, my blood does not flow through the veins of my children with Matrinka. That leaves only three possible first-line heirs." They all knew he meant his offspring with Xoraida: Barrindar, Calitha, and Eldorin. "We can't afford to lose any one of them."

The simple truth meant far more than Griff's words suggested. If anything happened to the current king, the Council would invoke the test of the Pica Stone on every possible heir until they found the one who could pass it. Since the ability to do so was believed to run only in the blood of the Béarnian royal family, they always began with those most closely related to the previous ruler. Only after the Pica failed all of the first-line heirs did they move on to cousins, uncles, and aunts.

Those whom the magic found unworthy nearly always went mad. Most committed suicide, others turned to drink or mind-altering substances, and the remainder flitted around, acted dangerously oddly, or became ghosts of their former selves. To her knowledge, Matrinka was the only living heir who had failed the test and maintained her sanity. Yet, despite the support of the best healers and friends in existence, she had still spent many years questioning everything she was or did. Two decades later, she continued to awaken from nightmares she knew, without understanding how, referred to a test she had no ability to remember.

Matrinka had no intention of allowing Marisole, Arturo, or Halika to take that test. The ascension laws of Béarnian royal marriage would explicitly exclude any of her offspring from ruling had their half-Pudarian parentage been known to the Council. They could rule without Griff's blood, so long as a Béarnide of suitable parentage had sired them, but that would not be true in this case. No one knew how the Pica Stone decided a man's or woman's worth; but all of the previous rulers throughout history had met the proper biological criteria. It was possible the Pica would reject her children solely because they lacked the proper bloodlines.

Matrinka suddenly realized something else, almost as significant. "There's also the issue of Darris' successor. Magic ties the bard to the ruler of Béarn. So long as Darris is alive, Marisole is free to come and go. But what happens if, gods forbid it, we lost Darris?" She did not add he had just volunteered for a dangerous assignment, assisting those missing on the Outworlds.

Another hush followed Matrinka's question. This time, everyone in the room seemed deep in thought. It soon became clear to Béarn's queen they had few options. It was possible Darris would outlive Marisole, and the baby in her womb would find its way home to take his place. Griff might remain on the throne until a grandchild or great-grandchild could replace him. However, depending on one or both of these to happen would be folly the world could ill-afford, even if any of them could stand to lose Barrindar and Marisole.

The silence intensified as they considered the terrible possibilities.

Griff spoke up softly, "There is only one solution to this problem, but it requires duplicity. I don't like it, but the only other possibility would tear apart Béarn and disrupt the balance. As I understand it . . ." He consulted Tem'aree'ay as he spoke. This was not her area of expertise, but she had more understanding of such things than anyone else in the room. ". . . if we lost that balance, the world would plunge into chaos. All structure and stability would fail, and every living thing would . . . die."

Matrinka pursed her lips, confronted with her own nightmares. If she thought about it too long, the madness she had avoided would consume her. The gravity of this danger explained why the peoples of the continent allowed the Béarnian ruler to retain primacy and also why Béarn risked the sanity of all its precious heirs when the time came to crown the next one. It seemed as if the laws of ascension ought to be suspended to account for this possibility, but they were even older than the knowledge the proper king or queen had to sit upon Béarn's throne for the balance to be maintained. Most believed those ancient edicts were the very reason Béarn's line had this remarkable ability, that it resided in the blood itself.

Only now did Matrinka truly realize the horrific gamble she and Griff and Darris had taken. They had been young, all still in their teens, and clearly foolish. Their own deceit had set the stage for this one. "Explain," was all she trusted herself to say.

Barrindar took Marisole's hand again, firmly. "It's still very early. If not for elfin magic, we wouldn't even know for sure. I've been told a lot of pregnancies fail at . . ."

Darris gave the prince a stern look that silenced him. Apparently, the bard did not believe a curse millennia old would fall so easily. If nothing else, ancient enchantment would see this child born.

Griff did not embrace the delay. "If Marisole swiftly married someone the Council approved . . ." He did not have to complete the thought. All of the human heads started bobbing, including Matrinka's. They understood.

It would be assumed the baby arose from the seed of her sanctioned husband. Babies often arrived a few weeks or even a month or two early. Usually, they were smaller, but not necessarily. Béarnides were a big-boned people, particularly the royal line, and they tended to have large offspring as well. No one outside this room would think to question.

Marisole's brow crinkled. "But who could we find who fits the proper criteria and would not mind a sham marriage?"

For a moment, Matrinka could not help thinking along the same lines. She and Darris had gotten lucky in a way she doubted anyone else ever could. Their "sham marriage" had been the sanctioned king's idea; otherwise, they would never have considered it.

Barrindar caught on more swiftly. "No one, Marisole." He tightened his grip on her hand. "It would be a real marriage, not a sham."

Xoraida added, "Your husband could never know the truth."

"But—" Marisole started, then stopped. She would have to sing to make her point, and that did not seem appropriate at the moment.

Barrindar made it for her. "We could never marry, not even if you became queen and were allowed multiple spouses. We're siblings."

Matrinka closed her eyes, fighting tears. The idea of her daughter forever unhappy felt like a leaden fist clutching her heart. She had hated the laws of ascension ever since she first heard the soul-wrenching strains of Darris' music, had looked into his perfect hazel eyes, but never more than at this moment.

Marisole kept her fingers entwined with Barrindar's and reached for his other hand. "How can I marry another man when I love you?"

Barrindar accepted her other hand. Clutching both, he pulled her so close they could see nothing but one another's eyes. They stared, clearly enraptured. "Darris is right. Our responsibility is to Béarn and her people, and we must do what's in the best interests of our country, no matter the cost to us. We've been rash and selfish, and look what it's gotten us." He let go of one of Marisole's hands to gesture around the room before grasping it again. "We had no right to cause so much trouble, so much grief."

Matrinka had always appreciated Barrindar but never so much as at this moment. She could see what Marisole loved about him . . . and something more. She suddenly realized, without any need to consider it further, Barrindar could pass the Pica test. Given the opportunity, he would become the next king of Béarn, the fulcrum on which the balance of the world rested. Banishment, never a good option, was no longer an option at all.

Barrindar released Marisole to turn to the rest of them. "I'm sorry," he said. "We made a terrible mistake, and I'll do whatever it takes to fix it."

Reluctantly, Marisole allowed Barrindar his hands. A moment later, she reached for them again, but they were gone, presumably for good. Her head fell forward, as if beyond her control. If she also wished to apologize, she gave no sign, clearly too aggrieved to speak.

As Marisole lost her composure, Matrinka forced hers back into play. "It's not as if you'll never see one another again. Siblings often talk privately, buoy one another's spirits, and there's no reason for a husband to feel suspicious or uncomfortable when a woman is with her brother."

Darris added warningly, "So long as you're not acting suspiciously or doing anything inappropriate, even in private."

Matrinka resisted the urge to hit him.

Marisole managed to raise her head, revealing a tear-streaked face. "How can I pretend to love a man I don't when the one I do is always within reach?"

"It's a big castle." Barrindar continued to face Marisole, though he did not reach for her. "I can avoid you if that's what you want."

"No!" Marisole said, tears starting fresh. Then, more softly, "No. That's not what I want. I would rather keep you as a sibling and a friend than lose you entirely. It's just going to be . . ." She stopped, balancing on a dangerous edge of informing without singing. Instead, she finished with a simple word rather than elaborating her feelings. ". . . hard."

Xoraida rose and walked to Marisole, placing her hands on the girl's quivering shoulders. "Consider yourself lucky to have experienced true love; not many do. We will pick you a kind, sweet husband, one who will treat you and the child well, who will appreciate your beauty and your talent. Believe me when I tell you you will learn to love him. Perhaps not with the white-hot intensity you do Barri, or perhaps with it. Either way, you can and will be happy if you don't dwell on what might have been." She looked at Matrinka as if she worried she had overstepped her maternal boundaries.

Matrinka turned a reassuring smile on Griff's third wife. No one else could have spoken those lines with the same enthusiasm.

The group set to picking out a husband for Marisole. After a moderately long discussion, they settled on Nomalan, a soft-spoken youngster who seized every opportunity to assist her during weapons training. Marisole had always liked this about him, although it had never occurred to her he did it out of a shy fondness. Most of the other boys and men seemed to either resent her presence or avoid her, especially when it came to sparring. It seemed no one wanted to risk getting bested by a girl, and politeness demanded they not dominate her, either.

When the women started discussing the how-tos of courtship, the men prepared to leave. But, before doing so, King Griff had a suggestion. "The current plan is for Darris to join the rescue crew as our Béarnian representative. What if I needed him here?"

Darris gave the king a quizzical look.

"Marisole's been saying she needs to test her mettle before she can feel comfortable guarding the high king. That's why she went on the mission to talk the elves into assisting in the war."

Darris opened his mouth, and his expression made it clear he did not approve of the idea.

Before he could speak, however, Marisole jumped in. "Please let me go. It's only fair for me to get as much experience as possible before I have to settle down with a husband and child."

Matrinka frowned, the suggestion counterintuitive. Marisole needed to marry as quickly as possible. It took a moment to see how sending her away from Béarn, even on an intermittent basis, could further that end. Then, the answer came, and she found herself blurting it aloud. "You're sending her *and* Nomalan in Darris' place."

Barrindar managed a smile, though it seemed a bit forced. "Nothing like a bit of danger to bring people together."

Griff added, "Despite his age, Nomalan's one of our better fighters. He's been hinting he'd like to train for the position of weaponsmaster when old Molo retires. What a great way to test his ability to handle duress."

Only then it occurred to Matrinka that, if she was right, if Barrindar did become the king, the curse assured Marisole would have to become his bodyguard and adviser. She found herself obsessed with the possibilities; and even the realization that, within weeks, she would probably have a son-in-law and, less than a year thereafter, a grandchild did not fully penetrate. The situation was not ideal. It required them to trick a sweet and sincere young man and the populace of Béarn, but Matrinka could not think of a way around it. Griff was the neutral point on which the balance hinged, and he always dispensed justice in a fair, impartial manner. If he felt comfortable with this idea, she was not worthy to question it. Matrinka only wished she could have found a better way, one that would allow the young lovers to marry and remain in good standing. Her heart still wrestled with the possibility long after her mind told it otherwise, wholly committed to the king of Béarn's plan.

CHAPTER 12

A man who can't keep himself alive is not worthy of that life.
—*Colbey Calistinsson*

THE FIRST GROUP OF RESCUED HUMAN SOLDIERS con-
sisted of seventeen Pudarians, seven Easterners, and three Northmen, each from a different tribe. Celebration of their return was
tempered by the lifeless bodies they pushed through the gate. The
survivors described suffering from perpetual storms and vicious
winds. In singles and groups, they had found one another, sheltering
in a series of caves carved into the side of a mountain by the same
weather that had caused them to require near-constant protection.

While trapped, the humans had found and worked with a dozen
elves to figure out which of the strange plants and animals were
safely edible. As they became more accustomed to the gales, some
ranged far enough to find the lifeless bodies and drag them to an
empty cave for examination. It appeared some had died during the
war, their corpses flung through the gates along with the living. Others had succumbed to squalls, though whether the terrible backlash
of magic on the battlefield or the ones on the Outworld, they could
only guess. Some of the soldiers had survived the transfer and even
found shelter only to starve or poison themselves with local vegeta-
tion or by consuming the meat of an Outworld rodent that feasted
on venomous plant life. Those lucky or wise enough to partner early
with the elves had the benefit of magic to help determine the safety
of their diet.

The people and elves gathered in the banquet hall hugged and
congratulated the twenty-seven human and twelve elfin survivors,
plying them for information. Others set to the gruesome task of
identifying the thirty-eight bodies, of which two were clearly elfin.
These names, too, were crossed off the list of the missing. As the
bodies had begun to decompose, they were swiftly moved to an outer

courtyard where servants and volunteers set to wrapping them in sheets and packing them in ice for travel or local services.

Tae took some solace in the realization his crude, nonverbal communication suggestions had done their job. The elves, mages, and Kentt had managed to bring up the image of one of the elves in the Pica Stone with a background of bleak stone cave walls. Using Tae's ideas, they had taught a quick and rudimentary form of sign language to the elf, which had resulted in a relatively simple rescue.

At Captain's urging, Tae now stood at the front edge of the massed magic users beside their leader. Imorelda perched on the table as if she had as much right to be there as the Pica Stone. Her two kittens crawled laboriously around her, unsteady on their paws, their chests and bellies dragging. She placed herself between them and the edge of the table, purring. He sent her a mental message. *I still think you should stay.*

You need me, Imorelda replied, not for the first time, though she brought up a new reason with each repetition. *Any intelligent beings on an Outworld won't speak a language you know. They might have a mental type of speech.*

It was not her strongest argument, and Tae let her know it. *Which I also won't speak. So what's the difference?*

Imorelda turned him a pointed look. *If they have only a mental language, I'll be able to let you know they're trying to communicate. You have a chance of figuring it out or, at least, using thought pictures. It's a lot faster and more useful than waving wildly and drawing in the dirt.*

Tae could not deny her logic. If not for those thought pictures and the leaking of ideas and emotion, he could never have learned to spy on and speak with the *Kjempemagiska.* The war would have been lost before they had known they were menaced. Still, he argued, wanting to keep Imorelda and her offspring safe. *The last time we went to Outworlds, nearly all of the creatures found a way to bridge the gap. Some even spoke our language.* He was not wholly sure if that was true, if they had used some sort of inherent translation ability or magic, or if it was some weird Outworld phenomenon generated by the gods. Perhaps it had something to do with the specific worlds they happened to visit on that occasion or some effect from the shards of the Pica Stone.

If you didn't think communication might be an issue, you wouldn't have volunteered. There are numerous better fighters in this room, and numerous NUMEROUS better thinkers.

Tae ignored the dig to address the salient point. *I do rely on you,* he admitted. *Sometimes, I wonder how I breathe and walk when you're not with me.*

Imorelda gave Tae a scathing look. Her tail flopped calmly. *I often wonder the same thing.*

Fine. I won't try to talk you out of accompanying me again. Tae hoped capitulation would leave him some space for negotiation. *But why can't we leave the kittens? You know Matrinka would be thrilled to take care of them.*

They're nursing.

Matrinka can use a dropper filled with goat milk.

Imorelda raised her head in a perfect imitation of human snootiness. *My children are not goats.*

I've seen you drink goat milk, Tae pointed out. *I have, too. We're not goats, either.*

Imorelda turned in a circle, then carefully lay down. The kittens snuggled in, their tiny noses questing her belly, seeking their chosen nipples. *My babies stay with me.*

Force accompanied the statement; on this point, too, she would not bargain. Something else slipped through their mental contact. She was hiding her true reason for being so insistent, and she had no intention of revealing it. Nothing Tae said would change her mind.

Tae had worn a specially designed tunic with wide, soft pockets for the kittens to snuggle into, tall enough even swift movement would not risk them falling out. He could throw a cloak over his outfit without harming them, but he still worried about their safety. A hard enough blow could crush them like eggs. *Your stubbornness may cost them their lives.*

Imorelda's tail lashed now. She peered directly into his eyes, her yellow orbs slitted and hard. *And your foolishness has nearly cost us yours and mine many times. This is my decision, and I have made it.* Working around the kittens took the heat from the gesture, but she still deliberately turned her back on Tae.

Tae knew when it was useless to argue. He redirected his attention to Captain, who had been peering diligently into the Pica Stone, allowing the other elves to handle the rescued and the dead. Unfooled by the elder's intensity, Tae put a gentle hand on the elf's shoulder. It surprised him to find it strangely angular and tense as any human's. "I'm sorry."

Captain sent Tae direct *khohlar*, as if afraid even a whisper might be overheard. *It seems callous to mourn our two too vigorously when you have lost so many more.*

Tae could not use *khohlar*, so he resorted to a murmur he felt certain only Captain and Imorelda could hear. "I understand. To humans, losing a life is a calamity. To elves, it is a holocaust of epic proportions."

Captain barely nodded. He did not need to explain; Tae knew.

Humans accepted death as a part of life; while they often hated or feared it, they also knew it, at times, as a blessing or even an event to celebrate. The Northmen, in particular, focused their entire lives on dying "correctly" to assure their souls a proper place in Valhalla. Many Easterners still believed in their one, nameless god and his divine afterlife for those who proved themselves worthy. Humans suffered illnesses, insanities, and infirmities from which death sometimes brought a welcome relief. For elves, there was no afterlife, no horrors to escape, only a soul to recycle or disintegrate. The two on the floor were lost for eternity, and no new elves could ever take their places. The number of elves in existence was forever diminished by two.

It took time to sort out the situation. The survivors were greeted, cataloged, and sent to the comforts they had missed: friends, familiar food, clean clothes, and beds in the royal barracks. Messengers were dispatched to let the proper authorities know which soldiers would soon find their ways home to their worried families and to ask what they wanted done with their dead. Slowly, all the bodies were removed, leaving the stench of rot to join the other myriad smells that filled the room. Servants cleaned where they had lain, expressions pinched with revulsion against the odor and the dislodged maggots.

Tae left Captain's side to whisper in the ear of the captain of Griff's guards. "Take care. We don't know if Outworld insects behave the same way as our own."

Seiryn turned Tae a look of alarm, then nodded and rose to discuss the matter with the handlers of the cleaning staff, then outside to those working with the dead.

As Tae returned to his place near the massed elves and mages, he realized no matter how many wise men assembled to guess what might happen, there were always unanticipated details, some large, some small. He leaned in to Captain again. "I think we should make some changes to the hand signals."

Captain sat up straighter, reaching for his quill.

Tae put his hand on the elf's wrist, stopping him. "Listen first. We may not want this . . . recorded."

Captain turned a curious look in Tae's direction but said nothing, allowing him to explain.

"I propose we ask them to hold up fingers for the number of dead they have knowledge of, first elves, then humans." Tae drew a deep breath, then suggested, "And we very quietly tell them to write down their names or descriptions, then leave the bodies behind."

Captain's brows rose in slow increments, each one further encouraging Tae to elaborate. When Tae did not, he finally asked. *Humans prefer to see their dead, to accord the bodies certain rites.* It was not a question, simply stated fact. Captain had enough experience on Midgard to know.

There were even more reasons to bring back the dead, but Tae would not argue against his own case. "True, but we have to balance that against other concerns. The bodies could be contaminated with Outworld creatures." He supposed it was also possible the living would bring back dangerous parasites. He had no desire to deal with intelligent or voracious fleas or ticks or lice; but that seemed unavoidable and far less concerning or, at least, far less creepy than magic-wielding maggots and dung beetles. "Béarn's resources are finite. Griff will feel obligated to deal properly with every corpse, at great cost in time and money much better spent on the living."

Captain nodded his understanding.

"We need to be subtle. Some people won't be happy, but it's definitely for the best." Soldiers despised leaving one of their own behind. Certain customs dictated the dead be handled in specific ways to assure the proper afterlife. Others would have difficulty accepting the deaths of loved ones if the bodies never surfaced. Some would surely be misidentified. Still, he believed he had made the right decision and he could far more easily justify it later than waste time pleading for it now.

The two spent the remainder of their waiting time refining the communication system and chatting. At one point, Imorelda leaped from the table and disappeared for nearly an hour, presumably to relieve herself or beg the cooks for food. Apparently still miffed, she gave no explanation, nor did she ask Tae to watch the sleeping kittens. Not that it mattered. Neither had done anything more than twitch in sleep the entire time she was gone, though both mewed wildly in welcome when she returned.

By late morning, the room had been cleared of the rescued, living and dead. Then, a page approached Captain. "Sir, King Griff would like to know if it's possible for you to continue. Do you have the strength to locate and save another group of soldiers?"

Captain sent a general *khohlar* that touched every mind in the room, though he targeted the elves, mages, and Kentt. Tae got the gist, though certain magical terms defied his understanding. The elf told them all to prepare for the imminent next round and asked anyone unable to assist or in need of more recovery time to contact him.

The page shifted nervously from foot to foot while Captain tipped his head to receive replies. If he got any, he gave no sign, merely looked at the mages, all huddled in a group. They could not use *khohlar*, so he needed a verbal or nonverbal confirmation from them. Chymmerlee caught his eye and waved assent. Captain next turned toward Kentt and Mistri. Receiving brisk nods, he finally responded to the page. "Please tell His Majesty we're ready as soon as he gives the signal."

The page scampered off to relay the message halfway across the room, which Tae found amusing. Captain could have sent *khohlar* to the high king much more swiftly, but he followed the human custom instead.

Captain rose and wound briefly through his contingent, sometimes relaying mental messages that made little sense to Tae, other times speaking directly to individuals or small groups. At length, he returned to his place beside Tae and put a hand on either side of the Pica Stone. Only the foggy prints his palms left on the sapphire revealed his anxiety. He looked toward the central table, waiting.

King Griff raised an arm, flexing his fingers to indicate Captain should begin the process.

Hunched over the Pica Stone, the oldest of the elves spoke harsh, sibilant syllables that little resembled the musical elfin tongue or his usual melodic tenor. All around him, magical voices rose and fell in a chant, filling the entire space with a wordless sound that seemed to vibrate through the walls, floor, furniture, and every being in the room. Though accustomed to the process from the previous trial, the humans still went fully silent, as if worried a single misplaced noise might interfere with the pooled magic.

As before, an image glimmered to life in the Pica Stone. Peering around Captain, Tae believed he saw the profile of an elfin face, including one delicately-pointed ear, an impossibly green eye, a high cheekbone, a pinched nose, and flame-red hair. A small, blonde elf gazed at the image from the opposite side of the table. If she and Captain communicated, they did so silently; and Tae had no idea what they might be saying. Imorelda took a position on one side of the gemstone, staring into it as well, her whiskers nearly touching it.

Captain leaned over. "Can you hear me, Tellurial Auzama Kahanath Shumaren Whir?" he asked beneath the chanting.

The elf in the image stiffened, head swiveling.

"It's Arak'bar Tulamii Dhor speaking to you through the Pica Stone."

Tellurial froze in position, mouth moving in silent speech.

"I can see you, Tellurial Auzama Ka-hanath Shumaren Whir, but you can't see me. I can project sound to you, but I can't hear you. *Khohlar* will not work. Nod once if you understand."

The elf raised and lowered his head in an exaggerated nod. His mouth did not move this time, but bits and pieces of more elves moved in and out of the picture. It was difficult to weed out what he saw, but Tae believed he could discern at least two others. Oddly, he found himself more focused on Captain's speaking than the picture in the Pica. Though Tae had picked up a few words of elvish—his facility with languages made that inevitable—hearing and understanding every syllable should have made him joyous the way mastering a new language always did. Instead, it felt terribly wrong, rousing the wariness that usually only accompanied danger.

Captain explained it as "new" magic, the same that had allowed Kentt and the elves to communicate. He had extended this temporary ability to Tae, obviously believing it a courtesy. Though Tae would have had difficulty assisting without it, he still could not shake the discomfort. He had spent most of his life unpuzzling foreign tongues, and the ease of his understanding felt unnatural and burdensome.

Captain continued addressing the image in the Pica, "You'll need to assist us with a gate."

The elf in the Pica started moving, apparently rushing to obey.

Captain stopped him. "But not quite yet. First, we need to exchange some information."

Tellurial went still again, waiting. He made a nonhuman gesture.

Captain frowned. "I'm going to ask some questions. To respond yes, bob your head up and down. To respond no, shake it side to side." He would not have had to explain those gestures to humans. They came naturally to most cultures, which was why Tae had chosen them. "Are you in imminent danger?"

Tellurial opened his mouth to answer, then apparently remembered Captain could not hear him, and closed it. He moved his head right once, then left. It was a "no," but not a firm one.

Captain moved away from the Pica to look at Tae. "I don't think they're entirely safe, either." He switched tactics. "Tellurial Auzama Ka-hanath Shumaren Whir, we are going to create that gate and bring all of you home. However, it's equally important we bring any and all humans sent to that Outworld home as well. When the last elf steps through the gate, it will close permanently. Any humans left behind would be trapped. Do you understand?"

Tellurial bobbed his head exactly one time, then made another uninterpretable gesture, at least to Tae. He looked askance at Captain, but the oldest of the elves kept his gaze on Tellurial, still frowning.

Captain muttered, "Something's wrong." Apparently, he could not read a whole lot more from the movement.

"Find out how many elves and how many humans are with him."

Captain gazed into the Pica. "Hold up a finger for each elf who arrived on that Outworld, including yourself."

Tellurial raised his hands, but they could not be seen around his shoulder.

Captain sighed. "Turn to your left."

Tellurial moved a bit.

"A little more."

Tellurial complied, finishing up so he appeared to face them directly. He had nine fingers raised.

"How many are alive and together at this moment?"

Tellurial continued to hold up nine fingers.

Captain breathed a relieved sigh, then caught himself, looking guiltily at Tae. Clearly, he had not meant to reveal emotions until after he knew the current state of any humans as well. "Now, how many humans arrived on the Outworld?"

Tellurial hesitated. He spoke silently for a moment, then pursed his lips. Finally, he flashed both hands, waited a moment, curled his fingers closed, then opened both hands and displayed all the fingers again two times. He fisted both hands, then held up only one. He ended with another nonhuman gesture.

Still hovered over the Pica, Captain interpreted, "Thirty-five, give or take?"

Tellurial nodded.

"And how many of the humans are with you now?"

Tellurial shook his head, not raising either hand.

"None?" Captain said, a touch of question and alarm in his voice. He looked at Tae for guidance.

"Ask him if the humans are not with him because they're all dead."

Captain repeated the question to Tellurial.

The elf shook his head, then shrugged.

Tae did not know how to interpret that. "What's he trying to say?"

"I'm not sure," Captain admitted. He addressed Tellurial again. "Are some of the humans dead?"

Tellurial's chest swelled as he sucked in a deep lungful of air. He held it several moments, then slowly deflated. Again, he shrugged.

"I don't think he knows." Tae leaned forward. "Ask him if he would need help to gather all the living humans."

Captain did so, receiving a brisk and definitive nod this time.

Tae hopped to his feet. "You prepare them for our arrival. I'll gather the troops."

Imorelda launched herself at Tae, landing heavily on his left shoulder and spreading herself around his neck. *Grab the kittens,* she commanded.

The time for argument had passed. With a grim sigh of resignation, Tae did as Imorelda bade, tucking the tiny mewling creatures into his pockets, and headed toward the prearranged staging area near the gate.

CHAPTER 13

*Most humans wouldn't know quality if it scratched their eyes out
and batted them around on the floor.*

—Imorelda

SAVIAR AND RA-KHIR insisted on being first through the gate,
followed swiftly by Chan'rék'ril and El-brinith, the same two elves
who had accompanied a somewhat different party nearly two decades earlier when they sought out the shards of the Pica Stone. Tae
knew Chan'rék'ril had lost his soul to spirit spiders, so it made sense
for him to volunteer and for the elves to send him. He could easily
have died then and there, proof a backup elf was needed to assure
the gate remained open and the rescue party did not become trapped
on the Outworld along with those they had come to save.

Marisole and Nomalan went next. The party had received no explanation for the substitution of those two for Darris. Ra-khir was
too polite and loyal to ask, and Saviar did not appear to notice or
wonder, probably believing it had something to do with competence
or age. Imorelda had informed Tae of the entire discussion, so he
also remained silent and accepting, especially after Matrinka gave
him a worried and significant look that suggested she did not want
to talk about it. He wondered if she had allowed herself and others
to speak freely in front of the cat because she trusted Imorelda, because concern had made her careless or because she wanted Tae to
know, certain he would keep their secret.

Last to go through, Tae hesitated long enough to assure multiple
warriors, most Renshai, guarded the gate to protect those gathered
from anything dangerous that might slip through from the other side,
then plunged through the nearly invisible opening. Tingling assailed
Tae's head and body, then subsided almost as quickly. He had closed
his eyes, prepared for the blinding flash and disorienting magic that
had overtaken him the last several times the elves had sent him to the

Outworlds, but it never came. Apparently, having elves on the opposite side changed the type of magic they used for the transport.

The rescue party stepped into a forest of bulbous, twisted trees that resembled *hadongo*s except these had darker trunks, nearly black, and were speckled with off-white markings Tae would have taken for scars had they not been so extensive and regular. They sported leaves as big as human feet, serrated and broad, nearly blocking the sunlight. Nine elves stared at the newcomers, their gemlike eyes registering no surprise or fear. Tae had no difficulty finding Tellurial among the others.

El-brinith spoke to them in elvish, and Tae realized his ability to comprehend it had returned to normal. He spoke the Northern tongue, which had significant overlap with elvish, and he knew Saviar did as well. Otherwise, he doubted any of his human companions could follow the discussion at all. It seemed to include a greeting, a request for information, and a promise.

Apparently, the Pica Stone had focused on Tellurial randomly because another elf stepped forward to do the talking for them. "My name is An'séarie." To Tae's relief, she stopped at four syllables. "I speak your human trading language, so I will explain what we know."

Tae saw tension leave several of his companions.

An'séarie continued, "We are very eager to return to our family, but we will remain until you have had time to ask your questions. It is the request of Arak'bar Tulamii Dhor."

"All of them are worthy of trust," Chan'rék'ril said. Apparently, An'séarie had addressed something to him with direct *khohlar*. Otherwise, his words had come out of nowhere. "The humans worry about their kin, just as we do. They have a right to get them safely home."

A hint of defensiveness entered An'séarie's tone. "Of course. But I'm not sure they can be saved."

Saviar's hand fell to his hilt so instinctively, Tae doubted he even realized it. "Are they in trouble?"

"We don't know," An'séarie replied, "but we believe so." She added quickly, "We tried to warn them, but they wouldn't listen."

Just tell us what happened, Imorelda sent.

Tae agreed. "Explain," he said simply, hoping his own pointed statement would encourage the others to avoid chatter and unnecessary verbiage. If the humans needed help, they should not delay unnecessarily, but it was crazy to charge in without knowledge, either.

An'séarie obliged. "There's something singing, more than one something, in fact, clearly magical. It's beautiful music, but also fae and dangerous. The humans made a camp near the shore, refusing to leave it. They say they're needed, but we have noticed fewer men every time one of us has dared to check on them. They won't come away with us. The last time we suggested it, they threatened violence. Since then, we've left them to their own devices."

"How many?" Tae asked. "Humans, I mean."

An'séarie hesitated, perhaps in silent consultation with the other elves. "We believe they started with thirty-five or forty. From what we can tell, fewer than two dozen remain."

Chan'rék'ril asked, "How often do you hear the singing?"

"Twice now." An'séarie considered. "Once within days of our arrival, and one time since. If the interval is regular, another singing time should come at any moment."

Marisole ran a finger along the side of her gittern. "How does the singing affect the humans?"

"It appears to entice them. The first time, we tried to reason with them, but they wouldn't listen. The second time, we tried to stop them, but they attacked. Between times, they are less excitable but still insistent they must await the next calling."

"And the elves?" Marisole again.

"We hear it, but we feel no need to rush headlong into danger. Some of us think it's only because we know better and aren't risk-takers by nature, but others believe the song has magic that affects some and not others." She stiffened suddenly. "There it is!"

Tae looked around, seeing nothing new. "There what is?"

"The singing!" An'séarie took several steps in a direction Tae labeled east based on the position of the sun and assuming a similar time of day to Midgard. "Don't you hear it?"

"I do," El-brinith said. She started walking, peering through the trees, Chan'rék'ril beside her. The rest of the elves remained in place or moved closer to the gate, clearly demonstrating An'séarie's point.

Another elf sent *khohlar*, *If you wish to save the humans, you should go now before more are lost.*

Be careful, another sent. *Or you'll be lost, too.*

Go, El-brinith said, waving toward the gate. *Chan'rék'ril and I will keep the way open for the humans.*

Most of the elves did not need a second suggestion. They rushed through the gate as quickly as they could in single file. Only An'séarie did not join the line. *I'm staying,* she announced. *A jovinay arythanik requires three.*

If this bothered any of the vacating elves, they gave no sign, focused on squeezing through the gate as quickly as possible.

El-brinith took An'séarie's hand and said something in elvish that resembled the Northern word *takk*, which meant "thank you."

As the group headed "eastward," Tae gradually began to discern the faint sounds of distant, rhythmical noise. At first, he followed the elves at their sedate pace. As they moved, the sounds grew louder and more discernible as singing. The words made no sense to him, nor did he care or bother to try to find meaning in their existence. There were several voices intertwined, definitely female; and, if they held only half the beauty of their voices, he would surely find them breathtaking. His pace quickened, beyond his control; and, within moments, he was running.

Stop! Imorelda shouted in his head.

The singing muffled the cat's urgent call. Tae ran faster.

Stop right now! Imorelda's voice echoed through his mind, an urgent command.

Still, Tae found himself charging, Ra-khir and Nomalan at either side and Saviar ahead of them all. Seized by the sudden fear the Renshai might hurt the singers, Tae accelerated to a breakneck speed.

Imorelda's claws sank into Tae's neck. The pain staggered him, tangling his feet, and he sprawled to the ground. He started to roll from habit, but Imorelda was all over him, slashing, spitting, hissing like an animated briar patch. *Move a muscle, and I'll kill you! Stay where you are.*

Tae curled into a ball, arms protecting his face and throat. *I won't move. I promise I won't move. Please stop tearing me to pieces.*

Imorelda's attack ceased, but she remained perched on the back of his head. He could feel every paw pinning him to the ground, and the hairs at the nape of his neck stood on end, drawn by the electricity of Imorelda's personal fluffing. At the moment, she was a massive ball of fur, teeth, and claws. *Listen to me, you moron. Let nothing into your head but me.*

Cautiously, Tae twitched the index finger of each hand, worried it betrayed his promise. Imorelda allowed him to use the tips to press the half circular bit of each ear flap over his canals, blocking all sound. The desire to rush toward the singing did not wholly disappear, but it diminished enough for him to think.

Leaving him on the ground, the elves and Marisole rushed past him. *Imorelda, we have to stop them! We're trapped without those elves!*

No, you fool. They're fine. They're trying to catch the other men.

Tae cringed. *They're not going to outrun Saviar.* Like all Béarnides, particularly those of royal lineage, Nomalan was a large man and Ra-khir was in his mid thirties; but the young Renshai was in peak physical condition. Tae had no idea of the relative speeds of elves and humans, but Marisole had little chance to catch warriors with a head start and an obsession.

She seemed to realize it as well, stopping suddenly and unlimbering her gittern. With his fingers in his ears, Tae had no idea what she was playing or if she accompanied the music with singing. He kept his attention on the three elves barreling after the running men, seeing no indication they were gaining ground, though they did not seem to be falling farther behind, either.

Imorelda filled in the gaps. *She's singing. Loud and . . . pretty.*

Tae doubted it could sound too pretty as she probably had not wasted much, if any, time tuning her instrument. He might have dismissed it as a waste of time had he less experience with Darris. Also, the running men seemed to be slowing, the elves definitely closing the gap.

Saviar was the first to whirl back the way he had come, his attention firmly focused on Marisole. Tae was too distant to appreciate the Renshai's expression, but he imagined it lax with confusion. Then, the other two men went still. Nomalan shook his head as if to clear it. They turned more awkwardly.

May I stand? Tae requested permission before daring to move. He did not relish the thought of having his eyeballs ripped out.

Imorelda sent him a positive, but wordless, thought. She bounded onto his shoulders.

Cautiously, handlessly, Tae clambered to his feet. *I'm going to try to hear. Be prepared to stop me again.*

Imorelda braced her claws into his shoulders and the side of his neck, hard enough for him to notice without drawing blood.

Tae unpinned his ears slightly, prepared to press his fingers back in place at the first indication he might lose control again. Marisole's sweet voice entered first, accompanied by the gittern and all partially muffled. The tone and timbre of the music was soothing, gripping, calling. He found himself taking a step toward her and stopped, wanting to assure he was still in control. She sang of the foolishness of running blindly into anything, of magical beings who caught their prey with illusion and lies:

> "Tin glitters as brightly as silver or gold.
> The most venomous snakes often patterned most bold.
> The ruby gleam of finest red could be the blood of newly dead
> Who dared to race to song so sweet
> And suckle at the monster's teat."

Monster? Tae found it nearly impossible to believe the perfect melodies that had sent him charging toward them could arise from something ugly or dangerous. Nothing so beautiful could harbor ill-will. Anything that drew him so inexorably could only . . . Tae checked his thought with great effort. *Could only what? Shower me with rose-scented dew and flowers?* As he listened to Marisole's song, the truth became undeniable. No good woman had to demand men's attention in such a way; men flocked to them without inducements. Only something truly dangerous resorted to drawing men in by trickery, to creating such desire and need, especially from a distance.

Soon, Marisole had gathered them into a group, placing herself and the elves between the men and the distant singing, and had coaxed the four male humans into lodging their fingers firmly into their own ears. Only then, she tucked the gittern under one arm and spoke to the elves. Tae had no idea what she said, but *khohlar* soon entered his head to explain.

There are creatures ahead whose singing enchants men. It does not appear to affect elves or human females. The four of you need to go back to the gate. Do not open your ears until you have arrived there safely.

Tae could see Ra-khir's lips moving, his head shaking slowly back and forth.

Chan'rék'ril sent more *khohlar* to obviate the need for anyone to hear. *Ra-khir doesn't like the idea of us trying to handle this without our warriors, but it is the only way. Marisole says we must attempt to rescue the remaining human soldiers.* He looked toward her briefly, then continued, apparently quoting. *"This is our battle, not yours, and you're wasting time. She says to go!"* The last word was practically thrust into Tae's mind. *If any of you attempt to follow us, she will fight until either she or you are dead. Your inability to control yourselves around these monsters makes you unpredictable and potentially dangerous to us as well as yourselves.*

Marisole jabbed a finger westward, glaring sternly.

Imorelda added pointedly, *Like it or not, she's right. None of you weak-minded men can help with this.*

Imorelda had never been one to mince words, and Tae knew taking offense would not help the situation. Trusting the cat to prevent him from running off again, he freed his hands. The distant singing funneled into his head, insistent and nearly inescapable. Seizing the shoulders of Ra-khir and Nomalan, Tae propelled them toward the gate. He did not attempt to touch Saviar, experienced enough to know a Renshai might consider it an attack and instinctively sever Tae's hand from his wrist. As soon as they took a step in the right direction, he plugged his ears again, certain his control would break if he allowed himself to listen too long. *Imorelda, follow the elves and Marisole, please. Call if we can do anything to help.*

The cat did not reply, but she did hop from Tae's shoulders and lope toward Marisole.

Marisole and the elves rushed toward the singing, certain it must have drawn any soldiers remaining on this world. The forest grew sparser, the ground rockier, then sandier as the whooshing sound of surf became a natural accompaniment to the lilting melodies that made the men so crazy but had little to no effect on Marisole and her elfin companions.

Then, the trees disappeared completely, and they found themselves on a low bluff overlooking a sandy, weedy stretch of shore. Five figures stretched across various large rocks near where the water met the land, a sixth lying in the open surf. They were woman, Marisole observed, all every bit as gorgeous as their voices. They appeared close to her own age, ranging from late teens to early twenties, with long thick hair shining in every human color from white-golden to nearly black. Their torsos were slender and graceful, perfectly formed and unselfconsciously naked. There, all resemblance to people ended. Below the waist, they all sported identical silver-scaled tails instead of legs, fishy but longer, more eel-like. Sunlight glinted from their lower halves, making them appear to sparkle with the same innocent light as their eyes.

Their song had no recognizable words, yet Marisole understood it and why it captured only men. They sang of crisis and passion, of a perfect world beneath the sea. Their music made them sound hopeless and in dire straits, appealing to the most masculine instincts of any man. It delved to that core, describing a deep and terrible loneliness that accompanies watching your kind become slowly extinct. Only females remained, it seemed, and they implored the men to fill the desperate need for creating offspring of both genders to continue their line. In return, they pledged delights of myriad types: sensual, gastronomic, and the choice of returning to shore or living forever as treasured royalty in their castle beneath the waves.

In response, a varied group of soldiers walked calmly toward the creatures, displaying none of the frenetic energy of the men with whom she had arrived. She recognized Béarnides in the throng, including Marstat, the blacksmith who had forged her sword. He looked like a gaunter version of his former self, aside from his eyes, which focused squarely on the singing creatures with a fanaticism that defied any possibility of noticing Marisole or the elves. He looked neither right nor left; none of the men did. They had eyes only for the fish-women. Not one of them carried a visible weapon. The men's mouths opened and closed, but she had to strain her ears beneath the music to understand them. It seemed as if they were all chanting the same words in cadence: "Pick me, pick me, pick *me!*"

El-brinith caught Marisole's arm. The instant she did, the creatures on the shore morphed into blubbery greenish-black creatures that no longer resembled any sort of human. They still had tails, now ending in paddlelike protrusions that gripped the rocks and sand on which they perched. They had a different sort of flippers instead of hands, and their corpulent necks ended in pointed, whiskered faces. Their eyes were dark, nearly black, with slitlike pupils. *Khohlar* rammed into Marisole's head. *They're mermaids, and they live to seduce and drown men.* *

The moment El-brinith released Marisole, the creatures returned to their previous forms. Or, rather, they appeared to do so. Now that she knew the truth, the bard's heir could see the illusions woven over their actual bodies, as if she had some sort of weird double vision. Grabbing up her gittern again, she started to play.

The men ignored the vibrant sounds of the strings; they had eyes for nothing but mermaids. Marisole forced herself to play louder, adding her voice to the mix and, unlike the mermaids, using a language the men would understand: the common trading tongue of the continent. She had become competent at ad-libbing words, but not adept, and she chose a complicated tune she knew well and believed most of them had heard, hoping the familiarity might work to her advantage. The tune originally belonged to a song evoking danger and fear, desperation and the need to pay close attention to one's situation, especially when feeling most secure. It also had an underlying theme of patriotism, a song soldiers knew and sang at the grave sites of their fallen.

Marisole changed the words and images, imploring the men to consider their wives and children, their siblings and the mothers and fathers who longed for their return. She promised to take them home, but only if they resisted the advances of the strange, fishy women who attempted to lure them into infidelity and immorality.

The mermaids' volume increased, their harmonies blending into a dazzling symphony, their voices twining expertly together, spinning emotion without need for comprehensible words. Despite having to overcome them, even though she despised them, Marisole found herself admiring their technique, unconsciously dissecting it for ideas on how to improve her own. They relied heavily on magic, she felt certain. A competent musician could extract emotion with nothing but proper, steady humming; but the detail their song evoked was too true and pure for tune alone. Music could bypass the brain to shoot directly at the heart, but it could not tell a story so full, so compelling.

Marisole sang louder, but she had little more to give. She already walked the fine line between volume and dysphonia. She plucked at the gittern with all the force she dared, and she had no second voice to add richness and harmony. The men had paused momentarily, but now they looked away from her, focusing fully on the mermaids. Their "pick me" chant began anew.

Desperate, Marisole sang on, seeking reserves, the most poignant tune, the most convincing words, the sweetest rhymes. She had the skills to influence, and she knew how to use them. Under ordinary circumstances, she would have had the attention of every man in Béarn. Here, she might just as well have been a cat screeching on a wall for all the good her talents did her. The men kept moving, relentlessly, toward their dooms.

Then, suddenly, a rhythmical noise started in several separate voices. *More of them?* The thought all but stunned her. She could not handle what she faced, let alone reinforcements. Then, slowly, she recognized the secondary sound for what it was: elfin chanting. Behind her, Chan'rék'ril, El-brinith, and An'séarie entwined their voices in *jovinay arythanik*, boosting her song and its effect on those around them. Again, the men of the continent stopped, their heads swiveling toward the single, human musician.

Marisole concentrated on her playing, every note perfect and clear, bent to her will and infused with all the emotion she could muster. She continued in her calmest, surest voice, choosing the best and most solid words to convince the men of their loyalty to their families, to twist their faiths to her will, to save them. Several of the men shook their heads, as if to escape a mental fog. A few actually started toward her.

An abrupt quaver in the elfin chanting was Marisole's only warning. By the time she noticed, the mermaid who had lain on the beach was nearly on her, strikingly quick for something so bulbous and lacking legs and feet. With no time for any other action, Marisole swung the gittern toward the charging monster. The bowl caught it squarely in the side of the neck, and the force thrummed through Marisole's fingers. The gittern made a horrible sound as it exploded into an unrecognizable mass of flying splinters and hunks of wood flopping at the ends of gut strings.

The hit threw the mermaid's aim off a bit, but not enough. Teeth closed on Marisole's left upper arm, and the bulk of the monster sent her sprawling. Unable to roll without risking her arm, she shimmied sideways, tearing her sword from its sheath, right-handed, in the same motion. The music stopped, not only her own, but the intertwined harmonies of the mermaids as well. Apparently, they had all decided to watch the battle, attack or retreat. The pain in Marisole's arm overwhelmed her, and she could feel the teeth grinding deeper while the monster attempted to use its blubbery body to pin her to the ground.

Marisole's combat training shed panic like beeswax did rain. Imminent death did not mean surrender; it only sparked her to fight harder, using more desperate techniques. Dodging wasn't working. The mermaid flopped over her legs, effectively pinning them, and worked its way slowly forward in a clear attempt to suffocate her. Its teeth remained clamped on her flesh. Marisole did not have the space to swing her weapon.

The elves joined her, battering the creature with punches and kicks that bounced harmlessly from its green-black hide. Marisole could smell its breath, fishy and putrid, like dead things washed up on shore. From the direction of the men came hurled rocks, some of which caused the mermaid to bellow and one of which struck Marisole's forehead so hard it dazed her. The mermaid raised its enormous body higher on its flippers as it prepared to throw itself onto Marisole's chest. The bard's heir attempted to fling herself sideways, without any result. Her legs were too fully pinned, her arm trapped. The thing was going to crush her, but she refused to die alone. As the great bulk descended, Marisole braced her sword against her side, point upward.

The mermaid's catlike eyes widened, but it was too massive to change its course. It impaled itself on Marisole's blade as it collapsed on top of her, slamming every bit of breath from her lungs and burying her rib cage in blubber. Darkness filled Marisole's vision, though whether because the mermaid covered her face or she had instinctively closed her eyes, she did not know. All that mattered were her empty lungs and the absolute need to fill them with air. They spasmed like bellows, shooting agony through her chest. Marisole felt her thoughts blurring. She fixated on the pain in her arm, trying to use it as an anchor. She gave no thought to breathing; her lungs were sucking desperately without any input from her wavering consciousness.

The mermaid started rocking. *It's still alive. Oh, gods! It's still alive.* Marisole struggled to wriggle out from under it, but the lack of air was making her weaker by the moment. She opened her eyes to a sea of men, some shoving the massive creature off of her, others cautiously shifting her from beneath it. Air funneled into her lungs with such sudden force she worried she had overfilled them and they would pop like an aged bladder. The men stepped back, clearly uncertain how to further assist. Marisole fought a battle with her own lungs as they shuddered into weird paroxysms, as if they had forgotten the simple act of breathing.

Gradually, her lungs and chest settled back into their usual cooperative rhythm. Her wits returned, and she realized the mermaid was lying lifeless on the beach, her sword thrust through its chest to the hilt. Her left upper arm felt on fire. When she touched it with her right hand, her fingers came away sticky with blood.

El-brinith shooed the men away from Marisole's arm, kneeling beside her to examine the wound. Several of the men studied the mermaid's body while others worked diligently to free her sword, and a few tried to collect the bits and pieces of the hopelessly shattered gittern. Several watched the sea, armed with rocks, prepared to pepper any mermaid who dared return to the shoals.

Though she wanted to rise, Marisole remained in place to allow El-brinith to finish her examination. Chan'rék'ril's *khohlar* filled her mind and, presumably, those of every nearby man and elf. **Quickly!**

Several of the men jumped, and all of them looked around. Marisole worried they would think the voice came from the mermaids and deliberately ignore or fight it. Despite El-brinith's ministrations, she sat up and pointed toward Chan'rék'ril with her uninjured arm. "That's the elf speaking in your heads. Listen to him; it's important."

Several of the men, most of them Béarnides, bowed at her command, apparently recognizing her as a princess. El-brinith muttered magical syllables, and the pain in Marisole's arm gradually lessened until it felt more like a bruise than a biting.

Chan'rék'ril continued, **Swiftly gather your things and head westward. We have four men waiting by a magical gate which will take you to Béarn. Stay together. If I see or hear the mermaids coming back, I will let you know. Then, you must drop everything, place your fingers firmly in both ears and run toward the gate. If we get separated, I will help you find us. I will not leave until all of you are safely through it. **

El-brinith stepped back. Two soldiers helped Marisole to her feet and another handed her the freshly cleaned sword. The remainder jogged toward the north, where they must have had some sort of camp. Likely, they had left their weapons there, instructed by the singing monsters. Marisole counted twenty-two living soldiers. Eight were definitely Béarnides, their thick black curls unmistakable. Seven looked Eastern, with smooth, straight hair as dark as the Béarnides and olive-colored skin. Seven were pale and blond, probably all Northmen of one tribe or another.

Marisole sheathed her sword and waved off her helpers. "Please go. We'll start heading slowly toward the gate, so you will know where to go once you have your things. Listen for Chan'rék'ril's call and immediately do whatever he tells you." She hoped the mermaids would not have a way to simulate *khohlar*. Since the elves seemed to have some understanding of the creatures, she believed they would have warned the men if that was a possibility.

The three remaining Béarnides bowed, mumbled something appreciative and supportive, then headed after the other men. Only then, Marisole noticed the silver tabby cat watching her from farther up the shore at the edge of the woodlands. She recognized Imorelda immediately. Her mother loved cats of all varieties but none so much as Tae's nearly-constant companion. Marisole crouched, reaching her right hand toward the animal. "Come here puss puss, beautiful kitty."

Imorelda stalked toward her, looking haughty and unhurried.

El-brinith stepped up beside Marisole, and the bard's heir looked upward without moving from her crouched position. "Thank you for tending my arm. Do I need to bandage it?"

"You won't bleed anymore, if that's what you're asking," El-brinith replied in her musical elfin accent. "But it may feel better covered and it could use some cleaning. I can only get the healing process started and take away the immediate pain."

"That's more than enough!" Matrinka was also a healer, and Marisole had seen her fuss over wounds many times. It currently felt as if she had suffered the injury days ago instead of only moments. Her arm was stiff, but the pain had receded to a dull ache. "I'm so glad you chose to come with us."

El-brinith dipped in a nonhuman gesture. "Arak'bar Tulamii Dhor asked, and I would not refuse him. He worried the rescuers or the rescued would require my services. My specialties are tracking, sensing, and travel, but I have some healing magic, too. Elfin wounds don't fester, so my understanding of that is limited. I would have your mother look at the injury when you get home."

"I will," Marisole promised.

Imorelda came close enough for Marisole to pet. When she did, the cat rubbed against her hand, then her legs, then leaped onto her shoulders. The sudden weight of the animal irritated her wound a bit, but she made no complaints. She had never seen Imorelda climb on anyone other than Tae and Matrinka, and she took it as a compliment, especially when the cat purred continuously against her neck.

Saviar, Nomalan, and Tae met them at the edge of the forest, apparently aware the mermaids had been silenced. Marisole did not know how they had learned it was safe to come closer. She could only assume they had allowed an ear to open at intervals, risking themselves but keeping abreast of the developments, at least from a distance. As the three elves and Marisole approached, Nomalan swept off his cloak and wrapped it cautiously around her. "You're hurt," he noticed immediately, his voice filled with honest concern and his gaze fixed on the cat as he clearly debated whether to push it off her shoulders.

Imorelda leaped from Marisole to Tae, obviating the decision, to Marisole's relief. She had seen Imorelda's temper in action when the cat had assaulted Tae, and Matrinka seemed to believe she understood more than any feline should and had the knowledge to become offended.

"Where's Ra-khir?" Chan'rék'ril asked, peering around them anxiously.

Saviar responded. "It took us a long time to find the gate again, and it didn't help that we couldn't communicate with one another with our fingers in our ears. We left Ra-khir beside the gate in case we had trouble finding it again. Hopefully, we'd wander within shouting range at least once."

Chan'rék'ril nodded, looking off toward where the soldiers had gone to get their gear, then at the shoreline. Marisole's attention followed his, and she saw no indication of the mermaids' return. "I forget humans can't see magic." His brow furrowed. "Marisole, what did those mermaids look like to you?"

Marisole finally spotted the soldiers rushing toward them at a brisk pace just shy of running. They still looked thin but relatively kempt for men living in the wilderness for weeks. They had clearly bathed, washed their clothes and tended their facial hair, she supposed for the benefit of the mermaids they had hoped to assist. "On my own, they looked like beautiful women with eel-like tails. When El-brinith touched me, I saw them as . . ." Words failed Marisole then. They resembled nothing she had ever seen before. ". . . blubbery blobs." She finished lamely. "When the one attacked me, I didn't need an elf. They all looked like awkward, fin-handed animals, kind of rounded in the middle and tapered on the ends."

An'séarie laughed. "A reasonable description of their true shape. When they stopped singing, their magic broke, and everyone saw them as they are, including those enchanted. Once they do, it becomes much harder for the mermaids to recapture their hearts." She gestured at Saviar, Tae, and Nomalan. "We need to get these three back first. They didn't see the regular form of the mermaids, which puts them at more risk."

Nomalan put a protective arm around Marisole, adjusting his enormous cloak over her thinner shoulders. As the mermaids still had not reappeared, the point seemed moot, but Marisole thought it best to heed the warning. The soldiers had come close enough she could now hear their voices engaged in multiple conversations, though she could not make out individual words. She paused to count them, reaffirming all twenty-two had come, then turned toward the gate. The arm around her felt warm and comfortable, but she found it impossible to press against Nomalan, to coordinate their walk until she pictured him as Barrindar in her mind's eye.

Then, it became a simple matter. Marisole felt the heartening warmth of a strong Béarnide at her side, took his free hand, and paced herself to him. It was an illusion, but one she currently needed to continue the charade. Barrindar's muscled arm encircled her, his callused hand held hers, his massive cloak embraced her. Snug and happy at the lead of a lost and found phalanx, she headed for the gate.

CHAPTER 14

A Knight of Erythane is honorable in every situation, not just when it suits him

—Sir Ra-khir Kedrin's son

THE WORKING DAY ENDED with the recovery of the men and elves sent to the mermaids' Outworld. Marisole's wounds needed tending, the elves wanted a rest, and the Council felt the rescue team should not attempt too much too quickly, no matter how eager they seemed. The soldiers required attention as well. They had lost a dozen companions to the monsters. On two occasions, the mermaids had selected one man apiece, claiming they would accompany the fish-tailed women to their underwater castle for feasting and procreation. With their deception magic, they had convinced the remaining soldiers their companions had not returned because they had chosen to remain either a bit longer, or for eternity, beneath the waves.

Once freed from the mermaids' spells, the men had had difficulty leaving their missing companions behind until An'séarie took them to a distant beach to show them a few of the partially-consumed corpses washed up on shore. Some of the men wished to stay and fight the mermaids, to demand justice for the dead and prevent others from succumbing to the same fate. It was a tempting idea, but practicality forced them to abandon it. Even after they had seen the monsters' true form, the men were potentially susceptible to their song. Marisole was in no condition to fight five more, and the elves knew little to nothing of combat.

After some argument, Tae had convinced the soldiers the odds of more Midgard men arriving there were astronomically small, and the mermaids might actually serve some mysterious but necessary purpose on their own world. But it was Ra-khir's pronouncement, as a Knight of Erythane, that finally convinced them to leave without retribution. Once the decision was made, they all seemed ultimately relieved and went happily through the gate and back to their own world.

The following day, the elves' first contact with the Outworlds resulted in a call for the rescue party. Ready, as always, Ra-khir kissed Tiega, smiled at Darby and Keva, then headed for the elves' gating area in Béarn's great hall. The room had grown more crowded since the previous day. Just as he had brought his fiancée and her children, others had convinced their families and friends to join the masses, many hoping to catch a glimpse of a missing soldier they loved or knew. Others were simply curious, wanting to watch at least one of the rescues and see magic in action.

Ra-khir worried about the crowds, especially the children. His soon-to-be stepchildren were teens, Darby a knight-in-training and Keva on the edge of womanhood. The recent successes had buoyed the mood. Everyone seemed to have forgotten about the maggot-riddled corpses some of the men had dragged out with them the previous morning. No one knew what might emerge from the gate: raving madness, soldiers with mutilations or grotesque injuries, dangerous creatures who managed to slip through the gate while they were distracted by the rescue. Any member of the rescue team could enter perfectly healthy and leave dead or disabled with wounds far worse than the one Marisole had suffered. Ra-khir took some solace in the knowledge that several warriors, mostly Renshai, routinely took positions at the gate, prepared to handle whatever monsters might slip through it.

Tae, Saviar, Nomalan, El-brinith, and Chan'rék'ril met Ra-khir at the faintly shimmering outline that defined the gate. A moment later, Marisole joined them, bereft of any musical instrument, her left arm bound in a sling. Ra-khir stepped forward to suggest she remain behind, but Marisole glared at him, speaking first. "I'm coming. There's nothing broken, and I'll do my best to avoid combat." She stopped there. Anything more would require song, which would waste time and could dilute her point.

Nomalan shrugged. "Don't bother. I've tried to talk her out of it all morning. She's determined, and she has more reasons than I can counter."

Certain Marisole would find the words or tune to convince them all eventually, Ra-khir nodded and stepped through the gate. At least, if there was danger, he could assure he was the first to meet it. The Outworlds could contain anything. The odds the rescue party

would discover another set of mermaids, or something else that inca-
pacitated only men, seemed unlikely nearly to the point of impossibility. Or so he hoped. Based on his last sojourn to the worlds beyond
Midgard, Ra-khir had sometimes wondered if these magical plains
of existence shaped themselves to make things as difficult as possible
for whoever appeared or—perhaps—to teach them a personal lesson. That went along with Captain's claim that gods had an interest
and a hand in the Outworlds.

Saviar followed his father, then Nomalan, Marisole, Tae with
Imorelda on his shoulders, and the elves. They found themselves in a
forest clearing on a crisp late autumn day much like the one they
had left behind. The gate always put them near the elf with whom
Captain had made contact, and this was no exception. Canted, gemlike eyes in an array of colors greeted them, a group of sixteen elves
standing amid the trees on the outskirts of the clearing. Ra-khir
turned to face a larger group of humans. This time, they had, apparently, chosen to remain together, which boded well for the shared
future King Griff had long desired. If these two disparate groups
could find common ground and remain together for several weeks in
a forest clearing, perhaps all of elfinkind could interact in positive
ways with the humans of Midgard.

"Hello," Ra-khir said. "You requested help, and we have come to
assist. Can you please explain what's needed?"

Several humans and a few elves started talking at once, and Ra-
khir raised his hands for quiet. It took a few moments, but everyone
stopped speaking, plunging them back into the previous silence.

Ra-khir assessed the group in front of him. It consisted mostly of
brown- and sandy-haired men. Their eyes ran the full spectrum of
human colors: from the ice blue of most Northmen to the deep, almost black of Béarnides and Easterners and several shades of gray,
green, and hazel between. Their builds also ran a gamut, although
medium and muscular predominated regardless of height. He believed the bulk of them were Westerners of various origins.

They did not appear particularly different than their counterparts
on Midgard. They had clearly eaten well enough, shaved and bathed
at reasonable intervals, and whatever injuries they had sustained
from the battle against the *Kjempemagiska* had mostly healed over
the past few weeks. He recognized seven Renshai by sight, three of
them female, a handful of Erythanians, two Béarnides, and four dark
enough to pass for Easterners. One of the Erythanians had a splint
on each arm, and two of the random Westerners walked with noticeable limps.

None of the other members of the rescue party seemed interested in taking over Ra-khir's role, so he tried again. This time, he directly addressed one of the Erythanians he had recognized, the scribe Liamar. He knew the man was educated, literate, and had a comfortable speaking voice. He also knew how to come to the point. "Liamar, can you please explain the situation to us?"

A small, slender man of middle-age, Liamar glanced around uncomfortably before speaking. Clearly, he wished Ra-khir had chosen someone else, but he would not gainsay a Knight of Erythane. "Well, sir. At first, we thought we were home and the rest of you had disappeared. The elves explained we had come through a magical gate, but we were . . ." He glanced toward the elves apologetically. ". . . skeptical. I mean, this looks exactly like the battlefield, sir, aside from the missing bodies and destruction."

Liamar singled out one of the elves with his gaze, a small female with enormous amber eyes and perfectly matching hair. Her face was a long oval, her cheekbones jutting, and her chin a sharp V. "Eth'eel'ya made some clear and poignant arguments, though, that kept us appropriately cautious. It's a good thing, too, because if we had all just dispersed to our homes, we could have caused enormous problems."

"Homes?" Ra-khir repeated. "You mean, if you had dispersed in the directions your homes would be?"

Liamar shook his head and looked to Eth'eel'ya for help.

The elf seemed to melt into herself, becoming even smaller, but she did speak. "This is what creatures of magic would refer to as a duplicate world. It's an echo of our own with certain differences: some large, some small. For example, this world seems to lack beings capable of manipulating chaos. Our magic still works; otherwise, we could not have created the gate. But there are no elves here and, it would seem, no *Kjempemagiska.*"

"The war didn't happen here," someone blurted out.

Ra-khir gave the speaker, a Westerner, a stern look. They needed the information, but if he did not keep order, the situation would degenerate into everyone speaking at once again. "But there are humans."

"Not just humans," Liamar confirmed. "It's . . . well, it appears to be . . . us."

Nomalan made a wordless noise. Shocked himself, Ra-khir did not scold him, not even with a look. "What do you mean by 'us'?"

"Us," Liamar repeated, gesturing broadly to include every human present. "Us, us. There's a King Griff in Béarn who is the identical twin of our king. There is a King Humfreet in Erythane." He added in a thin voice, "And there is a Liamar Carl's son married to Myrjela Hyamis' daughter."

Ra-khir attempted to speak, but his voice had disappeared. When it finally emerged, it sounded like a croak. "H-how do you know this?" He glanced around the group but did not allow his gaze to focus on any individual to discourage them all from talking. No one interrupted. They all wanted the information imparted as swiftly as possible.

Liamar swallowed hard, then pointed directly at one of the Westerners. "He can tell it best, Sir Ra-khir."

The indicated man stepped forward and bowed, apparently unaccustomed to dealing with knights. "Sir, my name is Broward of Corpa Schaull. I was among the six men sent to scout the area. At the time, we didn't know we were on a . . . a . . ." He gave Eth'eel'ya a searching look.

She supplied obligingly, "A duplicate world."

Broward nodded his thanks and continued. "We were following the river downstream, westward when we happened to come upon a group headed south who looked like regular men. At first, we hid ourselves, not certain if they were friendly. Then, I saw one who looked enough like the cooper of Corpa Schaull to be a lost brother. We met up with these strangers; and, to my surprise, Rowen, the cooper look-alike, greeted me by name and with great excitement."

A few others among the group nodded vigorously, and Ra-khir realized the scouters had consisted of a mixed origin lot of men, much as their rescue party did.

Broward continued, "Soon, I recognized the others, men of Corpa Schaull I had known all my life, including two we had left back at this very camp." He opened his arms. "These familiar 'strangers' demanded to know where I'd been, and when I reminded them of the war, they acted as if I was raving. They treated my companions with suspicion and offered to take me home, claiming my wife, daughters, and son missed me terribly."

Broward looked suddenly pained. "I have three daughters. No son, and that's when we realized something magical had definitely happened. The elves really had thrown us through a 'gate' as they called it. I volunteered to go with these men and promised to meet back up with the group the following morning, with as many supplies as I could gather. It turned out that 'I' or, rather, the 'me' who lived on this world had gone on a hunting expedition with two other men and never returned. The body of one was found, and we were all presumed dead." He looked up suddenly. "For the record, our versions of those other two men were alive last I knew and part of the twin cities army."

Broward paused there, and his expression went sad. Ra-khir did not rush him. On Midgard, the army of the *Kjempemagiska* had landed their massive boats near the twin cities, destroying them both and killing every man, woman and child in Corpa Schaull or Frist at the time. Then, suddenly, Broward smiled, though his voice had a catch that revealed his grief. "Corpa Schaull was very similar to how I remembered it before . . . before . . . well, before."

Every man, as well as some of the elves, the female Renshai, and Marisole bowed their heads in brief acknowledgment of the tragedy.

Broward's grin spread. "The people were going about their business as if the war had never happened. People I've known my whole life greeted me with great excitement, welcoming me home, and Varjerrah . . ." His mouth remained open, but no words emerged. He cleared his throat. "My wife was there. Haggard, but alive. Dusty, dressed in faded rags, but alive. So beautiful. My older daughters greeted me with warm embraces, but my youngest . . . Louisa, was a boy of the same age, Luka, with the same laughing dark eyes and carefree manner. A boy . . ." His grin wreathed his face now, and he fell silent in memory.

When the quiet stretched out too long, Ra-khir cleared his throat.

Broward said softly, "It was so hard to leave them. The look in Varjerrah's eyes. She was sure if I left again, I would never return. It was so hard to slip from her grasp, so difficult to go back to the others . . . I . . . must return to her." He turned Ra-khir a beseeching look. "She needs me, and my Varjerrah . . . my real Varjerrah . . . is dead. My children . . ." He sobbed, unable to continue.

Liamar took over again. "The scouting party brought supplies and the story. The elves explained the concept of a duplicate world. Then, we all wanted to rush home and see our own personal situations, especially the boys from the twin cities. After discussion, we decided that might cause more problems than it solved. Many, perhaps most, of us would seem like double-goers. Weird, magical twins of singleton men." He glanced at the female Renshai and added politely, "And women."

Eth'eel'ya supplied, "We call them *doppelgängers*. I've never seen one, but they're supposed to exist on some Outworlds, perhaps in rare situations exactly like this one or perhaps as some sort of shape-changing monster."

Liamar finished with, "Those whose doubles had died would seem like ghosts come to life. No one wanted to terrify loved ones, friends, and neighbors or risk being slaughtered as a monster. So we finally decided some or all of us would sneak home and secretly spy on . . . well, ourselves. Once we understood the details, we could decide whether to find ways to quietly reinsert ourselves individually or whether we should appeal to the kings en masse."

"So, we separated into groups, depending on our origins, and headed . . . um . . . home. We all agreed to return by yesterday, and the last ones straggled in shortly before you arrived." He indicated the Easterners who had traveled the farthest. "We've been debating since they got here, but now it all seems moot." He hesitated expectantly. "Assuming you can get us all home."

Ra-khir was glad to finally deliver happy news. "We can. Come with us, and we'll take you home."

A cheer erupted from the group, but not a unanimous one. A few stepped back or frowned, and Broward shouted. "No! I'm not leaving, and no one can make me."

Everyone turned toward him, and Broward backed farther from the group. "I have nothing to return to. My wife is dead, my daughters . . ." Tears rolled down his cheeks. "Here, they need me."

The pain in Broward's voice touched Ra-khir. He felt as if someone squeezed his chest until breathing became difficult. He looked directly at Eth'eel'ya, asking, "Would a person staying on a duplicate world cause trouble?"

Eth'eel'ya turned to address the other elves in their musical language. They exchanged words between them while Ra-khir watched Broward slip farther backward, arms folded tightly across his chest as he awaited the response. Finally, Eth'eel'ya faced Ra-khir again. "It depends on the person who stays and what you mean by 'trouble.'"

Ra-khir kept his gaze on Broward, worried the man might run. He did not want to have to chase or confine one of the brave soldiers who had fought in the World's War. "Let's say Broward, here, was the person. By trouble, I mean would his staying, in and of itself, cause a problem. Perhaps to the balance of the universe."

The elves exchanged just a few more sentences before Eth'eel'ya responded. "We don't know Broward well enough, or humans in general, to conjecture whether he might cause difficulties to others. Individuals with great power and the motivation to do so can affect the balance, but it has nothing to do with gating from one world to another. Apparently, this world has a fulcrum every bit as solid as our own in their King Griff."

Ra-khir considered that response. Just before the arrival of himself and his companions, the group had been considering ways to incorporate everyone into this duplicate world, including sixteen elves and their magic in a place previously lacking either.

Eth'eel'ya seemed to realize she had not answered Ra-khir's question exactly as he wished. "We're not sure precisely what you're asking, but if you're worried Broward remaining will cause issues at a catastrophic level, it is no more likely he could do so here than on our own world. His absence on our world would not likely affect it in any substantial way, no more than his death in the war would have. Does that answer your question, Sir Ra-khir Kedrin's son?"

It did, Ra-khir believed. It left him free to consider the decision in a strictly moral sense. He looked away from Eth'eel'ya to find every human in the clearing staring at him hopefully. He cleared his throat, trying to read their expressions. Different ones paraded across each visage as they considered the possibilities. Ra-khir could not help personalizing the situation. He had become almost catatonic with grief over Kevral's death; for months, the boys and knights had considered him all but worthless. He imagined himself in those tumultuous, terrible days, the black, hopeless cloud that had tainted his every action, the agony of every thought, the vast effort it took to do the simplest things: eating, sleeping, breathing. He could scarcely imagine all three of his boys dying along with Kevral, leaving him bereft and utterly alone.

Then, to find, on a duplicate world, Kevral's exact double, his three children alive, the youngest now a girl. He bit his lip to keep from smiling at the image of a female Calistin, then realized it probably would not have made much difference. Kevral had been stunningly competent, and he doubted a gender difference in any of their children would have changed much about their lives. Ra-khir clung to the significant. So long as he knew it would not damage either of the two worlds for him to stay, and Eth'eel'ya had assured him of that, no man, woman, child, or monster could have dragged him from her. He turned Broward a reassuring smile. "Anyone who did not arrive with me but wishes to return to Midgard, please step over there." He pointed to an area on the southernmost side of the clearing.

All of the trapped elves and most of the human soldiers did so, leaving eight Westerners, one Easterner and one male Renshai. Ra-khir could not help noticing one of the female Renshai looked back and forth several times between the one who wished to stay and the other Renshai, her right fist clamped over her hilt. Most would not have recognized that as a sign of discomfort, but Ra-khir had lived most of his adult life among Renshai.

Ra-khir swiftly explained his intentions. "Everyone who wants to return home shall."

A cheer went up from the massed soldiers in the larger group.

Ra-khir continued carefully, "As to these ten, I am not going to make any promises yet." He studied them in the morning light slanting through myriad branches: all men, all with serious expressions locked on their faces. "We need to understand, discuss, and consider each of their situations to make wise choices that won't cause harm to themselves, the natives, or one another. I would like a panel of judges to assist, people accustomed to deciding the most difficult cases." He considered his companions briefly. "If we can all agree on who those judges will be, can we also agree to abide by their decisions, regardless of our personal feelings?"

Ra-khir watched a sequence of emotions cross the ten faces. Surprise came first. Clearly, it never occurred to them the rescue party would do anything other than leave them behind. Most people probably would have without a second thought, but the morality driven into him from the moment he decided to become a Knight of Erythane forced Ra-khir to assure no one made a wrong-headed or dangerous decision. "You must realize anyone we leave behind is trapped forever. Without an elf on this side, gates to our world cannot be opened. We came to save your lives, not ruin them; most of you have people at home who might need or miss you."

To Ra-khir's relief, the expressions unanimously changed to ones of consideration. Not one of the ten rolled his eyes dismissively or seized a weapon. "As a knight, I'm accustomed to making judgments. Does anyone have an objection to having me on the panel?"

The ten exchanged a few words, then most shook their heads. Broward spoke for all of them. "No objections."

Ra-khir had not expected any. Cities and individuals frequently called on traveling knights to adjudicate their disputes. He looked around his companions, his gaze falling first on Marisole. "We are blessed to have a princess of Béarn among us. As the chosen heir to the bard, she will advise and guard the future king or queen. Any objections to her presence on the panel?"

This time, all ten bobbed their heads in ascent. Broward smiled. "No objections."

"Tae Kahn, king of the Eastlands is also here. He is the ultimate authority on justice in his lands. Any objections?"

Again, a bit of muttering followed, then Broward said, "No objections."

A three-judge panel seemed the perfect number. In case of a

deadlocked split decision, two could overrule one. Then, Ra-khir's gaze fell on Saviar, and he knew he had to speak.

The mood that had settled over his eldest son had grown uncomfortable to the point where it strained their personal relationship, which saddened Ra-khir. He felt certain the unknown status of Subikahn caused most of Saviar's distress, but his oldest son also seemed to have developed a fierce dislike of Tiega and her children, particularly Darby. Ra-khir could not, in good conscience, marry anyone without the consent of all of their offspring, and he doubted Saviar could give it, at least not in his recent state of mind.

Since they had both joined the rescue party, Saviar seemed more like his old self, and Ra-khir believed the distraction of a worthwhile responsibility was most of the reason. It could not hurt to add a bit more. "Saviar was chosen to become the next leader of the Renshai. He is known for his wisdom and competence, has assisted the knights in some matters of judgment, and has and will be making extremely difficult decisions regarding the future of his people. While he is my son, he has never blindly followed my suggestions or advice and has, in fact, opposed me on many occasions." He added facetiously, "Damn it."

A twitter of nervous laughter passed through the group of ten. They huddled together to discuss the situation, and Ra-khir had no idea what they would decide. It worked in Saviar's favor that their ranks included a Renshai and not a single Northman. Béarn had become a haven, especially since the royalty trusted Renshai to guard their youth. Valr Magnus' proclamation in the great hall had helped diffuse some long-held prejudices, but these men had not heard it or the applause that followed. Ra-khir found himself holding his breath. It would not matter to the situation whether Saviar assisted or not, but he believed it might mean more to Saviar than the young man would admit.

Broward finally spoke, "Some objections, but we have overall decided as a group to accept Saviar on the panel."

Ra-khir hid his relief behind a mask of knight's training. "If Nomalan and Eth'eel'ya would escort the others through the gate, I'd like to keep Chan'rék'ril and El-brinith with us so that we don't all become trapped here."

The two named elves stepped closer to the group. Ra-khir glanced at his son, expecting to see a sparkle in his eyes if not a casual smile. Instead, he found an expression that seemed more perplexed than happy. Ra-khir consoled himself with the knowledge that, at least, it was not overtly hostile.

Eth'eel'ya added, "The gate is right here, and the elves can handle the transfer if your rescue party would like to stay together."

Ra-khir looked at Nomalan, who nodded briskly. "I'd really like to watch Marisole in action, if it's no trouble."

"None at all," Ra-khir responded. He liked the young Béarnide; but, not for the first time, he wondered why King Griff had chosen him. Nomalan did not seem to have any particular skills the others lacked, nor did he represent an overlooked group. Griff surely had a good reason Ra-khir did not have the information to fathom. Clearly, some relationship existed between Nomalan and Marisole; perhaps it just came down to a doting father indulging his daughter's wishes.

As the soldiers and elves prepared to leave, Ra-khir caught one last glimpse of the same female Renshai. Her attention remained riveted on the male of her tribe who wished to stay, and she wore an expression of forlorn regret. For an instant, she hesitated, as if about to speak. Then, she turned quietly around and joined the line for the gate.

Ra-khir ushered the rescue party away from the group of ten who wished to remain on the duplicate world. As soon as they had gone beyond earshot, Tae spoke. "What's the purpose of this, Ra-khir? They're all adults who can make their own decisions. Do they really need us to judge their reasons for staying?"

Saviar responded before Ra-khir could. "It's not that simple, Tae. Some of them are still teens. That's a bit young to be making such a major and permanent choice. Others may be making quick, foolish decisions based only on emotion. It's one thing to make a bad choice, suffer the consequences and learn from it. It's quite another to make a fatal mistake or one that can't be reversed and destroys your entire life or the ones of innocents around you." He stopped there, his own words clearly giving him pause.

Ra-khir took over. "I think we can all agree Broward should stay. Perhaps some of the others have similarly legitimate reasons. But what if they all have exact and living duplicates? Frightened crowds do terrible things. Broward might die for his association with 'monsters,' and his widow and children would have to suffer his death a second time, as a violent execution."

Marisole considered her response. "I agree with them, Tae. We need to make sure we don't cause upheaval here or at home. Anyone who stays needs to fit in seamlessly." She added carefully, "What I don't know is why you want me involved in the decisions. If I make a new point, I have to sing it."

Nomalan put a comforting hand on her shoulder. "They know,

Marisole. But your input is always significant, worth the wait, and your music is a joy."

The others in the group voiced their agreement in two or three syllables, including Ra-khir's enthusiastic, "Yes, it is!"

Ra-khir finished with, "It's not just a matter of deciding who stays and who goes home. We do need to make certain they're making the right decision for the right reasons, but we also have to make sure the ones who do stay insert themselves in a logical and moral manner that doesn't risk the others."

"All right." Tae threw up his hands in surrender, carefully avoiding Imorelda, still wrapped around his neck. "I get it. The sooner started, the sooner finished." He headed toward the ten.

Ra-khir had intended to discuss the process in more detail, but Tae had a definite point. Knights did tend to drag things out too long, and they needed to get back home to help the elves locate more trapped soldiers. As they headed to the waiting group, he explained to all, "The panel will be the sole arbiters of whether an individual remains here or returns home. There will be no limit placed on the number of you who stay. However, if, in our combined wisdom, we decide some or all of you must go home, you must leave without a chase or a battle. Agreed?"

The ten exchanged looks, but they had obviously already discussed the matter. All emitted words of assent, though some looked more concerned than others. Broward added, withheld tears in his tone, "We will abide by what the panel decides."

Ra-khir accepted their word through Broward. "For those chosen to remain, we also need to approve how you insert yourself into this world. We need to keep the safety of all of you in mind, and you must realize the confession or lies of one might undo everyone."

Tae made an impatient gesture Ra-khir remembered from the days when they traveled together.

Ra-khir had one last point. "Whether or not we rule you can stay, you have the right to change your mind and come home with us instead. However, once the gate closes, every decision is, by default, final."

Marisole took a seat on a long deadfall, and the other judges joined her. The cat clambered from Tae's shoulders to crawl into his lap. Nomalan joined the group of ten, leaving a space for any man currently under judgment to stand between them. Those leaving through the gate did so in single file, allowing the ones in the back to turn and watch at least the initial proceedings, the female Renshai Ra-khir had noticed at the very end of the line.

Before Ra-khir could start the proceedings, Tae asked a pertinent question. "How many of you are from Corpa Schaull?"

Five of the Westerners jabbed fingers toward the sky. Among them, Broward pointed out, "And three from Frist. All of us lost our families to the giants." Every one of the remaining Westerners bowed his head or nodded agreement.

Tae continued to compartmentalize. "And how many of you have living duplicates?"

Two of the men from Frist and two from Corpa Schaull raised their index fingers. None of the others did, including the Renshai and the Easterner.

Ra-khir crossed his arms and sat back, allowing Tae to continue.

Tae separated those four from the others with a wave and focused on the remaining six. "Those of you without doubles, do any of you know what happened to them?"

Broward spoke for the Westerners. "We all do. In the burial ground for the twin cities, different areas are allotted for certain types of death: accidents, illnesses, childbirth, old age, unknown causes, starvation, violence, and heroes, which are usually those killed in war. A stone is placed on each grave, with the name and date of birth, if known, and the date and cause of death chiseled into it. There's a special area for unidentified corpses and another for those whose bodies were not recovered." He added, apparently for completion, "There's an area for infants and children as well, although they're often buried with a parent who died at the same time, for instance when we lose them both during childbirth or in a fire."

The Easterner spoke next, a heavyset dark man with the standard brown eyes and straight, nearly black hair of his kind. He had a round face and a hawkish nose. Ra-khir judged his age at about thirty. "My double died of blood poisoning. He had broken his leg in a fall, and it never healed right. It troubled him for many years before it became fatally infected."

Every eye went to the Easterner, and he fell abruptly silent under the intense scrutiny. Ra-khir asked the question on every mind, "How do you know that?"

The Easterner dropped his gaze, and his face seemed to darken, perhaps even adopting a slight reddish hue. "I spoke to my . . . his . . . the widow." He added defensively, "I used another name. I told her I was his cousin, that I'd spent the last twenty years living in the West. She believed me." He finished brokenly, almost in a whisper. "And she needs me." He pleaded his case. "Widows aren't treated well in the East." He fixed his gaze on Tae. "You know that,

Sire; and I know you've tried to help, but it's society. Ingrained. She's had a difficult time . . ."

Ra-khir frowned deeply. They had not started the individual trials yet, but he did not interrupt, allowing Tae to handle the only man still present who was one of his subjects.

Tae bobbed his head in a gesture of understanding. He kept his hands on Imorelda, but his gaze focused exclusively on the Easterner. "What's your name, soldier?"

The Easterner bowed low. "Sire, I'm Evrehar of Osporivat. My wife's name is Aditha."

"Rise Evrehar of Osporivat, husband of Aditha," Tae said, apparently cementing the names in his memory.

Evrehar straightened. "Yes, sire."

Ra-khir and Marisole exchanged glances, but Tae seemed to have the situation under control.

"If you stay here, you'll make the other Aditha, the one you love, the one you know intimately, a widow."

"Yes, Sire." Evrehar admitted. "But there is a difference. At home, I have a son and a daughter-in-law who will see to Aditha's care. The Aditha here was barren. She has nothing, no one to care for and protect her from . . . those who would treat her poorly."

Tae's lips pursed, and his expression turned thoughtful. His hands ran absently along the cat's furry sides, as if he had become so accustomed to the motion, he no longer recognized what his hands were doing. Ra-khir considered the situation, uncertain what to advise. They needed to consult with one another, to examine the matter from all sides. Perhaps one of the others would think of some detail he did not, but the case of Evrehar did not have the straightforward and moral solution he had hoped to find.

At length, Tae spoke. "Thank you, Evrehar of Osporivat." He looked around the ten. "You there." He gestured toward the Renshai. "What's your story?"

The Renshai stepped forward and bowed clumsily. Likely, he had never faced royalty in his entire life. Even the sinewy grace trained into him for swordplay failed him when it came to copying a motion he had only seen once. "Sire, my name is Falinir."

Saviar cut in, "Falinir is sixteen and still a boy by Renshai standards."

The flush on Falinir's pale face was easily visible. "I hoped this war would blood me, but my sword couldn't scratch those . . . those demons."

Sympathetic expressions touched several faces. Wounding *Kjem-*

pemagiska had required rare magical weapons, and the steel blessed by elves had done little or nothing to assist.

"I'm dead here," Falinir stated, "or at least my double is. I know he fell in valiant combat because my name's on the list approved for naming infants." His brow furrowed. "His name, I guess. Falinir, I mean."

The female Renshai had turned completely around, watching so intently a large gap developed between her and the departing warrior in front of her.

"You're not married, Falinir," Saviar pointed out. "No kids." He paused, eyes widening. "Right?"

Falinir inserted swiftly, "No kids. Of course, no kids. I haven't done . . . I mean I haven't slept with . . ." The redness returned to his cheeks, even more visible than before. ". . . anyone."

Saviar's features screwed into a knot of confusion. "Your parents are both living on our world."

"They are," Falinir confirmed.

"So why? Who's keeping you here?"

Falinir's eyes grew moist. He spoke a name so softly, Ra-khir did not hear it; but, apparently, the female Renshai did. Her lips pursed to bloodless lines, and she folded her arms across her chest.

"Gaelina?" Saviar said, apparently repeating Falinir. His brows knitted again. "But isn't she . . . and Warradon . . ."

"At home, yes, they're courting. But not here. Here, they're not together. Maybe here I have a chance."

"You love her?"

"I do," Falinir said, his gaze gone faraway, almost dreamy.

Ra-khir was watching the other Renshai who now wore a look of crestfallen sorrow. Her arms sank from her bosom to rest limply at her sides. It took him a moment to realize Saviar was looking at him.

Tearing his gaze from the woman warrior, Ra-khir addressed the Renshai in front of them. "Falinir, we seem to have established the couplings here match the ones back home. These men . . ." He gestured at the nine others awaiting judgment. ". . . all wound up in the same marriages as they did on our world."

Falinir glanced at the others. "That's true, but there are differences. You heard Broward say his youngest is a girl at home and a boy here. Our doubles' deaths don't match up, and this world has no elves or giants. For me, it's a second chance at Gaelina." He made it even more personal. "Could you pass up a second chance at having Kevral alive and well?"

Ra-khir had not wanted to go there; however, once raised, he had to admit he had considered it. "I may be doing exactly that, Falinir."

Saviar stiffened so suddenly, Ra-khir noticed, even from the corner of his eye.

He continued, as much for Saviar's sake, and his own, as Falinir's. "I haven't traveled to the Fields of Wrath here. It's possible Kevral is still alive on this world. I would love to have her back." A lump rose in his throat, and he had to speak around it. "Would love just to see her again. But . . ." He found himself incapable of saying anything more.

"But?" Falinir encouraged.

Ra-khir swallowed hard. "But my boys would miss me back on our world. And others, too. Why should the Saviar, Subikahn, and Calistin on this world have two Ra-khirs while the boys I raised and love back home have none?"

"But what if you have no double here? What if Kevral's pining for you? What if your children are fatherless?"

Ra-khir managed to speak again. "All of those things are possible and others as well. In my case, it's probably best I never know because I'm needed at home, not only by my children but by the Knights of Erythane, the kings I serve, my squire, and my father." He deliberately avoided mentioning Tiega. She had nothing to do with his decision, and mentioning her would dilute his point and might upset Saviar. "No world requires two of me; and, if I'm dead here, they've become accustomed to my absence."

Falinir had one last scenario to raise. "What if you and all three boys have died here? What if Kevral's all alone? Imagine if you could take her home."

Longing seized Ra-khir, but he shook his head sadly. "As much as I would love to end her suffering, the cost would be too high. I would have to travel to the Fields of Wrath and assess the situation. If it happened to be as you described, I would have to convince Kevral to come back with me. All of this would take weeks, during which this gate would have to remain open and the elves could not rescue other soldiers trapped on other worlds. It would be immoral to allow dozens to die for the tiny chance of one unlikely scenario to make myself, and one woman, happier." He tossed his head and the fantasy with it. "Kevral is a strong, beautiful woman who found the glorious death she sought throughout her life. To drag one exactly like her home would belittle her accomplishment and her memory."

Ra-khir paused, only then realizing the eight widowers of the twin cities were whispering furiously amongst themselves. Hoping to appease them, he said, "Not that others here don't have excellent and morally-sound reasons for remaining. I'm just not one of them." He turned Falinir a sad look. "And neither, in my opinion, are you."

Falinir looked stricken.

"Or mine," Saviar said.

Tae did not mince words. "The situations are not equivalent, Falinir. Ra-khir's a grown man who lost his wife, the mother of his children." He added facetiously, "And my son."

Ra-khir tried not to react but flinched a little. It could have become a sore subject; but, thus far, hadn't been except for occasional jabs. He never denied Tae's fatherhood and had made certain both of the twins visited him regularly as children. But, when the boys resided on the Fields of Wrath, he tried to treat them all the same and consider them all his.

Tae continued, "While you, Falinir, are a boy with a crush who's still too immature and stupid to realize his happiness doesn't lie with Gaelina here or at home."

Ra-khir sneaked a glance at the female Renshai who had become so engrossed in the proceedings she had gotten left behind. As the gate would remain open until El-brinith and Chan'rék'ril left with the rescue party, he did not prod her. She wanted, perhaps needed, to hear Tae's words.

Falinir's hand fell to his sword, knuckles blanched; but he did not draw it. Tae had spoken fighting words to a Renshai, but he was still a king. When it came to love, Falinir might be a fool, but he was not the total idiot Tae had just named him.

"And I know this because I've experienced something similar and acted just as stupidly."

That diffused at least some of Falinir's anger. His grip loosened, the knuckles regaining color.

Tae sat back, as if finished, then clearly thought better of it. It was not enough to leave the boy with sage words. In a situation that might require action, few Renshai had the patience to ponder something that might take months or years to understand. "I loved Kevral, too. I lost her to another man."

All eyes went to Ra-khir, but he found himself riveted to Tae's story. The three of them had always known Tae's obsession with Kevral had kept him unmarried far too long, but they never spoke of it. Ra-khir, at least, worried it might strain their friendship.

"For years, I plotted ways to steal her. Foolish, Falinir, because had I succeeded, I would have proven her a fickle and feckless woman, unworthy of my love. For many years more, I fretted over my bachelor lot in life only to realize recently, and nearly too late, another deserving woman loves me. Had I only let go of my bitterness, I would have discovered I loved her as well, hidden beneath my yearning for something I could never have. I should have married that other woman long ago, should have made her my queen and my life. We would have heirs now old enough to take my place, besides the one lost on some random world. It's not too late for me. I'm going home to court her, if she'll still have me. But I've lost far too much joy and too many years chasing a love that was never mine to begin with."

Touched by Tae's admission, Ra-khir bowed his head, his hands crossed over his heart. He had avoided the subject for decades, worried to upset Kevral, to enmesh the boys in an adult situation, to damage his friendship with Tae. Now, he wished he had broached it, wondering if he could have alleviated some of Tae's suffering, could have helped steer him in the right direction.

Marisole looked between the men. Young herself, she clearly had not noticed the discomfort of the female Renshai warrior near the gate the way Ra-khir and Tae had. "I'm afraid I agree with the others, Falinir, if not necessarily for the same reasons. Your parents here have already celebrated your double's honorable death, while those back home would have to mourn your disappearance, never knowing if you're alive or dead, if you're happy or sad, if you achieved the goal you abandoned them for. If nothing else, it's not fair to them." She looked about restively, apparently having said as much as she could without encroaching on brand-new ground.

Falinir's hand remained on his hilt, his lips pinched between his teeth. Frustration drove him to action he dared not take.

Ra-khir believed he knew Renshai and young love well enough to understand Falinir's internal struggle. All of the ten had agreed to abide by the panel's decision, and this one had been unanimous. Still, Renshai solved problems with violence, and desperation might drive him to dishonor himself and, quite possibly, die foolishly. He sought the necessary words to quell the budding fire.

The female Renshai appeared suddenly at Falinir's side and took his arm. "Let's go home." She looked up at Tae and mouthed the words, "Thank you."

Tae gave her only the barest smile and a spare hint of a nod. Imorelda purred so loudly Ra-khir could hear it.

Lips still firmly bitten, Falinir walked meekly alongside his companion. He hesitated a moment at the gate until she nudged him through it and followed. Both Renshai disappeared, leaving only the nine remaining soldiers and the rescue party.

Saviar murmured to his father. "Hit me if I'm ever that oblivious. I wish I had a woman that devoted to me."

Ra-khir delivered a playful but significant slap.

Saviar recoiled. "What was that for?"

"For all the young women throwing you the glad eye." Ra-khir shook his head but said nothing more. At Saviar's age, female attention had embarrassed and scared him, too. Though nineteen, Saviar was still as romantically naïve and confused as his father had been before Kevral turned his head.

Scarlet rose in Saviar's cheeks, and he looked away from his father.

Tae took over again, clearly wishing to move things along as swiftly as possible. "Evrehar, we haven't forgotten you. We're going to need some time to consider your case. Do you mind if we move on to the others for a bit?"

Evrehar made a gesture of supplication and stepped back, wringing his hands in nervous anticipation. The Westerners came forward as a group to replace him.

Usually, Tae discouraged the use of his title, but he had allowed Evrehar and the Renshai to address him as "Sire" without comment. Since rank had emerged, Ra-khir had no choice but to allow Tae to take over the proceedings. "Besides Broward, how many of you found your double's cemetery stones in the 'body not recovered' area?"

Broward indicated two men, both from Corpa Schaull. The three stepped in front of the other Westerners in the judging area. "When I visited Corpa Schaull, I asked about the others. Terrellis' double . . ." he indicated a short, stocky man with a bristly beard. ". . . disappeared a few months ago with a companion while tending goats. They think one of the two slipped through a crack in the western tail of the Southern Weathered Mountains, and the other fell attempting to rescue the first. The smell of rotting corpses was the only evidence. Not wanting to lose anyone else, they did not attempt to retrieve the bodies, and no one actually saw them to confirm both men had died."

Broward put a hand on the shoulder of the other, a tall muscular man of middle age. "Semarat's double disappeared just a week ago when a dam broke and washed him away. No body was ever found, but when he didn't return, they declared him dead."

Tae addressed the other judges. "Anyone have a problem considering these three men next and together?"

Ra-khir had planned to discuss each case individually in some random order but could see the wisdom in Tae's suggestion. He shook his head negatively, as did all of the others.

The three men whispered amongst themselves, then Broward stepped forward. "I'd like to speak for all three of us, if that suits you, Sire, sirs, and lady. My companions have agreed to answer any specific questions you might have for them."

Nods passed through the panel. Ra-khir considered aloud, "You've had time to discuss the possibilities while you traveled to your city and back."

"Indeed," Broward confirmed. "And with those two." He made a gesture toward the two additional men of Corpa Schaull, both of whom had indicated they had living duplicates.

Those two started toward the others, but Tae stopped them with a raised hand. "Let's not muddy the waters too much. I'd like to consider this group of three first." He explained his reasoning. "They all have two things in common: their presences don't cause duplication and their burial chambers are empty, which means their rise from the dead won't cause the same difficulties some of the others might."

The last two men of Corpa Schaull stopped, and the focus of the judges remained on Broward, Terrellis, and Semarat. The other six men showed various levels of discomfort, their cases clearly more complicated and, thus, more likely to get dismissed.

Tae turned his attention to Ra-khir, giving the floor back to the Knight of Erythane, who claimed it gratefully. "Broward, what plans do you have to integrate yourself back into society, and your family life, smoothly?"

Broward bowed briefly. "I believe I have a strong start. Many have already accepted me, including my family. We had decided I should bring Semarat with me, claiming the same people who nursed me back to health found him as well. I was going to use him as my excuse for why I needed to leave when I did. We were planning to use the trauma of our doubles' experiences, now part of our own history, to cover any mistakes we made in our memories of how certain events occurred, assuming they might be a bit different from our true experiences."

Ra-khir turned his attention to the third man of the trio. "And Terrellis?"

The three men exchanged smiles. "We thought that, given our experiences of being found after hope had been lost, Semarat and I might dedicate some of our spare time to helping others in the same situation. We figured Terrellis could hide out for a while, becoming more scruffy, smelly, and thin. Then, Semarat and I would pretend to discover the hole in the mountains where Terrellis had been trapped alive with his dead companion. If we actually find it, and the real corpses, we'll try to remove the other one for proper burial and make sure the duplicate Terrellis is never found. Again, we think any discrepancies between his other life and this one could be covered by memory issues brought about by trauma."

Ra-khir could find no significant fault with the story, though he did have some moral issues to consider with his fellow judges. "Semarat and Terrellis also have wives and children?"

Broward explained, "Semarat has the same wife and seven boys. Here, she's working hard to support them, with the older ones, one of them now a girl, taking care of the younger. As for Terrellis, he never married, but he was courting a widow back home with two children. I don't know if the here-Terrellis had been courting her, too, but I did look in on her. She's a widow here, as well, with one young child."

Terrellis stepped in to add, "I don't know if she'd welcome me here, but I have no way of knowing if things would have worked out on our world, either. At least here she's alive. Even if that relationship never works out, I have living sisters here and only dead ones back home. My parents are alive here, too; casualties of the giants at home." His voice went pleading. "I want to stay. Please."

Terrellis' desperation tugged at Ra-khir's heart. He understood the situation. These seemed like genuinely good men trying to make the best of several tragic situations. "Let me confer with my colleagues, and we'll get back to you as quickly as possible."

The panel withdrew a discreet distance and huddled together. Marisole spoke first, her voice pitched low and soft to prevent it from carrying. "I'm inclined to let all three of them stay behind. Do I need to explain?"

Clutching Imorelda in his arms, Tae shook his head. "Not necessary. They have good reasons and a logical plan." He gave Ra-khir a searching look, clearly expecting any divergent arguments to come from the Knight of Erythane and his rigid definitions of morality.

Saviar spoke before his father could. "Let them stay. It's good for so many, and I don't see how it hurts anyone."

Ra-khir hesitated. One thing bothered him about the whole situation, and he felt obligated to give it a voice. "I can't help wondering if it's entirely honorable to deceive widows and children, even to help them."

All three of the others turned Ra-khir scathing looks. Tae groaned.

That forced Ra-khir to explain. "I know they'll be overjoyed to have their lost fathers back, their husbands who were presumed dead. But these aren't actually the same men. They're . . ." Ra-khir used the elves' term, "*dopplegängers*." He addressed Marisole, the only woman in the group. "I mean, how would you feel if an Outworld creature magically assumed your husband's face, climbed into your bed and tricked you into . . . into . . . ?"

"Being loved?" Marisole inserted. "Acted in every way like my *deceased* lover and treated my children exactly as my husband would have had he survived?" She smiled. "I think I'd be all right with that."

Tae attempted to rescue her from song. "In her place, I would prefer never to know that he was not, in fact, my actual husband. I would, deliberately or unconsciously, overlook any behavior that seemed a bit 'off.'"

Marisole pointed at Tae and nodded briskly.

They seemed so certain Ra-khir wondered if they truly understood his argument. "So, it wouldn't feel like adultery to you? Not even a little bit?"

Saviar shook his head. "Papa, he's exactly the same as her husband who's never going to return."

"But it's dishonest. Don't you feel at all uncomfortable condoning blatant lying?" Ra-khir did not know why he felt the need to press a point that seemed clear to everyone else.

Tae sighed and rolled his eyes. He placed Imorelda gently on the ground, and she stalked back toward the log, tail lashing.

All the memories of their past interactions came flooding back. When they were teens, Ra-khir remembered how his every utterance had driven Tae near to madness, how Tae's casual lies and strange twists of ethics had made Ra-khir despise him. Both of them had mellowed with age and learned not only to coexist but to care deeply for one another. Now, it all seemed to strip away, bringing them back to those younger years when one's own opinion always felt like an ultimate truth and the need to convert the other person a desperate necessity.

Tae spoke softly, without any of the venom he had flung at Ra-khir in their youth. "My friend, if you truly believe lies of any kind are immoral, we will have no choice but to register your objection to any of them remaining here and decide each case among the three of us."

Ra-khir considered his companion's words and realized they were sound. This near-duplicate world contained no real magic, which left only fairy stories and superstition. If these men told the truth, they would, at best, be dismissed as crazy. Tae was also right, they did not need Ra-khir's approval. The three of them had already decided to allow Broward, Semarat, and Terrellis to remain, and their majority vote would triumph over his one objection.

Tae continued, "I divided them into the groups I did for a reason. This will be the easiest decision. When we start hearing from men with living doubles, it will get so much harder, their stories more convoluted and careful."

Saviar realized aloud, "Even the ones with dead doubles whose bodies were burned or buried will be difficult."

Everyone nodded grimly, including Ra-khir. He had suggested the trials, and he knew they would strain his sense of honor; but he had not realized just how much until this moment. He spoke carefully, "I don't actually believe lying is always immoral. There are rare situations where it's more moral than truth." He added in realization, Terrellis' pleading face filling his mind's eye, "And I do believe this is one of them. Please, make the vote unanimous."

Saviar said something even Ra-khir had not considered. "If it makes you feel better, Papa, I don't think it's a coincidence the gods sent a disproportionate number of Twin City soldiers to this particular Outworld."

It was not the first time it occurred to Ra-khir the passionate and unshakable moral foundation of the Knights of Erythane had nothing to do with religion. His father, the captain of the knights, was an atheist, although the repeated appearances of Colbey Calistinsson, who dwelt among the gods and spoke of them, had to have given him pause. Ra-khir's mother and stepfather had raised him to believe in the Western pantheon, and he had found his father's ideas on the subject interesting and worthy of consideration. Ultimately, most of the world had come to believe in the Northern gods, including Ra-khir who had heard firsthand stories from Colbey. Still, he did not allow religion to rule his life. It had not occurred to him to argue what the gods might or might not want, such as the possibility they had put these men on Midgard because that's where they wanted them and not as replacements for missing men on a duplicate world. As Saviar had just shown, the opposite side could be argued just as vehemently, which was why discussions that centered on the will of the gods tended to become contrary and dangerous.

Nevertheless, Saviar had a reasonable point. It did seem odd the very men who had nothing to live for on Midgard had gotten randomly sucked to this particular location. It did not change any of the details, but it did make him less determined to argue against them staying on vague moral grounds. *Interesting.*

Tae brought the session to an abrupt close. "If we're all agreed, let's not keep the men waiting in painful suspense." He headed back toward the deadfall the panel had occupied, the others scurrying after him. Ra-khir suspected no one wanted to miss seeing the joy on the men's faces.

Presumably to avoid a drawn-out process or pronouncement, Tae waited only until the others had retaken their places on the log. "Broward, Terrellis, and Semarat will stay here."

Cheers erupted from the group, and several men patted the three on the back or gave them exuberant embraces.

Ra-khir added, "We would ask them to remain until the proceedings have concluded. We need everyone to know who is staying and their stories, so no one compromises anyone else."

Broward looked over the shoulder of one of his well-wishers. "We wouldn't want it any other way." He clearly tried to sound neutral, but he practically sang the words. Tears of joy trickled down Terrellis' face. If anyone noticed his weakness, they gave no sign, patting and hugging him with the same excitement as his two companions.

Their reactions affirmed the decision for Ra-khir. These three Midgard soldiers had reason to live again. The widows would win back not only husbands they had already mourned, but a new chance at wedded life and an easier time in society. The children would grow up with a father, which could make substantial differences in their character as well as their happiness. Ra-khir's joy spiraled from there. Mothers and fathers, siblings and cousins, friends, employers, customers all gained. In the case of the men from Corpa Schaull and Frist, the only ones left to miss them on Midgard were fellow soldiers, some of those surely friends and brothers; but they would be buoyed by the knowledge their companions had found a better life. Nothing but good could come out of it, though that would surely become more of a balancing act as the cases grew less sure and obvious.

Ra-khir could not help glancing at Evrehar of Osporivat. The Easterner stood apart from the others, clasping his hands beneath his chin. He had pled his case first, the only one who had spoken and still waited. Ra-khir wished he could relieve the man's burden, but he knew they were not prepared to make that decision yet. He looked away, knowing Evrehar would attempt to read any tiny expression or movement that might suggest the group leaned one way or the other on his case. Since they had not yet discussed it, anything Ra-khir conveyed would be deceptive.

Tae took over again. At some point, his ever-present pet had climbed back into his lap. "Let's next consider the situations of the four men with living duplicates. Please step forward."

They did so. One was a broad-shouldered, square-jawed man in his late twenties. The second appeared about ten years older, short and skinny with squinty eyes and close-cropped hair. The third shuffled toward them uncertainly, an adolescent with a lanky frame and pimples marring his cheeks. The fourth was the oldest, his hair mostly gray, crow's feet around his eyes and wrinkles at the edges of his lips.

"You," Tae said, jabbing a hand toward the teen. "What's your name and where do you come from?"

The boy glanced to either side, then behind before shrinking into himself, clearly uncomfortable with his newly-grown height. "Leamond, Sire," he said in a quaking voice. "From Frist."

Ra-khir would have started with someone more self-assured, but he believed he understood Tae's strategy. The young man would likely state his case swiftly and briefly, setting the stage for the others. Also, he would have the least complicated situation and might get sent home immediately rather than needing to listen to all the others.

Tae encouraged, "Tell us about your situation, Leamond from Frist."

Leamond shifted from foot to foot. He cleared his throat once, twice, then a third time before speaking. "I'm not married, sire. I don't have a girl here or there, but I had parents, sire, two brothers too young to join the army and my baby sister. Cousins and uncles and aunts all dead back home. I was apprenticed to a tinsmith killed in battle at home but alive here. Everything I've ever known is gone there. But here . . . it's all still here. Please, if there's any way . . ." He studied his feet without looking up at those he addressed, then added hastily. "I know there's another Leamond, or Layamont as he's called here. I've thought about how to rejoin my family without displacing him, and I think I have a way."

The judges exchanged glances. They had expected him to leave the ideas to them, and Ra-khir feared Leamond's plan might sound silly, that it would only reflect the naïveté of his age.

Leamond plunged ahead, "I've heard the story of my birth many times. My father was a merchant who sold textiles from the West and brought back spices from the East. He had met my mother on one of his expeditions, married her, and brought her home. My birth was supposed to be nearly two months away when she talked him into one last trip East to see her homeland before she had to settle down to raise me in Frist. Of course, I was born early, precipitously, in a southern town so tiny it had no name. Strangers who spoke another language tended her. Blood loss and shock rendered my mother unconscious; she remembers little of my birth. By the time my father rushed to her side, it was over."

Leamond finally looked at the judges, dark eyes shining, face scrunched into lines of concentration. When they looked back at him intently, he dropped his gaze again. "I thought I might change my name, feign an accent and pass myself off as my own twin. I could claim, during the delivery, one of the women in the village whose baby had died stole me and raised me as her own. On her deathbed, she admitted the truth, and I came to find my blood parents."

Ra-khir kept his expression bland, though he wanted to smile. The story did sound implausible, but not impossible. In a world without magic, he realized, it might even work. Leamond's striking resemblance to his duplicate, and there being no obvious or logical reason for anyone to fake such a story, would work to his advantage. As weird as it sounded, it made far more sense than the truth.

Tae found the flaw Ra-khir had not yet considered. "You'd have to be an excellent actor. You'd have to keep track of what people told you and not react to things and people you know because of what you lived on our world."

Saviar pointed out, "You'd also have to pretend western and common were not your first languages."

"I thought of that," Leamond said. "I'm young, and I have a good memory. Also, I figured I'd tell them the mother who raised me made sure I grew up knowing other tongues, so I won't have to stumble too much. I think I can do it."

Ra-khir stroked his chin. "It's not like anyone's going to try to catch him making mistakes, and the truth is actually less believable than his story." He suddenly found all of the other judges staring at him and realized he had gone from the position of the most demanding to the biggest pushover. He smiled. "I guess I'm sold."

Tae laughed. "Well, the rest of us need to discuss it after we've heard the others in the group. We still have to make sure no one who stays interferes with any of the others. Having so many of them hail from the same place makes that a bit more difficult. We can't have eight unlikely appearances all happening at once."

The men with dead doubles who had not left corpses had dealt with that issue amongst themselves already. Nevertheless, Tae's point was viable. "Indeed," Ra-khir said. "Let's examine them in order of advancing age, if that works for everyone."

The other judges nodded. The four men looked at one another, then the man in his twenties stepped forward. Well-muscled and handsome, he appeared to have either been a career soldier, a guard, or a blacksmith. "My name is Ultaer from Frist. I had a daughter, and my wife was carrying my second child when those monsters killed them." He clamped his hands so tightly it appeared as if he might break his own fingers. "I thought the man who bears my name and resemblance here might have an unwitnessed accident. I could step in to take his place. No one would be the wiser."

Ra-khir waited for more information, but Ultaer said nothing more, simply looked from one judge to the next.

The knight pressed. "What makes you so certain your double will have some sort of 'unwitnessed accident'?"

The quick blue eyes darted to Ra-khir. "Well, sir, I supposed I plan to make certain of it." His hands remained blanched, but he seemed to knead them less forcefully. "Not cruelly, of course. Quickly and painlessly."

Abruptly, Ra-khir got what he should have understood from the beginning. Still, he had to ask. "You're planning to . . . murder your double?"

Ultaer finally unclamped his hands. "Quickly and painlessly," he repeated. Then, apparently sensing some discomfort in Ra-khir's tone, "Or I'm willing to face him in a fair duel if you think that's more ethical, sir. I have one wife, sir. It's not as if we could share her. There can be only one Ultaer. I'd like to be it, but if he can best me, I suppose he deserves it."

Ra-khir opened his mouth to remind Ultaer his double belonged here, that Ultaer himself was an intruder trying to fit himself into the other's world. He wanted the man to realize the inherent immorality in even suggesting such a course of action, but Tae seized his arm, head shaking ever so slightly. Before Ra-khir could say anything, the Eastern king spoke, "Thank you, Ultaer. We'll take your position under advisement, along with Leamond's and the others', and we'll let you know our decision."

Tae then reminded them all. "You do all remember you agreed to abide by our decision, even if you don't agree with it."

All nine of the men nodded and/or mouthed promises, including the ones who had already received their judgments.

"Very well," Tae said, gazing at the middle-aged man. "What do you wish to tell us?"

The short, skinny man took Ultaer's place, eyes so squinted Ra-khir could not make out their color. He ran a hand through his close-cropped hair before speaking, "I'm Kentarial, a scribe from Corpa

Schaull. Back home and here, I'm married with three handsome daughters in their teens. My double's name is Rentari." He smiled nervously. "I think I can change my appearance, quietly come to Corpa Schaull and become a part of it. I won't interfere with Rentari or his family, but I'll get to watch my daughters . . ." He amended with just a hint of wistfulness, ". . . his daughters grow up, marry, have children of their own. I'll watch them from afar."

Ra-khir saw how that plan could work, but only if Kentarial could handle the pain of watching another man sleep with his wife and raise daughters he considered his own, could stand his girls calling another man "Papa." "That's not going to be as easy as you're making it sound."

Kentarial shrugged. "I won't go into details except to say my marriage was not a happy one. She gave me three beautiful daughters, and for that I have to appreciate her. But there was no love lost between us. Rentari can have her with my blessing. I only want to stay to see the girls do all right. I can't imagine any double of mine treating them poorly, so I don't see us coming into conflict." He started to retreat, but Marisole's question brought him back.

"Kentarial, how do you see your future here?"

The question flummoxed Ra-khir.

"I'll get a fresh start," Kentarial said slowly, as if uncertain he were truly answering Marisole's query. "Perhaps I'll marry again. If I'm lucky, I'll find someone related and become an in-law to the girls. That will open the way for some sort of relationship with them. However, I'm not going to do anything to assure that outcome. I wouldn't trick someone into marrying me."

Marisole stiffened. Apparently, she had expected a different answer, but she sat back without prodding further. Ra-khir finally realized she had been trying to figure out if Kentarial would be truly happy here, basing his entire life on becoming a distant spectator to the people he loved. Ra-khir liked the man's reply, but something about it definitely bothered the princess.

Marisole dismissed Kentarial with a "thank you."

The last of the four men stepped forward, the elderly gentleman with the crow's feet. He bowed briefly to each of the judges in turn, then waited for one of them to speak.

Tae did so. "State your name, origin, and situation, please."

"Fitzmar of Corpa Schaull, Sire. I'm a lifelong bachelor who has had relationships with others like me over the years. No children. My only remaining relative back home was a niece who doesn't exist here. For me, it's not the people; it's the place. I've lived my whole life in Corpa Schaull. I know its ways and customs and how to conduct my . . . partnerships without causing discomfort to others or raising the ire of those who don't appreciate my . . . interests. I'm too old to rebuild. Probably was too old to join the army in the first place. I should have died with the city." He lifted a hand to forestall any argument. "But here I am, and I want to stay, Sire." He nodded at Marisole, "Princess." Then Ra-khir and Saviar, "Sirs."

Ra-khir suspected Fitzmar had just told them he preferred the sexual company of men, but he did not press. The morality of Fitzmar's bedroom was not Ra-khir's affair, and it did not influence the ethics of the situation itself.

Tae started speaking, which made Ra-khir cringe. In the East, homosexuality was punishable by death, and Tae had only recently come to grips with his own son's carnal desires. "Your so-called 'interests' don't involve inflicting anything onto unwilling partners, do they?"

Fitzmar's nostrils flared, but he gave no other sign of affront. Instead, he smiled. "No, Sire. My partners have all been adults and all willing participants. I can't guarantee I've pleased them all, but who can?"

A light and uncomfortable riffle of laughter passed through the group.

Ra-khir expected Tae to press further, but he did not. Instead, Fitzmar spoke again. "There are certain conventions among those of us with . . . less common desires. It took me a long time to learn those of Corpa Schaull, where men loving men is not considered a crime but flirting with the wrong one could be dangerous. It's hard enough for an older person to adjust to a whole new situation without adding the burden of some believing what I do in my relationships is a societal outrage or a capital offense."

"Indeed," Ra-khir said, mostly to forestall a discussion.

It did not stop Tae from speaking, and Ra-khir tensed in anticipation. But all the Easterner said was, "Thank you. All of you must remain here while we deliberate."

The four men who served as the topic of discussion stepped back among the others, and the judges returned to their quiet area to consider the information they had gathered. To Ra-khir's surprise, they came to four unanimous decisions after a few short tangents and a bit of convincing. They elected Tae to deliver the news when they returned to their places in front of the log.

Tae announced. "Ultaer, we agree with you that the only way you could stay would be to destroy your double. We find that to be an unfair or immoral act we cannot condone, so you will return with us."

Saviar subtly positioned himself in front of Marisole, clearly concerned about the broad-shouldered Fristin's reaction. But Ultaer
only groused to himself and anyone close enough to hear him and
sat on a nearby stone. Marisole backhanded Saviar in the small of his
spine, saying something about her capability to handle herself in a
fight. Ra-khir did not allow himself to smile. Renshai women fought,
and Saviar had probably chosen to protect her because of her status
rather than her gender.

Tae continued, "Leamond, we have decided to allow you to stay
as your own twin but caution you to pay attention. You may tell the
truth if cornered, but realize you probably won't be believed and the
others trusted to stay can't support your story without compromis-
ing their own. Also know that Layamont may not be as eager as you
to share his family with an unexpected brother."

Leamond nodded, quivering happily.

"We think Kentarial and Fitzmar should go to Corpa Schaull as
father and son, so they can arrive together without straining coincidence. Fitzmar could 'accidentally' discover the resemblance between
Kentarial and Rentari and 'remember' he is in some way related to
both of them. This should give Kentarial an opening to watch Rentari's daughters a bit closer without appearing to stalk them."

Saviar added, "Kentarial, just don't look too much like your double, if you can help it."

Kentarial nodded and glanced at Fitzmar, who also nodded.
"That should work. It will also give me some 'family,' which would
be nice now that I'm older and . . . um . . . slower." He smiled at his
new 'son.' "I've always wanted a son, and I can't think of a better one
than Kentarial."

The younger man beamed. "From mentor to father. I can live
with that. I only wish I could talk about your heroics during the
war." He turned to the judges. "He saved my life, you know."

Ra-khir did not, but now did not seem like the time to discuss it.
The two men would have their entire lives to talk about it, if only
with one another.

The judges all retook their seats and Imorelda her position in
Tae's lap before the king announced, "Now, we'd like to see the men
with dead and buried doubles." He glanced at Evrehar of Osporivat.
"Including Evrehar."

The two unjudged stepped forward, both looking pale and worried. Ra-khir had thought the ones with living doubles would have
the greater row to hoe, but three out of four of them were staying.
He hoped this group would fare similarly. He had become involved

with their stories and the tragedy that had destroyed the women, children, and elders of Corpa Schaull and Frist.

The other man, a Fristin in his early twenties, edged in front of Evrehar, who had already told his story. "I'm Blenhardius from Frist. Blenhardin, my double, died of the consumption along with several others, including his wife." The grief in his tone was so tangible, Ra-khir had to will himself not to cry. "My Hilda, and her double, both dead." Ra-khir succeeded, but Blenhardius did not. Tears coursed from his eyes. "My four children are orphans living with Hilda's brother, who has six mouths of his own to feed. He is trying, gods bless him, but he has to make choices. I can't wholly blame him for choosing his over mine."

Blenhardius broke down, sobbing, and had to stop speaking. Gradually, he regained control, wiping his eyes angrily with the back of his sleeve. "Sorry," he finally managed.

Marisole spoke through her own tears. "Completely understandable. Continue when you can."

Blenhardius nodded, looking down. He paused a bit longer before speaking. "My parents died many years ago, and I had no siblings. I intend to pass myself off as my older brother, conceived when my parents were courting and given away so no one would know their shame. I'll say I've heard about the situation, I have no children of my own, and I'm eager to raise those of my deceased brother. My brother-in-law will grill me to make sure I'm suitable and will treat them well. He'll probably insist I live nearby and he has access, but I don't think he'll fight me for them. He has too much to handle and has always been reasonable in the past. At least on our world."

Tae's attention shifted to Evrehar. "You've given us your story." He summarized for those who might have forgotten it beneath all the other heartrending ones that had followed it. "As I recall, your wife, Aditha, is a widow and maltreated. No offspring on this world. Back on Midgard, you have your Aditha, a son, and a daughter-in-law."

Evrehar nodded to indicate Tae had recapped the situation well enough. "I could do something similar to Blenhardius. Since we're going to entirely different parts of the world, no one would find it suspicious two men showed up in similar odd situations at the same time."

Ra-khir saw no reason to extract more information. With a few tweaks, the solutions could certainly work. It only remained to assure they had a consensus or, at least, a majority vote between the judges.

Once again, the judges conferred away from the waiting soldiers.

For once, Saviar spoke first. "I say 'yes' to Blenhardius and 'no' to Evrehar."

Marisole and Nomalan both looked to the Renshai, their faces creased in expressions of confusion. Technically nothing more than a bystander, Nomalan had remained silent throughout, but Marisole had seemed about to speak before Saviar's words pressed her into thoughtful silence.

Imorelda on his shoulders, Tae pinched his lower lip between his thumb and forefinger. "I'm more inclined to allow them both to stay. They have the same solution, so that's clearly not the issue. Is it because Blenhardius' situation involves children? Because, as an Easterner, I know how cruelly some of our societies treat their widows."

Ra-khir had come to the same conclusion as Saviar, and it had nothing to do with elevating children over widows. "It's because Blenhardius' wife and children are dead on our world. He has nothing to return to, and no one would suffer from his absence. Here, those children are alive, and they need him. Evrehar is rescuing one Aditha only to abandon another to the same fate."

"Except," Tae pointed out. "He's right that the son and daughter-in-law can alleviate some of the our-world-Aditha's suffering."

Saviar said softly. "But who will relieve the suffering of the son and daughter-in-law?"

Tae's expression mimicked Nomalan's. "They're a couple, Saviar. They can support one another."

Tae had a point, but Ra-khir recognized some surprising naïveté in his words. "They're a young couple, just starting out. That's difficult enough without adding the burden of a troubled widow. And the our-world-Aditha would have all the problems of the one on this world plus the added encumbrance of ruining her son's future."

Tae had clearly not considered that possibility. "Wouldn't the three of them work together to make all of their lives better?"

"Ideally," Ra-khir admitted. "But we have to deal with reality, not daydreams."

Marisole finally piped up, "But isn't Evrehar in the best position to decide where he belongs? To balance the way things will work best? He certainly knows Osporavat and its attitudes, his family and its abilities, better than any of us."

Ra-khir was not so sure. "If that were true, we would have no need for courts or judges. Kings would have a lot more time for leisure."

Saviar added, "Evrehar has just returned from seeing the Aditha on this world in all her suffering while his family back home is just a treasured memory. The emotion here is raw and visible. It's impossible to be impartial when you're comparing a loved one's visible pain to hypothetical future anguish."

Ra-khir bit back a smile. He knew Saviar was a thoughtful and intelligent man, but his own prejudices about youth and Renshai had made him believe they would not agree, at least initially, on these difficult situations. Now, he found himself standing on the same side as his son against two capable opponents whose opinions he also trusted. He had been at odds with his boys so many times since Kevral's death he had begun to wonder if they would ever agree on anything. He shoved that thought aside, suddenly concerned he might have biased his own arguments based on Saviar's initial opinion. Only the morality of the situation mattered, not who buoyed or opposed his assessment.

Tae tipped his head, clearly thinking. "In many Eastern societies, a widow is considered *frichen-karboh*. Many, including old friends, will ignore her even if she needs assistance. Few men would consider her suitable for courting or marriage. If she can't find a man or a job or a relative to care for her, she will likely starve."

Ra-khir avoided judging the culture of the Eastlands. It had changed a lot since Weile Kahn, then Tae, had taken over as king, but they could not make changes overnight. There were still a few parts of the Eastlands that condoned slavery. "A terrible situation indeed, but this Aditha has come to grips with the loss of her husband. She may die, or she could become a stronger person for the hardships she has already endured. A woman working for her money is not necessarily a bad thing, so long as the job itself is not degrading. Not all men can or even want to marry young virgins. There is also the possibility of her traveling westward into one of the cities where widows are not treated in such a . . ." He stopped himself from saying "disgraceful," which might offend. ". . . manner."

"Maybe," Tae said doubtfully. "It would help if we had the time and wherewithal to advise her." The corners of his mouth twitched. "I can admit I'm seeing the worst possible outcome if you can admit you're seeing the best."

"Agreed," Ra-khir said. "But there's still the matter of the wife and child on our world. If Evrehar stays here, their suffering is just beginning, particularly when they discover he chose this world over them."

Words fairly exploded from Marisole's mouth. "No one would tell them that!"

"We wouldn't," Saviar said, gesturing toward the gate. "But there are dozens of men, many of them from the East, who know he remained behind. Do you really think his wife and son won't beg news of him, that the truth will remain hidden?"

Tae shut his mouth with an audible click.

"Whereas," Marisole started, apparently unaware she might be considered to be imparting information, "the Aditha here has no idea he could have returned to her. She knows only he was the unwilling victim of death itself."

Ra-khir nodded.

Nomalan took Marisole's hand and whispered something into her ear before she spoke. "Evrehar needs to return."

It was now three against one. They did not need Tae's concurrence, but Ra-khir wanted it. It bothered him the only Easterner on the panel was the holdout. It might mean, or at least suggest, Evrehar had only lost his appeal because the panel judged him using Western standards. "Tae?"

"I can see both sides," the king admitted. "You all have definite points, but I also understand what Evrehar's saying. His son and daughter-in-law might prove a comfort to the Aditha on Midgard or her troubles might strain or destroy their marriage. The Aditha here could die in misery or she could parlay her suffering into making herself a stronger, more capable woman." He sighed deeply. "The problem is we can't see the future."

Ra-khir laughed. "If we could, we wouldn't do half the stupid things we do."

Saviar also chuckled, adding, "But we'd still do the other half. We'd want to so much we wouldn't care about the consequences, or we'd convince ourselves we could outwit the gods."

Tae looked at Saviar as if for the first time. "When did you get so smart?"

"Yesterday?" Saviar suggested, to Ra-khir's relief. For a moment, he worried about hearing something mildly funny and intensely disrespectful like, *"I've always been smart. You were just too stupid to notice."* Or, perhaps, something about the missing Subikahn no longer holding him back.

Tae released another deep sigh. "We've been unanimous on every other decision. Why not this one as well? You've convinced me, I guess. Evrehar returns with us." He turned Saviar an evil look. "So long as that brilliant young man has to tell him and explain the reasons."

Ra-khir studied Saviar. Less than a year ago, he and Kedrin had induced the young Renshai into judging a case brought before them as Knights of Erythane. At the time, Saviar had expressed a desire to join their ranks, so the Knight-Captain had chosen to test his sincerity in this manner. He had seemed so young and nervous at the time, though he had made a sound decision of which they both approved. Since then, Saviar had come a long way toward developing the qualities of a competent leader, though he had made no headway toward becoming a knight. Ra-khir would have liked Saviar to follow in his footsteps, but the young man had to make his own way and would surely do well in whatever pursuits he eventually selected. Ra-khir had gradually come to realize leading the Renshai seemed the most likely, and probably the best, future not only for his son, but for all of Midgard. Whatever course Saviar chose, however, Ra-khir would support it.

Saviar sucked in a deep breath, let it out slowly and smiled. "I accept your challenge, Sire." He headed toward the waiting soldiers.

CHAPTER 15

Mothers protecting their children aren't always thinking clearly.
—*Freya*

FOR NEARLY AN HOUR, Marisole found herself too engaged in burdensome thoughts to carry on a casual conversation with her mother. They sat in Matrinka's herbal room on small wooden chairs sorting medicinals into the press of drawers, bowls, and vials that nearly filled the room. The queen did most of the talking, explaining the uses and properties of the various dried leaves and corked liquids, the berries and seeds, the desiccated mushroom caps and bits of bark.

Matrinka's words washed over Marisole, mostly unheard. Since childhood, her mother had tried to get her interested in the healing arts. As a young child, she had attempted to learn the properties of dozens of remedies, the potential cures for diseases, how to tell when to use a poultice of perfringens root or bektal stem, mostly as a way to please her mother. The information refused to remain in her head, chased away by more interesting lessons from her various tutors, by childish pursuits but—more often—by music.

Their sorting days had grown less common through the years, more often a rare occasion to talk as mother and daughter without interruption or fear of someone overhearing. The walls of the tiny room were thick and windowless to maintain a constant temperature and chase away humidity that could temper the potency of several herbs. To some, it might seem like an airless prison; to Marisole, it would always be the place where she and her mother spoke frankly.

Matrinka's voice finally cut through the fog of Marisole's contemplations. "I heard about your adventures on the duplicate world."

Marisole looked up, clutching a handful of *garlet* petals contaminated with nonmedicinal stems. She found herself rubbing the side of her chin along the bandage on her shoulder and willed herself to stop. The bite from the mermaid no longer hurt, but she would have been absently scratching the forming scabs if not for the dressing and her hands being full. "From who?"

"Whom," Matrinka corrected absently. "Sir Ra-khir gave us the full report." She emphasized the word "full," which made Marisole smile. Although less formal than most of the Knights of Erythane, Ra-khir could become as tediously detailed as any of them if not rerouted by the king or queen. "And Tae gave me the abbreviated version."

Marisole appreciated that her mother already knew the entire story. That meant she could speak mostly freely, without fear of blundering into teaching territory and having to sing. The curse gave her some leeway with personal conversation, but it could become stingingly painful with small lapses and agonizingly driving with larger ones. "I'm sorry. Based on my judgments, I'm clearly not ruling-queen material."

Matrinka's brow furrowed as she crushed powder into a clay container. "They both said you did just fine. A bit quiet, perhaps, but that's only to be expected. They both traveled with Darris when he was your age. They understand the restrictions on the bard's heir."

It was not what Marisole had meant. "They did tell you about the last case, didn't they? The Easterner. I argued the wrong side."

Matrinka set the pot aside and patted her daughter gently across the shoulders, avoiding the wound. Marisole suddenly realized her mother's decades of healing had made her competent not only with potions and poultices and cures but also soothing touches and finding the right words. "That's the thing with moral situations, kitten. There's usually no right answer."

Opening her hand, Marisole routed stems and petals into different areas of her palm. "Well, this time there seemed to be. Once Saviar and Ra-khir explained it, I could see my error quite plainly." She sighed. "And you should have heard Saviar's explanation to Evrehar. I wish I could have memorized it. It would have made a beautiful, heartrending song. We were all in tears, and Evrehar came home without a single objection."

"I got to watch his reunion with his son. Touching. You could tell he knew he had done the right thing by returning." Matrinka added with a smile, "And you might want to talk to Ra-khir if you're serious about making it into a song. I believe he recited Saviar's words verbatim."

Marisole laughed. "A proud papa, and rightly so." She tipped her head in consideration. "I'm surprised no one has snapped him up."

Matrinka smiled and shrugged. "Do you mean Ra-khir? Or Saviar?"

Marisole had meant Saviar, but she realized it was a legitimate question. "Either, I guess. Both. But Ra-khir was married, so he was snapped up, at least at one time."

"And again soon, Tae and I believe." Matrinka bit her lower lip, her expression slightly guilty as she conveyed the gossip. "He brought his squire's widowed mother and sister from Keatoville all the way to Erythane, and he spends most of his free time with them, I understand."

Marisole considered the information. "Good. He deserves some happiness after what happened to Kevral." She knew the story well since her mother and Kevral had been close friends and had traveled with Darris, Ra-khir, and Tae. Everyone knew about the Renshai-Paradesian conflict, its outcome eventually positive thanks to the simple brilliance of King Griff. "I'm thinking more of Saviar, really. He's a strikingly handsome young man, if you like them ginger, with eyes like . . . like . . ." Marisole could think of nothing that matched their color.

"Sea foam," Matrinka filled in easily.

Marisole jerked her attention to Matrinka. Apparently, she had contemplated the beauty of a man young enough to be her son, scandalous for any woman, especially a married one with children of her own.

Her mother explained, "They're the same color as Knight-Captain Kedrin's. Surely, you've heard the playing rhymes: 'To their honor, always true. Their captain's eyes of sea-foam blue.'"

Marisole felt foolish for not thinking of that. She had studied so many songs, but that simple childhood verse had eluded her. "Most of the sea foam I've seen is white with chunks of flotsam. Saviar's eyes are more of a fierce blue as might be seen through a thick layer of ice."

"Sounds like your next musical project," Matrinka suggested.

Marisole had learned at least a hundred songs from Darris and had manufactured several from whole cloth to fulfill the whims of the bardic curse. She had not yet attempted a detailed, deliberate composition of her own, worried it might sound amateurish and immature, then get immortalized to embarrass her for all eternity. "That's all I need. A song of passion about another man."

Matrinka's brows shot up. "Saviar really impressed you."

Marisole forced herself to consider the possibility before casting the idea aside as ridiculous. "It's not often you find someone with looks, intelligence, brawn, and gentleness. He's a demon on the battlefield, quick with ideas in a crisis, speaks well, and seems so kind. What's not to love?"

Matrinka did not reach for more herbs. "Do you . . . love him?"

Marisole chuckled at the bare thought. "Under different circumstances, maybe." She could not deny an attraction, but it paled before the tidal wave of desire that assailed her whenever Barrindar was mentioned. "But not the way I love Barri. Mama, I know I'm young; but even I know the difference between lust and delight, between admiration and desire, between loving someone on a basic level and finding the man who . . . who completes you." Feeling the squeeze of the curse at her throat, Marisole stopped speaking, though she did not feel as if she were teaching anything. She added carefully, "You were younger than me when you and Darris . . ." She did not complete the sentence. "I know you love Griff, but Darris is the only one . . ."

Matrinka used Marisole's own words. ". . . who completes me. Yes. I would give my soul to him, if I haven't already." She sucked in a deep breath, loosed it, and explained. "The law would not allow you to marry Saviar, either, of course. You'd have to surrender your title and your position; but, at least you wouldn't be banished for all eternity for producing children with your brother."

Marisole did not doubt for a moment Matrinka knew those particular laws inside out and backward. "So . . . you could have married Darris if you gave up your title and left the castle." She had always assumed the consequences graver. She would happily live in squalor if Barrindar were by her side.

"Darris wouldn't allow it. He couldn't bear the thought of me suffering. I tried to assure him, but he would hear none of it. He said he would rather lose me to another man and watch from afar than condone such discomfort." Matrinka studied the floor, clearly uncomfortable with the information that followed but aware Marisole needed more. "And there was another important reason. You see, Griff's existence was unknown the last time Béarn invoked the Pica test, so the Council ran through nearly every heir. We lost so many, Darris worried the kingdom would collapse without my bloodline. Based on the absolute insistence of my marriage to Griff, apparently many others felt the same way he did."

Marisole considered her mother's words, carefully dumping the petals into a lidded vial and the stem pieces into an open bowl for dross. She rubbed her hands together to get rid of all the clinging bits, then reached for the water jar. Matrinka insisted on handwashing between various projects to avoid contamination. "Mama," she started slowly, uncertain how to word her next statement, even without the curse. She washed her hands with careful deliberation that had nothing to do with the process and everything to do with her thoughts. "They told you about Kentarial, right? He's the one who had had an unhappy marriage. Doubles of his entire family lived on the duplicate world, including himself, and he planned to watch his daughters' growing up from afar."

Matrinka nodded briskly. "I heard that story."

Marisole sighed, still reluctant to get to the crux of the matter. She set aside the water where it would not accidentally spill, then wound the drying cloth over her palms and between her fingers as she spoke. "He said he'd like to marry someone related in order to become an in-law to the girls, but he was very firm about one thing." She quoted him directly, assuming the tone of voice so as to impart the emotion as well as the words, "However, I'm not going to do anything to assure that outcome. I wouldn't trick someone into marrying me." She found herself incapable of meeting her mother's gaze.

Matrinka laid a heavy hand on Marisole's uninjured shoulder. "Your situations . . . are different. You do realize that."

Marisole shrugged just a bit, constrained by her injury on one side and not wishing to rudely dislodge her mother's hand on the other. A tear dripped down her cheek before she realized she was crying. "I just . . ." She regrouped. "The righteousness of his point was just so . . . so obvious. It's wrong to trick someone into marrying you."

Matrinka shifted, clearly trying to find a way to take Marisole into her arms. Their positions, and the precariousness of the surrounding medicinals, did not allow it. She settled for shifting her bulk to place her nearly right in front of her daughter. "Kitten, it's not the same thing at all. Kentarial was an intruder on another world where he already existed as a slightly different man. He . . . it . . ." Clearly frustrated, Matrinka finished lamely. "It's not the same at all."

Marisole understood the many differences, but none of them truly justified the dishonesty, the basic wrongness of trapping an innocent into a loveless marriage.

Apparently, Matrinka came to the same realization because she abruptly switched tacks. "In some places, marriages for love don't exist. They're arranged for convenience, for alliances, sometimes simply bought. Often, marriages are set up from the moment of birth. Mothers pray for a daughter to match with the neighbor's two-year-old son." She removed her hand from Marisole's shoulder and ducked her head to try to meet her lowered eyes. "These marriages work, Marisole. What is love other than proximity, shared experiences, and interests? Over time, nearly all couples come to love one another, their bonds unbreakable. I barely knew Griff when the

Council and the populace insisted on our marriage, yet I couldn't imagine my life without him now. I really do love him."

The last point did not impress Marisole. She finally met her mother's dark eyes. "You can afford to love him. You share your bed with the man who completes you."

Matrinka jerked backward, affronted. Even adult children did not speak of their parents' marital bed. She clamped her mouth closed, presumably to prevent herself from responding in haste, from emotion. She chewed her lip with diminishing fervor as she regained control. By the time she replied, she did so gently, without recrimination. "You're right, though you must know that bit of information never leaves this room."

"I know," Marisole reassured her. Unlike her mother, she had not managed to control her temper. "I'm sorry I . . ."

Matrinka took one of Marisole's freshly cleaned hands. "You have a valid point. I can try to put myself in your position, but I never truly can because I got unimaginably lucky."

Marisole had to make a point, and she hoped she could do it in few enough words to satisfy the curse, using information Matrinka already knew. "Barrindar and I made a foolish mistake and deserve to suffer any consequences. But Nomalan is innocent." To her relief, she got all the words out without even a mild prickle of discomfort.

Matrinka easily inferred the proper point. "I'm afraid that's the nature of consequences. People often think they're only harming themselves when they do something stupid or immoral, but that's rarely the case. Consequences expand to include everyone around you, particularly those who care the most. In particular, the baby growing inside you is entirely blameless."

Marisole closed her eyes. Knowing Matrinka spoke the truth did not make it any easier.

Matrinka squeezed Marisole's hand. "How are you and Nomalan getting along?"

Marisole found it easier to talk about that. She freed her hand to wipe her eyes, glad to find the flow of tears had already stopped. "He's nice enough. I like him, and I know he likes me. He hasn't really had a chance to do anything special. Speaking for myself, getting tossed in with the best and brightest of our world is rather intimidating under any circumstances, especially when you're young and inexperienced without a god-granted talent."

A gentle tap on the door startled Marisole. For a moment, she worried the elves had found another group of humans requiring help when she still felt exhausted from their previous excursions. Then, she remembered the *jovinay arythanik* had broken up for the evening and would not restart until after breakfast.

The door opened a crack, then a bit wider to reveal Halika's familiar head. Of Matrinka's three children, the youngest was the only one who bore a significant resemblance to Darris, her hair a full shade lighter than the others, more wavy than curly, and her build slender. "I'm supposed to call you both to supper."

"Thank you, Halika." Matrinka reached for the water jug. "We'll be right there."

Halika glanced at Marisole a moment before retreating, closing the door behind her.

Marisole rose and lidded the vial of *garlet* petals, placing it on the proper shelf. "Great. I'm starving."

Matrinka washed her hands. "Why don't you head out. I'll put things away and join you soon."

"You're sure you don't need my help with that?" Marisole asked from politeness, though she knew her mother would rebuff the offer. Matrinka preferred to perform the placement herself so she always knew exactly where to find what she wanted or needed.

As expected, Matrinka stood, shaking her head. "I'll join you very soon."

Marisole headed for the door.

Marisole had signaled Barrindar at supper to meet her in their private room, a seldom-used study on the highest floor of Béarn Castle. It had a single window and no furniture, every piece having been "borrowed" long ago by servants or various members of the family. The walls were gray stone, carved, like all of the castle, from the mountain itself but without a single remaining painting or tapestry. There was only the plush carpet that spanned the entire floor, the same one on which they had shared so many promises and secrets, where they had conceived the baby that grew inside her now.

Both of them had sneaked from their rooms after all the household staff, except the night watch, had gone to sleep. Previously, they had met any time of the day or night with little fear of reprisal. Now, they had grown even more cautious. They avoided one another, aside from passing pleasantries, shared classes, and meetings since they had learned about the pregnancy.

They sat in a far corner of the room, untouched by the moonlight slanting through the window, Marisole leaning against Barrindar's shoulder, his hand lying casually across her right thigh. She found it difficult to breathe, let alone talk. She could smell the alluring masculine scent that defined him on his sleeping gown. He nuzzled her hair, also sniffing, and his fingers tightened just a bit against her leg.

Marisole had brought him here to talk, not to find solutions that did not exist but to commiserate with him about the pain she knew they both experienced. Yet, now, she found his close silence more comforting than anything either of them might say. Her thoughts jumbled, but her mouth spoke the only words she needed to say, "I love you, Barri. I always will."

"I love you, too," he whispered directly into her ear. His breath excited her wildly. No one had ever told her the inner ear was an erogenous zone.

Marisole rolled into his lap, facing him, their mouths only a handspan apart. She could smell the herbs from the lamb on his lips, could feel the stiffening of his manhood against her inner thigh.

Barrindar went suddenly tense, though he did not pull away. "What are you doing?" he said tensely. "We can't—"

Marisole interrupted with a kiss, pressing her upper body against his until she could feel the muscles of his chest against hers, even through two thin layers of clothing. He started to respond, his tongue chasing hers inside her mouth. They remained in a passionate kiss for several moments, his fingers slipping in to massage her taut nipples. His touch sent waves of bliss through her, and desire pushed her further, shoving her chest against his questing hands, pressing her groin deeper into his lap. She wanted him with a hunger that went far beyond what she had experienced the first time.

Suddenly, Barrindar sprang to his feet, dumping her onto the rug. "Marisole, we can't do this. We're already in trouble." The moonlight outlined him, including his excitement. He wanted her as much as she did him.

Marisole rolled to her side, looking up at him teasingly. Even in the dark, she knew he could see the outlines of her nipples against her gown, which jumbled at her waist, not quite revealing places a true brother would never see. "Exactly. We're already in trouble. Why shouldn't we enjoy ourselves while we can? There's nothing more to risk." She added, running a finger along her lower lip, still wet from his kiss, "I'm already pregnant, and I'm not betrothed yet. How many more chances will we get?" She rolled onto her back.

Barrindar hesitated only a moment longer before dropping to the floor, eeling on top of her and reaching for the hem of her sleeping gown.

A knock sounded through Matrinka's chambers, so light and timid she was uncertain what had awakened her. Beside her, Darris tensed, rolling from beneath the blanket to crouch defensively between the door and the bed. Both of them remained still, ears sifting the silence. Darris had just risen and Matrinka rolled over to return to sleep, when they heard a series of two more gentle taps against the wooden door.

Darris glanced at Matrinka. Moonlight sifted through the gauzy curtains. The night was, at best, half over. She gestured toward the secret entrance that separated their rooms. "Go," she whispered.

Darris took one step toward the panel, then stopped, looking askance. "What if it's—" he started.

Matrinka waved him silent. "Assassins don't knock. Go!" She made a more enthusiastic gesture.

Swiftly, reluctantly, he slipped away, pulling the panel closed behind him.

Matrinka rose, smoothed the bed a bit, fixed her sleeping gown and checked to make certain the panel was perfectly positioned before making her way to the door. She opened it a crack. "Who is it?"

"It's me, Mama." Halika's thin voice wafted to her. "May I come in?"

Matrinka threw the door wide, beckoned her youngest daughter inside, then closed it behind her. "Of course, my love. I'm always available for you."

Without further invitation, Halika crawled into Darris' vacated spot on the bed, and Matrinka returned to her own. If Halika noticed the warmth, or any significance to it, she gave no sign. She pulled the blankets up to her chin.

Many years had passed since Halika had come to her room for comfort during a storm or after a nightmare. On those rare occasions, she used to crawl under the covers and they would talk about the problem until the fear or the thunder passed and Matrinka walked her youngest daughter back to her own quarters. In the last five years, Halika had either handled these matters herself or sought the comfort of one of her siblings instead.

Matrinka turned to face Halika, leaning on one elbow. The girl lay on her back, arms stiff at her side, staring at the ceiling. When Matrinka gave one hand a gentle squeeze, she found it clammy and trembling. "What's bothering you, my love?"

Halika drew in a deep breath, as if to speak, then loosed it slowly instead. Her fingers tightened around Matrinka's. "I saw . . . something I wasn't supposed to see."

"Something?" Matrinka asked encouragingly. She tried to keep her expression neutral, though her heartrate quickened. "Did someone . . . menace you?"

Halika shook her head, her hair rasping against the blankets. "It's not like that. I was somewhere I shouldn't have been and . . . saw it. Heard it." She sat up, leaning against the headboard. "Mama, I don't know if I should be telling you."

"You can tell me anything." Matrinka stroked the hair from Halika's forehead and eyes. "You know that."

Halika continued to focus on the ceiling. "Even if it might get someone in trouble? Someone I love?"

Concern squeezed Matrinka's heart. She tried to separate need from desire. She wanted to know what Halika had seen but did not want to obtain that information through deceit or wrongful advice. She sat up, too. "That depends. Is it something this loved one did that will get him in trouble? Or telling me about it?"

Halika considered. "Both," she finally said uncertainly. "Either." She sighed deeply. "Mama, I don't know. I'm so mixed up. I thought about talking to Arturo, but he's still recovering, and I don't want to alarm him. And Marisole . . ." She didn't seem to know how to finish that sentence.

Between the squeezing sensation and the quickening, Matrinka worried for her heart. It seemed poised to leap from her chest. "It's Marisole, isn't it?" She added carefully, wanting to put Halika at ease without revealing something that might have nothing to do with the girl's problem. If it involved the young lovers, Matrinka needed to know. "And Barrindar."

Halika jerked, turned her head to Matrinka. The expression on her face could have defined dread. "You know?"

Matrinka sighed, banning emotion from her voice and, hopefully, from her features. "Not what you saw, my love. Please tell me. It's the only way to protect them."

Halika nodded. Her brows lowered, her cheeks softened, and her eyes drooped back to their normal width. She looked almost relieved. "Mama, I didn't mean to see it. I couldn't sleep, so I went up to the old study, the one on the top floor where the furniture keeps disappearing. It has the softest rug and a soothing smell that never fails to help me sleep when I'm having difficulty."

Matrinka knew the room to which she referred, though she had not entered it in years. The finest rugs and clothing in the world were woven from special hairs combed from the wool of Eastern goats, a breed they called the *shaharin*. Several kingdoms, including Béarn, had imported *shaharin* goats, but the fleece never fully achieved the fine softness it did in the East, either due to diet, climate, or simply the process of removing the wool. The East had a special process; it was said it took weeks to properly harvest the right hairs, and they also had the most expert weavers. Household members had been removing the furniture and decorations from that room for years to replace broken or aging pieces, but no one wanted to risk ruining that gorgeous, expensive rug. Apparently, it still held the odor of exotic Eastern spices that had, apparently, traveled in the same merchant's wagon. Matrinka made a mental note to see if she could tease out the particular herb that gave off the smell that helped Halika sleep. It might assist others as well.

Oblivious to her mother's current tangent, Halika continued. "They came in while I was asleep in the darkest corner. I guess they didn't see or hear me because they started talking about loving one another in a way that didn't sound at all brotherly. I should have said something, let them know I was there, but I was confused from sleep. It took me a while to shake off a heavy dream and even remember where I was. I hadn't found my tongue yet when I heard Maris say something about being . . ." She licked her lips, obviously worried how Matrinka would react to what she might say next.

Matrinka had no doubt about the missing word. "Pregnant," she supplied.

Halika swallowed hard, then nodded, ". . . and in trouble, and I couldn't decide if it was better to let them know I was there so that they could stop talking or just stay quiet and pretend I didn't hear *anything* because I couldn't image them saying anything worse. But before I decided, they started . . . wrestling." She looked at Matrinka from the edge of her vision.

Matrinka hesitated. Halika was almost fourteen years old. Though she did not have experience with farm animals, she had certainly seen the cats in the palace copulating and likely her tutors had, at least, broached the subject. Matrinka and Halika had had a couple of conversations about where babies come from, but she had not gone into any detail about the actual physical actions involved. Still, she suspected Halika knew more than she was currently letting her mother know. "They weren't actually wrestling, were they?"

Halika sucked her lips into her mouth and avoided her mother's gaze. "I think it was . . . it had to be . . ." She clearly could not say the word. "I might have thought it if not for the odd sounds they were making. I sneaked out then, of course. I didn't know what to do." She freed her hand from Matrinka's only to enwrap it in her own and wring them on the covers. "Mama, Maris and Barri didn't really make a baby, did they? It's not possible, is it?"

Halika needed reassurance Matrinka could not give her. Clearly, she had to bring the youngster into their confidence, but it was only a temporary solution. She felt a raw, hot flash of anger at Marisole and Barrindar that faded swiftly. Their logic was hard to refute. They had only a couple of weeks to sort out their love before circumstances made it utterly and permanently impossible. They had probably gone to great lengths to keep their conversation and actions private and clearly had no idea Halika had seen and heard them. Matrinka understood, but Darris would not. She had no idea how Griff, Xoraida, and Tem'aree'ay would react. *Not well, understandably.* Only her desire to keep Halika guileless had kept her own anger and sorrow in check.

Matrinka wrapped her arms around her daughter and drew her close, wishing she had some magic way to restore her innocence. She did not deserve this burden. "Halika, thank you for telling me. I'm going to find a way to fix this, I promise. In the meantime, can you keep this terrible secret between the two of us?"

Matrinka could feel her daughter's tears soaking through her sleeping gown and onto her chest. She managed a nod.

"If you need to say something to someone, please come only to me or Marisole, and make absolutely sure we're alone." Matrinka knew Halika would heed that warning far more seriously after the mistake Marisole and Barrindar had made. "Can you do that?"

"I can," Halika said in a whisper muffled against Matrinka. "I don't want to talk about it, though. Not to anyone. Not ever."

Matrinka ran her hands up and down Halika's back in soothing motions, rocking ever so slightly. Griff's solution had seemed foolproof, logically flawless, but it had not taken into account the driving need that defined true love. Nor would it assuage Halika. Bad enough one daughter in eternal agony; Matrinka could never live with two. *Marisole and Barrindar made a terrible error, and they must live with the consequences.* It did not ring wholly true. *But none of this would have happened had I, Darris, and Griff not made one equally bad first.*

Suddenly, Matrinka knew exactly what she needed to do.

CHAPTER 16

Judging honor in hindsight is only condemnation.
—*Colbey Calistinsson*

PLAGUED BY MEMORIES AND CONCERNS, Saviar tossed and turned much of the night, so the call to action caught him half-way to the great hall. He quickened his pace, bursting into the room to find all eyes on him and the rest of the team assembled. Muttering apologies to everyone, but especially to his frowning father, he joined them; and the elves started their chant as soon as he took his place.

With a hand on *Motfrabelonning*'s hilt, Saviar watched hundreds of auras flare, bathing the entire room in crazy, echoing lights of myriad colors. The gate winked into existence almost immediately, in its usual location and looking even more solid than its predecessors. Saviar wondered if that had to do with more elves joining the *jovinay arythanik*, with repetition of a familiar task, or with improving collaboration between elves, *Kjempemagiska*, and Mages of Myrcidë. He could not help considering whether the growing cooperation of this unlikely triumvirate of magic might finally herald an end to the human conflicts of the continent as well, particularly the ingrained hatred for Renshai. It seemed like too much to hope for, but it did send his thoughts back to the cheers Valr Magnus had elicited when he named Saviar as the North's champion as well as representing his own people.

Ra-khir went first through the gate, Saviar on his heels. Before the others could follow, elves rushed in from the opposite side, plowing into Nomalan and Marisole in their haste. Apparently worried all the elves on the Outworld might dash through before they could get one on the other side, Chan'rék'ril shoved through the line of would-be escapees to join Saviar, Ra-khir, and a mixed group of elfin and human soldiers. A few more elves and even a couple of humans forced their way to the Midgard side before Nomalan, then Marisole and Tae arrived with Imorelda. By the time El-brinith managed to daintily elbow her way through the gate, only a single nervous elf, an elderly woman, a young Renshai male Saviar knew as Gazzinal, and an Eastern soldier remained in a stony, oblong clearing bounded by mountains so tall they disappeared into the clouds. A large heap of what appeared to be clothing lay at the opposite end.

Saviar drew his sword, searching for whatever threat had so terrorized the others they could not wait, but he saw nothing moving other than the three humans, one elf, and his companions.

"What's the story?" Tae demanded of the Easterner, while Saviar studied the elder. As far as he knew, the only female warriors on Midgard were the bard of Béarn and about half of the Renshai.

The Eastern soldier gestured toward a rocky cliff base, his gaze flicking from the indicated area to the wide-open gateway that would rescue him from this world. "Sire, a cave opens. One of us walks in. It closes." He was using as few words as possible, clearly trying to make his point as swiftly as he could so he could leave. "Once he's inside, a different cave opens over there and leaves what's left of the last person who entered."

"What's left?" Ra-khir repeated. His brows rose. "You mean he's dead."

"More often than not," the Easterner said, licking his lips in nervous motions and glancing toward the pile Saviar had first believed was clothing. "Or changed in some terrible way." Now, he glanced toward the old woman.

Ra-khir ran over to the mound. "They're dead," he announced. "Nine or ten at least."

The Easterner shook his head. "Not all dead."

Ra-khir added suddenly, as if in response, though he could not have heard the Easterner's soft voice from that distance. "Wait, some are alive. By the gods!"

Saviar wanted to look, but he was suddenly captivated by the woman. She seemed strangely familiar.

The Easterner shouted, "It's opening!"

All of the rescuers whirled toward the indicated mountain. A cavelike hole was taking form in the stone like a black maw.

"No one go inside!" Ra-khir shouted.

Everyone froze in place, but the Easterner shook his head sadly. "If no one goes in, it chooses someone."

Suddenly, Marisole screamed. She fell to the ground, writhing, as if fighting an unseen enemy. Some invisible force dragged her toward the cave.

Saviar moved first, seizing Marisole's arms. Something strong tugged against him with a force he did not have the strength or bulk to counter. He grabbed her tighter, wrapping his arms fully around her, but the force continued to tug her toward the opening, dragging Saviar with her. It heaved him to the ground, still clinging, scraping his extremities along the rocks, tearing his clothing and skin.

Chan'rék'ril, El-brinith, Ra-khir, and Tae ran to assist Saviar; but Nomalan was faster and closer. He darted into the cave mouth. "No!" Marisole shouted, too late. The opening shut off as swiftly as a snuffed torch, with Nomalan inside it. The instant it did, the force dragging Marisole toward it entirely disappeared. Saviar released Marisole and leaped to his feet, pounding his sword against the rock that had, a moment earlier, gaped open. Pain jarred through his arms with each strike. A lesser weapon would have shattered, but *Motfrabelloning* remained unsullied, the haft quivering in his grip.

It cannot be denied. The remaining elf used *khohlar*, either from habit or because he did not speak the common trading tongue. *If no one goes in voluntarily, it claims someone with magic far too powerful to resist.*

Around the corner from the first opening, another formed. Saviar ran toward it, prepared to face whatever emerged, and found the Easterner at his side. "It'll be Jharik. If he's still alive, don't hurt him."

A bedraggled man staggered out of the mountain. He clutched his chest as he moved stiffly into the clearing, eyes wide and rolling like a terrified animal's, his hair and clothing in chaotic knots, beyond windswept. As the Easterner ran past Saviar, Jharik collapsed into his arms, gibbering and sobbing like a man possessed. The Easterner clutched Jharik, patting his back soothingly and whispering something into the other man's ear. The door in the rocks winked out of existence.

The elf took over the explanation, apparently realizing *khohlar* allowed for swifter and fuller points. *The next victim has to go in before the previous one is released. This assures there is always someone trapped inside. If two try to enter, the door disappears behind the first. If they go in simultaneously, they both become trapped, but only one comes out at a time.*

Tae examined the rock, running his fingers over the edges where the opening had been, tapping it, studying it minutely. Shortly, he stepped back, shaking his head, then moved to check the exit from which Jharik had emerged.

"What happens inside?" Ra-khir asked, watching Tae. Imorelda leaned forward to bat at the rock with her paws as her master inspected it.

We don't know. Most come out dead, and those who've survived are changed in some negative way: some entirely insane, some missing body parts, Emissonr there. He waved at the elder.

Recognizing the name, Saviar jerked his attention back to the old woman. He knew a Renshai warrior called Emmissonr, a woman in her late twenties of great skill. The shriveled figure standing beside Gazzinal did bear a dogged resemblance to her grandmother. *Every elf who went in, whether voluntarily or forced, came out dead. Several of the humans have protected us, which we greatly appreciate.* He added raw waves of thanks through his sending, so much stronger than words. *They went in, so we did not have to. Yet, anyway; it seems determined to have us all. We banded together and tried to fight the magic of the cave, but it's much too strong. It's the work of a god or powerful demon.*

Apparently finding nothing useful, Tae returned to the group, Imorelda still perched on his shoulders. "We need to leave immediately." He herded the others toward the gate.

"Not without Nomalan," Marisole stated firmly. "We're not going to abandon him."

"Of course not," Ra-khir reassured her. "We'll wait until he comes out, then bring him home."

The unnamed elf pointed out the flaw in Ra-khir's plan. *Except someone else has to go in before it will release your friend.*

That shut Ra-khir up, but only for a moment. "Everyone except me can leave."

"You and me," Chan'rék'ril added. "An elf has to be the last one off-world. Otherwise, the gate will close."

Saviar saw the problem immediately. No matter how they arranged the escape, someone got left behind and, ultimately, it had to be an elf. They needed a coherent plan, one that would take time to form. The cave mouth opened. *Time we don't have.* He stared into the pitch-black maw and felt as much excitement as fear. *I'm the best equipped to survive whatever dwells within.* Before anyone could stop him, Saviar raced toward the opening.

"Saviar, no!" Ra-khir shouted. He heard other calls at his back, loud, shrieking, beseeching. Then the door disappeared behind him, and Saviar heard nothing more of his companions.

Saviar found himself in a vast room with paneled walls, not the least bit cavelike: dry, unweathered, and neutral in temperature. Sword in hand, he noticed colored auras reflected from every part of the room, scattered into tiny rainbows, reminding him everything was magical and nothing truly real. The room appeared empty except for something at the far end that outshone even the impossible walls, floor, and ceiling. Without hesitation, he headed toward it.

As Saviar drew closer, the thing of great brightness became more obviously a figure. It stood as tall as Kentt but without the relatively normal human proportions. A lizardlike tail curled around clawed legs, and its arms and hands looked more reptilian than human: short, closely-set, four-fingered with spiky nails. It had a long, slender neck with a relatively small triangular head perched atop it. Enormous eyes, pointed ears, and wide nostrils on the end of a scaled snout completed the picture.

Without hesitation, Saviar sallied toward it, prepared to strike its demonic head from its serpentine neck. Even as he moved, magic flared between them. He slammed full-run into an invisible barrier. Pain shot through his nose, stars filled his vision, and he tasted blood. Bounced backward, he had to take several small steps to regain his balance during which he kept his sword raised and what remained of his gaze locked on the creature in front of him. It did not appear to have moved.

The barrier remained clear as polished glass, but Saviar's grip on *Motfrabelonning* revealed its aura, a faint orange glow spanning from wall to wall. His nose and eye ridges throbbed, along with his left knee and shoulder; but he was trained to ignore pain in battle unless it threatened to incapacitate if not immediately tended. It would do no good to pound on the obstacle. The impact had made it obvious he could not burst through it physically, and he could see he could not go around it. He waited, prepared for anything and taking some solace in the belief the creature could not get to him, either.

As if to prove him wrong, Saviar felt a tickle inside his head. Having become more accustomed to *khohlar*, he anticipated words filling his mind and steeled himself to listen without allowing the voice to distract him. But, instead of speaking, the presence probed him, searching the deepest corners of his thoughts. He took another backward step, hand clenched to his hilt, seeking some way to expel the intruder. Short of stabbing his own face, he could think of nothing useful; and, as that would kill him, he did not attempt it. He fought to muster his thoughts like physical weapons, but they refused to organize in any corporeal manner. The being groped through dark recesses of his mind unimpeded while Saviar found himself incapable of any action other than examining and impotently attacking the invisible wall. "Get out!" he screamed. "Get out of my head!"

Saviar saw no reaction other than a slight smile raising the corners of the creature's lips to reveal the fangs beneath them. Then the thing in his mind seized it, upending his thoughts and reason, and he found himself locked in a tense *svergelse* against maneuvers he recognized as Renshai. Though hard-pressed to his defense, details trickled in to fill the blanks. The lithe, black-haired figure sparring with him was his beloved twin, Subikahn. His blood boiled with anger, most of it from other sources, Subikahn's taunts bringing it to the fore and making this battle too important to lose. They had selected a would-be fatal touch as the endpoint, the proof for which of them was the superior swordsman.

Saviar knew their battle had raged for some time. At the moment, he found himself wholly on the defensive, backstepping repeatedly as his brother's superior strength hammered him into a patch of nettles. As the needles stabbed the backs of his legs, he managed a desperate lunge for Subikahn's gut. His foot mired in detritus, sending his stroke low and opening his upper defenses. Subikahn's sword slammed his ribs, tossing him helplessly into the stinging plants. His own blade jarred through flesh, turned aside by bone, then was ripped from his hands as Subikahn staggered and fell.

Horror seized Saviar, like icy fingers reaching through him to dull all the fire that had previously filled his blood. He ran to his brother to find his sword jammed through Subikahn's thigh nearly to the hilt, the tip of the blade emerging from the opposite side. Blood seeped from the wound, dripping onto the wooded ground.

Emotions paraded through Saviar as he knelt to help his brother: guilt, terror, confusion, and self-loathing at the fore. He had done the unforgivable, goading his brother into a confrontation without a nearby *torke* to prevent such dangerous mistakes. It was forbidden for Renshai to spar others so evenly matched without a benign endpoint or an instructor able to step in and prevent the exact accident they dealt with now. A truly competent Renshai could pull or reroute any stroke, no matter how dedicated. They practiced with live steel knowing that to seriously injure a valued ally in *svergelse* was anathema.

And Saviar had not only done so, but the victim was his twin, the one person in the world he loved more than any other, more than life itself. The agony of that mistake was nearly beyond bearing.

The moments that passed as Saviar attempted to undo as much as he could of the unthinkable became a blur that passed into several days. The wound had started to heal, then festered, and it soon became apparent Subikahn would not survive much longer. They had tried every antidote either of them knew without success. Wracked by fever and weakness, it took every bit of Subikahn's strength just to stand and demand the battle to the death every Renshai deserved, that every other Renshai was honor-bound to inflict. To die of illness, age or injury meant a soul damned to the frozen pits of Hel.

Calistin had killed several Renshai; those nearing death often chose him as their salvation, trusting him to judge their condition and flagging abilities, to give them just enough of a battle before slaying them to assure one of the Valkyries escorted their dying spirit to Valhalla. Calistin also had a unique ability to determine if the Valkyrie had come, thus allowing the dead warrior's name to be placed on the list for future children. All Renshai babies became the ward of a deceased hero whose soul would look down on and protect them, reminding them to fight valiantly for the ultimate reward of joining their namesake in Valhalla. Of all the Renshai, Calistin was the most often chosen for what the tribe considered a great and difficult distinction.

No one had ever attacked Saviar in the hope he would prevent their ignoble death. He had never killed a Renshai warrior before, particularly one to whom he felt such an awesome attachment. But Subikahn needed to die in battle; all Renshai did. Saviar was the only one who could assure Subikahn's soul found Valhalla, to rescue him from an eternity in Hel.

Subikahn raised his sword, fighting for balance. Sepsis glazed his eyes, and he looked fragile as a blown glass figurine.

Saviar prepared for battle as a myriad thoughts battered his mind, all demanding access. How did one impale one's most beloved? How could he kill his own brother? Nearly two decades of Renshai training, knowledge and lore told him he not only could, but he must. Honor demanded he allow his brother the bliss Valhalla promised; but the idea of thrusting a weapon through Subikahn made him want to vomit. Was it barely possible they might stumble upon something, an herb, a healer, an elf before the blood poisoning wholly claimed him? What if Subikahn's body had one last rally that could overcome the infection which had been slowly claiming him over the last few days? If Saviar killed him, then discovered a means of rescue, he would prefer to die rather than live with the knowledge he had taken Subikahn's life even a moment prematurely.

Saviar fought these doubts with steady resilience. Similar thoughts had made him wait as long as he had. His eyes and mind told him the truth. If he did not fight Subikahn now, his brother would succumb, if not to death than to coma. Once he did, he would lose any opportunity to die in combat. He would drift away, his spirit claimed by Hel herself and doomed to an eternity of sloth and horror.

"Come at me!" Saviar shouted, as if he truly anticipated the fight of his life, even as he prepared to finesse, to give Subikahn enough time to attempt as many attacks as his strength allowed. Saviar would grant the Valkyries and gods a show, try his best to draw out every bit of mental and physical ability and energy Subikahn's failing body still possessed before delivering the killing stroke in the hope it would prove enough to earn him a right to spend his afterlife in Valhalla.

Saviar made it look as dangerous as possible, even as he realized he had never fought a battle so simple. Subikahn managed half a dozen strikes, none of which truly menaced a skilled Renshai but every one of which could have taken a life under other circumstances. Only when Subikahn dropped to his knees, winded and powerless, did Saviar thrust his blade between Subikahn's ribs and into his chest, assuring a quick and painless death.

It took power to drive a sword through flesh, and Saviar felt suddenly weak as a rag doll. He bulled through the thrust from training more than desire, feeling the familiar glide of flesh parting before perfectly honed and tended steel. Pain seared his own chest, as if the weapon cut through him as well as Subikahn, carving through skin and muscle to pierce his heart. Terrible grief and loathing overcame him. He heard himself howling in agony, overcome by unbearable loss. Every part of him became wet, then icy cold, other than the fiery pain in his chest.

Saviar wiped moisture from his eyes, a mixture of sweat and snot and tears. Images flitted through his mind of a life without his brother; the Fields of Wrath empty and strange, his innermost thoughts unshared, unspoken, the void left by the absence of his friend and confidante. Gently, he extracted his sword from his brother's body and dared to look upon it. Subikahn wore a blissful smile, his eyes closed, the breeze tugging at his inky hair as if to grant passage to one who would never move again.

Saviar forced a grin of his own. *Valhalla.* He felt certain Subikahn had reached it and took solace in the realization he had gone to the best imaginable place. One day, if he proved himself as courageous, Saviar would join his twin there for an eternity that would make their life in Midgard seem short and colorless in comparison. *Valhalla!* Suddenly remembering his brother carried a magical sword that allowed him to see Valkyries, he eased Subikahn's weapon from its sheath. A weapon in each hand, Saviar watched as a glorious, golden figure stepped toward Subikahn's prone body, saw his spirit rise to meet her.

A smile wreathed Saviar's face as he watched the Valkyrie approach. Even as he did, his mind faltered. Something was terribly wrong with the image. Motfrabelloning *is my sword, not Subikahn's.* That realization brought the world into different focus. Saviar fell to the ground, pain shooting through his knees. Instead of two swords, he held only *Motfrabelonning*, instinctively raised to guard the area between himself and any enemies. Subikahn's body disappeared, as did the woodland setting and the Valkyrie. Saviar found himself alone in a rocky clearing surrounded by the tallest mountains he could ever remember seeing. He scrambled to his feet and whirled.

With sword in hand, he could easily see the colorful, rectangular magic that defined the elfin gate. The only other being on the plane was the elderly woman they had called Emissonr. Saviar remained in place, utterly confused. Had he really killed Subikahn? He studied *Motfrabelonning.* The pristine blade showed no evidence of recent use, no blood, no entrails, not even a foggy line of condensation. His nose and eye ridges still ached a bit, along with his left shoulder and knee. When he rubbed beneath his nose, tacky blood stuck to his fingers. The crash into a clear, magical barrier had been real. Everything else, it seemed, had occurred only in his mind.

"Saviar." Emissonr's tone suggested she had already called him several times. "You need to come with me before—"

The abrupt break made Saviar suspicious. He wiped blood from under his nose onto his sleeve. It hurt, but not enough to be broken. Nothing made sense. The gate remained open, and only he and Emissonr remained. He spoke the next thought aloud. "You're an elf?"

Emissonr's brow creased beyond the permanently etched wrinkles of old age, and her eyes narrowed. "An elf? What's wrong with you, Saviar? I'm Emissonr. You know I'm Renshai. Now, hurry up or you'll ruin everything! We'll be trapped here." She ran to his side and grabbed his arm. Her tug was so slight, he barely noticed it. He took a single step toward the gate.

The opening in the mountain reappeared.

Emissonr gasped and pulled harder. "It's too late!"

Auras swept the plane, and Saviar felt the tingle of magic as something searched the stone clearing. Frustration touched his mind, then disappeared so quickly Saviar wondered if he had imagined it. His thoughts remained muddled, not wholly able to separate reality from fantasy. Then, the door snapped shut, and the other one opened. Chan'rék'ril emerged, looking no different than usual, his canted yellow eyes bright with determination, his elfin features oddly stolid for one of his ilk.

Emissonr stopped pulling, though she still clutched Saviar's arm, staring at the elf and blinking her rheumy eyes, clearly shocked to see him standing there. "You lived."

"I lived," Chan'rék'ril repeated.

Saviar looked from one to the other, still confused. "I don't understand."

Chan'rék'ril explained, "We couldn't stay because the demon or god of the mountain would continue to keep someone entrapped until every one of us had been tested. Based on the deaths and the terrible state of those who survived, we surmised the test forced each victim to experience his greatest fear. For most humans, that's death of one kind or another; so most of those who entered died. For others, madness or the deaths of loved ones, incapacitation or disfigurements actually worry them more than death itself." He turned Emissonr a sympathetic glance. Like most Renshai, she embraced death; her fear must have been becoming old instead of dying young in battle.

Saviar understood the common dichotomy of the Renshai way, one Colbey Calistinsson had lamented before he discovered his immortality. Becoming the best swordsmaster in existence meant surviving every battle; yet, to earn Valhalla, one had to die embroiled in combat. Saviar supposed many Renshai secretly feared becoming so competent they rendered their own death in war impossible and assured a cowardly one from age or illness instead.

Chan'rék'ril continued, clearly in none of the hurry that had driven Emissonr moments earlier. Her hand dropped away from Saviar. "For all elves, it's dying prematurely and permanently depriving us of a soul. Therefore, every elf who entered necessarily died. It became clear to me an elf had to be the last one tested. So long as that elf remained alive, the gate would stay open and you could leave. We left Emissonr behind because, of all the ones previously tested, she was the most capable of rushing you through the gate before the testing killed me, forever closing it. We correctly surmised the demon or god in charge would only demand one testing per individual; but Emissonr was willing to sacrifice herself if that did not prove to be the case."

Emissonr shrugged. "You have so much more to live for than I do now." She studied her weathered hands with a gaze that epitomized regret.

Saviar did not know what to say. He had no idea how to comfort someone who had lost nearly all the years of her life. He could see why she had feared it even more than death. What surprised him more was his own test. He had, apparently, relived Subikahn's struggle from his twin's point of view. Apparently, at the moment, his biggest fear was that he would react the same way Subikahn had, that his cowardice would doom the person he loved most in the world to Hel. A spark of anger rose within him. Unlike Subikahn, he had not relegated his twin's soul to Hel. He had done what needed doing.

One question remained in Saviar's mind. "Chan'rék'ril, you just told us all elves who undergo this test must necessarily die, yet here you are." The thought that struck Saviar next awed him. "Did you . . . find a way . . . to kill that demon?"

For an instant, Chan'rék'ril hesitated. He could lie, Saviar supposed. If he answered "yes," no one would ever know the truth, and he would earn the admiration of every Northman and Renshai, at least, and probably every being on Midgard. Saviar would feel indebted and embarrassed by his own failure to achieve the same result. The demon had manipulated him effortlessly.

"No," Chan'rék'ril admitted. "I volunteered to stay because, as the only soulless elf, my death would not affect my people. And it was precisely because of this realization I survived the test. I have already come to grips with the knowledge that my life or death is meaningless. Apparently . . ." Wistfulness entered his tone. ". . . that makes me Midgard's one truly fearless being."

CHAPTER 17

Integrity dictates that a man do the right thing even when it becomes inconvenient, even when it will result in the loss of one's own life.

—*Knight-Captain Kedrin*

THOUGH PAINTED IN CHEERFUL BLUES AND YELLOWS, Matrinka's room seemed grim and gray, sullied by the events of the last several months and the terrible thoughts accompanying them. She sat bolt upright on top of her blankets, Imorelda and the kittens in her lap. She stroked them incessantly, seeking the solace that usually accompanied that action, but, this time, it eluded her.

Nomalan was dead, along with several other soldiers sent to the testing Outworld, but his demise seemed all the more tragic because he had arrived with the liberators to save them. Everyone had braced for the fact that many or all of those blown to the Outworlds would never return, so the rescue of many overshadowed the loss of a few. But the heroic volunteers who risked their own lives to bring home those already gone should be untouchable, at least in Matrinka's mind. The loss of even one, rightly or wrongly, seemed so much more devastating. Nomalan's death, in particular, was personal on so many levels: a kind and competent man, the future son-in-law and father of her grandchildren, a cousin she had known since his birth; and, of course, the vital element in an elaborate and necessary plan.

A solid knock on the door barely stirred Matrinka from her solemn thoughts. She had sent for Marisole, so she called out, "Come in, kitten."

The door edged open, and Barrindar's bearded face poked through it, eyes tightly shut. "It's me, my lady. Is it all right if I enter instead?"

Matrinka sat up straighter; but, as she was decently dressed, she did nothing more. "Of course, Barri. Please come in, and shut the door behind you."

Barrindar did as the queen requested. Slowly, one at a time, he opened his eyes, then waited until she gestured toward a chair before seating himself. He fidgeted a bit, clearly uncomfortable meeting with Matrinka inside her bedchamber. "I know you were expecting Marisole, but she asked me to come in her stead. I hope that's all right."

Matrinka nodded, trying to guess Marisole's motivation. Decades of experience suggested her bardic daughter would have difficulty communicating the score of emotions assailing her, particularly when her curse limited her to musical explanations. "I imagine she's having trouble putting her thoughts and feelings into song. Did she manage to convey them to you?"

Barrindar studied Matrinka's expression as he answered, clearly worried he might offend. "She had planned to speak about it with you as well as me, but it proved a lot more difficult than she expected. I thought it best she try to rest or, at least, organize her thoughts and emotions before attempting to explain them again." He smiled conspiratorially. "I knew you, of all people, would understand."

Matrinka grinned as well, trying to reassure. "I do understand. Thank you for coming in her place."

Barrindar bowed his head briefly in respect.

Matrinka continued to stroke Imorelda, for once swiftly and intently enough the cat did not beg for more attention or even rub against her. "How did Nomalan . . ." She found the next word sticking to her tongue. As a healer, she had used it many times before in terrible situations; but, this time, it clung. ". . . die?"

Barrindar swallowed before speaking, as if this simple action could assist Matrinka with her own problem. "It would appear he drowned. From what I understand, the magical creature ruling that Outworld forced their greatest fear upon each person who confronted him. When Nomalan was three or four years old, he fell off the dock and inhaled a lot of water before his guardians could save him. He always had an excuse for not joining the cousins when we frolicked in the surf, and he once told me the reason in confidence. He never did learn to swim."

"I'm sorry," Matrinka said, the words emerging thickly. "He was a good man as well as a friend."

"One of the best," Barrindar admitted. "I was glad when Marisole chose him. Béarn is made poorer by his loss."

A few moments of silence passed between them before Matrinka said, "How is Marisole?"

"Sad." Barrindar said in a single word what would have taken Marisole at least twenty, accompanied by the most mournful tones any musical instrument could manufacture. "And guilt-riddled."

Matrinka thought she understood. "For bringing him along."

"That," Barrindar confirmed. "And also because she was the one the guardian of the Outworld had chosen to next undergo his test. Nomalan ran in bravely to take her place."

Matrinka made a pained noise. "Doubly the hero, then. He saved the life of my daughter."

"Quite likely." Barrindar shuffled his feet from his chair. "Marisole isn't entirely sure what her greatest fear is. She thinks it might be living her life without . . ." He clearly sought the right words, shook his head, then settled for, ". . . true intimacy. She worries she fears that even more than death, which means she would have survived the test had Nomalan not taken her place. She's concerned he died for nothing and it's her fault."

Matrinka could not help wincing. It was a heavy burden for anyone to bear, especially a young woman already wrestling with a god-created curse and saddled with protecting the life of the future king. If things worked out as Matrinka expected, Marisole would have to spend her life serving as the adviser and bodyguard of her one true love, forever forbidden to her in any other capacity. "Would the effects of the test carry over into our world? Because I would call rescuing anyone from a life devoid of intimacy a true act of heroism."

Barrindar did not address the intimacy issue, though it involved him as deeply as Marisole. Instead, he went to the crux of the question. "It would appear some effects do carry over. A warrior from the North feared amputation more than death, and his leg did not reappear on our side of the gate. One Renshai feared old age, and she is still elderly. Several apparently feared lunacy, or else facing their greatest fears turned them mad, and their sanity has not returned. Of course, none of the dead have come back to life."

Barrindar shook his head sadly. "However, the elves do not believe the demon or god in charge of the Outworld can affect events that take place after the testing or outside of his domain. Some of his victims faced hypothetical futures or situations; and, having conquered them, moved on without apparent effect. For example, one Béarnide most feared for the lives of his children. In his mind, they died, and he had to cope with the loss. When he returned to Midgard, he found them safely at home." He smiled again, this time broadly. "Never have I seen a man so relieved and happy. The elves believe that, had he responded to the perceived loss with suicide during his testing, he would have been found dead of a self-inflicted wound. Instead, he suffered his grief and survived."

Matrinka understood enough. She did not need or want any more details. "Did the rescuers know all this when they first arrived?"

"None of it." Barrindar's grin wilted.

"So Marisole could not possibly have known Nomalan was sacrificing his life for her happiness." Matrinka reasoned aloud. "She has every right and reason to suffer grief, but guilt is not warranted. It will only do her harm."

Barrindar nodded. "Quite right, and I told her that. But she pointed out Nomalan would never have been on that Outworld if she had not induced him to join the rescue party. And her reasons for doing that were, in her words: 'deceptive and self-serving.'"

Matrinka's petting grew even fiercer, if possible. Dislodged silver agouti hairs floated into the air. "All of us had a hand in that deception, and it was for the greater good."

Barrindar would not contradict the queen.

Matrinka met his gaze, suddenly tortured by the same guilt as her daughter. "Wasn't it?"

"I believe so," Barrindar assured her. "But I'm not sure Marisole ever will. Either way, she will have to learn to live with what happened because Nomalan is dead and the past cannot be undone."

While Matrinka considered his words, Barrindar spoke into the silence. "Perhaps it would be best if we pulled Marisole from the rescue group while she deals with these issues."

Matrinka appreciated Barrindar's suggestion. She wanted nothing more, knowing how such feelings had caused the death of many soldiers. Those who watched their friends die often became wracked with a guilt so intense they became heedless of their own safety. She worried for Marisole but did not know if she could explain the problem in a way the others would fully appreciate the danger rather than just dismiss her fears as motherly concern for her daughter. With Barrindar on her side, she had a chance of talking Marisole into remaining behind, at least for the next few rescue attempts.

Matrinka wanted to say so much more to Barrindar: how she understood the love her daughter felt for him and him for her, how she believed him not only the proper next king of Béarn but also the perfect husband for her beloved daughter; but she knew she could not and should not. Instead, she asked softly, as much for herself as Barrindar, "What will we do now?"

Barrindar sucked in a deep breath, then let it out through his nose in increments. "I thought perhaps we could still claim the baby as Nomalan's."

It was not exactly what Matrinka had meant, but she thought over his suggestion. Focused so intently on the tragic loss of life, she had not, until that moment, considered the need for a new plan now that King Griff's carefully laid one had unraveled. Though still dishonest, the idea had merit. Illegitimacy would taint the baby and Marisole, but not enough to force either from the palace since the father was a proper heir of Béarn. The Pica test had rendered the order of ascension moot as the magical stone chose the next king or queen. Higher placement in the testing order had some advantages if more than one heir proved competent; but failing the test had such dire consequences, in most cases, that it was not unusual for potential heirs to give up their turns to those more eager.

It was not entirely fair to Nomalan to tarnish his memory in this fashion, but it seemed more prudent than losing Barrindar and Marisole. The dead did not suffer embarrassment, and Matrinka guessed his parents would come to appreciate the existence of the infant as an echo of their lost son.

Apparently, Matrinka's thoughts radiated because Imorelda replied directly to them. *Except it would be a lie.*

Yes, Matrinka admitted. *A lie that might ease their suffering a bit, but still a lie.* She studied Barrindar. His face looked so young, yet his dark eyes seemed to have aged a decade since the announcement of the baby. She harbored no doubt he loved Marisole as much as she loved him, but she had to be sure. "Barrindar, if you did not have to follow the will of the king, what would you choose to do?"

Barrindar chewed his lower lip and looked at the floor. "I must defer to the wisdom of my elders. King Griff and Queen Matrinka know best, and I will do as you tell me, no matter the cost."

Matrinka delicately shifted the cat and kittens from her lap, rose, and left the bed. She walked to Barrindar and stood over his chair. When he did not look up, she put a hand on each cheek and tilted his face up to meet her gaze. "Let's say we decided to place the decision in your hands. What would you do?"

Barrindar met the queen's stare. "I would still do as you bade me. The king's wisdom is ultimate and legend, and he is correct. I won't put others' lives or well-being at risk for my own happiness."

Matrinka should have expected no other answer. She thought back to the plan she had considered the previous night, after talking to Marisole and then Halika. A fine point of law had delayed her from putting it into action this morning, but Barrindar's suggestion had given her a way around the problem. Before she exercised a dangerous possibility, though, she needed to assure herself her reasons were sound. She had to know exactly how Barrindar felt. "Let us suppose no other lives or well-beings were at risk, only your own. What does your heart tell you to do?"

Barrindar continued to look directly into the queen's eyes. "I have no doubt I love Marisole in a way I could never love another. She is my life, and the baby, *our baby*, is a blessing. I would abdicate any claim to the throne in a heartbeat and gladly leave Béarn to spend my life with Marisole and our child." He added carefully, "But, as lives and well-beings do hang in the balance, I know that can never be." Pain filled his eyes, and his jaw clamped shut.

Matrinka knew he spoke the truth. She released him and headed back toward the bed, this time perching on the edge. Imorelda remained in the center, still purring from her recent stroking. The kittens made tiny noises as they searched her belly for their breakfast. "Thank you for coming, Barrindar." She added, trying to sound calm and emotionless, "Would you mind letting the Council know I'd like a meeting with them this afternoon at their convenience?"

Though Barrindar did not share Darris' and Marisole's bardic curiosity, he did tip his head in question. He did not speak, however. The queen might have many reasons to call a meeting of the Council, most of them routine. Likely, he would assume she was arranging Marisole's reprieve from the rescue team, although normally she would discuss the matter with Griff and he would handle it further.

Matrinka continued, to steal all emphasis from her request. "Afterward, I'd appreciate whatever comfort you can give Marisole in this difficult situation. I'm confident you can do that better than anyone; but, if she changes her mind about talking to me, let me know. If she doesn't wish to come to me, I can always come to her; but I won't intrude on her solitude if that's what she prefers." She immediately saw the flaw in what she intended as a gesture of goodwill. "Of course, if you think I'm needed, if her desire to be alone has become unhealthy or obsessive, call me at once."

Barrindar gave a small bow. His own status did not require it, but it demonstrated his respect and appreciation. "She's a strong, intelligent woman; she's handling the situation as well as anyone could expect." He added, almost conspiratorially, "Singing her troubles to me drained her emotionally, and I just think she preferred not to have to perform something so painful twice in succession."

Matrinka managed a smile. "I understand." She also suspected

Marisole had sent Barrindar because she wanted her lover and her mother to spend time alone together, hopefully to bond.

Their business finished, Barrindar headed from the room, closing the door behind him.

Matrinka returned to the bed and absently gathered Imorelda into her lap, forgetting about the kittens until they mewed their protestations. Her gaze blindly fixed on the door, Matrinka scooped them up and added them to the pile. She stroked their mother, her mind distant.

What are you up to? Imorelda asked with clear suspicion as she rearranged the kittens.

Righting a wrong. Matrinka sent back, jaw set, hands balled into fists of determination.

Imorelda regarded her fixedly. *Be careful.*

Matrinka hesitated. She did not understand. *Careful of what, my friend? You don't even know what I'm planning to do.*

No, the cat admitted. *But I have found when humans commit themselves to righteousness, they often blunder into otherwise obvious danger. And, sometimes, the wrong they create is worse than the one they right.*

Matrinka did not believe that was the case. She had considered the situation for a long time, in some ways for the majority of her life. She sought words to assure the cat. Before she could speak them, someone knocked on the door. Knowing it would be a page sent to tell her the Council had gathered to meet her, she rose and headed for the door. "It'll be all right," was all she managed before slipping out of the room, leaving the door ajar so Imorelda and her kittens would not become trapped. *Everything will be all right.*

Matrinka felt a twinge of discomfort and uncertainty radiating from Imorelda before she moved beyond range of mental communication.

The Council of Béarn confined Matrinka to her quarters, placing a guard at the entrance and insisting she knock at her door for any assistance. As she had anticipated being locked in a dungeon cell, this arrangement surprised and pleased her at first. In her absence, Imorelda and the kittens had left, and she found herself wholly alone. In the past, she had considered her room a sanctuary. She enjoyed some alone time to nap or read or simply rearrange her belongings or her thoughts. Now, oddly, within moments it truly felt like a prison.

Matrinka went to the window and opened the shutters, immediately barraged by the early winter wind. For several moments, she allowed the cold to wash over her as she viewed the grounds five stories below. The gardens lay fallow, the benches empty, the stone statues that were the pride and joy of Béarn looking lumpish from this angle. At last, chilled to the bone, she reluctantly closed the shutters. She found her mind slipping back to the rare occasions in the past when Tae had climbed the walls of the castle, evading the guards, in order to visit her. The image made her smile.

Numbed by the cold, Matrinka opened her wardrobe and put on a thicker gown and hose, covering both with a heavy woolen cloak usually reserved for outdoor winter days. She did not intend to wear them long, only to reestablish her body heat; and it did not matter what she wore. No one could see her, and the guard would prevent any visitors. It occurred to her this might prove worse than standard incarceration; at least in the dungeon she might have a few interesting, if dangerous, neighbors and the antics and conversations of the prison guards to entertain her.

Three almost inaudible taps, in a familiar pattern, came from the wall of her room. She recognized the sound at once. Darris had come through the secret panel and wanted to announce his presence without the notice of others who might be in the room with her. When with company, Matrinka would ignore the sound and Darris would return to his own room to try again later. Now, she stepped to the proper position and responded with two delicate and deliberate beats of a single finger.

Darris pushed aside the panel to emerge into her room, then cautiously replaced it so no remnant or sign of it remained. Béarn Castle had several secret tunnels and openings created for the safety of its royalty. Matrinka knew a few, and the princes and princesses a couple of different ones; only the bard and his or her heir were trusted to memorize all of them. Sworn to secrecy, they were all taught not to share the information, except in times of greatest need. Rarely, a servant or visitor happened upon one, and it was usually sealed thereafter, especially if knowledge of it became too commonplace or if someone no longer trusted knew of its existence. Matrinka had always assumed new ones were fashioned on occasion at the whim of the king or the bard, the crafter also pledged to secrecy. If any opened to the outside or into the dungeon catacombs, she did not know about them. And, if the current queen was ignorant, she doubted enemies might know, either.

This particular passage between the quarters of the bard and the queen was supposed to be known only to Griff, Matrinka, and Darris. If anyone else had heard of it, they never indicated it in any way. In the twenty years since Matrinka had married Griff and he had deliberately assigned Darris and her these privately connecting rooms, no one had caught either of them using the tunnel nor found the two of them together inappropriately. She supposed, if any member of the Council knew about it, they would have placed a guard on it as well as her door immediately after her confession.

So many times, Matrinka had marveled at the craftsmanship, how the carpenter who created it left no lines or cracks to betray its existence. The granite walls looked no different than any other, and she would never have found it if Darris had not shown it to her.

Apparently satisfied, Darris crawled between the bed and the wall, where no one would see him if the door from the hallway opened without warning. Matrinka started to crouch down to follow him, but he waved her to the bed. She sat, legs dangling over the side, looking down at him. It seemed a particularly ridiculous way to hold a conversation.

"What have you done?" Darris demanded in a whisper. The need to keep his voice low took the venom from the words, but his dour expression combined anger with terrible anguish.

Matrinka replied just as softly. The stone walls of the castle rooms blocked sound well, but she could hear knocking on her chamber door and had called through it for people to enter enough times to worry for someone overhearing if their conversation became heated. If someone burst through the door, Darris would not have enough time to remove the carefully replaced panel and disappear. He could hide, but anyone hearing voices might become suspicious enough to search the room and find him. "I told the Council Griff was not Marisole's father."

Darris wrung his hands. "Why would you do that, Matrinka? We had a plan."

"A plan that protected our comfort at the expense of Barrindar and Marisole." Matrinka attempted to sound firm, unswayable. "My conscience couldn't allow this deception to continue."

"You should have discussed your intentions with the rest of us." Darris' words came dangerously close to imparting information. He did not currently carry an instrument, but his hands went instinctively into playing position. "We agreed no one would act without all of us conferring."

"You would not have allowed me to do what had to be done."

"So you did it without our consent or advice."

Matrinka set her jaw. Her feet were so close to him, she could easily kick him and pass it off as an accidental movement. She said only, "Yes," placing as much defiance into the word as she could without raising her voice.

Darris hesitated. Matrinka knew he wanted to tell her important things, ones he could not say without launching into song. He could not risk music; his voice would surely carry. Instead, he employed a technique that had worked in the past, forcing her to carefully contemplate a series of unrevealing questions until she discovered the cause of his concern by using her own knowledge and intellect. "At what price, Matrinka?" There was unexpected grief in his tone where she had anticipated anger. They were all deeply affected by Nomalan's death, but this seemed misplaced in the current conversation. Something else troubled him as deeply as the death of a beloved member of the royal family.

Matrinka believed she had considered every possible consequence to everyone involved by her confession and wanted Darris to know she had not acted out of impulse. "I'm incarcerated, obviously. I named a member of Béarnian aristocracy as Marisole's father. Angus, specifically." Her prior conversation with Barrindar had sparked the idea to select an appropriate partner who had died recently with no living parents or siblings who might be harmed by the false revelation. Angus had been killed in the war, his body located and appropriately mourned and disposed of, so he could not turn up after one of the expeditions to the Outworlds to dispute her claim. "Marisole will lose her status as princess, but she'll then become a potential, legal mate for Barrindar, which is her preference. They can marry almost immediately; night of marriage conceptions are a common phenomenon and babies frequently appear a couple weeks earlier than expected. It won't affect Arturo or Halika in any way, as Griff will still be presumed to be their father." Matrinka made a broad motion. "Problem solved. I can't believe it didn't occur to us to try that in the first place."

Darris stared at Matrinka as if she had gone entirely mad. "Didn't it?"

Matrinka hesitated. "We discussed the dangers of revealing our . . . situation, of telling the entire truth. My idea still requires deception, but it's a harmless one."

The grief in his voice was unmistakable. "Is it?"

Matrinka tried to understand. "I know you're concerned people will figure out Marisole is yours because she's the bard's heir, the way Barrindar and Marisole did when her talent first became apparent. But we've already explained that to the world's satisfaction. You have no heirs and don't wish to marry. The curse forced you to train someone to take your place, and you chose Marisole because she had musical talent and wanted the job."

Darris made an impatient gesture. He knew all that, and it clearly had little to do with his discomfort. Apparently, he did not worry for his own safety, which relieved Matrinka. When she had decided on this course of action, it had been her own biggest concern.

Matrinka frowned. The fact that she had acted unilaterally, without the input of the others involved, would understandably upset Darris; but it should not aggrieve him. He clearly worried for someone's life or sanity. "You're not worried for yourself."

Darris shook his head vigorously.

"Is it . . . Marisole?"

Darris continued shaking his head, if anything more actively.

"Barrindar?" she tried.

The movement continued unabated.

"Nomalan?" As that was still clearly not the answer, she tried again, though it seemed unlikely. "Griff?"

Darris shook his head one more time and stared at Matrinka. He could give her the answer with a single word, yet this particular name, in and of itself, apparently supplied too much information for him to even try to sneak it past the curse.

"It's me," Matrinka said with a laugh. She should have realized it from the beginning. "You're worried about me."

"Yes," Darris said, his voice a raw croak.

Afraid another laugh might alert the guard, she snorted softly instead. "No need. I picked Angus because he and I have the proper qualifications to marry so it keeps Marisole in the bloodline. I've studied history. I know the possible penalties for creating an out-of-wedlock royal. Mostly, it puts her at the end of the line for heir testing, which I think she'll actually appreciate. The penalties on me aren't harsh. I can handle them." Likely, by the time the Council determined the proper punishment, she would have spent enough time incarcerated they would consider the time served enough.

Darris practically curled around his absent lute, desperate to explain. Eyes closed, he sucked in a deep breath and held it so long Matrinka started to worry he had stopped breathing altogether.

Matrinka waited him out. She scarcely dared to believe such a mild punishment to her would upset him so badly. He knew something he could not tell her without music, and she did not seem capable of divining it on her own.

Finally, Darris expelled the breath and opened his eyes. He returned to strategic questioning. "Did you tell the Council Angus raped you?"

Matrinka's eyes narrowed at the bare thought. "Of course not," she responded indignantly. "Out of wedlock sex is stigma enough. I wasn't going to tarnish a war hero's legacy by accusing him of a vicious and unpardonable crime." She constructed an image of her distant cousin in her mind, and a nostalgic smile touched her lips. She added, "Besides, Angus was so mild-mannered, no one would have believed me. It might have called my whole confession into question. We can't afford to have the Council scrutinizing the situation too closely." Darris' question seemed like madness. "Why would you even ask such a thing?"

Darris loosed a breath he had probably been holding throughout her long response. "When did you and Griff marry?"

They both knew the answer; everyone in Béarn did, yet Matrinka did not fault him. If Darris asked something obvious, it was because the answer would help her figure out what preyed upon his mind. She quoted the precise day, month and year twenty years and several months earlier.

"And when was Marisole born?"

It was another unnecessary question, a miracle they had all celebrated. "Exactly one year and two months later." Matrinka smiled at the memory, still finding Darris' alarm unfathomable.

Darris repeated, "One year and two months after the marriage."

Matrinka nodded. Usually, she was patient with Darris and his curse, but these self-evident questions were becoming annoying even to her.

"And how far in advance of birth is conception?"

Matrinka's healer training put that information on the tip of her tongue. "Forty weeks." She added carefully, "Give or take four weeks. Sometimes babies are born earlier than that, but they seldom survive."

"Can they remain in the uterus longer than forty-four weeks?"

Matrinka's brow furrowed, and she shook her head. "I only know of it happening once. The baby had died inside, and the mother soon followed." It had occurred longer than a decade earlier, but she felt tears sting her eyes at the memory. "Of course, people get the dates wrong sometimes."

Darris frowned, indicating Matrinka had gone off on the wrong tangent. "A year is fifty weeks." It was common knowledge, so he could point it out without needing to sing. "No pregnancy can go longer than fifty weeks, can it?"

Matrinka did not believe Darris really wanted an answer. Instead, she considered the last several questions together, seeking the common thread. He was herding her as surely as a dog does sheep. She stated what seemed to be the significant fact. "Marisole was born sixty weeks after my marriage to Griff." She tipped her head and met Darris' hazel eyes. "So she was definitely conceived after we married."

Darris bobbed his head encouragingly.

"Which makes her illegitimate." Matrinka had already followed this tack. "Which doesn't matter." She quoted the law. "Children born illegitimately to ruling kings or queens are still accorded proper title, though they are considered lower in ascension lineage despite their ages. Since the Pica, ascension lineage no longer means much anyway."

Darris repeated, placing the emphasis on the important word, "Children born illegitimately to *ruling* kings or queens . . ."

Matrinka considered the significance of the term "ruling." When she read the law, she had assumed it referred to someone holding title at the time of the birth. Now, she realized, technically, the person who passed the Pica test, previously the staff-test and, prior to that, the one who ascended to the throne by virtue of birth order was deemed the "ruling" monarch regardless of gender. Matrinka was the queen of Béarn because she was the first spouse of the ruling king, making Tem'aree'ay and Xoraida "queen consorts." No one else had mothered children for Griff; but, if anyone had borne him illegitimate heirs, those women would take the title "consort." Their children would still be princes and princesses, but lower in the ascension line than the legitimate heirs. Some ruling kings and queens had produced illegitimate heirs, but she could not recall any references to a Béarnian king or queen *through marriage* doing so. She spoke the last thought aloud, "Historically, have non-ruling kings or queens produced illegitimate offspring?"

Darris squeezed his hands together, fingers blanching. "What do you call someone who betrays the king of Béarn?"

The question seemed unrelated. "A traitor?" Matrinka tried.

Darris studied Matrinka with an intensity that made her shift uncomfortably on the bed. That forced her legs to move in balance, and she nearly did inadvertently kick him.

"What do you call it when someone with a spouse sleeps with a person who is not said spouse?"

"Adultery." Matrinka believed she had all the information she needed, but things still refused to click into place.

"So adultery is a betrayal of one's spouse," Darris said.

Matrinka nodded in agreement, still thinking aloud. "Adultery is the betrayal of one's spouse. My spouse is the king of Béarn. Betraying the king is . . ." Her mouth flew open, and the word barely emerged. ". . . treason." She did not need Darris to ask the next question. "And the penalty for treason is . . ." She whispered the last word. ". . . death."

Matrinka's own words struck like a physical blow, and she suddenly understood why he had asked the rape question. She could see tears forming in Darris' eyes so quickly they rolled down his face before he could hide them or wipe them away. Matrinka found herself floating without realizing she had moved. Darris scrambled to his feet, catching her as she fell. She outweighed him, and the force of her collapse drove him backward. He managed to catch his balance within a stride, clutching her tightly in his arms.

"It never occurred to you," Darris said directly into her ear. Then, with evident surprise. "It *never* occurred to you?"

In all their conversations, no one had mentioned it as a possibility. Matrinka supposed it was so abhorrent not one of them could believe anyone would consider it. Or, if they did, they assumed the promise each of them made to the group would keep anyone from confessing. Matrinka had truly believed she found the last piece of the puzzle, that naming Angus as Marisole's father would solve every problem. The worst possibility she imagined was the truth would come out, that she and Darris could be banished from the kingdom. It had even briefly crossed her mind Darris might be at risk should anyone discover their ongoing relationship, but she had never contemplated her own life in jeopardy.

Matrinka pulled away. She had made the ultimate mistake and could not take it back; but she could, at least, save Darris. If anyone caught him here, he was as good as dead. "Go," she whispered. "Do what you can for me with the Council, but promise me you won't risk your own life no matter what they say, no matter what happens. Please, promise me that. Do not make my sacrifice worthless."

Darris hesitated just long enough for Matrinka to shake him. "Promise!" Admitting his own role in the situation would not save Matrinka; it would only assure they both died and prevent Marisole and Barrindar from marrying.

"Why not claim rape now?" Darris was clutching at straws. "You wouldn't be the first woman to protect a rapist out of shame."

Matrinka considered it briefly, then shook her head, certain it would only muddy the waters and assure such a close examination it would all unravel. The end result would prove dire not just for her, but for them all. She and Darris would die for treason, Barrindar and Marisole would be banished, and even Griff would not escape unscathed. She gave him her fiercest look and growled out through her teeth, "Promise, Darris."

Darris lowered his head, defeated. "I promise."

Matrinka forced a smile past her tears. "And one thing more. Don't come to me again while I'm incarcerated. It won't help me, and it's too dangerous for you. If you need to tell me something, send a message with Imorelda. Take her to any meetings with the Council, if Tae will let you."

"Imorelda?" Darris repeated in confusion. "You mean Tae's cat?"

Darris was one of the few people who had known about Matrinka's ability to communicate with Mior, although he had never fully believed it. "Are you suggesting you can speak with Imorelda as you did with Mior?"

Matrinka could not answer without implicating Tae, and he did not want anyone to know about his own ability. "Don't tell Tae; it might upset him, or he might feel obliged to give her to me, which would make both of them unhappy. But Imorelda is Mior's daughter, and we . . . have a similar connection."

Darris gave her a dubious look.

Matrinka would not waste any more time. If she was under threat of execution, Darris was risking his own life every moment he remained with her. "Believe me, she will get the message to me. Just go. Go now!"

"I love you," Darris whispered, then headed for the panel.

"I love you, too," Matrinka said as she shoved the stone into place behind him and set to making it entirely invisible once more.

CHAPTER 18

I have found when humans commit themselves to righteousness,
they often blunder into otherwise obvious danger. And, sometimes,
the wrong they create is worse than the one they right.

—Imorelda

AS THE RANKS OF the *jovinay arythanik* swelled from the rescued elves, Captain dismissed several healers to tend to the ill and injured humans liberated at the same time. So, when the surgeon arrived from Pudar to tend to Princess Ivana, Tem'aree'ay had assistance from four elves with whom she had already discussed the matter, including the two who had suggested she bring in a human healer with skull-opening experience to assist the process. Having explained the situation to the surgeon, named Tonaris, to the best of her ability, she brought those elves to the quarters Matrinka had arranged for him prior to her incarceration.

Initially terrified by the queen's inability to bridge the gap between the visiting Pudarian surgeon and the elves, Tem'aree'ay found herself up to the task. Like most healers, Tonaris had a curious and kindly demeanor that put Tem'aree'ay at ease. When she sent for him, Matrinka had explained the situation in a detailed note, so he had had time to prepare himself for meeting elves. When the group of elfin healers knocked on his door, he opened it immediately and politely ushered them all inside.

A shortish man of medium build, Tonaris sported dark brown hair a shade lighter than most Béarnides, a mustache, and a small neatly-tended beard all liberally flecked with gray. Top and bottom, his eyelids drooped in folds common to aging humans, surrounding keen, tea-colored eyes that radiated wisdom and inquisitiveness. He smiled and bowed at the group, stepping aside so they could enter. Tem'aree'ay did so without hesitation, hoping her assurance would spread to the other healers who had much less experience with indoor dwellings and their trappings, especially bedrooms, and found them confining, stale, and uncomfortable.

Tem'aree'ay introduced each healer as he or she entered, sticking to the shortened form of every name so as not to overwhelm and confuse the surgeon. "Ghy'rinith." The delicate female elf who entered on Tem'aree'ay's heels was also the one who had first agreed to work with a human healer when they had initially discussed the possibility. She had fine white hair, pinkish eyes, a rosy hue to her skin and could pass for a human albino should it ever become necessary.

Myr-intha came next, the one who had originally suggested the need for a human surgeon with knowledge of the brain. She stood a head taller than Ghy'rinith, with black hair that had a reddish sheen and canted eyes as brilliantly green as emeralds. Her angular features practically defined elfishness, and she would have been much harder pressed to pass for human. Tem'aree'ay introduced her. "Tonaris, this is Myr-intha."

"Lovely," Tonaris said, making another bow.

The last two practically tumbled through the door together, a male named Ath'erion with curly hair as red as a berry, a build nearly as slight as Ghy'rinith's and eyes that perfectly matched the color of his hair, with another female, Shar'iss'ah who sported inhumanly blue eyes and a mop of ruby-blond hair, the only one taller than Tonaris.

The surgeon made two more bows, then gestured the group fully into the room. Cued earlier that it might make his guests feel trapped, he did not bother to close the door but took a seat, cross-legged, on the wooden floor. Tem'aree'ay crouched beside him, taking over the proceedings. "This is Tonaris, the surgeon Matrinka requested from Pudar. Of all the human healers in the world, he has the most experience working inside the human brain."

Tonaris turned faintly pinkish. "I'm not entirely sure I have the most experience in the world, but I've had some success dealing with both penetrating wounds and abnormal growths inside the skull. You're the first elves I've met, though. Your construction looks quite similar to humans, at least on the outside, so I imagine we have some overlap when it comes to internal organs as well."

As the other elves sat, knelt, or crouched on the floor in front of them, Tem'aree'ay detailed some of the broad differences first. "We never become ill, so we don't suffer from wasting, plague, fevers, catarrh, cough, or similar maladies humans get. We don't mind any sort of weather unless it becomes intense and extreme, far beyond what would make a human miserable. When we die, it's of an advanced age unheard of in humans, usually three hundred to over a

thousand years, although we are susceptible to damage from violence and accidents."

Though her companions had known Tem'aree'ay would reveal
information the elves would rather keep secret, they stirred restively
at her recitation. By now, nearly all of the humans who had had regular dealings with them had either figured out or learned everything
she had mentioned. "Our healing is of a magical sort. We excel at
treating external injuries. We also can handle many internal problems, without opening the body, with a reasonable measure of success. Through trial and error, we have even discovered we can detect,
and often heal, many things humans suffer that we do not."

Tonaris nodded. Matrinka had explained some of this to him already, but he clearly appreciated the repetition. It was a lot of information for a human who had only just learned elves existed during
the World's War, where he had served with the other healers. Until
Tem'aree'ay, he had never met one up close. He added, "As I understand it, Princess Ivana is the only human-elf hybrid that has ever
existed, as far as anyone knows. She has some sort of growth in her
brain that damages her intellect as well as making her deaf to that
elfin mind-language that even I could hear quite plainly."

The elves stared at him, saying nothing.

Tem'aree'ay alone bobbed her head in a human manner, knowing he would need some sort of feedback. "It is our hope that you
can open her skull so that we could get a look at what some of us are
feeling with magic." Tem'aree'ay regretted she was not one of the
ones who could do so, being a weaker healer than many of her ilk.
"Working together, we may be able to remove the growth and restore
her to normal. But, if we do nothing, we believe it will continue to
grow, worsening her condition and probably resulting in her death."
Tem'aree'ay winced at her own words. Despite long and somber
contemplation, speaking them aloud never failed to bring home the
grim reality of the situation.

Tonaris rocked in place, considering. For a human, he remained
silent a long time; but the elves other than Tem'aree'ay did not seem
to notice. "I will help you," he finally promised. "But it is absolutely
imperative you understand: even under the best of circumstances,
opening any part of the body is dangerous and exposing a brain particularly so. Many patients die from the shock alone. Fatal blood loss
is always a possibility. There's sepsis, too, blood poisoning, and it can
occur days or even weeks after things appear to have gone perfectly
well. The surgery does not always work to cure the original problem
and can cause others, especially when things are removed and im-

portant parts have become attached or must be damaged in order to remove the defect."

Tem'aree'ay listened carefully to the list. He had mentioned nothing she had not already considered. "We have magic to keep her asleep through the procedure, which should ease the trauma of opening a body cavity and help keep her still and comfortable despite any pain. Between all of us, we ought to be able to contain the blood loss. As far as blood poisoning, we don't know if she's susceptible. Elves aren't; humans are. Throughout her eighteen years, Ivana's never taken ill, but that doesn't mean she can't." Tem'aree'ay could not speak to the other things as no one knew what they would find or the long-term effects of removal, if removal was even possible. "I understand there are enormous risks involved, Tonaris, and I will not allow anyone to hold you responsible if things go wrong." She steeled herself. Of them all, she had the most to lose, yet she was also the only one who could reassure Tonaris and hold him blameless, other than Griff, who had already placed the situation entirely into her hands.

Tem'aree'ay knew the surgeon needed to hear one more thing. "You come highly recommended by Queen Matrinka, a competent healer in her own right who has watched your work and others. If she believes you're the best, I do, too. Whatever happens, I'm certain the result would be no better with anyone else and you will have tried your best."

Tonaris rose, bowed deeply, then retook his seat on the floor. "I'm humbled by your praise. I will give Ivana my full attention and look forward to working with elves now and, hopefully, in the future. I am particularly intrigued by your ability to keep a patient asleep during the surgery and am looking forward to observing it."

Ghy'rinith sent direct *khohlar* to Tem'aree'ay, *Charming.* Surrounding that sending came a wordless understanding of how Tem'aree'ay had wound up married to King Griff.

Under other circumstances, Tem'aree'ay might have smiled. Elves did not pair up and, until recently, bonding to a human was anathema to nearly every elf. Of course, Ghy'rinith had shared the thought only with Tem'aree'ay, but that did not necessarily mean she was afraid to voice it to some of the others in the room. Indirect *khohlar* would have broadcast it not only to all the elves in range, but to Tonaris as well. *Human men have their allure, if you don't mind tying yourself to one partner for a few decades.*

Oblivious to the mental exchange, Tonaris continued, "When can I meet your daughter?"

"I don't want to rush you." Everything humans did seemed hurried to the near-immortal elves; but Tem'aree'ay had become accustomed to living at their speed. "After you're rested from your journey, please join us in the dining hall for dinner. I'll save a place for you at the royal table."

Tonaris put a hand over his chest. "Oh please, no, my lady. I'm just a common healer. I don't know the proper manners. I'll embarrass myself."

Tem'aree'ay forced a smile. "King Griff and Queen Matrinka despise formality." She mentioned the queen even though Matrinka would not be able to join them. "I'll see to it we have no Knights of Erythane at our table tonight, and no one will care how you eat."

Tonaris also grinned. "I promise not to spit, vomit, or throw food."

Tem'aree'ay chuckled. "That would be appreciated." She stood, preparing to leave, and everyone else scrambled to their feet as well.

Though slower and comparatively graceless, Tonaris raced to the door to hold it open for the elves. "I hope all of you lovely ladies will be joining us at the king's table."

Ghy'rinith, Myr'intha, and Shar'iss'ah giggled as they funneled through the door, and Ath'erion tossed a sour look over his shoulder. Tem'aree'ay waited at the open door until they had turned the first corner before looking back at Tonaris. *I've noticed it can be difficult for humans to tell female and male elves apart. To avoid future awkwardness, you should know, Ath'erion is male.*

Tonaris' cheeks blossomed. "I'm so sorry." He spoke softly so the elves around the corner might not hear. His eyes narrowed a bit, accentuating the lid folds. "The little one with the red eyes?" He shook his head. "No wonder people have trouble. Could you please send my apologies?"

"I will," Tem'aree'ay promised, "and don't worry. We're quite used to it, I assure you." With that said, she headed out the door to prepare Ivana for supper.

Dismissed from the rescue group in order to attend Nomalan's funeral, Marisole found herself in private conference with Barrindar, Griff, and Darris. Wracked with guilt, she sat numbly in a plush chair, Barrindar standing behind her, his hands resting on her tense shoulders, one still bandaged from the mermaid's bite. Griff perched in a matching chair, and Darris paced the room fretfully. Created for small meetings of royalty or guests, it had no windows, only stone walls and a thick door that blocked the penetration of sound. Still, neither Darris nor Marisole made any motion to draw an instrument. She did not know the bard's reason, but she felt too drained and defeated to create music, even of the most depressing kind. She also missed her favorite gittern, a casualty of the battle with the mermaids.

"You're the king, Papa." Barrindar pointed out the obvious. "You can't let them kill her. You wouldn't." His fingers bit into Marisole's shoulder but could not penetrate the bandage.

Griff hung his massive head. "It's not that simple, Barri. Believe me, I tried to pardon her, but the most ancient laws of Béarn are inviolate and beyond even my ability to change. They don't allow it."

"Why not?" Marisole managed to croak.

Griff looked directly at her, his expression soft with suppressed grief of his own. "'The victim of treason cannot pardon the perpetrator because there exists the strong probability that the victim is unduly influenced by the traitor.' In other words, the gods who created the law believed the reason a traitor is able to successfully commit a traitorous act is usually because he has some obvious or hidden power over the ruler: magic, a dangerous secret, a threat or, in this case, love or familiarity or the sharing of offspring. No matter how grievous the crime, few men would allow the mother of his children to be executed if he had the wherewithal to stop it. As I understand it, the gods felt if one traitor went unpunished, it would give the perpetrator even more power, perhaps enough to usurp the throne. It would also encourage others to put a real or proverbial knife to the throat of the king or queen. And, if Béarn falls, the nine worlds go with it."

"But you're the king!" Marisole could not let it go. "You rewrite law all the time."

It was not quite true, but Griff ignored the fallacy to address the real issue beneath her point. "What the gods set in stone even the ruler of Béarn cannot amend. You know that, Marisole. Otherwise, I could have revised the rules to allow you two to marry without Matrinka's sacrifice."

Marisole huffed out a sigh, then nudged Barrindar. "Ask."

Barrindar's hands went lax on her shoulders. "Marisole wants to know if she and I could go before the Council and claim Matrinka lied for us. We'd say she wanted us to be able to marry, so she made up an outlandish story to assist us."

Marisole nodded to indicate he had made her point aptly.

Darris frowned. He had skirted the edges of the curse in many ways and on many occasions, but he had never relied on singing in private so someone could speak for him. In no mood for a scolding, Marisole glared back. In this, she would find her own way.

"No!" The firmness of Griff's one-word answer left no leeway for argument. "I forbid either of you to do any such thing." He softened in explanation. "It would pit your word against Matrinka's about an incident that occurred before your birth. Even if I could convince her to retract her confession, it would be too easy to believe *you* were the ones lying to save *her* life. The whole situation would fall under intensive scrutiny, and the inconsistencies could no longer be overlooked. If the entire truth came out, the result would be catastrophic. We would still lose Matrinka, and also Darris. You'd be banished, both of you, which would make Matrinka's sacrifice worthless. Worse, she would know it. Marisole, Arturo, and Halika would have to leave the castle. My every word and action would become suspect, rendering me a useless king. I'd have to abdicate, placing Calitha, Eldorin, and probably countless others at the mercy of the Pica test, which would probably destroy them." He rose to make himself fully understood. "Neither of you goes to the Council unless I command you otherwise. Do you understand?"

All eyes went to the young lovers who nodded briskly.

Once certain he had made his point, Griff continued. "As soon as possible, I will announce your engagement and use it to delay Matrinka's sentencing. No one would deprive a condemned woman the opportunity to attend her daughter's wedding."

Darris finally spoke, as most usual, in the form of a question. "Won't the Council become suspicious of the timing and give the situation additional thought?"

"Perhaps." Griff shrugged. "But I doubt it. More likely, they'll assume Matrinka chose to speak out now because she knew Marisole and Barrindar were in love and didn't want her secret to stand in their way, which is wholly believable because it's true. I have no idea whether or not Matrinka knew the consequences to herself, but she clearly considered her actions carefully. She created a story no one could find evidence to contradict, that would keep you and all the children safe and titled yet still allow these two to legally marry. She's a clever woman."

Darris folded his arms across his chest. "She's a foolish woman who sacrificed her life for her daughter's love."

"She wouldn't be the first," Barrindar said softly. "But does she really think our marriage could ever be happy steeped in her blood? That we wouldn't drown in our own guilt?"

Griff turned his attention fully on Barrindar. "I don't think she considered that. Or else, she believed time would heal that wound. But I haven't given up on saving her. There's always an answer if you're wise enough to find it in time. The only way I can think to gain ourselves that time is to delay her sentencing until after your marriage."

"Which also cannot be delayed too long," Barrindar pointed out. "Because of the baby."

Darris and Griff both nodded. Marisole's head felt too heavy, and she let it sink into her palms. "I might as well have killed them," she moaned. "Nomalan and Mama. I don't deserve any happiness."

Barrindar shook her shoulders hard enough to elicit a shock of pain through the bandage. "Stop, Marisole. That two people chose to die for you doesn't make you a murderer, just a sweet, competent princess they considered worthy of their sacrifice. By holding yourself up as their killer, you demean them, stripping them of their well-deserved heroism and honor. A king celebrates the lives of soldiers lost in a necessary battle and only despairs if he sends them to a pointless death."

Darris and Griff both stared at him, silent and openmouthed at wisdom seldom espoused by one so young and inexperienced.

Marisole wrung her hands. "But Nomalan wouldn't have come if I hadn't invited him. And I wouldn't have invited him had we not been trying to trick him into marrying me." She made no attempt to sing the thought. She was not telling anyone in the room anything he did not already know.

Barrindar had a ready response, "No one was forced to go, not even you. Everyone in the rescue party recognized the danger and chose to join it anyway, including Nomalan. You could just as easily have died protecting him and the other men from mermaids." He added forcefully, "Besides, I agree with Papa." He managed a grin as he amended. "*My* Papa. We'll find a way to save Matrinka; and, if us getting married is the best way to stall, who am I to complain?" He walked around the chair and dropped to one knee in front of her. "I pledge my love to you forever and always."

Marisole had dreamed of seeing that gesture and hearing those words for longer than a year. The current situation paled them, but not enough for her to refuse. "I'm honored, and I accept you as mine."

The next words belonged to the bride's father. Griff and Darris glanced at one another, clearly at a loss. For so long, the king had been considered Marisole's father, but no longer. Darris had the correct blood in his veins but could never admit it. With Angus dead, the job ought to fall to the mother's husband; but, as he had fathered

Barrindar and the state of the marriage was in question, that seemed equally wrong. For a moment, it appeared as if Barrindar would remain forever frozen in position. Then, finally, the two men looked at one another and said simultaneously, "You have our blessing."

During the nightly feast, Tonaris met the off-putting Ivana who brayed a welcome that echoed through the dining hall and hugged the surgeon like an old friend, leaving a patch of drool on his linens. He handled the situation well, giving Tem'aree'ay an encouraging smile and wrapping his arms around Ivana in a display of affection. The young hybrid took his hand and solemnly led him to the seat beside hers, which Tonaris accepted with a hearty "thank you." Tem'aree'ay already trusted the surgeon because Matrinka had recommended him so highly, but his kindness toward Ivana, who openly horrified the other elves and caused most humans to politely avoid her, made Tem'aree'ay even more confident of his worth.

Tem'aree'ay missed Matrinka's presence at the meal. She knew too little of Béarnian law to realize the former queen's danger, and Griff had discussed it only in the most general terms. Her thoughts remained focused on Ivana and the upcoming surgery, as they should, and Griff took great care not to distract her with concerns of his own. Her singular attention to their only child gave him free rein to attend to the rescue mission, their guests, and the regular affairs of Béarn, at least those which could not be suspended until after the soldiers had returned from the Outworlds.

Tonaris requested a clean room for the surgery, including a high bed with disposable sheets and a firm pillow that no one would miss at the conclusion of the procedure. The servants chose a little-used bedroom on the fourth floor of the castle that had a single window, now shuttered, and a bed they had raised with broad and stable wooden blocks under each leg. They covered the ticking thickly with well-laundered, threadbare sheets and created a makeshift pillow on the end. They removed all of the other furnishings except a table Tonaris wanted to keep in the room for his tools. This, too, they covered with a throwaway sheet to protect the table and the implements.

Tem'aree'ay had kept Ivana awake most of the night, playing the princess' favorite games interspersed with talks as serious as the princess could understand. These included explaining what would happen the following morning, absent the gruesome details, and why it needed doing. Tem'aree'ay slept little even at the most stressful of times; some elves required none at all while others needed as much as humans. Ivana had always needed a humanly amount of rest. So, in the wee morning hours, when it became clear she could hold her eyes open no longer, Tem'aree'ay tucked her into her bed with an "I love you" and a gentle kiss, to spend the rest of the time until surgery alone with her thoughts, both hopeful and disturbing.

King Griff found Tem'aree'ay in Ivana's room the next morning. Wordlessly, he held her for a long time, then finally whispered in her ear, "I love you, Tem'aree'ay." His glance went over her shoulder. "And Ivana, too." He pulled away far enough to put his hand on her belly. "And this little one, no matter how he or she comes to us."

Tem'aree'ay wished she could supply the gender, but it was one of the weird holes in elfin magic.

"The baby seems normal to me, but Ivana did also at this stage. Would you mind if other elves checked? Some of them can delve deeper than I can."

"It won't harm the baby in any way?" Griff's expression turned almost pleading. He had to know Tem'aree'ay would not risk any life, but he also knew she had only allowed herself to become pregnant again with great reluctance. He might not coax her to do it again.

She forced a smile. "Certainly not, my love."

Griff stepped back and held her hand. "I'm needed in the great hall." His tone was filled with regret. "Do your best, and we'll deal with the will of the gods, whatever it may be."

Tem'aree'ay nodded. "Good luck to you as well. May your day be successful, and many elves and soldiers returned to Midgard."

A knock on the door interrupted their exchange. The panel slid open, and a slight young maid peered inside. When her gaze fell upon the king, she gasped and curtsied broadly. "I'm so sorry. I didn't realize I was—"

Griff crossed the room in a step and threw the door wide. "Please enter and give us your message."

The maid curtsied again, this time her attention on Tem'aree'ay. "My lady, the surgeon is asking for you and Princess Ivana."

Griff returned to Ivana's bedside and scooped the young woman into his arms. "Where do I need to take her?"

Tem'aree'ay described the proper bedroom, one floor below. The maid stepped aside so the king could carry his burden straight to the door, Tem'aree'ay trailing behind him.

Ivana slept through the transfer; and, when King Griff eased her onto the bed, she snuggled into the pillow with a sonorous snort that sent the four elfin healers scurrying away. To his credit, Tonaris did not react, studying the sleeping hybrid with an air of competence and curiosity. Griff and Tem'aree'ay also stared at their child. To Tem'aree'ay, her coarse features looked angelic in sleep, the picture of innocence despite the drool leaking from her open mouth to puddle on the pillow. Wearing a grin of paternal pride, Griff leaned in to kiss his daughter gently on the forehead before taking his leave.

Focused entirely upon Ivana, Tem'aree'ay did not watch him go, though she heard the quiet click of the door closing behind him. She stroked wisps of dark hair from her daughter's forehead, smiling at the memories of the games they had played the previous night. The long, thick fingers lay still, trained to make her needs known since she had no other capacity for language.

While Tem'aree'ay stared at the daughter she and Griff found beautiful despite any other opinions, Tonaris set a bronze medical chest on the bedside table and opened the largest of three compartments to reveal several trays. One held a neat array of scalpels: some stone, some copper and others steel, all honed to brilliant sharpness. Another held a collection of hooks, most blunt but a few well-edged. A third held a forceps, a small drill, a spathomele, and several curettes of differing sizes. He opened a smaller door in the portable chest to reveal several sewing needles and packets of thread. Apparently satisfied, he divided his attention between the elves. "Where do you suspect this defect lies? Which part of the head?"

All of the elfin eyes went to Ghy'rinith, the most competent and precise diagnostician. "Here," she said, touching the middle left side of her own head, then using the same finger to point to roughly the same location on Ivana. "I believe the source of the problem lies there, but it has grown and spread."

Tonaris examined Ivana's head from all sides but did not touch her. "Do you need to prepare in some way? Usually, I perform as quickly as possible to minimize the pain, but if you can really keep her asleep . . . ?" He turned Tem'aree'ay a hopeful look. "I can put caution foremost."

Ath'erion stepped forward. He was the one who worked the sleeping spell, with Tem'aree'ay and Shar'iss'ah to bolster it through any pain, noise or issue. Those three elves raised their hands and merged their voices into a *jovinay arythanik*, and Ivana's demeanor loosened further, if possible, her snores still filling the room. Ghy'rinith and Myr'intha moved to the head of the bed, leaving a space for Tonaris. "Whenever you're ready, surgeon," Ghy'rinith said.

Tonaris stepped up beside her, gently turning Ivana's head and watching closely, apparently to see if she showed any reaction to his touch. When she did not, he placed three fingers on the side of her head, close to where Ghy'rinith had indicated. "Will this work?" He explained, apparently to let her know why he had not chosen the precise position she had indicated. "I rarely find blood vessels or nerves here, although everyone's put together a bit differently and I've never worked on an elf."

"She's as much human as elf." Ghy'rinith shrugged. "And I've never sensed anything like this wall. There's nothing exact about my reckoning, so go in where you feel most comfortable."

Tonaris picked up a scalpel carved from black stone. Cautiously, he incised the skin, at first delicately and intently focused on Ivana's reaction. Then, when she slept on, more boldly. He used a piece of white cloth to mop up the blood, which stained it a rosy pink, and he looked askance at Tem'aree'ay. "Is this the proper color?" He held up the fabric demonstrating blood stains too light for humans and too dark for elves.

Locked into the *jovinay arythanik*, Tem'aree'ay managed only a single nod. She had cared for enough childhood scrapes, snot, and drool to recognize the proper appearance of her daughter's secretions.

Tonaris explained to Ghy'rinith and Myr'intha, "This just looks odd to me, but it's nothing for alarm. It's far more worrisome if it turns darker than normal, which usually indicates breathing issues. I need to know what shade's the right one for her to know if something goes wrong." He continued to cut through the skin until the white of bone appeared. At that point, he laid aside the obsidian knife, clamped the cloth onto the wound, and mopped his brow with his sleeve.

After several moments, he lifted the cloth. The bleeding had stopped, other than a minimal ooze, and he selected a larger instrument from his pile. Using an edge, he traced a circle onto the exposed bone, then with quick skilled movements, he scooped at the area until a crevice appeared, deepening a bit with each pass. Sweat trickled from his hairline, and he murmured, "How's the patient doing?"

Ath'erion merely nodded, while Tem'aree'ay and Shar'iss'ah continued their soft chant. It was a relatively simple task to boost natural sleep, especially when she was not the one directing the gathered chaos. Tonaris' actions looked brutal; cutting through bone could not appear otherwise. Yet Ivana did not seem to experience any pain and did not react to anything he did. Her eyes remained closed. She did not twitch. If anything, her snores seemed lighter, her breathing easier or, at least, quieter.

The sound of metal scraping bone filled the room, which did not soothe Tem'aree'ay. Silent, watching, everyone heard the almost inaudible pop as the tool finally penetrated the skull. Tonaris switched to his fingers, pulling out a tiny piece of bone and peering through the insignificant hole it left. "Hmmm," he murmured.

Myr'intha stood on her toes to try to peer over his shoulder. "Do you see something?"

Tonaris picked up the tool again. "Not much, yet. The membrane appears to be bulging, which usually means there's some sort of extraneous liquid under it. At various times, I've seen collections of blood, brain fluid, or pus do that. It can happen quickly; when it does, you have to make a hole, or the brain gets crushed and can even slide through the anatomical opening at the base of the skull."

"How do you know if it happened quickly or slowly?" Ghy'rinth asked the question Tem'aree'ay wished she could, but she dared not risk leaving the *jovinay arythanik* and allowing Ivana to awaken.

Tonaris scraped the edges of the skull hole, gradually enlarging it. Something huge has to have happened for the bulging to occur quickly. Usually, it's a serious injury: a hard, sharp blow to the head, something penetrating, like a spear through the eye, a long fall onto rocks. It can happen without trauma, but it's usually accompanied by a terrible headache. Ivana has a history of a gradual process over many years, so it is almost certain this is a case of slow, ongoing seepage. He continued working as he spoke, and Tem'aree'ay watched him enlarge the hole to the size of a small apple. Now, she could see the thin membrane bulging upward, clearly under tension. Beneath it, the fluid appeared dark, almost black.

The surgeon stepped back a moment, then looked at the elves. "Could I trouble one of you to get a lantern, a packet of salt and two buckets, one filled with fresh, clean water?"

Tem'aree'ay had to leave the *jovinay arythanik* to answer. She glanced at Ath'erion, who gave her a nonverbal signal elves used to convey she could leave for a moment without causing harm to the magic. He did not dare *khohlar*, which would have dropped the sleep spell entirely.

Tem'aree'ay seized the moment to speak, "There should be a guard or servant outside the door who can fetch things." She immediately returned to the chant.

Ghy'rinith moved toward the door. "I'll take care of it." She crossed the room, opened the door, and relayed their needs to someone standing outside.

Tonaris looked at the ceiling, sucking in a deep breath. He exhaled slowly, then turned his gaze to his portable chest of tools. Blood stained his fingers, but it did not look like a large amount. Tem'aree'ay had seen more from a simple nosebleed. She wanted to ask about his thoughts, but she could not speak and, this time, no one else anticipated her question.

It did not take long for a page to return with the requested items. He held a bucket in each hand, the left clearly much heavier than the right, which emitted light, demonstrating he had placed the lantern inside it. "Where would you like these, sir?"

"Put the full bucket there." Tonaris indicated the floor next to the table with a bloody hand, then reached for the other one.

Looking pale and unsteady, the page did as instructed, then handed the other bucket to the surgeon. "May I stay and watch, sir?" He added quickly, "Out of the way, of course."

"That's fine." Tonaris did not look at the boy as he spoke, instead placing the lit lantern beside his portable cabinet of supplies and grabbing the wrapped packet of salt from beneath it. He opened the paper, dumping most of the salt into the water, then put the wrapper and the remainder of its contents on the table with the lantern and equipment. The now-empty bucket went onto the bed beside Ivana. Putting aside the enormous implement he had used to carve the skull hole, he took out a delicate knife and addressed the elves again. "I'm not sure what's going to happen, but something's likely to come out. From the darkness of it under the membrane, I'm guessing it's a collection of old blood. Anyone squeamish shouldn't watch. Ivana takes precedence over fainters."

Tonaris flicked the smaller, sharp knife across the bulging membrane. Immediately, a viscous dark-brown substance seeped out, accompanied by a nearly overpowering rancid smell.

Bile filled Tem'aree'ay's mouth, but she managed to swallow the sour substance rather than vomit. The odor had affected her far more than the sight. The page turned away reluctantly. Ghy'rinith and Myr'intha stepped backward but made no sound or other motion. Ath'erion did not waver, but Shar'iss'ah emitted a slight gasp, then returned immediately to the *jovinay arythanik*. Ivana slumbered on.

Tonaris held the empty bucket at an angle, capturing some of the substance oozing from the opening. It resembled mud in color and texture, though it smelled entirely different, more like rotting meat. He gestured Myr'intha over. "Please hold this in place."

The elf complied, though her features twisted in revulsion and she made certain to hold it so nothing that leaked out could possibly touch her. Hands freed, Tonaris picked up the bucket of saltwater, pouring it into the opening a bit at a time, which diluted the brown substance and allowed it to flow out more quickly.

Tem'aree'ay watched in fascination and horror. Tae as well as Ghy'rinith had told her the barrier to *khohlar* was thick and becoming more so, yet she had not expected anything quite so intense and abundant could fit inside one small head. As the goop seeped out, becoming less pungent and lighter as more saltwater mixed with the foreign substance, she found her vision disappearing beneath a wash of helpless, anguished tears. Without meaning to, she left the *jovinay arythanik* to wrap her tortured daughter into a protective embrace.

A sudden sense of foreboding struck Tem'aree'ay nearly to the point of panic. She clutched Ivana tighter, realization dribbling through her as she clung. Ivana was too peaceful. She could feel no rise and fall of the broad chest, hear no thump of a beating heart, no movement whatsoever but the flow of watery goop from the manufactured opening in her skull.

Tem'aree'ay leaped backward with a scream of horror and dismay. Hurriedly setting down the now half-full bucket of saltwater, Tonaris ran to Ivana's side, shoving the elves out of his way. He placed an ear to the young woman's chest, then raised his head and slammed the side of his fist between her breasts. That caused the body to jump, but not in a natural way, only as an aftermath of the blow. Swearing, he struck her several more times, then blew air into her face. When neither of these maneuvers seemed to have any effect, he shouted toward Ath'erion, "Wake her! Wake her up, if you can!"

Ath'erion turned his attention to Tem'aree'ay, sending, *But there's a hole in her head!*

Apparently, he sent it as indirect *khohlar*, because Tonaris shouted, "The brain itself can't feel pain, so you won't hurt her much. But, if she doesn't wake up, she's dead!"

That mobilized everyone, except Myr'intha, who kept the bucket in place but did watch the others. Unable to do anything helpful, Tem'aree'ay stepped out of the way while Ath'erion attempted to work hyperalertness magic, Ghy'rinith stood by to assist with healing, and Shar'iss'ah joined Tem'aree'ay. The page remained in a corner, his skin tinged a greenish-gray.

A chill swept through Tem'aree'ay, running up her spine. She whirled to find herself facing a wispy duplicate of Ivana, her *ejenlyåndel* or immortality echo. Tem'aree'ay realized she faced the eternal soul of her daughter, and it stunned her. As a magical creature, she had seen spirits leave bodies before, though rarely. Elves who died of age nearly always demanded privacy in their final moments. When

Frey came to collect the souls destined for recycling, he refused to speak or respond in the presence of the living; so, if the newly dead wished to commune with him, they made certain to appear alone. The only time she had witnessed an elf dying prematurely was at the Ragnarok, when Alfheim had been utterly destroyed by fire and a huge number had been killed. Then, the desperate need to escape had consumed them all. Anyone who stayed to observe the lost souls had died with them.

Tem'aree'ay had seen a few human deaths since arriving on Midgard. In every case, a scowling creature that resembled a large, fierce human male had silently collected the confused and insubstantial creatures, disappearing without a word. She knew the Valkyries took the bravest warrior souls, those who died in battle. Before the Ragnarok, the goddess Hel had claimed all others; but she had died in the god's great battle and it appeared the male creature Tem'aree'ay had seen had taken her place. Or so she had assumed.

The soul of Ivana clung to Tem'aree'ay touching her with all the substance of butterfly wings. Accustomed to the large, heavy figure of her daughter, usually smashing into her with great exuberance, Tem'aree'ay had to use magic and imagination just to sense Ivana's presence. The girl's mouth moved in a way it never had in life, and actual words emerged for the first time, in a sweet higher-pitched voice, "Mama!"

Already surprised, Tem'aree'ay found herself utterly speechless in disbelief. She wrapped her arms around the ghostly form, using memory to recreate the feeling of her daughter in her arms.

"Mama," Ivana said again. "I love you, Mama. I love you."

"I love you, too," Tem'aree'ay said through a maelstrom of tears. "I've always loved you."

"I know it," Ivana said. "I've always known it. And Papa, too."

"Yes, Papa, too," Tem'aree'ay assured her.

Just behind the page in the corner, the scowling figure who had replaced Hel appeared. "Give her to me," he said fiercely. "She's mine."

Ivana held tightly to her mother, and Tem'aree'ay did not move her arms.

Almost immediately, a second figure appeared near the first, this one a portly female elder with a kindly, wrinkled face. White ringlets fell around a round head with sparkling blue eyes and pursed pink lips. "This one's not yours, Varthmathr. She belongs in Saklausshei-mili, with me."

"You!" The male's scowl deepened. "By what right do you claim this soul, Móthir? She's come of age, thus no longer a child, and belongs on the fifth plane of Hel." He took a menacing step toward her. "She's mine."

Móthir remained in place, which put the one she called Varthmathr so close they could share one another's exhalations, assuming these Outworld creatures breathed.

Tem'aree'ay clutched Ivana closer, wishing she felt more certain she actually held her child. Though frail nearly to the point of nonexistence, the soul appeared to cling and Tem'aree'ay needed to believe she could provide some protection, even after death.

Tonaris continued to try to bring soul and body back together. He shouted orders that were summarily ignored. Every elf now looked toward the collectors of souls, watching the drama unfold. Eventually, even the surgeon turned to see what so enraptured his assistants, although his human sight and ears would allow him to experience nothing other than Tem'aree'ay apparently grasping herself.

The being referred to as Móthir explained, "This one is not an adult, despite chronological age. She has always been, and always will be, a child, an innocent. She belongs to me."

Varthmathr took a small step backward, though he did not seem finished with his argument. It appeared he only sought a slightly more comfortable distance for speaking. He opened his mouth, but before he could say anything, a third figure joined them.

This one had to crouch to fit into the room, a massive ogre of tremendous proportions who held a war club in one hand. "Mine!" he said, raising the club as high as he could in the crowded room. If he could have gotten it above his shoulders, it might even have appeared menacing. "She's a creature of magic!"

"Why won't anyone help me!" Tonaris screamed in clear frustration. "She's dying . . ."

Ghy'rinith seized the surgeon's arm, granting him the ability to see and hear what already held the elves enthralled. Only the page remained in ignorance, and he looked from elf to elf, apparently believing they were staring at him. Ghy'rinith must have sent him direct *khohlar*, because he went entirely silent and stared with the rest of them, his jaw sagging and his eyes round as coins.

The three creatures of magic rounded on one another, arguing with such volume and vehemence that Tem'aree'ay could not follow the conversation. Ivana did not move, clinging to her mother, and Tem'aree'ay had no intention of letting her go.

Just as it appeared the three would surely come to blows, a crack thundered through the room and one more Outworld being appeared. This one glowed with a silver light unique to the gods, and Tem'aree'ay recognized him at once as Frey, god of rain, sunshine, and fortune, the creator and patron of elves. Strikingly handsome, with finely chiseled features that could pass for human or elfin, Frey sported a head of thick, straight golden hair, piercing blue eyes, and a sinewy body befitting his divinity.

As one, the elves gasped and dropped to one knee, except for Tem'aree'ay, who refused to abandon her child. She bowed her head low in acknowledgment, while Tonaris remained standing with Ghy'rinith's hand in his own, gaping.

The soul-claimers from the various levels of Hel spun as one to face Frey, the ogre a bit slower than the others, hampered by his size and the confines of the room. Varthmathr's mouth opened, and his features purpled, although he made no violent gesture toward the deity. Before he could speak, however, Frey did.

"Begone, all of you. Dead or alive, the affairs of the elves are mine alone."

Móthir backstepped, head bowed. The ogre remained in place, his club drooping. Only Varthmathr seemed to maintain his steam. "But she's clearly mortal. The blood of humans runs through her veins."

Frey glared at him. "Her mother is an elf. The dispensation of her soul is mine to decide."

The fearsome-looking man glanced around the room. Moments earlier, he seemed certain to fight the other supernatural creatures. Now, he clearly looked to them for support. When neither stepped up, his features opened a bit and his voice became less angry, almost neutral. "Of what use is her soul to you? It's at least partially mortal. If you put it into a new elf, it would be, at best, incomplete." Apparently, a bit unsure, he added, "Would it not?"

Frey hunched, placing himself at eye level with Tem'aree'ay and Ivana. Rather than looking at the creature who had addressed him, he kept his attention fully focused on the mother/daughter pair. "I am certain I can extract the elfin essence from the souls of those who carried the blood of my creation. It may take two such souls, in some cases three or four; but, if I combine them . . ." He let the thought trail into silence.

But the words stimulated every mind in the room, and Tem'aree'ay's raced with the others. Currently, no living elf hybrids existed, but another would soon enter the world and, hopefully, more would follow. One hand left Ivana to touch her belly and the life growing behind it. At one time, the elves had hoped such combination births might rescue both elves and humans from oblivion. Soon after, they had become certain creatures like Ivana would doom them. Now, it seemed, the tide had turned again. If Frey could do as he just claimed, the elves would no longer have to wait for one among them to die of age before another could be born. A premature death would no longer be a permanent loss to the elves. Instead of risking gradual or sudden extinction, the elves would finally have a means to increase their numbers, if only back to the original number.

The openmouthed expressions on the faces of the other elves told Tem'aree'ay their thoughts mirrored her own.

Móthir finally stepped into the fray, her voice gentler than Varthmathr's and so soft they all had to strain to hear. "But what of the human pieces of those souls? Can they also be combined to make a whole?"

Frey reluctantly tore his gaze from Ivana. "They're not constructed for reuse," he pointed out. "But, unlike elves, humans . . ." His gaze went to the ogre, and he added, apparently for his benefit, ". . . and most other magical beings, are not finite. The wasted bits of the soul will dissipate."

Varthmathr folded his arms across his chest. "So we'll get nothing."

Frey's eyes narrowed. As rage flared, his huge and gleaming aura turned crimson at the edges. "Of these rare souls, you'll get nothing; but that's the way it's always been and meant to be. Never in the history of the universe have souls been divided, nor has anyone demanded a piece of someone else's prize. What I do with the souls assigned to me is my business alone."

Móthir and the ogre both nodded, forcing Varthmathr to back down. Tem'aree'ay suspected Varthmathr would not have dared to pick a fight with any god under ordinary circumstances. This time, Frey had caught him hot, and his desire and concern for the dispensation of future souls had fueled his impetuousness. He did have one final argument. "You called them 'rare souls,' and, at the moment, that's clearly the case. But what if elfin and human societies become wholly intertwined? Hel could become . . ." He flailed around for a legitimate term.

"Empty" implied the current denizens might disappear, which did not seem likely. Tem'aree'ay knew when the goddess who ruled the cold under-realm for those who died outside of battle had still existed, before the Ragnarok, she had collected souls to use as warriors against the lighter gods and Valhalla's *Einherjar* in that final battle. Post-Ragnarok, apparently, a group of creatures collected the souls of the dead, each existing on its own plane of Hel and with its own requirements for entry. Clearly, they competed, each claiming as many souls for themselves as possible, but Tem'aree'ay had no clue what they did or planned to do with their collections.

Instinctively, her arms tightened around Ivana, though it only served to remind her she held something ephemeral and unworldly. Without Tem'aree'ay's knowledge, Ivana's soul had turned to face the confrontation.

Apparently finding no better word, Varthmathr finally resorted to the obvious one. ". . . empty. How could anyone consider that a just situation adherent to the terms or intentions of Odin's laws?"

Frey frowned. Tem'aree'ay could only guess the considerations racing through his head, and she dared not believe herself worthy of second-guessing any god, especially her creator. She knew Odin had also died at the Ragnarok, and the All-Father had never wholly approved of Frey's creation. Legend suggested Odin had believed the elves unfairly gifted with magic and near-immortality, thus had imposed strict limits on their survival, especially the system that regulated their souls after death. Now, Frey had finally found a means to prevent their extinction, and Tem'aree'ay hoped, for the sake of her people, he would not abandon it.

Frey bobbed his head a moment, then cleared his throat, while the three beings of Hel waited quietly for him to speak. The elves and surgeon also watched in silence, always patient, though their future, or lack of it, rested on the decision. "You have a valid point . . . as do I. Perhaps we can come to a workable agreement?"

Móthir finally spoke up. "Perhaps we could allow the soul a say in the matter. Argue our cases and let them choose their resting place." She looked directly at Ivana, and a beatific, motherly smile appeared on her features. Her sea-green eyes sparkled. "For example, this one would thrive on the first level. It's a paradise for innocents, especially children or those most childlike. She belongs with me."

"Hey!" the ogre said, his voice so rumbling, the entire room seemed to shake as he spoke. "That's not fair at all! We've never allowed the souls a choice; who wouldn't select Saklaussheimili over Niflhel? Kynstathr over Illrhel? Levels six through nine would get no one, and levels like yours would become overrun with sinners."

"Not everyone qualifies for Saklaussheimili!" Móthir pointed out. "How often do we quibble over who gets to claim a particular soul?"

Varthmathr made a gesture that encompassed the room. "We're doing it right now! And, if humans and elves keep interbreeding, it's likely to become more frequent. Ofriki's supposed to take the souls of the mortal magical. Do the *human* mages of Myrcidë go to him or to the level that suits their temperament and actions? Should he give up everything with human or elfin blood? And what's to stop other creatures from mating with one another? What happens to the soul of an elf-*Kjempemagiska* cross?"

The deities and monsters seemed to have forgotten they had an audience, which suited Tem'aree'ay and, probably, all of her companions.

Frey laughed, apparently at the image of slight elves and enormous giants attempting to breed. "I can limit my interests to souls at least half elfin in character, so long as all of those come to me. Believe me: anything less isn't worth extracting and saving; and it would result in too many patchwork memories for the infant elves to handle." He added carefully, "Realize now, when I say half elfin in character, I'm not talking about living bloodline. I don't care whose father is three-fourths human or seven-eighths elfin. The proof lies with the soul itself, in the nature of heart and mind as reflected in the spirit." He finally seemed to notice the gawkers, now that he had delivered information they might not know. Nevertheless, he continued dutifully, "We all have experience judging the recently deceased. I think we can find reasonable agreement on this, and I certainly don't want anyone, no matter how elfin, who would fit the criteria for the bottom four levels of Hel."

Varthmathr grumbled. "As usual, I'm the one sacrificing. The lowest four aren't losing anything. Kvikindi's only for animals, so the twins won't know the difference, either."

Móthir and Ofriki exchanged glances, and even the ogre's face seemed to acquire the monstrous equivalent of a smile. The woman spoke for both of them. "We're giving up at least as much as you. There will be elfin/human innocents and children who die, and as you already pointed out, they'll all qualify as magical beings. Sessgladr will also have to give up any hybrids with a kind, helpful, or charitable bent. Since you get the ordinary humans as well as the warriors not taken for Valhalla, you already take more souls than anyone else, that's why your level is in the middle and got to keep the name Hel. You're not going to miss the occasional crossbreed."

Varthmathr muttered. "You just wait. Over time, everyone will be a crossbreed."

Ofriki sighed, a sound nearly indistinguishable from a growl. Only the softness of his features and tone differentiated the two. "You're borrowing trouble, Varthmathr. If such a thing happens, it won't be for centuries or millennia. Only one of us in this room is immortal in the true sense of the word. By the time your concern is realized, we'll all be dead and gone or Hel reorganized. Frey's offered a fair compromise, and angering him isn't in any of our best interests. I, for one, am accepting the deal he offered."

"Me, too," Móthir added firmly.

With that, the two disappeared as suddenly as they had come.

Only Varthmathr remained. The ferocious-looking man licked his lips, glanced around the room, and scowled. "Deal," he finally said before leaving as abruptly as the others.

Frey finally turned his attention fully on Ivana and beckoned her to him.

Ivana paused, looking at Tem'aree'ay for guidance.

Tem'aree'ay gave her a reassuring smile. "Go," she whispered. "Frey is the father of all elves. No place is safer than in his arms."

Without further encouragement, the soul of Ivana Shorith'na Cha-tella Tir Hya'sellirian Albar headed eagerly toward the god of elves.

An abrupt and blinding light flashed between Ivana and her goal with a crash louder than any thunder. The soul stopped short with a shriek. The elves and Tonaris jerked backward, Tem'aree'ay stunned beyond words or action. As her vision cleared, she could see even Frey wore a startled expression as he faced an enormous, dark figure that had appeared between the god and Ivana's soul. More shadow than substance, it reached for the elfin hybrid with four clawed hands, but Ivana ran back to her mother, cowering into her arms.

Tem'aree'ay wrapped herself around her daughter's soul. She had no idea if she could hold the insubstantial thing that remained of Ivana, but she would never abandon her to whatever fate this demon promised. She would fight to the death, if necessary. "Go away!" she shouted. "This soul belongs to Frey!"

"Who are you?" Frey demanded. "And by what right do you dare to exist on this plane?"

The nebulous shadow-form appeared less to turn toward Frey than to develop a headlike protrusion on the god's side of its body. "Don't you recognize me?" The darkness coalesced into a vaguely human shape with a bulbous head, four arms and a pair of legs like tree trunks.

A light flashed through Frey's pale eyes. "Ondetar." They narrowed next. "You have no right."

The sound of deep and evil laughter filled the room. "I have every right. The souls of elves who die of anything other than age are mine. Odin decreed it."

Tem'aree'ay found herself clutching her chest with one hand, Ivana with the other. It did not matter what action Frey took. Tem'aree'ay would not allow this thing to have her daughter. She would sooner die fighting it.

Frey shook his head with a wry grimace. "Wrong on all counts, Ondetar. Odin made no such decree. You receive what I give you, and that only because I was forced to make a personal agreement with the All-Father."

Ondetar did not allow the argument to dissuade him. He enunciated each syllable, with greatest emphasis on the last. "The souls of elves who die of violence are mine to *eat!*" The face became more detailed, mostly toothy grin. "Mine to torture. Mine to utterly destroy."

Still in fighting mode, Tem'aree'ay did not allow the words to sink too deeply. She barely noticed the elves around her gasping in dismay.

The demon's proclamation rattled the observers but had no obvious effect on Frey. "You have no interest in anything other than pure elfin souls. And you have no dominion over anyone or anything. If you challenge me, I have the right and power to destroy you."

The darkness flared up like a freshly fed fire, hissing. "For the moment, Lord of Elves, but not much longer. My power has grown greatly as you can see." The blackness broke open in a gaping maw, its edges bowed upward in a parody of a smile. "And you gave me my followers."

Frey clearly did not agree. "Souls nourish you, but they don't add to your strength. Once destroyed, they cannot follow anyone."

"I'm not talking about the souls." Laughter accompanied the information.

Frey blinked. His pale features noticeably darkened. A single word slipped past his lips. "The *svartalf.*"

It literally meant dark elves. Tem'aree'ay could still remember when forty of their ilk who seethed in bitterness had become banished. Nearly all of the elves bore scars from the conflagration that had destroyed Alfheim and forced them to join the humans on Midgard, but a substantial group of them had become emotionally damaged as well, turning their rage upon the humans who had had nothing to do with the fire. Most had returned to the fold and their senses, but those forty could not be saved. Frey had sent them away permanently. Tem'aree'ay and the other *lysalf,* light elves, had heard nothing from or about the *svartalf* in the years since the split.

"They worship me," Ondetar rumbled. "And as their numbers grow, so will my power."

Still tightly wrapped around her daughter's soul, Tem'aree'ay felt her heart skip a beat.

But Frey only laughed. "Then they are fools. As you devour their souls, their numbers can only decrease and your power with them."

Ondetar mocked Frey's laughter. "Except we have enough souls to satiate me and add to their numbers."

Frey disagreed. "There is only one hybrid, and you haven't the strength to wrest her from me."

The demon made a gesture of dismissal with one bulbous hand. "Take her. I don't need her."

Frey made a beckoning gesture, and Tem'aree'ay loosed Ivana who raced around the vast bulk of the demon to settle into Frey's grip. Lowering his head, he whispered something to her.

Ivana's soul spoke one last time. "Thank you, Mama. I am safe." Then she dissipated within the protective circle of Frey's arms.

Only then, Frey's features went from smug to thoughtful. He speculated aloud, "Demons have no ability to travel between worlds. Even with the additional strength your witless followers grant you, you shouldn't be able to come here." He repeated more softly, eyes squinted in contemplation. "You shouldn't be able to come here. Demons must be summoned or pass through gates."

To Tem'aree'ay, Ondetar seemed to become a walking evil grin. No longer concerned with Ivana's soul, she found her stomach in knots over the realization the god she worshipped had become visibly troubled.

"Think," the demon instructed calmly. "Who might be building gates to Béarn Castle?"

Tem'aree'ay found her own thoughts racing, and the expressions on her companions' faces ranged from horror to confusion.

Ondetar did not wait for Frey to figure it out on his own. "Elves and humans blasted to random Outworlds. Sound familiar? Svartalfheim received seven usable souls. We divided six between us: three sacrificial and three for newborn *svartalf*. That left us one for bait."

Reality struck Tem'aree'ay like a physical blow. Their own *jovinay arythanik* had opened the way, not only for this demon but for a potential army of *svartalf*. "No," she whispered, then louder, "No!" *Warn them! Save them!*

Apparently, the other elves figured out the situation as well. They headed for the door, Tonaris, Ghy'rinith and Ath'erion at a panicked run, Myr-intha moving in the usual graceful and unhurried manner of elves, and Shar'iss'ah looking more confused than determined.

Apparently having recovered some of his composure, but still mostly ignorant, the page followed the others from the room.

Laughing uproariously, Ondetar floated after them, his shadow-form brushing Tem'aree'ay. Though usually impervious to cold, Tem'aree'ay suffered a chill that writhed through her entire arm before disappearing. She started to follow, but Frey's voice stopped her.

"Tem'aree'ay, wait."

The elf went still, then slowly turned her head toward her liege, afraid what he might say. Frey rarely deigned to speak to mortals; when he did, it usually heralded disaster.

"I can't help you," Frey said with tangible sorrow. "When gods meddle, even a little bit, it risks the balance of the universe. An attempt to help could destroy all life as you know it."

Tem'aree'ay swallowed hard. She understood but did not feel entirely certain utter destruction would prove less terrible than what the demon promised.

"And know," he continued. "No matter what happens, Ivana's soul is safe. She will remain with me until I can place her with an elf, no matter how long that takes."

Tem'aree'ay's hand went naturally to the bulge in her abdomen. She had so many questions she knew Frey would not or could not answer.

But Frey gave her some of the information she wanted. "The baby is male, well and normal at the present time. Ivana's abnormality arose because of the struggle between her elfin and human anatomy. Many, but not most, hybrids will have this issue, but elfin healers can fix it if it's caught near the time of birth."

Tem'aree'ay felt tears springing to her eyes. She ignored them, turning slowly toward the god. It was not in her nature to question their creator, but she needed to know. As she fully faced Frey, she expected to find him missing, but he met her gaze with concern in his inhuman eyes.

"I'm sorry, Tem'aree'ay, but gods cannot step in simply to prevent suffering. What sort of lives would you have if we did?"

Happy ones? Tem'aree'ay did not dare to speak the words aloud. She had never considered questioning a god before, particularly this one, but the horrors that had attended Ivana's short existence seemed too unfair not to consider breaking rules, even those laid down by the gods themselves. Tears blurred her vision entirely; by the time she wiped them away, Frey had disappeared.

Tem'aree'ay glanced at Ivana one more time. She had seen

human mothers cling to the lifeless bodies of their children, wailing, screaming, and raging at the world, yet she saw no reason. The remains on the bed were only the cruel vessel that had housed and restricted her daughter. Now, her soul ran free, promised companion to Frey until he procured another hybrid soul and brought them together to live again in a fully elfin infant. Wiping away the last of the tears, she raced from the room to join the *jovinay arythanik,* hopefully in time to save her people.

CHAPTER 19

*A couple dozen men seem like a hundred when you're fighting for
your life. And a hundred men seem more like ten thousand*
                                    —*Tae Kahn Weile's son*

ELVES AND HUMANS packed the great hall. As more groups arrived safely in Béarn from the Outworlds, curiosity seized the local
citizenry as well as the visiting dignitaries and even some of the previously liberated soldiers. Guardsmen kept the gawkers toward the
center and back of the room, apart from the *jovinay arythanik* and
the place the gate habitually winked into place at their magical urging. A small, fierce group of mostly Renshai warriors guarded that
area, including Rantire and Calistin, both of whom looked mostly
bored. Thus far, nothing untoward had slipped through the gate
along with the found soldiers and elves, even on those occasions
when they had needed to send the rescue party.

That group stood nearby, noticeably diminished. Nomalan had
died, and King Griff had pulled Marisole from the team, leaving
only Tae, Ra-khir, Saviar, El-brinith, and Chan'rék'ril. Tae hovered
near Captain, and Saviar stayed closer to the guardian Renshai,
making the group look even smaller and less effectual.

Kentt sat in his usual position behind the massed elves, his back
against the wall and his feet tucked under him to minimize the comparatively enormous amount of space he occupied. Thus far, he had
proven of limited use, though he had learned to add his piece to the
jovinay arythanik in gradually more helpful and powerful ways as
well as opened the path for communication and developed a better
understanding of elfin magic. Early on, everyone in the room seemed
determine to stare at him, and he attempted to win them over with
gentle smiles and quiet determination. He appreciated that, over
time, they had gradually come to accept him. Newcomers still tended
to watch him with suspicion, but those who had attended several

sessions ignored him to the point where he had come to feel like an invisible part of the wall.

Between sessions, Kentt spent all of his off-time with his daughter Mistri and Prince Arturo. The translation magic he and the elves had created worked wonders when it came to teaching the young man who intended to become a diplomat to Heimstadr. Over time, Kentt had come to see the Béarnian prince as something much more than the animalistic curiosity he had known back home. He only hoped he could convince the other Islanders to accept Arturo and the peoples of the continent as worthy associates and—eventually, hopefully—allies. To that end, he and Arturo spent hours discussing the differences and rare similarities of mindset and morality, gestures and other nonverbal forms of communication, images, emotions, and ways to bridge the enormous gaps between upbringings and experiences. It was going to be a monumental, but definitely worthwhile, task.

Captain announced to the room, using *khohlar*, *No rescue necessary. We're opening the gate.*

The process had become shortened since the first couple of days when Captain had needed to warn the humans about the forthcoming gate, instruct the guardians and rescuers how far to safely stand from the magic, and prepare the room for possible upcoming events. Now, the humans went silent, the elves began their chant, and the door-shaped form shimmered to life in its accustomed place.

In the past, Kentt had added his voice to the *jovinay arythanik*. As the number of elves had grown, his presence had become unnecessary. The last few times, he had found himself sitting in watchful silence, prepared to help with any emergencies that might arise.

The gate had barely formed when a shadow emerged from the opening. The elves did not seem to notice it, and Kentt might have believed his eyes had tricked him if not for the unusual number of human heads that followed its course outward and upward as well as his own sensitivities, which suggested the amorphous blob of darkness had an even darker aura. He started to rise, thinking to follow it as it floated toward an exit near the back, passing the king of Béarn without pausing or emitting any chaos energy.

Several moments later, the gate fully opened. Nothing happened for a long time. Finally, a tentative elfin head poked through it from the opposite side. He took a cautious look around the room, made a motion Kentt had not yet learned, then spoke too softly for him to hear. The head disappeared back into the gate.

Captain sent indirect *khohlar* to the room. *He says he needs a few moments to gather the others.*

It was not the first time this had happened. Much of the tension in the room disappeared, especially among the elves. Lapses in time rarely bothered them. Among the humans, the reaction seemed more mixed. Some relaxed while others seemed to become even more coiled and impatient. They whispered amongst themselves or remained staring intently at the gate.

The head reappeared, attached to a body that seemed a bit off to Kentt. It had a brownish aura compared with the light rainbow colors of most elves, and it moved with a heaviness he associated with the most somber of humans. Before he could ponder the figure too long, a sorcerous wave of sound blasted out from beyond the gate. Though clearly some sort of spell, it had no apparent effect on the *Kjempemagiska*. The gate widened exponentially, suddenly encompassing most of one wall.

Almost immediately, as one, every elf in the room charged toward it. Few humans stood between the elves and their creation, but those who did scurried wildly out of the way as the elves ran to embrace the gate with the speed and fury of a brokenhearted man called to his long-lost lover.

In an instant, most of the elves had disappeared through the gate, the rest following with the single-minded intent of rabbits darting through a hole to escape a pack of starving wolves. Though he did not fully understand what was happening, Kentt realized one important reality. Without elves on this side of the barrier, the gate would close; and no one he knew held the power to recreate it. He sprang to his feet, nearly braining himself on a ceiling built for humans, and dove for the mass of charging elves.

Kentt landed hard on the stone floor, his breath and half his wits jarred from him. One hand touched an elf, but it easily wriggled past his grasp and into the open maw of the gate. "Stop them!" he screamed in his best common. The sound emerging through the gate now resembled the hum of a *jovinay arythanik*.

Several Renshai attempted to come between the elves and their goal, but as the elves showed no fear of swords and seemed content to impale themselves, the maneuver had no effect. Kentt did see a couple of the humans duck through the gate amid the horde of elves; but none managed to stop a single one on the Béarnian side. "No!" he half-sobbed. Then, from the corner of his eye, he saw four more elves and a human rush into the room from an outside door. Once inside the great hall, the human skidded to a stop; but the chanting enthralled the new elves just as it had the others, and they rushed the gate as well.

Determined, Kentt dove on them, catching one tightly to his chest and another by an ankle. Both fought him, struggling wildly and viciously. Punches and kicks hammered his unprotected face and body, one slamming repeatedly into his groin. The one in his hand bit his thumb. Grip lost, pain aching through his entire body, the desire to stand disappearing, he instinctively wrapped both arms around the remaining elf, pinning her against him. With his prisoner held closely, the blows became ineffectual, but the icy agony gripping his body from the previous testicular kicks made his legs too weak to hold him. He collapsed onto the fighting form of the elf, knocking the breath from her lungs and stealing the last will to fight.

The shadow Kentt had seen previously swept over his head; he felt rather than saw it. It, too, entered the gate, which snapped shut behind it. The elf in Kentt's arms went limp, sobbing, and the room grew utterly silent. Only then, Kentt realized most of the human civilians had funneled through the exit doors. The guards of Béarn formed a protective pack around their king, who was clearly unharmed but shocked and uncertain. Eastern soldiers clung to Tae Kahn, who seemed miffed. Knowing him, Kentt suspected his mood had mostly to do with his adventurous nature; he had probably wanted to leap through the gate with the rushing tide of elves, perhaps not realizing he might find himself trapped on the other side. A few Renshai milled around the space where the gate had been, poking at the empty air. Where the elves had stood, nothing remained but Captain's table, which still held the Pica Stone. Whatever magical force had captured the elves had either not wanted or not recognized the artifact.

The elf under Kentt's massive body loosed a groan. He sat up, holding onto her arms, afraid she might run headfirst into the wall, still driven by the magical lure. When she only sat up dizzily and looked around her, he cautiously released her. It only required one elf on their side for a group on the other side to create a gate, but that presumed the other elves had the interest and wherewithal to craft one. To open a gate from this side, they needed a *jovinay arythanik*, and that required at least three. *Users of magic, but not necessarily elves.* For the first time since the gate had opened, Kentt felt hopeful. With any luck, the elf he had detained had the essential knowledge for making gates because none of the *Kjempemagiska* did. He also doubted any of the current Mages of Myrcidë held enough power to join a *jovinay arythanik* individually, even if properly taught. Given the dilution of their magic, it might take several to account for a single elf, but it was better than none at all.

Murmurs suffused the room as those remaining discussed what they had seen, the implications and the possible solutions. Kentt realized placing his hopes on a single elf, himself, and a handful of frightened barely-magical humans, presumably the weakest of the Mages of Myrcidë, highlighted the desperation. The previous rescues had required all of the elves, the Pica Stone, himself, the mages and a strong team to handle any danger. They still had the clairsentient sapphire, which boded well; but, at best, they had the ability to channel enough chaos to open a gate exactly where the old one had stood and back onto the world where the elves had disappeared. Doing that now would prove folly, only depriving them of their remaining elf. The situation on the other side needed to change so they had at least one ally capable of affixing the gate, hopefully in secret. Kentt also needed time to organize the dearth of magical beings remaining on the continent.

The elf Kentt had rescued and released looked around the room in quiet horror. Then, Tem'aree'ay arrived: disheveled, tears streaming from her eyes, her expression defining sorrow, dread, and despair. She ran toward Griff, and the humans parted in front of her, even the king's staunchest guardians. She all but disappeared into his arms, her slender form clutched to his massive body. He asked a one-word question, probably about their daughter, and her answer was equally short but entirely devastating. The king's leonine head wilted on top of hers. Smashed against him, her voice would never carry, so she used indirect *khohlar* to tell everyone in the room what they all needed to know. Princess Ivana was dead.

The instant the gate winked out, the magical noises stopped, and the elves went still and stupid. Hidden amongst them, Saviar Ra-khirsson fingered the hilt of his sword as he glanced around and between them, trying to take in the sights of the Outworld without revealing his presence. Whoever had captured them had taken great pains to assure all the elves and none of the humans responded to their sorceries. Nearby, and also surrounded by milling elves, Rantire watched him closely, apparently looking to him for guidance. He gestured for her to remain quietly hidden, then looked around for Calistin, whom he had also pegged to accompany the fleeing elves.

Saviar had chosen his companions with care. They faced an obvi-

ously magical threat, which meant they would almost certainly require weapons capable of striking magical beings. His mind had
immediately gone to the list from the war: himself, Rantire, Calistin,
and Valr Magnus plus a few others, like Ra-khir, who had sported
ill-suited and poorly-balanced objects such as *Kjempemagiska*-made
swords and utility knives. Though in the room, Magnus had seated
himself too far from the gate for Saviar to grab in time, and Ra-khir
had chosen a position in the back with Tiega, Darby, and Keva. That
had left only the three Renshai, and Saviar suddenly realized Calistin
no longer carried a magical weapon, only the crumbling Sword of
Mitrian with its new, non-magical gemstone eyes and a backup
weapon that was well-crafted but devoid of otherworldly properties.
That meant their survival might hinge upon the element of surprise.

Spotting Calistin amid the elves, Saviar approached him for a
whispered discussion. "Take my sword." He reached for his hilt.

Before Saviar could draw it, Calistin put a restraining hand over
his brother's. "No," he hissed back. "You keep it."

They could not afford to argue. The more they talked, the more
likely they would lose their cover. Saviar leaned toward Calistin.
"These are magical enemies. We need the functional sword with the
most competent warrior."

Calistin scowled. "I'll make do." He made a brisk motion that
commanded future silence. He also clearly realized the significance
of remaining hidden, at least until they had a chance to assess the
situation and their enemy.

Though against his better judgment, Saviar moved away, losing
himself among the elves.

Khohlar reached Saviar, its tone odd and clearly mocking. *Welcome, cousins, to our world.* Images accompanied that sending, of
dark, twisted elves with hearts filled with rage and bitterness. Without need for explanation, he knew they called themselves the *dwar-
freytii* and it translated to "the chosen ones of Frey." Despite this
information, the *khohlar* word evoked from the elves around him was
svartalf, meaning "dark elves" in both elvish and Northern.

Saviar had heard legends of the *svartalf*, about how they had attempted to destroy humankind and how Frey had banished them to
the Outworlds. Realizing they would slaughter any humans they
found, Saviar whispered to the elf standing closest to him, "Please let
all the good elves know we're here to help and to keep us hidden
from your cousins."

The elf responded with direct *khohlar*, *Will do; but please don't
call them our cousins. We claim no kinship to them any longer.*

Saviar returned a serious nod. He heard nothing around him that could pass for communication, no whispering chain, and he could only hope the true elves passed his message to one another in direct *khohlar*. He returned to Calistin, glad the *svartalf* had chosen to use mind-speech. None of the humans present, perhaps none in the world, spoke elvish, but *khohlar* bypassed the need for translation. Any hearer could immediately understand it unless the sender made a conscious effort to couch things into a specific language.

What do you want from us? someone shouted from the crowd.

Nothing much, came the purring reply of a *svartalf.* *Only your souls.* Laughter accompanied the sending, though only at the fringes. None of the transported elves joined the mirth. In fact, they stirred restlessly, clearly unnerved by the response. The *svartalf* explained further, *We have chosen to switch our allegiance from Frey, who abandoned us, to Ondetar, the demon who devours the souls of elves who die of violence.*

Someone immediately seized the bait, clearly startled, *Why would you do such a thing? What possible good could it do any of us?*

What other choice did Frey leave us? As it stands, he receives all the recyclable souls from you and from us. He passes them along to your off-spring while we're condemned to gradually disappear. Ondetar made us a deal we could not refuse. We grant him power by worshipping him, and he gains the ability to share the souls he receives with us. The *svartalf* speaker paused, allowing his listeners to contemplate the details.

Even Saviar understood. If the demon shared the souls equally, the *svartalf* stood to gain a fully-souled child for every two elves killed. Now that they held all of the *lysalf* prisoners, they could sacrifice the entire group. Half would get devoured, but the other half would be recycled into *svartalf* infants.

Captain's familiar *khohlar* followed. *It might be true that if you murdered all of us, you would get some of our souls. Some. The rest would disappear entirely. Over a short time, at least by elfin standards, you would continue to deplete the store of souls by whatever the demon consumed until, sooner than you understand, none of us would remain.*

The next reply came in a loud, verbal rumble that seemed to arise from the depths of the Outworld in a primitive language Saviar did not understand. He seized the elf next to him. "Please translate."

The elf nodded, feeding Saviar direct *khohlar*. *The demon, Ondetar, says that as the number of his followers swell, so will his power. Eventually, he will break free of the curse Odin and Frey placed upon him and will no longer be confined to elfin souls as sustenance. When that happens, the number of our souls will no longer dwindle. He "graciously" stated that any* lysalf *who disavows Frey to worship him is welcome to join the ranks of the* svartalf *and save his own soul and future.* *

Ice seemed to form in Saviar's chest. "Has anyone taken up his offer?"

**If anyone did, he used direct* khohlar, *so none of us could hear him.* *

Saviar bit his lip. It was a tempting offer. In the elves' place, at least some humans would take it. Since all of the light elves now knew they had three humans hidden among them, it put the Renshai at great risk. He could think of no better way for a traitorous *lysalf* to prove his loyalty to his new master than to reveal the secret of hidden and armed humans protecting the others.

The elf beside Saviar added, **Anyone who doesn't disavow Frey will be slaughtered, his soul either devoured or used to create* svartalf *babies. They're giving us until tomorrow to make the decision.* *

Another of the captured elves sent indirect *khohlar,* **How do you know he's not tricking all of us, that he won't just kill everyone and ingest all of our souls?* *

A murmur swept the elves at something Saviar could not see.

His translator explained, *Three pregnant svartalf *have stepped forward.* *

**When your war sent elves and human soldiers to our Outworld, Ondetar gave us a demonstration. We seized the seven elves and set to worshipping Ondetar. When he had the power we granted him as followers, we sacrificed six of them. He placed three inside our women. We've tested them; they are normal infants complete with* eyenlyåndel. * The *khohlar* gave Saviar the word as well as its meaning, "immortality echo," the magical indication of a present soul. **That earned him three to devour. The last we kept in order to trap all of you. As you know, Hy'astorion Kevtelent Ar'pero-miay Nor Shal'iend'tay has served his purpose as bait and now stands among you.* *

Captain asked the question on Saviar's mind, though no other elf would have thought of it at the moment, **What have you done with the humans sent with those seven elves?* *

Joy accompanied the next sending. **Oh, those we slaughtered, gleefully and slowly. They provided us with many hours of entertainment, I assure you.* *

Outraged, Saviar seized the arm of his translator. "Can you band together and contain the magic of the *svartalf* like you did with the *Kjempemagiska* during the war?"

The elf sent back, **They have us hemmed in with wards reinforced with spells that prevent anyone inside them from using magic. It's strong; they clearly spent time and effort preparing this trap.* *

Saviar frowned. That complicated the situation but did not surprise him. Once released from the spell that had summoned them so unreasoningly through the gate, the elves had not scattered, deliberately or in panic. Saviar had wondered why and now knew the reason. "Does it constrain humans, too?" His hand dropped to his hilt. "And magical weapons?"

The elf hesitated, tipping his head. At first, Saviar thought he might be listening to something, perhaps other *khohlar.* The *lysalf* as a group had remained remarkably quiet, and Saviar supposed they had resorted to whispered conversations and singularly directed *khohlar,* things that allowed conversation without concern for the enemy overhearing. He recalled someone telling him elves tended to think similarly and react in groups more than individually, so perhaps they simply required less discussion than a bunch of humans would in a similar situation.

Saviar's thoughts had gone off in their own direction, so the elf's reply startled him. *I don't know, but I imagine Captain might have answers to your questions that I don't. He's seen and heard more than nearly all of us together. He's at the center of the group, if you want to find him.*

"Thank you," Saviar whispered. He wanted to say more, but every word risked drawing attention to himself, especially that of the *svartalf.*

No further *khohlar* came from the captors nor did the demon speak. Apparently, they had made their offer and intended to allow the elves to discuss it amongst themselves through the night. Peeking around the elves, it appeared to Saviar as if the svartalf had disbanded and wandered off, presumably to their dwellings to rest. Likely, they left guards behind, though Saviar could not locate them without risking his own concealment.

Saviar wound through the *lysalf* with delicate caution, using the Renshai stealth maneuvers taught to him since infancy. Occasionally, he dared a whispered question to the elves, but this soon became unnecessary as those around him apparently knew his destination and directed him properly with light touches and rare *khohlar.* None of them appeared to wish him any malice, and a few turned him sympathetic looks, presumably because of the statement the demon had made about killing the human soldiers. One of the starker differences between humans and elves became crystal clear to him. Their loss of seven of their own struck them more prominently and deeply than the knowledge that many more human soldiers had died in agony did him. It was not that he did not care; but, so long as he did not know the identities of those killed, their loss remained academic and distant. To the elves, the loss of any one of their own was a devastation none of them could bear.

Sooner than he expected, Saviar discovered Captain in the densest part of the huddle with Calistin beside him. Both welcomed Saviar, the elf with a *khohlar* greeting and Calistin with an impatient gesture urging him to step closer. Saviar came as near as comfort allowed before whispering. "Can humans walk through the wards?"

Captain replied, his *khohlar* directed. *Not entirely unscathed, but certainly less so than any elves. Running through the wards would probably cause burns as well as drain us of our power. You would only have to deal with the wounds.* From the pause that followed, Saviar guessed Calistin, and possibly Rantire, received the same information. He did not like the thought of entering a battle with potentially serious injuries, but he would do so if no other option existed.

Saviar waited until Captain's attention came back to him before asking the next question. "What about magical weapons?"

Captain's brow crinkled, a humanlike affectation Saviar knew well. He was considering. *Items imbued with magic are more powerful than magical beings. It would probably depend on the type of magic.* He stopped suddenly, clearly not wishing to go into a long explanation they would not fully understand. *Your sword, for example, is* skyggefrodleikr. *The translation of "shadow magic" entered Saviar's head along with the unfamiliar term. *I believe it could penetrate the ward, but I'm not sure what effect the sword would have on the magic.*

Saviar had a bit of experience. "I don't know if this helps, but Subikahn was able to poke it all the way through an invisible magical window."

Captain's amber eyes flashed, and he spoke aloud, apparently too startled to respond to a verbalized question with *khohlar.* "Where did this happen?"

"At the compound of the Mages of Myrcidë when they held me prisoner."

"Through the window, you say?" The odd, canted eyes seemed to gain a life of their own as he considered the words. *Their compound is built on the ruins of the Western Wizard's lair. They incorporated his ancient magic into its construction. It's of the same source and power as the Pica Stone* His gaze went to Saviar's sword. *If it can poke through near godlike power, I have no doubt a swipe with the blade would destroy a ward, even one created with a* jovinay arythanik *and demon magic.*

For the first time since the capture, Saviar's thoughts soared. "So

Rantire or I or both could destroy the wards. The elves could band together to hold off any magic the *svartalf* threw at us while we cut them down."

Cut them down? Captain repeated. *You mean the* svartalf?*

That being self-evident, Saviar merely nodded. Then, he added, "And, hopefully, the demon."

The demon will prove a fight worthy of three Renshai. We can probably tamp down his magic for you. His every claw strike will age you ten years; and most demons have four per hand. Elves can spare forty years. Can you?

Though distinctly bothered by the idea, Saviar would not back down from a battle. *We'll just have to kill it without taking a hit.* He tried to sound utterly confident. While caution could serve a warrior well, fear or the contemplation of failure never did.

But you mustn't kill any of the svartalf.*

That took Saviar by surprise, but Calistin even more so.

"What?" the jewel of the Renshai hissed.

The svartalf *are fallen elves. We share the pool of souls with them. If any of them die by violence, their souls feed the demon and we have one less elfin soul for all eternity.*

"Making the demon more powerful," Saviar added thoughtfully.

No, Captain sent. *Making it less hungry. Its power stems from the number and fervor of its worshippers, not how many souls it eats.*

Calistin shook his head. "So you're telling us we need to kill a demon and defeat all of its followers without taking a single life?"

Captain made an apologetic gesture. *Renshai learn many ways to disarm and humiliate opponents. Surely there are ways to remove enemies from a fight without killing them.*

"Ways exist," Calistin admitted. "All of them far more difficult and dangerous to our opponents, us, and every innocent around us." He scowled, and Saviar knew he wanted to say much more. Noncombatants constantly suggested ways to make warfare less violent, never realizing the inhuman talent it took, the focus, and the risks involved. When warriors attempted to appease those preaching peace, the result was usually far more carnage and, far too often, the death of the warrior himself.

Please, Captain said, the emotion surrounding the plea desperate, genuine, and intense. *I can't imagine any warriors I trust more than the three of you when it comes to accomplishing the impossible. Just try your best to get us out of this with as few casualties as possible on either side. Other than the demon, of course.*

"We'll do our best," Saviar promised for all three of them, though he had little right to do so. Though the elves outnumbered the *svartalf* by a factor of five, the demon more than made up the difference. It, alone, would take all of the Renshai's attention, and the elves would have to focus every bit of their energy on binding magic. Saviar could see nothing that could stop the *svartalf* from using conventional weapons and random objects to slaughter the elves where they stood chanting or to assault the Renshai from behind. Unlike the *lysalf*, the *svartalf* had nothing to keep them from killing their cousins so long as the demon still lived. The next strategy practically wrote itself. "If we take down the demon, the *svartalf* can no longer risk killing elves."

"Only us," Calistin pointed out, and neither of them could honestly contradict him.

Now did not seem the time for historical questions, but Saviar had to know and realized *khohlar* could condense a long answer into moments. "I thought Frey loved the elves. Why did he create this terrible situation in the first place, and why hasn't he fixed it?"

Captain looked around the group a moment, clearly considering what he should impart in this situation. Elves rarely spoke freely of their strengths and weaknesses to humans for security reasons as well as the realization a secret, once told, could not be recanted. He rolled his eyes upward in more serious contemplation, then sighed sadly before launching into a story that imparted a lot of information into a short session of *khohlar*.

When it came time for the gods to create living beings to inhabit the nine worlds, they worked individually. Odin, the leader of the gods, made a creature in his own image, granting it a stolid form, a strong and warlike disposition, and vast quantities of wisdom. These he named "humans" and assumed they would have dominion over the lesser denizens crafted by the other gods just as as he did over them in Asgard. And, for the most part, he assumed rightly. The rest of the gods put most of their focus into the various animals, strong on sensation and speed while weaker in intelligence. *

Captain paused momentarily, presumably to pass the same information to Calistin and, possibly, Rantire whose location Saviar still did not know. He hoped she hid quietly among the elves with enough information and tending to prevent her doing anything rash.

Frey took the assignment differently, either thoughtless of the All-Father's moods or simply not realizing the effect he might have on his leader. In any case, he also created a being in his own image: handsome, lighter, and daintier than Odin, disinterested in battle and strategy. Because he went easy on the strength and wisdom, he could use more of the other . . .

ingredients. ★ He chuckled a bit and sent a wordless concept of vats labeled "intelligence," "chaos," "strength," "speed," "wisdom," and other attributes in a long and crooked line. ★*Thus, the elves were born, and they resembled humans in the same ways Frey did Odin: general form and vital organs, including, as we have discovered, the ones for procreation. But in other ways much different.* ★

★*Loki created the giants, beings of scant intelligence and far too little goodness, those things sacrificed for strength and size. Nearly all of the terrible monsters of the worlds came from breedings between gods and Loki's creation, yet those did not seem to bother Odin nearly as much as Frey's elves. To be sure, he kept the giants off of Midgard and Asgard, scattering them to the heat of Muspell and the horror of Jötunheim; but history would suggest he should have vetted them far more closely than he did the elves. For he did not fear Frey's creation; he envied it.* ★

Again, Captain paused a bit before continuing, and the confusion growing on Calistin's face suggested Saviar had been correct in believing he was telling the story in direct *khohlar* to each Renshai in turn. When Calistin opened his mouth to challenge Captain's last words, the elf leaped back into the story before the Renshai could speak. Given how quickly Calistin closed his mouth, he delivered this sending to Kevral's youngest son first, out of order.

It took less than two heartbeats, though, before he addressed Saviar again, ★*Remember, they had the same ingredients to work with; only the proportions differed. To be sure, Odin had placed the traits he valued most highly into his own creation, traits the elves tended to lack. However, the majority of the other gods, particularly the goddesses, voted to grant the elves dominion over Midgard. This angered Odin, who complained Frey had cheated. Frey, he said, had given the elves an unfair advantage over every other creature with their near immortality and magic, pointing out his humans had no magic whatsoever. He insisted the elves would use those things to conquer the humans and even challenge the gods. The argument that the elves had no warrior interests or abilities, little individual mindset, and no strategic concept did not sway him. Odin wanted what he wanted, and that mostly consisted of the praise and awe of his fellows and the acknowledged superiority of his own creation.* ★

Another minuscule lull followed while Captain caught up Calistin and, possibly, Rantire, then he continued, ★*So, the humans were given dominion over Midgard and all its creatures while the elves got Alfheim. But that was not enough for Odin, so focused was he on the inherent unfairness of the elfin lifespan and their magical abilities. So, Odin summoned Ondetar, designing in it the ability to digest nothing other than elfin souls. To assure control, he also made human souls deadly poisonous to it.*

Then, he came to Frey with an ultimatum. Either Odin released Ondetar, thereby assuring the destruction of all of the elves, or they found a way to limit the ability of the elves to procreate. I do not know the precise terms of their agreement, only that Frey got the souls of those elves who died of old age and Ondetar the ones who succumbed to violence. Frey had to gate the proper souls to Ondetar and got to keep and reuse the others. *

Captain hesitated again, then looked askance at the brothers. This time, he chose to speak softly, to address them both simultaneously. "I've known about Ondetar for some time because of my work with the Cardinal Wizards, the Outworlds, and the gods. To the rest of the elves, he was a ghastly surprise. They're reeling from the disclosure that Frey has been feeding our lost souls to a demon."

Saviar could see their point. "Couldn't Frey do anything to prevent this? Couldn't he stop it? Odin's been dead since the Ragnarok."

The look Captain gave Saviar combined surprise with inquisitiveness. Clearly, he expected the Renshai, perhaps all of humanity to know the reason. Nevertheless, he explained, **I don't know the terms of the agreement, but I'm wise enough to see Frey's indirect attempts to protect his elves. Alfheim had no predators, stagnant but perfect weather— a safe elfin paradise. Years ago, when he saw us taking a stand destined to destroy us all, he called out the bitter elves and sent them here to Svartalfheim. It's clear to me he wants us to thrive, but whatever terms Odin forced upon him ties his hands even after Odin's death.* He added, finally getting to the concept that perplexed him, *At least as severely as the gods' inability to interfere in the affairs of mortals because it would upend the balance and destroy our world entirely.* *

Saviar had known that; most humans did, at least the believers. He had always heard it applied to Midgard and mankind, so he supposed that explained why he had expected different things from Frey and the elves. Not that gods never risked interacting with humans. Thor, for example, had copulated with a Renshai, resulting in the birth of Colbey Calistinsson. Ravn had served as a playmate and adviser to Griff before he took the throne, though the king had believed him a figment of his imagination. Odin once took great pleasure and delight from stirring wars, presumably to alleviate his own boredom, though he had admittedly done it when the system of the powerful Cardinal Wizards still existed to help maintain the balance. Less provable stories abounded about how the gods descended to speak with or act among humans, though usually in small ways and often in disguise. Many of these could be dismissed as the overactive fantasies of the storyteller.

Unlike Saviar, Calistin remained entirely focused on the task at hand. "We can't harm the demon or the *svartalf* with nonmagical weapons, correct?"

Captain nodded, and Saviar frowned. The elf's *khohlar* beat his spoken response. *The demon is pure chaos, so nothing can strike it other than magic: spells, items, beings with infused chaos. The svartalf . . .* He hesitated just long enough to indicate a discomfort Saviar believed he understood. Whatever weaknesses he revealed about them applied to the regular elves as well. *Are susceptible to force injuries. If an elf falls from a height, he can break bones. A weapon without magical properties could still cause blunt damage, though it would not penetrate. A punch or kick would still hurt and, potentially, incapacitate.*

The Renshai exchanged glances. It should have been one of the first things Captain told them, but Saviar supposed nonmartial creatures might not realize the importance of such details. Or, perhaps, Captain had held the information so close for so long, it did not occur to him to reveal it. Despite the revelation, Saviar still remembered what he had planned to say. "I still think you should have the magic sword."

Calistin's voice remained soft but had an edge indicative of building rage. "I'm not taking your sword."

Saviar had to make one more plea. "We need every advantage. The best warrior should be the best armed—"

Calistin turned his brother a sudden, dangerous look, and Saviar backed down. "Can we at least agree Rantire and I will handle the demon?"

Calistin did not answer, and Saviar knew better than to press.

To warriors accustomed to swift action, the conversation seemed interminable, but Saviar knew its necessity. It kept them busy while the elves assessed and discussed their situation using soft conversation and directed *khohlar*, neither of which would carry to the enemy. It also gave the *svartalf* time to set watches and sleep cycles which gave some advantage to them but much more to the *lysalf*. Some elves needed sleep; others needed little or none. As Saviar understood it, the more "humanlike" the elf, the more likely the need; and the *svartalf* definitely more closely resembled humans than their lighter cousins. They seemed heavier, more ponderous and scheming, their expressions and movements more familiar and similar. An escape would force anyone sleeping to awaken before attacking, and a groggy enemy was an awkward, slow-witted enemy. Furthermore, given the situation and choices, he doubted any of the trapped elves would find himself or herself capable of sleep, no matter the desire or requirement.

I did not give Rantire quite as much information as you, Captain sent apologetically. *I don't know how much of her story you know, but she was once a prisoner of the elves. At the time, the elves were new to Midgard, angry about the destruction of Alfheim and persuaded humans had caused their misery. The* svartalf *had control, and I was having trouble convincing them to act like elves because they did not know or trust me. Most had never met me and knew me only as the ancient elf who chose to live on Midgard. They tortured her and would have killed her had I not eventually won them over and convinced them to release her. I don't know how much animus she still holds against us, but I thought it best not to explain our weaknesses to her as I did to you young men.* His gemlike eyes seemed enormous and childlike as he turned them to the Renshai. *I hope you understand and are not angry.*

"Not a problem," Saviar answered for both of them, and Calistin did not contradict him. "Now, if you could please explain the current situation. We can't get near enough to scout without revealing our presence, and that would remove any element of surprise, which we sorely need."

Captain turned all business. *What do you need to know?*

The answer came so instinctively, Saviar had to think about how to explain everything they needed. They had a reasonable idea of the terrain based on what they could see for themselves: the area seemed open and mostly rocky, indicative of nearby hills or mountains. The incomplete darkness and position of the moon suggested a time about halfway between dusk and midnight. He could not judge anything by the stars, which sprinkled the sky in an abnormal and wild array that little resembled a normal Midgard night. If the area had any trees, none stood tall enough to reveal itself over the massed elves, which further confirmed the likelihood of rocky hills.

"How far away are the enemy dwellings?"

Captain's brow knitted. *Elves don't make dwellings,* he reminded. *Although there's a surprising dearth of forest here, and most of the shrubbery appears to be scrub. It looked like they retired mostly to caves, and those are distant enough it would take a decent shout to rouse them.* He pursed his lips, a gesture that would indicate consideration in a human but probably demonstrated significant doubt about whether his words had proven useful in this instance.

Saviar encouraged, "That's helpful; thank you. How many remained behind as guards, and where's the demon?"

Captain bobbed his head, looking pleased that he had managed to convey something worthwhile. *Twenty remained, which is exactly half of their number last I knew. The demon is there.* Keeping his arm low, he pointed into a group of elves. *He moves from time to time, though. I'll make sure you're kept informed.*

Calistin asked the next question, "What sort of weapons do the svartalf have?"

Captain hesitated. He tipped his head, as if listening for something before replying. It occurred to Saviar, of all the queries to require assistance, this seemed the least logical, at least to the human mind. *No one has noticed any swords or large battle implements. They've seen quite a few knives, and they have access to plenty of rocks and sticks. Some have noticed rags that might work for slings. And, of course, they would rely heavily on magic.*

"Which you can neutralize?" Saviar asked hopefully.

Captain's expression did not pacify the Renshai. *We should be able to neutralize any cast spells by the svartalf or the demon. It won't undo any inherent magic, of course. And it will require us to band together, which means we can't assist you and we're essentially helpless to any physical attacks ourselves.*

"We will protect you." Saviar reminded.

We should be able to spare a few elves out of the jovinay arythanik to keep us apprised of the situation and, also, to warn you and us of any attacks. However, you need to realize none of us has much experience with warfare, and our spotters will be limited to their lines of sight as their magic would also be negated.

Calistin frowned but remained silent. Saviar understood his brother's concern. An inexperienced person shouting an inexplicable "watch out!" could be more distraction than assistance.

More reconnaissance was always better, but Saviar also knew elves did not handle time well. "If you could get Rantire closer to me, Calistin will work his way to the other side, and we'll get started. As soon as the wards go down, start your jovinya . . ." The elfin words would not come to him. ". . . your negating magic, please. We may not get the jump on the demon, but we sure don't want it getting off any spells before we're on it."

Though he barely moved, Saviar could tell Captain had already started connecting with his companions using direct khohlar. Calistin disappeared amid the milling elves, and Saviar waited politely until Rantire took his place. A few Renshai-taught gestures and words coordinated their attack, and both headed cautiously toward the edges of the gathered elves who kept them apprised of the demon's exact location and counted them down to the strike. On the khohlar number "one," Saviar thrust Motfrabelonning through the shimmering rainbow aura that surrounded them like a pen.

White light flashed where the steel met the ward, then the perimeter came alive with snarling, snapping lightning. A moment later, it vanished and went silent. Without pausing, Saviar rushed through the opening toward the black void of Ondetar. From the corner of his eye, he could see Rantire headed in the same direction.

Arms rose from the demon's mostly nebulous form, and a definitive head towered over it, scarlet eyes flashing and its mouth opening to reveal fangs as long as short swords. Captain had mentioned the claws but nothing about the teeth or the thick, yellow foam oozing from them that looked distinctly venomous. Its attention was fixed on the abruptly missing wards, and it seemed not to notice the two relatively small figures charging it from offset directions.

Saviar's steps never faltered. He reached Ondetar in six running steps, plunging *Motfrabelonning* into its central area. It looked so smoky, so insubstantial, he expected to feel nothing when the sword struck. Instead, something akin to flesh and muscle jarred his arm as the sword plunged into its body nearly to the hilt. A moment later, Rantire's blade sliced through an "arm" near the shoulder. The limb collapsed, dissipating as it did, and the demon roared with pain and outrage. "So you have magic, Little Ones. Toys for my worshippers after your deaths!"

Saviar did not waste time or effort on a reply. He ripped his sword from the depths of the beast, throwing steaming ichor over himself, Rantire, and the rocky ground.

The demon snarled syllables Saviar recognized as spell-words. Green light spewed forth, but before it could form, it was sucked toward the massed elves and dispersed en route. It shouted something in elvish, a warning or directions to its followers, Saviar presumed, but he did not understand a word. Once again, he plunged his sword deep into the formless creature in front of him. Again, he felt it jar through something solid, then the demon's fiery eyes fixed on him. What seemed like a hundred arms flared outward, all of them sweeping or grasping for Saviar.

The Renshai jumped backward, suddenly wholly on defense. Those claws did not need to strike anything vital to kill him. According to Captain, each nail that drew blood would steal a decade from his life; and, young as he was, he could not spare it. He found himself caught in an obstacle course in which a simple touch might prove his downfall. Ducking and weaving between those hands, he could spare no attention to attack, had no opportunity to build momentum without blundering into one of those deadly claws.

Then, the monster stiffened and whirled, presumably to counter an attack from Rantire on its opposite side. That gave Saviar a moment to reassess the situation, and he realized what had first seemed like a hundred clawed arms was actually more like a dozen. Heart pounding, sweat flying with every movement, he resisted the urge to back away and regain his bearings, driving in with a low cut intended to separate the formless legs from the remainder of what passed for Ondetar's body.

Soon, Saviar, Rantire, and Ondetar found themselves engaged in a lethal dance, charging in and out, whirling around one another, every precise movement potentially their last. The Renshai had scored several times, without noticeably slowing the demon, though its furious reactions suggested they had, in fact, caused injury. Thus far, none of the appearing and disappearing claws had met a mark, but it seemed like only a matter of time. Saviar had enough experience with Matrinka's cats to know if a paw got through one's defenses, it meant lines of multiple scratches, not just one. Captain had said four claws, forty years for every strike that hit, and Saviar dared not assume anything less. Rantire was already forty-five. One hit would definitely take her down.

Tarry blood speckled the ground and clung to Saviar's sword, so he knew he had done damage, but he had no idea how much. Vaguely, he wished the thing would show its wounds, that the ichor would flow from visible areas to give them some idea of the extent of the injuries they had inflicted. Then, multiple arms came at him again, and he had no thought for anything but his own defense, the lithe movements that saved him, once again, from death. Exhaustion pressed him, threatening to steal his lightning timing, urging him to flee, assuring a mistake he could not afford. His limbs felt on fire from the constant motion, sweat stung his eyes, and his head ached from the need to seize every opening, to anticipate and dodge. He had no idea how much time went by, but it seemed like hours. He only hoped the effort and pressure wore on Ondetar as well.

Seven clawed arms sailed toward him from several directions. Saviar dove between two, knocked one aside with his sword, swept under another, then rolled his ankle on a stone as he attempted to dodge the final three. He stumbled, dodged, overbalanced, and felt himself falling. He could attempt to catch his balance, tossing himself onto the claws and probably still failing or he could drop and roll. He chose the latter, realizing as he did he could eel his way past two of the strikes, but the third would definitely get him. Nevertheless, he continued moving, finding forty years preferable to a hundred and twenty.

As Saviar rolled, air hissed past him. Something shoved him askew, then he realized someone had thrown his own body between Saviar and the inevitable strike. The claws tore through the other's light tunic drawing four lines of blood, then the person rolled to his feet to reveal himself as Calistin. "No!" Saviar shouted, too late. Something flashed a deep and blinding yellow in the haft of the sword still at Calistin's hip. He held the other in his fist, crafted to Renshai standards yet wholly lacking magic. It was the gemstones in the wolf eyes in the corroding Sword of Mitrian that had caught Saviar's attention.

Saviar blazed to his feet, cursing his brother's impulsive heroism. He avoided Calistin's face, unable to deal with the certainty his little brother had become older than their father in an instant. What he did see was the laughing demon, the arms jutting from its bulbous body, and a golden aura radiating from Calistin's sheathed weapon. "Mitrian's sword!" Saviar shouted.

Calistin drew it as he moved and charged Ondetar.

Khohlar lanced into Saviar's head in Captain's voice. **My time! My time has come. Frey take my soul!**

The demon disappeared an instant later, magically, leaving nothing but lingering laughter. As the personal threat disappeared, realization struck Saviar. *Captain's dying. And the magic-negating net is down!*

That freed not only the demon, but also the *svartalf* to attack with chaos, and Saviar knew he could do little to nothing to defend or assist. Automatically, he sought out the current location of the demon. It had transported itself to near the center of the *lysalf*. He might not have seen it if not for its tendency to actively draw shadows the way a torch did moths. He ran toward it, Calistin and Rantire at his side. Whatever damage aging had done to his brother, it clearly had not slowed his pace.

From long habit, Saviar took in the details of the current situation as he moved. The elves remained mostly huddled in a mass where the wards no longer trapped them, the demon ensconced in their midst. Several *svartalf* watched from the periphery, some clearly dazed, others lying still on the ground, and a few tending their injured and possibly dead while others watched the demon work. As the Renshai drew closer, Saviar could see the demon crouched over Captain's prostrate form. A dark aura defined a bubble of space around the demon and the sluggishly moving form of the leader of the elves.

Calistin arrived first, slamming the Sword of Mitrian against the magical bubble. Light flared where the sword struck, sending sparks flying, but the magic remained intact. Apparently, whatever kept the elves at bay was stronger or, at least different, than the ward which had imprisoned them. Either that, or the ability to dispel it required an item infused with magic to strike it from the inside as Saviar's and Rantire's swords had done. An instant later, Saviar also made an attempt with *Motfrabelonning* and Rantire with her sword, without effect. Saviar cautiously probed the barrier with his hand, finding it surprisingly solid for something so entirely transparent. If not for the aura revealed by his sword, he would not have seen it at all.

"Keep an eye on the *svartalf*," Calistin instructed his companions.

For the first time since the claw strike, Saviar dared to look at his brother. Calistin had always appeared younger than his chronological age, just shy of nineteen, a common feature of Renshai with a significant amount of the old blood. He still looked fifteen at best, his blue eyes a bit large for his face, no hint of facial hair, his skin unblemished other than an occasional battle scar. A bloody flap of tunic dangled, marking the area along his left arm and shoulder where the demon claws had torn it. A golden aura surrounded him. Saviar had seen it many times, whenever he held *Motfrabelonning*'s hilt; yet it seemed to have flared into a yellow bonfire. The Sword of Mitrian had an aura of its own, just as it had in the war. Saviar had no idea how the weapon had come back to life without the benefit of the magical gemstones Colbey had borrowed from his wife, but it had apparently protected Calistin from the power of the demon's claws.

Rushing to obey Calistin's order, Saviar called out as he moved, "Tend to your injury, Calistin. You're of no use bloodless."

Rantire headed around the elves in one direction, Saviar in the other. He saw Calistin tearing a piece from his tunic and also Ondetar appearing to pull something from Captain's grounded body. The demon shouted in triumphant glee.

Khohlar followed in multiple voices, many accompanied by outrage or panic. *Leave him alone!* *That soul belongs to Frey!* *Stop it!* *Stop!* *That's Frey's soul!* It all blended into a cacophony that accomplished little more than a pounding headache. Saviar hoped, but doubted, it had the same affect on Ondetar, who remained focused on Captain, ignoring the other elves.

Then, suddenly, light flared within the transparent bubble, and a second figure appeared inside it. Tall, slender, handsome, it towered over the bending demon and the sprawling elf. The newcomer spoke softly, but his voice carried as if by speech and *khohlar* simultaneously, entering body, mind and soul. "That soul belongs to me."

A rumble of laughter escaped Ondetar, who barely bothered to glance at the creature who had joined him in his warded bubble. Saviar had no doubt he looked upon the god, Frey. His natural urge to drop to one knee passed swiftly. The elves remained on their feet, though several made gestures that appeared to indicate proper fealty. Saviar refused to let the *svartalf* go wholly unguarded, although even they seemed riveted by the drama. None of the elves or humans could penetrate the bubble to assist any of the players inside it, but they all seemed driven or compelled to watch.

Saviar could now see what appeared to be a second head emerging from Captain's body, identical to the first except it was translucent and ephemeral. When he removed his hand from *Motfrabelonning*'s hilt, the second head disappeared, the barrier turned invisible, and all of the auras winked out, including the one surrounding Frey. Not wanting to miss anything, he clamped his hand back onto the hilt, and it all instantly returned.

Frey spoke again, "All elfin souls who succumbed to age are mine."

"Not anymore." The demon's voice turned singsong with mockery. It rose to its amorphous legs, now taller than Frey. "Five of your elves gave themselves to me at the mere threat of annihilation. That grants me enough additional power to take what's mine . . . and yours. All elfin souls are mine. All of them! And you're constrained by the vow you made to Odin, so there's *nothing you can do!*" Howling with laughter, he dropped down to finish his work with Captain.

The laughter grew louder, stronger, and it took Saviar a moment to realize Frey had added his voice to the demon's mirth. Apparently, Ondetar realized it at the same time, because it stopped what it was doing, its bulbous head rising to meet Frey's gaze. Then, suddenly, the god was laughing alone.

Frey explained, "You didn't hear the condition I put on my vow to Odin, did you? I was bound not to interfere with your work, so long as you didn't interfere with mine. The moment you tried to take this soul, you released me from the vow that has bound me since the creation of human and elvinkind. Now, I'm free to do anything I want to you." He stepped over the body of Captain, the elf's soul still partially emerged.

Again, the demon rose, its body puffing outward as it did, looking half again as large as before. "You may find me more powerful now than even you can handle."

"I will have no trouble dismissing you to chaos and undoing everything you've done." Frey waved a hand, and the magic bubble that had surrounded them disappeared. With a cry of rage, the demon hurled itself at Frey, just as the god raised his hands.

A blur of gold passed through the demon's shadowy neck, then changed course and chopped downward through its body, cleaving it into two halves of amorphous shadow. Its pain-scream shot agony through Saviar's ears, and he could see the elves and *svartalf* gripping their heads, many collapsing to the ground at the aural onslaught. Then, the shadow dissipated. Nothing remained where the barrier had stood but Frey, Captain's body, and Calistin, the Sword of Mitrian already back in its sheath.

Frey's features turned a brilliant shade of red, and his hands, still raised, formed fists. "You stupid Renshai! Why did you do that?"

Calistin did not give ground. His own aura flared, nearly as large and brilliant as the god's. Ignoring the insult, he said so softly Saviar had to strain to hear, "Because it needed to be done."

"You didn't need to kill it!" Frey's voice sounded like a crash of thunder after Calistin's calm and quiet reply. "I was about to send it back to chaos. It would have become trapped there, unable to harm anyone."

"Until someone summoned it," Calistin pointed out. "Someone like its followers." He made a composed gesture that indicated the area beyond the elves where several *svartalf* remained. That reminded Saviar of his task. He glanced at the no-longer elfin creatures and realized not a single one showed any inclination to move. They looked deflated and hopeless, certainly not in any state to summon a demon.

Frey shook his head. "I would not have allowed that to happen. There are other ways to handle enemies than killing them, but warriors like you don't understand that, do you?"

A flare of Calistin's nostrils was the only thing to indicate his own building rage. "You have insulted me twice now, and I've allowed *you* to live."

Frey drew himself up, and he seemed to grow in front of Saviar's eyes. "You've *allowed* me?"

Calistin did not debate the question. "I'm sick to death of being denigrated as a 'killer' by those too weak-willed and foolish to see the truth. So many people and, apparently, even gods believe themselves special because they never personally took a life, even when they could have and should have, *especially* when they could have and should have. Every time you allow evil to live, the suffering they cause, the blood they subsequently spill is rightfully on your own hands. You wouldn't have allowed the demon to live because you're better or more righteous than me. You would have done it because you didn't have the guts to do what needed doing. Disguising that as heroism just makes you feel superior at the cost of innocent lives."

Frey glared at Calistin but said nothing, apparently rendered speechless, so Calistin turned on his heel and left the god with his charge and with his thoughts.

Frey muttered something Saviar could not hear, then called out into the clustered elves. "Chan'rék'ril Ar'temius Dal-ment'olian Mir'a Tam-möm'oly."

The summoned elf worked his way to the front. "Yes, my lord, Frey?"

"It appears you're in need of a soul, and I have one here. Would you be interested?"

The elves seemed to hold a collective breath, and Saviar understood. Chan'rék'ril had mourned his soul since the moment he had lost it to the spirit spider, had dedicated every day since to finding a way to restore it. But, now, his expression did not display the joy Saviar expected. Instead, he considered the offer for a long time before replying. "My lord, Frey, I thank you for the great honor you're offering me, but I must decline it."

Murmurs passed among the elves, and probably a lot of directed *khohlar.*

Frey cocked his head. "Would you please enlighten us as to why you've made this rather odd decision?"

Chan'rék'ril cleared his throat, then apparently decided against trying to speak loudly enough for all of the assemblage to hear. Instead, he used indirect *khohlar, *I won't deny I felt diminished when I lost my soul, along with bits and pieces of memory from the elves who shared it before me, but it didn't really affect me much. I had lived with it long enough for those remembrances to meld with my own, and any magic I knew because of them had become an integral part of my repertoire. The reason I've worked so hard to replace my soul is not because its lack damages me but because it harms the remainder of the elves. When I die, there will be one less elf we can never replace.* A grief so deep it pained wafted in with the words. *The soul you're offering me could go directly to an infant, a new life for us. If I take it, it may or may not eventually make it to a newborn elf. I would simply be a vehicle of delay.*

"Very noble," Frey said, his face a wreath of smiles.

Chan'rék'ril continued, *I appreciate your praise, my lord, Frey. But it's not entirely deserved. There's a second reason I refused this soul, one not so selfless.* He paused, but when no one, including Frey, seized the opening, he elaborated. *Arak'bar Tulamii Dhor is an elf of unprecedented age and accomplishment. A soul like that would prove far stronger than this vessel. * He made a gesture at his sides that encompassed his entire form. *If I accepted it, I would cease to be myself and would become, essentially, him. *

Frey prodded, "And if I placed it into an unborn elf?"

Chan'rék'ril looked at his feet. *I considered that, and I think it might work out well. Elves remember sometimes more, sometimes less, sometimes nothing of their previous incarnations. Until I lost my soul, I never gave it much thought, but I suspect the strength of the inherited soul has much to do with it. Placed into an infant, I believe the soul of Arak'bar Tulamii Dhor would shine through. That would serve the elves well, and I don't think it would harm the one his soul inhabits as he or she would have known no other personality, no other life, as I do. *

A golden figure glided up beside Frey appearing without fanfare and seemingly from nowhere. Saviar recognized him at once as Colbey Calistinsson, and the presence of the immortal Renshai at such a time surprised him. He seemed to have no stake in this particular matter. "This is not a safe time or place to converse," Colbey pointed out, loudly enough for all to hear. "Svartalf, your liege is dead. I suggest you gather your injured and stand aside until your creator has a chance to deal with you. Lysalf, you need to give Arak'bar Tulamii Dhor his privacy, and it would behoove you to surround the dark ones and keep them from doing anything foolish that might get them killed."

Frey added, "It will go better on those who betrayed me not to make it difficult for me to find you. I do not enjoy hiding games, and it will go harder on anyone I have to chase."

Colbey's gaze finally found Saviar, and a faint smile played over his features. He sent Saviar a mental message, different from khohlar. *You might want to listen in, but don't make it too obvious. I'm going to send Rantire and Calistin to watch over both groups of elves, but I doubt they'll encounter any problems. You . . . might learn something. *

Saviar nodded subtly. He wanted to know more about what Colbey meant, but he had no way to ask without everyone hearing. He suspected Colbey had singled him out because of his need to learn diplomatic skills either to become a knight, because what he learned might help the Renshai, or a combination of both. Easing backward toward a craggy area with a few scrub trees, he tended to his sword, keeping an ear cocked toward the interplay between immortal Renshai and god.

Paying no attention to the partially de-souled elf at his feet, Frey addressed Colbey. "So the worlds are lucky enough to have two immortal Renshai now?"

Startled by the proclamation, Saviar glanced toward them, whetstone scratched halfway along the blade. He knew Frey had to be referring to Calistin. Unless Captain had misrepresented the danger of the demon's claws, Saviar could see no other explanation for Calistin's unchanged features. Forty years to an immortal meant nothing. Saviar also felt suddenly and entirely certain the parallel scars he had noticed on Colbey's face resulted from a similar encounter. Frey's words might also explain the sudden resurrection of the Sword of Mitrian. *Calistin? Immortal?* Despite all the evidence, Saviar had to shake his head.

"It would appear so." Based on his tone, Colbey shared none of Saviar's surprise.

"I would not have thought a quarter god-blood would be enough, no matter what other skills and temperament he brought to the table."

A quarter god-blood? Saviar did not understand.

Colbey shrugged. "He carries the blood of both Aesir and Vanir gods; I calculate closer to 40%." He stifled an obvious grin. "Plus I like to think mine might have a little significance, too."

Nothing could have shocked Saviar more. He fumbled and dropped his whetstone.

"Aesir and Vanir," Frey repeated. A light dawned in his eyes. "Ravn? My little nephew is Calistin's father?"

"Blood father only," Colbey corrected.

"So I'm . . ." Frey pursed his lips in consideration.

"No relation," Colbey inserted. "As I said, in blood only. Calistin has a loving and rightful paternal parent named Ra-khir."

Frey apparently knew him. "The knight. The one who owned Frost Reaver for a time."

Saviar bit his tongue, not trusting himself to keep from gasping. He had no idea the gods knew Ra-khir personally, and he had believed Calistin shared every bit of his blood heritage. Ra-khir had made that abundantly clear. *Or did he?* Saviar recalled a time when he had disavowed his irritating little brother. Ra-khir had minced his words, assuring him his boys shared both parents, pointing out how children fully-related often looked and acted quite differently. It was the performance of an honorable man trapped between an unbreakable vow and the truth. Saviar had conducted a similar dance for Chymmerlee after promising Subikahn never to reveal their Renshai heritage to any mage.

Colbey nodded. "When I believed I was heading to certain doom, I did give Ra-khir my steed. You know how attached I am to that stallion, and I chose carefully. Ra-khir is a good man."

Frey made a wordless noise. "Does Freya know?"

Colbey laughed. "Do you think I could keep anything from my wife? Your sister? Of course, she knows. She approved it."

Frey glanced down at Captain's prostate form. "I'm sure there's an interesting story behind it."

"One you won't be hearing today, at least not from me." Colbey studied the ancient elf at Frey's feet. Even Saviar could see Captain was not truly dead, at least not yet. His chest continued to rise and fall, despite the piece of soul protruding from his chest. "Frey, what will you accomplish by reincarnating Arak'bar Tulamii Dhor? The elves thrive under his leadership, at least when they choose to follow it."

"It's his time to go," Frey pointed out. "He's had six thousand years. That's far longer than any other."

Colbey responded with a snort. "You're not talking to one of your elves here, and even they have more than an inkling you choose when old age takes them. Chan'rék'ril's right. If you stuff that primordial, gifted soul into a newborn, it's just going to be a younger version of him, frustrated for a few hundred years by his inability to work his magic and his limbs in the manner to which he's become accustomed. Besides, you're not fooling me. I know what you did."

"What?" Frey said, too innocently.

"You're never going to convince me you randomly chose the exact moment Captain was leading a *jovinay arythanik* of this significance to call his soul home."

Frey made another meaningless noise.

"It's not as if elves get heart attacks in stressful situations, the way humans do. Eventually, your followers are going to remember they have, in the past, had some choice in exactly when they pass. As I understand it, you point out their time has come, but it's not a sudden thing. Usually, they have plenty of time to tell the others goodbye, to select a private time and place where they gradually make their peace before joining you."

"It's not their way to contemplate strategy or situation," Frey said. "Humans muse; elves take things as they happen. To them, the passing of elves from age simply is and has always been."

"Chan'rék'ril's loss made him desperate enough to spend a lot of time considering every aspect of elfin death, souls, and reincarnation." Colbey continued to stare at Captain. "He will figure out you discussed the whole plan with Captain *before* he disrupted the *jovinay arythanik*. You knew Ondetar would try to claim his soul, that he would do the very thing that would break your vow to Odin."

Saviar did not bother to try to recover his whetstone or even cover his staring. The information about Calistin's blood parentage had stunned him, yet he suspected this was the part Colbey had actually wanted him to hear. To become a leader of Renshai, assuming Thialnir asked again, he needed to look beneath the obvious, to see the stealthy arrangements, the hidden strategies others missed.

"All right," Frey admitted, "you caught me. What do you intend to do with the information?"

"It just has me thinking," Colbey said conspiratorially. "If you're going to posthumously trick Odin again, why not do it right? I mean, this whole thing started because you wanted elves to be immortal, or nearly so, and Odin wanted to limit their lifespans as much as possible. What's the point of taking Arak'bar Tulamii Dhor now? Why not spite Odin entirely, restore the elf's soul, and stop the process. Make him a true immortal or, at least, the closest thing to it."

Frey looked down at Captain, head tipped to one side. "You don't think that might make the other elves less cooperative when their times come?" Without awaiting an answer, he placed his hands on the ephemeral head, closed his eyes, and muttered what sounded like magical syllables. As Saviar watched, the soul-head disappeared and Captain's eyes fluttered open. He looked around, apparently taking in his position, then latched his gaze onto Frey. He sat up swiftly.

"My lord, Frey." Captain bowed his head, hiding his expression, the barest hint of question in his tone. If he wished to know whether Frey had reprieved him for moments, years or decades, he did not ask.

Frey let him off the hook. "Thank you for your assistance, Arith'tinir Khy-loh'Shinaris Bal-ishi Sjörmann'taé Or. Midgard, and the elves, still need you; and I'm not yet ready for your soul."

When Captain's head came up, he looked entirely bewildered. He had waited so long for Frey to claim him, it must have seemed incredible. He still did not question, however, merely clambered to his feet, bowed, and joined the other elves.

Colbey rolled his eyes, head shaking. "Was that mouthful his original name?"

Frey maintained his unrevealing expression . . . almost. Saviar believed the corners of his mouth twitched ever so slightly upward. "Yes. Did you know Arak'bar Tulamii Dhor translates to 'He Who Has Forgotten His Name?'"

"I believe I heard that once." Colbey's casual response hid the likelihood he had actually been told multiple times. "I suppose after so many millennia of humans calling you Captain, one could lose track of a forty-syllable name."

"Seventeen syllables," Frey corrected, gaze tracing Captain's progress. At length, he returned his attention to Colbey, dusting his hands together. "Well, I believe I'm finished here. You coming?"

Colbey did meet the god's gaze. "What about Chan'rék'ril?"

Frey's brow furrowed, then rose. "What about him? I gave him an opportunity, and he refused it."

Saviar pretended he had no interest in the conversation, but he did. His mother had believed she lost her soul to spirit spiders at the same time Chan'rék'ril did, and the agony she suffered when she thought she could never go to Valhalla had nearly devastated her and Ra-khir both. Saviar now knew it had been Calistin's in-utero soul, not hers, the spider had devoured. Since even before his arrival in Béarn, Chan'rék'ril had made it his mission to discover how Calistin appeared to have recovered his soul, only to be repeatedly thwarted by Calistin's unwillingness to discuss the subject. Even Saviar did not know what had happened, though he suspected it bore some relation to the changes in Calistin's personality.

"You gave him an opportunity for a soul you never even collected," Colbey pointed out, without mentioning it was only because of his suggestion that the soul still inhabited Captain's body. "It seems to me you have a soul just waiting around doing absolutely nothing."

Frey's eyes narrowed, but he did not immediately reply. When Colbey also said nothing more, clearly waiting, Frey finally spoke. "But it's not . . . wholly elfin. If I tease out the elfin portion, there's not enough material for a complete soul. That's exactly why it's just waiting around."

Colbey shrugged. "You're the only one with incarnation experience, but I've been watching Calistin for quite some time now. The soul he received had little in common with him initially, but it seems to have adapted. Valhalla would have accepted it as his, and it didn't stop him from becoming immortal. In fact, I think it may have helped him. It clung to and infused a bit of Treysind's best feature, one Calistin desperately needed."

"Compassion," Frey said softly.

Colbey glanced at Saviar with a wink. The young man had a lot of information to process. This short conversation had explained so much.

Frey drummed his hands on his thighs, clearly in consideration. "I do have a lot of 'incarnation' experience, but it's exclusively with infants. They arise essentially blank, which makes me doubt the wisdom of inserting a partially human soul into them." He shook his head a bit. "I've seen what can happen when the more negative human traits become infused into my creation." He made a vague gesture, but Saviar knew he referred to the *svartalf*. "I can't risk a generation of part human souls in elfin newborns."

Colbey pointed out the obvious. "But Chan'rék'ril is not newborn, and the soul you'd be giving him isn't an unknown quantity. Ivana never knew a moment of spitefulness or cruelty or trickery. What could she inflict on him other than her tenacity and appreciation, even for those who shunned and despised her?"

A chill washed through Saviar. Though he was witnessing something profound, he found himself locked on the realization Ivana was, apparently, dead. Some in the castle might find it a respite, though they would know better than to voice such an opinion, especially amid Tem'aree'ay's and Griff's terrible grief. It also shocked him to realize Colbey Calistinsson, the consummate warrior, could offer profound advice to the gods themselves. And, sometimes, they would even accept it.

Frey nodded suddenly, mind made up. "Give me a bit of time to deal with the *svartalf* and award Chan'rék'ril his new soul. Then, would you mind stopping on Midgard to let any elves remaining there know it's time to recreate the gate to *Svartalfheim*? The *lysalf*, and their Renshai companions, need to go home."

The pleased look on Colbey's face told Saviar the words meant more than he could fully fathom, at least at the moment with so much information to ponder. He supposed it was a backhanded thank you to Calistin, Rantire, and himself. Also, there was significance in him calling Midgard the elves' home, perhaps for the first time. At least, it seemed the elves and their creator had finally found some positive feelings toward the half-human offspring of Tem'aree'ay and the king.

Colbey had one more question. "What will become of the *svartalf*?"

Frey frowned, and Saviar suspected Colbey had finally overstepped his boundaries. But Frey seemed to realize his immortal brother-in-law had contributed to the elves in a positive way and graced him with an answer. "Leaguing with a demon. Plotting against their cousins. They have gone beyond any ability for me to consider them elves any longer. A few may still retain enough of their original nature to remain here, and I will allow them to procreate from the common pool so long as they behave. Most, however, can no longer have 'alf' in their name. Those will become as twisted and lumbering in looks as in nature, shunning the light for the darkness of underground dwellings and caves on the currently empty world called Nídavellír.

"They once named themselves *dwar-freytii*, so I shall call them simply 'dwarf' as they do not deserve my name. They shall have no access to the pool of elfin souls, but neither will they need them as they will have no souls at all so can reproduce at will, like any animal. Hopefully, they will develop a skill that pleases at least some of the gods, so they will have a purpose to which to dedicate their lives. Otherwise, I fear they might disappear; and no one will mourn their passing."

Saviar suspected Frey had, deliberately or not, gravely insulted humans with his "reproduce at will, like any animal" comment, but he knew better than to take offense at anything spoken by a god.

Colbey gave no indication it bothered him, either. "It's about time Nídavellír had an occupant." He stretched lithely. A golden light flared around him, and he was gone.

Either oblivious to or not caring about Saviar's observations, Frey ignored him entirely as he headed toward the gathered elves.

Calistin appeared at Saviar's right hand so suddenly he wondered if his brother had already developed the magical skills of the other immortal Renshai. Then, he realized no flash had accompanied it. Nothing in the grim expression on Calistin's face seemed to suggest he had managed something beyond his previous abilities. Saviar also realized immortality and magical ability did not necessarily go together. In addition to his longevity and Renshai heritage, Colbey had served time as the Western Wizard, as a Knight of Erythane, and had lived for centuries among the gods.

"We have a lot to talk about," Saviar said, believing it vast understatement.

Calistin took Saviar's elbow, making no reply.

CHAPTER 20

A lot of knowledge is dangerous, a little knowledge even more so.
—Weile Kahn

LED BY KENTT and buoyed by the Pica Stone, the team of
Tem'aree'ay, Shar'iss'ah, and the mostly bewildered Mages of Myrcidë had no difficulty holding the gate open for the beleaguered elves
to return from their abrupt and unsettling visit to *Svartalfheim*. Captain disbanded his followers to recover from their ordeal, promising
to reconvene the following day in the usual place.

The rescue party demanded a summation of the happenings from
the only member who had attended: Saviar. After the overview, Tae
invited Saviar for a grilling session under the auspices of a walk and
meal. Cursing himself for not chasing the elves through the gate, Tae
was not content with the information Saviar provided the others. As
odd and fascinating as they proved to be, Tae could tell the young
Renshai was hiding details.

Seated in Tae's vast, private suite in Béarn Castle, Saviar lowered
his head to his arm, folded on the tabletop, and sighed. "I've told
you everything that happened."

Even Imorelda believed Tae was hounding Saviar too hard and
had chosen to take her kittens elsewhere under the auspices of a
quiet nap.

"You're leaving things out," Tae insisted. "Information that, in
the right hands—"

"Your hands?" Saviar huffed out.

Tae ignored the interruption, ". . . could be useful in ways you
might not imagine. Ways that could save lives."

"I assure you, I've told you every piece of information you could
possibly use. Anything more, you need to get from Captain. I wasn't
present when Frey addressed the elves."

Tae fairly whined. "But you're skipping details, Saviar."

"Of course I'm skipping details." Saviar raised his head and finally looked at Tae. "If I had some magical way to chronicle every
sight and sound exactly the way it happened, I'd have a talent even
the gods might never match. Imagine being able to make a gesture,
and a perfect duplication of an event appeared on a wall for everyone
to relive or to see and hear for the first time." He rose, raising his
hands grandly into the air. "I'd be wealthy and popular beyond belief. It would revolutionize the entire world!" He sat back down,
voice returning to its tired timbre. "A bird twittered on a tree branch
a moment before I dispelled the ward holding the elves prisoner. A
worm nibbled at a leaf, and the wind rose just enough to muss this
bit of hair . . ." He tweezed a hank of reddish bangs between his
thumb and forefinger. ". . . but not this one." He used the other hand
to pluck up another, then dropped both.

Tae knew a dodge when he heard one. He said with direct coldness, "Those aren't the kinds of details I mean, Saviar; and you know
it. I don't need a precise duplication. I need to know the big stuff,
the things you don't want to talk about."

Saviar sucked in a deep breath and held it. He let it all out at
once, in a noisy sigh. "Tae, I learned a lot of things today, most only
tangentially related to what happened. I'm not really sure what I
learned, but I do know I need to mull over the information and come
to some personal conclusions before I can share with anyone."

Again, it took surprisingly long for his gaze to find Tae's. "I'll give
you this much: my youngest brother selflessly saved my life and grew
to be something more, I'm not exactly sure what, in the process. Ivana
has apparently died, and her soul may or may not now dwell in
Chan'rék'ril. The implications for future elfin/human hybrids is
something I need to think about, as do the elves and the royal family,
among others." He finally got to the crux of the matter. "Colbey invited me to listen in on a conversation between himself and his
brother-in-law, who just happens to be a god. I found it humbling,
terrifying, and—in some ways—surprisingly similar to the way human
brothers chat, in-law or otherwise."

"You didn't mention that part to the others," Tae pointed out.

Saviar nodded. "It wasn't germane, Tae. It was personal, for
them and for me. I'm also not sure the decision of whether or not I
should replace Thialnir is mine any longer . . . assuming it ever
really was."

"The Renshai need your guidance," Tae said. "That's obvious to
anyone. Including you at one time."

"I turned Thialnir down in front of a crowd. He's searching for someone else." Saviar rubbed his hands across the tabletop. "Besides, I'm not ready."

"No one ever is." Tae thought back to when his father had handed him the title of king. Even at his most imperiled, he had never felt so stricken with panic. "Anyone who believes himself to be so isn't worthy of the job."

Saviar managed a weak smile. "I'm not fishing for sympathy, really I'm not. I know if Thialnir deigned to foist the responsibility upon me again, it's actually a great honor." He kept his head up, his attention on Tae. "I know you read people well, verbally and nonverbally, and that's the reason you think I have some juicy secret I'm keeping to myself. But that's really all there is. Just a lot of soul-searching and deliberation I need to do on my own."

Tae nodded. "The interrogation is finished, I promise." He rose and opened the door.

Saviar seized the opportunity to leap to his feet and head for the opening. "If I think of anything else that might prove useful for you to know, I'll come to you immediately."

"I appreciate that." Tae watched Saviar exit, then followed him into the hallway. He now had enough information, he believed, to face the king of Béarn.

Certain he would find Griff's quarters zealously guarded to maintain the king's privacy and not wishing to pull rank, Tae climbed the castle wall to a window of the royal suite and slipped inside. He did his best to do so unseen and unheard, silent and glued to the shadows, and believed he accomplished that goal; but he might never truly know. Ever since he had been near-fatally wounded on a spying mission, Béarn's protective forces looked the other way when he practiced climbing their fortifications as a form of therapy. Even though Tae had regained all of his previous strength and agility, he worried they still indulged him at Matrinka's urging. She did not seem to understand a large part of the remedy involved his ability to outwit and avoid the world's best security.

Imorelda had not yet returned from her jaunt, and she never approved of his climbing anyway, certain someone would shoot him off the wall and cause her to plummet to her untimely death. Tae appreciated her absence now, as her bulk in his arms made seizing handholds impossible and her weight on his shoulders not only limited his movements but tended to cause him neck strain and headaches when performing actions so detailed and precise. She would never admit it, but he also suspected she did not care much for heights.

Tae found King Griff alone at his desk, his back to the window and hunched over with his hands on the sides of his head, his fingers in front of his ears and his thumbs behind them. Tae approached quietly, so as not to disrupt Griff's contemplation. He resisted the strong urge to place a reassuring, steadying hand on the king's shoulder, concerned he might startle him. He could not step to the front as the desk broached the wall, but he did walk to its side, which would place him within Griff's visual field once the king raised his head. Only then, he realized the king was staring into the Pica Stone sitting on the wooden surface.

Tae made a gentle noise.

In response, Griff neither moved nor spoke.

Tae reached out a hand and hovered it over the Pica Stone directly into Griff's field of vision.

Only then, Griff looked up. He smiled, and it appeared weary but genuine. "Hello, Tae." He sat back in his chair. If he had any concerns about how the king of the Eastlands had gotten past his guards, he gave no indication.

"I'm sorry," Tae said, meaning it. He understood the loss of a child. As the searches grew longer and ranged farther, it had grown increasingly unlikely the elves would find Subikahn alive.

Griff bobbed his massive head. "Thank you. Parents aren't supposed to outlive their children, but it happens all too often." He reached out suddenly and caught Tae's still hovering hand. "Sometimes, not knowing is worse." He met Tae's eyes with sympathetic understanding.

Tae finally had to admit what had driven him to risk his life repeatedly for the other missing soldiers. Though he had chalked it up to his affinity for danger, it had more to do with finding his son and saving other parents from similar anguish. It also kept him too busy to dwell on the situation, except at night when his concern kept him wide-eyed and restless or haunted his dreams. "I miss Subikahn."

Griff tried to ease his thoughts. "I truly believe some of those we can't rescue will have a different but still happy life on another dimension."

It was a nice way to think about the situation, but Tae knew all too well many of the Outworlds were not compatible with life. Some humans and elves had been instantly or slowly destroyed, and no amount of courage, competence, or intelligence could save them.

Still, if they never found out the truth, he could draw some solace from the possibility Griff had presented.

Griff sat back fully and stretched limbs that had probably remained in their hunched position too long. "We knew Ivana would never have a full life."

"You gave her the best one she could possibly have." Tae felt certain he spoke the truth. He could not think of anyone who could have granted a child like Ivana as much, not only because of their wealth and power but because of their love for one another and for her. "You have nothing to regret, at least in regard to Ivana."

Griff did not take the bait. "Frey placed her soul into Chan'rék'ril. Did you know that?"

Tae did not lie. "I knew it was a possibility. Does that please you?"

"Very much." Griff managed another smile. "It means her soul has joined the elfin cycle. I can't think of a better tribute to her life. The elves have actually apologized for reviling her and have come to appreciate her soul, at least. They've opened the way for more hybrids. They've asked to call future elfin/human half-breeds 'ivanas.' I like that. I hope it sticks in the human vocabulary as well."

"I'm sure it will." Tae felt pretty certain of what he said. Humans tended to immortalize shortcuts, and ivanas was certainly easier to say than elfin/human half-breeds. He could not help thinking ahead and wondering if there would come a time when they would have to name half-human/half-ivana and half-elfin/half-ivana offspring. "Especially since the very next one will also be your son or daughter. People tend to follow the conventions of the high kingdom."

"Son," Griff said.

That seemed to come out of nowhere. "What?"

"Frey told Tem'aree'ay the unborn baby is a son, and it's healthy. The elves don't believe he will have the same issues as Ivana, although they promised to check him carefully at the time of birth. Apparently, it's a problem they believe will plague some hybrids . . ." He corrected with a half-smile, ". . . ivanas, but if they catch it early, they can easily fix it."

That brought many thoughts to mind, not the least of which was the significance of having a healer elf present at the birth of every ivana. Tae hoped, but doubted, male elves would keep that in mind before spreading their seed among human females. Hopefully, the newfound peace would mean more elves lived among humans so that it would not become a problem. Tae kept those thoughts to himself to address the ones more significant to Griff at the moment. "It's unfortunate no one knew that when Ivana was born, but it does provide some meaning to her death. Because of her, the elves know what the problem was, and they can save other children from suffering."

Griff added, "For someone considered worthless by so many, anathema by the elves, and tragic by all, she has accomplished so much, even if most of it was posthumously."

"The rest of us can only hope to change the world for the better as much as she did." Having assured himself Griff was not so devastated he could not handle other crises, Tae moved on to the real reason for his visit. "We have to save Matrinka."

Griff closed his eyes, sucked in a deep breath and held it.

That did not bode well. Tae's heart rate quickened. "What have you tried so far?"

Griff finally let the air out of his lungs. "Believe me, Tae. We've considered every possibility. Nearly all of the suggestions would only worsen the situation."

Tae tried the obvious, "Couldn't you just pardon her? There would be some repercussions, but at least she wouldn't be executed."

"Tried it," Griff moaned. "Ancient Béarnian law—the type I can't change—won't allow it."

Tae sighed deeply. "There has to be some way to spin the story that doesn't result in Matrinka dying."

Griff shook his head so slowly it practically defined sorrow. "I assure you there isn't. We've thought of everything believable and a lot that's ridiculous or beyond. In every case, she dies and, in most, Darris also. The way things stand, at least Matrinka gets her wish to see Barrindar and Marisole married."

Tae thought of something he doubted had crossed their minds. "What if I broke her out of prison and she . . . disappeared? I mean, the dungeons of Béarn are supposed to be escape-proof, but I'm up for the challenge." Tae knew the catacombs contained an impossible maze, but he and his friends had once attempted to rescue Kedrin from an illegal imprisonment through it. He would need Darris' assistance again. The bard of Béarn had an archaic song, passed from parent to firstborn, which could get them safely through it.

"Matrinka's not in the dungeons. She's under arrest in her own suite. Given your talents, you'd have little difficulty springing her, but it's expected someone of noble blood will display enough honor not to attempt escape, even under threat of execution."

Tae could have spit, glad he did not cling to his honor the way knights and most royalty did. "Are you going to stop me?"

Griff drew in a long breath and let it out at a snail's pace. "Not me, but I'm afraid Matrinka would. It's her honor at stake. Even if you could talk her into it, she'd be miserable. Darris' curse would force him to remain at my side. She could never see her beloved or her children again, and I don't believe she could live with that."

Tae could see ways around that problem, though only for short periods of time and only so long as no one saw through the necessary disguises. It would be untenable and impractical; but, at least, it meant Matrinka could live. If they came up with no better plan, he would implement it, even against her will.

Then, Griff said something so surprising all other thought left Tae's mind. "I'm abdicating the throne."

"What?" The word was startled from Tae's mouth.

Griff clearly knew it because he did not repeat what he had said, merely explained it. "I can't pardon Matrinka, but whoever succeeds me can."

"Well, yes, but . . ." Tae knew the king must have considered the downsides. "The world needs you. You're the fulcrum on which the balance of the universe rests."

"The proper king or queen of Béarn is the fulcrum," Griff corrected. "My successor will also have to pass the Pica test, which means he or she will serve as an equally competent neutral entity."

They both knew the Pica Stone would not pass anyone who did not fit that description. "But the risks, Griff!" Tae's thoughts slipped back to the months before the last coronation. Nearly every possible heir to Béarn's throne had been tested, and even the most accomplished found wanting. At the time, the prior king was dead. They had not known of Griff's existence, and it seemed as if the throne would sit empty, the world always on the brink of tipping into destruction.

Every heir who failed the Pica test plummeted into despair. Many had killed themselves, others went senseless or mad. Only Matrinka had been spared, though she refused to speak of how, and even she had suffered terrible doubts about her judgment forever afterward. "There aren't many heirs left, Griff, and nearly all of those your children. I love Matrinka, and I'd gladly risk my life to save hers; but is it worth destroying so many young lives?" Another thought struck Tae. "Béarn's royalty usually serves until death. It's possible the proper heir hasn't even been born yet; it might be a grandchild of yours. What if you empty the throne and destroy all the potential heirs in their youth?"

Griff pounded a fist on the table so hard the Pica jumped. "Don't you think I've considered that?"

Tae fell silent. Griff rarely raised his voice, almost never made an angry gesture. He finally considered what the king had been doing upon his arrival. "You're communing with the Pica Stone, aren't you? Trying to see if it will tell you who would pass."

Griff lowered his head. And nodded.

"Has it told you anything?"

"Not directly." Griff looked up. "I believe I know who would pass. If I tested him first, it would spare them all." He added plaintively, "Right?"

They both already knew the answer, but Tae spoke anyway, certain King Griff wanted to hear it, to reassure himself. "If the Pica passed the first heir tested, no one would be harmed." He glanced at the clairsentient sapphire. It did not look any different than usual, yet Captain had assured him its power was matchless. Griff had only two sons, and one of them was still recovering from amnesia. The other closely resembled him in looks and personality. "You think it's Barrindar?"

Griff looked askance. "What do you think?" Only then, he revealed the agony that clearly clutched his soul. Tae had watched him effortlessly render judgments that would turn young kings gray, yet this weighed on him like iron.

Tae understood why. "I can't make this decision for you. No one can." Realizing how entirely unhelpful that answer was, he added carefully, "Although, if I had to pick which of your children had a nature most like yours, it would be Barrindar." He did not point out what they both already knew. Some of the kindest, wisest people had failed the rigorous, hours-long testing. If human judgment could predict who would pass and who would fail, there would be no need for the test at all. "If Barrindar knew what you were contemplating, he'd insist on testing first."

"Yes."

Silence. Griff sighed again.

Tae allowed himself to consider the possibility of Griff's abdication. Béarn, the East, perhaps the entire world would miss him; but Tae had to admit, if an heir could be found, it would solve the problem. Matrinka would lose her title, and her marriage to Griff would become invalid; but he felt certain whoever succeeded Griff would issue the pardon and assure nothing worse befell her. It all came down to finding the appropriate heir. "Do you think if the elves banded together, they might get the Pica Stone to reveal the one who would pass the test?"

"Tem'aree'ay doesn't believe so. The Pica test exists for a reason, even if we can't understand it. It assures the properly neutral entity serves as high king or queen. It prevents would-be usurpers from stealing the throne, and it discourages . . ."

Griff hesitated just long enough for Tae to fill in the word. "Abdication."

"Yes," the king of Béarn practically whispered. "But I . . . I guess I hoped . . . if I communed with it . . ." He reconsidered, clearly running out of useful words. He lowered his huge head. "I'm being stupid."

Tae knew the massive king of Béarn never had much confidence in his intellectual abilities. A careful reading of history showed whatever magic selected the acting ruler of Béarn, and there had been several types of tests in the past, often picked ones who seemed a bit slow or guileless but who usually wound up making shockingly brilliant rulings despite all appearances. "I've never found reason to question your intelligence on any matter. Your past judgment has always been impeccable, as far as I can tell, and I'm not easily fooled."

Griff turned his companion a hopeful look. "I've asked the stone to give me a sign if Barrindar would pass its test. Of course, having received nothing, I have no idea whether it's telling me he would fail or simply ignoring me. As I suspect the latter, I'm still sitting here imploring it." Griff turned back to face the Pica Stone, wilting over it again.

Tae hesitated, then turned to leave. He found himself staring into another's face. What appeared to be a man had materialized directly behind King Griff.

Tae reached for his sword and opened his mouth in warning.

Before he made a sound, the other sent silent words directly into his brain. *I mean him no harm. Please say nothing.*

Against his better judgment, Tae remained quiet, but his hand remained on his hilt. The newcomer was as fair as any Northman, with tousled blond hair, eyes the color of the Pica and a sinewy form that promised strength and speed. He appeared young, perhaps in his late teens or very early twenties. Tae tried to address the other in the same manner as Imorelda. *Who are you?*

My name is Ravn. I'm Colbey and Freya's son. I've been Griff's guardian since childhood, and I would never hurt him.

Tae seized the opportunity. *He needs to know if Barrindar could pass the Pica test.*

So he can abdicate.

Tae knew it would do no good to deny the truth to an immortal who descended from and lived among the gods.

I don't want him to abdicate.

Ravn had asked no actual question, so Tae did not answer. Instead, he pled the king's case. *Griff's judgment is beyond question, but he cannot make the right decision without the proper information to base it on. He has asked the Pica Stone to give him a sign if Barrindar would pass.*

Ravn stared at the back of Griff's head, lips pursed, saying and doing nothing. But there was a fondness in his eyes.

Please, Tae said. *He gives all of himself every day and asks so little in return. There's a reason he's the neutral fulcrum on which the balance rests rather than one of the gods themselves. Trust his judgment, Ravn, and grant him this one piece of information to use as he sees fit. He may not make the choice wanted by those on high, but he will make the right one for the universe and its precious and precarious balance.* Tae had to believe he spoke the truth. He had no way of knowing whether or not having knowledge Griff could not personally attain would make a difference.

Ravn continued to study Griff. The affection Tae had spotted in Ravn's eyes now came through the mental connection, seeming much the same as his own for his missing son. Ravn clearly saw Griff as a younger brother and cared for him with a familial love gods rarely displayed for any human. *Tell no one what I've done, even that I was here.* Though worded as a command, it emerged more like a plea.

My father is to privacy what yours is to swordplay. Tae smiled. *Rest assured, secrets are always safe with me.*

The Pica Stone flashed so quickly Tae suspected, had he blinked, he would have missed it. His gaze went to it, then back to the empty space where Ravn had stood.

Griff did not react. Gradually, his head swiveled toward Tae, who held his breath, worried the king had closed his eyes at exactly the wrong moment. His voice emerged hoarse, uncertain. "Did you see . . . ?"

"I did," Tae said. "And I believe you have your answer."

CHAPTER 21

In war, I would rather have a single Renshai at my side than any army.

—Thialnir Thrudazisson

WHEN TAE ENTERED BÉARN'S GREAT HALL with Imorelda at his heels and the kittens secured in their tunic pockets, he found the room in pandemonium. Elves and humans, apparently freshly rescued, milled about, reuniting with colleagues or cornering servants, presumably for places to rest or eat. Apparently, Griff had returned the Pica Stone to the elves before retiring because Captain had it on the table in front of him, his hands clamped to its either side. At the sight of Tae, he brightened noticeably and gestured toward himself.

Tae threaded his way through the crowd to Captain's side. Imorelda bounded to the tabletop, twisted, then immediately leaped to his shoulders, settling into her usual position. "You started without me," Tae said with a smile, trying not to sound at all accusatory. Captain clearly suffered enough stress without him adding to it, certainly more than any elf was meant to handle.

Captain replied with *khohlar*, *I thought I'd bring in as many groups as I could that did not require the rescue crew. I was able to locate five of those, but I had to skip over one that begged for assistance. As you know, the information I can get from them is limited by the questions I can think to ask and can be answered with the code you created. This bunch seems quite desperate, although they did indicate they can hold out a while longer, if necessary.*

Tae tried to read any subtext beneath the *khohlar*, but learned nothing more. Captain's discomfort might stem wholly from concern about the group needing rescue. "I can go whenever you're ready. Do I need to gather the rest of the team?"

That depends on how you currently define "the team." Saviar and

Ra-khir say they're ready. Chan'rék'ril and El-brinith can go at at any time. I haven't seen Marisole since Nomalan died. Do we need to replace those two? *

Tae thought it best not to disturb Marisole. She may have already received word about Griff's decision to abdicate. Tae suspected, if he asked, she would return to the rescue team, if only from the overwhelming bardic curiosity, but she belonged at Barrindar's side.

Don't bother her, * Imorelda sent what Tae had already decided. *She has enough to deal with. If you need a bard, Darris would gladly replace her.* *

We don't, * Tae assured his pet. *And Griff should have his most significant adviser with him, especially the only one who truly understands what's happening and why. I also think Darris' worry over Matrinka might make him less cautious and predictable.* *

Cautious and predictable, * Imorelda repeated. *That defines Darris. I can't believe he could lose those traits and continue to exist.* *

Tae could not think of any other Béarnide who would agree to come and would benefit the group. "The five of us should suffice, Captain. If not, we can run back through the gate and grab a few more."

They all knew that was not necessarily the case. They might not have the chance to return for help, but neither voiced it.

Then we'll open the gate in a moment, but I think you should know something else. *

Tae nodded as much as Imorelda's position across his neck allowed, hoping he might finally discover the real reason for the elder's discomfort.

Captain's fingers went white around the Pica. *Once we bring this group in, I believe we've come to the end of the missing elves. I don't sense any more out there, not even with the jovinay arythanik, not even with the help of the Pica.* *

Tae believed he understood the problem. "We're still missing quite a few humans, then?"

And elves, * Captain added. *But, hopefully, you'll rescue most of those on this mission.* *

Imorelda asked, *Most of the elves, most of the humans, or both?* *

Tae used her exact phrasing aloud.

Though not a strictly yes-or-no question, Captain responded with a nod. *Exactly the issue, Tae Kahn Weile's son. You should find some of both. We can't account for thirty-six elves. I believe whoever is not here, or in this group you're going to rescue, has perished and will never be found. According to the lists, we're still missing almost four hundred humans.* *

Tae tried to reassure Captain. "Some of that is error: double-counting, deserters, and corpses missed or misidentified on the battlefield. It's a lot easier to lose track of humans."

Captain laced his fingers around the sapphire. *But will your people understand that? We may have left pockets of living humans on at least one Outworld, perhaps several. I don't know if we'll ever find them and, even if we do, we'll have lost the ability to retrieve them since we'll have nothing on which to ground a gate.*

Confusion radiated from Imorelda. *Why's he worrying about that now? Why not see what's left after this mission?*

Tae was there when Captain had mentioned this possibility before the rescues had started. *Humans build emotional attachments to other humans, much stronger and longer lasting than most animals.*

Imorelda lashed her tail. *I know that!*

Tae continued as if she had not interrupted. *And elves even more so. If they lost four hundred lives, it would mean permanently losing their entire race, nearly twice over.* Tae realized that might no longer be the truth; events of the last few days suggested the system for procuring elfin souls had drastically changed or, at least, would in the future. Nevertheless, the mindset of the elves through millennia could not change overnight. *He's upset about the humans, of course, but I know he's also worried our leaders might blame the elves for the lapse.*

But the elves have saved many hundreds of humans who would otherwise have died. Now Imorelda's discomfort leaked through the contact, and Tae found himself dealing with a double dose of foreign anxiety.

Tae reached up to give Imorelda a comforting pat. *I know that, and so do all the other kings, generals, and lieutenants. But Captain worries the humans might think the elves only saved those humans as an aside, while they were rescuing elves. Some humans could assume, once no elves remain on Outworlds, the elves are stopping their search because they don't care about the additional missing humans and refuse to risk themselves or their magic.*

Imorelda squirmed. *Is that really going to happen?*

The question could be taken two ways, that the elves really might abandon some humans or that the human leaders might blame the elves. He did not bother to take the time to differentiate. *Of course, it's possible. Especially if it involves a prince or a general's son or someone else considered particularly important.* That struck dangerously close to home. Tae had not seen Subikahn among the current crop of rescued, and he felt certain the young Renshai would have approached him immediately or, at least, someone would have mentioned it had his son been saved. If the team did not find Subikahn on this last mission, it seemed certain he would lose his son forever. Tae forced that thought from his mind, not wishing to sidetrack the conversation further. Either they would find Subikahn there or not. No amount of worrying would change the outcome.

Imorelda's claws sank through Tae's cloak, and he added as much to save his flesh as from truth. *But I truly believe the vast majority of the leaders, and even most of the followers, will understand the situation and give the elves credit for all the rescues they did manage. If not, I'm sure we can nudge them in that direction.* He added aloud for Captain's benefit, "All any of us can do is our best. It'll work out, Captain. Griff and I will see to it."

That seemed to help because Captain's grip on the Pica loosened, and he even managed a lopsided smile.

"What do we know about the rescue mission?"

Turning all business, Captain switched to speech. "As far as I can get from the one elf I spoke to, they started with twenty elves and thirty-seven humans. Ar'min'taé is confined in a physical structure, not bounded by magic, with three other elves and eight humans. Other human/elf groups are elsewhere on the world. He thinks most, if not all, are also confined. I could not get a good sense of who or what is doing the confining, but it does seem to be some sort of living beings. None of the ones in his confinement are significantly injured. Apparently, if we formed the gate near him, it would be inside this one confinement, and the twelve there could leave. However, without a rescue group, the others would be abandoned."

Tae considered. "If we brought them back, couldn't you build a new gate near another elf and keep doing that until we have everyone freed?"

Captain had, apparently, discarded the same thought. "Possibly, but I foresee a lot of problems. First, each gate would take an inordinate amount of energy, so the rescue would need to happen over several consecutive days. Beings intelligent enough to confine prisoners would have plenty of time to figure out what's happening and make changes dangerous to their prisoners, to the five of you and possibly to everyone in this room, if they position themselves right. There may be containments with only humans in them, which we would miss with gates. We can only open one gate at a time, but traces of magic remain whenever a gate is opened, so opening another anywhere near where a different one used to be can cause magic to fail or explode or worse. I don't know how large this Outworld is, but most are too small to risk such a thing happening." He made a throwaway gesture. "There's more, but it's technical. I think you get the idea."

Tae nodded, licked his lips, and considered. Mercifully, Imorelda settled back down without interrupting his train of thought. "I'll head over to the gating spot now. I'll give you the signal when everyone's together and ready to go."

"Thank you." Captain's face did not give away as much as his *khohlar*, but Tae felt certain the elf's anxiety would take a lot of reassurances before it faded.

Tae joined Ra-khir and Saviar. A moment later the two traveling elves came, Tae gave the signal, and the black maw of the gate formed in its usual place and manner. One by one, they stepped through it to find themselves standing on forest floor covered with fallen leaves, dirt, and detritus, and smelling of spring. Hemmed in by tangled tree branches and interwoven plants to a height of about one and a half average men, Tae could see a twilit sky overhead. Three elves approached El-brinith and Chan'rék'ril, speaking in rapid-fire elvish and gesticulating mildly, at least by human standards. The eight humans still had their weapons and war gear, but they seemed supremely uninterested in their surroundings and in the visitors who had suddenly appeared in their midst. Three slept through the gating, and the other five observed them with half-lidded eyes, as if bored by the process.

Saviar immediately began checking the perimeter in every direction, including up and down.

Tae seized one of the men, an Easterner by appearance, and hauled him to his feet. He remained standing, and his eyes narrowed, but he said nothing and did not seem to comprehend the situation. If he recognized his king, he made no gesture nor spoke any words of fealty.

"What's wrong with them?" Ra-khir demanded, clearly trusting Saviar to handle security.

One of the elves excused himself from the others to approach the humans. "You can call me Ar'min'taé," he said, apparently knowing enough about human convention and ability to shorten his name, as Captain had. He also spoke fluent common with barely an accent. "The creatures who hold us prisoner give us food and water that contains an herb that keeps them passive."

It doesn't affect elves? Imorelda sent.

Tae had several questions, but that seemed as good as any other to start with. "And it only works on humans?"

Ar'min'taé barely shook his head with the conservative gestures elves perfected, at least when it came to communication. "We have magic to counteract it. We don't use it on the humans, though, because they're much safer in this state."

Tae suspected the elf had no understanding of how offensive many humans would find that comment. Before he could ask, Rakhir stepped in to reveal it.

"You left the humans defenseless against an enemy and consider that safer?"

Until they had come to Midgard, elves had no concept of sides and dangerous hostilities. Ar'min'taé blinked eyes like polished rubies and turned to face Ra-khir. His head rolled upward. While the elf stood eye-to-eye with Tae, Ra-khir towered over them both. "Prior to them eating and drinking this herb, they were doing things that got them torn apart. None of them has died since the herb took affect. Should we not consider that an improvement?"

He has a point. Imorelda curled her tail under Tae's nose.

Tae could not deny it. Still, Ra-khir had an even better one. Dealing with helpless sheep might pacify the enemy, but it also granted them total control. If they decided to attack, the humans would have no recourse. In the meantime, they had no real life, no means to contemplate solutions or strategy. However, the rescue team did not have time to teach grand lessons about the differences between elves and humans nor should they expect the elves to understand.

One of the other elves interrupted, using elvish. Tae knew enough of the language to figure out he wanted to know if some of them could leave through the gate. He did not wait for Ar'min'taé to translate. "It would be nice if we could not tip our hands too early. Does the enemy know you as individuals? Will they notice if some of you disappear or get replaced?"

Ar'min'taé pursed lips that looked almost triangular. "I don't believe they know us individually. As far as we can tell, they're not checking in on us, either. They deal with anyone who escapes the boundaries, and they toss us food over the top once a day; but we're not seeing anything to make us think they're actually watching us. We believe the Outworld creatures were magically created, but we've had no indication they're capable of channeling or organizing chaos." Apparently noticing questioning looks, he explained further, "No one has used any magic since our arrival, except us."

Tae looked at Ra-khir for suggestions, then remembered the knight had no idea what the other elf had asked. He seized on that fact to make the decision himself. "Ar'min'taé, if you're willing to remain with us until we understand the situation, I don't see any reason why your three friends can't gather the humans and escape through the gate right now."

One of the other elves, a slight female, smiled broadly at this; but the other two clearly did not speak the common tongue. Ar'min'taé shifted his feet but showed no other signs of discomfort. Tae suspected the idea of remaining behind did not sit well with him, but he understood the need. He turned to the other elves, spoke briefly in elvish, then back to Tae. "I will stay as long as you need me." Even as he spoke, the other three elves started taking human hands and leading them toward the gate.

Ra-khir frowned but did not argue. "Did they say anything about their captors?"

"Just what you heard." Tae encouraged Ar'min'taé. "Tell us what you know about this world and, especially, your captors."

Ar'min'taé watched the other elves herd the drugged humans toward the opening and assist them to Midgard while he spoke. "This world's similar to what you called Elves' Island on Midgard: small, mostly forest, no towns or buildings. It appears to contain only animals: a variety of birds, rodents, and coneys. The storm threw us all around the Outworld, and those of us who survived it used *khohlar* to find one another. About the time all of the elves and humans came together, an enormous creature appeared. It looked similar to . . ." Ar'min'taé hesitated, glancing around the clearing and scratching his scalp through fine, white hair. "Well, most similar to that animal on your shoulders."

That magnificent animal on your shoulders, Imorelda corrected.

"Only much larger with claws as long as my fingers." Ar'min'taé spread his hands to reveal his slender, delicate digits. "And fangs like fat, ivory knives. Its coat was black with faint speckled patterns, and it moved with a grace even elves might envy. It crouched as if to spring upon us. Some of us hit it with a spell that made it sleepy. Then, the humans killed it with their swords."

Tae expected Imorelda to insist he extol her virtues, but she remained silent, apparently awed by Ar'min'taé's description. Uncertain what to ask, he allowed the elf to continue his story uninterrupted.

"Soon after that, we were assaulted by great numbers of similar beasts. Their colors varied a lot and their sizes a bit; but they were clearly related to one another and worked as a group. We tried talking to them, but they didn't respond. The humans killed a couple of the beasts, but a dozen of them were torn to pieces in the process. Using our magic, we discovered the natives were weaving plants and tree branches into a pen and figured out they intended to herd us into it.

Once we got the humans to move collectively toward it, the lethal attacks ceased. We were trapped, but we were alive."

"So they're intelligent," Ra-khir said to no one in particular.

Tae added, "Intelligent giant cats that cooperate in groups." Intrigued, he continued, "That's an ambitious project. How did they communicate with one another to organize it?"

Ar'min'taé shook his head. "Not in any way we could figure out. They growled at us, but not apparently to each other. A few of them roared, a terrifying sound that sends a man or elf scrambling; but, again, it always seemed to be for us. When struck with weapons, they whined in pain. They made no other utterances, nothing coordinated or back and forth. It seemed more as if they shared a mind, working seamlessly around one another."

Mental communication? Imorelda suggested.

Exactly what I was thinking.

Imorelda joked, *Oh. Then that can't be right.*

Tae did not rise to the bait. "You say you tried to talk to them. I assume you used a variety of languages. And also *khohlar*."

Ar'min'taé looked around the hemmed-in clearing. "The humans used languages I don't speak, so I'm not sure how many they tried. The beasts did not respond to any of those or elvish or even *khohlar*. Standard khohlar is automatically understood. Babies and animals hear and comprehend it, at least to the level their intelligence allows."

Tae knew that from his conversations with Tem'aree'ay, but he doubted Ra-khir did. Saviar had placed himself within the range of this conversation, probably listening even as he watched for enemies or intruders. "Eventually, they separated you into smaller groups, correct? And each group is in its own pen?"

The elf leaped on these new questions. "Yes. Once their herb took effect, they led off groups of humans. We tried to insinuate ourselves so at least three elves wound up in each group. That's enough for a *jovinay arythanik*."

Ra-khir said a few soft words to Saviar, who responded in kind. Then, he addressed Tae and Ar'min'taé. "Are you sure the other groups are still alive? They weren't led off for slaughter?"

Ar'min'taé's nod was so brisk, it rose to the level of human nonverbal communication. "We *khohlar* regularly. There's a total of seven groups, including this one. Six have elves and one only humans. Unfortunately, we have no contact with the last group, so we can't be entirely sure of their disposition; but the other six have not been harmed, so we believe the human group is all right, too."

Saviar finally spoke. "I think I could escape this confinement. It's woven tightly, and it contains brambles, but it's not indestructible."

To Tae's surprise, Ar'min'taé agreed heartily. "Our magic could get us through it, and a few of the humans chopped their way out before the herbs took their full effect. Also, this world has smaller cats, much like that one." He gestured toward Imorelda. "We're not sure if they're a distinct type of animal or the young of the bigger beasts, but one or two occasionally slip through the mess and visit us."

Tae could feel one of the kittens wriggling in his pocket. "What happened to the escapees?"

"The ones who didn't fight got tossed back over the walls of a pen, not always the one he escaped from. The ones who did got killed and, in at least one witnessed case, devoured." Ar'min'taé shivered. "It's safer inside the pens, at least for now."

Ask him about the cats, Imorelda demanded. The squirming kitten settled back down in its pocket.

Tae obeyed. "The smaller cats that visit you. Do you think they're spies?"

"Spies?" It was not an elfin concept. "You mean, you think they might be checking on us for the bigger beasts?"

Ra-khir's face screwed into a skeptical expression. He shook his head. "I doubt it if they're the larger creatures' young. Who would risk their children that way?"

Imorelda immediately sent, *I've seen people take stupid risks with children, especially ones who aren't their own.*

Tae had also, but another possibility seemed more likely. *Do you think the young of giant catlike creatures would look exactly like adult cats of our world?*

Imorelda placed a paw on Tae's chest and looked directly into his face. *Not likely, but I'd have to see them myself to know.*

Do you think you could squeeze through the woven branches without hurting yourself?

Imorelda jumped lightly to the ground.

Tae addressed Ra-khir's question. "They might risk their children, or it's possible the smaller cats are adults of a different breed working either for the larger animals or independently. Or, perhaps, the larger cats are intelligent, and the smaller ones aren't."

Tae anticipated an objection from Imorelda that never came. Though she considered herself smarter than any human, and he felt certain she surpassed many, she dismissed most of her ilk as morons. However, she rarely allowed Tae to get away with doing the same.

"I'm not sure any of that matters," Ra-khir said. "Right now, our best bet seems to be using *khohlar* to coordinate a breakout with the other groups, preferably in the middle of the night, and to have them all come to this confinement. Meanwhile, we'll take down one of the walls, which will give everyone access to the gate."

Tae saw merit in the overall plan, but he also found significant problems.

A cat could get through this tangle, no problem. You'd need a cutting tool and a lot of time, and you'd get more than a few gouges and scratches.

Thanks, Imorelda.

While Tae attended to the cat, Ar'min'taé addressed Ra-khir's plan. "A daytime breakout would be better. From what we've observed, the beasts are more active at night, and they don't seem to have trouble seeing. Dark doesn't hinder elves much, but it sure interferes with human vision."

"Noted," Ra-khir said, then smiled. "Who says elves can't handle strategy?"

Ar'min'tae flushed.

Tae spoke next. "Assuming we use that plan, the biggest issues will be getting word to the one confinement that contains only humans and getting all the humans and elves here safely."

Ra-khir explained further, "The pen with only humans could still hear and understand *khohlar*, they just couldn't reply. As far as getting everyone safely here, we'll have the element of surprise. The captors won't expect a sudden, mass escape. Plus, the prisoners are all warriors, at least all the humans. We'll probably lose some, but most should get back here. At least, we can rescue as many as possible."

Saviar added, "We can help, too. It's not the type of battle I'm trained for, but I'm up to facing giant cats."

Ar'min'taé found another loophole. "They are all warriors, but currently *drugged* warriors. The elves might make it to the gate, but I don't think the humans could."

They all turned to face the elf, even Saviar. Ra-khir voiced the question on every mind. "Didn't you say the elves have spells that can counteract the herbs?"

"We do," Ar'min'taé assured. "We use them daily. But these humans have been eating and drinking the herbs for weeks, so it's far more established in their systems. Also, magic works easier on creatures of chaos and we have more experience with elfin metabolism. One of the groups has only two elves and another none, not enough for the *jovinay arythanik* it would require to treat a group of humans, all of whom have imbibed a lot of herbs. It would also take us several days. During that time, the humans would have to avoid the drugged food and water, which might weaken them as much as the herb itself. It would also require a lot of *khohlar* to organize, which would surely alert the beasts, too."

"Except they can't hear *khohlar*," Tae reminded.

"I didn't say they couldn't hear *khohlar*. Only that they weren't responding to it. Over the millennia, we've found only one being who couldn't hear it, and she had a terrible medical defect. We have to assume the beasts do hear it and are either confused by it or are ignoring it."

Tae sighed. He had no doubt they needed to follow Ra-khir's plan in a general sense. He only hoped ironing out the details would not prove insurmountable.

I'm going to do some scouting, Imorelda informed Tae as she disappeared into the brush.

Wait! Tae sent. *I'll come with you.*

No you won't. Already, her communication became fainter. *If you try, and they don't kill you, I'll do it myself.* Then, the contact broke, and Tae realized the futility of attempting further discussion.

The idea of Imorelda alone among enemies made Tae frantic, but he reluctantly realized she was the only one who qualified for the mission. *Fare well, my friend. Don't take any unnecessary chances, and get back here as soon as you can.*

If she heard him, Imorelda did not reply.

So focused on his cat, Tae almost missed Ar'min'taé's next suggestion. "I could go through the gate and instruct any elves not holding the gate open to prepare some *atferth* food and drink. If we could get the humans to consume that instead of their usual fare, it would instantly energize them. That should be enough to overcome the herb, even given in large amounts over time."

Saviar added, "As long as you're going through the gate to gather things, you might want to bring back extra weapons for anyone who's either lost one or doesn't have a decent sword." Apparently, another thought hit him. "Also, suggest sending a bunch of Renshai."

Tae foresaw danger in that last idea. "Additional weapons, great. As far as the Renshai, you might want to organize them, but don't bring them back through the gate with you." He looked at Saviar as he explained. "If we can avoid a fight, it will be better, but if we need them to finish one, I can't think of any group I'd rather have by my side." He hoped Saviar would take the compliment and ignore the offense.

Saviar simply nodded. "Probably for the best."

Tae considered suggesting El-brinith or Chan'rék'ril should be the one to go through the gate so Ar'min'taé could tell them more, but he decided against it. The two who had accompanied the group were chosen because they had an adventurous bent rare in elves. "Can you think of any other specific information about what's happened so far on this world that might help us?"

Ar'min'taé shook his head, his gaze clearly on the gate. His desire to get through it as swiftly as possible was clear.

Tae decided to help him even more by not requiring his return. "El-brinith, would you mind accompanying Ar'min'taé? That way, you could bring back the magic food and drink, so your friend could be free of this place."

"I'd be happy to," El-brinith said, jumping to the task with unelf-like vigor. The two of them disappeared through the opening.

Only Ra-khir, Saviar, Tae, and Chan'rék'ril remained, and they moved closer together, allowing them to speak much more softly. The sky had gone dark other than an unfamiliar pattern of stars speckled across it, a quarter moon, and another just past new. Even with the double moons, their phases kept the sky blacker than average, and Tae could not help thinking wistfully about how that would work to his advantage in most circumstances. Given the beasts could see through it, however, the darkness could only work against them. He believed Ar'min'taé that a full breakout would prove safer in broad daylight.

Chan'rék'ril looked up at the sky thoughtfully before suggesting, "I need very little sleep, but the rest of you should prepare for what may prove an extremely difficult day. Why don't I keep watch? If I find myself drifting off, I'll wake someone immediately."

It seemed a reasonable suggestion, though Tae doubted sleep would come easily to any of them. They all had a lot to consider. The plan still had some enormous flaws, and his concern for Imorelda weighed on him like stone. That worsened when the kittens slipped out of their pockets and, not finding their mother, decided to use Tae's head as a plaything, batting mercilessly at his hair, ears, and nose.

Tae put up with the tiny paws, intervening only when a needlelike claw sank too deeply or a wandering paw strayed too close to his eyes or lips. He suspected by the time he found rest, if ever, they would have exhausted themselves. When El-brinith returned with the fabricated food and water, someone would have to secretly distribute it to the various confinements. Someone would also have to explain the plan to the pen holding only humans, so standard *khohlar* would not be necessary, and probably help them create a hole through which to escape. Tae suspected, as the only one with spying experience, he was the logical candidate for "someone."

Imorelda's voice in Tae's head awakened him, much to his surprise. *I'm back!*

Still outside of their protective pockets, the kittens ran to her, nearly bowling her over in their attempt to nurse.

Flopping onto her side beside Tae, Imorelda allowed the tiny creatures their breakfast. Dawn painted the sky in an array of subtle colors blending into one another. Tae's limbs had stiffened in temperatures that had dropped significantly since he had fallen asleep. He sat up, ignoring his body's complaints. A short distance away, Ra-khir and Saviar chatted softly, and Chan'rék'ril lay curled on his side near the gate. For an instant, Tae worried the elf could accidentally roll inside it or become startled into darting to its safety. Then, he remembered there were other elves on this world, separately confined, so the gate would remain open even if Chan'rék'ril crossed to Midgard. *What did you learn?* He kept his question general, hoping Imorelda would begin with the most pertinent information.

Cats are, indeed, the dominant people here. They use a mental language much like ours might be if we were both cats.

Tae's hopes soared as he contemplated the possibility he could communicate with the creatures holding the elves and humans hostage. It might change the entire dynamic, making it possible to talk their way out instead of fighting. Still, he did not press. Usually, allowing Imorelda to impart information in her own way shortened the conversation and kept it from devolving into worthless tangents. *Meaning?*

Imorelda purred, presumably due to the ministrations of her kittens as they ate and kneaded her belly to stimulate the milk. *They use only concepts rather than a combination of words and ideas, like we do. And rather than names for things, they use mostly scents, occasionally combined with pictures and sounds.* She demonstrated. *For example, the enormous cats are collectively called . . .* She sent a musty odor to his mind. *Then, each type has its own name. There's . . .* A smell accompanied by a gold-and-black–striped pattern filled Tae's head. *And . . .* This time, he received a scent too similar to the previous ones for him to differentiate, the image of a fringe of hair around the head, and a roaring sound. *And . . .* The smell again with a picture of tawny fur and oddly shaped black spots.

Tae did not need the full list. *What about the smaller cats, the ones Ar'min'taé said were your size?*

Imorelda quivered. Had she not been pinned down by her brood, he suspected she would have danced. *They're here, too. They call them . . .* This time, he got a clearly different scent, a purr and a concept of cat-sized. *They're similar to me. They're intelligent, unlike the cats back home, and we did a lot of talking.* She added excitedly, *I think it's possible, even likely, my mother somehow came from this world and got lost on ours.*

Gods! Tae sent, making no attempt to mask his surprise. *Imagine finding it this way. Any idea how it could have happened?*

None. Matrinka's grandfather found Mior as a tiny kitten stuck in a sewer grate. She was too young to remember the rescue, let alone anything that came before it.

Tae realized he had created the very side conversation he had been trying to avoid. *We can think about that later, preferably with Matrinka present.* His own words reminded him of her predicament, and sorrow filled him. He had to shake it off to continue. *Do you think I could speak to these cats the way I do you?*

Imorelda rolled onto her back to grant the kittens better access. *You have the ability to talk to them, if that's what you mean. I don't think you should talk to them like you do me, though. You don't know them.*

Tae believed he understood her point. *Ability, yes. That's what I meant.* He thought back over his experience with mental communication. *Would I have to find a way to talk to all of them at once?*

It doesn't work like that. They communicate singly with one another, then chain the message.

Tae scratched behind Imorelda's ears gently, careful not to disrupt the kittens. *Chain?*

One contacts the next who contacts the next who contacts the next until they're all working together. Another way is for one to speak to another, then a third joins with either the first or the second, which brings them together. They can do this with any number of listeners, but it gets confusing if they patch in too many, so they tend to use the other type of chain more often. Either way, they can communicate in groups even though they have nothing like indirect khohlar.

That led into the next important question. *Do they, in fact, receive khohlar? Have they heard anything the elves and humans said?*

They don't have a spoken language, other than the same basic cues animals on our world use. Warning growls, angry tails, purrs for the regular-sized cats, things of that type. They considered the sounds made by the elves and humans to be nonsensical. They do hear and understand the khohlar, *though. It's the only reason they didn't outright kill all the humans and elves. Apparently, the elves apologized for the murder and promised to try to keep everyone peaceful. Since the large cats don't differentiate between elves and humans, they don't know who promised and who didn't.* ∗

Probably a good thing, Tae realized. He addressed Imorelda again, ∗*I don't suppose they'd be willing to let all the elves and humans leave through the gate.* ∗

∗*They don't know about the gate, and I didn't tell them. They wove the pens, but they don't peer inside them regularly. They just toss in food and let rain fill the containers. Incidentally, those are made from a bark that sheds the herb Ar'min'taé mentioned. They also add a powdered version to the food. The cats that visit do it strictly on an individual basis and from curiosity, although they do occasionally share information with the bigger cats. Since the bigger cats sometimes eat the smaller cats, their interaction is somewhat limited.* ∗

That did not bode entirely well. If the enormous cats consumed their intelligent cousins, they would not hesitate to do the same with the elves and humans.

Imorelda continued, ∗*I did ask about releasing the elves and humans, and they would not hear of it. Apparently, they've penned them with the intention of domesticating them as a source of meat.* ∗

Tae stopped scratching the cat. ∗*Like the way we keep sheep?* ∗

∗*Exactly. Currently, they have enough meat from the ones they killed in their own defense. Eventually, though, they plan to harvest the prisoners. Also, to breed them.* ∗

∗*Breed them!* ∗ Tae could not contain a laugh, which he turned into a cough so as not to bring Ra-khir and Saviar into the conversation. Yet. ∗*Aren't they all males? I mean, the only female warriors I know of, besides Marisole, are Renshai; and I'm certain any Renshai who might have gotten sent here were the first to attack, escape, and eventually die.* ∗

∗*There are elves of both genders,* ∗ Imorelda pointed out.

∗*Elves who can't reproduce unless and until they have replacement souls.* ∗

∗*The people of this world don't know the elves can't reproduce, nor have they dared to examine the humans that intimately yet. Not until they're sure they've all been rendered safely placid.* ∗ Imorelda added, ∗*I'm sure the first humans domesticating the first goats had their issues, too. The difference between a wild boar and a tame pig is almost too huge to contemplate.* ∗

Tae could scarcely argue. He supposed the first person to befriend dogs and cats met more than his share of contentiousness, too. *Not unlike what we're facing with the beasts who rule this Outworld. *Did you explain our intelligence? Once we finally convinced the* Kjempemagiska *we weren't just animals, they became more willing to listen and, ultimately, we're making them allies. *

Imorelda had more insight into the matter than Tae realized. *The* Kjempemagiska *are magical giants, within the scope of "people." What we're dealing with here are intelligent animals with carnivorous diets. They eat whatever is edible, including my ilk if they can't find birds or coneys. Your intelligence, or lack of it, matters only in how difficult it makes you to catch and devour. *

*So, we're back to the original plan. * Tae sighed. *I don't suppose you scouted out the locations of all of the confinements. *

By now, the kittens had finished, so Imorelda clambered to her feet. Waves of offense tainted her sending. *Of course I did. That was my job, wasn't it? I sneaked inside each one and counted them, too, if you want to know. One group tried to grab me; they looked hungry. *

Tae knew the elves could code their *khohlar* into elvish so only those who spoke it could understand it. That would allow them to communicate with every confinement, except the one without elves, without revealing their plans to the enemy. It seemed like their strategy, such as it was, had finally come together.

CHAPTER 22

Your mind is elsewhere than battle? What good worrying about the future when you're dead?

—*Nirvinia, a Renshai torke*

TAE KAHN CLUNG TO THE SHADOWS and denser copses of bushes from habit, mentally cursing the decision to act in broad daylight, though Imorelda had assured him Ar'min'taé was correct about it being safer. As quiet and well-practiced as Tae was, Elbrinith moved more smoothly and quietly and through thicker brush and brambles than he could possibly handle, at least not without cutting them or making an inordinate amount of noise. Though she seemed calm and unencumbered, despite carrying a smaller share of the bundled foodstuffs and small but competent weaponry from Midgard, Tae spoke to her only when necessary so as not to risk disrupting whatever magic she was using to conceal the natural scents of their clothing and bodies. The elf and the cat had explained smell and sound were far more important than vision to predatory animals, but Tae could not shake the instinctive focus on hiding he had developed from years of avoiding his father's, and later his own, human enemies. The pack across his back seemed to grow heavier with each passing moment.

Imorelda took the lead, directing Tae with a steady mental prattle he tended to lose amidst overwhelming concerns. He had seen his feline friend seize and worry mice, tearing and devouring them without losing the train of conversation, and the idea of becoming dinner to cats fifteen times her size did not sit well in his mind. He tried not to imagine claws as long as his hand ripping through his abdomen or teeth like daggers penetrating his skull and started to wonder how any of the warriors had managed to dispatch even one of them.

Imorelda seemed to realize her information and reassurances were not reaching Tae, and she stopped talking except to give him necessary directional information when his searches for better cover caused him to stray. Shortly, she stepped aside, one forepaw stretched out in front of her. *There's a group in there. Two elves; ten humans.*

Tae saw only a wall of interwoven vines. He scuttled to El-brinith's side and whispered, "There's a group in there."

I know, El-brinith sent back. *Two elves and ten humans. I'm in contact using direct* khohlar *with one of them.*

Tae dropped to his haunches, examining the wall of foliage. It appeared impenetrable.

El-brinith ducked inside it and moved with relative ease. Tae could hear her mumbling magical syllables as she shoved her way deeper until she disappeared from his sight.

Tae remained entirely still, afraid her need to make more magic obviated his scentlessness. He did not want to add to his vulnerability by making a sound.

Imorelda suggested, *When I don't want to be smelled by things I'm hunting, I roll in stinky green stuff.*

Tae appreciated her advice but wished she had mentioned it sooner. *You could have told me that before we started. Now, I'm not making any unnecessary movements or risking potentially noisy actions.*

Imorelda flopped down on a patch of broad-leafed plants and vigorously rubbed her shoulders, back, and body against them.

Every tiny sound she made caused Tae to cringe. She did not have nearly as much to lose, as her presence here could be considered normal by the creatures from whom he and El-brinith hid. Imorelda had suggested, if the giant cats caught him, they would more likely toss him into the nearest enclosure than kill him, so long as he did not fight. But there was no guarantee a hungry giant might not choose to kill and/or eat him instead, even if Tae managed to suppress the instinct to struggle. Also, he worried the bundles he and El-brinith carried might cue the creatures to their plans or, at least, make the animals more vigilant or aggressive.

After what seemed like hours, El-brinith emerged from the foliage to announce with direct khohlar, *The humans are awakening and the elves are fully prepared for the signal.*

Tae nodded silently to indicate he had heard and understood. One enclosure down with five more to go, including the one with exclusively human occupants, which they would save for last. So far, things seemed to be going according to plan, but he knew it would become more difficult and dangerous as they proceeded, not only because more time and motion meant more chance for discovery. He drew solace from El-brinith's pronouncement the magicked foodstuffs appeared to be doing their job as swiftly as Ar'min'taé had promised.

Using the same caution and technique, El-brinith delivered four more packages, leaving only one in Tae's pack. Each time, she gave him the same positive message. The corners of her mouth assumed an upright position in the most neutral of circumstances, but they seemed to creep higher each time she emerged from another confinement. Tae tried to share her enthusiasm, without much success. He had known from the start the distribution would prove the easiest part of the plan. He, the light-footed elf, and a cat would have far less difficulty moving, unnoticed, through any situation than blocks of soldiers, especially ones recently awakened from drugging.

At last, Imorelda indicated the last of the enclosures. *This is the one with no elves,* she reminded him, sticking to the task with uncharacteristic single-mindedness that should have relieved him but, instead, discomforted. As they went about their task, she had become increasingly noncommunicative, the emotion that usually escaped around her verbatim sendings absent, presumably deliberately blocked. Whatever occupied his feline companion's thoughts, she kept it well and untypically hidden.

Yes. I need to get inside with El-brinith. Can you help me?

No. Imorelda turned him a slit-eyed look that suggested he had asked something particularly stupid. *But I'm sure the elf and her magic can.* She added without passion of any kind, *I'm going to leave you both here. I have some business to handle from when I went spying.*

Business? Tae sent, but Imorelda ignored the interruption.

I need to take the kittens with me.

Kittens? Caught up in the adventure, he had completely forgotten the little ones wedged into his pockets.

Kittens, Imorelda repeated impatiently. *My offspring. The growing creatures I made with a male of my species.* She sent an image of the calico and the tabby, still unaccompanied by any clues or emotion.

Tae's thoughts scattered. *What is she doing? What business could she have? What could she possibly have promised them?* Before he could contemplate any of those too long, his mind channeled back to a single, terrible possibility. *She's leaving me. By the gods, Imorelda is leaving me!* The idea struck with the force of a raging stallion, and tears filled his eyes before he recognized the terrible sadness that inspired them. *And why shouldn't she? She finally found a world where she is the norm, the place of her origin. Here, she's surrounded by her own kind, no longer forced to associate with witless cats or boorish humans. These are her people, and only a selfish lout would stand in the way of her joy.* Surreptitiously, he wiped away the tears. It did not surprise him she chose not to prolong her departure or even to admit it. She had to know it would upset him, but she did not have to suffer his pain or a long and heart-melting good-bye.

Though Tae tried to prevent it, images paraded through his mind. Imorelda had been his closest companion and confidante for eighteen years, longer than Midgard cats usually lived in total. He remembered her in a million places, her expressions ranging from quizzical to judgmental to contented, her purr a pleasure, her lashing tail a reminder of every mistake he ever made. He loved her as much as any human, he realized, more than most; and her absence would leave a void nothing could ever fill. Still, he had no right to influence her choice, to delay her decision. He looked up to find Imorelda staring at him, her tail twitching in irritation.

My kittens, she reminded.

Tae realized he had just spent the last several moments quietly staring at her. He forced a smile. *Yes, sorry. Lost in thought.* He reached into his pockets and pulled out first one handful of sleeping fur, then the other and laid them on the ground. They remained in place, blinking tiredly.

Imorelda's tail thrashed harder. She made no move to take them. *Help me out, would you? I can't carry them both at the same time.*

Shocked, Tae hesitated, uncertain whether to feel joyfully flattered or sick to his stomach. *You want me to go with you?*

The cat's tail became a veritable whip. *You mean, do I want you to become a snack for . . . ?* She added the generalized scent name for the enormous wild cats. *I was thinking more in terms of a scarf or handkerchief.*

Tae had neither. He unwrapped the food parcel, leaving its contents in the pack he would no longer need once they delivered the food and weapons to the last of the captured humans. He smoothed the now-empty cloth wrapping on the ground, placed the two kittens on it, and scooped them into a mewling bundle.

Without another word, or a backward glance, Imorelda seized the edges and bounded into the woodlands, the parcel of kittens dangling from her mouth.

Tae's vision blurred.

A presence touched his mind, and his heart soared until he recognized it as *khohlar*. *I'll need the pack,* El-brinith said.

Tae fisted tears from his eyes and turned to his remaining companion. He whispered back, "No elves in there, remember? We both have to go, but I'll need your help to get through the brush."

Stay close. * El-brinith led the way, seeming to crawl through the intensely woven foliage as naturally as breathing. Tae had experience with tight-packed forest but nothing deliberately and intensively knotted together, and he rarely escaped without abrasions, tears, and embedded splinters and brambles. Hyperalert to El-brinith's movements, he not only spared himself significant pain and injury, he also learned elfin motions and tricks that never would have occurred to him had he not so closely followed and mimicked her. At times, he felt as if something, probably magic, greased his limbs, causing the plant matter to slide over and around him rather than jabbing and sticking. The fluidity of her, the surety of her motion, seemed to open ways he otherwise would never have seen. He believed he did more than penetrate an enclosure; he learned a new way to approach the great outdoors. He only hoped he would live long enough to test this new knowledge.

Faster than Tae could have imagined, they found themselves in a leaf-strewn clearing with twelve gaunt human soldiers in various stages of repose, a few wandering aimlessly within the confines of the weeds-and-branches pen. Discarded weaponry lay scattered about, the bones of small animals in untidy heaps, and a dish made of bark held brackish, muddy water. Only a few of the men even bothered to look at the newcomers who had appeared suddenly in their midst, and not one spoke.

Tae pulled the pack off his back, removed the magicked food, mostly bread and jerked meat, and placed it on the pack which still held an assortment of finely made daggers. The men shuffled over and started eating methodically. Tae dared to say aloud, "How long before it takes affect?"

El-brinith looked up from shaking one of the sleepers. "Make sure they all get some, and watch. You'll be amazed."

Tae joined her, palming a couple hunks of jerky to assure distribution to the sleepers. Shortly, four more men had joined the others, and Tae forced the dried meat onto a fifth who seemed more reticent to come to his feet. Only then, he troubled to identify their countries of origin: four Northmen, seven Westerners and one Easterner who was not Subikahn.

With each bite they took, Tae could see results. They became more coordinated, less lolling and disinterested. Within moments, they were talking, questioning Tae and El-brinith about their presences, telling them about their experiences, which jibed with those of the men and elves in the first enclosure. Tae gave the soldiers general information, making sure he had the attention of as many as possible to avoid at least some repetition. When they had eaten all of the special food and avoided washing it down with any of the native water, he handed out the daggers, pleased to see most had longer weapons as well, mostly swords of varying quality.

Only then, Tae explained the plan. "We've met with all the captured groups; and, now, they all have at least one elf. El-brinith will let the others know that everyone has someone who can send *khohlar*, which is elfin mind-speech. When I finish explaining all this, you'll hear and feel her do it in your heads. She may or may not get a reply, which you'll also hear."

El-brinith nodded. Tae would have preferred the elves use direct *khohlar*, but it did not travel nearly as far. It also made sense to assure all of the groups heard essentially the same thing at about the same time. Of course, it also meant their enemies would hear.

Tae continued, "We'll all cut our way through the wall of this enclosure together." Ra-khir and the others had discussed the possibility of using magic to escape the fences but had decided against it. It did not seem prudent to waste the elves' power chopping foliage when they might face an army of giant cats. "Using *khohlar* for direction, with all humans following our assigned elves . . ." He added, "Our elf guide being El-brinith, of course. . . . we'll meet up at the gate and travel through it back to Midgard. Any questions?"

Several hands shot up at once.

Tae selected one of the Westerners, a man with reddish highlights in his dark hair which suggested an Erythanian heritage. "The last couple of men who went through the wall didn't return. One of them was eaten, at least judging from the sounds we heard. We don't know about the other."

The Easterner spoke without acknowledgment, "Sire, there're enormous cats out there, probably ten times our size, with claws and teeth."

"We know," Tae said calmly, trying not to reveal his own trepidations. "But we're going to come at them all together. We're hoping we can talk them out of attacking; but, if we can't, we need to be ready to fight."

One of the Northmen cleared his throat, and all eyes went to him. He said, "We're all warriors, Sire. We're brave and mostly strong and certainly trained for warfare, but it took nearly all of us at our best to kill one of those creatures."

"We know that, too," Tae said. "But we can't stay in here. They're penning you the way we do goats and sheep. They've kept you docile with drugged food and water with the plan of eating you at their leisure."

"Slow death; fast death," said someone in the back.

"Personally," the Easterner said. "I'll pick fast death over a drugged and worthless life anxiously awaiting my turn to become dinner."

"Hear! Hear!" several others called out in reply, most raising weapons to punctuate the words.

One older Westerner raised his hand.

Tae acknowledged him with a gesture.

"Sire, I'm just wondering how you plan to talk to these creatures. I remember our first encounter. They didn't respond to anything we said in any language, and they didn't even seem to hear the elves' mind-speech."

They all studied Tae. It had become common knowledge the Eastern king had an eerie command of languages most considered a god-given talent.

Tae pursed his lips to show he took the question seriously. "We're pretty certain they can hear and even understand *khohlar*." He did not go into the different gradations of the elves' mental language; since they had clearly heard it at the first encounter, they knew their own minds could grasp and translate at least one form of it. "We think the cats have chosen to ignore it, perhaps because they can't respond to it in kind or because the elves haven't said anything they want to acknowledge." *Such as that we're thinking beings they shouldn't be using as a food source.* He kept that last bit to himself. "I have good reason to believe I've found a way to communicate with them quite similar to how I connected with the giants and their servants."

Deep frowns scored the men's faces at the mention of their enemy. Tae suddenly realized they might not know the war had ended, so he added, "Which helped us, elves and humans, to destroy them."

The scowls disappeared, replaced by sudden conversation, which he cut off with a gesture. There was little time for conjecture.

"When you're home, that'll all be explained. For now, you just need to know I'm going to try to talk to these giant cats and find a peaceful end to this situation. If I can't, though, we need to be prepared to fight them with the goal of getting as many of us as possible through the magical gate and back to Midgard." Imorelda had seemed certain he could connect with these beings as individuals using the same technique he did with her, without need of her as a translator. He hoped she was right, they would listen, and he would find the words to get the elves and humans, including himself, safely home. "Any more questions?"

Every hand went up.

Tae amended, "Any more questions absolutely necessary to the success of this plan? Ones that can't wait until we're through the gate?"

All the hands dropped, aside from one Northerner.

Tae tipped his head toward the remaining man, who spoke.

"Once we're all embroiled in battle, how will we find the gate?"

El-brinith answered for him. "I'll be the last one through it, and I won't leave until I believe every man left alive has done so. If things get chaotic, we'll make sure to magically highlight it so that it can be seen from a distance. As a last resort, we'll keep up the *khohlar* calls, and you'll have to try to follow them or elves or one another."

Tae nodded. He could think of no better plan, and it bothered him it relied so heavily on one elf remaining behind to keep the gate from closing. He trusted El-brinith and Chan'rék'ril not to flee through the gate in panic, trapping any remaining humans, but as a group, elves were not known for courage under pressure. If either or both of their go-to elves was killed, anyone left, likely including himself, would have to stay on this world forever or, more likely, until claws and teeth ended their lives.

When no one else indicated a desire to speak, Tae gestured toward El-brinith. "Give the signal, please."

El-brinith's *khohlar* entered his head in an echoing shout. "All groups accounted for. Initiate escape."

Tae pointed at one of the enclosing walls of foliage, and the men attacked it with swords and axes. Behind them, Tae found a large rock, seated himself on it, and stretched his mental consciousness outward, seeking a mind capable of receiving his signal. To his surprise, he found one quickly and touched it in a friendly way, sending the concept of greeting.

Surprise wafted through the contact, then an aura of tentative questioning. Though he and the object of his contact exchanged no actual words, they were capable of basic communication. Tae read in the other's sending a desire to know his identity as well as confusion as to why such a thing was not instantaneously obvious. On his end, Tae found it exquisitely difficult to maintain a wordless conversation without revealing his every emotion and thought. His appreciation for Imorelda's talent and intelligence grew enormously.

Tae replied with an image of himself, then tried to mimic the general odor of giant cat Imorelda had supplied amid an aura of more uncertainty. The other corrected the smell routinely, then replied in the negative, supplying an image of itself that looked exactly like any standard black-and-white cat from Midgard. Then it added shock about Tae's ability to communicate and another question Tae believed meant it wanted to know why the humans, which it indicated with a heavy sweat odor, had waited so long to speak.

Tae suffered the familiar frustration of trying to communicate in a language in which he was not fluent. He felt hamstrung, confined by the simplicity of a tongue devoid of grammar, syntax and connotation. He had to rely on images, though he doubted the cats approached the situation quite the same way. He showed pictures of many humans sending out brain waves, accompanied by a negative sentiment, then one of himself with brain waves reaching a black-and-white feline receiver. He continued by a questing picture of the cat in his sending reaching out to larger animals in order to share his communication.

The cat paused in intense consideration. Tae could almost hear the gears of its mind spinning, see its head tipped to one side. Then, another presence seemed to meld into the contact. The two of them exchanged thoughts, mostly blanketed so Tae could only get a few general concepts; then, abruptly, the newcomer addressed him with the same sweat odor the regular cat had used to indicate humans, accompanied by question.

Tae sent it the image of himself, suddenly wondering if he was doing himself any favors. They could as easily single him out for death as for communication. Flashes of imagery and thought wafted to Tae. He tried to sort them, without success, then focused on it as a whole. In some odd manner he could not yet fathom, it had just asked him why he had waited until now to speak.

Outwardly, Tae sighed. Using simple pictograms that seemed childish compared to the smooth, fast sending of the large cat, he tried to outline the idea that he had only recently arrived in order to rescue his fellow humans. As the felines did not appear to separate elves from men intellectually, he did not do so, either. It would only make his explanation more difficult. He could feel others joining the contact as the newcomer brought in another, then that one chained in another until a long line of felines became capable of listening and responding to his sendings. Each time another joined, there was a short, blanketed side conversation, apparently bringing them up to the moment. At first, Tae tried to focus on these, but it made him dizzy with effort and lost him the thread of the main conversation, so he soon learned to ignore them.

Bombarded by questions, first in small numbers, then from every direction, Tae created his own narrative he hoped would address all of them and make his point before the situation drove him to madness. He felt like a creature with a hundred eyes trying to process a different image in each one. It seemed safer to just lower his head and put out the information he needed them to know. So, he sent an image of the humans and elves emerging from their prisons, with cats of every size quietly sitting back and watching them leave the world.

Outrage and questions pounded Tae's mind. Flashes of sounds, smells, and pictures struck him, all converging into the certainty such a thing would never happen. The giant cats of this world, represented by seven similar but distinct odors, would not allow their livestock to leave unmolested.

Tae waited until the bombast died to silence and they all awaited a reply. He attempted to radiate an aura of composure as he sent them an image of men and elves leaving peacefully until the citizens of this world attempted to stand in their way. At that point, he sent the bloodiest images of war he could remember, replacing the disembowelments and decapitation victims with pictures of giant cats with sword-ravaged tawny, speckled, or striped bodies, copying as well as possible the images Imorelda had earlier sent him. He did his best to send the concept that the people of his world preferred to go in peace but would kill viciously if pressed or assaulted.

The cats responded en masse with bloody images of themselves leaping upon the humans, bearing them to the ground, then tearing them into pieces with effortless slashes of enormous claws and single bites that could sever a man in twain, crush his skull or amputate a limb.

The pictures made Tae wince, and the urge to run seized him, but he had experience with hiding emotion and thought from Imorelda. He did not allow horror or fear to taint his sending. They could intimidate him to the point of panic, but he could not allow any sign of such feelings to leach to them from his mind. At least, he felt confident they could not see him, assuming they could read human body language, which seemed unlikely.

Instead, Tae impressed on them the enormous difference in size and population between their world and his, indicating humans as an endless stream of warriors pouring through the gate and into their feline Outworld. He mirrored their own sendings, showing them dozens of humans slaughtered by giant cats and trampled beneath the marching feet of hundreds more of Midgard's finest. He showed them cats of every variety fighting fiercely, then desperately, overpowered by sheer numbers of humans, cut down until the globs of meat on the forest floor became more feline than human and their rivers ran scarlet with their own blood. He used his clearest memories of Northmen diving fearlessly into the fray, cheering the very concept of war and death and destruction, never stopping until every foe lay dead in their wake.

Tae lost track of time, delineated only by the sound of swords striking leaves and branches, axes crunching through wood, the men swearing or crying out in triumph as more foliage disintegrated beneath their charge.

The cats hesitated. Many of them easily concealed their emotions, but Tae experienced some hesitation, discomfort, and even a bit of fear. They blanketed their discussions with one another, but Tae could feel the buzz of mental murmuring as they discussed the situation amongst themselves. Then, one voice came clear over the hubbub with flashes of scents, sounds, and images that suggested a one-on-one battle to decide the prisoners' fate.

It surprised Tae to find a concept he considered uniquely human came easily to the giant cats as well. He peppered his next images with question, showing first a human with a foot on an upside-down, clearly defeated large feline, then the same cat squashing that human's head beneath its paws.

Without using a single word, the speaker explained a human victory meant the sweat-scented ones would get to leave the Outworld, in total, without further problems. A feline victory meant the prisoners returned to their pens and did not attempt any more escapes.

Tae deliberately imbued his next sending with intense and unmistakable amusement. He showed a log balanced on a flat rock fulcrum, then put each of his prior images, human victory versus feline victory, on a side to demonstrate that, either way, the cats won. When he received puzzled responses, he pointed out the human victory left everyone alive and on his or her own world while the cat's victory resulted in every human dying. He showed the scale again, this time with what he considered equal outcomes. If the cats won, all the humans on the feline world would die. If the humans won, all the cats on the feline world should also die or, at least, they should have to come calmly to Midgard where the humans could display them in small metal cages.

This time, Tae found himself blasted with indignation, affront, and horror. His point had clearly struck home too deeply for all of them to hide their emotions.

"We're almost through!" one of the Westerners announced to the cheering of his fellow men.

Tae knew he had little time left to barter. Once the men left their prisons, the cats would either stand aside or attack. Whichever they did would determine what happened rather than his parlay. He had no idea how cats without clocks kept track of time, but he knew their intelligence assured they had some concept of it. Imorelda could count as well as anyone he knew, but she had also lived her entire life among humans, most of it in direct communication with him.

Thoughts of Imorelda brought welling sadness he quelled with all the other emotions fighting for his attention. He could not think about their parting now, not until after he returned to Midgard without her. He tried to send a concept of passing time using brief images that hopped to the future at regular intervals. He let them know the humans had had their agility restored, that they were all working together to break free of their enclosures. He had moments to command the humans: either not to harm their previous captors or to decimate them. He left the decision to the giant cats.

A branch broke with a sickening crack; and, a moment later, sunlight streamed into Tae's face. Based on the thoughts coming from the cats, Tae knew they realized they had run out of time. Dizziness crushed down on him, and he suddenly realized he was holding his breath, had been for at least a couple of minutes. He sucked in a deep lungful of air, stood, and placed a hand on his hilt.

Khohlar pounded his mind in several voices, all with the same general message: *Fight or flee? The men need to know.*

What should I tell them? El-brinith asked, all of her tension flowing easily through the contact.

Tae wished the elves would back off to let him more easily read the cats' intentions. The enormous and intense mixture of emotions threatened to overwhelm him.

Then, finally, the voice of the lead cat rose over the others. His message came in disjointed flashes; yet, this time, Tae's mind oriented it into common words, *Stand down, and let them leave. So long as they do not harm us, we will not harm them.* The contact between Tae and the cat people broke off.

Tae spoke aloud for El-brinith. "Tell them to run for the gate. The cats say they will not attack so long as no one does them any harm."

El-brinith sent the shout out to every mind on the feline Outworld, *Every human and elf is to go through the gate and back to Midgard. So long as no one harms or touches any inhabitant of this world, they will leave us alone.*

A verbal cheer followed her pronouncement, clearly from the men and, perhaps, the elves as well.

Tae slumped back to the stone, limbs shaking, cold sweat bathing every part of him. He had not realized how much physical and mental effort the conversation had taken from him. Not wishing the men to see him in this state, he forced himself to rise again and numbly followed El-brinith toward the gate.

By the time Tae arrived, he found a long line of men and elves entering the gate in single file. He sat beside El-brinith on a deadfall, his head in his hands, watching the others move through the portal. He tried to smile at the image, but it would not come. Exhaustion plagued him. He wanted nothing more than to stagger through the magical gate and collapse the moment he stepped onto Midgard. Not that he would allow that to happen. He had to maintain a strong image for the sake of the soldiers and all his many followers. He had to remain on this feline-controlled world until everyone except El-brinith had exited because he alone could speak to the inhabitants if something went awry. Apparently sensing his weakness, Ra-khir and Saviar took protective places beside him and El-brinith, not bothering to engage them in conversation, merely staring outward in the direction danger might come like well-trained royal bodyguards.

The giant cats kept their distance, but Tae sensed their massed presence just beyond what remained of the first enclosure. Twilight had descended on the world, and he could just barely make out faceless movement at a distance that would confound most bowmen. No elves remained behind, aside from El-brinith who had sent Chan'rék'ril ahead to assist the humans coming through the gate. Only a dozen men still stood in the line awaiting their turn to cross back to their own world. They were a study in alert fatigue, their gazes on the same distant movement as Tae's, their hands instinctively on their hilts, yet their heads bowed and heavy.

Then, from nowhere, a plushy paw touched Tae's arm. *I'm here.* Imorelda climbed into his lap as if she had never left him, the squirming parcel between her teeth.

It took everything Tae had not to envelope her in an embrace, worried the felines of this world might see it as an attack or attempted kidnapping of one of their own. *By all the gods, Imorelda! I thought I'd lost you forever.*

Lost me, she sent with abundant confusion. *I told you they wouldn't hurt me.* She dropped the bundle of kittens into his lap, and he blindly ladled each one into a pocket, his gaze locked on his long-time companion.

But you left on . . . on "business." With no indication you intended on coming back. I thought . . . I thought . . . Tae stopped, afraid to put ideas into her head, then realizing she had a right to consider what he already had. If he waited until they reached Midgard to mention it, he might deprive her of the opportunity to do what was best for herself and her family. He forced himself to finish, *I thought you had decided to stay here. With . . . with your own kind.*

Saviar prodded Tae's shoulder. "Time to go."

Tae glanced at the gate where the last two humans were disappearing.

Pet me! Imorelda demanded.

With those two words, she made it abundantly clear, at least to Tae. She belonged with him until the day one of them died, and he would not have wanted it any other way.

Rising, Tae cradled Imorelda with all the love in the universe and carried her through the gate.

CHAPTER 23

Penfruit doesn't grow on hadongo trees, and aristiri hawks don't hatch from lizard eggs.

—*Thialnir Thrudazisson*

TAE LAY IN ONE OF the most comfortable beds in Castle Béarn, exhausted from his recent excursion, yet sleep eluded him. He believed he had come to peace with the ordeal, but thoughts of Subikahn invaded his mind, poking it awake whenever the barest hint of slumber slid over him. The young man had not been among those rescued from the feline Outworld, which he realized in no way surprised him. Any Renshai forced into such a situation would not have allowed himself to become confined or would have escaped and challenged the giant cats until death. Tae made a mental note to ask about the humans who had done so, then decided against it. He would rather believe Subikahn lived somewhere beyond the reach of the elves' magic, doing something useful and heroic on one of the other Outworlds, that he was alive and happy.

Imorelda stretched out along Tae's side, purring. The kittens joined her, leaping back and forth along her furry length, batting the coverlet and pillows.

I can't sleep, Tae complained.

Neither can I, Imorelda pointed out. *Bothersome kittens. Still don't understand why Matrinka wanted them.* There was love in her sending, something Tae could not remember her allowing to slip through before, at least not in regard to her offspring.

So you really had no intention of leaving me? Tae ran his hand along her entire length, and the kittens seized his fingers with needle sharp claws. *It never occurred to you?*

Never occurred to me? Imorelda sent plenty of amusement with the words. *Only several times a day for my entire life. You're foul-*

smelling, half-foolish, mostly useless, and decidedly dangerous. Not an hour goes by I don't think about leaving you.*

Tae smiled, disengaged his flesh from the kittens and petted Imorelda again. *In other words, you love me too much to abandon me.*

Don't be absurd!

Tae's grin remained, and he focused intently on the conversation. Unlike his attempts to sleep, it kept images of Subikahn at bay.

I stay because you need me.

Tae had to know. Now that the feline world was permanently closed to them, he could afford to press. *You didn't even think about staying on that Outworld? Weren't you even curious to know what it would be like to live among intelligent cats like yourself?*

Imorelda rolled even more firmly against him, displaying her belly to his ministrations. *Here, I'm unique, a queen among cats with gobs of servants to attend my desires. There, I'd have been just one among many of the smaller servant class. They eat nothing but raw, unseasoned meat. They sleep on leaves instead of cushioned beds. They have to run or walk everywhere they go, using their very own paws.*

Tae had to admit he served as Imorelda's conveyance more often than not.

The tabby kitten charged up to his face, touching his lips and nose with a retracted paw. It tipped its head and gazed into his eyes. *Are you a bird?* The voice that entered Tae's mind was not Imorelda's.

Tae nearly fell off the bed.

The sudden movement sent both kittens scurrying over the side of the pallet, clinging to the blanket.

"He spoke to me!" Tae shouted, sitting bolt upright. "The kitten spoke to me."

He did? Imorelda barely stirred, her sending all innocence. *What did he say?*

"He asked me if I'm a bird." The absurdity of the question finally struck Tae. "Why would he ask if I'm a bird?"

Because you have two legs instead of four? Imorelda suggested. *Because he's only five weeks old?*

Tae shook his head, dispelling his current train of thought to address the more significant. He realized, though awake, his mind was not working to its full capacity. *I thought you said these kittens wouldn't be capable of speaking. You said the boy was a moron.*

Perhaps I made a mistake.

Tae tossed off the covers from the opposite side, careful not to bury Imorelda. He walked around the bed to where the two kittens still clung to the hanging blanket. He reached for the tabby, who fluffed up to a size tiny from a size super tiny and spit at him. Ignoring the threat, Tae grabbed the little body with one hand and disengaged its claws from the blanket with the other. He sat on the edge, plopping the kitten into his lap and petting it soothingly. The hair returned to its proper position, and a faint broken purr emerged.

Only then, Tae studied the kitten. It looked a little bigger and heavier, though that only made sense. Kittens seemed to grow by the moment. The white spot on its chest appeared smaller, the tail a trifle longer and more slender, the silver tabby pattern on its flanks more swirly and target-like than the regular rows he remembered. *This is a different kitten.* His mouth fell open, but no words emerged. He found his tongue too dry for speech. **This is an entirely different kitten. Isn't it?**

The calico freed herself from the blanket, dropping to the wooden floor with a tiny thump. Turning to face the bed, she climbed the blanket to join her brother in Tae's lap. He used one hand for each of them, stroking, tickling, scratching all the areas cats like best until he got both of the youngsters purring disjointedly.

When Imorelda did not answer, Tae added, **This was your so-called business? Trading your children?** He made no attempt to keep accusation from his voice. **Your own flesh and blood?**

Imorelda loosed a feline snort. **Get off your damned high horse. I've told you cats swap kittens all the time. It's no big deal.**

Tae could not let such a thing go so easily. **But you're intelligent, and so are the Outworld cats. Don't you have any sense of maternal responsibility?**

That seemed to confuse her. **I'm feeding them. I'm caring for them.**

*But they're not your *kittens!**

*They are *my kittens! They're the only kittens I have.**

Because you traded away the ones you made!

So?

That stopped Tae cold as he realized he was, once again, looking at the situation only from his own perspective, judging with a bias based on old-time Eastern values, the ones of a kingdom his father had overthrown because of its inherent immorality. The same thinking had caused a rift between himself and his only son, one he had worked hard to close and appreciated that he had. If he was doomed to never see Subikahn again, at least they had parted on good terms. Imorelda was highly intelligent and usually right, and Tae knew he needed to look at the situation from her point of view before casually and angrily discarding it.

Imorelda had not wanted to produce children in the first place; she had made it clear she found kittens annoying and abhorrent, that she did not see herself as a competent mother. Matrinka had practically forced her into it, and Tae had taken Matrinka's side. Imorelda had risen to the task admirably up until this moment. She had given them all the necessary care, kept them safe, and stepped in to help at the appropriate times without parenting them to the point of suffocation. She had brought them up healthy and self-reliant nearly to the point where they could live independently.

Colbey Calistinsson had once pointed out shared blood and love were not the same thing, luckily for all the married couples in the world. Colbey's Renshai parents had shared no blood with him, yet they raised him with at least the same pride and affection as any other parents, perhaps with more for having spent most of their young lives barren and wanting him so desperately. Tae knew of cases where new mothers whose spouses wanted a child of the gender opposite the one they bore secretly switched their newborn infants. He even knew of a mother devastated by bearing a baby with terrible defects who traded with a family overburdened with too many mouths to feed.

Tae forced a smile that soon became genuine. *I'm sorry, Imorelda. I'm tired and not thinking clearly.*

Imorelda twisted the knife. *And I was only thinking of Matrinka and you. She wants a replacement for Mior more than anything in the world. Now, she can have one.*

If they don't execute her. Tae kept that to himself. Imorelda already knew Matrinka's plight. She was trusting Tae and Griff, Marisole and Darris to rescue her. He was almost afraid to ask the next question. *How did you manage to talk them into trading?*

Imorelda carefully joined the kittens in Tae's lap, demanding stroking of her own, which he supplied. The kittens mewed their displeasure, both at being stepped on and losing his hands, climbing Imorelda and rubbing against his fingers as they moved along her sleek sides. She had lost some weight, he realized. Her nipples had distended beyond any normal proportions, and the fur around them had disappeared in circles. *It wasn't difficult. They have some regular cats there, just not many. They consider the regulars adorable oddities, basically pets. I had no trouble finding takers who promised to treat them well.*

Regulars? Tae could not imagine the creatures on the Outworld considering animal-level cats "regular."

They don't call them regulars, of course. That's my label. Remember, they don't speak or think in words like we do.

That got Tae thinking, *Do the regulars smell differently than other cats?*

Imorelda purred loudly, adjusting her position to get more of the stroking, which forced the kittens to move as well. *Not necessarily. They're not as discerning about what they eat, which can change the scent a bit. Mostly, they're distinguished by their inability to speak, other than basic verbal noises. And, of course, the way they act.*

Tae realized they had shifted onto a tangent and tried to right the conversation. *So the mother of these kittens had too many?*

The boy's mother did. She had nine in a single litter, almost unheard of, and she was worn out. The girl came from a youngster who had a litter of four. One was deformed and eaten, one wandered off and fell into a hole, and the third fell prey to a hungry turtle. She knew she wasn't a good mother, at least not yet, so she happily gave me the last one.

Tae finally found himself considering the upside of the trade. *And now we have two more intelligent, mindspeaking cats on Midgard.*

Mmm-hmmm. Imorelda did not seem as contented as she should, under the circumstances. *The hardest part was finding replacements that would fool Matrinka and, hopefully, you. It took me forever to get across the point I wanted kittens who resembled my trades in age, size, and coloring rather than by scent, activity level, and sound.*

That made sense to Tae, particularly after he had attempted to communicate with the Outworld cats. *Why did you want to fool us? I admit, I acted boorishly when I first figured it out, but I bowed to your superior decision-making fairly quickly.*

Matrinka's more . . . let's say sentimental. Also, it's important she believes these kittens are blood brother and sister and directly related to me.

Tae suspected Imorelda had gone to some trouble to assure the two did not share a bloodline. The mother of nine would probably have given up two as quickly as one, though, perhaps, only one had the proper coloring. He merely asked, *Why?*

Because, if Matrinka knew the truth, she'd insist on overbreeding them, and their offspring, like she did with my siblings and their kittens. The castle would become cat-infested again, only now with creatures far more capable of mischief.

Tae could see the problem. *You don't really think them being blood-related will stop her, do you? It didn't before.*

True. But then, she was desperate for just one who could communicate with her. Now, she'll have one, so she'll have less reason to breed indiscriminately. It should be easier to convince her of the foolishness of breeding *brother to sister when it's not necessary. We might even convince her doing so is what made the castle cats so particularly stupid and untalented.* *

Tae did not believe the castle cats were significantly different than any other regular cats, but he did not dispute the statement. *And yet, I notice you went out of your way to get unrelated kittens.* *

Imorelda hesitated. She seemed about to contradict his assertion, then chose to explain instead. *Despite your constant attempts to end your own life, your natural lifespan, and Matrinka's, is longer than mine. I want to see you taken care of forever, as well as any of your offspring who share your ability. If we ever need more intelligent kittens, we have a potential source, whether it's these two or the male with me.* * She allowed the kittens to steal Tae's hands, and he stroked the two of them for a bit while they twisted and turned to get his fingers into the best spaces.

Tae pointed out, *Mior managed to give birth to you even though your father was a regular cat. So, apparently, two intelligent cats aren't necessarily required.* *

To his surprise, Imorelda had an extensive answer. She had clearly thought the situation through, which explained her intentness on the Outworld. She had not gone mostly silent because she did not want to let him know she planned to leave him. She had done so to figure out the best and wisest way to swap the kittens. Suddenly, Tae felt extremely guilty about questioning her maternal instincts. Despite the disgust he felt for her trading off her own fur and blood, she had displayed far more compassion overall than he would have.

Regulars can only produce regulars. In order to get intelligents, you have to have at least one intelligent parent. They don't have much of a concept of numbers; but, from doing my own math, it appears that, when using one of each as parents, they produce about nine regulars to every intelligent. When two intelligents breed, the ratio is backwards, and the regular in such litters is usually abnormal in some physical way. I suspect it's really a matter of all the kittens in a litter of two intelligents are intelligent and they're counting abnormalities, like Ivana, as regulars because nearly all of those have intellectual abnormalities, too. *

Imorelda had given the situation so much thought Tae took his time responding so as not to sound foolish. *You're hoping we'll stick to breeding these kittens with regulars, so we only get an intelligent, on average, once every two litters rather than four or five intelligents each time.* *

Exactly. *

Because . . . * Tae started and stopped. He pursed his lips in thought, his hands still rubbing the kittens' tiny bellies and Imorelda in turn.

*Because I believe the ideal ratio of intelligent cats to mindspeaking *humans is one-to-one. And because feral intelligent cats on a mostly non-magical world would be extraordinarily dangerous.* *

Tae did not argue. Kentt had told him a story about a pair of rabbitlike creatures obtained from a tiny island and brought home by a sailor as pets for his son and daughter. Soon, all of the children wanted one, and as the pair reproduced swiftly, much like Midgard coneys, there were plenty to go around. Even many of the *alsona* boys and girls had island bunnies. The problem started when some escaped, by accident, carelessness, or the deliberate action of children tired of their pets or parents weary of reminding the children to feed, water, and clean them.

The adorable creatures had no enemies on Heimstadr; nothing hunted or ate them, but they developed a ravenous appetite for crops, open or stored, and reproduced at a fabulous rate. The *alsona* hunted them, the *Kjempemagiska* went after them with magic, but they could not satisfactorily contain the creatures. Finally, it was decided to import another creature from the same island, one that considered the pets a delicacy, a nasty carnivore they called a *jarfr*. Those, in turn, had no natural enemies on Heimstadr, though they did not breed nearly as quickly. Currently, the island home of the *Kjempemagiska* still had both of the imported animals in manageable numbers, although the *jarfr* occasionally stole some livestock, a few *alsona*, and even rarely attacked *Kjempemagiska* children when they found an opportunity, and the coneylike beasts still ruined the odd garden.

Arturo had told Tae he once killed a *jarfr* with his bare hands when it went after Mistri, a heroic action that had endeared him to Kentt.

At the time, Tae had listened mostly because of his curiosity about Arturo's time on Heimstadr and why the *Kjempemagiska* had kept the Béarnide alive when they had seemed so hellbent on slaughtering every man, woman, and child on the continent. Now, he took home another lesson: bringing non-native creatures to new worlds could cause unforeseen problems. Mior and Imorelda had become valuable assets to Midgard, if only because the mind-speech system, when combined with Tae's affinity for languages, had played a huge role in the defeat of the *Kjempemagiska*. A few more intelligent cats, especially bound to humans, did not seem like a potential burden; as Imorelda had stated, however, a large population of wild and uncontrolled intelligent cats could cause any number of issues.

Tae discovered he was bobbing his head the entire time those thoughts ran through his mind.

Imorelda apparently noticed. **So you agree.* *

I do, Tae admitted readily. He liked when he did not have to argue with the cat. *As much as I hate deceiving Matrinka, I can see the necessity. Of course, we'll have to keep whichever kitten we don't give her to replace Mior.*

Until her grandchild manifests its gift, of course.

"What?" The word was startled out of Tae, and he momentarily stopped petting anyone. He added mentally, *Do you know something I don't?*

Many things. It was the first time in a while Imorelda had said something characteristic. Though insulting, it put Tae more at ease. *But in this case, I'm just surmising. I think it'll be Matrinka's grandchild who can talk to cats because its mother is under the influence of a gods' curse and its father is one of the few people ever to pass the Pica test.*

Not yet, Tae pointed out.

Imorelda rammed her head beneath his stilled palm. *We're all counting on the fact he will. Otherwise, all the things we've said about Matrinka don't matter because she'll be dead. Béarn won't have a ruler. Midgard won't have balance. Ravn will have lied. Griff will —*

That's enough! Tae did not want to hear any more. He was having enough trouble sleeping without contemplating those terrible possibilities. *You're right. The baby has extraordinary parents and very well might have the ability to mindspeak. In the meanwhile, the other kitten should stay with us. Hopefully, once both of them wind up in this castle, as they probably will, the belief they're blood-related will keep Matrinka from kitty matchmaking.*

Unless and until it becomes necessary.

As that presumed Imorelda's death, Tae did not wish to process those thoughts, either. He had more questions and hoped their answers would not lead to more detailed conversation. Fatigue weighed heavily upon him, and he thought he might actually manage sleep. *How prolific are these intelligent cats, and how much do you think the kittens will remember from their original world?*

Imorelda chose to answer them in reverse. *The male is twelve weeks old, and the female only nine. They live longer, so they develop more slowly than regular kittens. I had to go a bit older to make them match the ones I had, which were only five weeks old. Still, they're infants. They won't remember much, if anything, of their old lives. As far as your other question, are you asking about their sexual habits?*

When put in those words, it sounded inappropriate. *I suppose I was, but only in a general sense. I mean, are we talking coneys or . . . or . . .* He could hardly compare them to humans given they gave birth in multiples.

Not exactly sure, but they seem closely in tune to their environment and intelligent enough to understand consequences, at least as well as humans. My mother only had one litter, and I had to be talked into mine. Apparently, that's not unusual. Most females reported one or two pregnancies in a lifetime was pretty normal. Their heat cycles and interest seem to synch up well with the availability of food and their population. *

Tae decided he liked those answers. If he thought anything else, he did not know it because he woke up hours later slumped over his own empty lap.

CHAPTER 24

There will always be hordes of jealous people who resent our
abilities and attribute our success to dark magic, trickery, or
deceit. But the truth of the matter is that we are willing to put in
an effort most are not.

—*Thialnir Thrudazisson*

BY THE TIME TAE AWAKENED, made himself reasonably pre-
sentable, and returned to the great hall, he found only a small number of humans seated in various places around the room and
conversing softly. He recognized a few, including a cluster of Béarn's
ministers, some off-duty guardsmen and servants, but there were
none he felt familiar enough with to join a private conversation. A
second inspection revealed his father sitting quietly in a shadowed
back corner with his bodyguards.

Tae came over to them and selected a seat beside Daxan, the
shorter and broader of his father's most trusted. "What's happening?"

Weile Kahn looked him up and down. "Where's your scarf?"

Tae put his hands to his throat, then recognized the joke and
dropped them to his lap. "If you're referring to Imorelda, she wasn't
with me when I woke up. She's most likely in the kitchen begging
from the cooks." He had no idea where the cat had taken her kittens,
probably giving them a castle tour while he slept. He repeated his
question, "So what's happening? Where is everyone?" He kept an
expectant gaze on his father who had a talent for concealing information, even while he milked people dry of theirs.

This time, Weile did not dodge Tae's question. "The elves ran out
of Outworlds."

"They're infinite," Tae pointed out, but he knew what Weile
meant. Captain had warned him before sending the rescue party to
the feline world that there might be no way to retrieve the last four
hundred or so missing humans. "So it's over? They're giving up?"

Alsrusett bumped Weile with his elbow, and the leader of criminals slowly turned his head to look at his bodyguard with an expression that could have curdled milk. It was not like his guards to gainsay their leader or even to speak.

Alsrusett's glare was ice.

Weile sighed in clear defeat. Tae had every right to know, and not telling him what had gotten decided was cruel, especially as it involved his only child. "They're not giving up. Captain gave an impassioned speech. I didn't know elves had that much emotional range, but he clearly meant every word. They're working closely with the Mages of Myrcidë and that *Kjempemagiska* . . ."

"Kentt," Tae supplied without thought. Weile had an eidetic memory, or so it had always appeared to Tae, so he surely could have used the name if he had wished.

". . . to try to come up with some type of solution to the problem."

Tae had expected nothing else. As suspicious as some humans found the elves, Tae knew them well enough to realize they truly wanted to help. The relationship between their peoples had reached an important stage, and Tae hoped they would come together rather than grow farther apart. The elves' future depended on it, and it would prove an enormous boon to the humans as well, whether or not they understood it. "Do you think most people believed Captain? Or do you still think the elves care only for themselves?"

Though trained for decades to remain silent, Alsrusett joined the conversation. "Either those elves are the best actors in the world, or they're really worried for the missing humans. The most skeptical cynic in the world believed every word he said." He tipped his dark head toward Weile, who flicked up a lip in a tolerant half-smile.

"It would appear I need a new, tighter-mouthed bodyguard."

Tae would not allow Alsrusett to suffer for him. "You do that, and you'll be looking for a new son. If you haven't figured out you can trust me, yet, you're beyond all hope."

Weile made a gesture of surrender. "Every single elf promised to stay and work on the problem, all of them definitely sincere." He turned the questioning onto Tae. "Do you think there's any possibility they might find the still missing humans?"

Tae shook his head, but he had pondered the situation much of the night and, now, shared his thoughts. "Most of the infinite number of Outworlds contain magic of one sort or another or of multiple types. It takes nearly all of the elves working in concert just to find the approximate location of one very specific sort of magic among all the background noise. When we went looking for the Pica shards almost two decades ago, the elves locked onto pieces of the broken sapphire, a unique object. This time, they've been locking on elves. With humans, there is no magic, hence nothing to lock onto. I don't know how they can possibly do it, with or without additional help." Something slid into his mind that he had not considered while tossing and turning in bed. "Unless . . ."

Weile and his bodyguards leaned toward Tae. When he did not continue, the father prompted with "Unless?"

Tae had not meant to trail off, but the need to think had caused him to pause mid-sentence. He could not help smiling at the realization, for once, he had information his father wanted and even the wherewithal to withhold it. "Never mind."

Weile reached out, as if to seize Tae.

Instinctively, Tae slipped off his chair and stepped beyond range. "Now you know what it feels like to have a conversation with you."

From the expression on his face, Weile was not amused. "Tell me what you're thinking."

"I will," Tae promised, backing further from the table. "After I've spoken with Captain and we've considered whether it's viable."

Weile's grin started small, then grew exponentially.

Tae watched him warily. "What?"

Weile rose. As if reading his mind, the two men on either side did the same simultaneously. It was difficult to tell who had initiated the movement. "Since you have no idea where the elves are cloistered, you'll need a guide."

A competent spy, Tae imagined he could find them eventually on his own, but the idea of wasting time, even to get the better of Weile Kahn, rankled. He forced a tight-lipped smile. "Very well," he said. "Won't you join me?"

Shortly after Tae's meeting with the elves, familiar excitement buzzed through the great hall once again. Saviar stood with the rescue crew: Tae, Ra-khir, El-brinith, Chan'rék'ril, and himself. Ra-khir had also quietly added Calistin to replace the missing Béarnides, a detail no one appeared to notice. Even the Northmen remained silent about the switch. Either Valr Magnus had convinced them Renshai represented the North or, more likely, they had become too tired or keyed up about the possibility of rescuing more humans to care.

Captain addressed the hastily gathered crowd with *khohlar*, **As you all know, we're gathered here to attempt to rescue a group of humans unaccompanied by elfin magic from the Outworlds. **

An enthusiastic cheer followed that pronouncement.

Captain continued, *Our first thought was to study the Myrcidians we have and try to lock onto the less familiar magic of their missing twelve. We had hoped to find them together along with any other humans sent to the same Outworld. As we were struggling with that, and having little success, King Tae Kahn pointed out some of our human warriors had access to magical weapons during the war.*

A murmur rose from the group. Saviar knew of only a few such weapons: his, Calistin's, Rantire's, and Magnus'. All of them had returned to Béarn. All, he suddenly realized, except one. When Calistin had taken up the Sword of Mitrian, he had allowed Subikahn to use his regular sword, the one Kevral had given him at the time of her death.

Subikahn. Saviar's heart rate quickened, and his thoughts returned to the Outworld where he had faced his worst fear. Then, he had relived the event that had severed his ties with his twin. Unlike Subikahn, he had done the right thing, chosen the honorable path, and allowed his brother to die with dignity and earn his rightful place in Valhalla. Yet that had been nothing but a simulation enacted in his own mind. In real life, Subikahn had been the one to make the choice. He had doomed Saviar's soul to deepest, blackest, coldest Hel; only the serendipity of running into Chymmerlee—only the grace of the Mages of Myrcidë—had saved him.

Subikahn, the filthy coward, had not even had the grace to tell Saviar until he believed he had suffered lethal wounds and the truth no longer mattered. *Subikahn.* Saviar's hands balled to fists. Though spoken only in his mind, the name left a bitter taste.

Apparently attuned to his brother's mood, Calistin placed a comforting hand on Saviar's shoulder, which startled him back to the present. Calistin showing any sort of emotion still shocked him, but the demonstration of empathy went so far beyond Calistin's previous character Saviar found himself incapable of other focus. His angst forgotten for the moment, he smiled at his younger, smaller brother, entirely missing the much larger grin on Ra-khir's face as he observed their interaction.

Captain was still speaking, explaining the elves' other plans for the future. Apparently, they had found a way to lock onto Subikahn's sword after studying Magnus', which had become magical in the same manner. After they rescued anyone on whatever Outworld held the sword, their next assignment would be trying to amplify the Myrcidians' magic enough to lock on it and rescue the twelve missing human mages.

Before the war, the elves had filled this same room with every weapon the human soldiers could collect and had chanted over them in the hope some trace of magic might cling to the blades and allow them to penetrate the *Kjempemagiska* enemies. It had been a desperate attempt that had garnered little or no success, but Captain clung to the ludicrous hope a tiny bit of that elf-summoned chaos lingered, enough that using all the magic at their disposal, they might find a way to lock onto the weapons of more of the missing humans.

Knowing Tae must have spoken with the elves recently and Captain tended to take the linguist king into his confidence, Saviar addressed him, "Is that last idea going to work?"

Tae did not equivocate. "No, but the elves promised the generals they would exhaust every possibility." He shook his head. "They may get the Myrcidians back eventually, though it's a long shot. Between the mages who didn't go to war and the promises King Griff made to the ones who did, I can't see anyone ever giving up. Creatures who live for centuries can get rather persistent when the need arises. We also considered the possibility some of our humans snatched up *Kjempemagiska* weapons. With Kentt's help, they could have locked onto that magic, but they had no luck. Only a handful of giants died before the blast, and their enormous weapons were beyond even the clumsiest wielding by our largest warriors. They tried but couldn't find any *Kjempemagiska* weapons on the Outworlds."

That did not surprise Saviar. He had collected a couple of those massive weapons himself, hoping to find continental warriors who could handle them. The only one who had tried was Ra-khir, and it had overbalanced him too much to be of much use except, perhaps, in some sort of clever trap. Saviar then considered their own recent experiences. "What about duplicate Outworlds? Couldn't they have their own *Kjempemagiska?*"

Tae smiled, apparently pleased by Saviar's consideration. "Apparently, each duplicate world has a slightly different flavor to its magic. Otherwise, while chasing down elves, we would have found infinite mirrors of our own."

Saviar had not considered that.

"Either that, or magical creatures don't mirror. Remember, the duplicate world where we left some of our men did not contain magic of any kind. No elves. No giants. Nothing."

Saviar remembered. It would make interesting consideration, though, ultimately, it did not matter. He only hoped all of the unfound soldiers had discovered happy duplicate worlds on which to spend all eternity. "Why is Captain going into so much detail anyway? Why not just announce they've found some human soldiers and get on with it?"

Tae had a ready answer. "Because he wants everyone to see the lengths the elves have gone to in attempting to find every lost soldier. Also, he needs them to understand why, in the end, several hundred will never be rescued through no fault of elves or humans or even *Kjempemagiska*. At least, not directly."

It seemed an odd thing to worry about, although Saviar figured it out quickly. As a member of the most hated tribe in the world, he knew what it was like to have every action, no matter how heroic and kind, twisted and distorted by history into something sinister and negative. Elves would never have the martial abilities and interests that had kept the Renshai alive. If they became an object of hatred, their only alternative was hiding. And, while they excelled at it, it would prove a terrible loss to both groups. He now knew elves needed the half-breed souls to prevent their own gradual extinction, and the magic of the elves would prove invaluable to humans, with or without the Myrcidians and *Kjempemagiska*.

Apparently, Captain had finished. The *khohlar* voice disappeared from Saviar's head, immediately replaced by Tae's spoken one. The Eastland's king waved in the rescue party and increased his volume to address them all. Saviar noted he seemed more agile than usual and realized the cat so often perched on his shoulders was missing. Apparently, she had proven enough of a burden on their last mission he had relegated her to remain in Béarn, which seemed like a wise choice to Saviar. He had never understood why Tae hamstrung himself with an unpredictable animal, especially on life-threatening expeditions. He had never seemed like the superstitious sort. "This is going to be a bit different than the other gatings." Tae looked around the group. "Ra-khir, do you remember the blind transports from when we were looking for the Pica pieces?"

Ra-khir groaned, then nodded.

Tae bit back a smile and continued. "The gates will only function one way until we have at least one elf on the other side." He looked at El-brinith and Chan'rék'ril who each made a single head movement that could pass for a nod. "There'll be a brilliant light, then a few moments of spinning blackness before the gate spits us out in some random location. I suggest you close your eyes tightly when you first step in, then get them open fast to face any danger. If you get sick easily, please make sure you're facing away from me."

Calistin scowled at what he surely took as an insult, but the others bobbed their heads.

Ready? Captain sent.

El-brinith fixed her gaze on Tae, who glanced around the group and, getting confirmation, gestured for her to respond.

The gate formed in front of them. Tae and Chan'rék'ril went through it first. Next, Saviar squeezed his eyes shut and stepped through with Calistin at his heels. Light stabbed right through his lids; he could scarcely imagine how brilliant the flare would have seemed with them open. Suddenly, it felt as if an enormous hand buffeted Saviar from behind. He stumbled and fell to his knees as a cold wind continued to pound him and ice filled his nose and mouth, chilling him to the bone. Wet breeks froze against his knees. Swiftly, he opened his eyes and found himself in a clearing covered with snow to a depth of his first knuckle. Patchy grass tips poked above it, and copses of needled trees hugged low, stony hills. Animal tracks crisscrossed the landscape: the strange off-center crosses left by coneys and their cousins, the triplet angled lines of a medium-sized bird, four-toed paw prints like those of a large dog, and something that looked like dragged logs, forming almost continuous furrows.

Chan'rék'ril held a wide-based stance and Tae a stealthy crouch. At Saviar's side, Calistin looked in every direction, his hand clamped to his hilt. When Saviar rose and turned to look behind him, he saw Ra-khir then El-brinith appear, staggering a bit but able to keep their feet. As the elf came through it, the gate disappeared.

"It's gone," Saviar said.

"We'll recreate it," El-brinith explained. "Arak'bar Tulamii Dhor will make contact at intervals, and we'll let him know when and where to reform it from his side."

Chan'rék'ril made a few broad gestures that seemed incongruous, and Saviar realized Captain must have spoken to him through the Pica in the same manner as the elves trapped on Outworlds. A bit embarrassed by his fall, Saviar stepped backward to assure he was not in the area around Chan'rék'ril visible in the Pica Stone. Brushing the snow off his breeks, he flipped up his hood, shoved his hands in his pockets, and pulled his cloak more tightly around him.

El-brinith had wandered off to study the tracks. The cold did not seem to bother her at all; neither of the elves had worn an overcloak, and she pointed without seeming to care that her index finger poked into the snow. "I've found boot tracks." She indicated a spot farther to her right. "Here someone killed a small animal."

The others joined her to examine what she had found. Blood and a bit of white fur marked the kill, and Saviar could see the boot trail leading up and away from it without much difficulty, though fresh or blown snow had partially obscured the tracks. Whoever had made them continued onward rather than turning back the way he came, perhaps to collect more food. That boded well to Saviar's mind. A single man could sustain himself for a day on just one coney, so it suggested he hunted for others, too.

Saviar hadn't realized he had spoken the thought aloud until Tae responded to it. "Either that, or he wanted to bring in more than a day's worth of food. Perhaps anticipating worse weather."

That got all of the humans looking around. Remembering elves originally came from a world lacking weather, Saviar realized they would probably get nothing useful from the elves in that regard.

"He . . . or she may not be one of ours," Ra-khir pointed out. "It could be a native."

Saviar looked into the distance, seeking anything to indicate they had arrived on a temperate world during winter. The entire area appeared to be ringed by distant mountains and devoid of any trees other than the withered copses protected from the wind by craggy hills. The tracks suggested some things lived here naturally, but he pitied anything humanoid that did. It was inhospitably cold in bright sunlight. At night, he suspected, any creature lacking thick layers of fur would suffer dearly.

Tae dropped to a low crouch, studying one print after another for a long time. "It's Subikahn."

Ra-khir took a position beside Tae, equally close to the ground. "How can you be sure?"

Tae stood up. "I know his boots. I bought them for him. Right size, right shape, and there's a familiar crack in the leather right here." He pointed toward one of the prints.

Saviar did not believe it possible to spot such a detail, especially with the tracks partially covered, but he did not question. Many *ganim* still attributed Renshai training and skill to demon magic. People could develop amazing talents; Tae's facility with languages, for example. Saviar suspected Tae's identification had more to do with hope and desire, but it was not impossible he actually saw something in the snow the others did not.

Ra-khir and Tae led the way, following the boot tracks backward toward the hills. Calistin and Saviar fanned out to the sides, ignoring the trail to watch for danger, while the elves took positions behind the leaders and inside the Renshai's watchful perimeter. Ra-khir and Tae kept up a steady patter as they came nearer the slopes and the copses sheltered by them. Looking outward, Saviar ignored their evidence, though he got the gist of their conversation, which seemed to consist of nothing other than indications they were following a useful path. Apparently, someone had gathered wood, and other shod human prints joined the first at intervals. Those caused a bit of a disagreement as to whether they belonged to multiple people or just several trips by the same individual who might or might not be Subikahn.

Saviar caught occasional glimpses of a quadrupedal, white creature slinking through the snow and watching them from a distance. As it never seemed to come nearer, he did not bother anyone with his observation, though it appeared large enough to cause significant problems if it chose to attack.

The tracks came to an end at the base of a steep hill. Ra-khir and Tae stopped, looking upward. Still trying to keep an eye on their stalker, which he now believed was a predatory creature, Saviar did not turn to look at what they did or to assess the cliff face. He kept his gaze turned outward, listening to their discussion.

"I imagine he's made himself a home in one of those caves."

"I would imagine so," Tae returned. "Hopefully with any other soldiers who wound up here."

"I was thinking about that." Ra-khir's voice echoed slightly around the crags. "No elves here, so no *khohlar*. People might not be able to find each other. We may have to search the entire Outworld to locate everyone sent here."

Saviar's blood ran even colder, wracking him with shivers and turning most of his skin to gooseflesh. He supposed his father had a point, but the idea of staying on this ice world a moment longer than necessary did not appeal to him. He could not see Calistin without turning his head, and he could not help wondering how his brother had reacted to the suggestion.

Tae dodged the point entirely. "I'm the one most used to climbing. Why don't I head up and check things out?"

Ra-khir did not respond for a moment. Saviar assumed his father was thinking, so the sudden shout, clearly between cupped hands, startled him again. "Halloo! Is there anyone up there?"

Saviar stiffened, gaze working double time in case the call brought enemies. From the corner of his eye, he saw Tae step against the base of the cliff face. Apparently, the Easterner assumed the greatest danger might come from above. It took Saviar a bit longer to puzzle out the possibility of frightened humans or humanlike creatures pelting them from the caves with rocks.

For several moments, nothing happened. Then, Tae called out much more softly. "There! I think I see someone."

A bit farther from the cliff, Ra-khir had a better vantage point. "Yes, I see it, too. Moving toward us." A heartbeat later, he added. "I think he's waving."

"Definitely waving," Tae concurred.

Saviar risked a longer look, cued by the direction of Ra-khir's and Tae's stares. What appeared to be a stout, milk-white human picked its way gracefully down the cliff face, headed in their general direction and throwing its arms in exaggerated arcs. Forced to look away to maintain their safety, Saviar went back to listening. He saw no sign of the creature that might have been stalking them. Either the shouts had frightened it, or it had found a more effective hiding place.

"It's human," El-brinith added. "Dressed in thick, white furs."

Tae announced at last, "It's Subikahn!" He shouted upward. "Subikahn! It's us! We're here to take you home!"

Saviar heard a distant, unintelligible reply.

For a moment, no one spoke, the only sound the rush of air and a few dislodged pebbles tumbling down the rock face.

Even stuffed inside his cloak, Saviar's hands hurt. The wind howled painfully in his ears. "What's going on?" he demanded.

Another brief silence, then, Ra-khir apparently realized his son's focus on their safety made it impossible for him to see what was happening on the cliff. "He's grabbed a vine or a rope and seems to be using it to climb down." He abruptly added, "Now he's using it to swing over. He'll be here in a moment."

Then, something large stirred the air, and Saviar turned just in time to see Subikahn land in their midst, a rope belayed well up the rocky hill clutched tightly in his mittened hands. He was covered head to toe in white furs sewed expertly into a one-piece suit that disappeared into his boots and left only his face exposed. A sword graced his left hip, and he clutched a leather mask in his hand. "Praise all of the gods." He looked around the group tensely, as if uncertain into whose arms to throw himself first.

Tae took the decision from Subikahn, embracing his son in a vigorous greeting that consisted mostly of pounding him on the back. Ra-khir went next. Saviar studied his twin. The last time he had seen Subikahn, his brother was lying on the ground dying of lethal wounds inflicted by a *Kjempemagiska.* The Myrcidians had been attempting to revive him when the explosion that killed so many and sent others to the Outworlds had occurred.

It all returned to Saviar in a painful assault of memory. Subikahn had just revealed the treachery he had committed against his twin, which he had kept secret until that moment when it was too late for Saviar to judge him, let alone to react in any way. Unable to cope with the information, Saviar had silently rejoined the battle, the ultimate Renshai betrayal like a fire consuming every part of him. His hatred for the cowardly Myrcidians, deserters all, had not helped the situation, especially after their leader had falsely accused him of raping his granddaughter.

As soon as Ra-khir released him, Subikahn started toward Saviar, who stepped backward and turned away. Calistin leaped into the void, seizing Subikahn tightly and gracing him with the enthusiastic greeting Saviar had denied. A look of surprise flashed across Subikahn's features, then a smile, and he embraced his younger brother fervently. Though Saviar had grown more accustomed to the changes taking place in Calistin, he still had not believed him capable of such heartfelt exuberance. It bothered Saviar his own snub seemed to go entirely unnoticed because of it.

The elves stood by patiently while the humans hugged one another, so it took Tae Kahn to ask, "Do you know if anyone else from our world got blown here?"

Subikahn turned Saviar a questioning look, and Saviar responded by scowling and crossing his arms over his chest. As this required him to pull his hands from his pockets, he suffered more than Subikahn; but he hoped he got his point across. His twin was not forgiven, not yet and probably not ever. Calistin's passionate greeting also revealed Saviar had not shared the secret of Subikahn's treachery. No Renshai could absolve another of the ultimate cowardice of dooming one of their own to Hel, and Calistin most of all.

Finally, Subikahn addressed the outstanding question. "The Mages of Myrcidë are in the cave above. Twelve of them, alive and well."

Saviar went rigid. He had known the elves would try to locate the Myrcidians on the Outworlds, but he had not expected to find them at the same time as Subikahn, although it made a certain amount of sense. They had been huddled together in a relatively isolated spot when the battlefield explosion had occurred. Saviar had no particular desire to rescue Subikahn or Jeremilan, but he supposed some of the other mages were innocent and did not deserve condemnation to a world that seemed like a pale echo of Hel itself.

Subikahn looked over the rescuers. "You must be freezing, and it's only getting colder. When the sun goes down, it's deadly." He turned his gaze upward. "It's warm in the cave. We have a fire going when I can get wood, and it's practically lined with fur. It's early enough their magic still works, too."

That piqued the elves' interest. "Early enough?" Chan'rék'ril asked. "Their magic is based on timing?"

"From what I understand, not usually, although it's always strongest after a good night's sleep. Something about this world having triplet moons. When they come up, it negates their magic somehow." Subikahn shook his head. "It's probably better if you talk to them."

El-brinith addressed Chan'rék'ril, at least Saviar assumed so. They could have used direct *khohlar*, so she apparently either wanted them all to hear or spoke aloud without thinking. "Do you think it might negate our magic, too?"

Chan'rék'ril raised and lowered one shoulder. "I've never heard of such a thing, but I suppose it's possible. If so, we need to get up there and make the gate as swiftly as possible." He added, cautiously, "Or I guess we could wait out the night and leave in the morning. Either way, we have to wait for Arak'bar Tulamii Dhor to contact us first."

Tae shivered deeply. "My vote's for getting out of here before moonrise. Even in a cave with fire and fur, I'm not excited about spending a night in lethal cold."

Calistin released Subikahn. "Then we'd best start climbing."

Subikahn looked at the elves, still standing together. "With my support, the Myrcidians kind of floated themselves up to the cave."

"We can do that, too." El-brinith looked at her companion. If they spoke again, they did it telepathically. Soon, she added, "Each of us can carry one other with us. If we make three trips, we can get everyone."

Subikahn had another idea. "Why don't you make two trips. I'm used to the climb, and I can tell my father wants to try it. We can save you a trip."

"I'll go with you," Calistin added eagerly. "That means just one trip."

Torn between appearing weak and trapping himself into cooperating with Subikahn, Saviar found the compromise. "Subikahn needs to get there first to let the Myrcidians know we're here to help. We don't want to scare them. They're extremely suspicious and tend to attack or hide before making proper identifications. While we're waiting for the others to climb to the cave, Papa and I'll keep the elves safe."

"Very wise." Tae acknowledged Saviar's suggestion, his gaze on the cliff face. Then, to his son, "Let Calistin use the rope. You and I need the practice on bare rock without a lifeline."

Subikahn laughed. "You're an idiot, but I'm game. In fact, I'll race you." Without hesitation, he started up the rocks alone.

Cursing, Tae followed, and Calistin grabbed hold of the rope.

Saviar did not bother to watch them, instead placing Ra-khir and the elves between himself and the stony hill and watching outward in all directions. He suspected the large white animal that had been stalking them was the same type of creature who had provided the fur for Subikahn's suit. If Subikahn had killed more than one, as he must have to make the garment, Saviar felt certain he could do the same.

But no creature of any kind bothered them before Chan'rék'ril announced Subikahn and Tae had reached and entered the cave, with Calistin almost there as well. El-brinith took Saviar's hand, Chan'rék'ril Ra-khir's. The elves muttered coarse syllables. In moments, they floated gently upward to the level of the proper opening. All four of them reached for outcroppings, the coldness of the stone burning Saviar's fingers, then they hauled themselves inside to join the others.

Magical light lit the cozy interior, and a fire burned cheerfully in an alcove near the entrance, its smoke funneled upward and outward through a neat stone chimney black with soot. Saviar recognized all twelve of the Mages of Myrcidë, covered in fur blankets ranging from a light brown to a pure and dazzling white. Tae crouched at the farthest end in quiet discussion with the mages' leader, the long-past elderly Jeremilan. Several other mages crowded around them, listening intently. Though some looked up as Saviar, Ra-khir, and the elves entered, they kept their attention mostly or wholly trained on the conversation.

Saviar found himself disgusted by the mere sight of them, though he kept this to himself other than to say calmly to El-brinith, "Let's gate out of here as soon as possible."

Clearly detecting no malice in his voice, El-brinith returned with *khohlar*, apparently so as not to disturb the other discussion. *We have to wait until Arak'bar Tulamii Dhor's next contact.* She added, misinterpreting his haste. *It'll come soon enough. Almost certainly before nightfall.*

Saviar schooled his features. If he ever did become a leader of Renshai, or a Knight of Erythane, he would have to deal with many people he did not like. The Northmen, and other haters of Renshai, regularly accused them of horrific, immoral, and far-beyond-criminal behavior, as Jeremilan had done to him; all of them would cheat and betray him at any opportunity.

A man of honor never allows emotions to control him. Memory of those words, spoken by Ra-khir, brought Saviar back to his long-ago meeting with Colbey Calistinsson. *Anger is a dangerous master. It saps a warrior of sound judgment and bodily control, both necessary in war.* Since that day, Saviar had tried to better control his rage and bitterness, with a good measure of success. He had learned to channel it against those who had actually done him harm and away from those who did not deserve it or, at least, at a lower level. Now, however, in the presence of the exact people who had wronged him, his self-control threatened to slip.

Saviar did not know how long he had crouched, staring out of the cave, alone with his thoughts. A long time, apparently, because when a loudly cleared throat brought him back to reality, the half of his body nearest the fire had become almost painfully hot while he still wore obvious and icy gooseflesh on the other side. He turned to face Jeremilan, with the other mages fanned out behind him, looking timid and nervous. Subikahn had come up beside Saviar, might even have touched him at some point.

When Saviar met Jeremilan's gaze, the leader of the mages started speaking, "Saviar Ra-khirsson." He rolled his attention to Subikahn. "Subikahn Taesson. I owe both of you an apology. You were right about so many things. I despised and distrusted you for no other reason than your heritage, consigned your abilities to demon-magic, even when pure evidence told me otherwise. I explained my motives then, and I'm not going to repeat them other than to say my main objective has, and always will be, to preserve and enhance the old magic once lost to mankind. That does not, however, grant me the right to do harm onto the innocent, which I have done.

"Now that I know the lengths the elves and the nonmagical humans have gone to to rescue us and others, I realize I have misjudged not only you, but so many others. When we return to Béarn, I will speak with King Griff and with the leader of the elves, this Arak-bar Tulamii Dhor, to attempt to renegotiate our relationship with the other intelligent beings of our world. If not for your . . ." He hesitated, seeking the right word.

Saviar mentally selected "pestering," which he suspected was precisely the one Jeremilan was trying to avoid.

". . . persistence, we would still be in hiding. That would have saved us from the considerable pain and angst we've suffered on this Outworld, and I confess I cursed you every day when I believed that the full and honest truth. But the elves have convinced me our contribution to the combined magic at the war, meager as it was comparatively, was necessary for victory. Without us, they say, the *Kjempemagiska* would certainly have won and all of us would have died. The giants had more than enough magic to uncover our compound."

Saviar knew his own sword, muted as its magic was, had allowed Subikahn to find it. The *Kjempemagiska* would have had no difficulty at all.

Jeremilan turned to face Subikahn directly. "Subikahn Taesson, I beg your forgiveness for all the wrongs any of us may have deliberately or unintentionally inflicted. You saved every one of our lives on the battlefield nearly at the cost of your own. You twice saved us from the pack of wolves that attacked us here and several of the huge, white predators that nearly took so many of us, one by one. When you told us to stay in the cave, that you would supply our basic needs, we thought you had abandoned us to die. Instead, you brought firewood and animals, from which we made these blankets and clothing and food. You could have gone your own way, alone, and survived without difficulty, yet you took care of us as well despite the cold, the hard work, and the many dangers. For that, I cannot thank you enough." Jeremilan ended with a deep bow of respect.

A chorus of murmurs from behind him expressed similar appreciation from the other Myrcidians who copied the gesture.

Saviar found himself staring past them to the back of the cave where the elves were doing something with broad gestures.

Subikahn looked panic-stricken for a moment. He glanced at Saviar who gave him nothing. Usually, he handled the fancy speeches, the politics, and anything more complicated than basic manners; but Saviar had no desire to make things any easier for his twin. Finally, Subikahn spoke, "I accept your apology. You saved my life as well; I know fatal battle wounds when I've received them. By helping you, I did nothing more than any civilized person would. You should know any Renshai in my place would have done the same."

Jeremilan smiled, then took Subikahn's hand in his own. "You have the gratitude and respect of the Mages of Myrcidë. If you ever need our assistance, and we can supply it, you need only ask." He released Subikahn and turned his attention to Saviar.

Saviar could feel his heart turning to stone, but he remained silent. Since the moment he had turned to face the Myrcidians, the cold half of his body, now near the fire, seemed to be slowly and painfully thawing.

"Saviar Ra-khirsson, I beg your forgiveness for all the wrongs any of us may have deliberately or unintentionally inflicted." He closed his rheumy eyes tightly, then opened them before continuing. "You never meant us ill, though we accused you of it. We thought you would harm

Chymmerlee, indicted you for a crime you didn't commit, attacked you, and kept you prisoner in isolation, not realizing the inherent cruelty of that punishment." Seeming to run out of words, Jeremilan lowered his head. The oration did not seem as enthusiastic as the one for Subikahn. Saviar had never directly saved the mages' lives, but their cruelty to him far surpassed whatever they might have done to Subikahn.

Jeremilan gave Saviar a significant look. He clearly wanted to say more, but the situation did not allow it. Whatever else he admitted to, he could not say that he or any other mage with his permission had raped his granddaughter. "I hope you can find it in yourself to forgive the Mages of Myrcidë, individually and collectively."

Saviar considered himself a reasonable and, usually, tolerant man. *How could anyone forgive what they did?* He thought back to the verbal cruelty and insolence the aged mage had heaped upon him. The assault in the woodlands had occurred because Saviar had cornered Chymmerlee knowing about her unreasonable anger toward his heritage, the lie she had caught him in, and the secret belief he had caused her pregnancy. For that attack, he could easily have forgiven them. But the solitary confinement that had driven him to the edge of madness had been a deliberate torture based on a known lie. True, the mages had only meant to confine him; once they realized the insanity that accompanied weeks without human company, they had released him, at least into their own companionship. Still, Jeremilan had continued to blame the rape on Saviar, had left Chymmerlee believing it until she had piled so much abuse upon him it had permanently ruined the budding love they had shared. Forgiveness would not come. Saviar started to turn away in silence.

Then, Colbey's words came back to him again, this time the ones he had not quite understood and promised to mull. *Anger has its place and its purpose, Saviar. It can change the world. The problem is it's far too easy; anyone can become angry. But rare the man who can channel it properly, who can use it to make himself stronger, better, wiser.* Saviar felt certain he had reached the moment, or at least one of them, to which Colbey had referred. He studied the Mages of Myrcidë, only to find each and every one of them staring back at him. Their expressions were grim, hopeful, their desperation evident and even stronger than that of their leader. Not a single one paid the slightest attention to the elfin magic they had to know was taking shape behind them. Despite the hardships they had endured, none of them considered bolting through the gate until this matter had been fully resolved. They did not just want Saviar's absolution; for some reason, they needed it.

Saviar doubted that need came solely from conscience, though some of it surely did. He had come to know several of them, and most meant well, many with a naiveté bordering on childlike. For many, their lot had never been simple. After Jeremilan had realized his own powers and surmised their source, he had scoured the West for adults, adolescents, and, mostly, infants displaying any hint of the Myrcidian power, the tiniest bit of the ancient wizards' bloodline. He had begged, bought, or stolen them from their families, then kept them hidden from the remainder of the world, convinced ignorance and fear would drive normal mortals to destroy them. Naturally, they followed him like a strict father; most of them had known no other. For the most part, his morality was their morality although some still remembered an upbringing that preceded his.

Even Jeremilan was not a bad man, despite some glaring blindnesses in judgment. He always did what he believed best for his followers or, at least, for the future of the Mages of Myrcidë. His cowardice stemmed from caution, his stubbornness from a grim certainty he could read the hearts and minds of others, his mistakes well-intentioned no matter how extreme.

Saviar sucked in a deep breath, then loosed it slowly and quietly to avoid a sigh. He channeled his anger and did his best to follow the well-reasoned path that would prove best not only for the Renshai, but for the mages, the elves, and the rest of humanity. "I forgive the Mages of Myrcidë for the wrongs they have committed against me, save one which is not mine to forgive. When you have corrected the unspeakable lie you told against me to the person who needs to know the truth, I will consider not only myself, but the Renshai tribe, a full ally of the Myrcidians from that day forth."

Every mage, including Jeremilan knew exactly what he meant, without need for explanation. Saviar had chosen his words to keep all others in ignorance. Although he had saved the mages great embarrassment, it was not the reason he did so, but rather for the sake of Chymmerlee. It was her story to tell or hide as she saw fit, hers and her unborn child's.

The mages seemed to stiffen as one, held their breaths, and looked toward their leader. Jeremilan pursed his lips and bowed his head ever so slightly, the closest he had come to contrition for as long as Saviar had known him. It suited him better than the angry haughtiness he usually assumed. "I will speak the truth to the wronged party, as you have requested."

As one, the Mages of Myrcidë relaxed. Smiles appeared on several faces, most of them tense, and most finally looked to see what magic the elves had wrought behind them.

Saviar did not allow himself to show emotion yet. Any indication of relief would make it appear as if Jeremilan truly had a choice and might drive him to reconsider reneging on the bargain. "Once that happens, I will do what I can to smooth relations between yourselves and all other humans to the best of my ability. I understand your concerns but truly believe nearly everyone will welcome you and appreciate, rather than revile, your talents. The protection you gain will more than offset the secrecy you've lost."

The conversation appeared to have ended, at least the public aspect of it. The mages dispersed to discuss the gate with the elves, but Jeremilan remained behind to speak with Saviar sotto voce. "I will tell Chymmerlee the truth but hope you understand I cannot sanction you courting her."

Saviar tried not to appear startled by the suggestion. Jeremilan clearly had no real idea of the effect his confession would have on Chymmerlee. The Renshai felt certain she would want nothing more to do with her grandfather at the very least. Courting anyone would probably be the last thing on her mind. "Whether or not we might have become a couple under ordinary circumstances, there's no love between us now. It would not surprise me if it takes her years, decades, or forever to trust a human male again." The thought of the pain Chymmerlee would suffer lifelong caused the worst of the anger to resurface, and Saviar walked away before he drew a sword or said something that would destroy all the peace he had created.

Ra-khir's voice rose about the others. "We can't leave yet, not all of us. Not until we've exhausted all possibility other humans got sent here in the blast. Once we leave, they're trapped here for eternity."

Subikahn spoke from beside Ra-khir. "I searched every part of this world. The only humans I found were a small group of dead Western soldiers, some partially eaten. I carried one of the bodies here, and the mages were able to determine he died fighting the wolf pack along with the others, and one of the white predators ate what the wolves left. I brought back the most portable of their possessions, including weapons, and we can take those back to their generals and families. If any others were sent here, either they were dead on arrival or they managed to hide themselves beyond my ability to find them and did not respond to shout-outs, even magically enhanced ones. I believe I can say with confidence, other than the Myrcidians and myself, there's no one here to rescue."

With that, Chan'rék'ril started filing mages, one by one, through the gate.

Saviar watched them go through, determined not to speak with Jeremilan, although he no longer felt as if he might harm the leader of the mages. Jeremilan had come a long way since his initial meeting with Saviar, and the other mages much further. They still had a rocky course to plow, especially their leader, but Saviar had lost nearly all of the irritability that had plagued him since Subikahn's confession. He realized Colbey had been right. It was not a matter of expressing or suppressing the rage, but of channeling it. He no longer bore any hatred toward the Mages of Myrcidë, not even toward Jeremilan himself. He despised what they had done to Chymmerlee, but he no longer had emotions invested in that battle.

Saviar found a position beside Tae so as not to purposefully or accidentally wind up beside Subikahn. He had not yet found any plausible way to reroute the rage that filled him at the mere thought of his twin and the evil he had inflicted. He doubted Colbey Calistinsson himself could forgive. The consummate Renshai would consider Subikahn's cowardice unpardonable, outraged by the horror of dooming any Renshai soul to Hel.

In the end, Calistin went through just after Subikahn, ignorant of his brother's crime. Then came Tae, followed by Ra-khir, then Saviar with El-brinith, and Chan'rék'ril bringing up the rear.

CHAPTER 25

Bloodline and love are unrelated. To love someone only because he shares your blood is as hollow and meaningless as loving someone only because he's young and beautiful. To a Northman, an unrelated blood brother becomes more important than kin, since the bond is based on honor and merit, not inescapable coincidence.
—Colbey Calistinsson

SAVIAR HAD LEAPED AT THE OPPORTUNITY to accompany Thialnir to the Council's and generals' meeting, despite the fact that it would prove interminably boring in so many ways. At least, it kept him from having to deal with Subikahn and out of Jeremilan's way while the mage tackled the most difficult chore of his two centuries. Saviar did not want to appear in any way to be looking over the old man's shoulders.

Now, as the sun spiraled toward evening and Saviar curled up on his cot alone in the bedroom he shared with Thialnir, luxuriating in the muscular pain and exhaustion that always followed a good sword practice, he considered the results of the meeting. King Griff had prepared his Council and the various representatives for Captain's arrival, so when the elf walked into the room, appearing haggard and worried, clutching the Pica Stone to his chest, they had all greeted him warmly, thanking him for the hard work and the many successes of his people rather than offering the condemnation he apparently anticipated.

Captain had explained the inability of the elves, even combined with all the Myrcidians and Kentt to locate any more humans on Outworlds. The humans had taken the news solemnly but remained appreciative for all the magical group had accomplished. Valr Magnus had pointed out that they had gone into the rescue mission with the understanding they would never find some men and some elves, and the approximate ten-to-one proportion well fit the ratio of humans to elves. If anything, it was in the humans' favor. Several pointed out this proved the elves had done everything possible, and Captain finally managed one of his radiant smiles before handing over the Pica Stone to its rightful caretaker, the king of Béarn.

The only surprise of the meeting came when Griff stopped Captain from leaving long enough to invite the elves to visit or live in any forest, city, or town throughout the Westlands. He vouched for their safety in any area under Béarnian rule in his name and that of any future king or queen in perpetuity. He assured their welcomeness in business or social dealings of any type. He specifically and personally invited Captain to consider sailing his tiny ship under Béarn's banner. The many ambassadors either promised the elves the same courtesies in their parts of the continent or, at least, to discuss it with their various rulers, whom they all felt sure would greet the elves with open arms as well. Though he made no vows, Captain exited the room beaming.

One by one, the generals and representatives of the various regions and countries still currently in Béarn thanked Griff, took their leave, and made their preparations to return themselves and their rescued men—and women in the case of the Renshai—home. The ambassadors from the Western regions had all restated their fealty to Griff and to Béarn before leaving, until only Thialnir, Saviar, Kedrin, and the Béarnian Council had remained. The Renshai and the Knight-Captain stayed because, as representatives of Béarn's closest allies, both geographically and politically, they were often considered an extension of the Council.

Then, Prime Minister Davian had made a gesture to dismiss the Renshai and the Knight-Captain of Erythane, but Griff stopped him with a word. "Wait." He added, "Let them stay. They'll know soon enough, and this affects them nearly as much as us."

Davian arrested his request mid-movement, bowed in deference to the king, and reclaimed his seat. "The Pica Stone has been returned, Your Majesty. How soon do you wish the testing to begin?"

Only then, Saviar realized just how momentous the situation had become. For whatever reason, Griff clearly intended to abdicate the throne, the only reason why his heirs would need to begin Pica testing. He hoped it did not mean Griff had developed a lethal illness. The Pica test always chose wisely, and King Griff had proven no exception to the rule. Saviar could scarcely imagine the world without the competent, fair, and neutral king who had occupied the throne since shortly before his birth. Historically, kings of Béarn retained rulership until their deaths or, at least, until their dotage. Griff was only thirty-five, a year younger than Saviar's father.

In lieu of an answer, Griff had wordlessly handed the magical artifact to his prime minister.

Still in the bedroom he shared with Thialnir, Saviar had just started to contemplate the terrible burden now placed on the young heirs to Béarn's throne when a gentle tap on the door interrupted his thoughts. Wondering why Thialnir was bothering to knock, Saviar called from his cot, "Come in!"

The door edged open to reveal Chymmerlee, who entered alone and closed it behind her before studying Saviar's lounging figure.

Startled by the impropriety of a young, unmarried woman in his bedroom, Saviar gazed at her as well. She looked much as he remembered, yet the overall image seemed strangely different. No longer blinded by love, or something akin to it, he could see faults he had overlooked in the past. He had recognized her face as oval, but now it appeared high and narrow to a fault that placed her eyes too close together. The pretty blue-gray of their color was difficult to see because of her tendency to squint. The freckles that made her look friendly and approachable had mostly disappeared, a summer phenomenon. Her nose and lips, just right to his courting eyes, now seemed a bit too generous. The cascade of auburn hair had lost much of its sun-bleached red, and she had it tied tightly behind her head, making her appear older and less approachable. She still maintained her lithe figure, but it had developed more prominent womanly curves and a decided bulge at the belly.

Saviar found himself fascinated by the idea a baby rested inside her. Someday, he hoped, a woman would love him enough to marry him and carry his offspring; he wanted a boy and a girl, he decided, and not necessarily in that order. The gods had blessed most of the animal kingdom with the wondrous ability to reproduce themselves, but only the most sapient of creatures did so with deliberation, passion, and for love of one another. It was the greatest gift a woman could give to any man, to agree to and want to accept his seed, to bear him shared children, to parent them together.

Then, Saviar recalled the circumstances of Chymmerlee's pregnancy and felt suddenly physically ill. She had had no choice in the matter. She had no romantic feelings for whoever had implanted the child in her womb; and, though the baby was innocent, he could not imagine the torrent of emotion that warred within her every moment of every day. "I'm sorry," he blurted out, climbing off the bed in the hope of comforting her.

Chymmerlee chuckled, much to Saviar's surprise, and he stopped midway to her, uncertain. "I didn't mean to laugh. It's just, I came to apologize to you, and you said it first." She tipped her head to one side, and her brow furrowed, all humor leaving her features abruptly. "What are *you* sorry for?"

Saviar nearly explained his words had come from sympathy for her plight, then stopped himself. He did not understand women well, but he did know human nature; and most strong people did not appreciate another's pity. He looked for a more personal reason to apologize. "I should have told you I was Renshai much sooner than I did. The moment I awakened from my coma, weak and confused, Subikahn made me promise not to tell any mage our tribe. My honor would not allow me to break a vow, even one made under duress." He wanted to add more in self-defense, to point out if two people truly loved one another, one's background or parentage should not matter to the other, but he did not. It would water down the apology and come out sounding more like a feeble excuse than explanation. Ultimately, her unwillingness to accept it had broken the deep bond that had once existed between them. That seemed like punishment enough.

Chymmerlee sighed deeply, head bowed. Either she intently considered his words or, more likely, her own forthcoming ones. "Saviar, I'm sorry. I was taught from infancy to hate Renshai, to believe they possessed devil magic and the obsession to brutally murder mages. Only today I discovered that, centuries ago, Colbey Calistinsson and the last of the great Mages of Myrcidë formed a blood brotherhood over the Pica Stone and declared our peoples one. Worse, despite knowing you as a sweet, wonderful, *honorable* man, I allowed myself to believe you used demon magic to rape me and wipe my mind of the memory. I treated you and your brother horribly, and neither of you deserved it."

Saviar had no trouble saying the words that had nearly abandoned him when confronting Jeremilan. "I forgive you for all of it, Chymmerlee. Under the circumstances, I even think I understand your reaction, though it wounded me deeply."

Chymmerlee shook her head, paused, then shook it more forcefully. "No, Saviar. Something terrible happened to me, and I had every right to be angry. But I had no right to take that anger out on you or on Subikahn."

Saviar found himself coming to Chymmerlee's defense. "Given your upbringing and what you found out I was hiding, it was not an unreasonable conclusion. I admit, you should have given me the opportunity to explain, to plead my innocence, but I really do understand why you didn't. When one is righteously enraged, it can be difficult or impossible to properly channel." He felt as if he were looking in a mirror. "I've done far too much inappropriate boiling over myself over the last few months."

Chymmerlee brightened. "So, you forgive me?"

"I said I did. And I meant it." Saviar wanted to ask who had fathered the infant, but he did not. If Chymmerlee knew that information and wished to share it, it was her decision entirely. If what Weile Kahn had suggested was true, and he was rarely wrong, one or more of the male mages had lain with Chymmerlee and forced her to forget. If several had done so, no one might ever know the blood father.

Chymmerlee finally managed a lopsided smile. "Thanks, Saviar. I forgive you, too. Do you think it's possible . . . we could ever be . . . ?"

She seemed reluctant to finish that sentence, and Saviar realized he could not allow her to do so. There would never be anything romantic between them again, he felt certain, so he had to assume she would have filled in the same word he did. "Friends? Of course." He had done a bit of research of his own. "According to Colbey and Shadimar, we're technically blood sister and blood brother."

If Chymmerlee had wanted something more, she did not show it. The grin became more natural. "Sister and brother. I like that. Especially since you're going to be seeing a lot more of me."

"Really?" Saviar had no idea what she meant.

"I have no desire to go back to the mage's compound, so I asked King Griff if I could stay in Béarn. He hired me as his court magician. I have permanent quarters in the castle, regular access to the Pica Stone, and everything."

"That's wonderful!" Saviar meant it. If nothing else positive came out of Subikahn blundering onto the hidden mages, this would more than do. "What about the rest of the Myrcidians?"

Chymmerlee finished the approach Saviar started, so they met in the middle of the room. "They're considering several options. Jeremilan's going back to the compound with anyone who chooses to join him. We left some of our people there, mostly the oldest ones. Nearly all the rest have decided to stay here and help me. I'm not sure whether it's actually me they want or just a chance to examine the Pica. And the elves have given us . . . an opportunity, of sorts."

Saviar had just reached out to embrace Chymmerlee, when he stopped to consider what she had just said. "The elves? An opportunity?"

Chymmerlee's eyes dulled, as if she suddenly wished she had not mentioned it. "Of sorts," she repeated. "Apparently, they want to make more hybrids, ivanas they call them. Not exactly sure why."

Saviar knew the reason, but he did not know if he had the right to share it.

"They know we're the only magical humans, that we have a scarcity of fertile women, and we're trying to infuse more magic into our line."

Suddenly it all made sense. "They're hoping your lot will interbreed with theirs to the advantage of both."

"Yes." Chymmerlee fairly spat. "As if children were experiments. I'm already carrying one created solely for the purpose of making another magical human with as much Myrcidian blood as possible, but no thought given to its loveless creation or my feelings. I've done my bit for science."

Now, Saviar found himself defending the elves. "I don't believe the elves think of it as experimentation, Chymmerlee. Elves don't pair up the way we do, and their babies are so scarce they consider them a shared blessing. Elfin children have about a hundred equal and loving mothers and another hundred or so proud and doting fathers." Another thought came to him. "I thought Myrcidians treated children pretty much the same way, as communal property."

"I was," Chymmerlee admitted. "But my mother died in childbirth and my father soon afterward. I'm not sure it was deliberate so much as necessary." She considered a moment. "I guess I don't really think it's such a terrible idea. It's just I'm the only fertile Myrcidian woman, and I want children within the confines of a loving marriage. It's not an unreasonable desire, is it?"

"I have the same desire," Saviar said. "Most humans do, or, at least, most choose to do so." He also mulled over the situation. "Elves have females, and few ever get to experience childbirth. Surely, some of the male mages might take up the elves on their offer. They wouldn't even have to share any of the responsibilities. I'm sure the elves would be happy to raise any ivanas who resulted."

"You're right." Chymmerlee bobbed her head. "Several of our men seem to be giving it serious thought. Of course, for it to actually expand our bloodline and enhance our magic, we would have to raise at least some of them as Myrcidians."

"Did the elves agree to that?"

"We haven't accepted the offer yet, so we haven't hammered out any terms. We do know at least one elf needs to be present at or near the birth. Apparently, some percentage of them will be born with the same issue that damaged Princess Ivana. If caught in infancy, it's supposed to be curable."

"That's great news!" Saviar realized it would put Tem'aree'ay's mind at ease, if she did not already know. Her future offspring with Griff would not have to suffer the way Ivana had. He finally reached out to Chymmerlee and caught her into an embrace. She felt warm and comfortable against him and, for a moment, he wondered if they could actually court again. Then, she pulled chastely away, and he realized the contact had not stimulated him to excitement the way it had in the past. Their relationship was well and truly dead, although a new one had been forged as blood brother and sister.

"Would you like me to walk you back to your quarters?" Saviar suggested, abruptly remembering Thialnir could come back at any time and it was not appropriate for the son of a knight to have a woman in his bedroom.

"Thank you, no." Chymmerlee headed for the door. "I'd like some alone time to think, if you don't mind. But I'll look you up tomorrow, if you'd like."

Saviar and Thialnir had already made plans. "Actually, we're going back to the Fields of Wrath in the morning, but it was great to see you, Chymmerlee. I'm so glad we talked. If you ever want a friendly ear or some assistance from me, you need only have me called."

"I will," Chymmerlee promised before slipping out the door.

Chymmerlee whistled a tune as she headed down the hallway. The meeting with Saviar had gone about as well as she could have hoped; and, although she still maintained a wistful desire for them to court again, she knew it had been highly unlikely. She still found him stunningly handsome and one of the kindest, smartest men she had ever met, but she had spent too many months despising him to ever feel fully comfortable with or desirous of him again. What she wanted, she realized, was a partner, someone she loved unconditionally and who felt the same way about her. A man who would willingly take on the burden of another man's child out of love for its mother, to father more children with her when the time was right. A man with whom she could live happily until the end of their excitement-fueled, passion-filled days.

As she walked, Chymmerlee thought back on the conversation she had had with the elves who had attended her. Three healers, all female, had examined her baby in the womb and proclaimed it a healthy human child with traces of budding magic. For weeks, she had loathed it, then suffered confusion, often hoping it would emerge early as a twisted lump of useless tissue the way most mage pregnancies did.

Since they all carried Myrcidian blood, they were all related to some extent, especially as they remained limited to the handful of magical humans Jeremilan had managed to find and bring together. Now, for the first time, she considered the being expanding in her womb her baby, and excitement about its upcoming birth began to grow.

Fear accompanied that anticipation. Jeremilan had finally admitted several of the male mages had raped her, including himself. He assured her they had done it with the full consent of ten elders, half of whom were female and the other half of whom were the potential fathers. He had apologized profusely but rationalized it with the understanding that it was the only way to keep the Mages of Myrcidë from dying out entirely. He believed he understood how she felt and she would eventually come to realize why they had needed to do it and forgive.

Chymmerlee doubted that either of those statements were true, though she felt certain he believed them both. As much as she wanted to, she found it impossible to hate the men and women who had raised her, especially the ones who had had no hand in the vile act. She did not wish to be around them ever again, but she was still one of the handful of mages existing in the world. She did not want to see the Myrcidians disappear from the world a second time, did not want to be the cause of their extinction even indirectly. The elves' suggestion did offer another opportunity to save the Mages of Myrcidë, so it needed to be taken seriously no matter her objections to it.

An additional thought intruded. The elfin healers had dropped another bombshell on Chymmerlee that had nothing to do with the pregnancy. Elves tended to have several relatively frivolous spells in common, but most also had an area of specialization. In the case of the three who assisted her, it was healing. Others could summon and control demons. Some focused naturally on transportation, such as gating. The three had informed Chymmerlee she had an unrecognized knack for what they called *litaska* or "seeking magic."

Apparently, that strength was why she among the mages chose to leave the compound most frequently and had the best luck finding various types of food. When she considered it, she realized she had discovered Subikahn, and, ultimately, the dying Saviar, because she had been focused on solving the procreation problem of the mages, which she had only learned about that morning. She had been wishing to find strangers who radiated magic, ones who might bring new blood to Myrcidë. Little had she known, only the day before, on her eighteenth birthday, the mages had tried to solve the same problem by using her as an unwitting breeder.

Now, a strange idea took shape in Chymmerlee's mind. Perhaps if she channeled her thoughts onto finding the soulmate she desired, her *litaska* would direct her. Once considered, the idea would not be banished. It grew stronger by the moment, and she allowed her legs to take her where they might, without deliberate guidance. She soon found herself walking down several flights of stairs and out into the courtyard gardens, dormant for the winter. Blindly, deafly, she wandered past staff and visitors, some of whom stared at her curiously or even called her name.

Chymmerlee rounded a gazebo and suddenly found herself face-to-face with the handsomest male she had ever met. Only a quarter of a head taller than her, he had hair the color of polished bronze and eyes like brilliant and shimmering citrines. The canted sockets and long-fingered hands identified him as elfin. Chymmerlee shook her head to clear it, her heart pounding in her chest. Only then, she realized she knew this elf. It was Chan'rék'ril, one of the two who had accompanied the rescue party to the various Outworlds. He had always seemed a bit different than his companions. Like her, he was the most adventuresome of his breed, and he demonstrated a stolidness that made him seem more human than his kin. Over the last few days, he had smiled more than he ever had in the time she had known him. She had noticed him and considered him attractive and likable, but she had never before thought of him, or any elf, as a potential mate. Now, suddenly, she knew it as surely as if the gods had pointed the way. She and Chan'rék'ril belonged together for as long as her mage-blood allowed her to live. She had never felt so certain of anything in her life. It only remained to convince him.

For his part, Chan'rék'ril withered under her scrutiny almost to the point of panic. His face reddened, which surprised her. She had never seen an elf embarrassed, and he seemed as uncomfortable as a smitten schoolboy. She hurled herself into his arms, and he embraced her, feeling warm and secure against her. She could feel his heart beating rapidly, in perfect time with her own. "What took you so long?" he whispered. Clearly, he had known even longer than she had.

Elves, Chymmerlee knew, believed in free love, sharing sex with the same ease humans did friendship. She would have to cure him of this notion, to assure he was hers and hers alone. For reasons only magic understood, she did not think it would prove too difficult.

CHAPTER 26

Families love each other, even when they can't stand each other.
—*Calistin Ra-khirsson*

TAE KAHN STOOD BENEATH the third-floor balcony of Béarn Castle amid the hordes of curious citizenry gathered to listen to the king's decrees. Imorelda curled around his neck, the kittens tucked into his pockets. No longer sleeping balls of fluff, both stood with hind paws braced against the fabric, forepaws looped over the top edges of his pockets fascinated by the antics of the humans around them. Vendors had turned the announcement into an event, selling everything from statues of bears and kings to Béarnian and Erythanian flags to foods of myriad varieties. The odors of sausages and pastries mingled into a delicate blend of grease and spices.

Griff had been speaking for some time, mostly about the blessed peace that had finally come to the entirety of the continent and how he and his heirs intended to make it last for all eternity. He had thanked everyone from the representatives of the various countries, now all gone home or preparing to do so, to the Mages of Myrcidë and the elves. He begged the populace to release any previous hostilities and prejudices, pleading for a new era of equality and tranquility between the peoples of every kingdom and country and proclivity, whether human sans magic, mage, or elf. Everyone on the continent had come together to fight a war that could well have spelled doom for every man, woman, and child. That goodwill needed to spread to encompass all of them in times of peace as well.

Quite the optimist, isn't he?

Tae found himself smiling broadly. **Indeed, but exactly what we need in a high king, don't you think?** He dared to wonder, *And maybe, just maybe, we can remember the horror of this war and use it to cement together the many and varied people who inhabit this world, at least for a while.*

Exactly, Imorelda agreed. *And yet, you and I know what's coming next.*

Tae could not deny it; but, for the moment, King Griff still personally addressed the crowd.

Griff went further yet in his plea for peace, introducing the *Kjempemagiska,* Kentt and Mistri, to the stunned crowd. Most of them had heard rumors of the surviving enemy and his young daughter, already the size of a full-grown man. Those who had entered the great hall during the proceedings had seen them, but Tae doubted most of the regular peasantry had believed their stories. Kentt then spoke several sentences in pidgin common. Apparently, he intended to sail back to Heimstadr with diplomats from the continent to create a relationship and open trade. The Heimstaders, he promised, produced many goods that would make their lives more pleasant and easy, and he would work toward the greater good of the Islanders and the peoples of the continent.

Murmurs arose when Kentt first showed his face; but, by the time he had finished speaking, the audience erupted in cheers.

Imorelda started, *Do you really think . . . ?*

Tae did not allow her to finish. *I really think, contrary to the view of a certain cat.*

Imorelda lashed her tail around his face and sent him a mental admonishment, finishing the sentence as if he had not interrupted. *. . . the giants will create peace with us? That they'll acknowledge us as something more than animals? That they can actually become allies?*

Tae had given it lots of thought already. *I think Kentt knows what he's doing. I've also seen some of their products, and they do have some clever and useful items we can't make ourselves. At worst, it will take the* Kjempemagiska *decades to rebuild their population. In the meantime, we're dealing with the least warlike of its people: women, children, the elderly, and men like Kentt. By the time they rebuild a fighting force, we should have treaties in place and strong diplomatic ties.* He concluded, surprising even himself, *I actually do believe we will create a lasting peace between Heimstadr and ourselves, Imorelda. Even on our own continent, the memory of this war and all its ugliness will last for a while. Old enmities might never fully heal, but I do believe we're ushering in an era of peace.*

Imorelda purred. *If the world's most virulent pessimist thinks that way, I suppose I can, too.*

Meaning me? Tae realized he did tend to embrace the dark side of situations. Hunted by his father's enemies nearly since birth, stabbed multiple times and left for dead as a child, he had good reason. Perhaps the time had come, though, to search for more rainbows and fewer meteors.

King Griff was still speaking and had, apparently, finally turned to the matter Tae had anticipated with some measure of dread. ". . . congratulations are in order. Prince Barrindar has passed the Pica test and will take my place upon the throne from this moment forward."

A shocked silence gripped the crowd. Every face seemed glued to the balcony and its occupants. There followed a collective groan, the rumble of questioning voices, a few desperate sobs. Griff took a step backward to stand among the inner guardsmen, and Barrindar came to the fore, the bard of Béarn beside him.

Another unnatural hush fell over the audience. Gently, Griff removed the crown from his own head and placed it upon his son's. Barrindar looked like a wounded deer: dark eyes wide, face pale, mouth moving soundlessly for a moment. Though tall, broad, and muscled like an ox, he seemed young and frail compared to his commanding and beloved father. Finally, he managed speech. "Believe me, citizens of Béarn. No one sees this as sudden and premature more than I do. I promise to do everything within my power to see to it you have wise, competent, and neutral decisions befitting the ruler of Béarn. As such, I vow to rely *heavily* on the advice of my father, the previous king, until such time as he believes my judgment has grown equal to his own."

A great cheer went up from below, along with multiple cries of "Long live King Barrindar!"

Barrindar waited until the shouts diminished, leaving only the usual murmured speculations and conversations of a gathered crowd. "My first act as king is to pardon Matrinka Talamaine's daughter of all wrongdoing."

The delighted cries that followed nearly deafened Tae. Matrinka had always been a favorite of Béarn's subjects. The populace had demanded her marriage to Griff, and they had loved and trusted the sweet-natured queen. Tae had simply not realized they had become so involved in the goings on of the high court. It only made sense for them to turn against someone branded a traitor and an adulterer, but the citizens of Béarn clearly had never lost their faith in Matrinka. That boded well for her, the kingdom, and the future peace.

Newly coronated King Barrindar waited until the noise died down to continue. "By Béarnian law, Matrinka must lose all of her titles and her positions, and her marriage will be nullified as of this moment. This cannot, of course, affect her bloodline or those of her progeny. Princess Marisole, as the daughter of Matrinka and Angus, and Prince Arturo and Princess Halika, as children of former King Griff and Matrinka, shall remain in the castle as legal heirs to the throne." He looked down at his feet for a moment, his expression grim. By the time he raised his head, the ghost of a smile appeared on his lips. "For my second act as king, with your forbearance and that of Béarn's Council, I would like to take Princess Marisole Angus' daughter as my wife and your future queen."

There was a moment of uncoordinated murmuring as the people followed the strange twists the saga had taken. It had only recently become public knowledge that Marisole was not the blood daughter of Griff and, thus, no longer inappropriately close kin to Barrindar. The announcement of marriage required them to divest the long-held image of Barrindar and Marisole as siblings. Then, as understanding spread through the crowd, another enormous cheer went up, including shouts of "Long live Queen Marisole!"

Tae released a pent-up breath he had not realized he was holding. Clearly, the citizenry of Béarn had not only accepted the change of rulership and the upcoming nuptials, but embraced it.

I can't believe they pulled that off.

Remember, my love. They've had the best minds in Béarn diligently working on it for a long time.

And yours, too, Imorelda added, nothing leaching through the contact to suggest she was anything but sincere. The insult was, apparently, unintentional.

Tae finished the thought, *The people of Béarn love their kings and queens and truly want them to be happy. The Pica test makes no mistakes. If it chose Barrindar, the people know he's the best one for the job and his judgment is flawless. They're willing to permanently overlook the obvious in certain circumstances, such as the true blood father of Matrinka's children.*

Imorelda made a noise halfway between a grunt and a single, short purr she apparently intended to sum up the positive and negative aspects of humans.

Tae focused on Barrindar's next words, spoken in a sad and wistful tone.

"Though our former queen no longer has a place at Béarn Castle, we will not toss her into the street. We will see to it she has a place to live and enough funds to keep her until such time as—"

Darris leaned in to whisper in the new king's ear, and Barrindar stopped abruptly. Even from a distance, Tae could see the smile broadening on his face. He said something inaudible back to Darris, they conversed briefly, then Barrindar explained to the crowd. "Now that Matrinka is no longer royalty, our very own bard, Darris, has requested her hand in marriage."

Another great cheer erupted from the crowd.

Barrindar lowered his head until the noise dissipated, then raised it and looked over the crowd as if to meet every eye. "Given the situation, and all its complications, I am leaving it to you to decide. If you approve of both of these marriages, I ask that you shout out 'yah' on my three count." He started immediately, "One . . . two . . . three."

An enormous cry of "yah!" followed in myriad voices, including Tae's own; though, as a citizen of the Eastlands, he had no real right to vote.

Barrindar followed with, "If you disapprove of either of these marriages, I ask that you shout out 'nay' on my three count." Again, he paused less than a moment, "One . . . two . . . three."

A spattering of "nays!" followed. Tae could see glares directed at the current shouters, mostly from the Béarnian women, and it died out much more swiftly.

Barrindar directed his next comment to Darris but easily loud enough for all to hear. "It would appear the populace approves of the marriages. And, as the bard of Béarn has quarters for self and family within the castle walls, we will not need to find housing for our former queen." He added, "If it works for you and Matrinka, I would like very much to combine the weddings into one. That will save the kingdom money at a time when the coffers are still recovering from a massive war and we have waived taxes from our allies to allow them to recover as well."

Women and their wedding plans. Tae considered. *I wonder how Marisole will feel about sharing an anniversary date.*

Imorelda buffeted his mind with waves of disdain. *Under the circumstances, she'll be thrilled.*

Tae supposed Imorelda knew better than he did. He recalled how guilty Marisole had acted when her ill-considered pregnancy had nearly resulted in her mother's execution. She had even offered to rescue Matrinka by placing her own head in the noose. Then, the bard's heir had compared her love for Barrindar with Matrinka's lifelong passion for Darris. Imorelda was right; she would be thrilled.

The crowd did not meet that pronouncement with the enthusiasm they had displayed for Matrinka's pardon or Barrindar's intention to marry Marisole. Tae felt certain they would have preferred two elaborate celebrations and ceremonies. Listening to the conversations around him, he knew they were gradually realizing the marriage between Darris and Matrinka, if celebrated alone, would not be a fancy gala, given both participants were now only minor nobility, at best. Barrindar had not only made a sound fiscal decision, he had found a roundabout way of making the Matrinka/Darris marriage the memorable event it deserved to be.

Tae's respect for Barrindar grew. He would miss having Griff on the throne of Béarn, but the younger man would prove a suitable replacement. And, in the end, it had been the only reasonable way to save Matrinka's life.

As the curtain closed around the balcony, and the crowd dispersed, chattering animatedly, Imorelda patted Tae's neck with a plushy paw. For the first in a very long time, genuine joy radiated across their mental contact. *And we have the best wedding present Matrinka could ever receive.*

Tae grinned, patting the tiny heads poking from his pockets. One thing he had noticed about the new kittens was he did not have to worry about losing or hurting them by accident. He or Imorelda could explain to them, in a way they fully understood, the necessity of remaining safely in the pockets during transportation. *Which one will we give her?*

They had debated the relative merits of each, without coming to a definitive conclusion. Matrinka would dote on either one, and whether the female's resemblance to Mior would raise expectations or would particularly delight the former queen was still unresolved. This time, Imorelda did not hesitate. *The girl. Girls deserve more spoiling. And, if anything happens to me, I'd rather the boy got stuck with you.*

Tae gave each of the kittens a final, fond scratch before tickling Imorelda's neck. *You're going to outlive me, my dear.*

Before Imorelda could respond, a breathless Darris caught Tae's arm. "They're preparing the diplomatic group for Heimstadr and want to know if you want to be part of it."

Tae had not realized it was leaving so soon. "Do they need me?"

"You're the only one of us who speaks the language with any fluency. Prince Arturo's got the spoken language down pretty well, but he can't do the mental piece and he's worried he's going to sound dim."

Tae sighed. His ability with languages had proven a colossal gift but also a curse. He had been preparing to return to the East. He spent too little time in his own castle to suit his citizenry, and something else was drawing him back as well, something soft and caring and feminine. "Who else is going?"

Darris' gaze fell on the kittens peeping from Tae's pockets. "Captain's piloting, of course, along with a Béarnian crew. He's the only one who currently knows the way, but others need to learn it. Prince Arturo, Kentt and Mistri, a couple of other elves, including Chan'rék'ril. And one of the mages is going, too, the one who helped in the Pirate War."

That surprised Tae. "Chymmerlee?"

"She's Béarn's magician now. And, between you and me, I think there's something between her and Chan'rék'ril."

From a Renshai to an elf. It seemed like quite a leap to Tae, but when it came to courtship, there was no accounting for taste. His first instinct, to accept the adventure delightedly, passed swiftly. The decision was not that simple anymore. He still had a taste for excitement and still secretly craved risk, but he had traveled to Heimstadr before, under far less positive circumstances. "They don't need me, Darris. Arturo speaks well enough, and the magical types have ways to translate for anyone now. They can fill in any lapses. *Anari* isn't necessary for communication, and the island peoples will have to get used to the fact our people don't use it. Kentt should have no difficulty explaining the situation."

Darris nodded. "I just thought you'd want to . . ." He broke off, clearly surprised by Tae's response. "I mean, you've always . . ." He stopped and started again. "Are you going back to the East?"

"I am." Tae found himself unexpectedly smiling at the thought. An image of Alneezah filled his mind's eye, all kindness and curves and smelling of cloves. "I've been glad to help; you know that, but a king can't rule from a distance. My people need me, and I deserve a permanent home." He had no idea if a romance would work between him and the castle maid, but he certainly intended to get to know her better. "You really don't need my services anymore. You have the elves' translation spell now. And if you require a mental speaker in the future, I believe your fiancée can stand in for me."

Now it was Darris' turn to blurt a name stupidly, "Matrinka?"

"She has the ability." *Or will once she bonds with her wedding gift.* "And, now, she has plenty of time on her hands to practice."

Darris bowed deeply, as if suddenly aware he addressed a king. Their friendship precluded such gestures in the past, but many things had recently changed. "Thank you for all you've done for Béarn. Let us know if there's anything we can do to make your journey as pleasant and easy as possible."

"I will, thank you. When are the weddings?"

"One week." The words seemed to startle Darris as much as Tae.

"The citizenry doesn't want us to wait and, quite frankly, I'm at least as eager as they are."

"It's been a long time coming, Darris. Congratulations."

Darris beamed like a child. "You'll stay for that, won't you?"

"Of course," Tae promised. "Nothing could make me miss it."

And you'll invite him to yours, right?

For an instant, Tae confused the conversations, stiffening. Then, realizing Imorelda had made the last statement, and no one else could hear it, he relaxed and sent back swiftly, *My wedding? Way too early to consider that, my love. Alneezah and I haven't even courted yet.*

But she loves you. And she loves me. What more could you want?

Tae did not wish to rehash the old argument. *Just because you love someone doesn't mean you can live with them. Let's give Alneezah a chance to really get to know me, to decide if I'm really worthy of her love.*

Imorelda's tail lashed wildly. *Wouldn't it be better to capture her while you can? Before she can change her mind?*

Tae did not allow a trace of humor to appear on his face. *No, Imorelda. If I love her, and I'm starting to believe I do, I couldn't do anything to hurt her. It would be wrong on so many levels. She needs to know exactly what she's getting if she decides to commit herself to me. It would be vile to return her devotion with misery.* He did not add he needed to assure himself she wanted him for the right reasons. Any woman might pretend to adore a king for the wealth and power the position accorded, whether or not she took the title of queen. Imorelda had vetted her, and the cat's assessment of human motivation was seldom wrong, but he had to make certain.

The tail ceased its angry motions to flop quietly onto his chest. *I suppose you're right. This time. But don't take too long or she may find someone better.*

Imorelda so rarely gave him a win, Tae threw her one of her own. *That wouldn't be difficult, but I hope she chooses me anyway.*

Darris caught Tae into a warm and sudden embrace, whispering into his ear. "I can hardly believe this is actually going to happen."

Tae ignored the nails Imorelda sank into his flesh for balance. "I know, my friend. And may all the gods bless it, I want only the best for both of you."

Thialnir and Saviar rode home from Béarn in a silence interrupted only by occasional bursts of casual conversation: about the many announcements, the weather, the successful conclusion of the rescues. Never one for deep discussion, Thialnir seemed jumpy and uncomfortable, measuring his every word and Saviar's responses. His rare smiles were strained. The last time Saviar had seen any display of true emotion from the leader of the Renshai was when Saviar had asked to accompany him to the Council meeting. Then, the aging face had registered clear surprise and a brief glimmer of delight. Since then, he had tiptoed around Saviar like a starving hunter terrified of frightening away a twitchy deer.

Saviar wanted to put Thialnir at ease, but he found himself incapable of speaking the necessary words. Until he resolved his issues with Subikahn and his feelings about becoming a Knight of Erythane, he did not have a definitive answer for Thialnir. Worse, he had little to no idea how to handle either of those problems. The mere thought of confronting Subikahn made his blood boil, and the issue of how to balance knighthood and Renshai teachings had plagued him for most of his life. Colbey's thoughts on that particular matter had proven of little use to him. The immortal Renshai could do both because the knights had essentially forgotten him and, even when they finally remembered, only dared to bother him in the most dire situation. Saviar would not have that luxury, even if he had wanted it. To become a knight meant dedicating himself to their honor and conventions, and it clashed impossibly with the Renshai training he had embraced since infancy.

All too soon, they arrived at the Fields of Wrath. The familiar sounds of clanging steel, shouted commands and curses filling the air, and the home-defining outline of simple cottages made Saviar smile despite his turbulent thoughts. Subikahn met them at the edge of town, where the woodlands touched the barren plains on which they had built their town, greeting them both with a delighted grin and happy gestures.

Nausea bubbled up in Saviar's stomach. Thialnir bellowed a welcome, Saviar silent beside him, lips pursed, gaze dodging his twin's. The leader of the Renshai did not appear to notice Saviar's reticence, instead speaking fondly. "I'm sure you two want some time alone to reunite. I'll carry all the news to the others."

Saviar wanted nothing less, but he did not contradict Thialnir. As much as he hated what Subikahn had done to him, he could not bring himself to tell anyone else what his brother had confessed. The penalty was just too harsh. While Subikahn deserved it, Saviar found himself incapable of being the mouthpiece for his twin's utter and terrible destruction.

Saviar paused while Thialnir rode on ahead, then shifted to urge his horse onward. As he did so, Subikahn caught the cheekpiece of his bridle, holding fast. He who controlled the head, controlled the horse. It occurred to Saviar if he kicked the beast hard enough, he might get it to either break free of Subikahn's hold or drag him alongside until he realized the prudence of releasing it. What stopped him was not the image of Subikahn bouncing over rocks at a full gallop but the concern the horse might be harmed in the process.

"We need to talk," Subikahn said.

Saviar gritted his teeth. "I have nothing to say to you."

"You don't need to speak, Savi. I need to explain."

Saviar continued to stare straight ahead. When he replied, he found his jaw aching from the strain of clenching. "You told me what you did. No excuse could justify such terrible cowardice nor the damning of another Renshai's soul. If you say one more word about it, I'm going to cleave your coward head from your coward neck."

They used the Renshai tongue, and the insult "*klaekir*" was the strongest, ugliest term Saviar knew in any language.

"I'd like to see you try."

Now, Saviar's fists went white on the reins, and the muscles of his jaw cramped to sharp agony. Fighting words he understood, and Subikahn had no right to utter them. Forcing words through the pain, he responded, "You're not worthy to dirty my blade. Not even in spar."

Subikahn fell silent; but, as Saviar refused to look at him, he had no idea what nonverbal expression or body language his twin revealed. From the corner of his eye, he could see the swarthy hand still clamped to his horse's bridle. "You won't hear me out?"

"Not one word."

"You're not even curious about why I did what I did?"

There was only one possible explanation. "Not in the slightest."

"Then I have no choice but to kill myself."

Saviar rolled his eyes; though, as he stared off into space, Subikahn could not see that gesture, either. "Don't expect me to deliver *tåphresëlmordat* to a *klaekir* who refused to do the same for me. Perhaps our dear brother would oblige, but not if he knew the reason, of course." Saviar realized the truth and spoke it, "No Renshai will oblige you because they'd all demand to know why any Renshai without a fatal wound or illness is requesting it. Would you lie to them, too? Feign infirmity? Because I'm not at all sure I could maintain my silence about what you did if you tried that." Saviar vividly recalled his test on the Outworld. In Subikahn's place, he had done the right thing, the moral and lawful thing, what Renshai learned from infancy. Subikahn could have, should have done the same.

If Subikahn took offense, his voice did not show it. "*Tăphresëlmordat?* That would send me to Valhalla. I trust my brother's judgment, and he's convinced I'm not worthy of a warrior's death."

That so startled Saviar he turned his head to look at Subikahn for the first time. "Calistin knows?"

Subikahn's features revealed nothing. "I was talking about you."

Me. Of course, me. If Calistin knew what he had done, he would not be here now talking to me. Certain Subikahn was bluffing, Saviar played along. He would not give the coward the benefit of concern or consideration. "You could throw yourself under the hooves of a merchant's cart."

If Subikahn took the suggestion anything but seriously, he gave no sign. "That takes some pretty specific timing that I've never practiced. I might just wound myself, and it wouldn't be fair to the merchant. He might lose his cart or his horse or wares. No, that won't do."

Saviar thought of several other possibilities. "Jump off a high wall."

"None near here."

"Weight yourself with stones and walk into the deepest part of the river."

"And ruin the drinking water for months?"

"Fall on your sword."

Subikahn glanced at his belt, where only one blade hung. Apparently, he had lost the other either in the war or on the Outworld. "The only one I have is Calistin's, which used to belong to our mother. She treasured it, and so does he. I can't dishonor someone else's sword that way, especially one so precious."

Saviar wasn't about to loan his disgraced brother one of his own weapons. Renshai never allowed an honored blade to touch the ground; and, if it happened, it required weeks of grueling atonement. It was one thing to allow Subikahn to take his own life and send his soul to Hel, quite another to assist the process. "Hang yourself."

Subikahn's head tipped to one side. His dark eyes brightened. "Excellent idea! Come on." He pulled at the bridle as he headed toward the woods.

Saviar sprang from the saddle as Subikahn led his mount to the trees. It did not appear as if his twin noticed his sudden absence, and Saviar considered going in the other direction, home to the Fields of Wrath. Then, curiosity got the better of him. No Renshai could kill himself outside of battle; even mired in deepest depression, Renshai always chose to die by the sword. His reasoning swept in an odd circle. Only a coward would condemn any Renshai soul to Hel, including his own, yet it took a weird sort of courage to deliberately kill oneself in a manner that must preclude Valhalla. He knew Subikahn had to find a way around it, yet he could think of no possibility that wouldn't make him look even more pathetic in his brother's eyes. Whether or not Subikahn actually killed himself, Saviar had to know. Otherwise, he would spend his life wondering, constantly looking behind him.

Subikahn did not go far before noticing Saviar's absence from the horse's back. His gaze found his brother briefly, then skittered away. Taking the reins, he tied the horse to a sturdy branch with them, keeping the head high enough to prevent it from stepping through the bridle. More than a few horses had broken legs attempting to graze with unsecured headgear. Sitting on a nearby deadfall, Subikahn removed a coil of rope from his pack and set to constructing an elaborate noose.

Leaning against a broad-limbed *mirack* tree, his arms crossed over his chest, Saviar watched his brother work in silence.

It did not take long for Subikahn to construct a noose suitable for a hangman. He actually managed a tight smile at his handiwork, then tossed the rope over a tree limb until the noose dangled. He tied the other end firmly to an adjacent branch. Leading the horse directly under the dangling noose, he climbed astride the saddle. Speaking gently to the animal, he raised one foot under his bottom.

The horse whinnied, stirring restively.

Subikahn spoke to it softly, patting its burnished red-brown neck. Then, he tried again, raising one booted foot into the saddle and placing the other onto its rump. This time, the horse stood firm. Balanced and standing on the creature's back, Subikahn reached for the noose.

Saviar watched his twin's antics, displaying only mild inquisitiveness, though he could not help wondering how Subikahn intended to get himself out of the mess he had created. He still did not believe his brother would go through with the actual suicide. It went against anything either of them believed or understood; yet, the moment that noose went around his neck, he was as good as dead. The horse was well-trained in Béarn; Saviar had intended to send it home with a simple command and a slap on the rump. But horses could become easily startled, even just by a human standing on its back. If it bolted or even ambled away, Subikahn would hang.

Still, until the moment Subikahn placed that rope around his neck, he was safe from anything more than a tumble and some bruises.

Subikahn took the noose in hand, then looked directly at Saviar. "Are you absolutely certain you don't want to hear my explanation?"

Saviar did not back down. "Absolutely certain." Even as he spoke the words, something of great consequence niggled at the back of his mind. He found himself chasing the concept, one that seemed strangely even more significant than his brother's suicide, mostly because he felt certain Subikahn had a foolproof plan to abort it. No way his brother would place that noose around his neck.

But then, he did. With familiar, measured grace, Subikahn ducked his head directly into the loop of rope.

And the thought Saviar had been chasing came to him verbatim, this time in words from his own mouth spoken just the previous day to Chymmerlee. *I admit, you should have given me the opportunity to explain, to plead my innocence, but I really do understand why you didn't. When one is righteously enraged, it can be difficult or impossible to properly channel. I've done far too much inappropriate boiling over myself over the last few months.* Most impressively right now. Whatever the certainty of Subikahn's cowardice, he had the right to explain his actions, deserved to be heard by the twin who had claimed to love him for all of his nineteen years.

Subikahn kicked the horse, and it bolted from beneath him.

Just as swiftly, Saviar drew and sprang. As Subikahn fell, Saviar's blade caught the rope a mighty blow, pinning it against the branch. For a sickening moment, Saviar thought the rope would hold, that the sharpened edge and his fabled strength would not prove enough. Then, the sisal parted.

Tensed for a sudden stop, Subikahn hit the ground hard enough that Saviar heard the slam of his body against it, the rattle of his teeth coming suddenly together. Whatever else, Subikahn had clearly not been bluffing, had definitely anticipated his death by hanging. In an instant, he was on his feet, throwing the noose from his neck. Drawing Calistin's sword, he charged Saviar in a bullrush of rage.

The blades met in an explosion of sound, actual sparks flying from the contact of one magical sword against the other. Saviar planted his feet, and the impact sent the smaller Subikahn bouncing backward. He recovered swiftly, and they came at one another again.

Subikahn measured his next several strokes, weaving in and out of Saviar's attack and defense like a black fly determined for a blood meal, despite the wild waving of its prey, the chance one lucky or well-timed blow would smash it. Saviar found himself battling a matched foe, a Renshai at his own level. Renshai law frowned on such contests, particularly without an end point called. Renshai sparred with live steel, and it was too easy for evenly experienced warriors at similar levels to harm one another by accident or for them to become so intent they forgot to pull a fatal blow. It was exactly the reason Subikahn had impaled his brother's thigh so many months ago.

A sense of twice-living invaded Saviar's consciousness, even as he concentrated as much as possible on give-and-take, attack and riposte, dodge and parry. Subikahn had claimed they sparred in wild anger that other time, a battle Saviar had found himself incapable of remembering and that the demon of the Outworld had forced him to relive in reverse facsimile. Now, the true details came back to him in snatches as they crossed swords once again. Both of them knew the same Renshai maneuvers, though each had his strengths and weaknesses. Both moved with swiftness and deadly accuracy. Saviar had the advantage of reach, bulk, and strength, while Subikahn had to rely fully on the speed, mobility, and agility they all aspired to perfect. Subikahn also had a quick and clever mind that forced Saviar to watch for unexpected actions that might stray into the realm of desperation or apparent insanity.

The battle continued, Saviar forcing as many parries as possible, knowing his superior power would eventually wear down Subikahn. Brute strength alone would not win this spar. The Renshai maneuvers never relied on it and taught them every lethal trick against it. But Saviar had to use his muscular superiority because he lacked any other. Both of them knew all the tactics and ruses taught to every Renshai, and they knew one another's personal repertoires as well.

More memories returned in a wild rush. They had both been in a foul temper, traveling through hostile territory, Subikahn harboring the secret of his homosexuality he worried would permanently end their friendship. So, when Subikahn claimed their mother had deemed him ready for the Renshai tests of adulthood, Saviar had belittled it as a lie. Under ordinary circumstances, they would have joked jovially about her strict and unreasonable standards. Both of them had become official Renshai men by killing enemies in battle, obviating the tests the tribe relied upon in peacetime. Then, petty bickering and negative dispositions had drawn them into a dangerous spar instead.

Saviar had tried for months to remember it, without success. He had believed his festering wound was inflicted by a Northman until Subikahn had told him the truth at the World's War, after taking fatal injuries of his own. Now, Saviar recalled the battle in detail and even its conclusion: Subikahn had sneaked away, hiding in the brush, only to catch Saviar by surprise. Saviar had recovered from that devious maneuver, had finally managed to score the first would-be killing blow when an errant stop-thrust from Subikahn found its way deep into the muscle of Saviar's thigh.

I won that spar, Saviar realized. *And I will win this one.* He leaped into battle with renewed enthusiasm, alert to Subikahn's every wile. When Subikahn attempted to disappear, Saviar anticipated it and bore in all the harder. Also a large man among mostly smaller Renshai, Thialnir had taught him some things in Subikahn's absence that he brought into action now. Subikahn relied on swift dodges and misdirection to keep himself from falling to superior strength, but he had no choice but to catch some strokes, to parry some closely cut attacks. And, each time their swords slammed together, Saviar gained the edge.

Openings came and went, missed or spoiled by the combatants until, after what seemed like several hours, a tight swing of Saviar's sword sang toward Subikahn's temple and seemed certain to land. Saviar remembered to turn the blade sideways, and Subikahn even got his between it and his skull as the distance closed. The side of Subikahn's own blade crashed against his head, pressed beneath Saviar's but unable to slow it enough. Subikahn crumpled wordlessly to the ground.

Saviar stood over his brother, panting, the warm glow of success sprouting through him. Twice now, they had sparred and twice he had proven himself the superior swordsman . . . eventually. The sun had slipped in the sky quite a bit since the whole ordeal had started. Saviar did not know how much of the time had passed during the near-hanging and how much for the spar, but they clearly were closely matched for skill. He recalled more about the past that, until recently, had eluded him. When Subikahn had pulled the sword from Saviar's leg, he had thrown it on the ground, deliberately dishonored. That was the true reason Subikahn currently carried only one sword, as penance for injuring and nearly killing his beloved brother.

For several moments, Subikahn lay still on the ground while Saviar tended his sword. When *Motfrabelonning* finally reentered its sheath, and Subikahn continued to lie perfectly still, a terrible thought entered Saviar's mind. *I killed him.* Uncertain which bothered him more, the fact that he might have dispatched his twin by accident or that he had done so in a way which allowed the coward's soul to find Valhalla, Saviar crouched at Subikahn's side. "Subi?" He shook the motionless form.

Subikahn sat up, grinning. "So you do care if I live or die."

Saviar turned away. "No, I don't. I just wanted to know whether I needed to finish you off."

Subikahn knew better. "If you wanted to kill me, you wouldn't have turned your blade. You'd have sliced off the top of my head."

"I should have done that," Saviar countered. "Then I'd know for sure whether there're any brains at all inside." Realizing he had fallen into old patterns of bantering when he still wanted to hate his brother, he scowled. "I only prevented you from hanging yourself because everyone, no matter how vile, deserves a chance to explain his actions."

Subikahn rose, walked to a deadfall and sat. He tapped the place beside him.

Saviar grudgingly realized he still harbored love for his twin. Still not ready to forgive, he ignored the invitation and crouched in front of Subikahn instead. "Start explaining."

Subikahn nodded. "I want you to know, as you were dying, you did everything possible to goad me into attacking you, to assure your honorable and heroic death in battle and to find your rightful place in Valhalla."

Saviar had worried about that. Although his memories of the events surrounding his coma had started to return, that part remained a hole and probably always would. Over the last several months, he had grown desperately concerned it was his own cowardice that had kept Subikahn from discussing what had happened. He would not give his dishonored twin the satisfaction of knowing that, though. "Of course. Any Renshai would; and, if he did not for some reason, it's the responsibility of the Renshai still capable of clear thought to goad him to do so."

"Yes." Subikahn looked at his hands, then, to Saviar's surprise, boldly met his gaze. "I refused your advances because I believed your body was strong enough to fight off the infection or I would find the right combination of herbs or I could drag you to a town and a healer. Love causes a man to cling to pipe dreams, even as time passes and all possibility dissipates."

Saviar listened; but, so far, Subikahn had not said anything that would change his mind about the situation. "If you truly loved me, you would have assured my place in Valhalla, not doomed me to Hel for any reason." He braced for another lame excuse.

"I was all set to deliver *tåphresëlmordat* when I realized Hel herself had died during the *Ragnarok* along with nearly all of the major, the most powerful, gods."

That was not at all what Saviar had expected. "So, you figured if

Hel was dead, she couldn't take my soul." He shook his head briskly. "Surely you assumed someone had taken her place. Even the weakest of the gods wouldn't leave the long-dead souls unguarded, wouldn't let the newly dead roam aimlessly or decree they all, automatically, went to Valhalla instead."

Subikahn screwed up his features in an expression approaching anger. "Give me some credit. Whether you believe it or not, I've quite a lot of brains in there." He touched the spot where Saviar's blade had struck, then winced in pain. A bruise was already taking shape over his left temple. "I knew I was holding a magic sword, which meant I could see whoever or whatever came for your soul. And if I could see it, I could fight it."

The sheer audacity of the suggestion shocked Saviar. Suddenly, all thought of his brother as a coward seemed madness. "You were going to fight Hel's replacement for control of my soul?"

Subikahn grinned evilly. Nodded.

Saviar marveled at a plan that never would have occurred to him, but suddenly made perfect sense. "You know, whatever replaced Hel has to be powerful. A lesser god, perhaps. A giant. Some sort of monster."

"Against me defending you from eternal damnation." Subikahn's mouth widened into a rictus. "No lesser god or giant or monster. No creature sanctioned by the gods themselves. Not even Hel, had she still existed, stood a chance."

Saviar studied Subikahn. His half-Eastern twin had his grandfather's and father's ability to hide his emotions—from anyone but Saviar. They had shared everything from the moment of conception, and no one knew him better. Subikahn, to all appearances, was telling the truth. "What if you lost?"

"How could the Valkyries resist the soul of a man who deliberately attacked such a creature? They would have fought each other to be the one to deliver me to Valhalla. And, the only way I'd agree to go with them was if they took your soul as well."

Saviar's mouth went cold, and he realized he had left it dangling open. "What if you'd won?"

Subikahn shrugged, the answer obvious, at least to him. "There'd be no one to take your soul to Hel, would there? The gods would have replaced the dead creature eventually, of course; but surely it would prove even weaker than its predecessor. The gods would have started with the most powerful successor for Hel they could find or create. If the replacement dared to come after your soul, I'd have killed it, too. Eventually, the sequential guardians of Hel would learn to leave us alone. I'd have had control of your soul, and I'd have found a way to get it to Valhalla, even if only at the time of my own death."

All the anger that had controlled Saviar for so long drained away, and nothing came in to replace it. He felt numb, icy cold, and stupid.

Subikahn reached for him, and they collapsed into one another's embrace.

"I've missed you," Saviar said, the only words that would come to him.

Subikahn had the right ones. "I love you, too, my brother."

CHAPTER 27

It is easier to fight for one's principles than to live up to them.
—*Colbey Calistinsson*

THE COMMON ROOM in the Knight's Rest Inn in Erythane remained mostly empty in the midafternoon when Ra-khir ushered the three grown boys he considered his sons inside it. Saviar took a place at the square table directly across from his father, Calistin to his left and Subikahn to his right. Saviar knew the room like a second home, the high-beamed ceiling, the neat arrangement of mostly rectangular tables with their spotless covercloths matching the curtains, today a soft light green. Adjustable lanterns on every table allowed the patrons to determine the preferred amount of light, although currently most remained dark. A few serving maids wound between the tables, disappearing and reappearing through a door behind the bar counter.

Having shared far fewer evening meals with Ra-khir, Calistin and Subikahn stared wonderingly around the room. They had been in bars before, in Béarn, Erythane, and the Eastlands, but most were dingy, dirty affairs with cluttered arrangements of rickety, ale-stained benches and stools. The Knight's Rest catered to the Knights of Erythane, the unmarried ones occupying most of the sleeping quarters, and the quieter wealthier travelers. The common room serviced families of all income levels, offering everything from simple fare to multicourse dinners. The king of Erythane was known to dine here with his family on occasion, and the idea of inflicting drunken havoc on such a place would have shocked the coarsest dockhand. The Knight's Rest did serve its share of alcoholic beverages, but revelry was confined to the lesser establishments.

When they had all pulled their chairs to the table, Ra-khir gestured the serving maid over to order the meal of the day for everyone, accompanied by mugs of quality ale. Only then, he leaned in to talk, a smile taking over his ruggedly handsome features, a gleam of excitement lighting his green eyes. "I can't remember the last time I've had you all together at the same time or described the treat it's become just to know I've raised three of the finest, most competent young men in all of Midgard. I'm so proud of every one of you."

Subikahn smiled broadly. Tae had shared in his upbringing, of course, but Saviar knew his twin had always appreciated that Ra-khir also considered him an equal son. Calistin tipped his head, far more accustomed to compliments. In the past, they had flowed off of him, too numerous to concern him or to stick. The Renshai tribe considered him the greatest living swordsman, excepting only the immortal Colbey Calistinsson, and even the most reticent found something positive to say about and to him. This time, he was clearly considering the situation and the source.

Saviar had become so focused on earning the approval of his many *torke*, on how he and Subikahn received only grudging "goods" and "that's the ways" compared to the effusive praise heaped upon their brother. Until this moment, it had never occurred to Saviar the much freer and more easily impressed Ra-khir found far less opportunity to spend time with, let alone to commend his youngest, emotionally-stilted son. Saviar even dared to wonder if Calistin had ever craved their father's approval the way Subikahn and Saviar did their mother's. In his youth, Calistin had shown little more than disdain for the Knights of Erythane, their abilities, and their honor. Now, things had clearly changed, and Calistin seemed to actually appreciate the compliment.

The effect on Saviar was not what he expected. He loved his father deeply, had often dreamed of following in his honorable footsteps. He treasured the time they had spent together in his youth, mostly after sneaking away from his sword lessons to silently watch the knights train. Now, Saviar found himself falling prey to the same wariness that had tainted all of his most recent dealings with his father. Ra-khir had called them together for a reason beyond expressing his respect for their achievements, and Saviar had the distinct feeling he was not going to like what his father was about to say.

The server, a tiny woman with long dark hair, brought their drinks, placing a mug in front of each of them. They thanked her as she scurried away to tend to the food.

Ra-khir took a long sip of his drink before speaking. Subikahn and Calistin did the same, but Saviar preferred not to have a mouthful of liquid when his father finally got around to his pronouncement.

Ra-khir did not leave them hanging. He delayed only long enough to swallow and clear his throat before getting to the point. "My sons, I have a question to ask. I don't want any of you to answer right away. I'd like you to take some time to consider and discuss it among yourselves before giving me an answer, no sooner than tonight and, preferably, no later than a month from today. I want you to know if any one of you does not give his consent . . ." He trailed off, apparently finding it harder to make his desires known than he had expected.

Subikahn looked at Saviar, who shrugged. The suspicion he had initially suffered was gradually turning to dread.

"What is it, Papa?" Calistin asked innocently, taking another sip from his mug.

Saviar found his mouth painfully dry and wished he had taken a drink along with the others. By now, he would have swallowed it safely. He had no idea when his father was going to make his point, so he continued to leave his ale untouched.

Ra-khir chewed his lower lip before continuing. "Tiega and I . . . would like your consent to marry."

The words fell like lead on Saviar's heart.

As all three boys met the announcement with silence, Ra-khir continued speaking. "I know it's less than a year since your mother's death, but so much has happened it seems much longer. We love each other and would like to be wed, but we've both agreed we will only do so if all of our children consent. If even one of you is unhappy with our decision, we will defer or abandon it." Ra-khir spoke matter-of-factly, but Saviar suspected he had rehearsed. There was still a note of sadness underlying his words.

Calistin studied his father, as if trying his best to read the emotions there, something he had only recently developed the ability to do. "I think it's—"

Ra-khir stayed him with a raised hand. "Don't tell me, Calistin. Not until you've discussed it with your brothers. Not before tonight, at least."

Subikahn turned his twin a knowing smile. The tone of Calistin's voice had given him away. He clearly had intended to express approval, perhaps even delight, and it seemed singularly weird to Saviar that the most taciturn of the brothers, the one who used to care nothing for the feelings of others, had nearly been the first to sanction a wedding.

At that moment, the server arrived to place steaming plates of shredded lamb with gravy, spiced beets, and boiled greens in front of each of them. She hurried off as the men enjoyed the intertwined aromas of the food. Saviar finally took a sip from his mug, only to find it sitting heavily in his stomach and churning up a nausea that ruined his dinner.

They had eaten mostly in silence, the boys contemplating the situation and Ra-khir avoiding what had to be a nearly irresistible urge to plead his case or, at least, prey on his loving sons' emotions. When they finished, he remained at the inn with his knight companions while the three of them retired to the cottage on the Fields of Wrath that had served as their home their entire lives to discuss their father's request, settling onto their individual cots in their familiar shared bedroom.

Calistin started the discussion, managing to look graceful despite his sprawled position and a sword at either hip. Though he, too, had worn swords his entire life, Saviar still had to adjust them carefully to keep them from twisting awkwardly on his sword belt or poking a hilt into his waist when he sat in anything but a straight-backed chair. "I don't see the problem. Why wouldn't we want Papa to be happy?"

Saviar had a ready answer for the simplistic question. "Happy isn't everything, Calistin. If people only did the things that make them happy, no work would ever get done and we'd be fishing a lot more bloated bodies out of our lakes and rivers. Parents have to say 'no' to their children often. It's what allows them to become useful, productive, and living members of society. Occasionally, grown children have to do the same for a parent who's about to make a terrible mistake."

Subikahn scoffed. "I hardly think Ra-khir marrying a nice and handsome woman will result in sifting corpses out of our drinking water."

Saviar turned his attention to Subikahn, a bit irked that, for the first time, his twin seemed to be taking Calistin's side immediately and without consideration. "I'm not saying it will. I'm just pointing out happiness isn't the primary, and certainly not the only, reason for doing something. We've all done things we thought would make us happy, only to find them miserable. Marriage is a permanent thing, a decision one should never make for the wrong reasons or in haste. How long has Papa really known Tiega? Is he ready for more children?"

"He's always wanted a girl," Subikahn pointed out. "Mama tried, but she never managed to get pregnant again after Calistin."

Saviar knew that but had never given it much consideration. It was a common problem for Renshai women, warriors all.

"Keva's a girl," Calistin pointed out unnecessarily. "She seems nice, and she's still young enough to need parenting."

Saviar said, "I've heard adolescent girls can be extremely difficult."

Subikahn and Calistin exchanged looks, then both started laughing. Saviar flushed.

Subikahn bounced on his cot. "As opposed to raising three male Renshai adolescents? She could be possessed by demons, and it'd still be a joy in comparison."

Saviar could not help smiling, though he tried to bite it back. His brothers had an undeniable point, but he still had an important one, too. "Papa loved Mama so much. And Tiega's so . . . so completely different. How could he possibly settle for someone so . . ." He searched for a word that would describe without condemning. He was not certain the marriage was a good idea, but he had nothing against Tiega Tiego's daughter personally. ". . . meek and mousy."

Again, Calistin laughed. "Compared to Mama, you're meek and mousy."

Those sounded like fighting words. Saviar surged halfway to his feet before he realized both of his brothers were laughing to the brink of gasping. Subikahn stammered out, "Me, too. Me, too!"

Saviar did not join their mirth. "My point's still valid. People tend to love a type, and I don't think Tiega fulfills Papa's."

Calistin spoke next, saying something the old Calistin would never have considered. "Perhaps Mama was the one who wasn't Papa's 'type.'"

Saviar lowered himself to the bed, "What's that supposed to mean?"

Subikahn stepped in to help. "Think about it, Savi. They were younger than we are now when they got married. Not exactly the age for wisest thought. Mama was pregnant, and Papa was a knight-in-training, the very definition of honor. Let's face it; they had no real choice in the matter, at least Papa didn't."

Saviar shook his head with vigor. "None of that matters. They clearly loved each other."

"I'm not denying that. I'm just saying, given a bit more age and experience, had they not been forced to marry so young, they might have found themselves less compatible and decided to end their relationship. Of course, once they actually married, they made the best of things."

Saviar repeated emphatically, "They *clearly* loved each other."

Calistin finally took Saviar's side. "They definitely loved each other. Even I could see that, and I didn't understand or care about those sorts of things until—" He broke off suddenly. He had never told them what had caused the gradual but enormous change in his personality.

Saviar knew, but he wanted to hear it from Calistin, to uncover some details that mystified him. "Until what, Calistin?" He glanced at Subikahn, who bobbed his head wildly in assent. "We'd really like to know."

Calistin looked from one to the other, and Saviar suddenly realized, whatever came out of this meeting regarding their father's potential marriage, it seemed to be bringing the brothers closer than ever, at least in Calistin's case. Saviar had only recently learned their youngest brother had several secrets he had never chosen to share. Subikahn deserved to know them, too.

Calistin seemed about to brush off the request as he had so many times before. Then, he cocked his head and said softly, "Colbey believes you deserve to know . . . things I haven't told anyone else."

The twins pinned identical expressions of encouragement onto their faces. Saviar provided verbal reassurance as well, "They're your secrets, Calistin. If you wish to tell us, we'd appreciate it, and you can bet your life we won't pass them along to anyone else without your consent." Saviar had not even told Subikahn what he learned in the conversation between Frey and Colbey.

Calistin seemed almost relieved to share his burden, "When Mama got bitten by the spirit spider, she was pregnant with me. The demon took my soul instead of hers." Calistin kept his description short and free of emotion, but Saviar easily imagined the agony anyone would feel at the loss of such an integral part of themselves. For a Renshai, or any Northmen, it took away any reason to live, for the attainment of Valhalla was overriding. That Calistin had lived with that knowledge and not shared his pain with anyone made him seem all the more heroic. Saviar felt a stab of guilt he had not made himself more approachable to the brother who had so peeved him in their youth. Even someone painfully annoying should not have to suffer such agony alone.

The twins staring, Calistin continued, "At the end of the Pirate War, Treysind died bravely. When the Valkyrie, Randgrithr, came for his soul, he chose to donate it to me instead." He swallowed hard. "She said I wasn't worthy of it, but she obliged. I wasn't sure whether to bless or curse him. I wanted a soul, but having one, especially one so . . . so different in personality, aroused things in me I'd never felt or even considered before."

Saviar found himself enthralled, considering every aspect of the story. As shocking as such a sacrifice seemed, he knew Treysind had dedicated his life to Calistin with the same fervor Renshai did to swordwork and the attainment of Valhalla, so it did not seem entirely impossible he might donate his eternal soul. Even so, Saviar might not have believed it had Colbey not previously revealed the same information. Saviar had to admit he had known little about Treysind other than he refused to leave Calistin's side and his presence seemed, more than anything, to infuriate Calistin. Now, Saviar wished he had gotten to know the orphaned Erythanian better.

Emboldened by Calistin's unusual forthrightness, Subikahn raised another touchy issue. "Ra-khir has always considered all of us equal sons, even though only one of us shares his bloodline."

That startled Saviar. They had known he and Subikahn had different fathers for as long as he could remember, but he had just recently learned about Calistin and only because Colbey had allowed him to overhear it. Thinking back, he had received a few clues, mostly mysterious comments inserted into unrelated conversations; but the most telling had been Colbey's lethal admonishment not to denigrate Calistin's parentage. What surprised Saviar most was Subikahn's knowledge. He wondered if his twin knew the truth or was surmising and had decided to test Calistin. "Are you trying to say I'm the only real son of Ra-khir and Kevral?"

Calistin turned defensive. "You don't have to share blood to be real. Kevral is mother to all of us, and Ra-khir is my real father, too. I'm not fake or artificial, and neither is he."

Saviar latched onto what he considered pertinent at the moment. "But you admit you don't carry his bloodline?"

Calistin evaded the question. "It's not for me to say."

Subikahn watched Calistin intently, as if concerned his younger brother might attack him. "Think about it, Saviar. Every one of us most closely resembles his grandfather. You're a dead ringer for Knight-Captain Kedrin, and I'm told I look an awful lot like a young Weile Kahn." He added sotto voce, "Assuming he was ever truly young." His volume returned to normal, "Who do you think Calistin looks most like?"

Saviar studied Calistin as if for the first time, seeing nothing new or unusual. Their youngest brother looked most like the stereotypical Renshai: blond, pale eyes, sinewy and younger than his chronological age. Even the claw strikes of the demon had not appeared to change that. "I've always thought he most closely resembles Mama."

"And who did Mama fashion herself after? Not only her look, but her walk, her talk, her fighting style? Whose wisdom was she constantly quoting?"

Saviar rolled his eyes. They all knew. "Colbey, of course."

"Ever seen a drawing of a young Colbey?"

Calistin stiffened.

Saviar considered. He already knew Subikahn had guessed correctly, but the question caught him flat-footed. He had read a significant portion of Béarn's enormous library, at least the part written in the common tongue, and everything he could find on the subject of Renshai. Some of it was illustrated, and many artists had drawn aspects of the legendary Renshai. To his knowledge, none of them was a posed or deliberate portrait, though. "Now that I've met him, I don't think most of the older drawings look much like him, old or young."

"Probably not," Subikahn finally admitted. "But I've always imagined he looked exactly like Calistin. Because he is, in fact, Calistin's blood grandfather."

Calistin and Saviar spoke at once, in nearly identical words, "How could you possibly know that?"

Subikahn did not leave them guessing. "Because my grandfather and my father had their hands in the situation. And, unlike your parents, they were not sworn to lifelong secrecy, although they mostly maintained it in deference to Ra-khir's request and his honor. I put together some of the information based on things I'd heard and learned, and wheedled the rest out of them."

Saviar had to know the details. "Tell me everything."

Subikahn looked at Calistin, who gave him a mortified look. "Later. When we're alone," he promised his twin, then Calistin. "And only with our brother's permission. As you said before, it's his secret."

There was a difference, and he needed to understand it. "Yes, but not one he revealed. You figured this out on your own, and I want to know how."

Subikahn gave his twin this much, "The final piece came from Captain, Saviar. He said after Calistin saved your life on *Svartalfheim*, the Sword of Mitrian, a rusted and crumbling relic of our people, cut through demon flesh like a scythe. I'm hoping Calistin knows the reason why because I'm not leaving this spot until he gives us some sort of explanation."

Saviar tried not to appear nervous as he peered between them. If Calistin did not wish to speak, he would not. If Subikahn pressed too hard, it would result in a battle he could not hope to win.

Calistin uncoiled his legs and unclipped the scabbarded Sword of Mitrian from his belt. "I'm not exactly certain myself, but I've given it a lot of thought. Colbey said a day might come when I earned my immortality and the gems I commissioned for the sword would restore its condition. It has always been my position a man or woman who can't defend himself in battle deserves to die, hopefully with enough courage to attain Valhalla. But, this time, when I saw Saviar fatally menaced, I acted from my heart or, perhaps, my soul rather than reason. It was the first time I felt truly bonded to my acquired soul as a single entity; it became an actual and integral part of me rather than something borrowed from Treysind."

Calistin shook his head, staring at the wall as if through it and a long distance beyond. "I've given it a lot of thought since, and I'm still not certain if that's the detail that explains how I earned my immortality. All I know is the event that was supposed to herald it, the restoration of magic to the ancient sword, happened." He held the sword out to Saviar. "I want you to try it."

Although Saviar already knew Calistin had become immortal, the words could not have shocked him more. The consummate Renshai, Calistin had only once allowed another to touch one of his swords, the one he had granted Subikahn to use in the war. Saviar was uncertain of his brother's purpose and still a bit untrusting of his motives despite the many changes the soul transfer had created. Gaze fixed on Calistin, Saviar accepted it and unsheathed the blade. Instantly, he assessed the balance, finding it no less than perfect, at least as far as he could tell from that simple action. All the pitting and rusting had disappeared. For centuries, the Renshai had kept their artifact as well as time and oil and restorative techniques allowed. Eventually, they had banished it to a case, afraid any touch would cause it to crumble to dust.

Now, the blade looked shiny and perfect, as if newly forged. The hilt, which had grown nearly formless with age was now clearly in the shape of a wolf's head, its once-empty eye sockets filled with glowing amber gems. With the sword in hand, Saviar could feel as well as see its magical aura as a golden light that hummed through his hand and surrounded the steel from its tip to its sculpted edge. He had seen better artwork in his lifetime, but no finer sword. After he had inspected it, Saviar tried a few tentative sweeps and stabs. It did not lead his arm in any way, responding only to his initiated movements, a sword that would do only what he asked but would strike true and remain sharp. It was a sword any Renshai would give all of his worldly possessions for, perhaps even his firstborn child. He wanted to communicate all of these thoughts, but none of them would come. Utterly speechless, he could only make a firm gesture of approval before returning it to its sheath and offering it back to Calistin.

But Calistin made no move to take it. "May I try *Motfrabelon-ning*?"

If anyone else had asked, or even Calistin under any other circumstance, Saviar would have politely but vehemently denied them. Now, he placed the Sword of Mitrian gently on his bed, unclipped *Motfrabelonning*, and handed the scabbarded sword to his youngest brother.

Calistin gave the sword a test similar to the one Saviar had performed, although with infinitely more grace and even more studious examination. Finally, he returned *Motfrabelonning* to its sheath. "Would you be terribly offended if I proposed a trade?"

Far more surprised than insulted, Saviar managed to stammer, "H-huh?"

Calistin explained. "The leader of the Renshai should wield the Sword of Mitrian forever onward."

Saviar started to protest, but he could not find the right words even then. Calistin was right; the Sword of Mitrian was an artifact of the entire tribe. At one time, it made sense for their best swordsman to carry it. However, if the Renshai were to follow a leader, and it seemed politically necessary, the one in charge should have their symbolic treasure. "I'll give it to Thialnir." He added with even more difficulty, "And you should keep *Motfrabelonning*." He felt as if he had just cut off an arm and given it to his brother.

Calistin clearly battled a smile. "To our leader. Thialnir. Right."

Subikahn had no choice but to jump in now. "Calistin, I promised to return this sword to you at the conclusion of the war. I should have given it to you as soon as I got back, but I kept waiting for you to ask." He started to unclip the sword Kevral had willed to Calistin. "Not terribly honorable of me, but then again, honor doesn't exactly run in my bloodline."

Calistin stopped Subikahn with a wave. "No, Subi. I want you to keep it. That way, we all still have swords that can assist against magic."

Everyone but me. Saviar did not voice his bitterness; but, as he had turned down the leadership position, the Sword of Mitrian did not belong to him. He left the sword lying on his bed while his brothers attached or reattached the legacies of Kevral to their belts. Reluctantly, he raised the proper topic of conversation again. "We're supposed to be deciding whether to approve Papa's marriage plans."

Calistin sat back down, shrugging. "I still think we should give him our blessing. The fact that he has promised to abide by our decision shows our opinions matter enough to him to sacrifice his happiness for us. I don't think we should squander that trust when really, legally, and honorably, it's his own choice."

Saviar had had no idea Calistin could speak so eloquently. In the past, he had confined himself to insults and sword training. Nothing else had interested him. Apparently, living with a Knight of Erythane had affected him more than any of them had realized.

Calistin had not finished, "However, I'm leaving for an extended period of time, so I won't have to deal with any consequences. So, if either of you decide not to consent, I won't interfere."

"Where are you going?" Subikahn inquired, and Saviar nodded to indicate he wanted the same answer. Born and raised on the Fields of Wrath, Calistin had shown little desire to leave it, even when his brothers had traveled to the Eastlands to visit Subikahn's father.

"Valira and I are going North with Valr Magnus. He's on a mission to reunite the Renshai with the other tribes of the North, and we've decided to try to help him."

Subikahn's mouth fell open, and Saviar supposed his must have done the same because he again found it difficult to speak. In a matter of moments, though, he managed. "You know you're going to have to overcome many centuries of ingrained and continually reinforced prejudice."

"I've never shied from a challenge," Calistin pointed out, his tone dangerous.

"Agreed," Subikahn said. "At least not from a physical challenge. But this is something entirely different, some would say utterly impossible, and, at least, not something one can win with sword strokes."

"New Calistin," he pointed out. "Freshly immortal and working on gods' time. Besides, I'm sure Colbey will give me some guidance."

Saviar decided not to point out Colbey had not managed the same task in the last two hundred years. It was a noble undertaking and, if it succeeded even a little bit, it was a far cry better than the relationship the Renshai currently had with the North. "I wish you all the best."

"As do I," Subikahn added. "And I suppose I should also butt out of the decision, given I'm also leaving."

Saviar's heart fell. He had only finally just reunited with his twin whom he had believed forever lost and remembered only as a sniveling coward. "You're leaving, too?"

Subikahn made helpless gestures with his hands. "My love has been waiting for me in the East a long time now and has responsibilities there. I have to go back, but I promise to visit soon. Or you can come visit me."

Saviar tried to swallow his anguish. "When are you leaving?"

"Directly after the royal wedding. I'm traveling with my father and whatever entourage goes with him."

It was inevitable, Saviar knew. Subikahn was the only heir to the Eastern throne unless and until Tae chose to marry, which had once seemed unlikely to ever happen. Recalling Tae's words to the misguided teen Renshai, Falinir, on the duplicate world, Saviar now had reason to believe Tae, too, would find his Tiega.

Once again, Saviar's thoughts went to his father's request. Calistin was right that Ra-khir had earned happiness and that Tiega seemed kind and loving. Still, whenever Saviar thought of the two of them together, it felt terribly wrong in a way he could not wholly define. He needed to search his heart for the answer that continued to elude his brain. He had a feeling it dwelt in emotion rather than logic.

Subikahn knew his twin well. "You're still not sure what answer to give?"

Saviar sighed deeply. "I'm having trouble with 'yes,' but I'm not sold on 'no,' either. I need just a bit more time, perhaps some more information."

"What about Keva and Darby?" Calistin suggested.

Something twinged inside Saviar. That made him wonder if Calistin had not hit upon something significant. "What about them?"

"Their mother probably gave them a speech similar to the one Papa gave us. Quite likely, somewhere else at the same time. Maybe if we all got together, we could find out how they feel about the matter. If one of them doesn't want the marriage to happen, the decision is no longer ours."

Saviar remembered Keva's excitement when she first realized Ra-khir and Tiega might start courting. Not only did it seem unlikely she would stand in their way, she might have been the driving force behind the marriage. As for Darby, he already looked to Ra-khir as a father figure, although marriage would change their relationship and not necessarily for the better. Ra-khir had made it clear when Saviar had asked that he did not feel it honorably appropriate for a Knight of Erythane to train his own son as his squire. If Ra-khir married Tiega, Darby would have to apprentice a different knight. At least, Saviar hoped that would prove true.

Saviar suffered a sudden surge of righteous anger. If Ra-khir did not divest himself of Darby as a squire, it would mean he favored Tiega's son over his own, a deep and terrible fear he could barely admit to himself. Saviar vividly remembered the time Ra-khir had berated him for disobedience. Shortly afterward, he had called Darby by Saviar's name and playfully ruffled his hair. That mistake had wounded Saviar to his core, reminding him the closeness between himself and his beloved father was waning, leaving a massive hole, and Darby seemed determined to step into his place.

Saviar caught himself gritting his teeth before he remembered Colbey's treatise on anger once more. It was not a matter of channeling; Darby was the very thing raising his ire. *I was the one supposed to follow in the venerable footsteps of Ra-khir, to stand in his stead once old age claimed him. I wanted his position and his approval more than life itself.*

And, yet, Saviar realized, he had allowed his Renshai training to derail his plans. For most of his life, he had struggled with that dichotomy. To become a competent Renshai meant devoting his life, soul, mind, heart, and honor to its edicts. The Knights of Erythane required equal dedication, and several of their mandates clashed. For so long, he had believed himself capable of both; well-meaning adults, including Ra-khir, Kedrin, and Colbey, had told him for almost two decades he had the ability to accomplish both if he only set his mind to it. Only now, Saviar finally realized to divide one's dedication to two such pure endeavors meant slighting both of them. The time had come to bury one of his dreams or, better yet, to pass it on to someone who could give it the proper time and commitment.

Saviar needed to stop seeing Darby as a rival and, instead, as a kindred soul, perhaps even as a brother. The boy was not stealing Saviar's dream; he was filling the void left by his inability to fulfill it. Ra-khir and Kedrin and Colbey had not lied or misled him. Saviar did have the ability to become a fully competent Renshai or Knight of Erythane, perhaps even both. But he finally knew for certain "both" was never going to happen, not unless the world itself changed in some significant way. And, most importantly, that was for the best. Saviar Ra-khirsson had a destiny as a Renshai. Because of Saviar's own misplaced temper, Thialnir would remain their leader, but Saviar would assist the aging Renshai any way he could.

In that moment, all the rage, all the jealousy and irritation that had plagued Saviar diminished to a trickle. For the first time in months, he felt like no one other than himself. Driven by a sudden desire to make amends to Darby, to pass the mantle of knighthood and embrace him as a brother, Saviar suggested, "I know where Tiega, Darby, and Keva are staying at the Knights' Rest Inn, and I suspect the youngsters are alone right now having a discussion similar to our own." He laughed at the oddity of what he had just said. "Well, probably quite a bit different but initiated by the same decision. What do you say we all go over there and welcome them into the family?"

Calistin and Subikahn exchanged looks, smiled, and nodded. Saviar's twin spoke first, "Just now, I can't think of anything I'd rather do more."

Saviar went to bed with the lightest heart he could remember in a very long time. He fell asleep quickly and slept soundly for several hours before a new concern awakened him, plaguing his mind until he had no choice but to sit up and take stock of the situation. He glanced over to Calistin's bed and, finding his brother also moving restlessly, he rose and tiptoed to the bedside before hissing, "Calistin?"

The youngest brother was up in an instant, free of any binding coverlet and with *Motfrabelonning* in his fist.

Saviar backstepped and raised his empty hands. "Just wanted to talk," he whispered, tipping his head toward the door. "Without waking up Papa and Subi."

Calistin sheathed the sword and nodded, indicating Saviar should go first.

Saviar led the way out the door and wound around a few similar Renshai cottages, stopping at the edge of the woodlands. There, he took a seat on a rotting stump and gestured at the overturned trunk beside it. He and Subikahn had used this particular spot for late-night conversations many times. It allowed a clear view in every direction, including through the trees. He did not believe anyone had ever overheard them there. "I hope I didn't wake you."

Calistin took the indicated seat. "I was having trouble sleeping. I need to talk to you about the Sword of Mitrian."

Saviar made a slight backward motion he suspected Calistin saw. It was the precise issue he had needed to raise. "I wanted to talk about that, too. I was hoping you'd present it to Thialnir instead of me. I don't want to take the credit for revitalizing it when I had nothing to do with it. It's your story to tell, your achievement."

Calistin chuckled. "Right subject, wrong problem. I was hoping I could convince you not to tell Thialnir how the revitalization happened, to keep me out of it."

Saviar stared for a moment before speaking again. "But it's a momentous accomplishment. I couldn't possibly take credit for it; I couldn't live with myself. And you should want to, Calistin."

Calistin placed his elbows on his thighs, folded his hands and lowered his chin to his knuckles. "I can't, Savi. Please. I've only just discovered I enjoy the company of people, that I can communicate with them in other ways than besting them in spar or killing them in battle. I have a girl I like a lot." He lifted his head and spread his fingers. "Look at me, Savi. I'm a man in a child's body. If the other Renshai discover my immortality, my life is over before it's truly begun."

Saviar did not understand. He studied his brother with beetled brows, seeing the master swordsman beneath the youthful exterior. Despite his features, no Renshai ever saw Calistin as a boy, not even when he had been one, before he passed his tests of manhood at thirteen. Now, Saviar also saw the resemblance to Colbey that Subikahn had mentioned. He wondered if he could ever look at his youngest brother the same way again.

"Colbey says once my situation becomes common knowledge, the gods will forbid my interaction with mortals except on rare occasions and on their terms. He holds dear the eighty-odd years during which even he believed himself entirely mortal. He had the chance to hone his skills, to learn some he would never have had the opportunity to experience had the gods claimed him early. He became the world's best swordsman, a Cardinal Wizard, even a Knight of Erythane for all the gods' sake. He had endless chances to die in battle, to earn the blessed eternity that is Valhalla, the missing of which he regrets to this day."

Saviar doubted that last comment. He had to believe the immortal Renshai could visit Valhalla on a whim and battle the *Einherjar*, at least the Renshai ones, whenever he pleased. Still, Calistin had an undeniable point. If word of his immortality spread, and it surely would if the tribe got wind of it, the gods might take him from the world of mortals from fear his actions might upset the balance.

Calistin's tone turned pleading. "I'm only just learning what it's like to have a soul, a girl, a purpose in life beyond dying. I believe in Valr Magnus' cause, in the possibility of bringing peace between Renshai and Northerners, maybe even joining them as allies someday. It will take a long time, but I have plenty of it, unless you or Subikahn reveals me."

Saviar knew the history of Colbey Calistinsson, how he had roamed the earth seeking death in battle, like all Northmen, despairing as it eluded him for so many decades. He had accomplished so much on Midgard, not always making it better but trying his best in his own inimitable, Renshai way. He had lived in a far more magical time, when Wizards had maintained the great balance between good and evil, before the gods had dared to allow chaos to exist on Midgard. But magic was chaos, and the mere presence of the Wizards had assured its arrival. Colbey had championed it or, rather, its opposite, and the world had not crumbled into ruin. If Colbey could remain on man's world without destroying it for so long, Calistin could surely do the same with no more magic than *Motfrabelonning*.

Of course, the world existed in cycles. With the elves and mages working together and the *Kjempemagiska* becoming continental allies, magic might rise again. It would not come quickly, not within Saviar's lifetime, but surely within Calistin's. By then, however, the gods would have plenty of time to discover his immortality, to notice if he did something earth-threatening or -shattering. Saviar also suspected Colbey would keep a close eye on his progeny, and probably Frey also.

Calistin continued, "It's not a certainty the gods will claim me as a ward. They might just choose to kill me or even to ignore me until I actually do something that threatens to tip the balance. In any event, I want to accomplish something bigger on the mortal world than just having gods' blood in my veins. Promise me you won't tell Thialnir or anyone else. And you'll do your best to keep Subikahn quiet as well."

Saviar did not have to think long. He knew Calistin regretted revealing the information, not realizing Colbey had already done so. He still operated on a level more immature than his years.

"I promise," Saviar said easily. He did not need to say more. Even Calistin knew how seriously he took his honor and his vows. "But what do I tell Thialnir? He's not going to believe a sword that's been decaying for centuries spontaneously healed itself."

"I know." Calistin looked askance at his brother. "You're the one with diplomatic experience." He tried to help. "Perhaps you could say Sif and Modi came to you in a dream and fixed it."

Saviar did not like that idea. Sif and Modi were the gods of Renshai, and lying in their names felt too much like blasphemy. "You know I don't lie."

The color drained from Calistin's face. "If you're going to become the leader of a hated band of people, dealing with friends and enemies alike, you're going to have to learn deception, Saviar."

Saviar had not expected such conjecture from Calistin, but he supposed his brother had a point. When he had believed himself a future knight at a tender age, he had adopted their extraordinary sense of honor. He still thought it the best and most ethical way to live, but he supposed he truly would have to learn to pick and choose his phraseology and what information he chose to share when handling diplomatic situations. Then, suddenly, he realized Calistin had manipulated him. "You're still talking as if I'm the leader of the Renshai when it's Thialnir. You even had me believing it for a moment. I turned down the position, remember?" A wave of guilt passed through him. At the time, he had been thinking solely of himself. Thialnir had never wanted the position, had reveled in the opportunity to pass the mantle to someone more suitable, only to have Saviar publicly humiliate him by shoving it back into the old man's face. He owed Thialnir a most humble apology.

Calistin shrugged. "Thialnir still depends on you to deal with treaties and tricky situations."

It was true, and Saviar had considered that exact thing moments earlier. He had learned a lot from joining the leader of the Renshai in various situations and negotiations. He had absorbed even more from watching Weile Kahn. It occurred to him that, despite Weile's crooked reputation, Saviar had never heard him lie. He could convey more with a well-timed silence than most could with a flowery speech. "Several people saw you wielding the Sword of Mitrian in the war, and they also know you've interacted with Colbey. I don't think anyone besides us knows the details. I could imply the gemstones currently in the eye sockets are the ones Colbey put there before the war and he's allowed us to keep them. Then I can truthfully say you surrendered the sword to Thialnir because you felt our leader should be the one to have it."

Saviar gave Calistin a significant look. He hoped his brother would realize the sword trade was not exactly fair, as it had left Saviar without a magical blade of his own. Swords long-carried, used, and important to Colbey eventually developed magical properties, and Saviar believed the same would prove true of Calistin. He did not really need *Motfrabelonning*.

But if Calistin had similar thoughts, he did not reveal them. "That works. It's practically the truth, doesn't change anything as far as the Renshai are concerned, and maintains my confidentiality. No wonder Thialnir relies on you."

It all seemed remarkably obvious and straightforward to Saviar, but he accepted the first compliment he could ever remember receiving from Calistin. The decision seemed comfortable and right. The Sword of Mitrian had returned from oblivion because of the actions of an immortal Renshai. The fact that it was Calistin rather than Colbey would not harm the legend or the tribe in any way.

All that remained was to place it in the hands of the rightful leader of the Renshai.

The following morning, the Fields of Wrath were alive with the familiar rasp and ring of swordplay. The first snowflakes of winter fell sparsely, each catching the sunlight and sparkling like a falling jewel. The land belonging to the Renshai, from wide open spaces to the areas between cottages to cluttered storage to forest, was alive with spars and lessons and *svergelse*. Men and women participated, ignoring the jobs other cities and towns took for granted. No one pounded an anvil, no one dug up the last of the harvest, no one placed gemstones into intricate settings. Everything they needed, the Renshai bought with the money they earned as soldiers or protectors or bodyguards to the heirs of Béarn.

Saviar had given the Sword of Mitrian to Thialnir that morning with a short explanation that did not require an outright lie but protected Calistin. In the many hours since, Thialnir had studied it from every angle, had swung it repeatedly, had practiced a myriad of maneuvers and participated in several spars. It captivated him utterly, absorbing his attention to the point where Saviar found it impossible to snatch a moment of it. Instead, he had practiced and sparred and performed *svergelse* on his own. The morning had dawned cold, and he was underdressed, but the effort of a full day of exertion had kept him warm enough he did not notice the chill until he stopped near sundown to grab some dinner at the family cottage.

Saviar found himself eating alone, and it occurred to him how strangely quiet it would seem after Subikahn and Calistin had gone, leaving only himself and Ra-khir to occupy it until the wedding with Tiega. They had scheduled that a few weeks after the new king's, when the celebrations had died down and the people returned to their normal schedules. From that time on, their cottage would once more hold a woman, Darby would take over Subikahn's sleeping pallet, and they would find a way to divide the room to give Keva sufficient privacy on Calistin's cot.

Saviar realized he was the only member of his family who had not moved on, and yet his circumstances felt strangely right. He belonged on the Fields of Wrath. It felt natural, proper, the way the gods had always intended. The entire tribe considered Calistin the quintessential Renshai, but Saviar abruptly understood he fit the picture better: wedded to his sword and to his tribe, dedicated to earning Valhalla, but also imperfect and needful in ways a man as talented as Calistin could never be. In his youth, Saviar had wanted everything; in his adulthood, he had found what really mattered.

Thialnir approached Saviar at the family's table, a hunk of parchment clutched in his fist. He had to clear his throat at least twice before Saviar noticed him, so thoroughly engrossed in thought was he. "I hope it's all right I came inside. You didn't answer my knock."

Saviar rose in deference, gesturing toward the table for Thialnir to sit. "I'm so sorry. I can't believe I dropped my guard that badly." Saviar doubted an enemy could have drawn so close; the ever-alert portion of his mind had clearly identified Thialnir and dismissed him as harmless. "You know you're *always* welcome. I just didn't hear you." He looked around the empty cabin. "Can I get you something to eat?" His own meal had consisted of cold jerked meat and dried, roasted seeds. Kevral had rarely cooked, Ra-khir had grabbed most of his late evening meals at the Knight's Rest, and the boys had become accustomed to helping themselves to basic necessities from the Renshai's stores that required no preparation.

Thialnir chose the seat across the table from Saviar. "I've already eaten," he said, to Saviar's relief. To his knowledge, there was nothing edible in the house, so they would have had to go fetch something and, possibly, cook it. "I was hoping you'd take a look at this. It's weeks old and no longer in effect, but it's been bothering me. I can't figure it out."

"Of course." Saviar reached for the parchment scrap, then spread it over the table. It was a scrawled copy, in Thialnir's hand, of what appeared to be the last page of a contract.

Saviar started reading aloud. "Parties further agree—"

Thialnir interrupted. "Just the last paragraph."

Saviar began again, in the indicated spot. "This accord agreed to and signed by the legal representatives of the entire Northlands, Eastlands, Westlands, and the Renshai this seventeenth day of the month of Engen—"

Thialnir jumped in again. "I got it the day you . . . well, when you wouldn't . . ." He sighed. "When you left me in Béarn."

"About that." Saviar studied his hands. "I owe you an apology for—"

Thialnir talked over him. "I kept reading and rereading, but you know how little sense these legal documents make to me. Then, Weile came looking for you. He crossed out the words 'and the Renshai,' nothing else in the entire blasted thing, and told me to sign it."

Saviar took another look at the parchment. "Did you do it?"

Saviar could feel Thialnir's attention steadily on him. "I didn't know what else to do. Was I right to trust him?"

Saviar finally met his leader's gaze. "I don't always like Weile's advice, but I've never known him to be wrong. Of course, right and wrong are relative states. Did it cause any trouble?"

"No." Thialnir tented his fingers on the table. "It didn't seem to make any difference at all, and as I said, the terms of the contract have expired, so it no longer matters." He looked askance at Saviar. "Since then, though, I've been trying to puzzle out his reasoning. All I can come up with is he found a way for me to sign the document without actually binding us to anything."

Saviar picked up the parchment and held it close to his eyes, as if the answer might leap out at him. He did not believe Thialnir's interpretation the correct one, mostly because it relied on every other party to the contract being either blind or stupid or choosing not to read Thialnir's copy. Apparently, if King Griff or any of his Council had questioned the validity of it, Weile had handled the answer rather than allowing it to come back to the old Renshai. "When did this contract come about, and do you remember its purpose?" Not having the entire document limited Saviar severely.

Thialnir nodded. "It was right after the first rescue, the one that brought home only elves. Captain had requested a two-week extension to try to bring together all the magical beings so we didn't leave humans on the Outworlds. The Council insisted on codifying everyone's agreement to the delay. As usual, it consisted of endless pages of flowery words."

Saviar looked again at the piece of crumpled parchment. ". . . signed by the legal representatives of the entire Northlands, Eastlands, Westlands, and the Renshai . . ." He read it the other way, ". . . signed by the legal representatives of the entire Northlands, Eastlands and Westlands . . ." Saviar started to laugh.

Thialnir grabbed Saviar's hands, still on the parchment. "What? Tell me."

Saviar explained, "Weile wasn't trying to get the Renshai out of the contract. Why would he do that? It was an unimportant, temporary little thing with a set expiration. Weile was simply pointing out the redundancy."

Thialnir tipped his head. "Redundancy?"

Saviar chuckled again. "By definition, the Fields of Wrath are part of Béarn, so the Renshai are citizens of the Westlands. Furthermore, we're still, technically, one of the Northern tribes. Magnus pointed that out when we chose the members of the rescue team and he allowed me to represent them. So, it's a double redundancy since we could also be included in the phrase 'entire Northlands.' Either way, 'and the Renshai' was an entirely unnecessary phrase." He handed the parchment back to Thialnir.

"That's it?" Thialnir sounded disappointed.

"That's it," Saviar agreed, "but it's actually a significant distinction because it's gotten Griff, the Council and us thinking, at the least. I'll bet they had a secret meeting, without you, just to puzzle out why you did it. It wouldn't surprise me to learn Valr Magnus took his cue from their discussion, the very reason he allowed me to represent the North." Saviar's mind drifted back to that moment in the great hall when everyone, even the Northmen, had risen and cheered. Suddenly, Calistin's and Valira's mission did not seem quite so grim.

Thialnir shook his head. Air hissed through his teeth, this time in admiration. "All this from crossing three words out of the last paragraph of a multipage document that had absolutely nothing to do with . . . it."

"Yes," Saviar acknowledged. He sat back, once again. "Weile Kahn is a wise man, Thialnir." He knew most kings would resist any type of alliance with a leader of criminals, would vehemently deny dealing with the man or anyone he represented. For the Renshai, however, he had proven a valuable ally time and time again. "And I believe the Renshai should maintain a positive relationship with him for as long as he allows it."

Thialnir nodded thoughtfully, his mind clearly on Saviar's words, but his gaze locked on the sheathed Sword of Mitrian. His lips bowed into a smile.

A warm feeling bathed Saviar as he realized the sword had found its rightful place with a man who had given so much for his tribe and his people. Thialnir may not have wanted the thankless position as leader of Renshai, but he had accepted it and dedicated his life to it for so many years without any consideration for payment or reward. That he had mulled over what must have seemed a tiny thing for so long made it clear he always gave his best. *Wield it with pride, old man. Long live the leader of the Renshai.*

Finally, the apology poured out, "I'm sorry, Thialnir. I treated you abominably when you deserved nothing but respect and admiration. My only explanation is I was wrestling with several weighty issues and did not have the wisdom or experience to handle them properly. It's not a fair reason, but it's the only one I have."

Thialnir could have reacted in any of a hundred ways, all of them appropriate to the situation. Not long ago, violence would surely have ensued, most probably a vicious spar that would leave them both winded and aching but with a fresh perspective, understanding and appreciation for one another. But Thialnir, too, had matured. He said only, "And now, Saviar?"

"Now." Saviar considered. "Now, Thialnir, I am finally at peace."

The following morning, Thialnir clambered onto the roof of a designated cottage in the center of town, crashing his other sword repeatedly against a mounted bell to command attention. Soon, Renshai throughout the Fields of Wrath ceased their sword work and gathered beneath him, many clapping their swords ringingly together in time with the bell, others shouting or stomping booted feet to protect the valuable edges of their blades. At length, Thialnir sheathed his weapon, raised his hands, and looked out over the group.

Saviar watched Thialnir curiously. The bell had been mounted many years ago in case of a major event requiring every Renshai ear. Children, including himself, often climbed to the rooftop just to show they could; a few even dared to hit the bell once or twice in a show of courage or defiance. Saviar could only recall a single time when anyone had used it as a real call to order: when his own mother had died in single combat with Valr Magnus, banishing the Renshai from the Fields of Wrath.

As the crowd quieted, Thialnir raised the Sword of Mitrian so nearly everyone could see it. "Behold! The Sword of Mitrian, the ancient symbol of our people, is whole and useful once again."

Most had already seen it the previous day, when Thialnir used it in a thousand *svergelse*, had sparred everyone who accepted his challenge. Still, at the official pronouncement, gasps of awe ran through the crowd in addition to cheers that echoed from every wall, every tree trunk, every rooftop.

Thialnir sheathed the sword, raised his hands, and silence fell over the Renshai. "Many of you know Colbey placed fresh magic into the gemstone eyes and gave the sword to our champion, Calistin, so he would have a sword that could strike our enemies during the war."

The statement was entirely true, though it missed a chunk of information that might remain forever lost to history. Saviar thought back to the shuffle of weapons between himself and his brothers. At the time of her death, Kevral had given him *Motfrabelonning* and Calistin the unnamed sword Subikahn now carried. Only one son of Kevral had been left without a magical weapon, she had only the two, and Subikahn had never once complained, though it surely must have bothered him. Now, Saviar was the odd man out, and he expected to suffer pangs of wistfulness, at least. Yet, oddly, he did not. He felt only a dim certainty all was right with the world.

More cheers erupted, then died to allow Thialnir to finish.

"Colbey and Calistin have decided it's in the best interests of our people for whoever leads us to wield this ancient, magical weapon. If anyone here feels I do not deserve this honor, you must speak now. Silence will be taken as assent."

The assemblage grew deathly still, as if some demon had stolen the breath from every Renshai at once. Saviar expected someone to challenge, if only for the opportunity to prove his or her superiority. Thialnir was a talented warrior with a lot of experience, but there were Renshai even more skilled than he. However, after several moments, it became clear no Renshai would contest the edict. The Sword of Mitrian belonged to Thialnir Thrudazisson.

More shouts rose to the heavens from every corner of the Fields of Wrath, only then followed by a chorus of people who wished to spar Thialnir, to pit their weapons against the great sword if only for the chance to have it touch their own blades as if in blessing.

Thialnir raised his hands once again. When the roar dulled, he said, "Now that we have agreed the designated leader of the Renshai will forever wield this venerated weapon, I would like to start a brand-new tradition: the passing of the Sword of Mitrian to the next great leader of our people."

This time, the silence grew so thick, a knife might have cut it. Saviar's heart started to pound as he watched Thialnir glance over the crowd, his eyes finally alighting on Saviar. He gestured the young man to him.

From his childhood exploits, Saviar knew the easiest and hardest places to scale the plank wall to the doubly reinforced thatch of the communal building. In moments, he had joined Thialnir on the rooftop, the crowd below them quiet. Some of them had been present the last time Thialnir had tried to pass the mantle, when Saviar had refused it. There was barely a sound below him, the scuffle of boots, a few whispers, the rustle of leaves in the winter wind. It occurred to

Saviar he was the only one surprised by the announcement, the only one who had not seen it coming, at least not so soon. So many people of significance: Weile Kahn, Calistin, Colbey, Thialnir himself had acted more as if Saviar had accepted the position the first time, despite a refusal that could only be described as rude.

In a display nearly as grand as a Knight of Erythane, Thialnir bowed, unclipped the Sword of Mitrian from his belt, and laid it across his palms, offering it to Saviar.

If possible, the crowd grew even more silent, straining to hear the words Thialnir spoke to Saviar. Surely, they expected ones every bit as grand as the gesture; but only Saviar was close enough to hear Thialnir whisper, "Take it, damn you, or I'll strike your stupid head from your even stupider shoulders."

Saviar did not allow himself a smile. With a formal bow actually taught to him by a Knight of Erythane, he plucked the weapon from Thialnir's outstretched hands and fastened it to his sword belt. He spoke loudly enough for all to hear, as if in answer to Thialnir's mumbled words, "I accept the position for as long as I serve well and the Renshai will have me do so. No man has ever been more honored."

Saviar suspected they could hear the cheering all the way back to Béarn Castle.

Appendices

Author's Note: For this last book of the Renshai, I have added a pronunciation key. This will change some pronunciation markings from previous editions but should make things simpler and more consistent.

Pronunciation Key for Vowels

Key	As In	Example
aa	relax	rih-LAAKS
ay	relate	rih-LAYT
ah	father	FAH-thuhr
aw	talk	TAWK
eh	medicine	MEH-dih-sihn
ee	oleander	oh-lee-AAN-duhr
er	lurk	LERK
ih	wish	WIHSH
iy	giant	JIY-ehnt
oh	bone	BOHN
oi	destroy	dih-STROI

Key	As In	Example
oo	balloon	buh-LOON
ow	bounty	BOWN-tee
uh	monotony	muh-NAH-tuh-nee

Pronunciation Key for Consonants

Key	As In	Example
b	borrow	BAH-roh
ch	chase	CHAYS
d	binder	BIYN-der
f	filter, rough	FIHL-ter
g	going	GOH-eeng
h	heaven	HEH-vihn
j	journey	JUHR-nee
k	cake	KAYK
/k/	Chanukah	/K/ahn-oo-kah
l	rally	RAA-lee
m	movement	MOOV-mehnt
n	never	NEHV-uhr
ng	nothing	NUH-thihng
p	purple	PER-puhl
r	river	RIH-ver
s	salivate	SAAL-ih-vayt

Key	As In	Example
sh	machine	muh-SHEEN
t	tatter	TAA-ter
th	thought	THAWT
t/h	this	T/HIHS
v	vote	VOHT
w	wading	WAY-dihng
wh	which	WHIHCH
y	younger	YUHNG-er
z	zipper	ZIH-per
zh	revision	ree-VIHYzhuhn

WESTERNERS

Béarnides

Aerean (AYR-ee-ehn): Minister of Internal Affairs
Angus (AANG-uhs): a nobleman (deceased)
Aranal (Ahr-ehn-AWL): a former king (deceased)
Aron (AHR-ihn): the current Sage
Arturo (Ahr-TOOR-oh): a prince; second child of Matrinka
Barrindar (BAA-rihn-dahr): a prince; first child of Griff and Xoraida
Calitha (Kuh-LEE-thuh): a princess; second child of Griff and Xoraida
Chaveeshia (Shuh-VEE-shuh): Minister of Local Affairs
Davian (DAY-vee-ihn): Prime Minister
Eldorin (Ehl-DOIR-ihn): a princess; third child of Griff and Xoraida
Franstaine (FRAAN-stayn): Minister of Household Affairs; in-law uncle of Helana
Galastad (GAAL-uh-staad): highest ranking infantry officer; a captain of the army
Griff (GRIHF): the king

Halika (Huh-LEE-kuh): a princess; third child of Matrinka

Helana (Hell-AHN-uh): Griff's mother; Petrostan's wife

Ivana Shorith'na Cha-tella Tir Hya'sellirian Albar (Ee-VAH-nuh Shohr-IHTH-nuh Shah-TEHL-uh TEER Hiy-uh-sehl-EER-ee-uhn AAL-bahr): a princess; half-elfin, only child of Griff and Tem'aree'ay (see Outworlders)

Jhirban (JEER-bahn): captain of the flagship Seven (deceased)

Kohleran (KAH-ler-ihn): a previous king of Béarn (deceased); Matrinka's and Griff's grandfather

Lazwald (LAHZ-wahld): a guardsman

Marisole (MAA-rih-sahl): a princess; first child of Matrinka; the Bard's heir

Marstat (MAHR-staat): a blacksmith

Matrinka (Muh-TRIHNK-uh): the queen; Griff's senior wife; mother of Marisole, Arturo, and Halika

Molo (MOH-loh): the weaponsmaster

Morhane (MOHR-hayn): an ancient king who usurped the throne from his twin brother, Valar

Myrenex (Miy-RIHN-ihks): a former king (deceased)

Nomalan (NOH-mah-lahn): a young noble

Petrostan (Peh-TRAAS-tihn): King Kohleran's youngest son; Griff's father (deceased)

Richar (REE-shahr): Minister of Foreign Affairs

Ruther (RUH-ther): a guardsman

The Sage: chronicler and keeper of Béarn's history and tomes

Saxanar (SAAX-uh-nahr): Minister of Courtroom Procedure and Affairs

Seiryn (SAYR-ihn): captain of the guards

Sterrane (Ster-RAYN): best-known ancient king (deceased)

Talamaine (TAAL-uh-mayn): Matrinka's father (deceased)

Valar (VAY-laar): Morhane's twin borther; Sterrane's father; a previous king murdered during his reign

Walfron (WAHL-frahn): supervisor of the kitchen staff

Xanranis (Zaan-RAAN-ihs): Sterrane's son; a former king (deceased)

Xoraida (Zohr-AY-duh): Griff's junior wife (third); mother of Barrindar, Calitha, and Eldorin

Yvalane (IHV-uh-layn): Kohleran's father; a previous king (deceased)

Zapara (Zuh-PAAR-uh): a guard

Zaysharn (ZAY-shahrn): Overseer of the Caretakers of Livestock, Gardens, and Food

Zelshia (ZEHL-shuh): a head maid
Zoenya (Zoh-EHN-yuh): a previous queen (deceased)

Erythanians

Alquantae (Aal-KWAHN-tay): a knight
Arduwyn (AHR-dwihn): a legendary archer and friend of King Sterrane (deceased)
Arner (AHR-ner): Perry's father
Aromay (AAR-oh-may): a knight
Ashtonik (Aash-TAH-nihk): a knight (deceased)
Avra (AHV-rah): a street tough
Braison (BRAY-suhn): a knight
Callan (CAA-lihn): a captain of palace guards
Castillon (CAHS-tee-ahn): a knight
Edwin (EHD-wihn): a knight; the armsman
Esatoric (ee-sah-TOHR-ihk): a knight (deceased)
Eshwin (EHSH-wihn): a horse breeder; Tirro's neighbor
Frendon (FREHN-dihn): interrupted battle between Kevral and Valr Magnus by jumping from a tree (deceased)
Garvin (GAHR-vihn): a knight (deceased)
Georan (JOHR-ihn): brother to Harveki; uncle to Frendon
Hansah (HAHN-suh): ranking lieutenant over infantry and regular cavalry
Harritin (HAHR-ih-tihn): a knight (deceased)
Harveki (Hahr-VEH-kee): father of Frendon; brother of Georan (deceased)
Humbert (HUHM-bert): crown prince; Humfreet's son
Humfreet (HUHM-freet): the king
Jakrusan (Jah-KROO-sihn): a knight
Kedrin (KEH-drihn): captain of the knights; Ra-khir's father
Khirwith (KEER-wihth): Ra-khir's stepfather (deceased)
Kovian (KOH-vee-ihn): a knight
Lakamorn (LAAK-uh-mohrn): a knight
Leicinder (Liy-SIHN-der): a knight
Liamar Carl's son (LEE-uh-mahr): a scribe; Myrjela's husband
Mandell (Mahn-DEHL): a palace guard
Myrjela Hyamis' daughter (Meer-HEHL-uh): Liamar's wife
Netan (NAYT-ehn): a palace guard
Oridan (OHR-ih-dehn): Shavasiay's father
Parmille (Pahr-MEEL): a street tough
Perry (PEH-ree): a spokesman for the Paradisians

Petrone (Peh-TROHN): a knight (deceased)

Ra-khir (Rah-KEER): a knight; Kedrin's son; father of Saviar and Calistin (see Renshai)

Ramytan (RAAM-ih-tihn): Kedrin's father (deceased)

Rayvonn (RAY-vahn): a soldier

Shavasiay (Shah-VAHS-ee-ay): a knight

Tellbastian (Tehl-BAAS-chihn): a knight

Thessilius (T/heh-SEEL-ee-uhs): a knight (deceased)

Tirro (TEER-oh): a farmer; Eshwin's neighbor

Treysind (TRAY-sihnd): an orphan (deceased)

Vellassir (Vehl-uh-SEER): a knight

Vincelin (VIHN-suhl-ihn): a knight

Yoneté (Yoh-nuh-TAY): a knight

Pudarians

Alenna (Aa-LEHN-uh): Prince Leondis' wife; mother of second Severin

Boshkin (BAHSH-kihn): Prince Leondis' steward and adviser

Cenna (SEH-nuh): an ancient queen (deceased)

Chethid (CHEHTH-ihd): one of three lieutenants

Cymion (KIY-mee-ahn): the king

Daizar (DIY-zahr): Minister of Visiting Dignitaries

Darian (DAYR-ee-uhn): one of three lieutenants

Darris (DAYR-ihs): the Bard; Linndar's son; blood-father of Marisole, Arturo, and Halika (see Béarnides)

DeShane (Dih-SHAYN): a captain of the guards

Eudora (Yoo-DOHR-uh): the late queen; Severin and Leondis' mother (deceased)

Harlton (HAAR-uhl-tuhn): a captain of the guards

Horatiannon (Hohr-ay-shee-AH-nuhn): an ancient king (deceased)

Jahiran (Jah-HEER-ihn): the first Bard (deceased); initiated the bardic curse

Javonzir (Juh-VAHN-zeer): the king's cousin and adviser

Larrin (LAAR-ihn): a captain of the guards

Leondis (Lee-AHN-dihs): the crown prince; second son of Cymion and Eudora

Linndar (LIHN-dahr): a previous bard; Darris' mother (deceased)

Mar Lon (MAHR-LAHN): a previous bard in the age of King Sterrane (deceased)

Markanyin (Mahr-KAAN-yihn): the general of the army

Nellkoris (Nehl-KOHR-ihs): one of three lieutenants

Severin (SEH-vrihn): first son of Cymion and Eudora; previous heir
  to the throne (deceased)
Severin (SEH-vrihn): Leondis' son; named for his deceased uncle
Tonaris (Toh-NAHR-ihs): a competent surgeon

Renshai

Alvida (Aal-VEE-duh): a young woman
Arsvid (AHRS-vihd): a man
Ashavir (AH-shuh-veer): a boy
Asmiri (Aaz-MEER-ee): a guardian of Prince Barrindar
Calistin the Bold (Kuh-LEES-tihn): Colbey's father (deceased)
Calistin Ra-khirsson (Kuh-LEES-tihn): youngest son of Ra-khir and
  Kevral
Colbey Calistinsson (KUHL-bay): legendary immortal Renshai now
  living among the gods
Elbirine (Ehl-ber-EE-neh): a guardian of Princess Halika; trained
  with Kevral
Emmissonr (Ehm-ih-SAHN-er): a woman
Episte Rachesson (Eh-PIHS-teh): an orphan raised by Colbey; later
  killed by Colbey after being driven mad by chaos
Erlse (ERL-seh): a man
Gareth Lasirsson (GAAR-ihth): tested the worthiness of Ra-khir
  and Tae to sire Renshai; Kristel's father
Falinir (FOWL-ihn-eer): a 16-year-old, male Renshai who has not
  yet passed the tests of manhood
Gaelina (Gay-ehl-EE-nah): Warradon's girlfriend; Falinir's crush
Gazzinal (GAAZ-ihn-ahl): a man
Gunnhar (GUHN-her): a guardian of Arturo (deceased)
Kevralyn Balmirsdatter (KEHV-ruh-lihn): Kevralyn Tainharsdat-
  ter's namesake (deceased)
Kevralyn Tainharsdatter (KEHV-ruh-lihn): aka Kevral; Ra-khir's
  wife; mother of Saviar, Subikahn, and Calistin (deceased)
Kwavirse (Kwah-VEER-seh): a man
Kristel Garethsdatter (KRIHS-tuhl): a previous guardian of Queen
  Matrinka
Kyndig (KAWN-dee): another name for Colbey Calistinsson; "Skilled
  One"
Kyntiri (Kawn-TEER-ee): a torke of Saviar and Subikahn
Mitrian Santagithisdatter (MIH-tree-ihn): foremother of the tribe of
  Tannin; Santagithi's daughter (deceased)
Modrey (MOH-dray): forefather of the tribe of Modrey (deceased)

Navali (Nuh-VAWL-ee): a torke

Nirvina (Ner-VEE-nah): a torke of Saviar

Nisse Nelsdatter (NEE-seh): a previous guardian of Queen Matrinka

Pseubicon (SOO-bih-kahn): an ancient Renshai; half-barbarian by blood (deceased)

Rache Garnsson (RAAK-ee): forefather of the tribe of Rache; son of Mitrian (deceased)

Rache Kallmirsson (RAAK-ee): Rache Garnsson's namesake; Episte's father (deceased)

Randil (Raan-DEEL): father of Tarah and Tannin (deceased)

Ranilda Battlemad (Raan-HEEL-duh): Colbey's mother (deceased)

Rantire Ulfinsdatter (Raan-TEER-ee): Griff's bodyguard in Darris' absence; a dedicated guardian

Raska "Ravn" Colbeysson (RAAS-kuh; RAY-vihn): only son of Colbey and Freya

Saviar Ra-khirsson (SAAV-ee-ahr): first son of Ra-khir and Kevral; Subikahn's twin

Sitari (Sih-TAHR-ee): Calistin's secret crush (deceased)

Subikahn Taesson (SOO-bih-kahn): only son of Tae and Kevral; Saviar's twin

Sylva (SIHL-vuh): foremother of the tribe of Rache; an Erythanian; daughter of Arduwyn (deceased)

Tainhar (TAYN-hahr): Kevral's father (deceased)

Talamir Edminsson (TAHL-uh-meer): a torke of Subikahn and his lover

Tanvard (TAAN-vayrd): a man

Tarah Randilsdatter (TAYR-uh): foremother of the tribe of Modrey; sister of Tannin (deceased)

Tannin Randilsson (TAAN-ihn): forefather of the tribe of Tannin; Tarah's brother; Mitrian's husband (deceased)

Thialnir Thrudazisson (Thee-AHL-neer): the chieftain

Trygg (TRIHG): a guardian of Arturo (deceased)

Tygbiar (TIHG-beer): a man; veteran warrior

Ulfin (OHL-fin): Rantire's father (deceased)

Valira Elforsdatter (Vuh-LEER-uh): a young woman

Warradon (WOHR-aa-dahn): Gaelina's boyfriend

Santagithians

Herwin (HER-wihn): King Griff's stepfather

Mitrian (MIH-tree-ihn): Santagithi's daughter (see Renshai) (deceased)

Santagithi (Saan-TAAG-ih-thiy): legendary general for whom the town was named; main strategist of the Great War (deceased)

Sutton (SUHT-ihn): general of the army; current leader

Mages of Myrcidë

Arinosta (Ayr-ih-NAHS-tuh): an elderly woman

Archille (Ahr-KEE-lee): a man

Blenford (BLEHN-fohrd): a man

Chestinar (CHEHS-tihn-ahr): a sickly man

Chymmerlee (KIHM-er-lee): a young woman

Dilphin (DIHL-fihn): a man

Eldebar (EHL-dih-bahr): older man

Giddion (GIHD-ee-ihn): a middle-aged man

Hevnard (HEHV-nahrd): a middle-aged man

Janecos (JAAN-ih-kohs): a middle-aged woman

Jeremilan (Jeh-rih-MIY-lehn): the leader

Lycros (LIY-krohs): a man

Netheron (NEH-t/her-ahn): a middle-aged man

Paultan (PAWL-tihn): a man

Roby (ROH-bee): an elder

Shadimar (SHAAD-ih-mahr): legendary Eastern Wizard who returned King Sterrane to his throne (deceased)

Valya (VAAL-yuh): an older woman

Ainsvillers

Burnold (Bern-OHLD): the blacksmith

Karruno (Kuh-ROO-noh): a farmer

Oscore (AHS-ker): the bartender

Keatovillers

Darby (DAAR-bee): Ra-khir's squire

Keva (KEY-vuh): Darby's younger sister

Tiega (Tee-AY-guh): Darby's mother

Tiego (Tee-AY-goh): Tiega's father

Corpa Schaullans (Twin Cities)

Broward (BROW-ahrd): a soldier; Varjerrah's husband

Fitzmar (FIHTZ-mahr): an elderly soldier

Kentarial (Kehn-TAHR-ee-uhl): a silversmith turned soldier
Louisa (Loo-EEZ-uh): youngest of Broward and Varjerrah's three daughters
Luka (LOO-kuh): youngest of Broward and Varjerrah's children on a duplicate world; a boy
Rentari (Rehn-TAHR-ee): Kentarial's doppelgänger on a duplicate world
Rowan (ROHW-ihn): a cooper
Semarat (SEHM-aa-raat): a soldier
Terrellis (Ter-EHL-ihs): a soldier
Varjerrah (Vahr-HEHR-uh): Broward's wife

Fristians (Twin Cities)

Blenhardin (Blehn-HAHR-dihn): Blenhardius' doppelgänger on a duplicate world
Blenhardius (Blehn-HAHR-dee-uhs): a young soldier; Hilda's husband
Hilda (HIHL-duh): Blenhardius' wife
Layamont (LAY-uh-mahnt): Leamond's doppelgänger on a duplicate world
Leamond (LEE-uh-mahnd): a young soldier
Ultaer (UHL-tayr): a young soldier

Other Westlanders

Howall (HOW-ehl): Sheatonian. the guardsman (deceased)
Khalen (KAY-lihn): New Lovénian. a fabric-seller
Lenn (LEHN): Dunforder. owner and barkeeper of only inn
Nat (NAAT): a highwayman
The Savage: New Lovénian. a brawly (deceased)

EASTERNERS

Aditha (Uh-DEE-thuh): Evrehar's wife
Alneezah (Aal-NEE-zuh): a castle maid
Alsrusett (Aal-RUHS-iht): one of Weile Kahn's bodyguards (with Daxan)
Chayl (SHAYL): a follower of Weile Kahn; commander of Nighthawk sector
Curdeis (KER-tuhs): Weile Kahn's brother (deceased)

Daxan (DIHK-suhn): one of Weile Kahn's bodyguards (with Alsrusett)

Evrehar (EEV-rah-hahr): a soldier from Osporivat; Aditha's husband

Halcone (Hehl-KAHN): high general of the Eastern armies

Jharik (ZHAHR-ihk): a soldier

Jeffrin (JEHF-rihn): an informant working for Weile Kahn

Kinya (KEHN-yuh): a long-time member of Weile Kahn's organization

Leightar (LAY-tahr): a follower of Weile Kahn

Midonner (May-DAHN-er): previous king of Stalmize; high king of the Eastlands (deceased)

Nacoma (Nah-KAH-mah): a follower of Weile Kahn

Saydee (SAY-dee): a server at the Dancing Dog

Shavoor (Shah-VOOR): an informant working for Weile Kahn

Shaxcharal (SHAAKS-krawl): the last king of LaZar

Tae Kahn (TIY KAHN): the king of Stalmize; high king of the Eastlands; Weile Kahn's only son

Tisharo (Tuh-SHAHR-oh): a con man working for Weile Kahn

Usyris (Yoo-SIY-ruhs): a follower of Weile Kahn; commander of Sparrowhawk sector

Weile Kahn (WAY-lee KAHN): Tae's father; father of organized crime

NORTHERNERS

Alsmir (AALS-meer): AERI; captain of Aerin's infantry

Andvari (Aand-VAHR-ee): NORDMIRIAN; warrior and diplomat

Avard (AAV-ahrd): AERI; a bartender in Aerin

Elgar (EHL-gahr): ERDAI; general of Erd's army

Erik Leifsson (EH-rihk): NORDMIRIAN; captain of the Sea Dragon, a warship

Griselda (Gree-ZEHL-duh): AERI; a server in the tavern in Aerin

Mundilnarvi (Muhn-dill-NAHR-vee): NORDMIRIAN; *Einherjar* killed in the war against the Renshai

Olvaerr (OHL-eh-vayr): NORDMIRIAN; Valr Kirin's son (deceased)

Olvirn (OHL-eh-veern): AERI; captain of Aerin's cavalry

Sigurd (SEE-gerd): NORDMIRIAN; a soldier

Sivaird (SEE-vayrd): AERI; captain of Aerin's archers

Tyrion (TEER-ee-ahn): ASCAI; an inner court guard of Pudar

Valr Kirin (Vawl-KEER-ihn): NORDMIRIAN; an ancient enemy of Colbey's; Rache Kallmirsson's blood brother (deceased)

Valr Magnus (Vawl-MAAG-nuhs): AERI; general of Aerin's army; the best swordsman in the North

Verdondi Eriksson (Ver-DAHN-dee): NORDMIRIAN; Erik's son

HEIMSTADERS

Bobbin (BAH-bihn): Mistri's pet human

Dillion (DIHL-ee-yon): an alsona (deceased)

Firuz (Fuh-ROOZ): one of the Kjempemagiska (deceased)

Fallon (FOWL-ihn): a general of the alsona (deceased)

Floralyn (FLOHR-uh-lihn): a Kjempemagiska; Mistri's aunt and Hortens' sister

Hortens (HOHR-tehns): a Kjempemagiska; Mistri's mother

Jaxon (JAAKS-uhn): an alsona (deceased)

Kalka (KOWL-kah): a general of the alsona (deceased)

Kentt (KENT): a Kjempemagiska; Mistri's father

Mistri (MIHS-tree): a Kjempemagiska child; daughter of Kentt and Hortens; owner of Bobbin

ELVES

An'séarie (Aan-say-AH-ree): a female elf

Arak'bar Tulamii Dhor (Ahr-AHK-bahr Too-LAHM-ee-iy ZHOOR): eldest of the elves; aka He Who Has Forgotten His Name; aka Captain

Arith'tinir Khy-loh'Shinaris Bal-ishi Sjörmann'taé Or (Ahr-IHTH-tih-neer Kiy-loh-shihn-AHR-iss Baal-EE-shee Syohr-MAHN-tiy Ohr): Captain's given name

Ar'min'taé (Ahr-MIHN-tay-yay): a male elf

Ath'erion (Aa-THEER-ee-ahn): a male elf

Captain: the common name for Arak'bar Tulamii Dhor

Chan'rék'ril Ar'temius Dal-ment'olian Mir'a Tam-möm'oly (Shawn-RAYK-rihl Ahr-TEEM-ee-uhs Dahl-mehnt-OH-lee-ahn MEER-uh Taam-MOHM-oh-lee): an artistic male elf who lost his soul to a spirit spider

Dh'arlo'mé'aftris'ter Te'meer Braylth'ryn Amareth Fel-Krin (ZHAHR-loh-may-aff-TRIHS-ter Tuh-MEER Brawl-THRIHN Ah-MAHR-ehth Fehl-KRIHN): former leader of the svartalf (deceased)

El-brinith (Ehl-BRIHN-ihth): a female elf with a good feel for magic

Eth'eel'ya (Ehth-EEL-yuh): a female elf

Ghy'rinith Ha-tarian Exar Myrintus Ashon'tae (Giy-RIHN-ihth Hah-TAAR-ee-ehn EHKS-ahr Muhr-IHN-tuhs Aash-ohn-TAY): a female elf healer

Hy'astorion Kev-telent Ar'pero-miay Nor Shal'ind'tay (Hiy-ehs-TOHR-ee-ahn Kehv-TEHL-ehnt Ahr-PAY-roh-miy-AY Nohr Shahl-ihnd-TAY): a male elf

Khy'barreth Y'vrintae Shabeerah El-borin Morbonos (Kiy-BAYR-ehth eev-RIHN-tiy Shah-BEER-ah EHL-boor-ihn Moor-BOH-nohs): a brain-damaged male elf

Ladori Ma'hellorian Naf-talis Ark Venarith Te (Lah-DOOR-ee Mah-hehl-OHR-ee-ahn Naaf-TAHL-ihs AHRK Vehn-AHR-ihth TEE): a female elf with a talent for locating magic

Myr-intha Tariash El'bar Kay Torrin'arka (Meer-IHN-thuh TAHR-ee-aash EHL-bahr KAY Tohr-ihn-AHRK-uh): a female elf healer

Shar'iss'ah (Shahr-ees-UH): a female elf

Tellurial Auzama Ka-hanath Shumanren Whir (Teh-LOOR-ee-uhl Aw-ZAH-mah Kaa-HAHN-ihth Shoo-MAHN-rehn Wer): a male elf

Tem'aree'ay Donnev'ra Amal-yah Krish-anda Mal-satorian (Teh-MAHR-ee-ay Dahn-EHV-er-uh Ah-MAAL-yah Kreesh-AAN-duh Maal-sah-TOOR-ee-uhn): a healer; King Griff's junior wife (second)

OTHER OUTWORLD CREATURES

Ámáttr (AH-maht-ehr): aka Terrible; demon who is ruler of Illrhel, the eighth level of Hel

Andskoti (Aand-SKOH-tee): aka Adversary; donkey who is ruler of Málsneidaheim, the seventh level of Hel

Hrimgirmnir (Hrihm-GERM-neer): aka Rime-Hooded; giant who is ruler of Niflhel, the ninth level of Hel

Móthir (MOH-theer): aka Mother; ruler of Saklaussheimili, the first level of Hel

Ofriki (Oh-FREE-kee): aka Overbearing; ogre who is ruler of Fróth-stathr, the fourth level of Hel

Ondetar (AHN-dih-tahr): an ancient demon

Sessgladr (SEHS-GLAAD-ehr): aka Full of Joy; ruler of Kynstathr, the second level of Hel

Sauthamathr (SAWTH-uh-maath-ehr): aka Shepherd (male); twin of Smalamanthr, co-ruler of Kvikindi, the third level of Hel

Senility Dotage: Hel's house slave and bond maid who served her before the Ragnarok; now ruler of Ósnjallrstathr, the sixth level of Hel

Smalamanthr (SMAHL-uh-maan-thehr): aka Shepherd (female); twin of Sauthamathr, co-ruler of Kvikindi, the third level of Hel

Varthmathr (Vahrth-MAATH-ehr): aka Watcher, ruler of Hel, the fifth level of Hel

ANIMALS

Clydin (KLIY-dihn): Darby's chestnut gelding

Frost Reaver: Colbey's white stallion

Imorelda (Ih-mawr-EHL-duh): Tae's silver tabby cat

Mior (Mee-OHR): Matrinka's calico cat (deceased)

Silver Warrior: Ra-khir's white stallion

Snow Stormer: Kedrin's white stallion, replacement for the horse of the same name

GODS, WORLDS, & LEGENDARY OBJECTS

Northern

Aegir (AHJ-eer): Northern god of the sea; killed at the *Ragnarok*

Alfheim (AALF-hiym): the world of elves; destroyed during the *Ragnarok*

Asgard (AAS-gahrd): the world of the gods

Baldur (BAWL-der): Northern god of beauty and gentleness who rose from the dead after the *Ragnarok*

Beyla (BAY-luh): Frey's human servant; wife of Byggvir

The Bifrost Bridge (BEE-frawst): the bridge between Asgard and man's world

Bragi (BRAH-gee): Northern god of poetry; killed at the *Ragnarok*

Brysombolig (Brihs-uhm-BOH-leeg): Troublesome House; Loki's long-abandoned citadel

Byggvir (BYOOG-veer): Frey's human servant; husband of Beyla

Colbey Calistinsson (KUHL-bay): legendary immortal Renshai; blood-son of Thor and a mortal Renshai; husband of Freya

The Fenris Wolf (FEHN-rihs): the Great Wolf; the evil son of Loki; also called Fenrir; killed at the *Ragnarok*

Frey (FRAY): Northern god of rain, sunshine and fortune; father of the elves

Freya (FRAY-uh): Frey's sister; Northern goddess of battle

Frigg (FRIHG): Odin's wife; Northern goddess of fate

*Frothstathr (Frohth-STAAT-ehr): aka Place of Magic; the fourth level of Hel ruled by Ofriki (see Other Outworlders); the destination for the souls of all magical beings except gods and elves; ruled by a massive ogre with powers of his own

Geirönul (Gay-EER-awn-uhl): Spear-bearer; a Valkyrie

Gladsheim (GLAAD-shiym): "Place of Joy"; sanctuary of the gods

Göll (GAWL): Screaming; a Valkyrie

Hel (HEHL): Northern goddess of the cold underrealm for those who do not die in valorous combat; killed at the *Ragnarok*

Hel (HEHL): the underrealm once ruled by the goddess Hel

*Hel (HEHL): the fifth level of Hel ruled by Varthmathr (see Other Outworlders); the destination for the souls of average humans, including warriors who die of illness or age; ruled by a fierce humanoid who keeps them in line, it is the most similar to the original Hel

Heimdall (HIYM-dahl): Northern god of vigilance and father of mankind; killed at the *Ragnarok*

Herfjötur (Herf-YOH-tehr): Host Fetter; a Valkyrie

Hildr (HEELD): Warrior; a Valkyrie

Hlidskjalf (HLIHD-skyuhlf): Odin's high seat from which he could survey the worlds

Hlökk (HLAWK): Shrieking; a Valkyrie

Hod (HAHD): Blind god, a son of Odin; returned with Baldur after the *Ragnarok*

Honir (HOH-neer): an indecisive god who survived the *Ragnarok*

Hrist (HRIHST): Shaker; a Valkyrie

Idunn (EE-duhn): Bragi's wife; keeper of the golden apples of youth

Ifing (IHF-ihng): river between Asgard and Jötunheim

*Illrhel (EEL-ehr-hehl): aka Hel for the Bad; the eighth level of Hel ruled by Ámáttr (see Other Outworlders); the destination for the souls of criminals; ruled by a cruel demon who enjoys torture and mayhem.

Jötunheim (YOH-tuhn-hiym): the world of the giants; destroyed during the *Ragnarok*

Kvasir (KWAH-seer): a wise god, murdered by dwarves, whose blood was brewed into the mead of poetry

*Kvindindi (Kwihn-DIHN-dee): aka Animal/Beast Home; the third level of Hel ruled by twins Sauthamathr and Smalamanthr (see Other Outworlders); the destination for the souls of animals who exhibit exemplary traits or deeds; ruled by male and female humanoid twins

*Kynstathr (KEEN-staat-ehr): aka Place of the Kind; the second level of Hel ruled by Sessgladr (see Other Outworlders); the destination for the souls of humans who exhibit exemplary behavior; ruled by a jolly man and filled with joyous activities and conversation

Loki (LOH-kee): Northern god of fire and guile; a traitor to the gods and a champion of chaos; killed at the *Ragnarok*

Magni (MAAG-nee): Thor's and Sif's son; Northern god of might

*Málsneidaheim (Maals-NIYD-uh-hiym): aka Place of the Noisome; the seventh level of Hel ruled by Andskoti (see Other Outworlders); the destination for the souls of gossips, busybodies and backstabbers; ruled by a rude and unfriendly donkey who is not inclined toward torture but is quick to put his charges in line

Mana-garmr (MAH-nah gahrm): Northern wolf destined to extinguish the sun with the blood of men at *Ragnarok*; killed in the *Ragnarok*

The Midgard Serpent: a massive, poisonous serpent destined to kill and be killed by Thor at the *Ragnarok*; Loki's son; killed in the *Ragnarok*

Mimir (MIH-meer): wise god who was killed by gods; Odin preserved his head and used it as an adviser

Mist: Mist; a Valkyrie

Modi: (MOH-dee): Thor's and Sif's son; Northern god of blood wrath

Nanna (NAH-nah): Baldur's wife

Náströnd (NAH-strahnd): aka Corpse Strand, a place of terrible punishment where serpents make a wickerwork of the walls and roof with their venom dribbling; to arrive, souls must wade through the river Slithr

Nidhogg (NIHD-hahg): dragon who gnaws at the root of the World Tree in Niflheim

Niflheim (NIHF-uhl-hiym): Misty Hel; the coldest part of Hel to which the worst of the dead are committed

*Niflheim (NIHF-uhl-hiym): aka Misty Hel; the ninth, lowest and worst level of Hel ruled by Hrimgrimnir (see Other Outworlders); destination for the cruelest and meanest souls; ruled by a horrible giant; souls there must live in Náströnd

Njord (NYOHRD): Frey's and Freya's father; died in the *Ragnarok*

Norns (NOHRNS): the keepers of past (Urdr), present (Verdandi), and future (Skuld)

Odin: (OH-dihn): Northern leader of the pantheon; father of the gods; killed in the *Ragnarok*; resurrected self by placing his soul in the empty Staff of Law prior to his slaying, then overtaking the leader of the elves (deceased)

Odrorir (Ah-DROHR-eer): the cauldron containing the mead of poetry brewed from Kvasir's blood

*Ósnjallrstathr (Ohs-ehn-YAHL-ehr-staat-ehr): aka Place of the Foolish; the sixth level of Hel ruled by Senility Dotage (see Other Outworlders); destination for the souls of the foolish or insane; ruled by the woman who used to serve as Hel's house slave and bond maid, it is chaotic and generally odd

The Ragnarok (RAAG-nuh-rahk): the massive war prophesied to destroy the gods, humans, and elves; partially thwarted by Colbey Calistinsson and Odin

Ran (RAHN): wife of Aegir; killed in the *Ragnarok*

Randgrithr (RAWND-greeth-ehr): Shield-bearer; a Valkyrie

Raska Colbeysson (RAAS-kuh): son of Colbey and Freya aka Ravn (RAY-vihn); see Renshai

Ratatosk (Rah-tah-TAHSK): a squirrel who relays insults between Nidhogg and the eagle at the top of Yggdrasill

Rathgrithr (RAATH-greeth-ehr): Plan-Destroyer; a Valkyrie

Reginleif (REHG-ihn-leef): God's Kin; a Valkyrie

*Saklaussheimili (Sahk-LAWS-hiym-EE-lee): aka Home of the Guiltless; the first level of Hel ruled by Móthir (see Other Outworlders); the destination for the souls of children and the childlike; ruled by a plump motherly figure, it is always sunny, and the souls play

Sif (SIHF): Thor's wife; Northern goddess of fertility and fidelity

Sigyn (SEE-giyn): Loki's wife

Skeggjöld (SKEHG-yawld): Ax Time; a Valkyrie

Skögul (SKOH-guhl): Raging; a Valkyrie

Skoll (SKOHWL): Northern wolf who was to swallow the sun at the *Ragnarok*

Skuld (SKUHLD): Being; the Norn who represents the future

Slithr (SLIHTH-ehr): aka Fearful, a river of knives and sharp swords through which the most evil souls must wade to get to Náströnd

Spring of Mimir: spring under the second root of Yggdrasill

Syn (SIHN): Northern goddess of justice and innocence

Surtr (SERT): the king of fire giants; destined to kill Frey and destroy the worlds of elves and men with fire at the *Ragnarok*; killed in the *Ragnarok*

Thor (THOHR): Northern god of storms, farmers, and law; killed in the *Ragnarok*

Thrudr (THRUD-ehr): Thor's daughter; goddess of power

Tyr (TEER): Northern one-handed god of war and faith; killed in the *Ragnarok*

Ugagnevangar (Oo-gaag-nih-VAYNG-ahr): Dark Plain of Misfortune; Loki's world on which sits Brysombolig

Urdr (ERD): Fate; the Norn who represents the past

Valaskjalf (Vahl-AAS-kyahlf): Shelf of the Slain; Odin's citadel

Valhalla (Vawl-HAH-luh):the heaven for the souls of dead warriors killed in valiant combat; at the *Ragnarok*, the souls in Valhalla (*Einherjar*) assisted the gods in battle

Vali (VAWL-ee): Odin's son; survived the *Ragnarok*

The Valkyries (VAWL-ker-ees): the Choosers of the Slain; warrior women who choose which souls go to Valhalla on the battlefield

Verdandi (Ver-DAHN-dee): Necessity; the Norn who represents the present

Vidar (VEE-dahr): son of Odin destined to avenge his father's death at the *Ragnarok* by slaying the Fenris Wolf; current leader of the gods

The Well of Urdr: body of water at the base of the first root of Yggdrasill

The Wolf Age: the sequence of events immediately preceding the *Ragnarok* during which Skoll swallows the sun, Hati mangles the moon, and the Fenris Wolf runs free

Yggdrasil (IHG-druh-zihl): the World Tree

*The nine layers of NuHel after the death of the goddess Hel

Western

(now considered essentially defunct;
mostly studied for its historical significance)

Aphrikelle (Ah-frih-KEHL):Western goddess of spring

Cathan (KAY-t/hehn):Western goddess of war, specifically hand-to-hand combat; twin to Kadrak

Dakoi (Dah-KOY):Western god of death

The Faceless God:Western god of winter

Firfan (FEER-faan):Western god of archers and hunters

Itu (EE-too):Western goddess of knowledge and truth

Kadrak (KAH-drahk):Western god of war; twin to Cathan

Ruaidhri (Roo-AY-dree):Western leader of the pantheon

Suman (SOO-mahn):Western god of farmers and peasants

Weese (WEESSS):Western god of winds

Yvesen (IHV-eh-sehn):Western god of steel and women

Zera'im (ZAYR-uh-eem):Western god of honor

Eastern

(though more common than the Western religion,
it is also considered essentially defunct)

Sheriva (Shuh-REE-vah): omnipotent, only god of the Eastlands

Outworld Gods

Ciacera (See-uh-SAYR-uh): goddess of life on the sea floor who
takes the form of an octopus

Mahaj (Muh-HAHJ): the god of dolphins

Morista (Moor-EES-tuh): the god of swimming creatures who takes
the form of a seahorse

FOREIGN WORDS

a (AH): EASTERN. "from"

ailar (IY-lahr): EASTERN. "to bring"

al (AYL): EASTERN. the first person singular pronoun

aldrnari (ohld-ehr-NAHR-ee): HEIMSTADER. "fire"

alfen (AALF-ihn): BÉARNESE. "elves"; term created by elves to
refer to themselves

alsona (aal-SOH-nuh): HEIMSTADER. "person" or "people"

alsonese (aal-soh-NEEZ): TRADING. Tae's made-up name for *usaro*

amythest-weed: TRADING. a specific type of wildflower

anari (uh-NAHR-ee): HEIMSTADER. the mind language of Heimstadr

anem (AHN-uhm): BARBARIAN. "enemy"; usually used in reference to a specific race or tribe with whom the barbarian's tribe is
at war

åndelig mannhimmel (AWN-deh-lee mahn-hee-MELL): REN-
SHAI. "spirit man of the sky"; an advanced Renshai sword maneuver

aristiri (aa-rihs-TEER-ee): TRADING. a breed of singing hawk

årvåkir (awr-vaw-KEER): NORTHERN. "vigilant one"

atferth (AAT-ferth): ELVISH. magically enhanced food that ener-
gizes and counteracts certain herbs

baronshei (buh-RAHN-shiy): TRADING. "bald"

bassana (buh-SAW-nah): HEIMSTADER. "bed"

bein (BAYN): NORTHERN. "legs"

berserks (BAYR-sayr): NORTHERN. soldiers who fight without emotion, ignoring the safety of self and companions because of drugs or mental isolation; "crazy"

bha'fraktii (bah-FRAHK-tee-iy): ELVISH. "those who court their doom"; a *lysalf* term for *svartalf*

binyal (BIHN-yahl): TRADING. a type of spindly tree

bleffy (BLEHF-ee): WESTERN/TRADING. a child's euphemism for nauseating

bolboda (bawl-BOH-duh): NORTHERN. "evilbringer"

bonta (BAHN-tuh): EASTERN. vulgar term for a male homosexual

brawly (BRAWL-ee): WESTERN. street slang for gang-level protection racketeers

brigshigsa weed (brih-SHIHG-suh): WESTERN. a specific leafy weed with a translucent, red stem; a universal antidote to several common poisons

brorin (BROHR-ihn): RENSHAI. "brother"

bruni (broo-NEE): NORTHERN. "fire"

brunstil (BRUHN-steel): NORTHERN. a stealth maneuver learned from barbarians by the Renshai; literally "brown and still"

butterflower (BUH-ter-FLOW-er): TRADING. a specific type of wild flower with a brilliant, yellow hue

chrisshius (KRIHS-ee-uhs): WESTERN. a specific type of wildflower

chroams (krohms): WESTERN. a specific coinage of copper, silver, or gold

corpa (KOHR-puh): WESTERN. "brotherhood", "town"; literally "body"

cringer (KRIHN-jer): EASTERN. gang slang for a person who shows fear

daimo (DIY-moh): EASTERN. slang term for Renshai

demon (DEE-muhn): ANCIENT TONGUE. a creature of magic

dero (DAYR-oh): EASTERN. a type of winter fruit

djem (dee-YEHM): NORTHERN. "demon"

djevgullinhåri (dee-YEHV-guhl-ihn-HAHR-ee): NORTHERN. "golden-haired devils"

djevskulka (dee-yehv-SKOHL-kuh): NORTHERN. an expletive that essentially means "devil's play"

doppelgänger (DOH-puhl-gaang-er): NORTHERN. double-goer, a look alike or double of a living being

doranga (door-AYNG-uh): TRADING. a type of tropical tree with serrated leaves and jutting rings of bark

drilstin (DRIHL-stihn): TRADING. an herb used by healers

dwar-freytii (dwawr-FRAY-tee-iy): ELVISH. "the chosen ones of Frey"; a *svartalf* name for themselves

Einherjar (Iyn-HER-yahr): NORTHERN. "the dead warriors' souls in Vahalla"

ejenlyåndel (ay-YEN-lee-AHN-dehl): ELVISH. "immortality echo"; a sense of infinality that is a part of every human and elf; the soul

eksil (EHK-seel): NORTHERN. "exile"

erenspice (EH-rehn-spiys): EASTERN. a type of hot spice used in cooking

ernontris (er-NAHN-trihs): HEIMSTADER. a specific gruesome and magical type of torture

fafra (FAH-fruh): TRADING. "to eat"

feflin (FEHF-lihn): TRADING. "to hunt"

fegling (FEHG-lihng): ERYTHANIAN. "coward"

feuer (fee-YOHR): BÉARNESE. "fire"

floyetsverd (floy-EHTS-wayrd): RENSHAI. a disarming maneuver

formynder (fohr-MYOON-der): NORTHERN. "guardian", "teacher"

forrader (foh-RAY-der): NORTHERN. "traitor"

forraderi (foh-RAY-der-ee): NORTHERN. "treason"

forsvarir (fohrs-vahr-EER): RENSHAI. a specific disarming maneuver

frey (FRAY): NORTHERN. "lord"

freya (FRAY-uh): NORTHERN. "lady"

frichen-karboh (FRAATCH-ihn kayr-BOH): EASTERN. widow; literally "manless woman, past usefulness"

frilka (FRAYL-kah): EASTERN. the most formal title for a woman, elevating her nearly to the level of a man

fussling (FUHS-lihng): TRADING. slang for bothering

galn (GAHLN): NORTHERN. "ferociously crazy"

gamin (GAH-neem): RENSHAI. "a non-Renshai"

garlet (GAAR-leht): WESTERN. a specific type of wildflower believed to have healing properties

garn (GAHRN): NORTHERN. "yarn"

gerlinr (ger-LEEN): RENSHAI. a specific aesthetic and difficult sword maneuver

gloik (GLOIK): TRADING. slang erm for oaf

gloop (GLOOP): a sound effect created by an elf to describe the action of a semi-solid substance filling in gaps

glorbit (GLOYR-biht): a sound effect created by an elf to describe the action of a semi-solid substance filling in gaps

granshy (GRAAN-shiy): WESTERN. "plump"

gullin (GUH-lihn): NORTHERN. "golden"

gynurith (guh-NAHR-ayth): EASTERN. "excrement"

hacantha (huh-CAAN-thuh): TRADING. a specific type of culti-
vated flower that comes in various hues

hadongo (hah-DAHNG-oh):WESTERN. a twisted, hardwood tree

handelegg (HAHN-deh-lehg): NORTHERN. "arm"

HandeleggColbyr (HAHN-deh-lehg-KUHL-bay-ehr): NORTH-
ERN. "the arm of Colbey";Valr Magnus' sword

harval (hahr-VAWL): ANCIENT TONGUE. "the gray blade"

hastivillr (hahs-tih-VEEL-ehr): RENSHAI. a sword maneuver

herbont (HER-bahnt):TRADING. a specific type of gnarly tree that
tends to grow with multiple trunks

hervani arwawn telis braiforn (her-VAHN-ee ahr-WAHN tehl-EES
bray-FOHRN): ELVISH. "joining together that which normally
has no true focus"; adding magical strength to solid objects

hyrr (HIY-ehr): ELVISH. "fire"

ivana (ee-VAH-nuh): ELVISH. negative slang term for "half-human/
half-elfin creature"; named for Ivana (see BÉARNIDES)

jarfr (YAHR-fahr): HEIMSTADER. a specific, ferocious predator
(akin to a wolverine)

jeconia (jeh-KOHN-yah): TRADING. a specific type of venomous
snake

jovinay arithanik (joh-VIH-nay ahr-ih-THAAN-ihk): ELVISH. "a
joining of magic"; a gathering of elves for the purpose of amplify-
ing and casting spells

jufinar (JOO-fihn-ahr):TRADING. a specific type of bush-like tree
that produces berries

kadlach (KAHD-lah/k/):TRADING. a vulgar term for a disobedient
child; akin to brat

kathkral (KAATH-krawl): ELVISH. a specific type of broad-leafed
tree

kenya (KEHN-yuh):WESTERN. "bird"

khohlar (KOH-lahr): ELVISH. a mental magical concept that involves transmitting several words in an instantaneous concept

khohlar, direct: ELVISH. khohlar sent to an individual; aka singular
khohlar

khohlar, indirect: ELVISH. khohlar sent to everyone

kinesthe (KIHN-ehs-teh): NORTHERN. "strength"

kirstal (KEER-stahl): HEIMSTADER. a specific type of towering,
thickly-branched tree that grows on Heimstadr

kjaelnabnir (kyahl-NAAB-neer): RENSHAI. temporary name for a
child until a hero's name becomes available

Kjempemagiska (Kee-YEHM-pay-muh-JEES-kuh): HEIMSTA-
DER. "magical giants"; "the masters"

Kjempese (kee-YEM-peez): TRADING. Tae's made-up word for
anari

klaekir (klay-uh-KEER): RENSHAI. coward; the most vile insult in
the language

kolbladnir (kohl-BLAW-neer): NORTHERN. "the cold-bladed"

krabbe (KRAAB-eh): NORTHERN. "the crab"; a Renshai sword
maneuver

kraell (kray-EHL): ANCIENT TONGUE. a type of demon dwelling
in the deepest region of chaos' realm

kyndig (KAWN-dee): NORTHERN. "skilled one"

lasat (lih-SAHT): HEIMSTADER. "apple"

latense (lah-TEHN-seh): RENSHAI. a sword maneuver

lav'rintir (lahv-rihn-TEER): ELVISH. "destroyer of the peace"

lav'rintii (lahv-RIHN-tee-iy): ELVISH. "the followers of Lav'rintir"

lessakit (LAYS-eh-kiyt): EASTERN. "a message"

leuk (LOOK): WESTERN. "white"

litaska (lee-TAHS-kuh): ELVISH. "seeking magic;" a magical spe-
cialty that enhances the ability to find needed or desired objects

loki (LOH-kee): NORTHERN. "fire"

lonriset (LAHN-rih-seht): WESTERN. a ten-stringed instrument

lynstriek (LEEN-strayk): RENSHAI. a sword maneuver

lysalf (LEES-aalf): ELVISH. "light elf"

magni (MAAG-nee): NORTHERN. "might"

mehiar (mih-HIY-er): HEIMSTADER. a tea-like drink flavored
with milk and honey

meirtrin (MAYR-trihn): TRADING. a specific breed of nocturnal
rodent

menneskelik (mehn-EHS-kuh-leek): ELVISH. "humanized"

mermaid (MER-mayd): NORTHERN. a seal-like magical creature
that seduces, drowns and feeds on human males; takes on the illu-
sory appearance of a beautiful woman with a fish-like tail

mermelr (MER-mehl): HEIMSTADER. a specific squirrel-like animal with a flat tail (akin to marmoset)

minkelik (mihn-KEHL-ihk): ELVISH. "human"

mirack (mer-AAK): WESTERN. a specific type of hardwood tree
with white bark

missy beetle (MIH-see BEE-tuhl): TRADING. a type of harmless,
black beetle

mjollnir (MYAHL-neer): NORTHERN. "mullicrusher"

modi (MOH-dee): NORTHERN. "wrath"

Morshoch (MOHR-shahk): ANCIENT TONGUE. "sword of darkness"

Motfrabelonning (maht-frah-behl-AHN-ee): NORTHERN. "reward of courage"

muldyrein (MUHL-dih-rayn): ELVISH. "mule"

mulesl om natten (MYOO-sihl-ohm-NAHT-ihn): RENSHAI. "the night mule"; a Renshai sword maneuver

musserёnde (myoo-ser-EHN-deh): RENSHAI. "sparkling"; a Renshai sword maneuver

mynten (MIHN-tihn): NORTHERN. a specific type of coin

nådenal (naw-deh-NAHL): RENSHAI. "needle of mercy"; a silver, guardless, needle-shaped dagger constructed during a meticulous religious ceremony and used to end the life of an honored, suffering ally or enemy, then melted in the victim's pyre

nålogtråd (naw-LAHG-trawd): RENSHAI. "needle and thread"; a Renshai sword maneuver

noca (NOH-kuh): BÉARNESE. "grandfather"

Nualfheim (Noo-AALF-hiym): ELVISH. "new elf home"

odelhurtig (ahd-ehl-HYOO-tih): RENSHAI. a sword maneuver

oopey (OO-pee): WESTERN/TRADING. a child's euphemism for an injury

orlorner (oir-LEERN-ahr): EASTERN. "to deliver to"

pen-fruit (PEHN-froot): WESTERN. an edible fruit that is the seed of the pen-fruit tree

perfrans (PER-fraanz): WESTERN. a specific scarlet wildflower

pike (PIYK): NORTHERN. "mountain"

placeling (PLAYS-lihng): ANCIENT TONGUE. a creature with Outworld blood placed magically into a human womb

prins (PRIHNZ): NORTHERN. "prince"

ranweed (RAAN-weed): WESTERN. a specific type of wild plant

raynshee (RAYN-shee): TRADING. "elder"

reipfrodleikr (riyp-FROHD-liyk): ELVISH. "trace magic"; an impression of magic on an object that is not magical but has had magic cast directly upon it

rexin (RAYKS-ihn): EASTERN. "king"

rhinsheh (raan-SHAY): EASTERN. "morning"

richi (REE-chee): WESTERN. a specific type of songbird

rintsha (RIHNT-shah): WESTERN. "cat"

Ristoril (RIHS-tohr-rihl): ANCIENT TONGUE. "sword of tranquility"

sangrit (SAAN-griht): BARBARIAN. "to form a blood bond"

sannrfrodleikr (saan-FROHD-liyk): ELVISH. "true magic"; an item that is inherently magical

sarvenna (sahr-VEH-nuh): TRADING. a specific type of plant that has anesthetic properties

sawgrass (SAW-graas): WESTERN. a specific type of grass

shaharin (shuh-HAYR-ihn): EASTERN. a specific breed of goat

shucara: (shoo-KAHR-uh): TRADING. a specific type of medicinal root

skjald (SKYAWLD): NORTHERN. "musician chronicler"

skulkë i djevlir (SKOOLK-eh ee dyehv-LEER): NORTHERN. "devil's brutal fun"

skulkë i djevgullinhåri (SKOOLK-eh ee dyehv-guhl-ihn-HAHR-ee): NORTHERN. "golden-haired devils' brutal fun"

skyggefrodleikr (skihg-eh-FROHD-liyk): ELVISH. "shadow magic"; an impression or echo of magic on an object that has been in long and close proximity to, and/or greatly treasured by, one or more powerfully magical beings (or to raw chaos)

stjerne skytedel (STYAARN-eh skih-TEHD-ehl): RENSHAI. "the shooting star"; a Renshai sword maneuver

sugarberries (SHOO-ger BEH-rees): TRADING. a specific type of edible berry with green and orange striped skin

svartalf (SWAHRT-aalf): ELVISH. "dark elf"

svergelse (swer-GEHL-seh): RENSHAI. "sword figures practiced alone"; katas

take (TAYK): TRADING. a game children play

takk: (TAAK): NORTHERN. "thank you"

takudan (TAHK-oo-dahn): HEIMSTADER. "sewer rat"

talvus (TAAL-vuhs): WESTERN. "midday"

tåphresëlmordat (taw-FREHS-ahl-MOOR-duht): RENSHAI. "brave suicide"; leaping into an unwinnable battle for the sole purpose of dying in glory for Valhalla rather than of illness or old age

thrudr (THRUHD): NORTHERN. "power", "might"

tisis (TIHS-ihs): NORTHERN. "retaliation"

torke (TOHR-keh): RENSHAI. "teacher", "sword instructor"

tre-ved-en (TREH-vehd-ahn): RENSHAI. "Loki's cross"; a Renshai sword maneuver designed for battling three against one

trithray (TRIHTH-ray): TRADING. a specific type of purple wildflower

tvinfri (TWIHN-free): RENSHAI. a specific disarming maneuver

ulvstikk (OOL-steek): RENSHAI. a specific sword maneuver

usaro (oo-SAHR-oh): HEIMSTADER. spoken language

uvakt (oo-VAHKT): RENSHAI. "the unguarded"; a term for children whose *kjaelnabnir* becomes a permanent name

Valhalla (Vawl-HAHL-uh): NORTHERN. "hall of the slain"

valkyrie (VAWL-ker-ee): NORTHERN. "choser of the slain"

valr (VAWL): NORTHERN. "slayer"

vesell argalfr (vih-SEHL AHR-gahlf): ELVISH. "wretched woman-elf hybrid"

Vestan (VAYST-ihn): EASTERN. "the Westlands"

vethrleikr (VEHTH-er-liyk): HEIMSTADER. "weather magic"

villieldr (VIHL-ee-ehld): ELVISH. "the great fire"; the *Ragnarok* fire that destroyed Alfheim

vitanhvergi (veet-ehn-HWER-gee): ELVISH. "understand a nowhere"; a "non-concept" beyond elfin understanding that does not translate from another language or culture

waterroot (WAH-ter root): TRADING. a specific edible sea plant

wertell (wer-TEHL): TRADING. a specific plant with an acid seed used for medicinal purposes

wisule (WIH-sool): TRADING. A foul-smelling, disease-carrying breed of rodents that has many offspring because the adults will abandon them when threatened

yarshimyan (yahr-SHIHM-yuhn): ELVISH. a type of tree with bubblelike fruit

yessha (YEH-shuh): HEIMSTADER. a type of animal that resembles a brown-and-white striped horse

yonha (YAHN-uh): HEIMSTADER. "wild animal"

yrtventrig (ihrt-VEHN-tree): RENSHAI. a specific sword maneuver

PLACES

Northlands

The area north of the Weathered Mountains and west of the Great Frenum Range. The Northmen live in nine tribes, each with its own town surrounded by forest and farmland. The boundaries change.

Asci (AAS-kee): home of the Ascai; Patron god: Bragi

Aerin (Ah-REEN): home of the Aeri; Patron god: Aegir

Devil's Island: an island in the Amirannak. A home to the Renshai after their exile. Currently part of Nordmir

Erd (ERD): home of the Erdai; Patron god: Freya

Gelshnir (GEELSH-neer): home of the Gelshni; Patron god: Tyr

Gjar (GYAHR): home of the Gyar; Patron god: Heimdall
Nordmir (NOHRD-meer): the Northlands high kingdom, home of the Nordmirians; Patron god: Odin
Shamir (Shuh-MEER): home of the Shamirians; Patron god: Freya
Skrytil (SKRIY-teel): home of the Skrytila; Patron god: Thor
Talmir (TAHL-meer): home of the Talmirians; Patron god: Frey

Westlands

The Westlands are bounded by the Great Frenum Mountains to the east, the Weathered Mountains to the north, and the sea to the west and south. In general, the cities become larger and more civilized as the land sweeps westward. The central area is packed with tiny farm towns dwarfed by lush farm fields that, over time, have nearly co-alesced. This area is known as the Fertile Oval. The easternmost portions of the Westlands are forested, with sparse towns and rare barbarian tribes. To the south lies an uninhabited tidal plain.

Almische (Ahl-mihsh-AY): a small city
Béarn (Bay-AHRN): the high kingdom; a large mountain city
Bellenet Fields (Behl-eh-NAY): a tourney field in Erythane
Corpa Bickat (KOHR-pah Bih-KAY): a large city
Corpa Schaull (KOHR-pah SHAWL): a medium-sized city; one of the "twin cities" (see Frist)
Dunford (DUHN-ferd): a small village east of Erythane
Erythane (AYR-eh-thayn): a large city closely allied with Béarn; famous for its knights
The Fields of Wrath: plains on the outskirts of Erythane; home to the Renshai
Frist (FRIHST): a medium-sized city; one of the "twin cities" (see Corpa Schaull)
Granite Hills: a small, low range of mountains
Great Frenum Mountains: (FREH-nuhm): towering, impassable mountains that divide the Eastlands from the Westlands and Northlands
Greentree (GREEN-tree): a small town
Hopewell (HOHP-wehl): a small town
Keatoville (KEY-toh-vihl): a small town east and south of Dunford
The Knight's Rest (NIYT's rehst): a pricey tavern in Erythane
Myrcidë (Meer-see-DAY): a town near the Weathered Mountains that consists entirely of a magically hidden compound
New Lovén: (Loh-VEHN): a medium-sized city

Nualfheim (Noo-AALF-hiym): the elves' name for their island
The Off-Duty Tavern: a Pudarian tavern frequented by guardsmen
Oshtan (AHSH-taan): a small town
Paradise Plains (PAAR-uh-diys): an Erythanian name for the Fields of Wrath
Porvada (Pawr-VAH-duh): a medium-sized city
Pudar (Poo-DAHR): the largest city of the West; the great trade center
The Red Horse Inn: an inn in Pudar
The Road of Kings: the legendary route by which the Eastern Wizard is believed to have rescued the high king's heir after a bloody coup
Santagithi (Saan-TAAG-ih-thiy): a medium-sized town
Sheaton (SHAY-tuhn): a small town northeast of Dunford
The Western Plains: a barren salt flat
Wynix (Wiy-NIHKS): a medium-sized town

Eastlands

The area east of the Great Frenum Mountains, it is a vast, overpopulated area filled with crowded cities and eroded fields. Little forest remains.

Dunchart (DOON-shayrt): a small city
Ixaphant (IHKS-font): a large city
Gihabortch (GIY-hah-bohrtch): a city
LaZar (LAH-zahr): a small city
Lemnock (LAYM-nahk): a large city
Osporivat (Aas-poor-IY-veht): a large city
Prohathra (Pree-HAHTH-ruh): a large city
Rozmath (RAHZ-mihth): a medium-sized city
Stalmize (STAHL-meez): the Eastern high kingdom

Heimstadr

An island far out into the Amirranak Sea which is home to the *Kjempemagiska* and their servants, the *alsona*. The giants live in family units, their technology, magically based, significantly advanced over that of the people of the continent.

Beach of Flotsam: an inlet where the currents tend to carry nearby flotsam onto shore

Bodies of Water

Amirannak Sea (uh-MEER-uh-naak): the northernmost ocean
Brunn River (BRUHN): a muddy river in the Northlands
Conus River (KOH-nuhs): a shared river of the Eastlands and Westlands
Icy River (IY-see): a cold, northern river
Jewel River (JOOL): one of the rivers that flows to Trader's Lake
Mahajian Ocean (Muh-HAHJ-ee-ehn): distant extension of the Amirannak Sea southward; surrounds the island of Heimstadr
Perionyx River (Peh-ree-AHN-ihks): a Western river
Southern Sea (SUH-t/hern): the southernmost ocean
Trader's Lake (TRAY-der): a harbor for trading boats in Pudar
Trader's River (TRAY-der): the main route for overwater trade

Objects/Systems/Events

Bards, the: a familial curse passed to the oldest child, male or female, of one specific family. The curse condemns the current bard to obsessive curiosity but allows him to impart his learning only in song. A condition added by the Eastern Wizards compels each bard to serve as the personal bodyguard to the current king of Béarn as well.

Cardinal Wizards, the: a system of balance created by Odin in the beginning of time consisting of four, near-immortal, opposing guards of evil, neutrality, and goodness who were tightly constrained by Odin's laws. Obsolete.

Great War, the: a massive war fought between the Eastland army and the combined forces of the Westlands

Harval: "the Gray Blade" the sword of balance imbued with the forces of law, chaos, good, and evil. Obsolete

Knights of Erythane, the: an elite guardian unit for the king of Erythane that also serves the high king in Béarn in shifts. Steeped in rigid codes of dress, manner, conduct, and chivalry, they are famed throughout the world.

Kolbladnir: "the Cold-Bladed" a magic sword commissioned by Frey to combat Surtr at the *Ragnarok*

Mages of Myrcidë: a society of genetic human mages once feared and revered. The greatest and strongest of the Cardinal Wizards came from this society before the Renshai killed them all and left their dwellings in ruins. Always reclusive, after their destruction, they were all but erased from human memory

Mjollnir: "Mullicrusher" Thor's gold, short-handled hammer so heavy only he can lift it

Necklace of the Brisings, the: a necklace worn by the goddess Freya and forged by dwarves from "living gold"

Pica Stone, the: a clairsentient sapphire. One of the rare items with magical power. Once the province of the Mages of Myrcidë, it became the totem of Renshai, was returned to the "last" Myrcidian by the "last" Renshai, then was shattered. The shards were regathered, the stone remade, and it now tests the heirs of Béarn to assign the one worthy of rulership.

Pirate War, the: a recent mostly ship-based war fought between the *alsona* of Heimstadr under the direction of one *Kjempemagiska* against the armies of the Continent in the sea and on the shores of Béarn.

Ragnarok: "the Destruction of the Powers" the prophesied time when men, elves, and nearly all the gods would die. Because of actions by Colbey Calistinsson and Odin, things did not go exactly as fated. The current flashpoint of religious differences comes in the form of those who believe the *Ragnarok* has already occurred and those who believe it is still to come.

Sea Seraph, the: a ship once owned by an elf known only as Captain and used to transport the Cardinal Wizards. Obsolete.

Seven Tasks of Wizardry, the: a series of tasks designed by gods to test the power and worth of the Cardinal Wizards' chosen successors. Obsolete.

Staves of Law and Chaos, the: a pair of staves each representing one of the two opposing forces and hidden from the world by the gods until the two Cardinal Wizards representing neutrality were felt to be strong enough to champion one apiece in opposition (defunct).

Sword of Mitrian, the: an ancient sword commissioned by Mitrian and forged by the Western Wizard, Shadimar, using magical gemstones for the eyes of the wolf's head pommel. For the last several centuries, it has remained a crumbling treasure of the Renshai tribe.

Trobok, the: "the Book of the Faithful" a scripture that guides the lives of Northmen. It is believed that daily reading from the book assists Odin in holding chaos at bay from the world of law.

World's War, the: the most recent war fought between the *Kjempemagiska* of Heimstadr and the combined armies of the Continent in the Westlands.

The Knights of Erythane

(in child's rhyme order)

Kedrin (captain)   Edwin (armsman)
Garvin   Bennardin
Harritin   Vincelin
Kovian   Braison
Jakrusan   Tellbastian
Ra-khir   Vellassir
Aromay   Alquantae
Shavasiay   Yoneté
Esatoric   Ashtonik
Tylan   Castillon
Lakamorn   Petrone
Thessilius   Leicinder

Colbey (missing from the rhyme)

NuHel

(Nine layers of Hel after the Ragnarok)

	Name	Ruler	Who Goes There	Meaning Name of Ruler
1	Saklaussheimili	Móthir	Children, Innocents	Mother
2	Kynstathr	Sessgladr	Kind, Charitable, Helpful	Full of Joy
3	Kvikindi	Sauthamathr Smalamanthr	Animals	Shepherd (twins)
4	Fróthstathr	Ofriki	Magical Beings	Overbearing
5	Hel	Varthmathr	Ordinary Humans/ Warriors no Valhalla	Watcher
6	Ósnjallrstathr	Senility Dotage	Foolish, Insanity	House Slave & Bondmaid of Hel
7	Málsneidaheim	Andskoti	Gossips, Busybodies, Nosies, Backstabbers	Adversary
8	Illrhel	Ámáttr	Sinners (thieves, liars, drunkenness)	Terrible
9	Niflhel	Hrimgrimnir	Worst Sinners (murder, oathbreakers, psychopaths)	Rime-Hooded